MW01230154

Thanks to my friends and family for all the help they have given me.

The Dragon's Eye

Nathan Baird

Chapter 1-The Color of a Dragon's Eyes

The moon was high in the sky as Airria, a young man in a long, dark green cloak with faded patches, crept into the slaver's camp. He was as tall as a warhorse with long sandy-red hair which had a slight curl at the top of his neck.

He had come to see the new selection of slave women, as had become a practice for him when a slaver came through town. Airria's goal was to free one or two of the more beautiful women. He had been sneaking into slaver's camps since he was ten. He was especially sneaky and time had taught him well which slave caravans he could get into and which ones would be worthwhile.

The slaver's wagons were set up in their typical pattern, three slave wagons and a guard wagon on the outside. Airria had no trouble penetrating the loop of wagons because the slobs guarding the outer rim seemed to be paying more attention to their ale than to their jobs. Airria almost laughed as one of them tripped on a stick and then lay on the ground, drooling and snoring.

Inside the ring, as expected, was Henrik the slaver's wagon; the guards were leaning against the wagons sleeping. Unlike their under-dressed counterparts, the inner guards were armored with hard leather. These were the guards Henrik referred to as his elite guard; a laughable thought.

To his surprise, there was a second wagon in the center ring. It had guards on both sides of the door and one patrolling around it. The wagon had no windows and a very nice lock on the door; a sure sign of valuable cargo. Airria's curiosity piqued.

The sun's light would soon start to creep over the distant town of Tark-Ancia. Airria had found this time in the morning the best for releasing slaves, there was enough light to pick the locks and still enough shadows to hide him.

Airria first retreated back to the outer ring of wagons then made his way to the guards' wagon. Quietly he wedged a small stick into the latch and smiled as he thought about the guards bumbling around, trying to get out. When he was satisfied that the guards were secure, he crept back to the center ring and looked in the windows of the slave wagons. All of the captives were sleeping. He decided on the wagon with the most slave cargo. The lock was well made, but Airria had many years of practice and picked it quickly. He quietly went through and picked the cankered lock on each person, then woke up one, placing his hand over the slave's mouth to prevent a scream. Together, they finished waking up all the others in the wagon. The only noise was a single whimper from one of the young girls.

Airria could hear a two-man patrol of guards, in their drunken state, clumsily making their rounds. He listened as the guards passed. "E won'd ev'n let us look! Id ain't wite!" one of the guards said.

"I zaw er once. E' ad me beat," the other one replied. "Oh, ws id worth id!"

"Really?" the first responded. "Cun I zee?"

"No!" The second yelled in panic, "We will bote be tilled if you do!"

"Sscchhh! Don't wake up the boss!" The first said far too loudly. Airria thought to himself *I will make it out of here without even being seen. This is almost too easy.* He waited until the guards were out of range, then he opened the door and helped the slaves out, warning them to be careful.

When the slaves were gone, Airria closed the door and waited. He heard exactly what he expected, the drunken guards trying to catch the slaves. He didn't expect many of the slaves to make it far, but he knew they would be the distraction he would need. He had to laugh at the simple minds of the guards.

As he had anticipated, Airria could hear the guards in the center of the rings as they left their post to see what was going on. This was his chance; Airria slipped back to the center, to the wagon with no windows.

He had never seen a lock that looked so complex. It was like the legendary Dwarven treasure locks. It took a six sided key and the tumblers would not set for him to move on to the next one. His determination was reinforced by the complication. Realizing the lock was too complex for him to pick before the guards returned, he began looking for other avenues of access into the wagon. No luck; the hinges were riveted on and there were no visible vents. There was not a weakness on the whole wagon; it was obviously designed to transport a great treasure. He also knew that this slaver was not good enough to afford such a wagon. *If there is a slave inside, she is one the slaver was planning on selling for a true fortune. He is risking everything for this one. Definitely not one of the run-of-the-mill, dirty, abused slaves he normally carries*, he thought to himself.

He admired the quality of the wagon, but not for long. He'd already wasted too much time. He pulled out his lock picks and went to work again. It took him a while, but once he got the hang of holding the tumblers the picking went much quicker. Every once in a while he found himself grunting and shuffling around as he twisted his body to hold the picks and lock. Just as Airria had determined that he didn't have much time before the amount of shadow wouldn't be enough to make his retreat, the lock snapped with a loud pop.

Airria looked to see if anybody was around to hear the unnatural sound. He could see no one, but could hear the faint screams of the slaves who had been caught and were now being dragged back. Airria

10

knew he would have to hurry.

Before removing the lock he had to disarm two noise traps and one poison stinger. When the door was finally open he stood for a moment in awe. The inside of the wagon was plush velvet with padding everywhere. The light was beginning to stream in through small slits in the ceiling. In the faint light he could see a soft seat and even an empty, yet used, plush bed. *This looks like a coach for royalty*, he thought.

His eyes continued scanning the wagon until they caught hold of the most exquisite creature he had ever beheld. She had long, thick, red hair flowing down her strong and confident shoulders. Her eyes were like emeralds well set in a perfect face. The woman was crouching in the shadows of a corner, but her clean white slave dress stood out in the dim light of the morning.

The slave girl cowered for only a moment in the back corner and then jumped past Airria, crying out, "Stay away from me!" Airria turned to follow her and discovered the slaver standing in front of him trying to grab the girl. Airria quickly used the stick, which he had forgotten to use on the slaver's door, to club the slob. The fat man's cry of pain alerted the four sleeping guards, who came running to their boss' aid. Airria quickly rolled under one of the inner carts. He jumped up on the other side of the wagon and quickly looked around to see where his best escape would be. He could hear the slave boss yelling to the guards to get the girl. He could see her running from the guards as well as dodging the arms of the drunken guards returning with only two of the younger children.

Airria enjoyed the young woman's speed, mobility and her hourglass figure. What he admired most was how she used the drunken guards to distract the sober ones. She would get close enough to the drunken ones to make them reach and then she would swerve out of the way causing the drunken guards to smash into the sober ones. She seemed to think well under the pressure of her escape.

Airria made his way to the woods, shocked that the guards had completely ignored him. He smiled, thinking about the agility, determination and exceptional beauty of the girl. Moving through the woods he thought to himself, *this morning was a welcome distraction.*

11

For months his mind had been plagued with much weightier matters. Now it was time to make his way back to town.

****

It took him almost until midday to circle the barren area around the town and enter it from the other side. Then he made his way to his favorite place to sit and think, the Drunken Mad Man Tavern. The scent of ale and stench of vomit seemed to calm his nerves. This had been his father's favorite place as well. They had come here together for most of Airria's life. It still felt strange not to have his father with him. The ruckus inside helped him to feel a little more at home and let him know everything was normal.

As he took his seat he noticed something very unusual, there was a bard setting up. Bards never came to Tark-Ancia, known on the island as the Town of Chaos. The town was made up of mostly thieves and thugs. Bards normally wouldn't stop here, there just wasn't enough profit in it and it was too hard to sing or talk over the crowd. This bard, old and grey, didn't seem to care.

The bard stood on the splintered stage and began his tale. "Dragons, the myth of myths, the terror of dreams, the reality of true darkness..."

Airria used to love hearing stories of dragons, but after seeing one kill his father and uncle the stories just didn't measure up and were only real enough for a vague reminder. As the bard continued on Airria only half paid attention until he noticed this bard was telling a tale as few others had. He did not tell of the speed or strength of the dragon. He was talking of emotions and thought. They were feelings and thoughts Airria remembered from his encounter.

Airria looked around the tavern. For the first time that he could recollect the tavern was quiet. There was such emotion in the bard's tale, real feelings, not the typical melodrama. Airria began to shake, he could remember the fear; he could smell the darkness and heat.

He looked into the bard's eyes; there was something more. Airria finished listening intently to the bard, then went and offered to buy him a drink. "Your story, I find it very interesting that you told nothing of blades and armor, but only of fear and pain."

"That is how I learned it, boy," the bard smiled.

"I know the feelings and thoughts better than that. You told the story as if you'd experienced it," Airria responded.

"Experienced it?" The bard was still calmly grinning, but was now making eye contact with Airria. "Dragons are myths, stories of legend. Only children believe in them."

"I know that you know that they are not just fables. If you look closely in my eyes you will see I know dragons are real too." Airria was starting to lose his patience with the old man. Deep in his heart, he knew the bard was testing his belief.

"You really want to believe, don't you?" The bard's smile was now showing some teeth.

"I really wish I could go back to just wanting to believe, but I know they are real!" Airria put a strong emphasis on the "know" to punctuate his point and with the pain evident in his voice he said, "I am going to kill one."

"How old are you, boy?" asked the bard, taking a leisurely sip of ale, now paying more attention to the bustle of the bar than to the boy right in front of him. His rough boney fingers stroked his long, grey beard.

"Eighteen! That's old enough to fight!" Airria growled, putting his right hand on the hilt of his sword and standing, trying to use height for intimidation. It was surprising how effective this tactic usually was, considering his lack of bulk, but it didn't seem to be working on the bard.

"Calm down, boy. I can tell you little more than I have already." Taking another sip of ale, the bard allowed his annoyance to show a little. For a moment he stared into the fire.

"What do you mean, you can't tell me more?" Airria protested, his eyes flashed almost red in the mild firelight as if the rage in his heart were burning through them. He could feel his temperature rising. "The way you tell the story could only come from someone who had seen a dragon." The other people in the tavern didn't even seem to notice the disruption.

"No." the bard's fingers continued stroking his twisted beard, "It is just a story I heard. I will tell you where to find the man who told me; maybe he can tell you more." His grin was gone.

"Only a man who has seen a dragon first-hand could tell the tale with that kind of feeling and fear." Airria's fists clinched, his well-defined shoulders became rigid, showing the strength of his slender build. A wave of tension rippled down his frame, his worn-out deerskin trousers making it easy to see his muscles tighten down his thighs. Airria felt the emotion of the story and unwillingly recalled his feelings as he watched the dragon take his father's soul several months earlier. He remembered his mind screaming for him to get up, move, do something to help, but all he could do was sit by helpless, paralyzed with fear.

"The color of the dragon's eyes, the smell of her breath, the length of her claws and the blackness of her evil heart." The bard said as he let out a sigh of relief. As Airria began to relax, he continued, "There is only one man who can truly tell you about these things. His name is Jammar, the Light Bringer, a holy warrior from the Land of Ice. He is the only person to face an ancient Black Dragon in over a thousand years and live to tell the tale. This is the man you should seek. He now lives northwest of the Fire Mountain Pass, on the other side of the Great Forest, near a city called Droir. You must travel there for the information you are seeking." His gray eyes filled with doubt. "When you find him, if you still feel like you want to face a dragon, he will help you." Then he chuckled, "Besides, how would an old bard like me live though an experience like that?"

"Thank you for your time," Airria said as he stood, throwing a bronze coin on the table. After what seemed like countless months, night after night, watching his father's soul being torn from his body in his dreams and waking in a cold sweat, he finally knew of someone who might know where to find his father's killer. He strode out of the bar with determination. His intentions were to mount his massive gray steed and ride directly towards Fire Mountain Pass.

As he passed through the tavern doorway, something caught him just under the chin. A familiar voice came from his right, as he hit the ground. "I know that this isn't the first time you stole something from me." Henrik, the greasy, fat slaver from this morning's adventure stood over him, a gnarled tree branch in hand.

Rage burned in the slaver's voice as he continued, "You cost me an easy life for the rest my days, releasing that girl. You will repay the debt with your flesh." People in the tavern were beginning to notice the disturbance.

"Not if I have anything to say about it," the strong deep voice drew Airria's attention to a familiar and welcome sight; his cousin.

"Stay out of this. It doesn't concern you. This boy stole the most valuable slave I've ever come across," snarled the slaver as he spun around to see the man who had just spoken. His confident shoulders slumped as he recognized the famed mercenary, Joskin DeAveron.

Airria had to smile as he could see what was going on inside the slaver's head. The stories of Joskin, his cousin, had flooded through the town. It was said that a battle could be determined by which side he fought on. Yes, Joskin was not a person to trifle with.

The double-bladed head of Joskin's pole ax glistened in the light of the sun, the Dwarven-quality steel etched with the scratches of many battles. The haft reached from the ground to Joskin's shoulder. An armor gouged spike protruded out of the top of the ax.

"I'll make it my business. Don't touch that boy, or you will find your hand on the ground." Powerful shoulders rippled under worn, hardened leather shoulderguards as the warrior repositioned the weapon in his hands. Joskin was far less intimidating in his "casual wear"; a light leather vest, a knee-length leather strap kilt, hardened leather shoulderguards and shin guards, with soft leather boots. Every piece of his outfit was a blaring testament that the stories were more than bards' tales.

It had been a while since Airria had been struck and he'd forgotten how much it hurt. Slightly stunned by the slaver's blow, yet comforted by his cousin's presence, he pondered the situation he had gotten into for a girl, just this morning. She hadn't even thanked him. *I'm always doing that*, he thought. *I'm always getting into messes for pretty girls. Why do I do that?* Though not terribly shocked by his cousin's

15

return, Airria was surprised to see Joskin at that moment and was grateful for his cousin's timing.

Joskin had been away fighting yet another battle for a man he didn't know. His fame had spread to the point that when warlords would send for him they would send several gold coins (each worth a hundred bronze) in hopes of getting the contract before the competition.

"I don't want any trouble," whimpered the slaver, sweat running off his dirty, bald head and down his oily face as the afternoon sun beat down on him. Henrik had travelled through town enough to know he would need more men to fight this battle. "This boy took something that belonged to me and I'm just here to retrieve payment," the slaver said. He became more courageous in his justification and reached a fat hand toward the boy.

Two of the slaver's men came around the corner, swords drawn. Airria decided that with Henrik's back turned and all the attention on Joskin, it was a good time to stand up and be ready for a fight.

"Might I recommend you deal with me first," Joskin growled. His well-toned thighs flexed as he stepped within obvious striking distance of the slaver. A group had begun to gather to see the fight, like vultures waiting for their next meal to die.

The slaver muttered under his breath, "She was valuable, but not worth my life." Then he hissed at Airria, "This isn't finished, boy," and stormed off, beckoning the two shaking henchmen to follow.

"Thanks, cousin." Then to change the subject, Airria casually asked as he dusted off his backside, "Have you seen your mother since you got back?"

"Yes, she's doing fine." Joskin continued casually, "Let another slave girl go?" A hint of disapproval showed in his rich brown eyes. When they were younger it had become regular practice for Joskin to save Airria from such trouble.

"Joskin, it's evil to steal and sell girls like that. They should be free!" Airria said, angrily throwing his rusty-blond hair behind his shoulder.

Intentionally speaking down to his cousin, Joskin said, "My dear boy, when will you learn that it is the deities who decide what is righteous and what is evil, society then decides what is right and wrong and individuals decide what is good and bad. Now with that, I just gotta know, did you at least get a little something from this one?"

"Just a fat lip," Airria rubbed his sore jaw, a trickle of blood now showing where the club had hit him. He was glad to see Joskin. Joskin had been more of a big brother to him throughout his life. This time though he finally had a lead on where to start searching for the dragon and knew his cousin would not approve. "Well, I have some place to get to, so, I'll see you later."

Joskin grabbed Airria's arm to stop him. "Your mother asked me to come find you, see what you were up to. To make sure you weren't trying to track down that dragon." His face became much less serious and he added, "Besides I couldn't let you have all the fun." Joskin, though a finger length shorter than his cousin, had twice the shoulders.

"So you have come to join my expedition, eh?" Airria allowed a childish smirk to cross his face. "In that case, only if you can keep up." Quickly walking over to his horse he threw himself up to the saddle, turned and said, "If you want to come you'd better hurry, I'm leaving now." Then, kicking the animal in the ribs, he darted off.

When Joskin realized what was happening he ran across the street and jumped on his own steed, turned and raced after his younger cousin.

It didn't take long before Airria could hear the hoofbeats of his cousin's horse. Not only had Joskin had the opportunity to learn what made a good horse, he had the money to afford the best warhorses he could find.

"Keeping up has never been the issue. It is hard to follow someone as slow as you," Joskin yelled over the rush of the horses, slapping Airria's horse on the rear with the flat of his axe.

Together they raced through the dirty, twisted streets of town. People dodged out of the way of the oncoming charge then went on about their business as though this happened daily. Near the edge of town, Joskin's large bay warhorse easily jumped a small girl playing with sticks and a jug in the middle of the street. They continued out of the city, into a huge patch of bare land which circled Tark-Ancia and continued out until it reached the forest. There were only a few dead trees standing sparsely on the desolate ground and only mild ruts to signify the true path to the forest. The road did not become apparent until the two men were almost to the trees.

The rough, dark gray bark ran into the black-streaked leaves. Many of the local ruffians used the forest as a place to rob passing travelers. This was one of the reasons that this side of the nearby mountainous ridge was known as the "Dark Side" of the island.

A little while later, at a dusty little clearing, they decided to rest their horses. In a concerned tone, Joskin asked, "Why do you insist on this crazy pursuit? Isn't the loss of our father's enough strain on our mothers?"

"I know you can't understand, so I'm not even going to try to explain," said Airria. His mind wandered again to the night his father was killed. He could still see the look on both of their fathers' faces as the enormous creature ripped their souls from their bodies.

"It got my father, too, remember!" Frustration radiated from his face but was concealed in his voice. "You're not the only one that was hurt. Our mothers were hurt as well. If you keep going, you'll hurt your mother even worse." Joskin visibly tried to calm down by taking a deep breath.

"But I was there! I saw it all!" Airria could feel his heart harden and become icy, "The cruel way they were tortured and then how it pulled out that crystal and stole their souls." He could see a new level of concern form on Joskin's face but didn't really care at this point. "I saw the torment in their souls as it stroked the crystal like petting the thing gave that dragon an extra thrill and then it swept its hand over it making it vanish."

Airria had seen both of their fathers' agonizing demise. Worse than that, he relived it every night. Deep in his heart Airria couldn't stand the thought of any soul existing in the pain he had seen on his father's face. He didn't like to admit he had a big heart. "If you aren't going to help, then get lost!" Airria really did want his cousin's help. If nothing else, Airria wanted Joskin's company. They were not only cousins, but had been raised as brothers and best friends, so he quickly calmed his voice down to an almost playful tone. "If you'll come, you can have any treasure we find."

A female voice exploded from somewhere in the distance, "My clothes are just fine the way they are and they do not need your help!"

Joskin found the plea a welcome diversion from the argument and said, "Hey, what's that?" His relaxed tone told Airria that he was tired of arguing. Such a plea was not so uncommon in these woods. Usually they would let such a situation alone, it was just a part of living in the area. Airria's frustration melted quickly as he recognized the voice as the valuable slave girl he had freed that morning.

Joskin looked in the direction of the sound. These woods were filled with ruthless thieves, but Airria and Joskin had helped cut the bandit population down considerably while making trips from the nearby town to the Fire Mountain Pass. There wasn't a thug in the Dark Forest Airria feared. Airria and Joskin were often hired to give safe passage through the forest to wealthy merchants.

"No! Stay away!" The girl's voice shook, pride replaced by terror. A plea for life would have rung with less fear.

A glint of excitement reflected in Airria's eyes, "Let's check it out." Maybe this time she would be more grateful.

Chapter 2- Faith

Faith woke up to the sound of commotion outside, the predawn light beginning to glimmer through the slits in the roof of her wagon. The guards were definitely drunk again. However, it sounded as if some of the slaves were taking advantage of this and were escaping. The caravan must have made its way to Tark-Ancia, a town rumored to be without laws or peacekeepers. Henrik, the slaver, had complained the only road to the port on Ramsal Island ran so close to this town.

Realizing where they were, her mind raced with stories she had heard of a young man who rescued slave girls as the caravans passed this way. Some rumors claimed he took the girls for his own, adding them to his 'harem'. Others said he helped them escape in exchange for sex. While most of the other slave girls would gladly pay such a price to escape their captors it was different for Faith. Faith was still untouched. Even the devious slaver had afforded her privacy to change when she had been taken. The "dress" he had given her was far too small and tight for her comfort. She was used to most of her body being covered. The only reason she had agreed to put it on was to avoid the grubby and eager hands of the guards who would be 'helping' her.

While several of the slaves may actually escape this morning, Faith knew there would be no such luck for her. She knew the wagon maker well and had seen the lock used to "secure her safety" in the wagon. It was curiously akin to the unused prison cells of Droir, her home town. No, there would be no escape. There was one way in and only one key.

She thought how nice it would be to run away, run home back to her family and guard training. Her father had lost her to the slaver. There was nothing to be done about gambling with the life of your daughter if she was still underage. At seventeen, a beautiful daughter brought rich men. In her city, Droir, you did not dishonor your parents. Even though gambling was shunned, if things did not go your way you still paid your debts. Then, if you did not have the money or sufficient property, your family was used to pay the debt, however reluctant and repulsed you may be. The only way for her father to pay his debt was to let the slaver take her. She had later learned the slaver had cheated, but that would make no difference in the eyes of the council. Even if she managed to escape she now had nowhere to go.

The rattle of the lock surprised her back to reality. It was not the sound of the key, but the futile sounds of someone trying to pick the lock. She crouched in the corner breathless, wondering who would even try to pick such a lock, the sound stopped. She could hear someone walking around and inspecting the outside, then the lock picking began again. Eventually she heard the unexpected and sickening pop of the lock yielding to the meddling fingers. When the door suddenly cracked open, she saw a handsome young man peeking in with long, rusty blond hair fading into the scarce morning light. He looked slightly barbaric with his bare chest and cloak, like stories of bad men sneaking in to steal children.

How she wished she had some real clothes just then. She had wished as much since she had been required to put on her slave outfit. Even the dirty, worn-out dress her father had made her wear for farm chores would do.

She did not recognize the guy, but she had not seen all the immoral brutes that passed for guards yet. Of one thing she was sure, she was not going to be used as she had heard so many of the other girls were.

She hesitated only a moment then darted past the man. The slaver was right behind him, but she easily dodged his fat, slow hands. She had been training as a town guard before her enslavement. Making it out of the caravan would be easy with most of the guards drunk and scattered. She darted back and forth, zigzagging, using the drunken men to distract the sober ones; usually tripping them both up.

The wagons were on the edge of a strangely dark and intimidating forest. Even though the sober guards were faster and stronger than her, navigating the forest would be a feat of dexterity and her smaller frame would allow her to cut through the dense forest much more easily.

It was almost midday before she was able to put enough distance between herself and her pursuers to find a place to hide. She had never been so grateful for all the long hours of running and agility practice she had had to do as a guard.

It was funny to think that Droir even had guards. There was no crime and there had not been an invasion as far as anyone had known. Still, she had been training as an archer. Well, kind of training. She was the most naturally skilled archer anyone in the city had ever seen. She may have excelled at everything, but archery was like breathing. It came so naturally. Within the small space of only a few months she had been instructing other guards. Despite her extreme beauty the men, both young and old, were intimidated by her skill. They would say, "It is not the natural order for women to be more skilled at fighting than men."

She often wondered what life could be like on this side of the island. What little she had discovered today made her want to go home. Yet how could she return home? The city council would never allow her back. Not only was she an escaped slave, but she would unjustly be considered a harlot, as well as a disruptor of the peace. No, there was no way she could go back.

In the silence she sat for quite a while, contemplating her options. She had just decided to leave the island for a free port to get employ as a guard when she felt four strong hands, two on each arm, grab her and pull her to her feet. A rough looking man in tattered deerskin trousers stepped out of the bushes.

"There is a nice reward for you," a rough looking man with dirty, ratty hair said.

"She's too perty ta' just turn over!" the man holding her right side said. This one was half bald, scarred and only wearing a loincloth, if you could call it that.

The man at her left sounded torn, "She a'nt worth near as much if we bag her first."

The three thugs argued back and forth for quite some time, completely ignoring Faith's pleas. She struggled to break free of her captors, but their iron grip held tight. As the argument continued it became heated between the first and second, with the third switching sides often enough to add fuel to the argument. After awhile the man wearing the loincloth thrust her into the full grip of the other. "I'll settle this once and for all!" he exclaimed. The third began to laugh maliciously, clearly enjoying himself as he positioned to hold her arms from behind. The only man actually wearing trousers, which appeared to be enough to grant him leader status, weakly protested. The loincloth man grunted and pawed at her so hard she began to cry. She struggled, but the grip on her arms was too tight.

Faith was not going to fall victim to these men. Her quickly rising knee found its mark in the man's loincloth. She brought her foot down squarely on the foot of the man holding her. Though the knee to the groin was not as effective as she had anticipated, both injuries proved an adequate distraction for her to make an escape.

She darted in and out of the trees for the second time today, but these thugs didn't give a direct chase. One ran carefully behind her while the other two ran alongside, giving her only one path. Within a short distance she broke into a dirty little clearing, walled by bushes with three fist sized trees in the center acting as a palisade for three horses.

As she darted to untie the horses the men cut in behind her. The knots on the ropes were tied too tight for her to manage. The men surrounded her like a pack of wolves circling a deer. In her brief search she found nothing useful on the horses. As the men circled she watched for an opening. When she darted for freedom the man in trousers grabbed her by the arm. Using her momentum, he spun her around and launched her toward the other two, as though this were a well-practiced routine. She could not believe how fast they had her against a tree. While the uninjured man held her, the others untied and moved the horses to make room.

Shortly after the rustling sound of rummaging through the saddlebags stopped, her arms were pulled back tightly around the tree and tied. Her hands were bound first and then the rope was wrapped and tied up to her elbows pulling her back tightly against the rough bark. As she continued to struggle she could feel the blood on her wrists and back began to run. When her arms were secured, they stood just beyond her reach in front of her,

"Thank you for settling our disagreement," drawled the trousered man with a smile which made Faith sick. "You see, we were not sure if we should turn you over to the slaver or keep you for ourselves. Fortunately, you have shown that you are in need of some discipline. Because you offended us directly, we will gladly teach you your place."

Faith contemplated the distance closing between them. When he was close enough she kicked. He dodged as if it were all part of his plan. The man with the loincloth reacted just as quickly, tossing a loop around her ankle which he pulled around the next tree, spreading her leg out.

The third man carefully bent down to loop his rope around her other leg. She hopped, kicking at him. He also caught her foot and tied it around the tree on the other side, successfully suspending her from the trees with her legs splayed outward.

"You see," the leader continued, "we don't care for pain." His smile widened as he looked her up and down hungrily. "Let me correct that statement. We don't care to experience pain ourselves. We will, however, enjoy your experience."

Faith could feel the pull on her shoulders. The bark eating into her back and the ropes chewing into her arms and wrists and ankles provided her with all the experience she needed. "All right, so you got even. My shoulders and arms hurt tremendously. Is this not enough?"

The group laughed and the leader replied, "These ropes are just an introduction to the lessons we'll teach you. Understand, I'm the only one who likes it in front. When I'm done with you," his eyes again canvassed her body, "then the boys'll teach you a new type of pain."

Faith pleaded, "I understand there is quite a reward for me if I am untouched."

The leader ignored the comment and sneered out loud, "This dress covers way too much for me. I think it should be adjusted."

Faith, now in a total state of panic, tried hard not to show it. "My clothes are just fine the way they are. They do not need any help!" she yelled angrily.

All three men chuckled as if her fear and anger added to their entertainment. Enjoying Faith's sobs, the leader pulled out a small skinning knife. "These straps are in the way." he said as he slipped the knife under one of her shoulder straps.

Faith could feel the cold metal of the blade against her skin. As the man began to slowly pull the blade against the strap she screamed, "No! Stay away!" She could hear the shaking in her voice. The strap made a pop as it gave way. For the first time Faith was truly grateful the dress was so tight, as it kept the cloth from falling.

With her senses on edge, she wasn't sure if it was her shaking breath or if she was hearing rustles in the bushes, but she searched the edges of the clearing anyway. She didn't even dare hope that help would come. Suddenly she noticed the young man from this morning. He seemed to step out of nowhere.

It didn't matter what he demanded, it had to be better than what these thugs had planned. "If he helps me out of this, I will do whatever he wants," she promised in her mind. She tried not to show any excitement and hoped he would not just join in. As she felt the cold metal touch her shoulder she winced again and was instantly brought back to the hell facing her.

"Is this a game?" the handsome stranger asked playfully.

The leader did not flinch. "Yes this is a game, one we like to play ourselves," he started slowly lifting the knife's blade against the remaining strap.

"That's not fair! Why can't I join?" Airria taunted.

Faith breathed a small sigh of relief as the blade pressure backed off and slowly slid out from under the strap. The leader's face now showed his displeasure as he turned around. Even with all three men pulling out their daggers the young man kept his sword sheathed. The men began to form a semicircle around the boy and still he did not budge. He simply stood there with a joking grin ornamenting his face. She could not decide whether the boy was crazy or completely unaware of how serious these men were.

The leader spoke, "Airria, you never learn! This time I'll teach you right!"

When the men were within cautious striking distance of the boy, a huge double bladed ax flew into the clearing knocking one of the thugs to the other side of the glade. With unbelievable speed the young man drew his sword and slit another of the thug's throat and then blocked a thrust from the leader.

"I warned you what'd happen the next time I caught you threatening my cousin!" a deep voice exclaimed from a nearby thicket.

The leader's body went pale and his shoulders hunched. "Joskin, when did you get back?" The leader fidgeted, his eyes dropping to the ground as an extremely well-muscled, lightly armored man stepped into the clearing.

Undaunted, the muscular man the leader had called Joskin asked more calmly, "How should we do this?"

The leader started to straighten with a small burst of courage, "I think I have something here worth my offense." He said bowing and pointing to Faith. Though his body had almost returned to its natural shade, his face was still ghostly white.

"If I so much as see you again I will finish this!" Joskin threatened in a voice that made Faith shudder.

The leader took his cue, grabbed his steed and left. Faith looked at the two new men hoping they were not replacements for the terror she had just survived.

"Before we release you," Airria said, "I would like to introduce us. I am Airria DeAveron," he paused and motioned to Joskin, "this is my cousin Joskin DeAveron."

26

Faith nodded, still concerned, but feeling the adrenaline wearing off. Pain was shooting through her shoulders; blood was dripping from her wrists into her hands and she could feel the cuts she had up and down her legs from her running through the underbrush all day.

Airria used his sword to cut the ropes tying her legs. It felt so good to take the pressure off her arms she almost cried. She did not even mind Airria staring at her legs. Joskin walked behind her. His deep voice was much gentler as he spoke, "I wouldn't recommend you run away again."

"Are you going to take me back to Henrik?" she asked, her voice still shaky. She could just imagine her punishment when she got back.

Airria smiled a playful smile and looked into her eyes. "What do you think, cousin? Should we turn this lovely creature over to that disgusting ooze of a man?" He paused only for a moment, but did not receive a reply. "No, I think not. She's far too beautiful to belong to something like that."

She could feel Joskin's strong hands untie the ropes. When he was finished, Joskin handed her a cloak. By the look and smell of it, it had belonged to one of the thugs. It was extremely dirty and full of holes. Nevertheless she was grateful to have something to cover up with.

While she quickly wrapped it around her, Airria spoke up, "By the way you handled those guards this morning, I would guess you have played with weapons before. By the way you stand, I would guess you've not been a slave very long."

She smiled the best she could. The more she began to trust these two men, the more she could feel the strain of the day. "I was in training to be a town guard in Droir."

Airria looked excited, "Do you know Jammar the Light Bringer?"

She started to smile as she realized she had a little leverage, small, yes, but it would ensure her safety back to the other side, the safe side,- of the island. Or at least she hoped she did. She said slyly, "I do know Jammar. He lives on the outskirts of Droir. Would you like to meet him?" As she heard herself say the name of her lifelong tutor and friend she began to smile; she may not be able to return to her home, but maybe

Jammar would take her in. She would have a good life as his servant.

Airria responded very eagerly, "Yes! Will you take us?" His smile and excitement showed a touch of concern for Faith's well-being.

Joskin interrupted, "Whatever we are going to do, we'd best get started." His tone was calm but carried a hint of urgency.

Faith felt a little guilty taking the reins of one of the horses. After all, it was something that belonged to the thugs. However, considering the circumstances, she did not dare refuse. She followed the two men to their horses and pulled herself up as they did. Together they rode in silence.

Faith watched intensely as the two men moved forward as fast as their horses would walk. The forest was too thick with underbrush, too dense to run through on horseback. Now, out of the clearing and not running from people, she noticed it was as dark as it would be at dusk. With the canopy as thick as it was it could have been dusk and she would not have noticed.

It was a very long time before the canopy broke into another small clearing. It was far less dusty than the one she had been tied in, but even the dark green of the grass seemed to negate the diminishing light as the sun disappeared over the ridge of the ominous mountain range in the near distance.

This is the range which splits the island! This is the range I have to cross! She thought as she pulled her horse to a stop. Discouragement ran through her as she looked at the steep rocky face. *How do I get across?*

She had not noticed the men getting off their horses until she heard Airria reply to what she thought was an unheard question. "Trust us; you'll be able to see your home again." Airria's voice was playful and comforting, "We will show you how to cross the range."

Joskin was already digging a fire pit when she dismounted. Her legs hurt so badly from running and riding that she collapsed on the ground. Every muscle in her body hurt! She looked down at her legs and ran her fingers over several of the now scabbed scratches. The motion brought the pain and fear back. For some time she stared at the dry blood on her hands, running her fingers over the bloody rope burns on her

28

wrists and elbows. Her mind raced over the day's events, her escape from the slaver, her almost rape and even her rescue.

"They won't touch you again," Airria's voice pulled her back. She had not noticed the tears running down her cheeks, but could now see their streaks in the blood on her legs. She looked up at him. The humor of his eyes had been replaced with honest concern. He held out his hand, a small open box of salve in it. He smiled, "This should help some with the pain. Joskin picked it up the last time he left the island."

All she could muster was a dry, "Thank you," as she took the salve. She had no idea how long she had been crying and staring at her wounds, but she noticed a large pile of wood and a small fire with two large rabbits roasting over it. She looked around the clearing and up to the now star-lit sky. The sun had finished setting. There were two bedrolls on one side of the clearing behind where Joskin was sitting. On the other side of the fire there was a bedroll with an extra blanket on a smoothed out pile of leaves.

Airria offered a hand, "We thought you needed a better place, somewhere a little cleaner." Faith looked at it blinking. He continued, "We don't want those cuts to get infected."

She painfully stood. Leaning heavily on Airria, she was escorted to the blanket. She sat fairly hard finding the leaves a great comfort. Her muscles and wounds hurt terribly, but she was feeling numb inside after the events of the day. She sat there holding the box.

"Would you like me to put some salve on your back?" Airria asked. At first she defensively recoiled, causing Airria to take a step back. Then she remembered her promise, if they would get her away from those thugs she would do what they wanted. Even if they did not hear the promise, she felt obligated to comply. She nervously reached into her cloak and made sure the cut side of her slave dress still covered her breast. Her other hand slid the dirty cloak off, then reached for the remaining strap but was interrupted when Airria placed his cloak over her front.

"This cloak is much warmer," Airria smiled at her.

She looked up at him, grateful for the much cleaner and less hole filled covering. She leaned forward, nervously allowing Airria to put the salve on her back.

His touch was warm and gentle, no demands, no anticipation. His hands felt like those of a caring physician. He leaned near to her ear, "Don't worry. The only advantage I plan to take is to have you guide us to Jammar's house," he whispered. "You are safe and free to go after."

She could feel the relief wash down her from the words. She was glad he did not seem to enjoy her pain. Even though she could still see the desire in his glances, it was a relief to know he would not expect her to do anything she did not want.

When he finished her back, he handed the box to her and whispered with a slight chuckle, "For the sake of my promise, you should do your own arms and legs." She turned to watch him stand up with a jovial smirk on his lips, but a hint of nervousness in his eyes.

Joskin stood up and bowed courteously to her, "I'll take my leave." He turned to Airria, "Wake me up for my turn at watch."

Airria stood up as Joskin lay down. He also gave a courteous bow, picked up a metal plate she had not noticed Joskin had prepared and handed it to her. "Eat, then put the salve on your wounds. Get some sleep, you'll feel better in the morning." He then took up his post with his back to her.

She again appreciated the opportunity to keep her dignity intact and how they both honored her modesty.

The food was very good for trail food and the salve helped with the pain. When she was finished, she took one more look at the men and lay down. She was reveling in the security and warmth Airria's cloak brought to her as she drifted off to sleep.

Chapter 3-The Cave

Faith woke up to the sound of a sizzling rabbit breakfast. She slowly sat up enjoying the warmth of Airria's cloak in the cool morning air. She was surprised to realize how little stiffness there was in her joints and only a slight pink around her deepest wounds.

The horses had been saddled and both men's bedrolls were already packed. There was an air of excitement. For the first time since she discovered she was to be a slave, she felt reasonably normal.

"You look like you're feeling better," Airria said with a smile. "Are you ready to move on?"

Faith felt so normal she started to unwrap herself from Airria's cloak. When the cool air caught her, she was brought back to the events of the day before. She looked up at Airria and bashfully asked, "Do you mind if I hold on to this for a while?"

The chill was obviously making him uncomfortable, but nonetheless he replied, "It's warm enough for me without it. Hold on to it."

She smiled gratefully, then stood up and turned around and adjusted the cloak to make it more suitable for riding. When she turned back, her bed was already rolled up. She stood for a moment in amazement at how quickly the camp was cleaned up. "You have done this often?" she joked.

"A few times," Airria returned the jest.

Joskin rolled his eyes, but smiled and chuckled. After a moment he became more serious, "We have a full day's journey ahead of us. We'd best be going."

Airria offered to help Faith on her horse. She lifted her leg to his hands, placing her foot securely. The way he admired her leg made her feel uncomfortable. She trusted he would not touch her against her will, but she still did not like it. In an attempt to bury the feeling she asked, "Why do you want to meet Jammar?"

"I heard a story and wanted to confirm it," Airria answered. He was having trouble meeting her eyes.

"It is such a long way to go to confirm a story," she laughed, wishing she could tell if he was only nervous or just trying not to look at her.

"He's on a quest," Joskin laughed. Then he nudged his horse and started down the trail.

"A quest? How exciting," she giggled. "I will warn you there is nothing exciting on the other side of this mountain range."

"Oh, don't worry. He will find some excitement," Joskin jested.

"Of such I will trust you," she giggled back. She took the middle place in the line. "The question is how much excitement and how many others will be a part of it? What kind of excitement am I in for?"

"Dragon hunting!" Joskin blurted out from the front.

Faith laughed as she heard Airria groan behind her. "Dragon hunting? I'm sure I would know if Jammar was a dragon."

Airria did not answer for quite a while and Faith did not know what to say. She was relieved when he finally did speak.

"Will you be glad to get home?" Airria asked.

Now it was Faith's turn to be quiet. It seemed like forever that she watched the ground beneath her horse. Finally she let out a sigh, "I cannot go home."

"Why not?" Airria queried carefully.

"I was a slave. I can never return home," she said sadly.

"So? Why can't you go home?" Airria asked, truly confused.

Faith was silent, but Joskin answered for her. "There are a lot of social rules that you haven't learned. You've never been past this range. For that matter neither have I, but I've talked to some of the merchants we have guarded through this forest. I've traveled a fair bit. As strange as it is, on this island each separate city has very different cultures. Faith seems to come from a town that won't accept runaway slaves," he looked back at Faith for confirmation.

She nodded as tears started rolling down her cheeks. Hearing the confusion in Airria's voice, she knew that not everyone believed in such strict laws. Her parents did and they were the ones that mattered. She was relieved when Joskin changed the subject.

"As I understand it," Joskin said glancing over his shoulder, "each city on this island, even though they are so close, rarely have relations with each other." He paused only for a moment then continued, "Each town is also fanatical about their respective beliefs."

"Tark-Ancia is not fanatical about anything!" Airria laughed.

"At first glance, you're right," Joskin's voice was beginning to sound more like a schoolteacher than a warrior, "but you've traveled enough to see that Tark-Ancia is zealous about staying in a state of chaos."

Airria replied like a little brother trying to pick a fight, "Wouldn't chaos, by definition, not be fanatical?"

"Being a fanatic has nothing to do with chaos," Joskin had taken the bait. To Faith they sounded more like brothers than cousins. "You see, it seems to be the town itself that is fanatical. The people come and go. Many die; somehow enough survive to keep the town alive."

"The town is fanatical?" Airria laughed mockingly, "You make it sound as if the town had a will beyond the people in it."

"I know it sounds odd to someone of your limited travel, but it's the only thing that makes sense," Joskin sounded slightly frustrated. "Think about it. How many times have you ever traveled to another city? How many townsfolk have you personally killed?"

Listening to the debate Faith had to admit Joskin had a point. Even though her home was only a couple days travel from Gentrail, the nearest town, she had never been farther from home than Jammar's place. Jammar was the only outsider. Other than merchants and a couple of

34

bards, she had never seen anyone other than Jammar who had been out of town and Jammar lived on the outskirts of her hometown.

Airria interrupted Joskin's lecture. "Hey, I only ever killed anyone in self-defense!" he protested

"Why get defensive?" Faith asked. "Isn't it all just a part of your culture?"

"Mom," both men said together.

"She is not from Tark-Ancia?" Faith queried.

"The story of how our mothers came to Tark-Ancia can only be rightfully told by them." Joskin answered her question in a gentle yet serious tone. "This story is as personal to them as yours is to you. If you meet them someday, you can ask them."

Faith was trying to avoid talking about herself, so she could understand how personal the story could be. She still wanted to divert the conversation away from herself so she decided to ask, "How often have you traveled this path?"

Airria answered, "This is the trail we bring single wagon merchants on when they come. It takes a little longer, but we don't have to work as hard. The caravan merchants have to travel the main road, but they usually bring their own escort."

"And how often do you make the trip?" Faith continued.

"Once or twice a month for the past few years," Airria answered. "When Joskin's gone I travel it on my own. We rarely meet anyone this close to the mountain range until we get near the main road.

Joskin added, "We also camp in this area regularly."

"So we will get back to the main road?" Faith felt a little nervous about the prospect. "Will it not increase the chance of bandits, or even of running into Henrik again?"

Faith could hear the smile in Airria's voice, "Don't worry. We won't let anything happen to you, at least until you get us to Jammar's place.

For the rest of the morning and well past midday the conversation was mostly Airria and Joskin telling Faith about their adventures on the island together. Airria was much more vocal. From time to time they would tell a story that would embarrass the other. Faith even encouraged it by asking as many questions as she thought was appropriate, but for the most part she was content to just listen. It was extremely fascinating to her how different their lives had been from hers.

The conversation quit abruptly when Joskin stopped his horse to look at something. It seemed to Faith as if he were looking at a bush or a caterpillar or something relatively insignificant that she could not see. After a moment he dismounted and began to kick methodically at the ground. Eventually he uncovered the edge of a pit. He got down on his belly and looked inside. He got up without a word; his eyes crept out to the forest floor and into the woods. Finally he said something, "They're getting better."

Airria chuckled and said in a half serious tone, "Should we set it off and see what comes running?"

"It's dangerous to just leave it," Joskin replied. "I also don't like the fact that they are getting better and each trap we spring gives them reason to improve."

"Then we go around and find a new route?" Airria questioned.

"Yeah, I think on the way back we can find a new route," Joskin replied. "For now we'll have to backtrack a bit and walk through the forest.

Though Faith did not know for sure what they were talking about, she guessed that bandits would leave traps from time to time to catch them and the merchants they were escorting. She was tempted to ask if this was the case, but she felt it was an inappropriate time.

Together they rode back a ways then dismounted and left the trail. The underbrush, fallen branches and trees were much more difficult to get through with the horses. The sun had vanished into the thick canopy. Soon there was no underbrush, only fallen logs and sticks. They moved on, following any trail they could find. It was rough going but eventually they came out into a clearing next to the mountain range. There were little outcroppings that would work as a shelter, small and cozy. They could see the trail; the one she supposed they had been traveling on. She felt some relief just to see a real trail.

The men jumped off their horses and tied onto a log which at first glance looked like it had fallen in place, but further inspection

36

showed it was tied in place. As she was tying her own horse, Faith overheard Joskin talking to Airria, "That trap was meant to take us out of the way and capture her."

"What do you mean?" Airria asked.

"They knew we would be protecting her front and rear. There was a pit for me and a log for you. They had a net overhead for her," Joskin sounded somewhat worried.

Airria replied with less concern, "Are you sure you're not just being paranoid? I mean, we're the only ones who travel that trail and that's how we guard the merchants."

"Maybe, maybe not," Joskin sounded unconvinced, "either way keep an eye out for a better cave while you're hunting.

Airria nodded to Joskin then turned to face Faith, "I'll return soon with your dinner, m' lady," with an elaborate bow he disappeared into the thick brush.

Faith looked around for some way to help, but Joskin looked like he had things so well in hand she did not know what to do, "Is there something I can do to help?"

"Find some wood. But do me a favor, don't wander far," Joskin smiled at her.

She smiled and started up the trail she thought they would be traveling in the morning. Once back in the thick forest it was not hard to find wood, it was everywhere! It was nothing like the well-manicured and beautifully organized forests her father had taken her camping in. The wood here was dark, streaked and very heavy for its size. The wood she was used to gathering was lighter and much easier to break.

She was glad to be alone for a bit. She took some time to check on her wounds from yesterday and also the new wounds she had acquired today. The travel through the thick branches had left many new cuts and scrapes, but the ones she had rubbed the salve on were completely healed. Not even a hint of pink.

The more she wandered around the forest the more she thought she could see thugs around every tree. She really wished she had her bow. It would also be nice to have some real clothes, not that she was not grateful for Airria's cloak, but she would really like to have some actual protection for her legs.

She was pulled out of her thoughts by a distant crashing sound. She hurried back to camp to see Joskin standing, ax in hand and ready. Her lungs felt like they were frozen when Joskin whirled around on her as if he were going to hit her, but relaxed when she saw the recognition in his eyes and turned back to the sound.

A moment later Airria came crashing into the clearing. "I found a better place!" he exclaimed.

Faith almost laughed when she realized the sound had been Airria racing back to camp. She also wondered if he had heard her.

"Are you sure it's not trap?" Joskin asked curiously.

"Well, it's much more defensible than here and far enough away that anyone who knows us will have a hard time finding us." Then Airria darted back in the direction he had come from.

Joskin and Faith followed as quickly as they could. Airria stopped in front of a small cave just big enough for all three of them to be comfortable with a small fire. The walls of the cave were rough but clean. "Come on," Airria said.

Together they quickly threw together a camp. Joskin collected rocks into a circle while Airria and Faith gathered wood. Gathering wood went very quickly as it was a very short trip to get a lot of fallen branches. When the wood was gathered, Airria went hunting while Faith went to get the horses. By the time she returned both Airria and Joskin were sitting next to the fire cooking some rabbits. A bed of leaves was made for her in the back. They even had a rock for each of them to sit on around the fire.

She found separate trees to tie the horses to and turned to thank the men for all they had done. When she turned around she froze as she noticed an opening in the back wall. Both men had their backs to it.

"What is it?" Airria asked.

She could only bring herself to point, with a squeaky gasp as torches lit in the opening revealing a hallway. Both men slowly turned around, bringing their weapons to the ready.

Airria edged forward, carefully looking around the frame of the new opening. As he advanced, so did Faith until she was between the men.

"No edges?" Airria said curiously. "If there was some sort of sliding door, there should be edges, ridges or spaces. It is solid and there is a hallway. It's definitely handmade. It looks like the Dwarven halls you were telling me about." He continued forward to a corner. When he peeked around the edge he dropped his sword. He stepped around the turn in a hypnotic daze. Faith tried to hurry forward to see what was going on, but felt Joskin's strong hand grab her shoulder. She looked back to have Joskin pull her behind him. He cautiously advanced and peeked around the corner then proceeded into the room. Faith was close behind.

It was a room, perhaps a little like a tomb, with no windows. The walls were decorated in low relief depictions of battles and fights. It was filled with weapons of varying types and sizes. Faith, along with Joskin, watched as Airria made his way around the room admiring the weapons. Most of the weapons looked to be plain but in excellent condition. There were several fancy axes and swords as well. Airria ran his finger over each one individually until he came across one so unusual he picked it up. Faith was no expert on swords or craftsmanship, but this one took her breath away. "May I see it?" Faith asked. When he hesitated she added, "You will get it back. I only want to admire the craftsmanship." Airria reluctantly relinquished the sword. The first thing Faith noticed was the power she felt just touching the sheath, which was glossy white with golden vines decorating the edges. The hilt was the neck of a dragon, white with scales so real she expected them to move. The pommel was the smooth head of the dragon with a white gem in its mouth. The cross piece was an equally perfect depiction of dragon wings, though she thought they were proportionally small for the dragon, they were of perfect size for the sword. In the center, where the wings crossed the hilt and on either tip of the wings, there were gems matching the one on the pommel. When she pulled it, she saw the rest of the dragon's spike free body continuing down the blade. It almost appeared as if the dragon were alive, the tail slowly swishing from side to side of the blade. The blade itself was smooth with elegant patterned lines edging it and seemed to be forged of the most intense fire. It was fascinating to see the white dragon body on the blade. It seemed so alive yet left no ridges on the blade.

Dragons were folklore and legend for most, but she had spent enough time at Jammar's to believe they were a real part of the world history. All the dragon statues and tapestries Jammar had around his place, as exquisite as they were, they could not rival the artistry of this sword.

She handed it back to Airria, half expecting him to snatch it from her. He took it as if receiving a delicate gift from royalty, though the respect seemed to be more for the sword than her. He smiled at her and continued to admire it. Soon he pulled it and began testing its usability.

She turned her attention to Joskin. He was running through some drills with a large double bladed ax. The ax itself was, by shape, very unremarkable. It was similar in design to the ax Joskin had been wielding, except the whole ax was one piece. There were no frills or fancy decorations on it. It was quite remarkable though, by color; it was violet, with black and white marbling. The haft seemed smooth and yet as Joskin swung it it seemed secure in his hands.

She watched the men for a while, they were like children. She could not bring herself to take any of the weapons, but she was not going to say anything to them. After a while she went to the front of the cave and sat by the fire. She pulled out the salve and began rubbing it on her new cuts and bruises. The salve felt good, which allowed her to get lost in thought for a while. When she looked up both Airria and Joskin were watching her. She promptly covered up her legs and asked uncomfortably, "Do you like your new weapons?" Then she noticed just behind them. She almost fell into the fire as she tried to get up and back away. The wall was back to the way it was before, solid, no cracks to indicate there was ever a door.

Airria turned around and started to press his hands on the wall. Joskin watched Airria for a moment and then went to sit down by the fire. His simple words brought little comfort, "If they wanted to kill us we would be dead. If they wanted to trap us we would be trapped."

Airria muttered, "B-but why?"

Joskin replied with concern in his voice, "I would guess they want to hire us for something."

Airria was obviously still panicked, "Hire us for what?"

Joskin answered, "Don't know, but I'm sure whoever it is, they will let us know when the time is right for them."

Airria was starting to move toward the fire, "I'm not a mercenary for hire to the highest bidder."

Faith could see Airria's words cut into his cousin. She had not known him long, but he seemed honorable and as respectful as possible. She also knew he was a mercenary, but seemed to her his acts were not merely for the cause that sent the most money, after all, the most money would have been taking her back to the slaver or selling her himself. They were both good people. Thinking about this, she said, "Whatever it is; whoever wants your help, you will have a chance to accept or reject what they have to offer." She smiled at Joskin and turned to Airria and gently added, "Not all mercenaries fight for the biggest pile of silver. Sometimes their price is more than money can bring."

Airria gazed into the fire for a moment then gave Joskin an apologetic look and offered to take the first watch. Joskin nodded at him and went to his bedroll. Faith did not feel tired, but she could tell Airria wanted to be alone. So she went and lay down.

For awhile she admired Airria's physique, he was not as muscular as Joskin, but somewhat better looking. She realized that she was looking at him the way he did when her cloak slipped. She rolled over and tried to put the last few days out of her head. So much had happened to her, so much in her life was going to change....So much had changed. What bothered her most, other than the thoughts of her new well-built friends, was that she had a feeling her friend and lifelong mentor, Jammar, knew something about what was going on. As she was drifting off to sleep she thought she saw a strange creature in the shadows; half bull, half man. She quickly dismissed it as paranoia and fell into a restless sleep.

Chapter 4-Hard Roads

      Airria's mind raced. He had spent the day following the most beautiful woman he could imagine with a determination to protect her and help her. He knew the slaver wouldn't stop following him this time. Even more plaguing was the fact that someone had manipulated him and gotten the whole group into this cave.

      Whoever had directed them here knew them well enough to understand how they would react to the trap and how he liked to hunt in order to bring them to the spot. *How many times have Joskin and I passed here? Why haven't we seen this cave before?* he asked himself.

      Still more intimidating was the fact that whoever had brought them here had power to remove the back wall and replace it without him knowing. This person had given him his choice of the most amazingly crafted weapons he had ever seen. According to Joskin this mage, as Airria supposed, was expecting him to do something. Airria pondered on this for some time. He had no idea how long the thoughts rattled around in his head, but eventually the sound of Faith's restless sleep pulled him out of it. He was about to check on her when he thought he saw something, a huge creature with bull-like horns and head with a body much larger and more muscular than Joskin's. It was only visible for a moment and then was gone.

Airria jumped to his feet and pulled his new sword. The creature was nowhere to be seen. He began to wonder if he had really seen anything or if he had imagined the whole thing.

When he heard a rustle behind him, he spun around. It was Faith again, she was tossing and turning. He really couldn't blame her. The last few days must've been hard on her. She'd become a slave, been chased, almost raped and now had to depend on two strangers to take her back to a home she didn't believe wanted her anymore.

She turned again and the cloak slid off her. For a short while he sat admiring her long athletic legs. His eyes moved up her body admiring the perfectly firm yet womanly shape and tone.

His eyes stopped on her face. She had a strong, yet feminine jaw; full, yet well-defined lips; a smooth, yet perfectly curved nose; and, though he couldn't see them now, he could remember the emerald green of her eyes. Tonight though, her eyes showed she was troubled. He badly wanted to chase the trouble away from her. It was not like he knew her well. Actually, he had just met her, yet he wanted to protect her. He did enjoy the sparkle of her eyes and the curve of her lips when she smiled.

She was different than any of the girls he had ever met. He could tell by her posture and the way she always spoke like the bards and scholars he'd met that she was educated and proper. She was strong-willed, even when she was painfully tied up she didn't submit. She had morals. Even when the room of weapons was open before her and both he and Joskin were taking weapons she refrained.

As the thought of her moral standing entered his mind he thought she would likely not appreciate him ogling her. Besides she was starting to look cold. He got up and pulled the cloak back over her. He wanted one more good look at her face so he gently brushed the auburn hair out of her eyes. He half expected her to wake up but instead some of the trouble left her eyes. He smiled and turned back to his post. Joskin was sitting up in his bed roll with approval on his face.

"She is a very beautiful woman," Joskin said softly.

"Yes she is," Airria replied.

"She's not like the girls you're used to," Joskin sounded concerned. "She is a better person than both of us combined. I have seen

43

only a few women like her and none so beautiful. Be careful what you do." Airria was about to explain his actions, but Joskin cut him off. "Is it time for my watch?"

Airria understood Joskin was talking about more than he was saying and that it would take a while for him to figure it out. So, he only responded to the last question, "I'm not tired yet. I'll wake you up when I'm ready."

Without another word Joskin rolled over and laid back down, leaving Airria to his thoughts. He looked back down at his new sword and started thinking about the day's events again, especially the cave and the power he felt when he picked up the sword. Though he had enjoyed the feeling, he had never worried so much. Even in a place that was as well protected and hard-to-find as this was. And why shouldn't he worry? He'd never even heard of anyone who could make a doorway disappear or reappear without a sound.

Even more difficult to accept was the belief that someone this powerful could want anything of him. Airria had also seen the treasure in that room. He could feel power emanating from all of it. The sword he had picked didn't seem to be made of metal. It was lighter in his hand than softwood, yet he knew that he would be able to cut through a leg sized tree with little effort. What could such a powerful being want him to do so badly that he would offer such an exceptional item as payment?

Nothing more than what you are setting out to do, an inaudible voice whispered in his head. He thought it was his own mind until he realized that the words did not follow his own thoughts.

He drew his sword, waiting for someone in robes or a pointy hat to appear before him.

Do not worry; I will help you, as long as your intentions and actions are pure, the voice continued.

"Who are you!" Airria exclaimed out loud.

I cannot speak out loud and I promise other people will believe you crazy if they see you talking to your sword, the sword said. Airria heard a chuckle in his thoughts.

Who are you? Where do you come from? How can a sword talk? Airria queried in his mind.

You will soon learn. For now, just know you are not the only one who wishes to see you succeed. And do not worry-- I will not interrupt your thoughts unless it is an emergency, the sword finished.

None of the thoughts Airria directed towards the sword the rest of the night got an answer. By the time the sunlight began creeping over the forest he began to believe he had imagined it.

Joskin got up. He stretched and said," I'm glad to have my sleep, but you need some rest, too."

Airria smiled wearily at his cousin. Joskin had always taken care of him and had been even more protective since their fathers had died at the hand of an ancient Black Dragon. "Sorry. I kind of got lost in my thoughts."

Joskin asked, "Anything you want to discuss?"

Airria replied, "Just a lot to think about." He began stroking his sword.

"Don't worry about who wants to hire us or what they want," Joskin comforted. "We will have the chance to accept or reject any offers."

"I know," Airria said as he ducked out of the cave. His concerns were more about what the sword had said. He knew in his heart he would not get a good night's sleep until he killed the dragon or was dead himself. Part of him was glad that someone influential enough to give him such an exceptional weapon would be on his side. Part of him was concerned that such a powerful being wouldn't be willing to face the dragon himself. He didn't want to burden his cousin any more and wasn't sure what he could tell Joskin. Airria smiled his most comforting smile, "I had better get some breakfast."

As Airria walked to check the traps he'd set the night before his mind raced. The thought of avenging his father helped him feel better for not being able to help his father. Being on this quest helped him sleep a little at night, but knowing that others were counting on him to succeed made the whole thing less personal.

These thoughts raced around in his head as he collected the rabbits his traps had caught and disarmed the ones that hadn't been successful. Without thinking he began to wander back to their old camp site. The sound of unfamiliar voices pulled him out of his thoughts. He crept to the edge of the clearing. The slaver was there. He had brought his entourage of what Henrik would call his elite guard. There were two others with them that Airria didn't recognize. One was in black leather with a long black cloak and sitting atop a wolf that stood as tall as a warhorse. The other wore black robes and held a black staff. He was mounted upon a tiger that was just as tall as the wolf. Both had leather bracers with an insignia Airria couldn't make out. After observing them for a few moments Airria realized that the two new men couldn't be working for the slaver as they were ordering Henrik and his guards around.

The group seemed to be looking for tracks. Panic crept into Airria's mind as he remembered they had not covered their tracks; they had been too distracted to even think of it. He glanced around to start covering the trail to the cave. He was amazed to see that even he couldn't see their tracks.

Eventually the slaver and his allies headed back on the trail.

Airria breathed a sigh of relief when the last one disappeared back into the forest. He quickly yet stealthily hurried back to Joskin and Faith. Joskin already had the fire going. Airria tossed Joskin the rabbits. In his heart Airria was grateful his cousin could make a fire so well that no smoke could be seen. He was trying hard not to let his urgency show as he helped Joskin skin and prepare the rabbits because he didn't want to alert Faith to the trouble behind them.

The rabbits were sizzling over the fire when Faith woke up. Even with her hair in a ratted mess and red lines across her face, her smile stole the worry out of Airria's mind. It amazed him that anyone could inspire such peace in him. He knew he would already do everything he could to help. Except, that is, stop his pursuit of the dragon.

"You look distracted," Faith's angelic voice pulled his thoughts back to the camp.

Airria smiled his best smile and replied, "I didn't sleep well last night, still a little nervous about the cave." Though he was embarrassed to admit he was nervous, he would be more embarrassed to admit she distracted him so.

46

"Didn't sleep at all," Joskin stated with a hint of frustration.

"I've got a lot on my mind," Airria responded, trying not to let the defensiveness he felt show through.

Faith thanked both of them for breakfast. While she ate Airria prepared the horses.

Joskin asked, "Are we in a hurry this morning? No one should know we're here."

Airria shrugged. "It's a long trip up the switchbacks to Smandler."

"I guess we could make it that far," Joskin said.

Airria allowed a little urgency to show through. "I don't think we want to spend the night at the base of the road." He hoped it was enough for Joskin to notice, but not enough to panic Faith. "The slaver is quite a bit upset with me and is still looking for Faith."

Immediately Airria knew he had failed as Faith stopped eating and came over to help him finish getting horses ready, an expression of distress marring her face. Joskin took the hint and began to clean up.

Together they pushed through the forest. There were no paths, only small deer trails too small for the horses. Often they had to go around fallen trees or jump small logs. The horses were well lathered by the time they emerged onto the main road.

Faith stopped her horse in the middle of the road and stared up the slope. Airria understood her awe. The difference was he knew the ride was even more daunting than it looked. The switchbacks were only slightly wider than a wagon. At the bottom the rock was smooth and worn; only the most sure-footed horses could climb it without trouble. At the top the rock was covered in ash; the journey was dangerous on a rested horse and they would have to make the trip on tired animals.

"If we are going to make it alive the horses will need to rest for a bit," Joskin said.

Faith had a nervous look on her face but said nothing.

"Don't worry, the slaver will have to stop here for the night," Airria said, trying to reassure Faith. "Only someone with a death wish will try to bring a wagon up this in the dark."

They all got off their horses and let them graze in the clearing.

Together they sat down and ate some of the rations Joskin had brought. The jerky and cheese tasted good after the hard day. Airria wanted to take a nap but was afraid to close his eyes. He was afraid of resting too long and allowing the slaver to catch up, or of having to finish the trip in the dark. Even more he was afraid of his dreams. Ever since he had witnessed his father's death he had been forced to relive the tragedy in his dreams.

Without thinking he got up and began brushing his horse with a clump of grass. The motion helped him forget his troubles for a short while.

Faith began rubbing her own horse. Airria began brushing slower as he watched Faith work. He became so distracted that he almost forgot what he was doing.

"We should be going if we're going to try to make this trip," Joskin's voice pulled Airria back to the task at hand.

After checking the saddles Airria insisted that Faith take his horse. She reluctantly agreed and the three headed up the road.

The switchbacks were every bit as bad as he remembered and the horse he was on was not as sure footed as he was used to. The beast was far less careful than his own steed. He knew he could handle the trail even on this inferior horse. He was not sure how Faith would do, though he was not happy with this horse it was better for him to be on it than for Faith; even if Faith did look uncomfortable on his horse.

The group stopped well over halfway up the slope. The horses were thick with lather. The horse Airria was riding stumbled, almost throwing both of them off the edge. The forest floor looked like a patchwork carpet with the ocean stretching into the distance. The main road was like a snake stretching out through the forest whenever they caught a glimpse of it through the trees. There was only one little caravan on the entire stretch. Even at this distance the squeak of the wagon wheels could be heard and by the look on Faith's face it was clear she could tell it was Henrik.

Airria wondered if the slaver could see them on their perch or hear what they said.

Joskin dug into his saddlebags and pulled out some strips of cloth. "Wrap these around your face," he said, handing the strips to the others. "Until we are in town the air will be hard to breathe." He said this more for Faith's benefit than for Airria's. Airria had been to Smandler several times, but it made him feel a little more secure to have Joskin worry about him.

Joskin pulled out masks for the horses too. The two warhorses allowed him to put the mask on. The third, the one they had acquired from the thugs, protested; throwing his head and squealing. In the end all the horses were muzzled.

Airria looked up warily, "Hope the rest is enough to get us to the top of the ridge." He knew the warhorses had the strength, but had his doubts the smaller horse could make it. Looking back down the slope, he was even more certain the slaver would stop at the bottom. With cautious confidence he mounted and followed the other two. The forest floor was already dark and storm clouds were moving in as the steep slope and switchbacks tapered into a gentle curve. The ash was over the horses' hooves. The smell of sulfur was almost unbearable. Worst of all, the horse Airria was riding was barely able to lift his own hooves.

Raindrops started to fall as they began crossing the bridge outside of town. The heat from the flowing river of lava evaporated the dark droplets as quickly as they hit the surface. The coolness of the rain made crossing the bridge bearable. The horse Airria was on was too tired to care about either the rain or the bridge. Faith slowed down only a moment to admire the river and then moved on.

Once across the bridge, they entered a pocket or bubble where the rain fell clear onto the ash free ground. Airria was excited to be inside the magical barrier. The magic was the only thing that made this town livable. It always amazed Airria how this place could survive. With Joskin's theory about the island and towns being alive and magically sustained the town's survival finally made sense.

The stable master had a serious look of disapproval on his face when they entered the stableyard. The warhorses looked extremely tired. The third horse looked dead on its feet and nearly tripped on the flat ground. The master came out to chastise them for pushing their horses so hard, but before he opened his mouth Joskin flipped him a bronze coin, a

49

good week's wage for peasant labor.

"That is for the care of our horses," Joskin smiled. "Feed and other stabling fees will be paid in the morning."

"That one won't be ready to move on by morning," the master protested, pointing to the horse Airria was riding.

Airria looked at his purse; all he had was two copper coins. That would be enough to cover the fee for his horse, but only for the night. He looked at his cousin who seemed to understand.

"Do you have a fresh horse we could trade?" Joskin asked.

"I have three good saddle horses, but it would take more than this half-dead creature to get me to part with any of them," the stable master replied.

"Then care for the horse tonight and on the morrow we will discuss the appropriate fee."

When the group was satisfied the horses and tack were secured and being properly cared for they headed to the inn. They were greeted at the door by a jolly-looking man who welcomed them excitedly. Airria and his cousin had always been generous and the innkeeper had always taken good care of them in return.

The innkeeper called to his wife who brought two plates filled with thick stew and heavy bread. She set them on the corner table and turned to address the men. Her mouth opened, but nothing came out while her eyes scrutinized Faith. She finally spoke, "This is different."

Her husband looked at her as if to warn her not to offend their clients, but Airria stopped the innkeeper by saying, "You're right. This is the first time we are escorting someone all the way across the island."

The innkeeper's wife looked from Airria to Joskin suspiciously, "And how is she paying for such a service?"

The innkeeper and his wife had known Airria and Joskin for many years. They were like the aunt and uncle the men wished they had. Airria knew the tavern-maid, Lorinda, was not usually so nosy nor insistent on courtesy. Still she had always wanted what was best for the boys. Lorinda knew the town the boys grew up in and the reputation the men there had.

Airria smiled big, "Information! You know we'd never take

advantage of a damsel in distress."

"Hmmm," was her only reply to the men, but they knew by the twinkle in her eyes that she believed them. She turned to Faith and asked if she could get her something.

"I have no money," Faith smiled sweetly at Lorinda.

Airria spoke before the tavern-maid could say anything, "Put it on our tab." He looked at Joskin who rolled his eyes, but nodded.

The innkeeper ran a frustrated hand over his dark bald head as his wife led Faith out of the room. When they were clear of earshot the innkeeper apologized for his wife.

Airria smiled at him, "It's all right. Given the state of Faith's clothes and her beauty I understand your wife's suspicion."

"You mean you really are just escorting her for no pay?" The innkeeper asked.

Joskin nodded and the innkeeper rocked back on his heels. He got a look of admiration in his eyes and continued, looking at Joskin. "Your cousin freed a slave like that and has not taken advantage of her?"

Joskin laughed as Airria blushed and tried to think of something to say. Until now whenever he had freed a slave girl she had offered herself to him. The slave women were used to it and hadn't seemed to mind.

The innkeeper slapped both men on the shoulder and then went into the back room. As the men began to eat they could hear the innkeeper call for his wife. She warned her husband to stay and tend to the inn and for him to make a plate for Faith.

Once Faith finally entered the room with the innkeeper's wife she had changed into a lovely, plain peasant dress. The chest and hips were tight as the dress was made for someone more petite, but she looked far more comfortable than she had before. Her hair was pulled back in a ponytail and her face and hands were washed.

Airria didn't notice his jaw drop when she walked into the room. Faith blushed, "Lorinda said she would loan it to me until I can get some better fitting clothes."

The tavern-maid was standing in the kitchen door with a motherly warning across her face. "I'll make sure the seamstress is open bright and early in the morning so you can get her some real clothes."

Joskin smiled at Airria, "Looks like the adventurer treasury on this trip is one big expense." His words were filled with jovial sarcasm. Then he turned to the maid and said, "She will have everything she needs."

Faith blushed again and quietly sat to eat.

They ate together and were given all three rooms in the inn. Airria was a little sad as the others went to their rooms. He had enjoyed having them around when he couldn't sleep, but was glad his cousin would get a good night's rest tonight.

Chapter 5-Bad Dreams

Airria was a little sad to be away from his companions, even if it was only for the night. He felt alone. He often wanted to be by himself to think, but had found peace in having Joskin around. Joskin had been a protector and a mentor even before their dads' deaths. This protection had always given Airria a sense of security. Even knowing his cousin was two rooms away didn't help him feel safe tonight.

Faith was a welcome distraction. She was very nice to look at. More pleasurable perhaps, was that her questions over the last few days had reminded him of happier times. He was able to remember the wonders and pleasures of his youth.

Unfortunately, he was also reminded of his dad's death. He was tired of remembering his dad. He especially hated seeing his dad's torment every time he closed his eyes. He hadn't had a good night's sleep since that event.

In an attempt to drive the negative thoughts from his head he decided to concentrate on the rain outside. The pitter-patter of the drops on the wood shingles and shutters created a rhythm of peace and renewing. He closed his eyes and made himself see the rain falling, washing the earth. It took some time, but eventually he pictured himself standing in the downpour. He could feel the rain washing the pain from him. Now he was peacefully alone.

In time the peaceful drumming faded into the bitter crackle of a fire. The tranquility he had surrounded himself with blew away on a hot breeze. He opened his eyes in a panic and found himself in the dark forest next to a clearing, near the mountain range.

It was a place he knew well. It was almost a day's ride from Tark-Ancia. No one lived nearby. His dad and uncle had been coming here for months to test potions from a black leather-bound book they had stolen from a dark robed traveler. This night's experiment was supposed to bring them great power and knowledge.

Airria had overheard them talking about their plans to try it. Their women had futilely tried to change their minds. Airria was not supposed to be there.

They had ordered some special Black Wood through a merchant. This was unusual, they never ordered anything. They had stolen a black, scale-shaped plate from the same traveler from whom they had stolen the book. They were preparing sacrifices of various animals.

As they ran back and forth getting everything ready Airria sat in a bush and watched. He was filled with a horrible sense of dread and wasn't sure why.

Even the stars and moon seemed to sense what was coming as they hid behind rumbling clouds. The trees seemed to bend away as the flames of the raging fire faded from their bright orange-red light to an abysmal black. At some point the fire seemed to be sucking the mild light right out of the air.

This was truly not a night to be out here, but Airria couldn't pull himself away. The tree leaves had changed from a rich green to a blood-soaked red.

The angry roar of the fire beckoned to him, taunting him. It promised only pain, pain of body and pain of soul. The torment of the flame was the peace Airria wanted most. All he wanted was to join the rage.

For only a moment he noticed his dad and uncle reaching into the fire, the excruciating flames licking their hands. Their eyes showed only anguish, but they reached deeper into the small infernal. Together they grabbed the plate in the middle of the flames and the smell of burning flesh filled the clearing.

A blast of black energy exploded from the plate, knocking the men to the edge of the clearing. Airria's body could feel the unbearable heat of the fire, but his soul was encased in its deadly chill.

He was trapped in this contradictory state for a short while when the flames began to grow, consuming trees and underbrush. They danced around, tickling the two dazed men and expanding the clearing away from them until it was the size of Tark-Ancia. Then the flames began to gather, forming into a monstrous Black Dragon.

The beast's long body was taller than any building Airria had ever seen and was covered in black plates like the one his dad had used. Its arms were like rough barked trees, its claws like spears, its tail was extensive with long, cruel spikes running its length ending in a blade-like tip. Its head was framed by three sets of cruel horns and its eyes were filled with the same torturous glee as the flames it had erupted from.

When it was fully formed it roared so loudly the ground shook. Then it laughed with a cruel tone that matched its eyes. "You have called for knowledge and power," the creature mocked, revealing its great sword length teeth. "There are none who compare to mine. Now you have summoned me, what should be done?"

Airria was frozen with terror. He couldn't run. He couldn't scream. He couldn't breathe. All he could do was feel the desire to join the creature, but he couldn't make a sound.

With a massive claw it reached out and snapped each of his dad's legs, then his uncle's. Airria wanted to get up to help his dad and his uncle, he wished they would fight back or run, but they were as frozen as Airria. They were only able to scream as their bones snapped.

The dragon shuttered with glee at the sound of each scream. It then broke their arms, laughing all the while. When the men were sufficiently helpless the dragon picked them up and shook them. Its eyes danced with delight for the pain of its victims.

"This is a game I like to play," the dragon gloated. "For the greedy and the proud are easy prey," it continued as its enormous claws delicately pulled small chunks of flesh from its victims' bodies. "I send one of my servants to a town. I have them brag about the potions of their books. The greediest and proudest will steal or buy the book and one of my scales." It stopped its torment of the men for a moment while it picked up the book and began again, "In time their lust for power consumes them. That is when the book shows them the spell to summon me."

While the dragon was talking Airria wished his dad and uncle would pass out, but they stayed conscious groaning and screaming in pain.

"You see," the dragon continued, "I cannot come here on my own, not yet anyway. It was your greed that brought me here. If it were not for your lust, I could not touch you. It is your foolishness which has allowed me to come."

Airria had seen enough dismemberment and pain in his life to know both his dad and uncle should be dead, or at least unconscious. Somehow they were both still awake and aware. He could feel the dark energy radiating off the dragon and supposed it was keeping them alive so they could feel every bit of pain.

When the dragon had finished its speech, it waved a dark claw in the air over its victims. A hut sized crystal appeared, filled with tormented souls. It was emitting the same deceptive light as the dragon's eyes. As the crystal came closer to his uncle, Airria could see his uncle's soul being slowly and painfully ripped from his body and dragged into the crystal. Next his dad was forced through the same process.

When finished the dragon held the crystal between itself and Airria. Airria could see the tormented faces of his dad and his uncle. They stood out only because he knew them. They seemed to be pleading for his help.

For a moment he glimpsed another who stood out, the woman was not wailing and moaning, but was standing strong. When their eyes met she smiled, not a cruel smile, but a kind of sympathetic comforting smile. Her eyes carried a majesty and honor Airria had never seen before. After a quick moment a large black claw grabbed the crystal and lifted it into the air.

The dragon was caressing it tenderly. "This is a treasure of all treasures," the dragon said to Airria. "All who are trapped inside will pay for eternity. All my enemies will end up where I can watch them forever. They will never know peace. Even the brothers I just acquired will never know they are in their prison together."

Airria's rage finally overcame the fear that had frozen him. He dashed forward, rushing the monster. His foot tripped over a rock around the pit where the fire had been and the dragon's form began to wisp into a smoky cloud until only the eyes remained. The freezing white burned into his mind. In his heart he knew this white was a black so dark it reversed itself to deceive with promises of comforting pain.

Airria awoke in a cold sweat. His blankets were twisted around him like a snake. He could still fill the panic of facing the dragon and the shame of knowing he'd sat behind a rock in a bush while his dad's soul was ripped from his body.

He decided to take a walk. He got up and put on his torn deerskin pants and shoes and left. The rain was still pouring down but it had lightened some. He let the warm rain wash over him, calming him, washing away his guilt; until the next time he went to sleep. Tonight he just wanted to forget. He wandered the snaking street with thoughts of his father racing through his head.

When he looked up, he found himself in front of the stable. He went in and began brushing his horse. As his hands repeatedly passed over his horse's withers his mind relaxed and drifted to pleasantries of years gone by. He could remember Joskin teaching him how to properly take care of his horse. It was a much simpler time.

It wasn't long before the lantern appeared in the doorway. A familiar yet rough voice asked, "What you doing here?"

Airria turned around to see the stable owner's disapproving face. "You know we don't normally push our horses that hard," Airria said, attempting to justify his actions. Both Airria and Joskin had been coming here for quite some time so he figured he knew what the disapproving look was from.

"You should never push a horse like that," Foris, the keeper, replied. "It will take months for this poor creature to recover, if it recovers at all," he said, pointing to the near dead horse Airria had ridden up the road.

"It was kind of an emergency," Airria insisted.

"What can be so important as to make you push that hard?" There was a little more openness in his voice.

"Henrik, the slaver, is after the girl we brought with us," Airria explained. He was about to continue but was cut off.

"After her, not you?" The keeper asked suspiciously. "You've been giving him grief for years."

"Okay, maybe he wants me dead," Airria conceded, "but he wants the girl more." Airria paused to examine Foris' thoughtful face. He knew the keeper didn't like, or even approve of Henrik, but the slaver had brought a lot of business to this town, especially to the stable keeper. "I think we can agree that the girl, Faith, is far too good for Henrik." Airria had added her name to make her more than a slave to the innkeeper.

After some time Foris replied, "This Faith is a beautiful creature...far too beautiful for the likes of Henrik." A gracious look crossed his face as he continued, "As I said earlier the poor creature you rode in on will not be ready to depart for some time, but I have a few saddle horses for sale. I'm afraid I can't give you much for trade value of this horse as I'm not sure it will survive." He began walking to the back of the stables. "What you will need is a horse that can keep up with your warhorses. Not an easy task."

Airria wasn't sure what to expect from Foris. The look on his face was that of someone doing a service. What he was saying sounded more like the windup for a sales pitch. "We only have a few more days; then she will be safe at home in Droir."

"You don't know Droir. Even the great Jammar won't be able to stop Henrik if he comes to claim her." Foris' voice had a hint of concern. "No, she will have to keep moving. For that I have the horse she'll need." He opened a blind stall door and led out the most beautiful white horse Airria had ever seen. "This horse is the perfect accent for Faith and the only animal I own that has a chance to keep up with your horses."

Airria gawked, "Where did you get such a creature?"

Foris smiled so all his teeth were showing. "A merchant who passed this way traded it to me a few months ago. He traded straight across for basic saddle horse," he paused and shrugged, "A deal I thought too good to pass up."

"You thought?" For Foris to offer such a magnificent horse meant the creature was likely very difficult to handle, but it was standing and leading like a dream. Nevertheless Airria could tell this horse was special, somehow.

"Yes and here's your warning," Foris furrowed his brow and put a thoughtful finger to his lips. "The horse is different than any I have come across...smarter. The merchant traded her to me because he couldn't control her. I get the feeling this horse picks her owner, not the other way around.

Airria chuckled a bit, "If anyone could convince this horse to behave, it would be Faith."

"I promise you'll know soon after they meet if this horse will accept the girl." The stable owner patted the horse on the shoulder.

For being such a difficult horse it was standing perfectly still and acting well behaved. "I'll have to discuss with Joskin as to what we can pay," Airria said.

"I'll charge you no more than I would for any other saddle horse," Foris smiled. "If the two of them get along then the deal is done. If not, then you can choose from my other stock."

"Thank you. I'll discuss it with Joskin when he gets up." He bowed gratefully and left.

It was still too soon to wake up Joskin so he decided to look down the mountain to see if the slaver was getting ready to start his assent. The rain had stopped and if they were determined enough they might start early, so he quickly retrieved his mouth cover and jogged to the top of the switchbacks. To his surprise there were lantern lights halfway up the switchbacks. From the noise and argument he could hear it sounded like they were fixing the wagon's wheels and had lost two of Henrik's elite guards. By the wagon's lanterns he could tell they were only bringing one wagon.

From his vantage point he could see the sun cresting the mist over the distant ocean. He decided it was time to wake up Joskin.

When he arrived at the inn, he was surprised to see Joskin sitting at a table. He had a small plain chest and a beautiful silvery bow with

60

gorgeous silver vinework sitting on the table next to him.

"I didn't think you would sleep the whole night," Joskin was dressed and ready, "Breakfast will be prepared soon. I'll leave it up to you when to wake up the sleeping beauty."

Airria tried to smile, "The slaver is on his way already, he's halfway up."

Joskin furrowed his brow, "Never seen anyone survive the switchbacks at night, not without serious problems."

Airria chuckled, "From what I can hear they broke a wheel and lost some of the guards."

Joskin chuckled, too, "Looks like it will take them as long to get here as if they'd waited."

Airria ran his fingers over the silver vine pattern on the bow, "Where did you get this?"

"The elves," Joskin replied simply.

"No, I mean you didn't have it at the bottom of the mountain. Do you have a place to keep things here?"

"That is my secret. Didn't want you breaking it," Joskin said with a wink.

Airria was going to protest, but was interrupted by the innkeeper's wife. "Hope you slept well. Tamina, the seamstress, will be waiting when you're ready," Lorinda said.

Airria smiled as nicely as he could, "Faith has had a very hard few days. I think we will let her sleep as long as she can. When she gets up, she'll need breakfast. Then we'll get her some better clothes."

Satisfied, Lorinda nodded approvingly and left the men to their food.

As they ate Airria told Joskin about the magnificent horse and the price Foris had offered. Joskin gave little indication of his opinions. He seemed to eat with his typical stoicism.

When Joskin had finished he excused himself. "I have a few things I want to do before we leave." Then with brotherly jest he added, "You'll be all right showing Faith to the seamstress?" He laughed, "I will meet you there."

Chapter 6-New Things

Faith awoke the next morning in the warm comfort of a bed. For a moment she thought she was at home and had dreamed the whole adventure. In her heart she knew she was in a strange town in a room between those of two strange men, Airria in the room to the right and Joskin in the room to the left, making a strange journey. She closed her eyes tight and tried to hold on to the moment of hope before pulling herself from the comfort of her bedcovers.

As she slipped on and tightened the dress the tavern-maid had lent her reality crashed in all around her. Though it was not as good as what she had back home reality was not so bad. The men had been unexpectedly courteous and generous. They had been very respectful of her modesty and had told her they were happy to get her some new clothes. She felt bad Lorinda had pushed them into buying her stuff; she already owed them both so much. Joskin had told her it was in their plans anyway. "You need something more suited to riding," Airria had said with a blush. When she had left the room with the tavern-maid, Lorinda had made sure the men were treating her respectfully while lending her the dress.

Still trying to hold on to her sense of normalcy she made her way down to the tavern. The smell of good food filled the air. She found Airria sitting alone at the table. Across from him were a couple of plates; one piled with ham and eggs the other with buttered bread. In front of the plates was a flagon of fresh goat's milk. She stood basking in the wonder of such marvelous smelling food.

Airria smiled big as he said, "Good morning!"

Overwhelmed by the moment, she could only ask about what was not there. "Where is Joskin?"

"He said he had some errands to run and then he'd meet us at the seamstress'," Airria replied.

She opened her mouth to begin to explain how bad she felt, but Airria cut her off. "It will be all right. Besides I want my cloak back," he said with a wink.

Faith took a deep breath of approval, the fresh rain and the smell of morning filled her lungs. "It was a nice storm last night," she said.

"Yes, it was. The sound of rain helps me sleep," Airria responded. Then he added, "It also made it impossible for the slaver to travel last night, and it will make it slow going for him this morning."

By his face she could tell she had not covered her own fear at the mention of the slaver. Her mind churned to find something to say to reassure him she would be all right. "The downpour combined with the steep trail should give us plenty of time to get something for me to wear."

Airria smiled an apology, "We'll make sure you have what you need."

Faith ate quickly listening to Airria's tales of Joskin. The way he told the tales was much funnier than the way Joskin told them. More than once she had to put a napkin over her mouth to stop from spraying Airria with eggs.

When breakfast was over they headed for the clothier's place. They enjoyed the fresh smell of the rain washed streets. The sun was constantly dimmed by the perpetual cloud of ash and soot hanging over the magic dome, but fortunately the air inside smelled fresh and clean. The whole town smelled fresh and clean. The town itself was made up of only one short snaking street with a couple dozen houses and a dozen small businesses.

Town, she thought, *more like a blacksmith haven*. With four blacksmith shops and two jewelers she could see why all orders for farm implements and metal wares came through here. They did have a blacksmith in Droir, but he only did basic repairs and horseshoes.

The walk to the clothier's was short; it was just across the street. They were greeted by a proper looking woman with her daughter. The woman said, "That dress was not made for you."

The girl smiled sweetly at Faith and then turned to her mother, "Of course not, Lorinda loaned it to her. They're very different people."

The woman looked crossly at her daughter and back to Faith. "Let's see what we can do to get you some properly fitting clothes."

Faith smiled back at the two nervously. "I will not have time for a proper fitting."

"What a shame. You have such an unusually nice hourglass figure. It would be a pleasure to make you a custom ball gown," Tamina said, smiling more sweetly.

"I wish I had time for such a treat. Perhaps someday I will," Faith said considerately. "For now, I just need something to cover me." She walked over to a stack of flax cloth, pullover type of dresses, "One of these, perhaps."

Airria laughed at the seamstress's snort and then spoke up. "Faith, you'll need something a little better suited for travel." He then turned to the seamstress and added, "Something that'll be comfortable enough to sleep in and strong enough to survive the rigors of traveling with me and Joskin."

The young girl laughed out loud. "This isn't an armor shop," she blurted out. From what I hear, metal is the only thing durable enough to survive your travels."

Faith looked questioningly at Airria who shrugged his shoulders. She looked at the seamstress who had a thoughtful smile.

"This may not be an armor shop, but we have some wares that will last better than this dress," the seamstress said as she took the flaxen dress from Faith.

Faith had made up her mind to be as little of a burden on her companions as she could. Yet they seemed more determined to waste their money on her than the boys back home. Both Airria and the seamstress were quite insistent Faith get something in leather, at least to cover her legs and feet. She had enough sparring to know her best asset in fighting was her agility and all other armor would slow her down. She didn't even have a weapon to fight with. In time she consented to a lace-up leather vest and short-sleeved cotton tunic.

The seamstress and her daughter took Faith into the back room, helped her out of her dress and took her measurements. They then provided her with a robe.

"I really do not have time for custom clothes," Faith said hoping the urgency did not come too strongly through her words.

"Don't worry," the girl said. "Your new clothes will be ready before midday." She then disappeared through the door with the dress Faith had borrowed.

Tamina laughed a little, "We'll have to customize what we have. They will not fit as nicely as if I had started from scratch, but they should serve your needs."

Faith began wandering around the back of the shop admiring the seamstress's work. She was very talented. Most of what was in the back was very fancy with multiple colors and decorative accents. Her eyes stopped on an elegant gown. It reminded her of a dress Jammar's wife, Tarsa, had worn to a ball she had attended.

By the time the girl had returned, Faith was dressed in her new clothes and emerged so Airria could see them. Joskin was sitting next to Airria with a new sword, new bow and a quiver of arrows. He leaned over to Airria and whispered so low Faith almost could not hear, "That's not going to help much."

Faith responded defensively, "It should offer much more protection and make it easier to ride."

"You're right. It will help a lot," Airria said smiling.

The seamstress handed Faith a brown wool cloak. "I would have preferred to make you a lovely gown, but as long as you are with these two you can use all the protection you can get," with that she winked at the men.

Joskin grabbed the new weapons and said, "Now that you look fit to travel, here are some weapons."

"I cannot take such expensive gifts," Faith protested.

"With those we have on our tail you may need to join the fight," Airria reminded her. "We made a promise to get you home safely. You may need to help us accomplish this." Airria had more concern in his voice than expected.

Joskin looked at Airria quizzically, but Airria just ducked out of the store saying, "I'll pay you back cousin. I promise."

Joskin turned back to the seamstress, "How much do we owe you?"

"Thirteen bronze," came the reply.

Both Faith and Joskin gasped at the cost. Faith had seen the excellent quality of materials used in the back room. She had seen the beautiful gowns. She had no doubt in the quality of the workmanship of her clothes. Even though the seamstress had declared it a rush job the clothes were a perfect fit; not too tight and with no extra hanging to get caught on stuff. The dress she had picked out would have cost a few tin pieces. At most, it would have been less than one percent of the cost.

"That is not cheap leather she is wearing," The seamstress continued. "Here it is hard to come by any leather and hers is exceptional leather. Airria asked for something that was comfortable enough to sleep in and durable enough to travel with you."

Joskin looked over the pants. His eyes stopped at the lacing which stretched from her mid-thigh all the way up over her hip.

"She is more shapely than most of my customers," the seamstress added, "and she made it clear she did not have time for me to make custom clothes."

Joskin looked Faith in the eyes and asked, "Is this an outfit you can sleep and live in for the rest of the trip?"

Faith felt conflicted. A silver piece, or ten bronze pieces, was enough money to feed her family for more than two months. On the other hand the clothes fit and felt so nice. In the end she decided to be honest, "Yes, they are very comfortable. I believe I will be fine in them."

Joskin nodded, first to Faith then to the seamstress, "She will also need a sword belt of equal quality and fashion."

The woman hurried to the back and returned with the belt explaining it would add one copper or the equivalent ten tin pieces to the price. Joskin fished in his pouch and produced two silver pieces. He looked sternly at the seamstress and her daughter. "You've always taken care of us in the past. There is a very upset slaver after us. If he asks, you haven't seen us in months." The woman and her daughter nodded in acknowledgment.

Joskin handed the weapons to Faith. First was the sword, it was polished and balanced. Faith was no expert on swords, but this one seemed very nice. She belted it on. Joskin handed her the bow and said, his voice soft yet stern, "This is only a loan. This bow is one from my personal collection. It was a gift from the elves of Buzlin Isle, as were the arrows."

Faith had never heard of Buzlin Isle. She doubted if she would ever know what or where that was. In the past elves were little more than legends and stories Jammar had told her. Now in her hand was a bow they had made. The wood of the bow was a silvery white with leafy vines of pure silver tangled and weaving into an intricate pattern up the bow. The string was a tightly woven thread of silver. She had never seen such a beautiful bow. As they walked to the hitching rail outside she pulled on the string a couple times. It was a very difficult pull, but manageable.

The shafts of the arrows were made of the same material as the bow without the silver vinework. The tips were of a design she had only seen sketches of in Jammar's archery books. The fletchings were as soft as a feather but appeared to be made of silver. She carefully placed the fancy leather quiver over her shoulder and began unstringing the bow.

Joskin stopped her. "This bow you do not unstring," he said.

She had been taught how to properly care for a bow and knew that if she did not unstring it it would lose its spring. "Why not?"

Joskin smiled playfully, "You would have to ask the elves. All I know is that it should never be unstrung."

She nodded consent then stopped in amazement. Tied to the

hitching rail where Joskin and Airria's warhorses were tied was a stout, yet sleek white horse. She looked at Joskin questioningly. She was unsure what to do. Joskin, she knew, had paid for all of it. She felt overwhelmed with gratitude.

Joskin smiled, "Airria picked it out for you and will pay me back."

Airria mounted as if nothing had happened. Faith fought back tears as she strained to understand. She had offered what she would have thought Airria was after from her and he had rejected it. Joskin had made no indication of wanting anything from her yet had spent enough in this town to buy a small house. *Why,* she thought, *why would anyone do this?*

While she was deep in thought a familiar squeak dimly made its way over the rise. Fear gripped her. She threw her cloak over the horse and leapt on. Without a word they took off.

Chapter 7-The Gate

Once outside of the magic barrier the rain of ash continued, but only for about a hundred strides. Though the other two continued, Airria stopped his horse to watch the breeze blow the ash back into the bubble. The ground quickly faded from ash to dirt to bright green grass in only a couple paces. He'd always assumed both sides of the town were the same, but was amazed to find it so much cleaner and brighter on this side.

Even though he knew the other two were leaving him behind Airria enjoyed a much more casual pace. Birds were singing in the trees and flowers were blooming beautifully on this side of the mountain. The white bark trees had funny round leaves that fluttered like silver in the breeze. This was the most peaceful place he had ever been.

The road was wide enough for two wagons and, though the hillside was steep enough to use switchbacks he felt safe going straight down and by-passing the road altogether. In doing so he quickly caught up to Faith and Joskin who had slowed to a walk. The trees were tall and made it impossible to see up or down the mountain.

When they had traveled about halfway down the slope the road cut through a ridge, creating a small valley. In time it turned and the side became more steep and jagged. Shortly after turning the corner they could see a large wall with a double door gate in the center of the road.

A scrappy young man who appeared to be about fourteen years old, wearing both a black eye and rusty sword guarded the gate. The group approached slowly. When close enough to communicate the young man yelled, "You must pay to go through!"

While the words were still in the air six thugs shuffled down the steep incline to the side taking up positions behind the group. Each of them was as poorly dressed as the young man. Their ages seemed to range from about twenty to forty. Each had a gnarly beard and oily, ratty hair. As they brandished their weapons it was obvious they did not take proper care of themselves, though none looked as bad as the boy in front. They all stared hungrily at Faith but said nothing.

Joskin asked, "What is the price for passage?" His voice was louder than necessary to talk to the boy, even while facing the slope the men had come down.

An overweight man with a mangy red beard, breakfast still hanging from it, appeared on the ridge. His hair looked as though bugs were living in it. His sword appeared bright and new. On either side of him two archers positioned themselves with arrows nocked.

The obese figure left his entourage on the ridge and followed a narrow path down to the boy who was cowering. When he reached the boy he said far too loudly, with artificial anger, "I told you to get the money and let them through! I wanted to rest!" Without waiting for a reply he backhanded the boy, knocking him to the ground. All the thugs laughed.

Airria could see immediately this was a game they all liked to play. He could feel his blood boiling inside. He had watched behavior like this his whole life and tried to let it go. Nonetheless, it still bothered him incurably. His own father never beat him for entertainment though he knew plenty of fathers who did.

Faith jumped off her horse to see if the boy was all right. Airria leapt quickly to stop her. She had Joskin's Elven bow in hand and was to the boy's side in the blink of an eye. Airria was close behind.

Joskin asked again, this time putting more impatience in his voice, "What is the price of passage?"

The leader reached down and grabbed Faith by the cloak and jerked her to her feet, "This will do!"

Airria drew his sword to attack, but Faith's bow had already found its mark deep in the leader's mangy beard knocking him back and forcing him to let go. Airria glanced around to see how the other thugs were going to react. He had enough experience to know that many groups of thugs depended on their numbers to intimidate their victims. This group seemed stunned. Airria guessed no one had ever fought back.

The leader bellowed, "Kill the men! The woman is mine!" Between his teeth he added, "You will pay like that insolent little girl in camp!"

Airria sidestepped one arrow and deflected another with his sword. He knew Joskin would be all right so he ventured a glance at Faith.

She brought her bow up with an arrow in it and the leader knocked it away. Airria dove in sword first. It wasn't a fair fight. Airria was much faster than the leader and Airria's sword found its mark in the leader's heart, the blade sizzling as it entered.

Before the archers could reload two twangs came from Faith's bow, sending two of the archers flying off the hill. Airria had to dodge arrows from the other two. Before they could reload, Faith dispatched them in the same way as she had the other two.

Together Airria and Faith turned to Joskin. All that was left were six piles of gore. As was expected Joskin was covered in blood, but surprisingly he had a look of shock on his face as he stared at his ax. Airria wanted to question Joskin on his surprise, but didn't feel it was the time.

Airria looked at the boy. He had caught one of the stray arrows in the chest and was gasping for air. Faith rushed over to him just in time for him to die in her arms. A moment later her head spun to the side and she threw up. After a few heaves she stood up in a daze. Wobbling and weak she said, "I have to find those arrows."

Airria helped her sit back on the ground. He gave his most comforting grin and said, "Don't worry about it. I'll find them." He motioned for Joskin to sit with her. As much as he longed to help her, Joskin had more experience helping people deal with their first battle.

Faith smiled back weakly and said, "Thank you." Then she continued dry heaving.

Airria waited long enough for Joskin to come stand with her before heading up the trail the leader had come down. From the ridge he could see all four bodies at the base. He ran down to retrieve the arrows, but found only holes through the men. He followed the path he thought the arrows would travel and stumbled into a village-like camp.

The huts in the camp were of the shoddiest workmanship. They were basic bundles of sticks lashed into huts. Only one of them had a roof that might keep out rain and it had two large holes in its side.

That is one powerful bow! Airria thought to himself. The arrow had flown over the hill, through a man and through a thin wall over fifty paces past the hill. *At least I can retrieve those two arrows.* As he neared the door he saw the other two arrows sticking in trees at the edge of camp. He used his dagger to dig them out. While digging in the trees he heard a rustle coming from the largest hut.

He kept a cautious eye out for bandits and as he approached the hut, he drew his sword. The door creaked loudly as it swung open. When the opening was wide enough for him, he carefully slipped inside. He found a small room with a bed, little chest and a young girl tied uncomfortably to the center support of the hut. The girl was wearing a torn slave's dress. Her legs were covered with welts and bleeding cuts, both eyes were black and her lips and cheeks were split and bleeding. Her chin was quivering with fear, yet her eyes still held a sense of defiance.

He felt a tear run down his cheek when he looked in her eyes. He had seen many children with a similar look. His heart broke when she whispered, "Please do not hurt me."

Something in the girl's eyes and face held a familiarity that engendered more sympathy than it should have. Somehow he knew he had met this girl or a relative of hers before. Perhaps he had seen her in a

73

dream, but it had to have been from a long time ago for all he dreamed about anymore was his father's death. Nonetheless, this awareness made him want even more to help and protect her.

He slid his sword through the ropes with ease. He was surprised she just stood there, not running away, while he grabbed a blanket. She did step away when he tried to put the blanket around her.

"I won't hurt you," Airria said as comfortingly as he could. He extended his arm, handing the blanket to her, "I'm here to take you away from this place."

He glanced around the room trying to keep himself from scaring her anymore. He spotted the arrows, one on each end of the bed. He grabbed them as well as the small chest. In an attempt to encourage her to come he said, "If you'll follow me, I'll take you where you'll be safe."

The girl followed him at a cautious distance through the forest and down the trail. Faith was still sitting on the ground. Joskin was standing nearby, but giving her distance.

"Who is this?" Joskin asked.

"I've never felt so good about killing anyone as I do about killing him." Airria spat, pointing to the leader. "She was in his hut." He looked back at the girl who was looking from him to Faith and back. He motioned for the girl to go to Faith.

The girl ran as fast as her emaciated legs could carry her. The two girls sat for some time on the ground hugging and crying. Airria wasn't sure why the girl ran to Faith; he assumed it had something to do with Faith being a woman who also seemed traumatized, some kind of kinship.

To take their minds off the girls the men picked up the moneybags and opened the chest. Most of the bags contained a few tin pieces, about enough for a week of evenings at the tavern. The leader's bag had a couple silver pieces worth of assorted coin, a key to the chest and a key to the gate. The chest had a few gems, some necklaces, a few brooches, one fancy dagger and an assortment of coins.

They loaded the valuable coins in Joskin's saddlebags and then hid the bodies and weapons of the thugs over the hill. They covered them with branches and left them to rot.

When they were done and ready to go, Airria gently touched Faith on the shoulder. "We need to get moving," he said as softly as he could.

"I will be all right," Faith replied and then gently pushed the girl out of her embrace. With sincere concern she asked the girl, "Can you travel?"

"May I travel with you?" the girl asked in a shaky voice.

"Of course," Faith replied. She helped the girl to her feet and onto her horse. Then she climbed on behind her.

Joskin had the gate opened and his horse already on the other side. When they were all through the gate he closed and locked it and threw the key into the woods. "With no other way to get a wagon down this road that should slow them down a little," he said.

Airria thought back to what he'd seen in the clearing the other day. He didn't think Joskin knew about the mage or the trained fighter. Thinking of it made him shudder and he didn't think the gate would slow the slaver down much. Hopefully they were still dragging that wagon which would slow them enough.

It took the most of the day to get to the campsite at the base of the range. The girl held tightly to Faith the whole time. There were no stories, no laughs, not a word the whole way. Airria didn't mind the silence. His head was full and swirling with thoughts of the day's events.

The campsite was an opening in the trees, the flat area big enough for three wagons to circle the fire and in the back area, a small cave. In a nearby tree there was a lookout blind to watch the road.

Joskin insisted the girls take the cave and Airria offered his bedroll to the child before he left to go hunting. He didn't wait for a reply, just left it on the ground and went hunting.

He was happy to be alone with his thoughts. Over the last few days he had had several epiphanies. His life was quickly changing, more than it had since his father's death. For the first time he felt bad about the way he had treated most of the women in his past. He never forced himself on any of them, most of them had offered, but many of them had been taught to offer by abusive masters or parents.

There was something about the situation with Faith and the look in the girl's eyes. It let him know that most of the women he had been with had been abused. Their offers were the only thing they had to pay him with. Abuse was not uncommon where he was from. His father had raised him to take care of himself. His mother had taught him to look out for more than just himself. Somewhere in the middle he had found that he helped those he hoped to get some form of payment from. "How dark is my heart?" he asked out loud.

The sound of his voice brought movement out of the trees. Without a thought, he pulled his dagger and implanted it in the back of the young doe's head. For the first time he felt a little bad about killing an animal, but knew it was for the good of the group.

As he carried his prey back to camp he thought more about the new girl. He wondered how long she had been a slave, how long she had been with the bandits, where her parents were, how long she'd been away from home. He thought he might ask her and then thought again.

Airria arrived in camp to see Faith in the cave sobbing and holding the girl. He looked at Joskin for an explanation.

Joskin took the deer and began skinning it. Without looking up at Airria he said, "They have a lot to work through. Faith killed her first person today and I don't want to know what the child has been through. It is best to let them deal with it."

Airria wanted to help and he let Joskin know as much.

"The best help you can give is to let them work through it." Joskin stopped working long enough to look up at Airria, "When, and if, they are ready for your help they will come to you. Until then, let it be."

Airria nodded and began assisting Joskin. When the deer was skinned Airria used the brains and some alum powder to treat the hide and stretched it between a set of trees for the night. Joskin started cutting the meat into strips. First he made some small steaks, skewered them on sticks and began cooking them and then he made thinner strips to cure later over the coals. Fortunately, it was a small deer so it didn't take too long.

When the steaks were cooked Airria took some food, as well as Joskin's healing salve to the girls. The girls quieted at his approach. "I'll take the watch so you can help your new friend," Airria said to Faith, smiling weakly at her. He hated to see anyone suffer, but it was hardest when you knew why they hurt and weren't able to help.

Faith's eyes were puffy and bloodshot, but she managed to smile back. "Thank you. Thank you for everything." The young girl looked at him and forced a smile then quickly looked at the ground.

Airria nodded and went to his post. He had no more than sat down when Joskin put a hand on his shoulder. Joskin's voice was deep and understanding as he asked, "Would you like me to take the first watch?"

"Not tired," Airria replied flatly.

"You need to sleep," Joskin's voice was somewhat insistent.

"I did sleep. Last night," Airria's voice was just as insistent.

"One night a week is not enough," Joskin half jested.

"My eyes will be open whether I'm lying on the ground or watching for Henrik and his men."

"You'll come get me if you start feeling tired?" Joskin asked.

"If I think I might start dozing, I'll come get you. I promise."

"That's not what I requested."

"I am tired, I'm always tired. Since our dads died even when I am asleep I don't rest. And more than usual I have things I need to deal with." Airria tried not to let his annoyance show through. He was grateful for Joskin's concern.

"Now you see why I knew to tell you to let the girls deal with their problems." Joskin smiled a weary smile. "If there's anything I can do to help, let me know."

"Thanks, you're already doing it." Airria returned the smile and Joskin headed off to his bedroll. Airria continued pondering.

It was near midnight when Airria was pulled from his thoughts again. This time it was by Faith. She sat down beside him beneath the tree blind. Her eyes were still puffy.

"She finally went to sleep," Faith sniffled. After some time she spoke again, "Her name is Carrita. She was stolen from an orphanage almost six months ago. She was used to purchase a year's passage through the gate." She looked at Airria more earnestly. "How could anyone be so cruel?"

77

It took Airria a while to answer, but Faith looked like she needed one. Finally he said, "It truly takes a dark heart to do something like that." His heart was filled with self-loathing as he said it. He'd spent a lot of time pondering his own part in similar situations. He continued to consider until he noticed a tear crawling down Faith's cheek as she rubbed her hands together. In an attempt to offer some comfort he placed his hand on her shoulder.

She leaned into him and sobbed, "How do you get the blood off?"

He knew she was talking of her first kill. He remembered his first kill as well. He had been twelve. His father, his uncle and Joskin were away from the house. Three men had come to the house to loot and pillage the goods and women. Even at this age he was very proficient with the sword. Though his was lighter than most he wielded it with incredible speed.

The three men had burst into the house. One by one they found their way to the room he, his mother and his aunt were hiding in. As neither woman was willing to take up arms he was forced to. When the fight was over and the adrenaline was gone, he, like Faith had puked. The bruises and cuts didn't matter; he had blood on his hands. The women told him he did well. His father and uncle were proud of him. No matter how many times he washed the blood never seemed to go away. Airria rubbed lightly on her shoulder. "I wish I could tell you," He paused to remember what Joskin had told him. Not that it made him feel better, but it had helped keep him from going bitter. "Many people try to cover the blood of the first kill by embracing the power they felt taking the life, convincing themselves that the next kill will wash away the blood of the last kill."

Faith pulled away looking into his eyes. "Does it help? Does the next kill help?"

He really hoped he was saying things right. "In my experience, no. I still cry over my first kill. The others may fade, but your first will stay with you."

"How will I live with myself?"

"One day at a time." Airria could remember his own struggles to deal with his first kill. It was not pleasant. At the time he didn't know if he could handle it. Joskin had been there to help him through it.

"How?" she asked again.

"You hold it close to you so you never forget. Every human life is precious. If you forget the pain then you cease to be human and become a monster." Airria forced himself to smile, "Or, at least that is the way Joskin tells it."

Faith let another tear fall, "I do not know if I can."

"You won't have to deal with it alone."

Faith leaned back into Airria. They stayed like that the rest of the evening.

Chapter 8-New Friends

For Faith the day had been a long, hard and draining day. She had killed four men, watched the boy die in her arms and took responsibility for a severely abused girl. Though she had not caused the death of the boy his blood was on her hands. No matter how she washed, rubbed or scrubbed she could still see the blood.

The girl had run to her, expecting Faith to protect and help her. Moreover, she felt like she needed to help and protect Carrita. Part of it stemmed from her inability to help the boy, but it was more. The girl's eyes held a sorrow deeper than the abuse she had suffered. Much like Airria, it was deeper than Faith could comprehend. In a way, she knew she had taken the girl in to help because she could not help Airria and he had helped her.

The campsite at the bottom of the range was a welcome sight. The last time Faith was here she was in the wagon, a prison she would not soon forget. She was forced to listen to the other girls as they were used as payment to the guards. The guards had enjoyed each scream.

Just as disturbing was listening to Henrik talk about how much money he was going to make off her. He already had a buyer, a mage of the Order of the Black Claw, whatever that meant. The slaver's voice always quivered with fear as he talked about this client. "I hate to think what dark things he is going to do to you!" Henrik would say every night when he brought the food. She wasn't sure if her imagination of what life would be was worse than reality would have been or if the slaver was right and the horrors were truly beyond her imagination. Either way she could feel her sense of self and sanity slipping away, just as it had from the slave girl who she was tending.

The men insisted Faith and the girl take the cave. Airria had offered his bedroll to the new girl. It was sweet of him, but it meant Airria was not intending to sleep that night. Faith doubted she would sleep either. It had been a very trying day and her mind was racing over the events.

Faith guided the girl to the cave while carrying the bedrolls. After she had set them out she collapsed. The girl dropped beside her. Now that they were not moving the burden of the day overwhelmed her and she began to cry. She needed to feel someone, hold someone, be held by someone, so she embraced the girl and together they sobbed until it was almost dark.

Airria interrupted them. At the sound of his approach the girl silenced her sobs and Faith followed suit. He had brought some steaks on a skewer and Joskin's box of salve. As he handed a steak to each girl and the salve to Faith he said, "I'll take the watch so you can help our new friend." He smiled at them both. It was weak, but still made Faith feel a little better. Faith appreciated the sentiment and though she did not feel like it she forced herself to smile at him.

Airria nodded and headed to his post. Joskin got up from the cooking fire and followed Airria.

"Why do you travel with men?" The girl's voice was bitter. "They only want one thing; to hurt you!"

"Not all men," Faith responded. Her eyes stayed focused on the men for a moment then shifted to the girl. "They have had plenty of chances to hurt or use me. So far all they have expected of me is to stay safe."

"Your faith in men will change!" the girl's cynicism was far beyond her years.

"Yes, it will," Faith said. "Soon they will expect me to lead them where they want to go."

"And what will they expect when you arrive at their requested destination?" The girl asked suspiciously.

"Then I will have to evaluate my life and go from there." Faith was amazed; this girl was immersed in such bitterness. She dreaded to think about what the gate thugs, and likely the slaver, had done to her. Faith thought about how cynical she herself had been becoming before running into Airria and Joskin. In fact it was that cynicism that pushed her to offer her body to Airria.

"In time they will expect more," the girl snapped, "and if you don't give it to them they will take it!"

"I don't think so." Faith was trying hard not to let her voice rise. "Not these two."

"All of them!" the girl snapped again.

Faith said sympathetically, "All of them? Has your life been so terrible? Have you never met a man who wanted only to help?"

The girl stared at the ground.

Faith could see the girl was remembering at least one good man in her life, but before she continued on such a hard topic she asked, "What is your name?"

"Carrita," the girl answered, her countenance softening a little.

Faith smiled more sincerely at her softening, "Carrita? It seems you remember something? A man who was nice to you?"

"Before the orphanage, in the town where I grew up." A twinkle came to Carrita's eyes as she spoke of her life before, "My mother had many men visit who treated us both very well."

"How long has it been?" Faith pushed a little.

"It seems like a lifetime ago." Carrita seemed to be deep in thought, "Let's see. I was given to the gate man as payment for one year's passage two weeks ago. The slaver stole me out of the orphanage about five months before that and I was in the orphanage less than a year," her

The Dragon's Pain Trilogy

****

The Dragon's Eye
****

The Dragon's Claw
****

The Dragon's Heart

voice was cracking and tears were running down her face as she started picking at the meat Airria had brought.

Faith wanted to stay off the subject of the slaver and the gatemen, so she asked, "Was the orphanage hard to adjust to?" She began picking at the meat as well.

A smile crept across Carrita's face. "No. My mother's friend ran the orphanage. As much as I missed my mother, her magic library was huge and she let me spend as much time as I wanted in it."

It seemed talking about magic helped to pull the girl's mind off the pain she had dealt with for the last six months. "Magic? You know magic?"

Carrita almost giggled, "I understand much better than most old mages." There was a sense of smugness as she said it.

Faith risked asking the question that popped into her head. "If you knew magic why did you not use it against those men?"

As Faith had feared the sadness and bitterness returned to the girl's face. She glanced to make sure the men were not watching and pulled up her clothes to reveal her navel. Embedded in the hole was a brownish crystal with symbols in it. "The slaver had a very powerful mage place this crystal on me. It keeps my own ability suppressed."

Faith could feel the power emanating from the crystal. "Is there no way to remove it?" she asked.

"Yes, there are ways," Carrita's face became calculating. "It would take many years for you to learn enough magic. There are not enough of the proper alchemy ingredients on this island for me to remove it. The quickest and best way would be to find a Life Priestess."

Faith's attention was caught. "Did you just say I could learn magic?" Faith waited breathlessly for the answer.

The glimmer returned to Carrita's eyes, "You do not know magic?" When Faith did not respond she continued, "Then I will teach you. Every woman should have the chance to learn."

Faith knew it might be a bad idea to ask, but she did anyway, "Why just women?"

Surprisingly Carrita only got a little defensive, "I know it sounds like I was demeaning the rougher gender again. I do believe I am at least somewhat justified. In this case, according to my mother, women carry an affinity for magic. In circles of physical combat men excel and far outnumber women. When it comes to magic, because men often control society, men still outnumber; but given equal training a woman will be much more powerful."

Faith was amazed at Carrita. She was talking as though she were an adult. In fact, Faith was having a hard time seeing the little girl.

Carrita continued, "By the way you keep rubbing your hands I would guess you killed your first person today."

"Yes actually, four of them," Faith could feel her heart drop, "also, a boy was killed, he died in my arms. Every time I look at my hands I see the blood." She heard her own voice crack.

"How many did the men kill?" Carrita asked.

"Airria killed the fat one, the leader. Joskin killed the others." Faith wanted to change the subject.

Carrita smiled weakly, "Then perhaps I should be a bit less prejudiced toward them. I guess I owe them such courtesy." The smile turned more real as she said, "Their rescuing me and putting their lives on the line to save you does nothing to prove my point."

Faith was able to return the smile. "I trained as the town guard. I exceeded even the guard masters at archery."

"There it is!" Carrita said as though she had a grand discovery. "Your ability to excel so far beyond the men in an area which by all natural order you should not have, the area of which I speak is magic."

"I was trained by a man, Jammar. He is another good man who lives close to my home." Faith pulled out the salve and began putting it on Carrita's wounds.

"Jammar?" Carrita asked as though she were speaking more to herself. "The name is familiar, but I cannot place it." She stopped for a moment then got back to her point, "Whether you knew it or not, you were tapping into magic."

"Is this why you assumed I knew magic?"

"Part of it, but the rest we can save for another day." Carrita yawned, "Thank you, for the food. Thank you for saving me. Thank you for reminding me there is good in this world. Please, for now, keep the whole magic thing our secret."

Faith nodded and Carrita placed her head on Faith's lap while Faith rubbed the salve on Carrita's facial wounds, shortly after Faith finished applying the salve Carrita drifted off to sleep. Faith waited until Carrita was sound asleep and then she went to sit by Airria. She had a lot more on her mind than she ever had before. She did not know what she dared tell Airria, but she knew she could not keep it all to herself.

"The girl finally went to sleep," Faith said sniffing as she sat down. She sat next to him for quite some time just wishing to feel a warm touch. After a while she blurted out, "Her name is Carrita. She was stolen from an orphanage about six months ago. She was used to purchase a year's passage through the gate." She turned to look at Airria's eyes. They were filled with concern. "How could anyone be so cruel?" She was already afraid she had said too much of what Carrita had confided in her. She hoped it would help Airria be more patient with her. Not that he had been pushy or mean, he just seemed to want to help and he, being a man, could not help her.

"It truly takes a black heart to do something like that," his voice was filled with bitterness and disdain.

Faith could feel the tears starting to trickle down her face as her thoughts jumped from the gatekeeper, to the deaths, to the slaver. She blamed the slaver for all of it.

Airria placed his arm around her, putting his hand on her shoulder. As soon as she felt his warm touch emotions flooded through her and she leaned into him and began to sob. Her mind fixated on the deaths, "How do you get the blood off?" Her mind kept jumping back to the blood.

Airria rubbed lightly on her shoulder, it reminded her of when she would come to her father as a child. For a moment she felt safe.

His words were not so comforting. "I wish I could tell you," he took a deep breath and then continued, "Many people try to cover the blood of the their first kill by embracing the power they felt taking the life, convincing themselves that the next kill will wash off the blood of the last kill."

Faith pulled away to get a better look into his eyes. She wanted to know if he was being sincere. His eyes looked directly into hers. She could see the pain in his eyes which she felt in her own heart. While she could see into his eyes she asked, "Does it? Does the next kill help?"

"In my experience, no. I still cry over my first. The others may fade, but the first will stay with you," Airria said nervously.

Faith was not sure she wanted to go on being reminded of her part in the massacre. "How will I live with myself?"

"One day at a time."

His advice did not seem practical and made no sense. It was not the answer she was looking for. "How?" she asked again.

Airria's face was gentle as he answered, "You hold it close to you so you never forget. Every human life is precious. If you forget the pain then you cease to be human and become a monster." He smiled with effort, "Or, at least, that is the way Joskin tells it."

Faith could not hold back the tears. "I do not know if I can."

"You don't have to do it alone." Airria's words brought her some comfort. She leaned back into him enjoying the security of his warm, firm body. There was no expectation in his touch, only comfort. When she began to get overwhelmed with her thoughts she reminded herself of his last words. She thought about Airria and Joskin and all they had done for her. She thought of all Carrita had been through and how young, yet strong, she had been. She was so wrapped up in her thoughts that she did not notice the sky getting bright until she heard Carrita scream, "No! No! Do not take her!"

Faith rushed over to see what the problem was. Carrita was tossing and turning. Faith touched the girl on the shoulder and she woke. Sobbing, the girl grabbed Faith. Faith looked around not knowing what to do. She saw Airria and Joskin standing by, willing to help where they could. "What do we do?" Faith asked.

Joskin, in a concerned tone said, "We need to get her to a priestess."

Faith ducked her head. She did not want to trust someone else with the child, but both Joskin and Carrita had suggested the same thing. "There is one in Gentrail," Faith conceded, "we should be there in a couple of days at the longest."

Chapter 9-Life Lessons

"We need to be going," Joskin said with a concerned look. "If Henrik didn't stop in Smandler he will be on his way."

Both Airria and Joskin hurried to get the horses ready. Faith stayed behind to console Carrita.

"I cannot live like this!" Carrita sobbed. "The dreams, I do not know how long I can deal with them."

"If it makes you feel any better you are not the only one in this group who has dreams which cause a fear of sleeping," Faith told the girl while holding her close. "Airria is afraid to sleep."

"What does he dream of?" Carrita asked with pleading eyes.

Faith hoped she was not betraying Airria. "He says he saw a dragon kill both his and Joskin's fathers."

"As bad as the abuse was, the helplessness and pain," Carrita gulped back more tears, "as bad as it was, the nights when I have to relive my mother's death, they are the worst."

"What happened, if you do not mind me asking?" the last thing Faith wanted was to cause Carrita more pain.

"She was taken by the biggest and cruelest of the Black Dragons." Carrita began to sob uncontrollably again.

Airria and Joskin came over to prepare the bedrolls. "We need to go!" Joskin said with more urgency. By the way he said it Faith could tell he was worried about more than just escaping the slaver.

They pushed hard through the morning. Everyone made an effort to lighten the mood with pleasant stories of childhood fun, in spite of the pace. Before the sun was at its full height Faith stopped. She spied a clear pond near a small campground. "I think it is time for a bath," she said.

"We really don't have time for this," Joskin reminded her.

Faith looked at the dried blood on her clothes. She glanced at the dirty young girl behind her. She looked again at her hands. Even though she had washed them several times she could still see the blood. "I know this is your excursion and therefore have the final say. I would prefer not to face a Priestess of Life covered in blood."

Airria opened his mouth to protest. Faith could almost hear the words which would be coming. She had been the one to push them, to run from the slavery awaiting her in the wagon relentlessly pursuing them. To her surprise no words exited Airria's mouth. He just sat there, mouth hanging open.

Joskin was more obvious with his concerns, "Henrik is coming. He didn't stop at the base camp on the other side and I doubt the gate will slow him much."

Faith looked at the stains on her new trousers again. She adamantly wished she could get the blood off them.

Airria finally spoke, "Perhaps we should go see if they are coming down the trail?" He flipped his head as if he had a secret to tell Joskin. At this point she did not care if they had secrets; she knew they had many together. She was glad Airria was taking her side.

Joskin furrowed his brow and then said, "Fine, we will go see if we can see where the slave party is," then the two men left.

Faith and Carrita tied their horse to a tree and found a secluded place to disrobe. As soon as Carrita pulled off her clothes Faith could feel the power again. It made her body tingle slightly.

"Why do I feel it when you uncover the crystal?" Faith asked.

"What you feel is magic," Carrita said matter-of-factly. "More accurately, what you are feeling is a drain on your magic. This is what the crystal does, or more precisely what the ward in the crystal does."

"What is a ward?"

"A very powerful magical symbol or collection of symbols," Carrita said looking a little discouraged. "It drains me enough I cannot use my power, but not so much I will pass out."

"It is safe for me to be around you?" Faith asked as she began washing her clothes, relieved to see the blood slipping way. She knew so little about magic and was interested in learning it. With what Carrita had said she was afraid the crystal would diminish her potential.

"As the crystal is linked directly to me, the amount it drains from you is negligible," Carrita said as she began washing her rags.

After the clothes were washed and hung to dry, the girls stepped into the cool water. Faith asked, "If we have the crystal removed will your magic heal?"

Carrita got excited, "Yes. I will heal." She sat on a rock, which put the water up to her neck. "It is time for your first lesson," she said thoughtfully.

Faith was surprised, "How? Can you teach me without the crystal interfering?"

Carrita giggled slightly, showing the child she was. "There is much which will be more difficult to teach you without my own magic, but I can teach you the basics and give you a start." Carrita ducked her head under the water and shook it. The water around her became murky. When she pulled her head from the water her hair was much lighter. "Manna, or magical energy, is what mages call the life force or magical essence or power in every living thing. Like this pond it can be influenced by outside forces. Unlike this pond you have a choice, for the most part, whether or not something influences you and your manna. Also like this pond, there is always renewed power flowing in. This is why when the crystal is gone I will be able to use my magic again."

Faith was not sure if Carrita's hair washing was part of the lesson or not but was amazed at how mature the girl sounded. "Will you return to the same level of power you were at before or will your capacity for magic be diminished?"

The twinkle in Carrita's eyes grew brighter with each question. "The ability to use and hold manna grows with use. The crystal is constantly draining my manna, in effect forcing me to use my magic. When it is removed my capacity will have greatly increased. Putting this crystal on me was good and bad for the slaver. He made it so I could not use magic on him, but if it were ever removed I would have access to even more power. The slaver was counting on my dying."

"Where did you learn all this?" Faith asked. She was not as curious about the where as to why Carrita sounded so mature.

Carrita's countenance fell, as if a cloud were crossing her face, "My mother taught me. She was a great enchantress."

Faith felt bad about taking the light out of the girl's eyes. "I will bet I can influence this pond, at least a little." Carrita looked confused so Faith splashed her with water. Carrita returned the gesture and play began. The two played and swam, forgetting about the slaver following them for a short while. By the time they decided to get out, Carrita's hair had gone from a ratty-brown to cornsilk blond.

As they stepped onto the shore, Carrita said, "Thank you. It has been a long time since anyone has played with me like this."

Faith could not help herself; she went over to Carrita and gave her a hug. Carrita hugged her back. After a moment, they let go and got dressed. They sat on the side of the stream. While Faith filled the waterskins and prepared her horse, Carrita stared contemplatively into the ripples of the stream.

"When Faith was finished Carrita said, "It is time for another lesson," with importance in her voice.

Faith had been trying to figure out what was taking the men so long. The sound of Carrita's voice startled her, "Yes, yes, go ahead."

"When you felt the crystal, where did you feel it?" Carrita asked almost as though it were a statement.

"In my head, I guess. Why?" Faith was only half paying attention to the girl. She was still wondering what had happened to the men and why they had been gone so long.

"It was more than your head; it was your entire body!" Carrita's voice showed she was getting a little frustrated at Faith's lack of concentration.

Faith felt her attention drawn to the girl's words, "You are right. Why was it more than just my head, or hands, or heart or something?"

"Look at the stream," Carrita said pointing to the stream that fed the pond. "Do you see the ripples in it?"

"Yes?" Faith was confused by the question.

"Do you see how unfocused they are, tossing to and fro on the whim of the bank and the rocks the bottom?" Once Carrita received a nod from Faith she continued, "The magical energies flow through you the same way, giving you extra strength or energy or even making food taste better when you are hungry, but nothing major. The energy is unfocused, mostly countering itself. If you could channel this stream and control its flow this water could eat through stone in a relatively short amount of time. It is the same with the manna or energy inside you. The first thing you will need to do is close your eyes and imagine your body is filled with thousands of small streams flowing in all directions." After Faith had laid flat on her back and closed her eyes it was not hard to imagine. Carrita continued, "Try to force all of the streams to go in the same direction. Many great wizards say you should start at your fingertips and toes and begin moving towards your head."

Faith found the task which Carrita had given her was much more difficult than she had thought. She worked at it for some time and felt like she had done well, but it was not long before the sound of hoofbeats brought Faith to her feet. She grabbed her bow and arrows and then she began looking for a good place for defense.

"Are you two dressed yet?" Airria shouted from a safe distance.

"Yes!" Faith yelled back to Airria then turned to Carrita, "I will practice as often as I can."

"Practice always; this is our edge over men." Carrita gave Faith an impatient look and placed her finger over her mouth, indicating to her to keep it a secret.

The men rode into the clearing. Both of them sat and stared at Carrita. Faith smiled when she realized that they had noticed a drastic change in the girl's appearance. "Amazing the difference a little water can make, is it not?" Faith asked. "Best of all, I no longer smell like you two."

The men laughed and Airria responded, "Wish we had time to rectify the situation. Unfortunately Henrik is on his way." The tone of his voice started jovial, but quickly faded to slight urgency.

Alarm filled Faith. She grabbed Carrita and helped her onto the horse. She was glad she had gotten it ready.

"Don't panic too much," Joskin said in a much calmer tone. "With the wagon they move much slower than us. It will be dark before they reach this point."

Faith got on the horse, "I can do the math. The slaver should have been reaching last night's camp tonight. He is not stopping so we need to get moving. If we push hard we should reach Gentrail by sundown."

Joskin looked at Carrita and asked her, "Can you handle pushing that hard?"

The girl smiled shyly. "The horses will have to do most of the work. I should be fine."

Faith knew they had to get to Gentrail with enough of a lead to make sure the local Life Priestess could help Carrita. After her bath and fun the girl looked much better, but there was no telling what the evening would bring and there was no way she was going to stop for a night's rest until she got to Jammar's house. She looked into the girl's eyes. "We will make sure you are taken care of." She felt a little embarrassed to be making promises for the men, but felt confident they, at least to some level, shared her sentiment. "Now hold on," she said and began galloping her horse down the road. The men followed closely behind.

Together they galloped until the horses started to lather and then slowed to a walk. Now at a pace where the girls could talk Carrita asked, "Do you think Henrik will run his horses too?"

Joskin answered matter-of-factly, "He is pushing his horses as fast as he can already."

There was no doubt who "he" referred to. "I do not know if he had his prison-wagon when you were with him, but it is very heavy." Faith stopped when she realized anything else she said would only be speculation.

Airria backed her up though, "With the weight of the wagon he is dragging and the fact that he's not resting his horses it will take at least a day to get to this point."

Faith was not sure if Airria was just trying to comfort them or if he was telling the truth. Either way she was grateful.

As they continued down the road the trees grew thicker and greener and the grass grew rich and tall. Soon the trees formed a tunnel. Though the sun could not be seen the light seemed to penetrate the tunnel, which stretched on for quite some time.

Without warning the trees thinned and the roadway went from dirt to cobblestone. Tall, white stone buildings, most of them reaching three levels high, shimmered in the fading sunlight. The buildings in the streets were lined with lush green vines and trees. The well-kept streets wound up the small hill crossing at least five streets as they went. The group stopped in amazement, admiring the beauty and majesty of the city.

Chapter 10-Help

From well before where the trees grew into a tunnel, Carrita could feel the power of Life magic in the area. It was as intense as the Water magic near O'queen on the coast, the Chaos magic around Tark-Ancia or the Fire magic surrounding Smandler. Her mother had told her this island was different. The people here worshiped the Rarstocks, the high deities. The rest of the world worshiped their subordinates, the low deities or Treasents. Each town she had been near had a very powerful enchantment on it. The incantations were specific to one facet of magic and yet so complex that she could not even begin to comprehend the scope of its power. The island's name was a humanized draconic word which translated as both forgetting and remembering. Like a book, it had been lost for centuries only to be found and read. For all of her thirteen years Carrita had been intellectually advanced and sometimes she felt bad she did not fit in with the other children. But whenever she saw how proud her mother was the sadness faded. By the time she was eight years of age she realized she was as advanced as several of the old mages who visited her mother. Once she had asked her mother why she was able to learn so quickly. "I taught you before you were born, when it was easy. Now you just have to remember," her mother had responded.

Because of her advanced understanding Carrita had always felt more comfortable around adults, acted more like a grown-up than a child. Over the last year, she had been forced to grow up even quicker, especially in the last several months and in ways no girl should.

Now, here she was riding a horse, holding tight to a woman traveling with two warrior protectors. From the first time she laid eyes on Faith she knew Faith was a powerful yet kind person. Her aura emanated as strongly as a middle-aged Life or Order Priestess. That was why Carrita ran to Faith and supposed she had been trained in magic. From what Faith had said about how she was raised Carrita could not figure out how she had developed such a strong Life aura. She was raised in Droir, the town of Order on this island. Her confusion about Faith may be tied into this Jammar, a familiar name she could not recall. Perhaps he had taught Faith something about the Life religion.

Faith's affinity was not as odd as the men's auras. They had been raised in a town of Chaos, yet their auras were heavy in many different facets, including both Life and Death. Joskin's was by far the most balanced.

Carrita pondered on all these things as they passed through the tunnel made by the trees. The rest of the group conversed about their childhoods. Anytime Carrita's mind wandered to the painful memories of the last year she began listening to the others. When they all went quiet she leaned around Faith to see what was going on.

She had seen bigger cities, but this one was made entirely of white stone. Even the cobblestone of the streets was bright white. Rich green vines climbed lighting poles, pillars and trellises. Each building had a manicured patch of grass separating it from the road. Even in the fading sunlight this town was a sight to behold.

As the group watched in amazement, the dimming sunlight was replaced by street lights. As the main street dipped into a small valley and rose on a nearby hill, the lights gave the illusion of starlight. From where they were the town seemed to climb into the night sky.

Carrita was so enthralled with the magic of the optical illusion she did not notice herself sliding off the horse. Fortunately, Faith caught her.

Faith smiled as she made sure Carrita was secure. "Perhaps we should get to the temple," Her voice had a touch of unease.

Slowly they rode through the town admiring the beauty. Carrita especially felt a sense of peace and hope emanating from the buildings. Even the tavern and stable they passed were clean and bright.

When they reached the temple, they hitched their horses to the rail. A monk greeted each of them each individually. Dressed in white robes he was young, charming and eager to help. Carrita could feel him reaching out to understand what kind of people they were.

He greeted Faith first, "Welcome lady." He bowed low, as Carrita would have expected if he were greeting a priestess. It was obvious he felt the same thing Carrita had.

Faith took a step back and put her hand on her chest because of the respect of his greeting and simply said, "Thank you."

Both men received a nod and a, "Welcome," which they returned with, "Thank you."

The monk stopped at Carrita. He began to nod, then paused and paled slightly and stared for a moment. Carrita knew he could feel the crystal. He probably thought it was her own power. To relieve the boy's tension she said in a voice that cracked along with her heart, "I need help."

The color returned to the boy's cheeks and he finished his nod, "Please come in."

The young monk led the group to a dining room. Each table was set with mounds of various uncooked fruits and vegetables. "Please, sit, eat. I will get the High Priestess; she will tell you what needs to be done." He bowed before exiting the room.

"Lady?" Carrita teased Faith.

"Have you been here before?" Airria asked.

Faith shrugged her shoulders and glanced at Carrita, "I guess my presence just commands respect."

Carrita giggled, "Powers beyond understanding."

Airria blushed slightly. Joskin chuckled. Faith laughed out loud.

It felt good to laugh. For the second time in many years Carrita felt like a thirteen-year-old girl, both times had been because of Faith.

The feeling was contagious, laughing and joking ensued and continued until Carrita noticed the womanly figure at the door.

When Carrita stood up the figure stepped forward smiling, "If you can laugh, no problem is too big." The woman had a presence of elegance and power. She had a face of kindness and knowledge. The group turned to see who was speaking. The woman nodded politely at each of them, "I am Valnicia, High Priestess to Mellinatia, mistress of Life. I am honored to meet you..." Valnicia's voice trailed off when Faith stepped forward. After a moment of looking into Faith's eyes she said, "I am truly honored to meet you. Jammar has told me much good about you."

Faith bowed courteously, "It is kind of you to say, but I am in a bit of a hurry to visit Jammar. Is there something you can do to help our friend?" Faith asked as she encouraged Carrita forward.

The High Priestess gasped when she looked into Carrita's eyes, "It is truly a rare honor to have you visit my temple."

"Why?" Carrita asked. When she was with her mother she was used to such greetings, but never on her own.

"I have never met your mother, but I know her work," Valnicia said warmly. "You are truly her daughter."

Carrita could feel herself blush. She knew her mother was a very powerful enchantress, but had no idea her fame had reached so far. Even more amazing was the fact this priestess who had never met Carrita's mother, could tell she was her daughter.

Faith spoke up, "The more I learn of this girl, the more I wish I had the opportunity to know her mother."

"According to all those I have met who have had the chance, it is unforgettable," the Priestess said humbly as she picked up Carrita's hand, "much like looking into the eyes of someone who has seen a dragon." The priestess' eyes jumped from Carrita to Airria and back to Carrita. "If you know what to look for you can tell when someone has witnessed her work."

Joskin spoke up, "Can you help her?"

"It is true, you will need help," Valnicia said looking at Carrita. "I am honored to be the one you ask. I will do all I can to ease your suffering."

"She has a crystal," Faith said. "It needs to be removed. Can you remove it?"

"It will cost me in both pain and coin, but I will remove it," Valnicia hesitated in her speech, almost stuttering.

Joskin walked over to the priestess and placed his money bag in her hand. "This will ease the coin issue. Please make sure she gets some clothes." Without another word he walked out.

Airria thanked the priestess and headed for the door, but stopped and waited for Faith.

Faith gave Carrita a hug, "I will come back for you in a few days." Then she hugged her once more. Again Carrita felt her own age. She did not want to let go, but she knew Faith was in danger and needed to get somewhere safe.

"I will wait here," Carrita smiled. She knew even with magic it would take a very intense week to overcome the abuse enough for her to function normally in society.

Faith said farewell one more time and headed out with Airria.

Carrita already missed Faith, but knew she needed help beyond what Faith could provide.

"I can see much trouble in your young eyes. Tell me about it," Valnicia said as she indicated with her hand for Carrita to walk with her. Carrita started weeping. Just thinking of the events she had been through was enough to cause her to cry. She knew she could trust the Priestess, but it was hard to get any words out. Side-by-side they walked into a room filled with glass beakers and tubes and walls filled with books. Carrita stopped and looked at Valnicia. What did she want? Why bring her here?

The priestess reached up on a shelf and grabbed a white vial. "You will need to sleep and this will help you heal," she handed it to Carrita.

Without another word they began walking again. After a while Carrita found the strength to talk. She started at her introduction to Airria and explained what had happened all the way back to her capture at the orphanage. By that time they were in front of a wooden door. As Valnicia opened it she asked, "What about the dragon?"

Carrita was shocked. She had thought she had hidden her dragon encounter well. "This is something which I must keep deep within me,"

Carrita said trying not to sound too bitter. The bitterness was not at the priestess, it was focused on the dragon and the memories. "I will confront the dragon again."

Valnicia bowed her head respectfully, "Tonight rest and heal. When you awaken, we will remove that crystal." With that, the priestess closed the door and Carrita was left in the room.

The room was simple, a writing desk, a bed with warm and comfortable blankets and a plain white robe hanging on the wall. At least while she was at the temple she would have something dignified to wear. She walked over to the wall and replaced her tattered reminder of pain with an unsoiled white robe. It felt good to have something clean on.

While the fresh robe helped her feel a little better, inside she still felt very dirty. She had been through a lot in the last few months. She did not want to hold on to it, but knew she had to hold on to at least a piece of the memory. Even with magic it would be impossible to erase it all.

Deep in her heart she knew there was more to her story than a simple abduction by a crooked slaver and pedophile. She had been chosen out of all the children in the orphanage only six months after the dragon claimed her mother's soul. The slaver was not affluent enough to have afforded the insertion of her crystal by a powerful sorcerer. There was more which she did not know. In the back of her mind she knew she would see both the slaver and the sorcerer again.

She climbed into bed and pulled the covers up to her chin. They were as soft and warm as they looked. There was even a magic comfort in them. She could tell the blankets and sheets had been enchanted to help troubled minds rest. Even more comforting than the enchantments on the sheets was the fact she knew she was surrounded by the most merciful of magics. Filling her mind with that thought she drank the potion and drifted off to sleep.

Chapter 11-Jammar

A day and a half after leaving Carrita at the temple the party was exhausted. They had not slept, nor had they rested their horses for long. Though Faith was not aware, Airria had spoken to Joskin about the mysterious mage and warrior. After learning this even Joskin encouraged the faster pace.

The trees in the nearby forest had gone from wild growth to a perfectly manicured and pruned grid. The side of the road was lined with well-tended rose bushes. The road had a line where it changed from dirt to square yellow stones.

Airria could see Faith relax when her horse set foot on the stone road. "We are almost there," she said.

They came to a road on the right of the main. It was the width of two wagons. The road stones were octagons and squares. The octagons were one of eight colors; snow white, sky blue, bronzed brown, silvery gray, onyx black, forest green, golden yellow and blazing red. The squares were dull gray. Together they made a beautiful mosaic all the way up the hill.

Evenly spaced along both sides of the road were beautiful statues. Most of them were basic gray stone, but dispersed within the gray statues were eight larger statues each one carved from the stone that matched one of the octagon tiles of the road. Each statue, whether colored or plain gray, was so well carved it looked as if it were alive.

Of all the figures Airria recognized only one. It was one of the larger ones, the one made of white stone. He recognized it from the Life Temple. It was a representation of Mellinatia, Mistress of Life. He supposed the other colored figures were the other Rarstocks.

The top of the road circled around a large fountain. Inside the fountain, just below the water line, were statues of eight different dragons chasing one another. Airria felt himself begin to shake as his eyes locked on one figure; it looked like the dragon that had killed his father. The ripples of the water seemed to bring the figures to life.

Airria pulled his horse to a stop. He stared at the figure of the dragon. Images of his father's soul being ripped from his body reached into his head. He could see the dragon's satisfied grin. He could remember the dragon's sheer size. All of it came back so realistically; Airria could smell the sulfur and feel the heat.

"Are you sure you still want to meet him?" Faith asked, jolting Airria back to the group.

Airria was still shaking but answered, "We've come this far. It would be a waste to stop now."

The group crossed the road to the marble stairway at the crest of the circle. The stairway was Airria's height and flooded down from the decorative door at the top. The door was a dark hardwood that had beautiful silver and gold vinework framing it.

It was the most expensive and elaborate house Airria had ever seen. The gray stone walls reached as high as the trees next to them with pointed turrets on the roof. All the windows were stained-glass and large enough to walk through. Even Joskin stared for a moment in awe.

"I can see why he'd live on this side of the island," Airria said out loud, surprised to hear his own voice. "This place wouldn't survive near Tark-Ancia."

Faith snickered, "The house would survive, the town would not."

103

Joskin spoke, "If he can afford to build such a place, he can afford to magically protect it."

Faith snickered again but said no more.

Airria admired the house a little longer then rang a head-sized bell. The door was answered by a man who looked to be in his late twenties and was dressed in an elegant gray tunic and equally neat trousers. Although he looked nice, he didn't look nice enough to own such a place. Without checking with Faith, he assumed this was a servant.

"How may I help you?" the servant asked. He gave no acknowledgment to knowing Faith.

"I'm here to see Jammar, the Light Bringer," Airria said as properly as he could.

"Please come in," the servant said. When all three were inside the house he shut the door and quietly led them to a large gathering room. The room had a few bookshelves and several sofas and chairs. Some of the couches and chairs were against the walls. Many of them were in groups, presumably to facilitate conversation. The room had a gray rug which covered the whole floor and eight tapestries that hung on the walls depicting in incredible color the same beings the larger colored statues outside depicted.

Airria admired the tapestries while the servant seated Joskin and Faith on the couch facing a table with a head sized crystal ball on it. Faith was smiling, her eyes sparkling. Airria figured she was excited to be there.

"Please follow me," the servant said to Airria.

Airria followed the servant down the hallway. The walls were covered in tapestries of such fine weave and intricate detail they almost seemed to be alive. Each tapestry was twenty to thirty paces in length and reached from the floor to the extremely high ceiling. They depicted grand battles. Airria wished he could take the time to study them closer, but the servant was not waiting.

Soon they came to a circular stairwell. The outside wall had only torches. The inside wall had alcoves with different styles of armor on sculptures of men and women. Again all of the artistry was incredible.

104

Airria knew the house was made of stone blocks, but he couldn't see the seams between the stones.

The stairs went farther than Airria thought possible. When they finally reached the bottom the servant opened the door to a massive room. Torches lined the walls in two layers that extended as far as Airria could see. He continued to follow the servant until the doorway behind him disappeared.

"Stop," Airria insisted. "I have followed you long enough without receiving any explanation." He couldn't see an end forward or back. "I'm here to speak with Jammar, the Dragon Slayer and it doesn't appear you are taking me to him." He used the different title to emphasize his reason for being there.

The servant stopped and turned around. "Dragon Slayer?" his voice was somewhat distant. "It has been a very long time since anyone has asked for the Dragon Slayer."

Airria was already tired and irritable. The servant's charade was not lightening his mood. "May I speak to Jammar or not?"

The visual expression and tone of the servant never changed, but he raised his arm over his head and threw a red sphere Airria hadn't noticed in his hand.

When the sphere hit the ground is shattered. A red mist quickly filled the room. Airria pulled his sword as the mist began dancing away to reveal that he was now in a gigantic cavern.

The walls were rough and the cavern edges were cluttered with damaged armor and broken weapons. Towards the center were a mound of gold and a sleeping Red Dragon. Airria could feel the heat emanating from the dragon. He could smell the ash of its breath.

Airria snuck slowly up on the dragon. He'd practiced since he was very young and knew well how to make no noise, but today everything seemed to echo. His heart was pounding so loudly in his ears he couldn't even hear the rasp of the dragon's breathing. The dragon didn't move except for the expansion and contraction of its chest.

Things may not be what they seem. The thought went through his head in a way he vaguely recalled from the cave a few days ago, but the fear and excitement of being so close to a dragon pushed any sane thoughts to the back of his mind.

This dragon was much smaller, perhaps a tenth of the size of the one who had taken his father. This dragon was red instead of black. Nonetheless he felt the thirst for revenge.

Airria struck with his usual speed and precision, but the dragon moved so quickly and naturally as to cause its dodge to appear that it was just getting up, oblivious to Airria's presence. It began to scratch its head on the side of the cave.

Airria had missed a strike before, but it had been many years since even Joskin had been able to make such a casual dodge. Frustrated, he dove in for another swing. This one was slightly wilder.

Again the dragon moved with casual ease and began scratching its shoulder on the wall, "Nothing like a good scratch after a long nap."

Even with Airria's skills and the powerful magic sword in his hand the dragon was showing its disregard for him, which fueled both his anger and his frustration. In the back of his mind he could hear the voice telling him it was all an illusion, but he ignored it.

With each swing Airria lost more and more control. His swings became wilder as the dragon, near Airria's height at the shoulder, made its way around the room scratching, sorting armor or gold, or laying back down for a rest. It didn't even acknowledge Airria's presence until Airria's sword landed deep in the dragon's golden bed.

The dragon let out a rumbling laugh the made Airria's jaw vibrate. "Now where am I supposed to sleep? You have ruined my bed." It spoke to Airria in a voice that made Airria's ribs resonate. It glanced at Airria with a look of mock frustration.

Airria couldn't pull his sword free of the bed. It was like the sword was holding on to the bed. *Calm down boy*! The voice shouted in his mind finally cutting through his rage.

As Airria tugged at the sword he realized he could feel no power in it. It was at this epiphany he realized it had been the sword talking to him.

The sword continued, *This is all an illusion. Look at the situation. That dragon has not even tried to touch you. Only a White or Gold Dragon would ever be so courteous.*

The words made enough sense to pull Airria out of his rage. He had always listened intently to stories of dragons, though for most of his life he had thought they were just interesting legends. Red or Fire Dragons were, by all the accounts, extremely fond of igniting intruders. This one had only danced around the cave. As his mind grasped and held on to these thoughts the sword slid free.

Airria took a few breaths and pondered what had happened. He had lost control and allowed this illusion to push him into carelessness. If this dragon had been real he knew he would've been dead of his own stupidity.

After a moment Airria began to wonder why Jammar would put him through this. It occurred to him that the whole thing may have been a test. He had come to Jammar for help and had been given a test. Jammar had no right to test him. All he wanted was some information and this man had sent him here.

The thought occurred to him that he was irrationally tired and his anger at Jammar's test was unjustified. Right now he didn't care.

Airria could feel the anger returning, but this time he kept it in check. He took a few breaths to calm down again. He knew he still needed Jammar's help. He looked around and saw no openings to the cavern. The only thing he could think to do was call for him."Jammar! I'm ready!" he shouted

Chapter 12-Disappointment

Faith was excited to see her old mentor. She remembered the first time she had come to Jammar in hopes of becoming a better archer. He had taken her to a room full of fluttering bats and scurrying rats. She could not hit a single one. Her test was so frustrating she almost quit before she started. She knew the test was different for each person. That was how Jammar weeded out the ones not serious enough for him to train. He seemed to know the best test for each candidate.

Standing at Jammar's door again she knew she would not help Airria if she let him know what was going on. When Airria glanced at her she shrugged, both to not show her excitement at seeing Jammar and to hide her anxiety over the test Airria would have to face. She could only guess at how Jammar would test him. She really wanted him to pass, but Jammar would not accept him to be trained if he suspected she had warned him. Airria would have to give up and walk away to fail. Faith had seen four others come to Jammar for training and none of them ever came back.

Jammar ushered them to the greeting room, as much a she wanted to give her mentor a hug and ask him the questions racing around in her mind she knew his dutiful servant act was a part of the test. She knew she had to pretend she did not know him. She was not sure how well she was doing. Not to mention, she had talked quite a bit about Jammar and did not know if the men would believe she really would not know one of his servants.

She could not look Airria in the eye before they left the room. Fortunately he was intrigued by the tapestries representing the Rarstocks, or High Deities, of the world.

When Jammar and Airria were out of earshot Joskin asked Faith, "I thought you had trained here. Why didn't the servant know you?"

Faith did not look Joskin in the eye. She looked at the carpet and focused on the intricate gray design. She did not want to give away anything she should not. "Airria needs to understand some things before he talks to Jammar."

"What things?" Joskin's voice was a little suspicious.

Faith thought for a moment. She really did not know what Airria would have to learn. She did not know what his test would be. "I honestly do not know."

"Airria can be a little hot-headed at times. I'm sure you've noticed," Joskin chuckled nervously. "I know this isn't a trap. You worked too hard to get him here safely to want him dead now." He sounded as if he were trying to convince himself. "Where did they go?"

In her travels with the men she had learned many things about them. Joskin was a little paranoid and was very protective of his cousin. Airria often rushed in without thinking and he had a lot of enemies, most of which were kept at bay by Joskin's reputation.

"You trusted me this far," Faith looked up from the rug to make eye contact with Joskin. She did not know if Jammar was planning on testing Joskin or not, but she had to comfort him in some way, "will you trust me a little further?"

"Always a good idea," Jammar's voice came as a wave of relief from the doorway, "she is an honest and helpful woman." He held out his arms in welcome.

She seized the opportunity and jumped up and gave him a hug. "I know I have only been gone a couple of weeks, but I have missed you terribly."

"It has been almost a month since you visited me last," Jammar said with a chastising grin.

"It is not my fault," Faith explained. "My father had a debt to pay." She did not want to go down that road again.

Fortunately Jammar cut her off. "I understand," his voice was gentle. She knew at that point he had been jesting with her, a month ago she would have understood it. The last few weeks had changed her more than she thought.

Joskin interrupted the reunion, "Where is Airria?"

"Do not worry," Jammar's tone was partially amused, the voice of a man well familiar through long experience with the situation at hand. He gave Faith a wink and then nodded to Joskin, "Would you like to see him?"

Joskin was standing, ax in hand. He was not in a threatening stance, but he had such a powerful figure. Faith felt a little ruffled. Jammar showed no signs of fear or intimidation, he waved his hand and an image of Airria walking down the hallway appeared over the nearby crystal ball.

Joskin sat back down, a humble look on his face. It was surprising to see how easily Jammar had abased Joskin, even if it were only a little. Faith had seen Jammar's artifacts and she knew several of them came from a dragon's hoard. She knew Joskin had spent a lot of time off the island and had dealings with mages. It was not hard to guess why he did not press. Besides, he seemed to be satisfied to just watch.

She turned back to Jammar, "You know they will never accept me back into the town guard." She hoped she would not have to ask for work, but was ready to.

"They will see you only as a slave. If the slaver comes looking for you they will turn you over." Jammar's face showed an uncharacteristic glimmer of excitement, as if something about the situation made him happy though his voice sounded of sadness. "I could not even hire you. I cannot protect you."

"Could you not purchase me and then let me work the debt off?" Faith felt her stomach drop with despair. Though she noticed the glimmer of excitement in his eye, the sadness in his voice and unwelcome words hurt too much for her to wonder. "Is there really nothing you can do to help me?"

"Me?" Jammar said. "There is nothing I can directly do, but it would appear you have found friends who can and have helped you thus far."

Faith looked at Joskin and thought of Airria. "They assisted me in getting here because Airria wanted to meet you."

"This," Jammar said pointing to the crystal, "is only part of his test. Airria will want your help with the other part."

Faith was confused, "My test was only the illusion," she cringed as she realized she had told Joskin more than she thought she was supposed to.

Jammar remained unfazed. "I knew this day would come. The training you received was to help Airria through this."

She was not sure if Jammar was talking about the second part of Airria's test or the quest Airria desired Jammar to help him with. "What can I do?"

The corners of Jammar's lips rose, "Trust yourself." His face quickly faded back into a somber look. "If he accepts the second test and you help him through it. There may be a way for you to not go back to the slaver."

Faith gave Jammar another hug, "Thank you!"

"This test will not be as easy as yours was," Jammar said, "it will not be safe. Thank me when you get back, if you can get back." The glimmer left Jammar's eyes.

Joskin's booming laugh turned Faith around. "Is this really an illusion?" he exclaimed. "I wish I could play pranks like this on him back home."

Airria was in an impossibly long hallway with only Jammar and rows of torches either way. "Can I speak with Jammar or not?" Airria yelled.

Joskin chuckled, "You got him on a good day for this. He hasn't slept in a few days. Soon he'll lose it."

The illusion of Jammar threw the sphere and the mist rose. When

111

it cleared both Joskin and Faith gasped at the dragon.

As Airria crept up to the creature, Faith was amazed at his ability. He made no sound. When he swung his sword it was with his usual speed and precision, but the dragon's ease and fluid motion made it look awkward.

Suddenly tense Joskin asked, "This is an illusion, right?"

"Airria is the only dangerous thing in the room," Jammar said.

Together the three of them watched Airria recklessly attack the dragon. Joskin shook his head with each stroke of Airria's sword.

When the sword finally got stuck in the golden bed and Airria struggled to pull it out Joskin breathed a sigh of relief, "Maybe he can get his head back on his shoulders." Then he began to hold his breath.

Airria finally pulled his sword free and stood staring at it. After a few moments he began looking around. Then he yelled, "Jammar, I'm ready!"

The other four candidates Faith was aware of who had come to Jammar to be trained had worked themselves into such a frenzy they had knocked themselves out. She was surprised Airria had done so well.

"That did not take long," Jammar said waving his arms in the air. He began to chant in a language Faith did not recognize.

Soon Jammar stopped his chanting. Then there was a loud pop, a bright light and Airria was standing with them. He looked as though he were struggling to keep his frustration under control.

Before Airria could get a word out Jammar said, "That is a beautiful weapon. Where did you get it?" Jammar stared at Airria's sword as though it were an old friend he had not seen in a long while.

"I found it in a cave on our way here," Airria's tone became defensive. Faith knew he had no intentions of giving it up.

"A weapon like this finds its owner, not the other way around." Jammar's gaze shifted from Airria to Joskin and back.

Joskin was standing, rolling his ax haft in his hands. His eyes shifted from his ax to Jammar and back. After a moment he spoke up, "Were you the one who opened the cave for us?"

"Cave?" Jammar queried. "No. I know a little magic and have a few parlor tricks and illusions. I have neither the power nor the authority to contain such weapons."

"Do you know who would have such power or authority?" Joskin asked. "You seem to know our weapons without even touching them."

"It is true I believe I know both of your weapons. Your ax I have never seen in battle, I have only read legends of it. This sword," Jammar said pointing to Airria's weapon, "has slain dragons before. I will tell you more in the morning. For now all of you are tired and famished. Perhaps you would share a meal with me?"

Faith had never seen Jammar in armor and it did not seem as though he had seen any battles outside of his books. As far as she knew he had never even left the island. Now she was thinking about it he had looked the same age for as long as she could remember. Some things he had said today made him sound much older. The way he looked at Airria's sword indicated he had a personal attachment to it. She was about to ask how old he was when a familiar voice distracted her.

"Dinner is ready." Tarsa, Jammar's wife walked in the room.

Faith could not help herself, she squealed with delight at the sight of another dear friend, whom only two weeks ago she thought she would never see again. She ran and gave Tarsa a hug.

Though her face beamed with excitement Tarsa's voice was calm and gentle. "It is good to see you and in such fine spirits." Leaving one arm around Faith she added, "There will be baths ready for each of you in your rooms when you are finished eating."

Both Joskin and Airria kept rubbing their weapons and looking around. It was understandable why they were nervous, but Faith knew she was safe, at least for now.

Dinner was drake tail in butter sauce with all of the trimmings. As per usual, Jammar's cook had done an outstanding job. Even Joskin and Airria stopped twitching and enjoyed the harp music playing in the background. Not a word about dragons or weapons, just pure contentment. With everything she had learned about magic and what she knew about Jammar she wondered if the room was enchanted to help them all feel peaceful.

After dinner Jammar led the men to their respective rooms, Tarsa

113

led Faith. While they walked Tarsa updated Faith on all the gossip of the town. Faith truly felt like herself again. She gratefully listened.

Tarsa made sure Faith had everything she needed, including a book covering the basics of magic which Faith had not asked for. When Tarsa was gone Faith soaked in the tub and read. The longer she was in the tub, the further away her troubles seemed.

After some time she got ready for bed. She set the book on the desk next to her bed and crawled under the covers. For the first time since she laid eyes on the Henrik she slept restfully.

Chapter 13-Real Pain

Carrita woke up the next morning with Valnicia sitting next to her bed. She felt well rested, but was still sore from the previous day's push. Her physical scars and bruises had been healed days ago by Joskin's salve. The emotional scars would take much longer, though the potion and the magic in the bed had healed overnight what would have taken months. It still hurt to think about the last several months, but it did not force her to break down.

"You are looking rested," Valnicia said.

"Yes." Carrita appreciated Valnicia's help, but was still thinking about the crystal. She knew Henrik was not far behind them. She knew Faith had headed back to Droir. With knowledge of Order followers as well as what Faith had told her Carrita knew the slaver would not need guards to abduct Faith again. Airria and Joskin, she figured, would abandon Faith as soon as they got what they wanted. All three of them had been great to Carrita, but she still did not trust the men. Faith had mentioned the Order of the Black Claw, or at least a mage from the Order had already paid for her.

These thoughts remained at the foremost of Carrita's mind. "I would like to remove the crystal as soon as possible," she said to

Valnicia.

"I have already sent Bronak, my son, to purchase the spell components we require. He should be back soon." She sighed, "It is good you are rested. This will take a lot out of both of us."

"I am not worried about the pain," Carrita said as strongly as she could. "I am worried for you and just as much for what will happen to my friend." She knew the crystal not only drained her manna, but carried a dark curse for anyone who tried to remove it. There was a good chance Valnicia would lose her mind in the process causing the island to lose their Life Priestess. Also, if Valnicia's mind went before the removal, Carrita would have no chance of getting it out.

"As I promised we will do what we can to remove it," the tremor in the priestess's voice was not comforting, "as soon as Bronak gets back."

"While we wait do you mind if I try something?" Carrita felt awkward trying to comfort the woman who was to heal her, but she was used to knowing more about magic than many great mages. "I would like to do something which may help you."

Valnicia looked intrigued, "I don't believe there is anything you can do. The magic in the crystal is strong and you do not have your magic."

Carrita almost giggled, "I may not be able to access my manna, but I definitely can help. My mother trained me not only in spell casting, but also alchemy."

"You are so young," the priestess protested. "How can you know enough to help?"

Carrita felt giddy to be able to talk a little about magic. Magic was the one subject she knew well. It had been her escape from the trials of the last year. She would prevent herself from screaming during the months of torture and abuse by contemplating magic, both spells and alchemy. She had figured out how to make a potion which would safely remove the crystal, but was sure Ramsel Island did not have access to lightning water or ground unicorn horn, much less the bottled blue drake's breath. Such rare components would take months, if not years, to track down and a small fortune to purchase. Neither luxury did she have

117

at this time. As much as Carrita did not want to risk Valnicia's mind, she knew they would have to make do with what they had on hand.

The night before she had seen ingredients in the alchemy room she would require to create a potion to help Valnicia stay grounded. She smiled at the priestess, "If I may use your laboratory I may be able to help. My mother trained me well."

Valnicia said, "I don't know if you can help or not, but if there is a chance you can I will give you everything I have."

Carrita hopped out of bed, though her muscles protested and allowed Valnicia to lead her to the laboratory. It was full of books and ingredients. Valnicia watched Carrita's every move with intense curiosity. Carrita felt good getting her fingers dirty mixing a potion. In a laboratory as well-equipped as this one she could make a very powerful potion. Unfortunately, a very powerful potion might not be enough, but she had to try.

Valnicia asked Carrita why she added each ingredient and why she would use a different refining process on each ingredient. Carrita did not mind; she always loved to teach about magic, especially to women she knew would use it to help others. Talking slowed the process a little, but Carrita was confident her work would greatly increase their chances of success.

The process took much longer than she thought it would. Though the time flew by as she worked her stomach began to hurt with hunger. She looked around the room while the potion cooled. Bronak was waiting at the door with two small baskets of ingredients. He was slouching slightly and glancing casually around the room, but said nothing.

"Were you able to get everything?" Valnicia asked as she approached her son.

"Yes, Mother," he held out the baskets.

"Then we shall eat," she turned to Carrita, "after which we shall remove the crystal." She still sounded as though she were headed into a losing battle.

"I believe," Carrita spoke up, "my efforts this morning will help you." Even Carrita could not make her heart feel confident. This was an absolute gamble. Either she would walk away a free girl, or the priestess would lose her mind or even her life. If the priestess failed, Carrita would have little to no hope of ever getting off this island, nor of obtaining the items she would need to remove it herself.

They all walked to the dining hall and had a light meal. Carrita had been hungry when she had finished the potion, but when the priestess had reminded her of the stakes her appetite had lessened. Watching the other two picking at their food she assumed they felt the same way. Carrita hated to take such a chance with such an important woman. She felt very selfish, but she had her own mission and she could not accomplish it with the crystal still bound to her.

It did not take long for them to finish. Carrita went to the laboratory and poured most of the potion into a vial. Valnicia and Bronak went to prepare the room. When Carrita arrived at the room her bed resembled a sacrificial altar. There was a huge circle of snow white crystal around her bed. Several symbols were painted just inside the circle with exotic herbs and juices. White rose and lily blossoms covered the bed.

Admiring the priestess's handiwork Carrita thought, *This woman really knows her trade.* She walked around the circle slowly, trying to think of anything that might help. "Do you have some golden crystal or powdered gold?" she asked, an idea forming in her mind.

Valnicia looked a little puzzled. "Have I done something wrong?"

It still felt a little strange to have a High Priestess question her work based on Carrita's word, but it was not unexpected. Carrita smiled at the priestess, "Everything looks to be in order. I just had another thought which might help us."

"There is not much crystal, but what I have you are welcome to." The priestess waved a hand and her son, the young monk, ran down the hall. "If you were anyone else's child I would doubt you. I am a High Priestess of Mellinatia. I have been blessed with a tremendous knowledge of the powers of life. You were trained by Tarsella, the Fairen of the Blood Range and an immortal in her own right. There is no telling what secrets are in your head."

119

"Immortal?" Carrita asked. Tarsella was just her mother to her. She knew her mother was a powerful enchantress, mages and clergy showed her respect. She had never thought of her mother's age. She was just mother.

The priestess simply smiled and began walking around the circle. She was looking intently at the symbols. Carrita guessed she was double-checking the work and possibly trying to figure out what Carrita had in mind.

Carrita was happy to see the boy come back with a small pouch. "There's not much here, but if it will help..." clearly Bronak also realized the gravity of the situation.

Carrita accepted the pouch gratefully. She turned to the priestess, "Where do you plan on standing through the ritual?" Valnicia indicated a spot on the side of the bed and Carrita drew a small circle with a triangle in the middle. It was a very basic order symbol as far as symbols went, but Carrita hoped with all the magic which would be traversing the room it would help to protect the priestess. "If you carefully stand on it the symbol should help keep you grounded."

"Of course, Order to counter the Chaos."

"This," Carrita said as she handed the priestess the buttery-looking potion, "will also help." She removed her robe and lay down in the middle of the bed. She was concerned about the twelve year old monk seeing her naked, but she knew he had a purpose to perform and her robes would interfere with the magic. They needed all the help they could get.

The monk went about his task of lighting opposing candles, walking from side to side around the outside of the circle. He was precise and specific with the candles. He didn't even seem to notice Carrita in her vulnerable state.

The priestess disrobed and drank the potion. Gently Valnicia stepped into the circle and stood on Carrita's symbol. Soon she began to chant. Carrita could feel when the Life magic began dancing around the room. When the last candle was lit the boy left the room. The candles erupted and a brilliant white flame spread around the circle creating a white wall at the edge of the circle. The symbols began to light up one after the other.

Carrita could feel the magic being yanked from the crystal. She could feel that it should have hurt her. By the whimpers coming from the priestess Carrita could tell the priestess was accepting the pain for her. Carrita wished the priestess would let Carrita carry the pain; this was going to be hard enough without the extra distraction.

Beads of sweat began running down Valnicia's body. Death and Chaos magic could almost be seen as they began swirling up from the crystal in her navel. Carrita tried to reach out with her mind and catch onto it, to help control and direct it. As Carrita reached out she could feel Valnicia's struggle with trying to simultaneously hold on to her own magic and her sanity. The woman began glowing golden-white. Carrita knew her potion was helping but had severely underestimated the power of the crystal. Valnicia's face became more twisted with pain as the glowing protection from the potion wore off. Her words became slurred and distant. Her eyelids twitched, as did her hands. Blood began running out of her nose and the corners of her eyes.

It was a long while before enough of the magic was out of the crystal for Carrita to control even a small amount of it. As soon as that happened, she began changing the Chaos and Death magic into Order magic and funneling it into the crystal at the priestess' feet. Slowly the crystal began to glow. As Carrita gained more access to the wild magic she changed it and continued to funnel into the crystal powder. The glow intensified. In time the glow became a bright yellow wall around the priestess. The brighter the glow, the more of the pain Carrita could feel.

The pain intensified until she could feel blood running out of her own nose and eyes. Not only did her head feel like it was caught in a vice, but her whole body felt like it was slowly being torn apart.

As if the pain were not enough, her mind was having a hard time focusing on anything. The magic, normally invisible, began to show itself from time to time in black or bronze and then disappear. The walls of the room were gone, solid and crumbled all at the same time. The priestess was a young girl, an old woman, a pile of bones and dust in a breeze all in the exact moment. Nothing made sense. She felt like eternity was only an instant and each instant was an eternity.

In the deepest and most painful times she could see her mother's face in the flashes of magic. Though she did not know if the face was real or a product of her degrading mental state she held onto the feeling and thought of her mother being near as long as she could.

There was no way to tell how long she remained in that condition. A bright flash and a loud boom finally brought the golden shield down. Carrita could feel the priestess reclaim the pain. Valnicia looked better for a short while and then the sweat and blood began to run down her again. She looked as if she would soon collapse.

Carrita could now grab much more of the magic being released by the crystal. She used what she could to heal Valnicia and herself by changing it to Healing magic, then converted it to Order magic and began weaving it around the room. She could see the priestess' face; Carrita's efforts were not in vain. The blood slowed and her face became less twisted.

Carrita was becoming so tired she was about to give up. Valnicia was shaking again, on the edge of collapse. Blood covered the ground. Carrita knew if she had not done what she had, the priestess would have bled out and died. She also knew if she stopped the crystal would recharge using the manna it sucked from her.

With one final effort Carrita took all of the magic she could grab from the air, converted it to Earth magic and forced it back into the crystal. She ground the magic around in the crystal until it cracked. She felt as though her body had split in two and she could not die, being stuck in a place outside of time.

She had no idea how long she was like that, but eventually there was a flash of green light and a loud rumble. Then things went dark.

When Airria woke up that morning he felt rested. For the first time since his father died he hadn't had to relive it. He felt peaceful. If it weren't for the gnawing at his stomach, he would have been happy to stay in bed all day. He had forgotten how restful sleep could be. It was nice, but he had come for a purpose. Today he would get the information he needed from Jammar to find the dragon.

He forced himself to get out of bed and strapped the sword on. Then he headed out to find Jammar. A servant boy was waiting for him and led him to the most exquisite breakfast he had ever tasted. There were flatbreads with exotic fruits on top, with smoked and spiced meats on the side. He ate until he thought he would burst.

When he was finished the servant led him to a monstrous library. Not that he had ever been inside or even seen a library before, but his entire house could fit inside the room.

Faith was sitting in a chair reading a book. Her clothes appeared clean. Joskin was looking over maps with great interest. Jammar stood up from his chair as Airria entered the room.

"Forgive me for asking, but I would like to make sure I am correct about your sword. May I hold it?" Jammar asked.

Airria was not sure it was a good idea to give up his weapon. "You seemed pretty sure of yourself yesterday. Why do you need to hold it today?"

Jammar grinned, "Do not worry, you will get it back. I already have my own." He pointed around the room to the weapons decorating the spaces between the bookshelves.

Airria realized if Jammar wanted the sword for himself he could have taken it by force. Reluctantly he gave it up.

Jammar received it with both hands and a bowed head. "Do you know what kind of sword this is?" there was a hint of adoration in his voice.

The only things that came to Airria's mind were the power he felt holding it and the voice in his mind. "I know it's a magic sword. I think it talked to me," both Joskin and Faith laughed.

"A talking sword?" Joskin asked.

Faith's eyes flashed playfully when Jammar looked at her and she bit her lip to try to stop laughing.

"Well it did talk to me!" Airria protested. It had been hard for him to accept at first. He could understand his friends not believing, but it still hurt when they laughed.

After a long moment Joskin said, "It has to be a sword made with Order magic. Its golden color says as much."

Airria remembered the religious color code. Gold did mean Order, but this was not gold, it was a golden-white fire.

Jammar's voice was reverential, "Not quite. It was forged for far greater purpose than helping a single religious facet. It is a true holy sword." His eyes focused on something distant, as though he were looking back to the days of its creation.

"Each Rarstock decides what is holy for their facet and what is not," Joskin protested. "That may be a holy sword for Order, but Chaos would consider it unholy."

Jammar's eyes locked with Joskin's. Even though the gaze was not directed at him, Airria could feel the power and authority. By the way Joskin's skin lightened it was obvious he could feel it, too.

"I once thought as you do," Jammar said. "After I killed the dragon I went around in my new-found glory, doing as I pleased. I thought I could save my soul by accepting whatever deity fit my mood or accepting only the teachings I wanted to. One day I realized there were many people suffering. I decided I was going to take the place of one of the Rarstocks which would give me the right and ability to end the suffering; I believed I had the means," irony edged Jammar's voice.

"That is, except for how to find the Rarstocks. An old man told me to search the edges of this island to become aware of what was really going on. I found four shrines which told the history of the existence of both Rarstocks and all of the human-like creatures. The shrines told why dragons existed, why the Rarstocks cannot help more than they do and what will happen to our souls after we die." His voice tapered off as if he were tired from the weight of all the things he had learned.

Faith interrupted, "It sounds like you have been around for thousands of years. I knew you were different, but I just thought you were little older than you look. With everything you have said in the last couple of days it would seem you are much older than thirty or even forty. Why the pretense of youth?"

"I am a little older than I look," Jammar said with a playful gleam in his eyes. "There is no pretense; I simply am myself and allow people to draw their own conclusions."

"How is it done?" Faith asked.

Jammar gently handed Airria back his sword and put his fingers together under his chin. "In a dragon's heart there are four stones made entirely of magic. These gems naturally grow in proportion with the dragon's magical ability, her dedication to her alignment, her skills and her knowledge. While touching these gems a being will be able to access a portion of those traits. If a person were to touch them too long or too often without magic protection he would go insane; even with magical help the gems will often flood those who are not ready with too much knowledge and drive him insane. I have three of the four gems from the dragon I killed. The magic from the gems keeps me looking young."

"Why did you refer to dragons as female?" Faith asked. Airria hadn't even noticed.

"Because they are, but you will learn more about that at the shrines, if you really want to know," Jammar chuckled.

"You promised to tell me about my sword," Airria insisted.

"Of her history from after her first owner until now, I can tell you little. I can only tell you the Rarstocks and High Dragons of Life, Order and Nature created it from pure sunlight. One of the Elder White Dragons donated her life. It was crafted for a man named Theilord who lived outside the boundary; it was created to limit the Black Dragon population. Esnie, the only true God, punished all of them for interfering with such power."

Joskin, with a look of disbelief asked, "Why were they punished? Isn't it their right to do as they please?"

"No," Jammar said with a relaxing grin.

"Why not? They have limitless power." Joskin's teeth were grinding slightly, but his tone carried a small amount of tension.

Jammar raised an eyebrow. "They are only Rarstocks, not Gods. Rather than argue with you about it you can read about it at the shrines. If you have any questions afterwards, I will be glad to answer them then."

Faith frowned, "How were the Rarstocks punished? I am sure they were just trying to help."

Jammar's smile expanded, "They were just trying to help, but this world runs on a balance of all eight facets and the sword would throw it out of balance. They were punished by being banished to another dimension where they could see the destruction happening in the world, but could do nothing to stop it. Theilord, his wife and a few others were all that stood between total destruction of the world outside the boundary. It was a dark time. Fortunately the great powers of Death, Chaos and Fire were busy creating a weapon of equal destructive power as yours."

Faith asked, "What is this boundary you speak of?"

"It is an area set aside by the entirety of the Council: all the Rarstocks, High Dragons, Treasents and Terisents. It is protected by powerful magic. No dragon, Titan, or any being of great power can enter except certain of the Council and Guardians. This also will be better described at the shrines," Jammer said.

Airria was excited to know more of the original owner of the sword. If he guessed right the gems in his sword were dragon gems. They should have granted Theilord eternal youth, if he understood Jammar right. "Tell us more about Theilord, or is that on the shrines as well?" He was also tired of Jammar telling them the answers to their questions were at the shrines.

Jammar got a distant look in his eye as though he were looking back on his childhood hero. "Theilord is the only being ever to defeat an Elder Black Dragon with only a magical dagger. His is also only one of three non-Titans to live through an exclusive fight with one." Looking back down at Airria's sword Jammar's eyes became misty. He continued, "He was the one who inspired me to hunt dragons, regardless of his warnings." He had to chuckle to clear a knot in his throat.

"What happened to him?" Airria sensed there was more to this story.

Jammar paused for a moment, "They killed him."

"How?" Joskin asked. "If he could slay an Elder Dragon with nothing but a magic dagger, how could they touch him with such a powerful sword? I mean, he was so good and he had this amazing sword. So, how?"

"Sword, great armor," Jammar reminisced. After a moment of silence, he slammed his fist on the table. "After Theilord disposed of the owner of the other sword and hid it, the High Black Dragon raised the most powerful army ever assembled, the Death Army. As a High Dragon she could not participate in the fight, but she instructed them on what to do. They ambushed him when he was alone. He killed many of them before he was defeated, but there were just too many. As if it were not enough to kill him they placed his body on a pole for archery practice," his teeth ground together as he spoke.

Faith put a hand on his shoulder as a tear ran down his cheek. "Did anybody do anything about it?"

"Theilord had many powerful friends," Jammar's tone softened as he continued, "They raised an army to destroy what was left of the Death Army, but the Death Army caught wind of the coming attack and ran to a large bowl deep in a dark mountain range. There they made a stronghold."

"The leaders of the army raised to destroy the Death Army, or Army of Light as they called themselves, knew the strength of their enemy's position. They sent a messenger under a flag of truce to challenge them to a fair fight in the nearby open plains.

By this time Faith, Airria and Joskin were all on the edges of their seats.

Jammar continued, "The Death Army did not trust anybody. They not only would not let the messenger in, they shot him and let him tumble back down the slope. The note attached to the arrow said they would only accept Theilord's wife, Viehasia into their camp."

"It was obvious to everyone what the opposing army would do

128

with Viehasia if they captured her. They would use her for their own torturous pleasures until they grew tired and then kill her and raise her as undead."

"She was in the Army of Light's camp, being there to witness the avenging of her husband. She suggested they make a suit of armor for her to help her defeat the army. It took almost a year, but all the magic users and a few dragons worked together with the greatest of armor smiths to create a suit of armor unequaled anywhere. To make sure it would be enough two powerful mages and one of Theilord's dearest warrior friends allowed their souls to be placed into it."

He continued on as he started to pace, "She put it on and marched up the hill with an ancient bow and quiver with four arrows in it, trophies from Theilord's adventures. All I saw was a red and black mist rise on the mountain. All I heard were the cries of pain. When she came down carrying her husband's body we all cheered. After the ordeal was over she took both suits into the boundary and hid them. The last I heard they were still hidden there."

Joskin asked, "Did anyone ever go check out the scene? Or go pick up the gold?" His eyes were bright and he was sitting on the edge of his chair.

Jammar chuckled, "You were raised Chaos, were you not?" Without waiting for a reply he continued, "I did go see what had happened. Many of the bodies had holes in them large enough to stick my head through. Their entrails covered the ground and every swell and gully was running rivers of blood. I could only find half the numbers we had thought to be in the army."

"And nobody has taken the armor?" Airria saw an opportunity to gain an extremely good suit of armor.

"I know of many who have tried and I'm sure there have been many more, but the Ward is strong," Jammar said shaking his head.

"Ward?" Airria's lack of magical understanding showed once again.

"It is a magical symbol having a permanent effect," Faith felt as surprised as Airria looked to have such information come out of her mouth.

"I did not know you knew so much about magic," Jammar smiled proudly.

Trying to hide her own surprise at the answer Faith replied, "Just something I picked up from a young friend on the trail." Then with an obvious attempt to put the subject somewhere else she asked, "Where is this place?"

"I will tell you after you get back from the shrines. If you still want to know," Jammar spoke with a dare in his voice.

"Why are all four of the shrines on this island?" Joskin asked. "Or are there shrines like this everywhere? And why were you searching this island for a way to get to the Rarstocks?"

"As I told you an old man pointed me in this direction," Jammar explained. "The shrines were placed on this island because the island was made by the Rarstocks to stay separated from the outside turmoil. All eight of the basic facets of existence are represented; each facet has its own town here. You see this island was created by the Rarstocks as a reminder of the history of this world. Each one of the Rarstocks created a town and filled it with people dedicated to them. Humans are the only intelligent race allowed on the island. There will never be any other races without the Rarstocks consent."

Faith interrupted, "I thought I knew this corner of the island pretty well and I have never seen a shrine."

Jammar smiled as he handed a rolled up piece of parchment to Airria. "I assure you the shrines are here on this island."

Airria asked with a touch of impatience in his voice, "Why travel around the island when you could just tell us what's in them."

Jammar glanced over at Joskin, "As was shown earlier, you have your own belief system, the way you understand the world. It would be much more difficult for you to accept such a paradigm shift from my words. Besides, the shrines are more than words. Hopefully you'll understand when you see them."

Joskin's legs were shifting under his chair. Airria had seen this before when one of their mothers would say something Joskin did not agree with, but Joskin did not want to say anything about it. In an attempt to help his cousin now Airria suggested, "It will take us some time to make the trip around the island, I'm sure. Perhaps we should get started."

Chapter 15-Faith's Truth

When the group left Jammar's place they decided to head to the nearest shrine. The path led them through Droir. They knew passing through Droir was a risk, but even Faith agreed the risk was worth it and Faith wanted to see her parents.

The slaver had insisted her father had been playing a game of chance, using her as a betting chip. Faith struggled to believe this. Games of chance were forbidden in Droir and her father was careful to live as exact as he could to the laws of the town. She knew he had a debt with the seed store, but Furlin, the owner, had always been kind about allowing farmers to pay when they could. Her father's farm had not been producing well the last few years no matter what he tried.

Garrett, the general store owner, had been less understanding, but her father's debt there was not big enough for the law to require a member of his family as payment.

Faith knew the law, having been trained as the town guard. Part of her training included cases of law. If a debt of five silver pieces or greater was taken and the creditor demanded payment, the debt must be paid. If the debtor could not pay, then the debtor, the spouse, or one of the children could be taken as compensation. The creditor could choose which.

Faith was sure her father had been careful to avoid any single debt in town reaching this limit. Yet the slaver had insisted her father had gambled into such debt.

As the group rode, Faith pondered how she became a slave. It was not long before the stone walls of Droir came into view. At the sight, her already confused heart became a cacophony of emotion. She was terrified the slaver would be waiting. She desperately wanted to see her family again. She also wanted to find out how her father could have acquired such a debt. She had promised to help Airria and was not sure if he would be willing to stop.

As they passed through the gate Faith expected to be halted, but all she saw from the guards were their usual looks of jealousy. At least she did not notice any strange looks when they saw her. She did notice confused and disgusted expressions when they noticed the men.

She had grown accustomed to seeing Airria and Joskin in their rough clothes. When she met them she had been more concerned with what she was wearing. In the time she had been with them she had admired their bodies, but she was starting to see their lack of attire as a basic part of being around them. "Perhaps it is time you two got some clothes," Faith suggested. She really did not want trouble and this town had moral standards of dress.

"What's wrong with what we're wearing?" Airria asked, which earned him a frustrated look from Joskin.

"Around here your current dress is considered unacceptable," Faith insisted.

"I'm comfortable the way I am," Airria said.

"No, Faith's right. Especially considering who is after us," Joskin glanced around. "We don't want to have to fight the whole town as well as Henrik and any guards he is bringing with him to keep Faith."

Joskin's reminder made Faith even more nervous. "The general store is just up here," she pointed up the street.

She was happy when the two men followed. She wanted to talk to the shop owner, maybe he could help her find out what happened.

It was a short trip to the store. Everything was just as she remembered. Barrels of wheat and molasses were stacked in the front.

The inside was clean and well-organized. Clothing and textiles were on the right, leathers and basic tack were on the left, food and sweets were straight ahead. Joskin led Airria into the leather clothes section as Faith went to the counter deep inside the store.

Garrett was hard at work measuring bags of flour. When his eyes lifted he had a look of both shock and shame on his face. "You weren't gone long," he said as he set down the scoop.

"Nice to see you too," Faith said sarcastically. Garret's confused look reminded her sarcasm was not a part of the culture here. She had to laugh as she realized Joskin and Airria's culture and mannerisms were becoming a part of her paradigm. Before she met them she would never have said anything like that. She knew she had little time before the men would have their clothes and be ready to pay so she asked Garrett directly, "Did you sell my father's debt?"

"It is acceptable to sell a debt so I can get paid," Garrett responded defensively.

"Yes," Faith was trying to hide the hurt and betrayal she felt, "such is our law. How much was the debt?"

"It is no longer my problem. Your father's credit has been restored," Garrett responded almost proudly.

"How much?" Faith's demand came out louder than she had intended.

"Is everything all right?" Airria poked his head out.

"Everything is fine," she said, trying not to alert the men more. Fortunately Airria seemed to take a hint.

Garrett looked concerned, though Faith could not tell if it was for his reputation or conscience. She was sure he knew of her fate; this town was not big and news traveled fast.

The shopkeeper dropped his head, "It was twenty-two bronze and I needed to keep my own family fed."

"We have established you were within your rights," Faith sighed. Her father had not been able to pay. "Do you know who else sold my father's debts?"

"Karon, the Ferrier, and Furlin, the seed merchant, both sold." Garrett's eyes pleaded for Faith's forgiveness, "We didn't know the men who offered to take the debts worked for the Henrik."

Faith had been betrayed by people she counted as trustworthy and kind, but she understood they had been tricked as well. She also knew, between the three of them, her father had more than enough debt for the slaver to claim her. It was the law.

"I will be all right," Faith was not sure how well she was hiding her anger, but her words brought comfort to the storekeeper's eyes.

"What do you think?" Airria came out of the clothes area, Joskin close behind. They were both wearing leather trousers and cotton shirts. They looked so proud of their pick. Faith giggled, releasing some of her resentment. "You both look so handsome," Faith said, trying to keep a straight face.

Even funnier was the look on the poor shopkeeper's face. He was horrified. Faith knew his expression was not from the men trying on the clothes. It was from his realization both of them had changed in the open, right in the middle of his store. He had rooms specifically for that.

"They are from out of town," Faith whispered to the shopkeeper.

"How much do we owe?" Joskin asked.

"Twenty-three tin," the shopkeeper replied, shyly glancing at Faith.

Joskin reached for his coin bag, realizing he did not have one he blushed slightly. "I will get that for you," he said ducking out of the store.

Garrett raised his hand and opened his mouth to call after Joskin, but Faith stopped him. "He will be back. He always pays his debts. At times he even pays other people's debts. You have nothing to worry about."

It did not take long for Joskin to return with a fist full of coins. "I also need a coin pouch, if you have one," Joskin smiled, still a little embarrassed. He handed the shopkeeper two copper and five tin pieces. Garrett looked content and Joskin put the other coins into the pouch.

As the three walked out of the store Faith asked, "May we stop one more place? I would like to see my family."

"We do still have Henrik behind us," Joskin said.

Airria thought for a moment, "We should still have a day's lead on him. We could stop for short while."

Faith led them through the town to her family's small farmhouse outside the walls. Even at a distance they could smell the fresh bread and beet stew. She could see her younger brother and sister playing in the yard. Her father was off to the side chopping wood. It was her mother who noticed her arrival and came running out of the house, arms wide and shrieking with joy.

After her mother's grand display the rest of the family came to greet them. Her mother and siblings gave Faith a big hug.

Her sister, the youngest, held tightly to her leg. "Please do not go again," the child pleaded.

"Dear Natalya, I wish I could stay," Faith said. The pleading in the child's eyes broke her heart. She could see the same plea in the eyes of her entire family. "I have come to tell you I must go away for awhile. When I come back I will be able to stay."

Faith's father, though his eyes pleaded for her to stay, also carried a heavy conflict. "Did these men purchase you?"

"They have definitely paid the price," Faith said, smiling appreciatively at her companions.

"Hmmm..." was all her father said. This was his indicator that he really did not want to know any more. He knew there was more to the story, but because of his religious beliefs he would be more conflicted if he knew what it was. Finally he gave Faith a hug and said, "I am glad to see you are all right."

"This is Joskin," Faith said pointing to him. "He is a famed warrior as well as the one who bought me these clothes," She gestured to her outfit.

"It's a true honor to meet you," Joskin said with a polite bow.

Faith's mother just stared at the flesh showing through the laced up slits on the sides of Faith's trousers. "Is this the way we taught you to dress?"

Faith looked at her sister's dress, reaching from her neck to the ground. She thought it was funny; it had only taken a couple of weeks to change her views on moral dress and practicality. The dress was fine for the girl and worked well for her mother, as long as she was not working

136

in the field or walking in the grasslands. Faith remembered how hard it had been to keep up with her younger brother when they played in the tall canary grass to the north. She also remembered the cuts and scrapes.

"No Mother," Faith said respectfully, "this is far more moral than what the slaver had me wear. More to the point, this is much better for what I need to do to have any chance of returning home in peace."

Two weeks ago she would have never spoken in such a way. Spending a week in a prison wagon where the only human contact was a gawking, fat, greasy man and the young, abused slave girls had made her re-evaluate. Spending almost a week with Joskin and Airria had taught her some practicality. "You taught me to care to be covered. These two taught me more." She pointed to the men, "They taught me, as did my guard training, a covering should help protect from more than prying eyes."

"That does not protect from prying eyes," her mother said as she pointed to the slits.

"Sorry, I was both blessed and cursed with your body shape. It was the best the seamstress could do under the circumstances," Faith chuckled as she placed her hands on her hips. In an attempt to change the subject to something more comfortable she asked, "Is it bread and soup I smell?"

"Yes dear," Her mother still looked frustrated. "Would you and your...friends care to have some?"

"Is there enough?" Faith asked.

"Dear, it is soup. As long as we have water there is always enough," her mother smiled. This was the humor Faith remembered from her childhood.

Airria cleared his throat.

Faith took the hint, "This is Airria, he helps Joskin sometimes."

Airria scowled at the comment, but the scowl quickly faded as Joskin laughed.

As her family continued to question her about the last two weeks she realized she did not dare tell that much of it. She was changed. Not all the changes would meet with their approval. Some of the changes she did not like. She had killed men. She had been taken as a slave. She had been betrayed by several she had trusted. She had almost been defiled and tortured. She was definitely not the same person she had been when she left.

She now knew the world outside Droir was a scary and dangerous place. Carrita had told her many more stories of pain and woe. A part of her wished she could go back to the innocence, but a bigger part of her was glad to know the truth. She wanted to share what she had learned, yet part of her wanted to allow her siblings to remain in peace in their innocence.

Faith let Airria and Joskin regale the family with their tales of the games they had played growing up. She was grateful they kept to tales appropriate for her family. Though Airria pushed the edge from time to time. Joskin would stop him with a look before finishing the story.

The group enjoyed the meal, though it had only been a short time since they had had breakfast. It was the company and opportunity to be in a comfortable family setting they hungered for. Though Faith did not want to leave, eventually she got up the courage to say, "We need to be going. We need to get to the first shrine."

"Must you leave?" Natalya pleaded. "Can you not stay the night?"

"I wish we could, but we need to finish this journey so I am able to return here in peace," Faith's heart was breaking again. She did not want to leave, but knew she must.

The group walked out to the horses. Airria and Joskin mounted. Faith hugged each member of her family, her father last. She hugged him hard and whispered in his ear, "I do not blame you for my enslavement. You and several in the town were tricked. Henrik had it all planned out. He may even have had something to do with your failed crops." She gulped hard to stop the tears, "I love you." Before anyone could see her cry she leapt on her horse and headed north, the men close behind.

Chapter 16-Soul Destination

Airria found it interesting to meet the family Faith had come from. He learned that her father had actually taken responsibility for his family, both their upkeep and education. Her mother seemed to not only care about the children, but she cared what they did and how they did it. Both her brother and sister were very happy in the security the family rules had given. Faith's home looked like a wonderful place to be raised, but Airria wasn't sure he could handle it, not enough freedom.

As they rode through the farmland Faith would point to a field and talk about chasing mice and gophers or playing with her family. Sometimes she would talk about her father and the work he had done to keep the farm running. It sounded like a lot of work, but Faith talked like it was paradise.

The grass just past the farms reached up to the horses' bellies, but it didn't take long before the group found themselves in grass so tall they couldn't see the horizon. Canary grass, as Faith called it, was tall and rough, with stalks as big around as his fingers. As the rough blades scraped against his legs he was glad he had gotten new leather trousers.

As the day wore on Airria realized the map was worthless in this grass jungle. There were no landmarks. Even the great mountain range or even the mighty forest could not be seen unless he stood on his saddle.

From that vantage point, all he could figure out was that they were close, but he could see no structure anywhere.

By the time the sun was disappearing into the nearby grass, Airria was so frustrated he'd determined to turn back and give Jammar a piece of his mind. He climbed off his horse and declared, "We are camping here tonight!"

Joskin shrugged, "If you're sure." He climbed off his horse and began pushing the grass out from the center point.

As soon as Airria realized the pattern Joskin was using he joined in. It felt good to press the stalks down. They were hard but green and hollow. He put all his frustration into the work. His muscles began to ache, which made him push even harder. As his energy began to run low he realized that his anger was at the dragon, not Jammar. As soon as that thought hit him he began to relax a little.

Only then did he notice Faith was attempting to help. She was not heavy enough, nor muscled enough, to quickly push down the stalks. She would grab a bunch as wide as her and lean with all her weight and push with her legs. When the stalks were halfway to the ground she would sit on them and bounce.

Airria couldn't help himself, he had to chuckle. She looked like a child playing. He became so enthralled he forgot to continue his own labor.

It took her some time, but when she stopped for a break she had made a space just big enough for her to sleep. She stood up and declared, "I am finished!" She looked around at what the men, especially Joskin, had done and pouted charmingly, "I tried."

"Yes you did," Airria said with a chuckle.

Faith's face changed to one of embarrassment. "Excuse me," she said as she disappeared into the grass red-faced.

"Sorry!" Airria shouted after her. He wasn't sure what had upset her, but he hadn't meant to hurt her feelings. He was sorry to see her go, though he knew she would be back.

"Don't take it personally," Joskin said, chuckling as well. "She probably had to relieve herself."

Together the men hobbled the horses and set up the bedrolls.

141

Airria made sure to smooth out the area Faith had laid down and placed her bedroll on it. She had been so proud of her little space and he just wanted her to enjoy it, even if it was for one night.

A loud crashing noise pulled Airria from smoothing Faith's bedroll. It sounded as if it were coming from the direction Faith had gone, as if she were being chased by a group or herd. Both men drew their weapons and stepped forward, ready for a fight.

Faith burst into the clearing. She was out of breath and her arms were scraped up, there were even a few small cuts on the exposed part of her thighs. She ran straight up to Airria. To his surprise the breathless look in her face wasn't one of concern, but one of excitement.

The men waited, eyes shifting, while she caught her breath. The first words out of her mouth were, "I may not be able to push down grass as well as you two, but I did find the shrine."

The frustration of the day burst into relief and excitement, but looking beyond her Airria could hardly see the trail Faith had made. He glanced around for a torch. They hadn't even lit a fire. Even if he had a torch, he would have to light it and he didn't have time for that.

His mind wandered back to the cave on the other side of the range and to his sword. Airria had spent several nights admiring the appearance of the weapon and the way it burned: like white-hot fire. He had never used it as a torch before, but it might just work. It gave plenty of light to follow Faith's tracks.

Airria followed them to a small white pedestal with shifting black slithering within. It looked like a white prison with souls trying to escape, leaving black streaks in their wake. The area around the pedestal had been cleared so Airria had no trouble seeing all the way to the base.

On the pedestal was a plaque. Looking at it was like looking into his own soul. He could see his own reflection with all of his deeds dancing and swirling inside. He blushed with embarrassment, hoping no one else could see.

Though Airria had only a cursory understanding of reading the words on the plaque were clear to him. In fact, after a moment he realized he was not seeing words but somehow understanding the concepts.

142

The first task given to the Rarstocks upon their appointment was to create a place for their dedicated followers to exist after death. Each Rarstock was given the opportunity to have four children and an army of their choosing to assist.

Each Rarstock created a realm which exemplified their belief in paradise. Some of the Rarstocks also worked together to create another paradise which was less extreme.

As Airria then read through the description of each realm he could see in his mind's eye what each one was like and many of the actions that would bring him to each place. In total, there was one extreme realm for each of the eight Rarstocks and several other realms created as a compromise between two or three of the Rarstocks' possible destinations. Of all, two of them really caught Airria's attention.

The first place was a Chaos-Death combination realm. He could see in his mind that it was a place of selfishness and deception, filled with souls who had been given semi-mortal bodies and whose purpose was to rise to the greatest power. They would cheat, scheme, seduce and kill to get as high as they could on the ladder. Eventually someone would kill them and they would be reborn at the bottom of the power struggle.

This place caught Airria's attention because the actions and motives to get to it were those that governed his life. Though oftentimes he'd killed or stolen to help others, he also had done it to acquire favor, show how good he really was, or for some other self-serving desire.

Although he had been raised in a town that would believe this place to be near enough to Paradise, he had known enough peace in his life to know what he wanted. His mother and aunt had changed his father and uncle enough to create a more safe and nurturing home than in any other around Tark-Ancia.

The peace and safety he felt at home was part of why the second place that caught his attention was so attractive. It was a realm shared by Gattono, Lord of Order; and Mellinitia, Mistress of Life. This realm was not as structured as the realm Gattono had made as his personal providence, but was more organized than the realm Mellinitia had created as her personal paradise. He could see it was a place where people respected each other, worked together and kept laws for the good

143

of everyone. This was what he had wished for his own family.

To decide the best eternal reward for each individual the Rarstocks each chose one of their children to sit on a council. This council became known as the Council of Souls. It is the charge of this council to decide the place you will be the most content.

Airria stepped back deep in thought. While the plaque had been written, the words had appeared as a vision to his mind; as his eyes crossed the closing line the whole thing became very personal to him. In his mind he wanted to disagree with some of the claims, but he knew every word on the plaque was true and real. He almost felt as though his mind and body were being pulled apart.

For a time Airria wondered if he really wanted to change his ways. He liked who he was, but he was not sure he liked who he was becoming. Other than his time with Faith he had led a relatively selfish life. Maybe the time he had spent with Faith had changed him, maybe more than he had realized.

The waxing moon was high overhead before he had the courage to look at his companions. They both had the same reflective expression on their faces. Airria couldn't imagine what Faith would have to reflect on, but she looked as condemned as he felt. The three of them slowly and quietly made their way back to the campsite. Airria had never thought about what would happen when he died. From the silence he could guess neither of the others had either. He expected Joskin to debate what was on the plaque. Of course, if he had read it the same way he would have nothing to argue with.

When they got back to camp they all sat around the empty fire pit Joskin had dug until Faith broke the silence. "What language was the plaque written in?" she asked.

"The Common Trade tongue," Joskin replied.

"What language did you see, Airria?"

What he saw was not exactly a language. There were words and they were in the Trade tongue, but he more saw what they were saying than read. He answered the best he could, "Common, I guess."

Faith furrowed her brow. "Many of the words I saw were in Elven, words which have no counterpart in Common."

This was the first indication that the others saw something different. Airria asked, "Did you have to read the words?"

Faith got a nervously excited look, "I read the words, but I saw the meaning."

Joskin looked even more solemn, "How is it possible? How can we read the words but see what they're saying."

"Magic?" Faith sounded unsure.

"Of course it was magic," Joskin's face broke into a smirk. "If it wasn't magic, Airria wouldn't have been the able to read it at all."

Faith burst out laughing. Airria was embarrassed, but it felt good to think of something else. Playfully he jumped to his feet. As if on cue Joskin followed suit. Airria lunged at his cousin. He knew Joskin could end this quickly if he wanted, but they all needed a release. Joskin took the hint and they wrestled for a time. In the end there was no winner, just two tired men and one laughing woman.

When Faith finished laughing and the men had caught their breath, she stood up, "It is time to sleep. Do you mind if I take the morning watch?"

"I'll take the first watch, if you don't mind," Airria said.

Joskin jumped in, "I mind. I think you need some rest."

"I slept last night," Airria grinned. "I'm good for another week." Airria really didn't think he could sleep, even if he wasn't worried about the dreams. His view of life and death and the ends of his every action had just been forcefully exploded. He needed some time to sort through things. "I promise to wake you up for your watch," he said hoping to satisfy Joskin.

"As long as you two let me start pulling my weight around here," Faith said as she headed to her bed. She stopped when she noticed the little room she had worked so hard to set up. "Someone messed with my bed!" she exclaimed.

"Fixing your little room would have been too much work for me," Joskin said as he pointed at Airria.

Airria was a little embarrassed that he had adjusted her work and was not sure if she was joking until she turned around and said, "Thank you."

145

Airria didn't know what to say, so he just nodded and avoided eye contact.

It was not long before Airria was alone with his thoughts. Though it was not a comfortable place to be, he was glad to have the time to think.

Chapter 17-The Great War

True to their word, the men woke up Faith for her watch. She expected Airria to be awake, but she had been awakened by Joskin. From the looks on their faces they had been talking about something Faith assumed she did not want to know about. In context of the day before, they were likely discussing the shrine. Both of them had been extremely shaken up by what they had read.

Faith, on the other hand, was not even sure if she could really call what she had done reading. She remembered seeing words in both Elven and Common script, but as her eyes had crossed the words her mind had seen the destinations. One comfort was she was on a path leading to a happy place.

It was the magic behind the shrine which captured Faith's attention. How could they all have been able to see everything so clearly? How could the words paint such a picture in her mind? It was like she had been to each place.

Though she could not get the questions out of her mind, she resolved to ask Carrita the next time she saw her. Instead she contemplated the stars and how her world, or her understanding of the world, had changed so drastically. Though the shrine had not changed her views about existence after death, it had opened to her the possibilities of magic.

Her mind deep in thought, she did not notice the sunrise until Airria brought her back to reality. "Where are you this morning?" he asked playfully.

Faith knew Airria had many worries, but he usually found a way to smile and almost as often found a way to make her do the same. "Just thinking," she said smiling back at him.

Airria nodded and handed her some breakfast. Faith ate it gratefully though she really did not feel hungry, and after breakfast they got ready for the ride. As usual her bedroll was rolled up and tied to her horse before she had finished eating.

The group rode through the day, but this time it was Faith's turn to tell her stories. It was easy to talk and as they passed through the tall grass she could remember the fun she had as a child. She almost did not need the prompting from the men to continue for the next few days. Even her watches were spent telling stories to Airria.

As they traveled the fauna changed from canary grass to basic tall grass and the conversation stopped when they reached the forest. The trees were taller than those of any other forests and larger and more densely packed, yet the underbrush was soft and full of lush ferns. The canopy was so thick no sun could be seen, but the light did not diminish. This forest was another testament of how strange Ramsel Island was.

Though there was game everywhere, no one felt to draw a weapon. Fortunately there were plenty of fruit and berries for them to eat. There was a strong feeling of reverence for the trees and animals. Before long the group dismounted, feeling a reverence even for their horses.

They walked the rest of the day, enjoying a feeling of peace. As they set up camp they were careful not to crush any of the plants unnecessarily. There was no fire pit and no deadwood anywhere.

After all day riding and walking, Faith felt a tremendous thirst. She also had not had a bath since Jammar's place and with all of the greenery she figured there had to be water somewhere. With a quick explanation, she excused herself.

It did not take long to find a small fresh pond. She looked around to make sure she was alone and then she disrobed and eased into the water. The cool water helped relieve the pains in her muscles from her journey. She closed her eyes to enjoy the feeling of the dust and sweat lifting.

149

She soaked there until the light in the sky began to fade, which was not long enough for her, but she did not want to worry the men. As she neared the edge of the pond she noticed a green and brown marble pedestal with a plaque on it. The pedestal blended into the forest perfectly and was behind a tree she had walked right past.

She quickly got dressed and ran back to the camp where the men were contentedly conversing. When she rushed in they jumped to their feet. "I found the shrine!" Faith said, somewhat out of breath. Then she turned around and headed back.

When they reached it together, they first admired the green stone with brown marbling. It looked like a stump with a rich, green vine covering it. The plaque was exactly like the other shrine, except the words on it were different.

After the dragons were banished from a large area of the world, humanity divided into two factions; the Matradom and the Men...

Faith could instantly picture the two groups. The first group, the Matradom, was led by two exceptionally powerful women who shared only one belief, men should not rule. One of the women had started the Elven and Dwarven races, the other had created a bloodthirsty, monstrous race called the matrataurs. At first they worked together to try to magically replace men and improve on the races. In their attempts they created sprites, fairies, dryads and all manner of creatures which looked half-human and half-animal. Together they raised a huge army of both women and creatures of their own construct.

It was the Matradom who named the second set; Men. The Men consisted of any group of humans who allowed men to rule over them.

The group of men who resided closest to the Matradom began to fear for their safety. They began their own experiments to create Guardians...Faith could see them mixing potions and forcing others, mostly children, to drink them. Most of the experiments were deadly failures. Among the more successful experiments were the dark bloods, kobolds, goblins, hobgoblins and orcs. Also among the successes came the minotaur and many different types of giants.

The alchemists and trainers for the men worked night and day to create an army to rival the Matradom. To their dismay, due to their ruthless choosing of children for the experiments, many families sided with the Matradom.

A war of magic and metal broke out between the factions. The Matradom had better magic and loyal followers. The Men had created many creatures of power and had far greater numbers, but none of the creatures they created were dedicated to their cause.

As the war raged on it became obvious the Matradom were winning and they began to split. The more brutal and bloodthirsty group retained the name Matradom. The more peaceful group took the name Fairenkin.

After hundreds of years of war some of the Fairenkin began working with a fair-minded warrior to enchant an ax created by the dragons...Faith could not help but gasp; neither could the men. The ax they had enchanted was the same ax Joskin had in his hand.

With his ax and an alliance with the Fairenkin, he unified the other groups...Faith became sick as she watched the war rage on. The death toll was staggering.

The leader of the Matradom worried she would lose her power, so she created a potion to transform herself into a creature of the night.

As bloodthirsty as this leader had been before, it was nothing compared to her bloodlust after. Each evening she and a handful of her matrataur minions would slaughter thousands. It was while watching the slaughter Faith realized this vampire was none other than Rantail, Mistress of Death.

Faith watched as one day an Elven woman whom Faith recognized as Mellinatia, Mistress of Life, trapped Rantail while she was still asleep in a crystal coffin and hid it. Then to make sure no one would release Rantail, Mellinatia created a crypt for the coffin and magically sealed herself inside as a guard.

Without their Empress the Matradom were driven into a deep cavern and sealed out of the area.

The immense destruction of both mankind and the world they inhabited brought great sadness to all. Many blamed magic and started a war on any who would practice the magical arts. The leader of the Fairenkin had used magic to preserve many of the great beings and

151

powerful commanders of the war. She knew there must be a time of forgetting, a time for man to forgive the destruction.

In an instant Faith saw thousands of years pass as humankind forgot about magic and technology. Many of the more magical races were hidden in the deep forests, the oceans or the high mountains.

After thousands of years of forgetting, Esnie, the one and only God of this world, decided to release eight of the most outstanding beings who had been trapped; eight to lead the humans out of their self-induced darkness. These he called Rarstocks, or Supreme Governors.

Faith recognized them from the statues outside Jammar's place. As each one was named, a list of their accomplishments appeared. Faith could not help but notice the similarities between the actions of each Rarstock and the actions necessary to be sent to their respective realm.

Even as powerful as the Rarstocks were, educating the protected area of the world was a great task. Each Rarstock was instructed to choose a mate and have four children. The children were called Terisent, or Choosers of Educators. Three Terisents from each Rarstock convened in a meeting to choose Treasent, or High Educators.

As each Treasent was chosen, Faith recognized them from the statues outside Jammar's.

These have been chosen to educate and govern the education of the mortal races. They are not to govern or interfere in the affairs of the races, except to educate and maintain a basic balance. This is their governorship and belongs to no one else.

When Faith looked up from the plaque she realized she was holding her breath. All this knowledge had been found within the reaches of a short trip, yet Jammar seemed to be the only one on the island who knew anything about it. She thought about how Jammar worked so hard to find the shrines. *It would seem the knowledge is here and available to those who would work to find it. It would also seem few are willing to look*, she thought.

She glanced at her companions. Joskin was shaking and twitching. He looked as though he was fighting a battle within himself and it was the most brutal battle he had ever fought. She knew he had spent more time and effort than most learning about deities and their roles. Now everything he thought he knew was being reshuffled.

Airria, on the other hand, looked ponderous. Surprisingly, he almost looked excited. Finally he said, as if the plaque had vindicated some aspect of his life, "One God means one ultimate morality. We may choose to live in shades of gray or dance between many different colors, but there is a definite right and wrong."

Faith did not understand exactly what Airria was talking about or why it made him so energetic, but she was happy to see him excited. She had never heard him talk about moral colors nor be so philosophical, but she did not care at this point. She had more than enough to think about.

She glanced back to Joskin. He looked like he was about to collapse. "Will he be all right?" she asked Airria. He looked almost as vulnerable as Carrita had when they met.

"His whole understanding of this world has been completely shattered. He went through this when he learned the dragons were not just myth. It will take a little time before comes to terms with it."

Airria's words were comforting. They let Faith know the men had been through this before. "This time it may take several days before he's back to normal," ignoring Joskin's glare, Airria grinned. "We may have to nurse him along a bit until then."

"I'll be fine. I don't need your nursing," Joskin said with a shaky growl, returning Airria's jest.

Together they made their way back to camp. Then Airria went to pick some berries. Faith sat on her bedroll and watched Joskin as he sat muttering almost incoherently to himself. Faith did catch phrases such as, "Why?" or "I should have known!" as they escaped his lips, but none of it made sense to her.

When Airria returned, he and Faith ate and talked about what they had read and seen. After a little discussion Airria asked, "Did the leader of the Fairenkin look familiar to you?"

She had looked a little familiar, mostly her eyes. Her eyes had shown both understanding of pain and the strength to keep her pride intact. She really hadn't noticed until Airria pointed it out. "She did have a familiar look to her, but why would she seem so to both of us?"

"For me, it was more than that. It was as if I had seen her

somewhere before." Airria did not wait for Faith to say anything, "I'm sure I've seen her somewhere before. I mean, I recognized each deity, except Esnie, from the statues at Jammar's, but I cannot place where I know that woman from."

It was terribly odd that any of the beings they had just seen and read about should carry that kind of familiarity. She racked her brain trying to figure out whom they both knew who looked anything like that woman, but came up empty.

After some time Airria suggested, "Maybe she just has a common face." His voice sounded unconvinced.

His suggestion did not feel right, but she could not find any other explanation, "Perhaps you are right."

These were the last words they spoke before Faith went to bed. Sleep did not come easily that night as her mind was plagued with thoughts of what she had learned, yet eventually it did come.

Chapter 18-Return to Sanity

The whole night Airria was awake and thinking. How could he sleep? Through the magic of the shrines he had witnessed things few had even heard about. He now knew what happened to souls after death and was very glad he was not on the Judgment Council. Thanks to the second shrine, the one about the Rarstocks, he now understood what the role was for each deity and who each one was.

To him the most important thing he had learned was why the deities didn't do more to create peace and equality in the world. Each being in the world needed the opportunity to choose the path they would walk. It was the deities' job to give everyone an opportunity to learn the cause and effect of their actions. It was up to the people to accept the teachings.

More prickling to his mind was the information he'd gained about the leader of the Fairenkin. She had been more powerful than Rantail, yet had not been chosen as a Rarstock. She was familiar to both him and Faith, yet neither could place her.

These thoughts rattled around in his head until the sun rose. Then his mind turned to Joskin. Joskin was always up early, making sure things were ready. This morning he was sitting on his bedroll mumbling. He had been there all night.

This shrine had really shattered Joskin's view of reality. He had worked so hard to understand the deities and he had worked even harder to defend his views. Now he had to re-evaluate his entire paradigm, not an easy task.

If Airria didn't know better he would think Joskin broken. Fortunately Airria had been through this before when he'd convinced Joskin about the dragon. Joskin would spend a few nights putting the new pieces of information in place and rearranging his thoughts to accommodate. For now he would need a break and something else to occupy his mind.

"It's nice not to have to cook breakfast, isn't it?" Airria said, watching Joskin's response carefully.

"Yes," Joskin said, looking up. "We can get an early start today."

"An early start may be good," Faith said. "I do not think Henrik is going to give up."

Joskin's face changed. The wrinkles on his forehead shifted to a thoughtful squint. He put his hand on his chin and began stroking his beard. Faith had already found the best way to get Joskin back...the threat of battle. Airria could almost see the strategy forming in Joskin's mind.

After Faith's comment it didn't take long before the group was on their way walking through the forest. To help keep Joskin's mind on the group pursuing them Airria asked, "Do you think the slaver's party will be riding through this forest, or will they lead their animals as well?"

The question sparked a conversation of the possibilities the slaver would take in his pursuit. Theories ranged from the likelihood of the slaver being a few days behind to the absurdity that he knew where they were going and was setting up an ambush. The latter was brought up mainly so Joskin would stay alert.

The conversation lasted until Faith stopped the group. "I do not believe it," was all she said. Then she started pointing into the trees.

"What?" Airria began to ask and then his eyes followed her finger into the trees. Branches had grown into paths and there were people on them. None of the buildings looked like buildings. It was like the forest had grown simply to house the people.

Even with the ever-present threat of the slaver on her trail the group quickly and unanimously decided they would spend the night here. It took some time to find the stable, but it looked comfortable and well-stocked. The owner greeted the horses warmly with carrots and then he acknowledged the group.

"Your horses look like they could use a rest. Don't worry about a thing. I will take good care of them." Without waiting for a reply he grabbed the reins and tried to lead them away.

Joskin's steed stood staunch. Airria expected this. It was a well-trained warhorse and wouldn't let just anyone take it.

Faith's horse nuzzled her and began to head towards a stable, leaving the keeper in a quandary.

Joskin laughed, "We'd better help. This horse doesn't react well to strangers."

The keeper stared deep into the horse's eyes for some time. Eventually he said, "Very well, if that's what you want." His words seemed to be more to the animal than the group.

The group went to the stable, which had no rails or fences. Each horse seemed content to mill around and pick at the fresh grass. They needed no borders or hobbles.

After securing the tack and watching for a moment while the keeper brushed and treated the horses to more carrots the group followed a winding set of branches that formed a ramp up a tree. Smaller branches created a railing of sorts which made them feel safe as they ascended.

At the top of the ramp there was an inn. It was open-topped, with walls of weaving branches covered in white and blue flowering vines. The tables were branches that had grown to form a flat top before curling back to the wooden floor. Squirrels and monkeys of varying sizes and colors were picking through dishes of nuts and fruits on each table. The people all seemed to enjoy the presence of the scurrying animals.

As they walked in, a cheerful, generously rounded woman bounded up to them. "How can I help you?" she asked sweetly.

Airria waited a moment for Joskin to speak, but there was only silence. So he said, "We will need rooms and a meal."

The hostess smiled broadly, "It will be my pleasure." Then she

158

led them to a table where, as a group, they sat down. To their surprise the birds didn't flinch. A couple of them even hopped closer and began watching the group curiously.

It wasn't long before the hostess returned with some nut bread and a variety of fruits and berries to eat and some sweet berry juice to drink. Airria and Faith ate ravenously. Joskin ate a few berries and a little bread. After a short while, Joskin grabbed a bunch of grapes and walked to the center of the floor. He began picking off the fruit and setting it around him.

"Are you sure he is all right?" Faith asked.

"I'm hoping this is a part of his healing process," Airria replied. He was becoming increasingly concerned about his cousin.

It was looking like Joskin was becoming more pacifistic. He'd even left his ax behind, something he never did. If he truly became a pacifist he would be killed. For years punks and warriors had tried to make names for themselves by trying to kill him.

On the other hand, Joskin looked so tranquil playing with the birds. Maybe he could stay here and live in peace. He'd definitely earned it. He had defended Airria and both of their families for years. He had fought countless battles and wasn't even thirty yet. Yes, Joskin deserved some rest.

It was so pleasant watching Joskin they completely forgot about Henrik. As the sun began to set Joskin stood up strong and tall his eyes were clear and sharp as he glanced around at the people in the inn. Finally he spoke, "It works!" Then he walked over grabbed his ax and sat back at the table.

"What works?" Faith asked.

Airria wanted to ask the same question, but was afraid to. Joskin smiled broadly, "All of it. It makes sense now. The why, what and how."

Though there was nothing in his demeanor to be feared his voice was filled with a zealous sanity that left the other two speechless.

After some time Airria spoke up, "Perhaps we should get some rest," he suggested in an attempt to change the topic.

"True," Joskin replied. "This may be the last peaceful place we have to rest for a while."

He got up and talked to the hostess. She led them to some rooms. "Rest well," she said to each of them with a knowing smile as she left.

Airria's room was very simple. There was a little walking space and a bed-size patch of clover on the ground. He put his hand down to feel it; it was soft and warm. He found it odd that there were no blankets, but when he crawled in he felt no need for covering.

Even with the warm comfort of the bed sleep did not come easily. When it did come he found himself in the same dark grove he had every time he closed his eyes. This time something was different and rather than the fire catching his attention he looked to the sky and saw an army of angels approaching. Then an army of devils and demons cut them off. The words, "to maintain balance," echoed through the air.

"How can there be a balance to such a cruel and destructive force?" he said out loud to the echo, but there was no answer.

This night he was not bound with fear, but rather curiosity as he watched the battle. He still could not move to help his dad or uncle, but for the first time he was free to pay attention to his surroundings and the conflict above. He realized the dragon knew he was there from the beginning.

When the time came, he was able to concentrate on the woman in the crystal. He now recognized her as the leader of the Fairenkin. In that instant he realized she was not the only one standing proud and honorable as someone who accepted the punishment of another. He had not noticed the others for the chaos and pain of the suffering souls around them. This group of noble souls was standing together, staring at him with pleading eyes. Though he could see they were suffering unfathomable torment they had the presence of mind to look out of the crystal directly at him. These were the true enemies of the dragon.

When he woke up, both Faith and Joskin were watching him. The sun was up and he felt more focused.

"I have never seen you sleep so relaxed," Faith commented.

"Other than at Jammar's, it's been years since he slept this late," Joskin added.

"How late is it?" Airria asked.

"Late enough we should be going," Joskin said. With a smile he

160

added, "It's good to see you rest."

Airria leapt up and grabbed his stuff. "Will there be time for breakfast?" he asked as he strapped on his sword.

"I think we have time," Faith said looking between the two men.

After they ate they descended the long ramp. Faith's horse was waiting at the bottom, its tack clumsily stacked next to it. There was a small bare spot where it had been pawing. Faith ran up to it and petted it's nose.

"Looks like your horse knows that it's time to go," Airria laughed. He wasn't sure he would ever get used to this horse's intellect. It also had an uncommon attachment to Faith. This attachment was both disturbing and comforting. Foris, the stable owner in Smandler, had warned him, so it wasn't unexpected. Still, it was unnerving to see a horse so dedicated to its owner.

It was not long before they all had their horses saddled. Joskin made sure all the bills were paid and then they continued on their journey.

Chapter 19-Healing the Physician

Carrita awoke in a new bed and comfortable robe. Her whole body hurt so much she didn't want to move. Her head was pounding so hard she wished it would split open and let whatever was banging inside out. There was no sunlight, only one candle, but even that was blinding. For the first time she had pity for the guards in her hometown when they had hangovers.

Valnicia's voice, though Carrita knew it was soft, sounded like an avalanche, "I am glad to see you awake. You have been asleep for days. In your malnourished state I was afraid you would never wake up." Painfully Carrita rolled over to look at the priestess. Valnicia's arms were bruised and she moved very slowly as she sat down beside Carrita. Her eyes wandered around the room and occasional tremors shook her body.

Carrita sat up straight in her bed in spite of the pain. "How did you get those?"Carrita pointed to some of the bruises.

The priestess smiled, "From you."

"Why have you not healed yourself?" Carrita knew Valnicia was an accomplished healer.

162

"I cannot remember how," Valnicia looked down at her hands. She was holding several vials of white liquid, each with a slightly different viscosity and clarity. "My son says one of these might help, but I don't know which one." Carrita accepted the vials as the priestess handed them to her. She began examining them as she asked, "How did I hurt you so?"

"Most of the ritual is very fuzzy." Valnicia narrowed her eyes. "I remember trying to remove the crystal. I remember fading into the Astral Plane, but only partly. Then you somehow raised the wall that protected me from the magic. The wall broke and the pain, as well as the insanity of the Astral Plane returned. Again you amazed me by converting some of the pain to relief. Even with your assistance, I was about to give up when the crystal exploded."

Bronak appeared behind his mother and spoke, "When I entered the room you both were unconscious. The bed you were on had been destroyed. All of the crystal symbols had been burned up and the only thing left there, besides you two, were these." He held out his hand to reveal three shards of the crystal Carrita had unwillingly carried.

Carrita painfully flinched when she saw the crystal. "Please dispose of those. I would prefer to never see them again," then she looked at Valnicia. The woman looked terrible, but the worst part was she could not remember any of her magic. Seeing the priestess like this was worse than the light or her bruised and stiff body. "I am sorry for your loss and pain."

Valnicia smiled gently and even mustered a hint of gratefulness in her voice, "I may not remember clearly what happened; I may not remember how to use magic, I may never remember, yet this I do know; you saved my life."

"I would not have had to save you if you were not so busy saving me." Carrita was a little discouraged with herself, she could remember knowing magic but looking at the potions she could tell nothing about them. "I am not even sure I am able to help you heal."

Valnicia's shoulders slumped as her eyes dropped to the ground. Bronak stepped forward. "I don't know much of magic or potions, but I did realize something from your request of the crystal and my mother's story. The healing we are used to providing may not be effective. When I was cleaning the laboratory I found a small amount of the potion you made and put it in a vial. Will it help?"

"It cannot hurt." Carrita could only remember she had made a potion, but could not remember the steps she had taken, nor what it was supposed to do.

The boy ran out of the room. Hope flashed across his mother's face, "You must be the one to try it."

"I appreciate your noble sacrifice, but you have responsibilities." Carrita could still remember watching the priestess take on her pain as long as she could.

"If it works, you can make more," Valnicia pleaded.

"We do not even know if it will help," Carrita said with a shrug.

"If it does not work, then it will not help me either." The priestess was insistent, "Either way, it should be you who drinks."

"But, mother," Bronak protested as he entered the room, "you need to heal, too!"

Valnicia motioned for him to give the vial to Carrita. Reluctantly Carrita took the vial. It was less than half-full. Even if it could help, she was not sure it was enough. Of course, she was not sure of anything at the moment. She swirled the vial for a moment and drank it down.

At first she was not sure if there was any change. After a while the fog in her mind began to clear and she began to remember what she had mixed and how she had processed it, though she still could not recall the theories behind what she had done. She also considered how dangerous alchemy could be if something were to go wrong. She sat for some time, the other two watching her intently. Finally she got up the courage to speak.

"I think I remember enough to recreate the potion. It seems to be helping some." Without thinking she grabbed one of the vials off the bed where she had placed them and handed it to Valnicia.

"What will this do?" Valnicia asked.

"I-I am not sure," Carrita was surprised she had even picked it up, much less that she had given it to the priestess.

"I guess it makes as much sense as the rest of this," Valnicia said. Then she drank the potion. Immediately she began to wobble. Bronak and Carrita helped her into the bed. Bronak was worried, but Carrita remained unconcerned.

"She will be all right. Do not worry," Carrita was surprised to hear the words come out of her mouth.

"How do you know?" Bronak asked with concern in his eyes and voice.

"I am just sure," Carrita stood and began walking.

Soon she found herself in the laboratory. She did her best not to think about what she was doing but rather let her body go through the motions. As Carrita crushed, distilled and mixed things small flashes of reason came to her mind. While the solution was cooling she realized it was not the same one she had made a few days ago. It was meant to restore order to the mind, rather than protect from Chaos and Death magic.

While the solution was still too hot to be safely consumed, she poured herself a small teacup's worth. With one swift motion, she drank it in one gulp. She felt the burn as it went down. What little she could taste made her grateful for the burnt taste buds.

It took little time before the potion began to work. It felt like a dam burst in her body. The pain was intense and she was only vaguely aware when she fell to the floor and began screaming.

When the pain had passed, her muscles continued to spasm for some time. Afterwards, she just laughed to think of the comparatively mild muscle and headache pain she had when she woke up. She could remember everything in great detail. "It worked," she whimpered.

"I guess it is my turn." Carrita had not noticed Valnicia and Bronak enter the lab. The priestess was looking much better. Her eyes were focused and the muscles spasms had stopped; the bruising and stiff movement apparently still remained.

"It hurts to drink this," Carrita informed her.

Valnicia chuckled, "So I see, but as you said earlier, I have responsibilities. As you should know better than most, I will not let a little pain stop me."

Carrita got off the floor and poured another teacup full of the potion. As she handed it to Valnicia, she added, "It tastes terrible, so drink it fast before you change your mind."

The priestess took it and gulped it down. As expected, she soon dropped the cup and slumped to the floor. She grabbed her head and began screaming. Her hands pressed hard against her head. A trickle of blood began to stream out of her nose. After some time she began panting, then her breathing slowed and her muscles began to sporadically shudder. Eventually she sat up slowly and said, "This has been the most painful week of my life." She looked around and asked, "Where's my son?"

Carrita had been watching Valnicia so intently she had not noticed Bronak slip out. "I am sure he just did not want to see you suffer," Carrita said trying to comfort the priestess.

"He has little aptitude for the magical art, except Mellinatia has blessed him to know when people are coming,"

Valnicia got up, walked over to the shelf and grabbed two vials of white liquid. She handed one to Carrita and drank the other, "This will help with the pain and bruising." Immediately Valnicia's bruises began to fade and her movements became stronger and more graceful.

Carrita drank hers. It tasted like honey but felt like slime. It almost rolled down her throat. She could feel a tingling in her muscles and her head stopped throbbing. "This is a wonderful potion. I would love the recipe."

"It will take months to get the ingredients I will need to replace these," Valnicia said as the two began walking down the hall.

As they approached the dining room Carrita heard some familiar voices. One belonged to Henrik, the slaver and the other belonged to the mage who had placed the crystal in her navel. Carrita did not notice her own gasp. Even with the crystal gone, she felt like a helpless child compared to the enormity of dark power she could feel. She cowered in a small alcove in the hall.

"What is wrong?" Valnicia asked concerned.

"Be careful with these men. They both contributed to my being here." Carrita was not sure if she should run or test her magic against the mage. Though she was sure she was more powerful, he would have the

166

advantage of his staff. "The mage, the one in black robes, is the one who placed the crystal in me."

"How do you know?" Valnicia asked as her face went white.

Carrita realized if she were to kill the mage, or even the slaver, it would dishonor the priestess's efforts as well as desecrate the sanctuary. "You do not quickly forget such a taste of magic, nor the voice who wields it." She looked up at the priestess, "Do not worry. I will stay here, unless something goes wrong."

While Carrita hid there, the priestess ran to her room. Carrita pulled her magic close to her. She did not want to let them know she was there.

Bronak exited the room, also ghostly pale. With panic in his voice he quietly asked, "Where is my mother?"

Carrita pointed in the direction the priestess had gone and Bronak dashed off. Carrita stayed right where she was and listened.

"The people of Droir were not as cooperative as I had expected," a tremor sounded in the slaver's voice. "I'm just glad you were able to persuade her family to tell us where they were going."

"It is a simple matter of knowing what they want most," the mage bragged. "Her father was a devout follower of Order. It was not hard to guess his weakness."

"Now the question is, which shrine'll they go to next and how'll they choose to get there?" Henrik said ponderously, still somewhat shaky. "There are many ways they could go. Perhaps we should split up. I could check the shrines and track them while you and your guards go to the docks and make sure they don't leave the island," his suggestion almost sounded like a question.

"Do you believe your miserable little force will be enough to recapture her?" the mage asked cruelly. "After all, it was you and your guards' incompetence which allowed her to get away."

"That arrogant boy caught us by surprise and my mage was spending the night in town," the slaver whined. "He'll not catch me off guard again."

"This is not the first time that boy has stolen from you," the mage said coldly. "His arrogance is well-earned. You should have been ready for him this time!" He ground his teeth loudly as he spoke.

"I won't be so careless again," Henrik promised, "and if I can't handle them this time or if they get by me, someone will need to stop them at the docks."

"How will you find them?" The mage's tone was very condescending.

"This island isn't so big," Henrik said with growing confidence. "Eventually they will need to head back to Smandler. This means we can ambush them on the way."

"Will you try to ambush them at the gate?" the mage asked.

"No," Henrik replied, "they'll be expecting us there. We'll ambush them at the road fork. That way it won't matter if I'm right about where they will be coming from or not. They'll have to pass the fork."

The mage grumbled, "Your plan is almost intelligent, but how will you deal with her guards?"

"There are only two of them and only Joskin is a trained warrior," the slaver gave a short laugh. "He's a merc. If he gives us trouble, I'll buy him off."

"What of the child," the mage asked, continuing in the same condescending tone, "the one you sold to the gate master?"

"Faith's family did not mention the child, just one more reason I believe she's dead. I'm sure of it," Henrik snorted. "That buffoon of a gatekeeper never could keep a slave girl alive very long. He likely beat her to death the first day and then fed her to the wild animals."

"Hmmm," the mage did not seem convinced.

The thought of the slaver believing her to be dead brought Carrita a sense of relief. She thought for a moment on what the two had said about Joskin. First, it was obvious the slaver knew Airria and Joskin were still traveling with Faith. Second, Faith had not been taken in, as hoped, by her friend and mentor. Finally, she realized the group was not traveling the road and the slaver was not sure where they were.

She was left with several questions in her mind, some of which she doubted she would ever know the answer to. Had Faith's family really betrayed her and if so, what had the mage used as persuasion? Why had Jammar not taken her in? How much payment would it take to get Joskin to turn on Faith?

These questions pounded in her mind, until she heard the mage say, "I will leave two of my guards with you."

"My guards will be enough," Henrik protested.

"For your sake I hope so. Nonetheless, I will send two of my warriors with you."

Henrik grunted his consent and the mage stormed out. Carrita flattened herself as tightly as she could against the wall. Fortunately the mage was very intent on leaving and did not notice her. She could hear him outside barking orders.

Valnicia set a hand on Carrita's shoulder. Carrita jumped and squeaked involuntarily. When she regained her composure she said, "The mage left."

Valnicia nodded and breathed a sigh of relief, "I will take care of the slaver."

"I need to go," Carrita said softly. "I know I am not ready, but I need to go."

The priestess smiled understandingly, "Bronak is already preparing a bag for you. Please be careful." After a quick hug Carrita ran to find Bronak.

Chapter 20-Henrik's Return

It had been a restful evening followed by a peaceful morning. Only her horse had any sense of urgency. Faith supposed it had missed her through the evening.

This horse had a mind all its own. Yet sometimes it seemed as though it could read her thoughts. On occasion Faith could almost read the horse's thoughts as well. Airria teased her about taking so long to give her horse a name. The one that had settled well was Persephone.

It was such a beautiful day she decided she would not think on her horse. She soaked in the sunlight and warm breeze. She was dreading the thought of leaving the city's magic.

All too soon it happened, the trees began to thin and shorten and the rich fern underbrush faded into sparse grass. The peaceful feeling lingered a bit longer but slowly faded to nothing but a happy memory.

It was tempting to go back. She could see both men were feeling

169

it, but they pressed on through the day until a little after midday when Joskin started looking at the woods suspiciously. His horse was continually adjusting its ears. Her horse was also pointing its ears around. She could feel tension in the air. To help ease her fears she pulled out her bow.

As the road fork came into view, a familiar voice came out of the trees, sending a shock of terror up her back. "There you are," it was Henrik's voice. "You've caused me too much trouble already. If you come quietly, I'll let the others go; otherwise I'll kill your friends and let each guard have a turn at you!"

The cruel threat almost caused her to drop her bow. She did not want Airria or Joskin to get hurt. She also did not want to go back to slavery. She glanced at her companions to see what they were doing.

Joskin was warming up his ax arm by swinging it in both figure eight and circular patterns. Airria had taken up the rear defensive position; his sword was out and had erupted into flame.

Henrik's guards streamed out of the woods and surrounded them. Some had bows, some had shields. All of them were well-armored and moved as if they were trained. Once the circle was solidly formed, two warriors strolled out on warhorse-sized black wolves. They were covered from head to toe in black plate armor. They were carrying long black lances and shields painted white with an emblem of a Black Dragon's claw crushing a vampiric skull.

Behind the black warriors strode out a mage in black robes lined with red. He had a fireball hovering between his hands and a cruel grin across his face.

Finally Henrik came out of hiding looking very confident in his superior numbers. In his hand he held a money pouch. He rode between the two giant wolves and spoke, "Joskin, you are a brave and honorable warrior. This woman is mine by law. Before the end of the day she'll be mine by possession," his voice was smooth and alluring, but his words sounded rehearsed. "I'm offering forty pieces of silver to you if you'll simply walk away," he paused only a moment while waiting for a response, then continued, "there is no need to throw away your life this way. You're a skilled fighter, but even you have no chance against two elite warriors from the Order of the Black Claw. No one has ever defeated them. Be smart, take the money and leave. I will even let your worthless cousin leave in one piece."

Faith's heart skipped a beat as Joskin's ax tip was lowered to the ground, his hand lightly holding the haft. "Forty pieces of silver is a fair bit of money for such a simple task," he sounded very subdued.

She wished she could see his face to know if he really meant to give up and leave her to the mercy of the slaver. She wanted to turn around to see Airria's reaction but could not pull her eyes away from Joskin. She did not want either man hurt. If they were to take Henrik's deal she would not blame them, but hoped and partly believed Joskin was playing with Henrik.

Joskin continued, "And you brought the Order of the Black Claw. They're very dangerous. A few years ago I witnessed one slaughter a whole village just for the fun of it. They are absolutely ruthless."

Henrik was standing a little straighter. His smile was getting wider. He stepped forward and held out the coin purse.

"You're wrong about one thing though," Joskin said, anger seeping into his voice. "Someone has defeated one of them. The butcher who destroyed that village, I left his head on a spike," as his last phrase exited his lips he slammed his ax head into the slaver's horse. He used the momentum of the horse's lunge to bring his weapon around. In one swipe he cut through three of the guards, armor and all. Several arrows almost hit him and a couple glanced off his leather vest. Almost immediately Faith lost track of Joskin. Her own horse jolted to the right, throwing her to the ground as two arrows scratched her shoulder. Her own arrows spread across the ground. Even through the adrenaline she could feel the hard road crashing into her shoulder as she tried to roll out of the fall.

She grabbed an arrow off the ground and nocked it. Then she looked around for a target. There were four piles of ash around Airria, who was scanning for another target. His horse was next to hers, kicking, biting and spinning in a whirlwind of blood.

The three guards who had survived Joskin's charge were advancing, shields held forward toward her. Though pain shot from her shoulder and down her arm as she drew the bow, the present danger was more important than the pain. She let the arrow fly. It ripped through the fighter's shield, through his body and disappeared into the distant forest. The man's body flew back several paces.

The other two guards hesitated for only a brief moment, which bought Faith the time she needed to reload. As fast as she could she dispatched the other two leaving them lying next to their friend. She grabbed another arrow and looked for the next target. Henrik had retreated behind the Black Claw warriors. The warriors on the giant wolves were keeping Joskin busy, forcing him into a retreat. Though it was hard to find an opening, she let an arrow fly.

This time the arrow shattered on the guards shield, knocking him back, but not off his wolf. At least it gave Joskin a short break from one of the two.

By this time Airria was charging into the fray. Faith chose to bring one of the Black Claw fighters down to Airria's level so the next arrow drove deep into one of the monstrous black wolves, dropping it to the ground. The rider easily rolled out of the fall and to his feet.

The grounded Black Claw warrior charged Airria, almost knocking him down. For a moment Faith saw the image of a fiery White Dragon helping Airria as the fight turned into a blur of flame and black metal.

Though her arm throbbed with pain, Faith glanced around again to discover the robed figure pointing his staff in the direction of the fight, gritting his teeth as he stood rigidly in place. He had a flame at the end of his staff which lit and fizzled out in bursts. He was clearly the only enemy she dared shoot at. She had talked enough to Carrita to know mages could be dangerous and she was grateful this one had not joined the fight. He might not even be a real mage, but he was one of Henrik's allies.

She let her arrow fly. There was a flicker of bronze around him, which exploded as the arrow passed through. The robed figure flew back into the woods and lay still.

With each shot the pain in her shoulder had become much more severe. Her last arrow, though it had done its job, was almost a hand's length off its mark. The pain was too much for her to draw again. She stood holding the bow at the ready. As much as she wanted to kill the cowering slaver, she could not pull her arrow.

Neither Airria's nor Joskin's fight seemed to be slowing and both were too fast and furious for her to attempt to interfere. Like a loyal dog, Airria's horse had joined him.

Faith's horse had gaping wounds, but was now protectively at her side. Faith stood, wishing there was something more she could do, but glad there was no one else to fight. She was having trouble holding her bow.

Behind the slaver, a small, white-robed figure emerged. Faith panicked and attempted to draw her bow. Her arm gave out, sending her hand painfully into her own nose. She collapsed, blood rushing off her chin. Her eyes watering she glanced up just in time to see the burly slaver raise his hands above his head and throw something on the ground. A silvery blue mist encompassed him and he was gone.

The robed figure raised her hands above her head and let out a fiery blast towards the warrior fighting Airria causing him to fall to the ground, his armor glowing red. Airria quickly rammed his sword into the warrior's back.

The final Black Claw warrior dropped his sword and reached for his belt. He never made it. Joskin's ax barreled into him, lodging deep in his black armor. As the warrior tumbled to the ground it ripped Joskin's weapon out of his hands.

The wolf leapt for the weaponless Joskin. It erupted into a ball of fire as a wall of transparent gold rose to protect Joskin. Confusion and fear struck Faith's heart. The robed figure was obviously a powerful mage.

"I can help now," the robed figure's voice was familiar and most welcome.

"Carrita!" Faith cheered as Airria pulled his now flameless sword out of the corpse.

Carrita pulled her hood back and ran to Faith. Still on her knees, Faith did her best to hug the girl but could not even bring her arm up. Her good arm held her young friend close. "What are you doing here?"

she asked. "I'm glad to see you, but I thought you would be healing at the temple."

Carrita pulled away and gently set her hand on Faith's shoulder. "I thought you could use my help."

Faith could feel magic flowing into her as the pain in her shoulder diminished. "Your help, as is your presence, is always welcome." She glanced down at Carrita's navel region. "You were able to remove the crystal?" she could not hold in her excitement.

Carrita glanced around at the destruction she had helped cause, "It feels good to use magic again." Her smile weakened slightly, "Still, it is sad my first spell in so many months was used to kill."

"It's good to see you!" Airria said, trotting over to them with his horse in tow.

"You look better!" Joskin was a few steps behind Airria, "We obviously left you in great hands."

"Yes," Carrita said looking gratefully at the men, "Valnicia, the High Priestess, was incredible. Please understand she paid a great price to heal me, though."

"Is she all right?" Faith asked, concerned.

"She is fine, but I do not think she would like to deal with a trauma of such magnitude again," Carrita replied with a troubled smirk.

"I expected it would take longer for her to help you," Joskin said as he picked up the coin purse the slaver had dropped.

Carrita walked over to Faith's horse and began petting it. As she did so the cuts began closing up. "She would have liked to have had more time to help me, but she agreed I was well enough to help you." She glanced at Joskin, "I am well enough."

Joskin nodded.

When Faith's horse was healed Carrita wandered over to the other horses and held them the same way as she told the group what she had heard in the temple.

When she brought up Faith's father telling where they went, Faith's heart filled with protest. "My father willingly told the black mage where I was going?" she questioned.

"I do not know how willingly he talked," Carrita said as

comfortingly as she could. "In my experience black mages lie, even to themselves. It could be someone else in town saw what direction you went. The mage may have known there were few possible destinations for the direction he was given for your departure. To make himself appear more intimidating to Henrik, he told the story the way he did," though her voice was that of a child, Carrita sounded more like an old sage.

Carrita turned to the men, "You are fortunate those black weapons did not touch you. Just a small scratch from them and even Valnicia would be unable to heal you."

She began levitating the broken lances over to one of the black armored bodies. Then she brought the other body over, creating a pile. As she set it down she got a distracted look, "If this armor had been made of anything less than dragon scale, it would have melted in my blast." She looked Faith directly in the eye, "These are two of the Black Claw's elite warriors. They must want you very badly."

Joskin spat, "They'll not touch you!"

Faith ignored Joskin for a moment. She brushed Carrita's hair back, "You mean they want us badly." She knew she did not have to bring up the crystal, nor the mage that put it there.

"Both of you?" Airria interrupted. "What makes you think they want both of you?"

Though Faith's mind was swimming, she kept her voice calm. "I would dare to say Carrita's enslavement was as orchestrated as was my own."

"They do not want me anymore," Carrita's voice carried a hint of a laugh. "They think I'm dead."

"Why?" Airria asked, adding to the pile the bodies of the others who had died.

"I may have been, had you not saved me from the gatekeeper." She began waving her hands over the pile. Then she began to chant in Elven.

Faith only understood a few words, but she understood Carrita was asking, ordering the earth to swallow the pile. It was not long before the ground opened up and consumed the whole pile.

175

"They don't deserve a burial," Joskin protested.

Carrita smiled weakly at Joskin. "Those weapons and armor are powerful tools only for the worst forces. Destroying them is almost impossible and far beyond my power. Burying them deep in the rocks is the best way to keep them from those who would use them."

Faith looked around. She could still see signs of the battle, burnt trees, ashes on the road and blood. Tears filled her eyes as she once again realized she had caused men's deaths. She knew the world was a better place without those who had died, but she hated the idea of killing them anyway.

She felt a firm hand on her shoulder and looked up to see Airria trying to comfort her. Somewhat embarrassed to be the only one crying she looked around for another excuse. When she noticed Joskin it came to her, the arrows. "I am sorry; I have lost some of your precious arrows."

For a moment Joskin's rock-hard physique seemed to melt into softness, "A small price to pay." He glanced around for a moment then added, "What about Henrik? Where did he go?"

Carrita furrowed her brow and ground her teeth, "He got away!"

Faith was glad to have something else to think about; though she was furious the slaver had escaped. "There was a cloud of smoke and he was gone."

"He left the island, the coward. We will not likely see him again." Carrita kicked the dust, for a moment looking like the girl she was, "Both Faith and I owe him severe pain."

At the mention of pain, Faith was brought back to the battle and the death she had caused. She wept for some time and then asked, "Can we leave this place?"

Carrita glanced at each member of the group, "You have seen I know some magic. I would ask you to keep it between us." Both Joskin and Airria promised.

Without another word they all mounted and rode well into the evening. They stopped at the campsite at the base of the range.

Faith unsaddled her horse, grabbed her bedroll, went to the cave and cried herself to sleep. Carrita sat behind her with a comforting hand on her shoulder.

Chapter 21-Rooms and Baths

Carrita was glad to feel her magic flowing again, but she had not expected to use so much of her energy. Nor had she expected the mage to be so well-trained. Henrik should not have had access to such powerful magic; he was just not a good enough slave trader. Even with the strain the mage had been on her, it was the burying of the armor which drained her most.

The armor, she remembered, was made by Jarmack'Trastibbik the oldest and most powerful of all Black Dragons. She had used her own scales for the elite guards of her order, the Order of the Black Claw. Even touching the armor would cause the most excruciating pain to any except the most cruel and blood-thirsty. The weapons were also formed by the dragon. To her knowledge, they were some of the most dangerous weapons ever formed. Their blades were lined with the darkest of poisons, which never ran out of potency.

Basic foot soldiers in the Order of the Black Claw would be considered elite in any other army. To have an elite Black Claw warrior here meant Jarmack'Trastibbik wanted Faith in the worst way.

The fight Joskin had waged with the Black Claw guards gave Carrita a new respect for his martial skills. He had defended himself against two of the brutal warriors for some time. There were few who could.

Even more impressive was both men had had a chance to abandon Faith for a fortune, as well as the promise of their own safety, but they had both stayed. They had turned down payment to defend a woman they had met just a few weeks earlier.

Carrita had known from the first time she had felt Faith she was someone very special, but she could not have expected her friend to inspire such loyalty from mercenary men.

Of course, as she was already aware, these men were not ordinary either. She knew they had been raised in a place of greed and brutality, yet they had tenderly cared for her and Faith. Without a thought and without even knowing her, Joskin had paid a small fortune to help her. She knew Airria would have done the same if he had had the means.

As Faith helped Carrita onto the horse, Carrita realized this group had been brought together by a force beyond her comprehension for a purpose greater than anything she could understand. Though the thought overwhelmed her, she was glad to be in such elect company.

From the back of the horse she looked at each member of the group. The amount of magic and power she commanded was a secret she guarded adamantly. For some reason, she was almost happy the group knew what she could do, but she did not want anyone else to know if she could help it. "You have seen I know some magic. I would ask you to keep this knowledge between us.

Both men had promised. Faith had promised before. Carrita was satisfied they would all take her secret to their graves if they had to.

That night was spent in the same place she had spent her first night with the group. Faith was in tears as she removed the tack from her horse. Without a word she grabbed her bedroll and took it into the cave. She lay down and began to sob. Carrita sat on the ground and set a soft hand on her shoulder to let her know she was not alone.

Shortly after Faith had fallen asleep, Airria brought a bedroll for Carrita. "Thank you," she said as she rolled it out. Then she lay down leaving one hand on Faith's shoulder.

Whether or not she slept she did not know, for her mind was caught up in her thoughts of her companions and where they might be going. She was awake, but deep in thought when Airria brought

179

breakfast. Faith looked better. She was dry-eyed and smiling.

"You still don't sleep at night?" Carrita asked Airria.

"More than I used to," he half smiled. "It looked like Faith could use the rest, so I took her watch."

"Thank you," Faith said graciously. "I did need it."

"Besides," he joked as he turned to return to the fire, "someone stole my bed."

The girls laughed, then ate a quick breakfast.

As she pondered the steep rise in front of them, Carrita worried about what would happen through the day. Though she was not sure she had slept, she knew she had not rested that night and was still feeling the drain. If there was to be another fight, she would be near useless.

As they approached the location of the gate, her stomach began to knot up. Hideous memories flooded into her mind. She tried to keep her fear from showing but lost control of herself once, almost falling off the horse. Faith caught her. Not bothering to ask what was wrong, she instead held her tightly.

The large solid gate had been shattered. Splinters and metal scraps were scattered down the road. More frightening was the sheer enormity of the dark magic residue left by the mage who had destroyed the gate. The bitter remains of magic made her feel as if her flesh was rotting on her body.

She looked around at the others. They all looked nervous. The men had taken a position on either side and had their weapons drawn. Their skin had paled significantly. It was obvious, even with their lack of magical training; they could feel the magical remains.

Faith's eyes fixed on the spot where the boy had died. She was shaking. Her right hand fidgeted with the reins, while her left gripped tightly to Carrita's robe.

Even the horses seemed affected. Their ears were constantly shifting. Their pace slowed as they approached the gate, then quickened once they passed.

No one spoke until they reached the ash barrier outside Smandler.

"Put these on," Joskin said, handing a cloth to each of them.

180

Then he put one on each of the horses. "The barrier is much thinner on this side, but we still shouldn't breathe the air."

As they passed to the other side color finally returned to the group's skin, as if the magic barrier was keeping out more than ash. The overall mood of the group lightened greatly.

The group made its way to the stable. They were met by a wild-looking, muscular stableman. "Your horses look much better this time," the man said in a rough voice.

Airria responded, "That side is less steep and we had all day to climb it." He was almost smiling at the other man, "It makes a difference when you don't have to push."

The man turned to Faith and asked, "How are you getting along with your steed?"

Faith responded after a slight hesitation, "We get along well, thank you for asking."

"Foris," Joskin said getting his attention, "we'll need to stable for the night."

Foris smiled, "Of course. You know I always take the best care of your animals."

"You guys get our rooms," Airria said hopping off his horse, "I'll take care of the tack and help Foris brush the horses."

Joskin dismounted and handed Airria a few coins before beckoning to the girls. They helped Carrita off the horse and then the three of them made their way to the inn.

As the group entered through the front door, a jolly looking man came out from behind the counter. "I thought you were taking this one home," the man said with a slight smile.

Faith laughed, "They kept their word. They did escort me to my home. I have made the choice to continue traveling with them for a while longer."

"And who is this charming young woman?" the balding stranger asked, pointing to Carrita. Without waiting for an answer he continued, "It's good to see you again, Joskin." He had rosy cheeks and a pleasant smile. It was not hard to tell, especially by the mixture of food and woodchips on his apron; this was the innkeeper.

Before anyone could answer, a woman came bursting out of the back room. "You've added another girl?" the woman sounded slightly suspicious. "Not only have you not taken Faith home, you brought another young girl back." The woman was happily round, with auburn hair pulled into a messy bun. Once she was standing next to the man, she placed her arm around him. Her eyes danced between Faith and Carrita.

"My apologies," Faith replied with a chuckle, "I have been spending too much time with these two." She shifted her hand to Carrita, "This is our new friend..."

Faith paused to look at Carrita. Carrita understood what Faith was asking through a glance; if it was all right to tell these people her name. She nodded her approval.

"...Carrita," Faith concluded. "She also has joined our little adventure."

Faith then turned to Carrita, "This is Lorinda and Brian. They run this wonderful little establishment."

Carrita curtsied elegantly, "I am pleased to meet you," she said with all the courtesy her mother had taught her.

Both Brian and Lorinda bowed clumsily, but with sincerity. They said in unison, "Pleased to meet you as well."

Lorinda added, "It is been a long time since we entertained anyone with such manners."

"Thank you," Carrita responded shyly. "It is been some time since anyone has noticed."

Joskin interrupted, "We will need rooms again tonight."

"Of course," Lorinda said kindly, "and perhaps a warm bath for the ladies?"

Carrita smiled childishly at Joskin for a moment and then opened her mouth to thank Lorinda for her kindness and let her know she did not need the luxury. Before she could, she was cut off.

"If the ladies want to bathe, then they may," Joskin said, his eyes shifting curiously between the girls.

Faith responded in a sheepish tone, "I hate to add to your expenses. I have already lost some of your precious arrows and you have purchased these fine cloths and a beautiful horse for me..."

Joskin smiled and cut her off, his voice booming, "Then you shall have it! Take them and bathe them to their hearts' content. As for me, I'm tired of trail rations. Bring me some of your best stew!" Joskin almost seemed silly. It was refreshing to see him is such a fine mood.

"Right this way ladies," Lorinda said.

Carrita's gaze darted everywhere as she followed the woman to a large, clean, humid room with a steaming stone pool in the middle. The water was clear with a thick mist rising from it. There were four reddish stone channels where water ran off to a drain.

"The water is naturally warm," Lorinda said proudly. "You can soak undisturbed for as long as you like."

"Do Joskin and Airria not want to bathe?" Carrita asked.

"Like most people around here, they wait for the rain to wash them." Lorinda's voice was very smooth with a slight giggle, "We rarely charge for people to clean themselves, if they even bother to ask." She then bowed slightly and left the girls to their bath.

"Now we are alone I wanted to ask you a few questions," Faith said excitedly as she began removing her clothes. "You told me you knew magic, but what you did in the skirmish yesterday was amazing! What you did burying the armor...is it something you can teach me?"

Carrita giggled, trying not to show the pride she felt inside. She knew she was far beyond what she should be for her age. She also knew it would take Faith months, if not years, to do some of the simple magic she had done. Having the earth swallow the armor would take Faith decades to learn, especially armor like Carrita had buried. "I will be glad to provide the education if you promise to receive it," she responded as she slipped into the almost-too-hot water.

Carrita could feel her tensions drain into the pool, loosening her muscles. The troubles of the day slipped away leaving her with only fatigue. She did not know how long she could stay awake. In an attempt to prolong her time alone with Faith she asked, "Have you been practicing controlling your magic?"

Faith averted her eyes and blushed slightly, "We have been busy." Faith began to sum up what Jammar had shown her and what she had learned about Henrik and her enslavement. When Faith began telling about the shrines and tree city intrigue filled Carrita's mind. She listened intently to every word. Though there was little new information, it felt good to know her mother had taught her correctly. She wished with all her heart she could have seen the plaques. The part about the Fairenkin and their leader tickled her memory, but only enough to seem like an almost forgotten dream.

When Faith finished her story she moved to the edge of the bath, "I am tired and would like to eat before I go to bed. Lorinda is a wonderful cook."

Carrita hesitated, she was enjoying the bath and the time alone with Faith, but her stomach was beginning to grumble. With a sigh she followed Faith out of the water. They dressed quickly, but when they arrived, wet haired, in the dining area all the other patrons were gone. Airria and Joskin sat at a corner table enjoying the fresh bread and stew. Both of them seemed a little distracted.

"How do you feel?" Airria asked the girls as they approached.

"I feel much cleaner, thank you," Carrita responded.

"Is everything all right?" Faith asked.

Joskin looked at the stew he was eating, "There was another mage with Henrik when we crossed this way last time. I'm a little worried that he wasn't with the slaver when we fought."

Carrita smiled slightly as Faith gasped, "Another mage?"

"One in long black robes," Joskin continued, "I would guess a mage of the Order of the Black Claw. A mage that would make the last mage we saw look like a beginner."

"I believe I know where he is," Carrita interrupted. A chill went up her spine as she thought back to the temple. She knew more about this mage than his order.

The other three looked suspiciously at her. Joskin broke the uncomfortable silence, "How would you know where he is?"

Carrita reluctantly launched into her near-encounter with the mage. The group listened intently. She finished with, "I believe he is waiting at the port. He sounded very sure Faith was going to leave this island."

Joskin's brow furrowed, "If he went to talk to your family," he

184

said to Faith, "he may go to see Airria's and my families. I had better go check on them." He chewed his lip thoughtfully, "I'd best leave in the morning."

Airria looked conflicted but said nothing. The group quietly ate and went to bed. Carrita enjoyed, once again, sleeping in a real bed. She kept thinking of what Faith had told her but could not focus on any one thing. Finally, she surrendered to sleep.

Chapter 22-Dragons

It was sad to see Joskin disappear over the ridge the next morning. He had left a small coin purse with Airria, as well as purchased a pony for Carrita. He told them he was going to make sure his family was safe. No one wanted him to go, but they were not about to try and change his mind. So they all watched as he rode away.

Once Joskin was out of sight, Airria led the group up a narrow path through the barrier and around the volcanic rim to the ridge. The innkeeper knew nothing of any shrines but had been kind enough to instruct them on the path they would need to travel to Breece, the Air City. Carrita had seen less of the island than the others, but she was intrigued to see people living in a city with little trade. More to her curiosity was how the city would be designed to honor Air. Each town she had seen truly honored their facet of existence. From what Faith had told her about the other towns she was sure they fit the profile. Moreover, as she neared each town, she could feel its purpose.

Once they reached the ridge, she began to wonder how people could live in such wind. Any tree which dared peek its head over the ridge was now bowed and twisted to conform to the intense air movement. It took most of her concentration just to stay in the saddle.

It was hard to look toward Tark-Ancia and into the humid wind, but the view was incredible. She could see the ocean, the port city of O'queen, the huge dirt area around Tark-Ancia, even a huge blackened area near the mountains.

The view on the other side of the range was just as beautiful, but in a different way. It was lush and green, well forested. Though she could not see the actual cities because of the rich green, she could tell where they were by the distinct change in flora.

The awe-inspiring views helped her to pass the day. Near sundown they reached a place to camp. The path dropped beneath the ridgeline and led to a small cave. Though there was no fire pit, the cave was warm and comfortable.

About the time the group began settling in, they heard a booming crack. It forced the three of them outside the cave for a look over the island. Low dark clouds rumbled around, lightning dancing over them. The unbelievable power and loud noise gripped Carrita's heart with fear. Even more disheartening was watching the clouds swirl around the monstrous blackened area.

"What am I seeing? Why have those clouds amassed?" Carrita caught herself saying out loud.

It was as though Airria could tell what Carrita was feeling when he replied, "That's where it happened."

"What?" Faith asked.

Carrita pointed to the center of the swirling clouds, "This storm is not natural. It does not move. It hovers over the same place."

"What happened...?" Faith's voice trailed off as understanding crossed her face.

Carrita opened herself up to feel the magic of the storm. Even at this tremendous distance she could feel the dark energy fighting to escape. It felt as though the magic of the island was trying to suppress some incredible dark magic. She could tell the storm would rage for a time then subside for a few weeks before exploding again.

As a group, and without a word, they all watched the storm through the night. As the sun's rays touched it the lightning faded and the clouds melted away until there was nothing left but a blackened circle.

187

As they rode through the day, Carrita could not help but keep an eye on the darkened land. She could feel the resolve of the dragon which had destroyed the place. There was no doubt in her mind that the dragon who had claimed her mother had also claimed Airria's father and uncle. Only Jarmack'Trastibbik had such incredibly cruel power.

Unlike Airria, Carrita knew what this dragon was and what the dragon was capable of. Airria had already shown he was an exceptional fighter, but he was no match for the creature he was pursuing. She could not imagine how even an army of Airrias could survive this quest.

Nor could she fathom how they would get off the island. It was one thing to defeat a couple of warriors of the Black Claw, but she knew they were facing a small army led by a mage so powerful even she could not compete. Yet with the futility of the quest, Carrita knew she had to see it through to the end.

As the sun began sinking into the ocean, the wind slowed to a pleasant breeze and the rocky, narrow trail opened into a grassy field. Many tall stone buildings quickly came into view. The buildings were tall pillars with open stairs and open living areas; no walls of any kind. As a group, they stood in awe for a while before deciding to camp on the outskirts.

Their rest was peaceful and morning came quickly. After breakfast they headed for the shrine. There was no trail, so they followed the ridge.

The shrine was, not surprisingly, in the open. It was blue with silver marbling twisting into images of hordes of dragons flying through the midday sky. There was a landing around it upon which to stand.

The plaque was exactly as Faith had described the others, except the writing Carrita saw was not in Common nor Elven, it was in the Draconic language, a language few even knew existed. As Faith had described, she could see, more than read what the plaque was saying.

"After all else was created, the God, Esnie, created dragons of the pure essence of existence."

Carrita watched in awe as Esnie pulled the raw essence of each of the eight elements and formed them into magnificent creatures, three of each. Each type was slightly different reflecting its individual element.

Each one was created as a female.

"For thousands of years the dragons isolated themselves from the humans, but eventually created alliances with the people who shared their beliefs."

"Being made of the essence of the elements, magic came naturally to the dragons."

Carrita watched as the dragons began teaching the humans to read and write and then selected a few, mostly women, who excelled in their studies to learn the basics of magic. Each of the dragons chose five apprentices. Among the chosen were Rantail and Carrita's mother. As part of the training, they were required to create a potion to give them immortality.

Carrita stopped reading for a moment. The notion that such a powerful potion was considered "basic" redefined the potential of magic. Her mind was slammed with the realization of how little she knew and she wondered what other things there were to learn. *I guess you cannot understand how much you do not know until you have tasted what else is out there,* she thought.

As confidence in their own ability and fanaticism grew within each sect, a war broke out. She watched as the humans and dragons joined in battle. The whole face of the land was changed by the ferocity and magic of the wars. Each dragon learned to use her own scales, first to make weapons, then to augment metal for more powerful weapons. More devastating to the humans was the fact the dragons learned to morph into human-like creatures, which were able to procreate with the humans, giving them the ability to have offspring. With this ability the dragon population was able to grow beyond the initial twenty-four.

Carrita watched as the dragon population grew rapidly over the thousand years of war. As the dragon population increased, the human population decreased and the war shifted from fighting factions to an attempt to destroy the dragons.

Seeing the devastation the war had caused on both sides, the original dragons and their surviving apprentices constructed a wall to give the humans a place to flourish.

She watched as sixteen of the great dragons placed their own souls into the barrier to empower it, creating a magical barrier which repelled the most powerful beings. Only the apprentices were allowed to pass. She watched as the wall was enchanted; all of the dragons were banished from the area. Much of what her mother had taught her about the history of dragons and why people did not believe in them finally made sense. Dragons had not been part of this portion of the world for tens of thousands of years.

Carrita had always known her mother was special, but was struck with awe to know she was an Immortal. Even more, she was among the first Immortals and had been taught by the oldest and most powerful White Dragons. It finally made sense why so many people she had never met knew her mother.

While her mind was swimming around immortality and education, she heard Airria and Faith discussing the Fairenkin. It was not the first time they had talked about this woman, but as they talked Carrita realized the Fairenkin was her mother and the creator of both Elven and Dwarven races. Her mother was once a colleague and later became a nemesis to Rantail, the great Mistress of Death. It was no wonder the High Black Dragon wanted her soul. This piece of knowledge she opted to keep to herself.

She glanced around to see how the others reacted. Airria was shaking, his face filled with anger and confusion. His eyes were blinking in disbelief. His mouth kept opening as if he wanted to say something and then closed again.

"How could there be so many..." he finally squeaked out."How could there be so many dragons, so much destruction and yet the world still exists?" his strained voice drifted like the wind.

Carrita understood now why she could see the words as well. She was also thankful her mother insisted she learn Draconic, the only language she was aware of which was complex enough to capture the ideas. She realized she was able to understand more than the other two.

She knew she could not adequately convey this extra knowledge to the others without first teaching them Draconic. Draconic was so much more complex and many of the concepts could not be well conveyed in Common, or even Elven. In time she would be able to teach some of it to Faith, through magic, but for now she would have to keep many of her thoughts to herself.

Chapter 23-The Stars

The next few days were very tense. Not only was Airria dealing with the reality of hundreds of dragons, but there was the ever present possibility of running into more warriors from the Order of the Black Claw. When there was conversation, the three of them made a superficial attempt to keep it simple.

By the time they reached the dark forest at the base of the range, Carrita could tell Airria was feeling more comfortable. His eyes were sharper; he even smiled a little and sat straighter in his saddle.

As quickly as they could they left the road. It was almost a relief to see the restrictive road disappear and the random deer paths open before them.

That night was spent with no fire and very light conversation. To sleep Carrita nestled into Faith's arms. When she closed her eyes she felt as though she were back with her mother.

The next morning Carrita looked around and relished the comforting solitude the thick forest afforded the group. She carried this feeling of security as the group rode on.

It was not long before the feeling of the forest faded into the wet stench of an open swamp. The air was filled with a deadly chill which made her skin crawl.

"Perhaps we should go around the swamp," Carrita said much more loudly than she intended. A small part of her wanted to see the Death City, but the magic she could feel left her cold and empty inside.

"But it's the shortest way," Airria said.

Faith was a little pale. "It may be the shortest route, but the swamp would be more difficult for the horses."

Airria gazed into the swamp. His eyes carried both fear and longing. Carrita watched him closely, his brow furrowed and flattened. She was starting to understand the lengths this man was willing to go to face his dragon.

She could not blame him for his fervor. She had been equally obsessed in her pursuit of magic. Even with the strong determination from both, she knew they had no real chance. Jarmack'Trastibbik, the greatest and most powerful of the Black Dragons, had only one rival, Larist'Nastyalna, the greatest of the White Dragons. However, according to what she had once thought of as mere legends, though the Rarstocks did not dare interfere, the mighty dragons needed to be fought.

She considered what they were up against in this quest. She had been worried the Order of the Black Claw would catch up with them. They were mere pawns, base-level lackeys by comparison to what they would have to face. *Would he still be so determined if he really understood what he was up against?* she wondered to herself. As she looked deep into Airria's eyes and saw the struggle at the idea of not rushing through the swamp, she could see the scars on his soul left by the encounter. She knew nothing would break his resolve. Carrita actually started to laugh as she thought, *We will need all the drive we can get and so much more.*

Airria conceded and followed a faded trail not far from the swamp's edge until dusk. As the sun set, mist rose from the still water nearby and began to dance in a hypnotic elegance. Carrita could almost see people peacefully gliding and twirling in a graceful waltz.

"It's odd," Faith whispered as the girls were lying down, "I can feel the chill of death here, but the movements in the mist remind me of an elegant dance. It is as though the spirits which inhabit this place are happy to be dead."

"Is it surprising?" Carrita replied softly. "In each town we have visited all of the residents were content to live there."

"I guess you are right...mostly," Faith said.

"Mostly?" Carrita asked. "Have you seen anyone in any of these towns who was not glad to be there?"

"Three come to mind," Faith said, smiling mischievously. "I was never really content living in Droir. Joskin has traveled extensively. Even Airria has spent more time outside his hometown than inside."

"You're right," Carrita conceded, almost letting go of her whisper, "as a group we are somewhat unusual." Faith giggled lightly in response. Carrita pondered the implications as she drifted off to sleep.

The stench in the morning breeze quickly reminded Carrita where she was. Faith and Airria already had the horses ready. A small flap of soft leather held her breakfast of cold, smoked meat.

It was not long before they were traveling again. They moved on with minimal conversation until dusk, stopping only when they could not see the trail. Quickly they dismounted and lay out their bedrolls.

As a group they sat and watched the dancing mist until one strand of the mist blew out of the swamp and into their camp. It caressed each of them and then blew into the thicket nearby.

Airria sprang up, drew his sword and followed. Faith was close behind with her bow. Carrita quickly conjured a sphere of light and followed. He broke through the thick curtain of trees and vines into a clearing. In the center of the clearing was a pedestal of gold and bronze.

Carrita stopped in amazement at the scene portrayed on the metallic shrine; planets were spinning in a cosmological dance around a golden sun. It looked just like it had in the books, except with impossible detail. She could see the worlds spinning in the pedestal. The constant state of change, as the cosmos swirled, seemed almost chaotic and yet at the same time she could see the order which kept it all together.

"Can you see it?" she shouted in amazement. Then she noticed the other's eyes darting around. Understanding of planets and the cosmos was generally limited to higher magic studies. Faith had an introduction and Airria had no idea about it.

"Where did it go?" Airria demanded roughly.

194

Carrita shrugged, "I am unaware of where it went, nevertheless it led us to the final shrine."

Carefully they all approached the pedestal and gazed at the plaque.

"Eons before time began there was a powerful ruling body of immortals called Gods. Together they would create worlds and inhabit them with mortals."

Carrita could see hundreds of beings working together to create more mortals than she could count. No one God was greater than another. And each had their own idea of how the creation should be used. Some were sadistic, tormenting the mortals. Some were kind and generous, with mortals who worshiped them. Still others were indifferent to the mortals and only gave attention to their personal contributions, like the plants, oceans or animals.

Each deity carried a strong pride in his or her own contributions. This pride created conflict. The Gods who had created the land were continuously fighting with those who created the water and those who created the oceans tried to claim the land. Even the deities who had created the mortals bickered over how to care for and use them.

Each world began peacefully, but slowly each of the deity's subjects would try to expand into the other deity's territories. First it twisted into conflict between the creations, which escalated into wars and then the Gods would get involved, which led to the destruction of the world. For a long time afterward nothing would happen. Then they would create another world and start the cycle over. Each time a new world was created the Gods would become more devious and overtly supportive of their own creations, claiming their contributions were the most valuable. Each one was striving to become the supreme God.

In course of time, a war broke out between the Gods. Each fought with immensely powerful weapons of his or her own creation and design. For the first time since the Council had been formed, Gods died, his or her immortal soul destroyed.

Carrita watched as each God was destroyed and the Council destroyed by unspeakable weapons and magic. One of the Gods, Esnie, less proud than the others, retreated and let the war run its course. When

195

he returned, he witnessed the last two slaying each other.

In his loneliness he attempted to create a peaceful world where he could walk among his subjects. He quickly saw the natural conflicts between the elements.

Carrita could see Esnie pondering every interaction, element by element. He started with the conflict of fire and earth; in time he realized this conflict allowed each one to grow and shape and become.

He continued through each of the elements finding the same thing. Air did nothing without fire, water or earth. Earth would not produce without heat, water and air. He needed all of the elements to work in unifying conflict for the world to be more than a big rock.

After countless revolutions, the elements reached an uneasy equilibrium. They shifted back and forth like a battle line in an unyielding war, but the changes were minor.

Esnie placed a portion of his essence in each element, giving them a form of immortality and potential. He did the same with each of his creations. Only humans and dragons received enough of his essence to have the potential to become Gods, but not so much they could become Gods on their own.

Many of the souls were so greedy and selfish he did not want these to be allowed to continue to Godhood, but decided he would keep them as servants. He used his world as a place to separate the few he would find worthy to teach and exalt to the status of God.

When Carrita pulled her eyes from the plaque she could hardly breathe. This world was Esnie's first and an opportunity for each mortal to become greater than all of the dragons and Rarstocks combined. More so, she realized the incomprehensible games the Rarstocks and their lesser deities were playing were even less significant. Even all the plotting done by Jarmack'Trastibbik to destroy the life of this world, in the end, amounted to nothing.

For some time she contemplated the ramifications of what it all meant. Eventually her mind twisted around to thoughts of her mother and a conflict started within her. She could live her life, grow up, have children and ignore the whole game. If she chose to ignore all Jarmack'Trastibbik was doing there was no telling what catastrophic things could befall the world. She knew Esnie would not let it run its course to the world's destruction. She also knew she did not want her mother to suffer one moment longer than she had to.

The thought ran through her mind, *Countless years are an insignificant amount of time, yet each moment is worth more than everything else.*

With that thought, the sun hit her eyes and she glanced around for her companions. Both of them were staring at the pedestal, their eyebrows rising and lowering independently.

Carrita watched the other two for some time then touched them. "Airria has a quest to complete. We should be going," she said in hopes of a response

Both Faith and Airria walked slowly back to camp and readied for the journey back to Jammar's without speaking a word.

Chapter 24-Decisions

It had been over a week since the group had left the final shrine. Carrita still had not come completely to terms with everything she had learned, but for the last several days it had not consumed her thoughts. Faith had spent the last few days regaling the group with stories of her training.

Carrita was looking forward to meeting Jammar. Not only had Faith talked about Jammar, but she had talked about some of the rooms she had been trained in. Many of the rooms she had spoken of could only exist in and through magic.

Now here they were at the base of the colored cobblestone road lined with statues of every deity…except Esnie. *Jammar is more than a retired adventurer*, Carrita thought to herself as she admired the lifelike detail of the statues.

When they rang the ornate doorbell her palms became clammy. She had never been nervous to meet anyone, but this was different. From Faith's description, Jammar sounded like a Guardian, a demi-deity with stewardship over a region of life aura race. Unlike most deities, they walked among the mortals and were never worshiped.

If she were correct about the role Jammar played in the grand tapestry of existence, this encounter would prove to be an education.

Faith did not seem to know. She found it odd. Then again, Guardians were known to lead relatively normal lives. As she looked at Faith, Carrita wondered how many of the people who had come to visit her mother had been Guardians without her recognizing them as such.

The door eased open to reveal a well-dressed gentleman. "Welcome back," he said as Carrita shyly ducked behind Faith, "I trust your journey was educational."

Faith spoke, "Why did you not teach me about all of the deities and their history?" frustration sounded in her voice.

The well-dressed man hesitated, more as if he was distracted rather than nervous. Carrita could feel him reaching out to her, magically trying to identify something. She reigned harder to keep her magic buried deeply.

"In reading the plaques you have learned the history which was important to you. What I would have taught you would have been a history which was important to me and much of the information would have directly conflicted with what you were raised to believe."

"But…" Faith's voice trailed off. After some time she continued softly, "I guess you are right."

Between the way Faith was talking to him and the magical probing she could feel, Carrita realized this man was Jammar. His youthful face added validity to her assumption. Jammar had to be a Guardian. He appeared to be in his mid-twenties, yet Faith talked as if she had known him since her childhood.

"Who is this you have brought to meet me?" Jammar asked.

Faith glanced at Carrita with questioning eyes.

Without waiting for a response Jammar dropped to one knee, bringing him to Carrita's eye level, "You are the daughter of Tarsella, are you not?"

Carrita knew her mother had been visited by many powerful beings and had lived a very long life. Even so, she was still surprised when important people knew her mother. Even more surprised when they knew she was her mother's daughter.

"H-how do you know?" she finally squeaked out.

"You have her eyes," Jammar replied, his eyes dropping to the

199

floor. "I was truly sorry to hear about your mother."

Carrita could feel anger boiling up inside her. She knew the anger was at the dragon who had taken her mother and she tried hard to focus the anger into determination. "I will get her back!" she snapped much louder than she had intended.

"You have her body preserved?" Jammar asked.

"Yes," Carrita replied, "her body is safe."

"Good," Jammar said grinning. "You are in fine company to get her back."

Jammar stood, took a step back and bowed low, "Please, will you not enter?"

As a group they were led into the waiting room. A beautiful woman with long blonde hair and dark blue eyes was sitting on the couch. Faith ran over and embraced the woman, who stood and embraced her back.

The woman then bowed respectfully to Carrita, "I am Tarsa, Jammar's wife. It is a true pleasure to meet you."

Carrita took a step back. Even understanding her mother's place in the grand tapestry, she felt off guard when people greeted her with such respect. Even more strange was, unlike most, Tarsa's greeting seemed to be directed to Carrita, not her mother's daughter.

To Carrita's relief, a girl about half her own age came running into the room. "Faith!" The child cried as she sprinted, lengthy red hair flowing behind her as her long dress almost tripped her.

Faith squatted to receive the child. "Natalya!" Faith said excitedly as they embraced.

Carrita could see the child's tear-filled eyes over Faith's shoulder. They were tears of pain Carrita knew well, the tears of loss. It was all Carrita needed to know how the mage had gotten his information. The child's family, at the very least her parents, had been mercilessly tortured and brutally murdered in front of her.

It was not hard to tell this was Faith's sister, which meant Faith's parents were both dead.

Carrita's heart filled with pity and fear. The pity was for the child. No child should be a witness to such brutality, especially one so

200

young.

The fear in her heart was a fear of how Faith would react and more so, how she would change when she found out.

"They are all dead!" Natalya cried.

"Who?" Faith asked, pushing her sister away slightly.

"Mother, father, brother! All dead!" The child replied sobbing.

Faith's head jerked to look at Jammar, whose eyes had dropped, filled with sadness. "It is true," he said after some time.

Faith studied her sister's eyes. After a long while her eyes dropped and she asked, "Who did this?" Her eyes rose to meet her sister's again. Then she looked at Jammar. "Who did this?" she asked again spitting through her teeth in a cold and bitter voice which made a chill run up Carrita's spine.

"All which has been taken from you can never be returned," Carrita said calmly. "If you seek only revenge, your sister will lose even more. Henrik has left this island for good. Our exit is blocked by the Order of the Black Claw."

"Stay," Natalya sobbed.

Faith's jaw unclenched and she grabbed her sister in a tight embrace.

"By the laws of the city you still belong to Henrik," Jammar said in a calculating tone. "If what your friend said is true, I will only be able to protect you so long. When the time comes you will have a choice to make."

Faith looked back to Jammar, "What choice? She is my sister."

"You are being hunted by the most ruthless and relentless order in existence," Tarsa said. "They will stop at nothing to acquire you. They will use any means to hurt you. They will murder anyone who gets in the way." She walked over and put a hand on Faith's shoulder, "We can help and protect Natalya, but we cannot protect you."

"Why not?" Natalya asked. "Why can you not help Faith?"

Realization settled over Faith, "You are Guardians?"

Tarsa and Jammar smiled. Calmly Jammar said, "For us to protect your sister you have to relinquish your claim on her. The City Council has already declared her our ward."

201

Tarsa kept her hand gently on Faith's shoulder, "If you choose to allow us to take care of your sister, it would only be until you can convince those who have claim on you to relinquish their claim."

"How can I give up my sister?" Faith asked.

"You need not decide now," Jammar said. "You may choose to take her with you. You may choose to leave her with us. The choice is yours. In the time we have we will train you, to give you the best chance of success. Either way, we need to start some intense training."

"Now?" Faith asked.

"No," Tarsa said. "We shall eat; then you'll have time to spend with your sister. When you feel ready, training will start."

Jammar gently ushered the group into the dining room. The table was set with a rich meal of drake tail and blackberry sauce with all the trimmings. All of the plates were of solid silver as were most of the goblets. Only Carrita, Faith and Airria were seated next to plates with golden goblets as well. The golden goblets were filled with a dark gray, foul-smelling liquid. Carrita could feel the neutral magic coming off it and she recognized none of the ingredients by smell.

Before they began eating, Jammar stood before them. "Airria you have come to me for direction to the dragon who stole your father. I will not send you to certain death." Airria opened his mouth as if to speak, but Jammar continued, cutting him off, "I will provide you with the means and set you on the path you will need to travel."

He turned to look at Carrita, "Carrita you wish to find the means to free your mother. I am sure you have realized Airria is questing for the same dragon. Your success is tied directly to his."

"Faith," Jammar continued as he turned to Faith, "you have a choice to make. If you wish to free yourself from the claim of the slaver of the Order of the Black Claw, you will need to quest with your new friends. If you wish to attend to your sister, you will need to be ready for anything."

"For all three of you, I will provide training. In order to provide enough guidance for you to have any real chance to leave this island, you will need to work on your lessons all day every day. No mortal can handle such stress. The drink in the golden goblet is provided to grant

202

you the ability to handle the rigors of your preparation. Drinking the beverage will be as binding as a signed contract between you and me. I will provide you with training and start you on the path to accomplish your goals."

Immediately Airria reached for his cup. Carrita stopped him by asking, "How will it make us able to accomplish this rigorous instruction?"

"As the potion is bitter, yet sweet, so it has a bitter yet sweet side effect. The only way to give you the ability to handle the rigors of an immortal training is to make you immortal. This is a gift I cannot take back if you choose to accept. You will, possibly for many years, only taste the sweet, you will need no food or drink and you will need no physical rest. The bitter comes when loved ones grow old and die."

"It will make us so we can't die?" Airria asked excitedly.

"Not exactly. All life and un-life in this world can taste death. A sword will still have power to drain the life from you. You will not age, hunger, nor thirst, but you will still get fatigued. If you use magic you will still feel drained and may need to sleep. Because you will recover more quickly, we will have more time to train you."

Carrita would accept Jammar's offer regardless of his answer, "I realize the quest Airria and I have accepted will likely end in our demise. In the case it does not, I do not relish the thought of remaining in this youthful form."

Jammar smiled, "You will age in a relatively normal manner until you are eighteen years of age. This is when your aging process will be stopped."

Faith was staring longingly at her sister, "Is there no other way to keep my sister safe?"

"None we can find," Tarsa said sadly.

Airria wasted no time. He grabbed his goblet and gulped it down. For some time afterwards he shuddered. Finally he sat confused.

Carrita picked up hers and brought it to her lips. Jammar was truthful in what he said; it was very bitter and sweet. As the fluid slid down her throat, it filled her with the chill of a dark winter and then a rush of flame filled her veins. The whole experience seemed to last days, though she knew it was only a few moments. She expected to feel different somehow, but at this point she felt the same.

When the pain stopped and Carrita could see clearly again, she looked over at Faith. Faith and Natalya were looking at each other. "What do you think?" Faith asked her sister.

Natalya turned to Jammar, "Will the drink make her stop loving me?"

"Dear child," Tarsa answered, "nothing could make your sister stop loving you. It will only make her better able to learn and spend time with you."

"Will it hurt her?" Natalya asked Carrita.

"Yes," Carrita answered honestly, "but the pain lasts for only a short while."

"What do you think?" the child asked her sister.

"I believe we have no option," Faith sounded defeated. Natalya nodded to Faith. Faith picked up the goblet and drank. She did not shudder nor cringe, just drank. Carrita guessed Faith was numb inside.

The rest of dinner was quiet, but very delicious. Afterwards they all went to bed without a word.

Chapter 25-Training

The next morning, Faith woke up feeling different. She was awake and refreshed, which she expected, but this morning she felt more alive. Colors seem more vivid, shapes crisper, even the bed felt softer. Though the eggs and bacon breakfast smelled divine, she felt no hunger. Deep inside she knew sleep was no longer required, it was now an option.

Natalya was still asleep in the same bed lying next to her. Faith watched her sister for some time. She looked so peaceful. The magic woven into the bed had afforded the child rest. The peace on Natalya's face made the news of her family's demise seem like yesterday's bad dream. Faith knew Airria had found such peace at Jammar's place. His bad dreams had also returned when he had left. Natalya would have a life of peace here and she would have a life of terror if Faith took her along.

With these thoughts Faith wandered to the dining area. Tarsa was at the table eating some of the delectable food. Faith watched Tarsa for a moment. Finally she asked, "How will this work?"

"Train your sister in what you know best," Tarsa responded. She had stopped eating. "You have an uncanny ability with the bow. In teaching your sister, you will better learn for yourself."

"I will have to train for the fight ahead," Faith stated, concerned she would not have both the time she wanted with her sister and time for the practice she would need.

Tarsa smiled gently, "If you will trust us, I will train you in the morning. At midday Carrita will instruct you in magic. The rest of the time, your sister will be awake for you to both play with and teach. While she sleeps Airria will train you in the sword and Carrita will further your understanding of magic."

"Will it be enough?" Faith asked desperately. "Will Natalya understand why I am leaving? Will I see her again?"

Tarsa's expression reassured her as the woman stood up and put a hand on Faith's shoulder. "We cannot be sure of the future. All we can do is our best. Then we just have to hope it will be enough."

Faith desperately wanted a guarantee that everything would end well. Deep inside she knew what Tarsa had said was exactly right.

"Come," Tarsa said, "let us start your training. Then I will personally make sure your sister is cared for properly."

Together they walked to a hall full of doors a little over a pace apart. They stopped at one, the familiar sign of a target and the bow pressed into the wood.

Tarsa paused before opening the door. "This will be your room," Tarsa smiled as though her words had more meaning, "you will train and play with your sister here as well."

The door opened into a large meadow surrounded by a thick forest. Faith stood in the doorway smelling the fresh air. "No matter how many times I come here, the immensity of space inside this closet amazes me," Faith said as she stepped through the door. "It truly looks and feels as if we are in the wilds."

"It should," Tarsa replied, "it would take centuries of training to start understanding the magic principles involved. Even with all the time I spend here, I, too, am still amazed every time I step through the door."

Together they walked over to the archery range and picked up bows and quivers of arrows. Faith began walking to her position to shoot the targets.

Tarsa stopped her, "This range is for beginners. It is where you can train your sister. Today we work in the forest."

Faith did not realize there were any targets in the forest area, but she did not doubt Tarsa. Curiously she started walking toward the trees.

"I can only guess what you will face in your travels. Of two things I am sure," Tarsa sounded more like an instructor than she ever had, "first, you will need to hunt. Not for yourself, nor for Airria, nor Carrita, but you will need to hunt. Second, you have not taken your last human life. The Order of the Black Claw will not hesitate to kill you and you will not have the luxury of hesitating to kill them."

Faith's heart broke as she approached the forest and a bandit jumped out. Tarsa quickly dispatched it, "You cannot hesitate, not at all."

"I am afraid of what I will become if I keep killing," Faith said, her voice full of concern.

"Fear the day when taking a life is easy," Tarsa explained. "Don't ever let it become so. When it is necessary, feel the pain, but don't let it cloud your judgment."

Tarsa's words did not help. For some time Faith simply looked at the ground pondering what Tarsa had said, she thought of what Airria had told her and what she had felt.

Tarsa continued, "When you are out in the real world, you will need to live in order to return to your sister. In here, all targets are only illusions so you need feel no guilt. All of these exercises will help you not to hesitate when you need to take a life."

Faith conceded and practice began. She quickly found hitting moving targets who shot back was not as easy as she had hoped. She oftentimes missed and when the bandit hit her, she felt the full pain, knocking her to the ground. The pain would quickly fade, but the memory helped her move more quickly.

The rest of the morning was spent dodging arrows and shooting illusions of thugs. Before long she could almost feel when a bandit was going to appear behind a tree.

At midday Tarsa led Faith to a room with the moon and a star on it. Carrita was inside, a brightly glowing crystal near her.

"What is she doing with the crystal and what is it for?" Faith asked Tarsa as they came into the room.

208

Tarsa picked up the crystal, "This is a tool to help Carrita focus her magic better. Carrita will explain," Tarsa smiled and left.

Carrita stood up and said, "May I assume by your being here, you have accepted the proposed schedule?"

Faith was still reluctant to give up her sister, but knew either way she needed training. "Yes, I am here to learn from you."

Carrita gave Faith a strong hug before grabbing her hand and pulling her to the center of the massive room. "I hope you have been practicing," Carrita said as she bounded a little way off.

Faith nodded her head.

"Now close your eyes and focus your energy," Carrita said excitedly.

"Before we start, what was the crystal for?" Faith asked.

"I have told you, as your energy flows, some of it seeps into the area. The crystal shows me how much of my energy is escaping. If I minimize the magical energy, or manna, escaping it will reduce the likelihood another mage will be able to identify my power," Carrita said.

"Will I have the opportunity to train with the crystal?" Faith asked.

"Yes, but you have much to learn before then," Carrita responded. "Shall we begin?"

Faith looked in amazement at Carrita. She still looked like a thirteen-year-old, but all Faith could see now was a schoolteacher. When Carrita frowned at her she closed her eyes.

Faith began imagining her energy flowing as clearly and focused as she could. She made it flow around her whole body. She could see ways to make her magic energy flow more efficiently. She also found ways to keep better control of it. From time to time she would force a change of direction.

Without a word she stopped and opened her eyes as the realization hit her, she had learned more in the short time she had been in this room than she had learned since Carrita had first taught her magic.

Carrita opened her eyes. "Yes," Carrita said as if she could see what Faith had realized, "these training rooms enhance our abilities to learn. In the time of a few months we will be able to learn what should take us years, if not decades."

Carrita excitedly looked Faith up and down, "I believe you have sufficient understanding to begin learning to cast spells." She pulled Faith's hands out, palms facing each other. "This time push the manna, or magical energy, into the space between your hands."

Faith closed her eyes and hurriedly pushed the energy between her hands. It was her manna, it was safe for her. It was protection for her sister. It was death for her enemies. When she felt she had pushed enough energy into the pool between her hands she imagined it burning Henrik alive. After a moment she yelled, "Fire!" commanding her pool of magic into flame.

Burning heat flooded over her from the front. Even before she opened her eyes, she could tell her cotton blouse had burned off. Her chest and stomach were badly burned. *So much for my magic being safe for me,* she thought to herself.

"Here," Jammar's voice startled her, "I thought you could use this." He wrapped a soft cloak around her shoulders. As he did so, the pain began to dissipate. "You taught her more than I had expected," he said to Carrita.

Carrita responded, "The magic of this place will help us learn very quickly."

"The enchantments will help, but your ability to educate has but one rival; your mother," he said.

Carrita grew a sad smile for a moment and then said, "She truly was a great instructor."

Jammar smiled, "Then I will leave you to your teaching." Without another word, he left.

After Jammar had closed the door Faith asked, "Why did my own magic hurt me?"

4

Faith could feel her cheeks flush, "Thank you. Jammar said something similar when I started with the bow." Her eyes searched the room for something to relieve the discomfort, but found nothing. "I'm sure you have given insufficient credit to the enchantments here."

Carrita gave a nod of acknowledgement and let it go. For the rest of the time they had together Carrita continued teaching Faith about energy flow and elements.

Carrita was in midsentence about constellation alignments when the door sprang open and Natalya bounded through. "Tarsa says you can play with me now!" Natalya yelled.

Tarsa was outside the door looking apologetically at Carrita.

Carrita looked oddly uncomfortable, "I will continue your education when you are finished with Airria."

Faith thanked both Tarsa then Carrita for everything they had done for her. Then she grabbed her sister's hand and led her to the archery range.

Chapter 26-Education

Faith led her sister to the archery room. She opened the door and allowed Natalya the opportunity to stare in amazement at what the magic of the room had created and then she led her sister over to the bow rack. On the rack was a small, light bow, perfect for Natalya. Faith grabbed the bow and handed it to her sister. "It is time you learn to use this."

"It looks just like yours; the one you had when you were a guard," Natalya noted enthusiastically.

"Yes, it does," Faith responded. She was filled with emotion. She was excited to finally have the opportunity to teach her sister. Yet she was worried for her sister after Natalya's traumatic experience. She was afraid of the way Natalya would react. "Today you will have the opportunity to learn how to use it."

"Mother said I should wait until I am older," sadness covered Natalya's young face.

Faith knelt down to give her sister a hug. "You will see them again," she said as comfortingly as she could. She wanted to share everything she had learned about the afterlife.

"I know," Natalya said. "Tarsa told me."

After a long moment Faith stood up. "I say you are old enough to learn." She smiled down at her sister, "You are the exact same age I was when I started. This means, if you start now, when you are my age you'll be as good as I am."

"Really?" Natalya asked, her sadness melting into excitement.

"Really!" Faith responded. Then she began teaching her sister the basics of stance, posture and breathing.

When Natalya took her first shot Faith understood why everyone said she was a natural. Natalya missed the entire target. Faith, on her first shot, had hit the target center. She always had.

Faith was also very proud of her sister, for in spite of the failure Natalya simply picked up another arrow and drew back. "Do not worry, I will make you proud."

"You already have," Faith said.

Faith coached Natalya until her sister's arm was too sore to pull the bow. Then they played games in the open meadow. When Natalya became hungry Faith escorted her to the dining room where the table was set with some of Natalya's favorite foods. It was no surprise Tarsa would know what Natalya liked; Tarsa had known Faith's family for years.

After dinner, Faith escorted Natalya to her room and found a happy tale to read. Her sister got ready for bed and then Faith read her to sleep. For some time Faith sat by the bed watching her sister sleep, wishing the child had also drunk the potion so they could be together forever.

After watching her sister sleep for a time Faith went to the window. In the courtyard Airria was training with a monstrous creature. It had large, black-tipped horns and the head of a bull. It towered over Airria. It had enough muscle to make even Joskin seem scrawny. The monster looked familiar, almost as though she had seen it in a dream. She only tried for a moment to place the beast, for she knew she had never met any non-humans. Then her mind turned to the oddity of seeing Airria in full plate armor.

The creature, despite his enormity, moved as gracefully as a dancer. Airria on the other hand, moved rigidly. She was used to seeing him move quickly and with precision. It was quite a surprise to see the difference the armor made.

When it was time for Airria to train her in swords, the first words out of her mouth were, "Why have you decided to use armor?"

"Salle'allak says I need to learn," Airria looked beat.

"Salle'allak?" Faith asked. Though she assumed this was the name of the creature Airria had trained with, she wanted to be sure.

"You don't know him?" Airria asked wide-eyed

"Before I brought you here, I believed I knew Jammar and his household well," she said, thinking of all she had learned about her friend and mentor over the last while, "Now everything is a surprise."

"Apparently he's one of a handful of non-humans allowed on this island," Airria said, still breathing hard. "I guess, like Jammar, he's a Guardian, though he didn't say."

"It looks as though he worked you extremely hard," Faith said admiring Airria's dedication.

Airria smiled at her, "This was easy compared to the White Room."

"The White Room?" She asked

"It redefined pain and torment," Airria said as his gaze fell to the ground.

Faith could not tell if the fluid running down Airria's nose was a tear or sweat. She wanted to know more but did not feel it was a good time to ask. She changed the subject, "They say you are training me with swords."

"Are you sure you want to learn?" he asked.

"Tarsa says I need the training," she was feeling a little too excited to spend time with Airria and hoping he did not notice. "She says training me will also help you as well."

"Then we'll start," he said standing up. "The only training I have comes from defending myself. I'll give pointers where I can, but you mostly just have to keep me from hitting you."

"Will you need to remove your armor?" she asked hopefully.

"No, I'll stay in it for now," he said almost laughing. "It will help me prepare for tomorrow's beating."

Airria handed her a wooden practice sword. As awkward as Airria looked in his armor she felt more so with the bladed club in her hands. It did not take her long to gain an appreciation for Airria's skill.

Though he easily sliced and poked past her defenses he only hit her hard enough to sting a little.

Though she could see a tremendous improvement in her own skill with the sword by the time she was finished, she could see she still had a long way to go to be considered good.

When Carrita came to get her, Faith was soaked in sweat and covered in dust. She badly wanted to just rest and bathe. Carrita would have none of it. They went directly to the library. "Your sister was excited to see you," Carrita said as they passed into the reading area.

"As I was to see her," Faith replied. She knew Carrita wanted to know about her decision but was trying not to push the issue.

"How was your time with her today?" Carrita asked.

"Far too short," Faith responded. She could feel her friend's anxiety, so she let Carrita know, the best way she could think to, "It will be hard to let her go when I leave with you. I am trying to figure out how to tell her."

Carrita grinned broadly, "You'll think of something."

Faith did not want to think of such things right now, so she changed the subject. "Why are we not in the practice room?"

"I get two opportunities to teach you magic. Earlier today we worked on the practical aspects of magic," Carrita again sounded like a schoolteacher, "now we will discuss the theories of magic."

"Theories?" Faith asked confused.

"To learn fencing and archery from books will help a small amount," Carrita replied, "for them you need the physical motion and feelings."

"The practice with Airria was very educational," Faith cut Carrita off. "I was amazed how much mental strain it was."

"The more you learn of your swordplay, even as you analyze your archery, you will see they both require extreme intellect. What I am hoping you understand is, magic requires even more." Carrita kept the thoughtful look on her face, "I will require you to spend hours reading and asking questions."

"What questions would you have me ask?" Faith queried.

Carrita smiled knowingly as she held out a book, "Just read, the

215

questions will come."

Faith sat down and began to read, she had always excelled in studies. Painfully, this book was not only written in High Elven, but also described Order as an element, as tangible as Water, Wind or Earth, rather than the philosophy of organization. As Carrita had predicted, questions began swimming around her head, first about translation, as she was not familiar with High Elven, then to more meaningful questions. It took her some time to narrow them down to one. "If order is tangible, why have I never seen it or felt it?"

Carrita answered, "You have."

"When?" Faith asked, but even as she did so, she could see how it was Order which made a rock fall or held the metal in an anvil together. Before Carrita could answer, Faith asked another question, "Would manipulating Order be similar to manipulating Fire?"

Carrita looked proud. "Similar, yes. As you learn how the elements work, you will better see how to manipulate and summon them."

Faith continued researching, studying and asking questions until the sunlight crept through the high windows. When Tarsa entered the room to get her, Faith realized the regimen of the last day would be her life for her duration at Jammar's.

Over the next few months she learned more than she could have imagined about swordplay, magic and even her specialty of archery. She relished every moment she spent with her sister and entertained herself in the evenings after her sister had fallen asleep by first watching Airria train, then making his training more difficult by casting small spells.

One morning while training with Tarsa, Natalya burst into the forested room. "Faith," she demanded, "we need to talk!"

Faith felt her heart fall. She had been dreading telling her sister she would be leaving. She guessed Natalya had somehow found out she was planning to leave.

As they walked through the nearby trees Natalya grabbed Faith's hand. "You know I love you and want you to never leave? Right?"

Faith could see the deep conflict on her sister's eyes. "Yes, dear one." Before the child could speak again, Faith asked, "Are you aware, you are dearer to me than my own life?"

To Faith's surprise the conflict in her sister's eyes grew and a tear ran down her cheek. "Yes, I know," Natalya answered as she held more tightly to Faith's hand. Together they walked for some time before she finally blurted out, "You have to go!" Her breathing was labored; her voice was splintered with grief, "As much as I do not want you to go, you must!"

Faith's heart shattered to see her sister hurt so, "I can stay, if you want."

"No, you cannot!" Natalya said brushing her long skirt, biting her lip. "You must go!"

"Who has requested you to speak with me in such a way?" Faith could not believe her little sister would be so adamant about her leaving.

"I know you think I am a kid and you do not think I know what is going on," Natalya's voice was shaky, but her eyes were solidly fixed on Faith's. "Though Tarsa and Jammar will not tell me anything, I know I was spared by those men to keep you from going."

"Where am I going?" Faith also wanted to know how Natalya knew what was happening, but the child had indicated she figured it out on her own. To ask "how" would be insulting. So Faith settled for the "where."

"You must go with Airria and Carrita," Natalya's fists were now clenched.

"Do you know where they are going or what they plan to do?" Faith was trying hard not to be condescending.

"They were far too focused on training not to have a serious reason for it. When I realized they were training for a quest," Natalya's face grew into a weak smile as she went on, "I decided to ask them why they were training so hard." Another smile crept on her face. "I have to say it was a little scary talking to Carrita. She looks like she is only about thirteen, but when she talks she reminds me of Grandma or Tarsa."

"Yes, she has the same effect on me," Faith returned the smile; grateful to see some of the conflict go away.

"Both of them talked to me like I was a grown up." Natalya's voice was clearing. "They never talked like you were going with them, but something in what they did not say made me think of what was not said."

"Are you saying I should go with them because they did not say they wanted me to?" Faith asked.

"I apologize; I'm not making myself clear." A hint of frustration crawled into Natalya's eyes. "I am trying to explain months of thoughts, ranging from mother and father's deaths to your travels and incredible skill with the bow. Even what Carrita and Airria told me," for a moment the girl seemed almost grown-up. "I know you want to take care of me. The only way you can is to help your friends. Then we can be a family again."

Faith realized her sister was also very gifted at deducing facts.

"Do you understand," Natalya asked, "without you, they will fail and if you stay with me, you will fail."

Faith could find no words of relevance so she hugged her sister tight. "I will come back for you," she whispered in her ear.

"And when you do, you will be able to protect me," Natalya whispered back.

Chapter 27 Departure

After three months of the most mind-bending, emotionally distressing and physically draining training Airria had ever been through, he decided it was time to leave the island and start the next stage of his journey. Rather than going on his customary early morning run when Carrita came to get Faith, he began wandering the halls of Jammar's mansion. He was trying to figure out how to tell Jammar he was leaving.

It had been a very long time since he had admired the tapestries. He paused at one of them he now recognized as Theilord's Last Stand. It depicted a well-built man in beautiful armor surrounded by piles of bodies in an army of mixed humanoid creatures. His shield was fending off fireballs so real Airria could almost feel the heat. His sword, the one sitting in Airria's room right now, was blazing through the skull plate of a goring minotaur. In the design and posture of the image Airria thought he could almost see a dragon fighting instead of the man.

"Airria?" a voice pulled him out of the tapestry. Startled he looked around.

When his eyes locked on Natalya he almost jumped, "What are you doing up?"

"May I speak to you?" the girl looked so determined.

"Of course," he said, hoping his question would be answered soon.

"If Faith stays here with me, what will happen to her?" Natalya asked.

"You know your laws better than I do," Airria pointed out, "your sister was used to pay a debt. What do your laws say should happen to her?"

"She belongs to the person who bought her," Natalya responded looking at the ground.

"Have you seen the man who would own her?" Airria asked.

Natalya spat at the ground and looked up, her teeth grinding as she spoke, "He cannot have her!"

"But it's your law," Airria said calmly.

"Why do you not buy her?" Natalya asked. "Even I can tell you like her."

"Your laws say I can only buy her if her owner will sell her to me," Airria was trying hard to help the child understand.

"I know the law!" Natalya's voice was filled with frustration. "Can we do nothing?"

"You know your law better than I do," Airria said placing his hand on her shoulder in an attempt comfort her.

"What do you mean 'my laws'?" A glimmer of hope crossed Natalya's face. "Are laws different in other places?"

"Yes, laws are different in other places," Airria responded.

"Then why can she not take me to a place where the bad man cannot take her away?" Natalya asked. "Why can she not take me to such a place?"

"The same laws that give her protection allow the slaver to take her," Airria was struggling even to make sense of his own words. "If you two moved to a place where the bad man doesn't own Faith, the laws of such a land will also not protect you if he came to claim her."

"The laws did not protect my mother or father or brother!" Natalya snapped angrily.

"The bad man is using, and will use, the laws that work to his advantage and ignoring the ones that won't," Airria felt very proud of his wording.

"How can he do that?" Natalya asked as she folded her arms across her chest.

"Each place has different laws," Airria explained. "He claims only the laws that will help him. Because he doesn't live in any one place, he gets away with it."

Little Natalya got a furl on her brow. "That is not fair!" she finally exclaimed.

"No, it's not," Airria agreed, "but that is what is going on." Then a thought came into his mind, "My cousin told me of a place where the laws would protect you and your sister. The slaver wouldn't be able to use any laws to claim her."

"Really, where's this place?" Her arms swung down to her sides.

"I don't know, exactly," Airria responded. "I do know it's far from here and it will be a dangerous trip."

"Will you find this place and come get us and take us there?" Natalya's pleading eyes locked Airria's heart into a vice.

"I have something I need to do first," Airria said sadly. "If I survive, then I will find the place and send for you."

"You want to kill one of the High Dragons, correct?" the girl asked.

"Yes." Airria was surprised, "How did you know that?"

"I did not know until now," the child said cryptically.

"Did Faith tell you?" he asked

"No, it was my mother," the girl responded. "Until now, I thought it was a dream." Before Airria could ask another question, Natalya ran down the hall. Airria figured she was headed to see her sister and hoped Tarsa wouldn't mind the interruption, he had other things to do. He turned to go the other way down the hall, only to be startled by Salle'allak. His massive frame loomed over Airria, who was instinctively reaching for his sword.

"Come. Jammar would like to talk to you in the study." Even after all this time the deep gravelly voice of the minotaur still gave Airria chills.

Airria was doing everything he could not to show his intimidation, "Do you know what he wants?"

"Yes," Salle'allak said with his grinding chuckle, "but you will have to come and find out for yourself." The minotaur laughed again as he walked away.

The monstrous laugh was plenty to make Airria nervous, but knowing that Jammar wanted to talk to him the same morning he had decided to leave and the same morning Natalya had chosen to talk to him, really sent his skin crawling.

Suddenly Airria wasn't in such a rush to talk to Jammar. He wandered the halls admiring more of the tapestries. He got lost in another depiction of Theilord fighting. Again he swore he could see a dragon in place of the man.

"Airria," Faith's voice pulled him out of his trance, "Tarsa said Jammar wanted to speak to all of us."

"Salle'allak said the same thing," Airria said, wondering how long he had been. "I guess it's time to get to the study," he couldn't help but notice how tightly Natalya was holding Faith's hand.

The three of them slowly and quietly wandered to the study. When they arrived, Carrita was sitting cross-legged in a chair reading a book. Tarsa was sitting next to her husband waiting wide-eyed. Salle'allak was standing in a corner, like a massive statue. The room was completely quiet.

The silence made Airria even more nervous. "You wanted to speak to us," he said after a moment.

"Yes," Jammar stood; his long gray robes flowed to the floor. A single piece of trim starting at one end in white and running through all eight colors and culminating in black indicated he was talking officially as a Guardian. "All of you have learned much since arriving here. You are all very gifted. We've educated you with magic and personal experience. All of you have been receptive to what we have taught."

Airria realized Jammar was in his official Guardian robes. Though it was very intimidating, it was also comforting to know that his quest was being assisted by Guardians.

Jammar continued, "When you arrived, you informed us you are on a quest to dispatch the oldest and most powerful of all Black Dragons. We have given all the training and information we could to help you in your quest. Now it is time for you to start your journey anew."

"Do you think we are ready?" Carrita asked. Her book now lay closed on her lap.

"We could instruct you for thousands of years and I would continue to have reservations," Jammar said, looking into Carrita's eyes, "nonetheless, it is time for you to move on." His eyes drifted to Faith.

As Jammar spoke, Airria had the realization that the Order of the Black Claw had challenged Jammar's right to shelter Faith. Over the last few months he had learned many things, one of which was that Jammar was a Guardian and as such couldn't keep Faith safe. Though Jammar's words gave no indication of the Black Claw's involvement, only such a protest would cause Jammar to send Faith away.

"Then we move on," Airria said.

"Before you go," the minotaur in this corner boomed, "here is the shield Theilord used." He slowly pulled a kite shaped shield out from behind him and handed it to Airria.

Airria was speechless. The shield was warm to the touch. Like his sword, it seemed to be made of blazing fire. The front had a dragon pacing back and forth, so alive he could imagine it flying off. Finally he squeaked out, "Thank you."

Without a reply, Salle'allak stepped back to his place in the corner and Tarsa stood up. She reached behind the couch and pulled out her bow, plain white in appearance except for some scratches artistically scrawling up the entire length and a pearly white quiver with only four arrows in it.

"Three of these arrows will always be there. The fourth is to make sure you will always be able to find your way," Tarsa said. "The bow and arrows are the same Viehasia, Theilord's wife, used when she went to rescue her husband's corpse."

"Thank you," Faith said as she pulled one of the arrows from the quiver. It seemed to be made of green stone with brown marbling.

"This arrow will morph its target into a matching marble statue," Tarsa said pointing to the arrow.

Faith carefully put it back and pulled one which had a flaming red tip and blazing red fletching. It had a light red-bone shaft.

Tarsa explained, "This arrow will explode in a ball of fire."

Faith reverently put it back. The next arrow she pulled was icy

224

blue.

"This will shatter into thousands of icy splinters. If used correctly, it has the ability to be as equally destructive as the red one," Tarsa said.

Again Faith replaced it and then pulled out the final arrow. Both shaft and fletching were grey and it ended with a golden tip.

Tarsa focused more intently on this one as she explained, "This is the one arrow which will not return when used. The other three Viehasia had when she went up the hill. This one Jammar found. It will always point your way."

"Thank you!" Faith exclaimed.

Carrita spoke up, "You have been so kind as to provide the weapons which will be of greatest benefit. For this we are all grateful, but I am driven to ask, why have you not provided the armor of which I am sure we will have need before the end?"

"Both Theilord's and Viehasia's armor, even I cannot touch," Salle'allak boomed from the corner. "Only someone who will emulate Theilord and his wife can retrieve it."

"Where is it?" Airria asked.

"It is hidden in the Arstock Range, near the Frozen Waste, far to the North," the minotaur said. "I will warn you, if you are not chosen by the armor, you will die the most agonizing death."

Carrita gave a rebuttal, sounding far too grown-up, "If we fail our quest, we will suffer an even more agonizing fate." Then, shrinking back into her childish face, she added, "I am just glad it will not be me testing the armor's acceptance." She then stood up as if to leave.

Jammar stopped her by saying, "You asked for armor. Here is yours," he held up a small package that had been sitting on his lap.

Carrita opened it carefully. Before Airria could even see the cloth, Carrita gasped and tears began to flow down her face.

"Your mother gave me that years before your birth. She told me the time would come when I was to pass it to someone very special," Jammar said a crack in his own voice.

"I recognize my mother's work," Carrita sobbed.

Jammar gave her a soft smile, "I'm sure it is magical, but have no

225

idea what it does."

"Magically, I could not even guess at its purpose. For me, it will be a reminder my mother will always be with me," Carrita said. After hugging the package tightly she rushed out of the room. Faith and Natalya followed.

Airria stood to leave, but before he could pick up the shield, Salle'allak held out a scroll. "This is for Joskin. It will tell him the history of his ax. Also, I give you this warning. If you flaunt such miraculous weapons you will attract unwanted attention. When you are safely away from the island procure some common weapons and armor for your travels."

After safely tucking the scroll into his coin pouch Airria bent over to pick up his new shield again. Jammar stopped him by handing him a sealed letter. "This is for your mother," Jammar said.

Airria asked, "What does it say?"

The words are for your mother and Joskin's mother," Jammar said with a bright smile. "It will be up to them whether or not they will share it with you."

Airria again thanked Jammar, Tarsa and Salle'allak for their gifts to the group. He then he made his way to the stables and began preparing the horses. When he had almost finished, Faith and Natalya walked in smiling.

Faith asked, "Are we ready?"

Before Airria could answer Carrita walked in. She was in a new, seemingly plain gray robe that fit her perfectly. As she moved, a very light shimmering of the movements of battles, wars and peaceful existences brushed across it. He was filled with fear to harm the girl; yet even having seen her kill soldiers, he couldn't imagine her being any kind of a threat.

Carrita must have noticed him staring. "My mother was an amazing seamstress as well as an enchantress. I may never know the exact nature of the magic, but this robe will always fit me."

"I can guess at another magical effect," Airria said slowly, "you will never be considered a great threat."

"Such will be of immense assistance to us," Carrita said twirling around.

"I guess it is time to get moving," Airria said this as he mounted his horse. Faith gave Natalya one last big hug and followed suit. Carrita packed some books into her bags and then hopped on her pony. Together they headed back across the island.

Chapter 28-Black Claw

Airria appreciated the welcome sight of his hometown. It had been over a week since they left Jammar's and over four months since he had left the bard at his favorite place to unwind. It struck him as odd that he was returning only to leave again.

So much had happened since that day. As the people in the streets came into view he began to realize just how much he had changed. He noticed how dirty and ill-dressed the men were. Their tattered pants and loincloths seemed like lazy protection from the elements.

A bloody-faced woman was tossed into the streets with a torn and tattered dress. As she stumbled down the street she knocked over a bottle. Next to the bottle was a small skull with a couple of random bones. Airria's mind flashed back to the day he raced out of town and the child they had almost hit. Now he wished he had stopped and taken the child to his mother's care.

He had originally brought the girls into town to show them all the things he loved about it. Now he could see nothing to show. He nudged his horse to hurry through the streets and was relieved to see his companions do the same.

It didn't take long to leave the small town and enter the dusty waste surrounding it. Airria was relieved to see the buildings shrink behind them. His relief was short-lived, as a small, yet well-armored caravan, filtered out through the trees. Twenty guards in full black armor on warhorse-sized, barded wolves spread across the path. Two soldiers were driving the wagon Airria had freed Faith from. Behind them were three black-robed figures on equally large tigers.

Airria struggled to imagine how he was going to deal with the situation. He had been training to fight the dragon by fighting Salle'allak and groups of illusionary thugs, but he remembered how much trouble a couple of these guards had given Joskin.

Even more disconcerting was watching terror cross Carrita's face. After what he had learned from and about the girl, he knew the central robed figure would be as powerful as a small dragon. He knew Carrita could feel exactly what she was up against.

"So the girl did survive!" The central robed figure, obviously the leader, spoke, his voice as hollow as death. "I will give you a choice boy! Leave and live or die like this one's family!" he pointed to Faith.

Before Airria had a chance to fully understand, an arrow was released from Faith's bow, exploding on a fast-formed black magic wall in front of the mage.

The figure laughed, "I have been waiting centuries for the opportunity to acquire these weapons. My master will reward me greatly!" He laughed again then yelled, "My offer is withdrawn!"

Airria still had no idea how to fight from horseback, so he dismounted, pulled his sword and readied his shield. His horse stayed on his heels like a dedicated guard dog.

As the gap closed between the two groups, Faith released arrows as fast as she could, each one exploding into the same wall as before. Airria marched on, wondering how he would penetrate the barrier.

He dared to quickly glance back to Carrita who seemed to be bombarded by invisible forces, almost as if she were crazy. Even he could feel the immense magical struggle going on.

Faith was doing all she could and Airria didn't know how much time Carrita had before she would be worthless, so he charged in.

The wall absorbed into his shield and when they touched, Airria was suddenly crazy sick with energy. He began swinging and blocking in a fury even he couldn't follow. All he knew was the sword and shield were keeping him from harm. More times than he could count, a sword or wolf's teeth nearly struck him, only to have the shield jerk him out of the way or fly in front of him.

He could vaguely hear the explosions of Faith's arrows and the yelping of dying wolves and horses. He could feel Faith and Carrita keeping his back clear. No matter how hard he pressed forward, he could not get past the guards to the mage. Even when the walls fell he didn't have enough to get through.

He knew it was taking everything Faith and Carrita had to keep the mages busy and his back clear. Though his shield was absorbing any spell that came near him, giving him energy to continue the fight, he was wearing down. The energy wasn't enough. Even with his intense training and the energy the sword was giving him, he was out of breath and ready to collapse.

"Hands off my cousin!" Joskin's welcome voice roared over the battle, piercing Airria's battle haze and mildly renewing his vigor. What added more hope was that Joskin was fully suited for battle.

The leader, the mage Airria had kept his eye on, spun around throwing up a wall. The wall shattered as Joskin's ax drove through it and ripped through the mage.

The other two robed figures turned their attention to the back. Carrita let out a burst of magic that shook the earth, making both robed figures fall to the ground.

Unfortunately none of the dozen remaining guards were affected. Half of them closed in and took up position around the fallen robed figures. Two of them took a position around the leader, his tiger and Joskin's ax.

Now that he had time to look, Airria noticed Carrita was covered in sweat and the horses in blood but there was not time to figure out nor ask whose blood it was. Three of the guards attacked Airria, while the remaining one attacked Joskin. The two tigers became focused on Carrita.

The earth shook again and a half dozen fighters as well as the two robed figures were swallowed up in the earth. Faith launched a deadly arrow at one of the now pouncing tigers while Airria dove to intercept the other. Though Airria couldn't see anything of what was happening he knew his mass wouldn't be enough to divert such a huge creature much, but he hoped it would be enough. His sword sizzled loudly as it dove deep into the creature's rib cage. He could feel the creature twisting in pain. He could hear Carrita's pony squeal with the impact and tumble to the ground.

He tried to get up. He knew there were still guards to deal with. He desperately wanted to help his friends and know they were all right. All he could manage was to roll over on the now lifeless tiger and defend himself. All he could see from his vantage point were the two guards that were pounding on him. He struggled with both hands to move his shield to block their attacks. At this point he was so fatigued from the fight and sore from the heavy blows of his adversaries he was losing the will to continue.

As he was about to give up hope, one of Faith's arrows exploded behind them, throwing both of them over the tiger. Airria lay there stunned with fatigue and soreness.

The next thing he knew, a very weary Joskin was helping him to his feet. He hurt from head to toe, but he forced himself to look around.

Faith was sitting on the ground next to Carrita, who looked like she was about to pass out. Everything was covered in blood. Giant wolf corpses were ripped apart and smoldering. One tiger looked like it had half its coat ripped off. The one he had killed was still lying on Carrita's squealing pony. Armor and body pieces from the guards were strewn about.

He looked up from the carnage to see most of the town standing in a semicircle around them. Many of them were splashed in blood. All of them were frozen with wide eyes and open mouths. Airria struggled to his feet. His horse was limping from large claw marks and had blood dripping from its mouth. Slowly he picked up his shield and pulled his sword free. Then he wandered over to Faith. She was clean. Her beautiful white horse looked like she had been splashing in the blood, but

Faith had no blood on her. How she had remained clean when even Carrita was covered was a mystery he was too tired to question. Airria collapsed at Faith's side and watched Joskin use his magical ax to roll the tiger off Carrita's pony. "Is it over?" he found himself asking.

Carrita answered very weakly, "This battle is over, but the fight has just begun."

Faith interrupted. "What can we do about the armor and weapons? I remember you buried the last set, but you are in no condition to do so now."

Carrita forced a weak smile, "Either you will have to figure out how to bury them or lend me some of your strength."

"What little I have left, you are welcome to," Faith said in a voice much stronger than Airria expected to hear.

Carrita closed her eyes for a moment. Faith began to droop as badly as Airria. Then Carrita struggled to sit up and asked Joskin to slide all the armor together. While Joskin pushed the armor around to the place Carrita had instructed, Carrita closed her eyes and meditated. When Joskin was finished and walking away, the ground split into a small yet deep fissure, funneling into the heart of the monstrous stone.

The armor tumbled into the hole and the earth closed around it, then the ground began to shake. Carrita was straining. When she stopped, she said breathlessly, "They will not be found," then she collapsed to the ground, completely spent.

Joskin helped the girls onto Faith's horse then helped Airria onto his own horse. He grabbed all the horses by the reins and began to lead them into the forest. They continued this way most of the rest of the day, too tired to even talk.

Airria knew the sword and shield had given him more strength and speed throughout the fight than was normally his to command. Yet now he was almost too tired to ride his own horse. He wondered what would happen when they ran into a bigger group; this one was almost too much for them to handle.

Faith was the only one not showing extreme signs of fatigue. Yet even she was looking tired. She was handling the gore much better than she had in the past.

It was almost sunset when they came into a small clearing with a crawling brook. "We'll stop here for the night," Joskin said as he began to set up camp. We will need to wash and heal the horses and ourselves. You know how our mothers hate the sight of blood, or any indication we've been fighting."

Airria slid off the horse and collapsed on the ground. After a moment he collected himself. "Yes I know. Give me awhile to get my strength back and I'll help." Seeing Joskin set up camp by himself, ax in hand, reminded Airria of the note Salle'allak had sent him. He didn't know how to explain the minotaur's presence, so he said, "Jammar has sent one note for you and one for our mothers." Though he could feel his strength returning, he was still too weak to stand.

Joskin nodded in acknowledgment and finished setting up. By that time, the girls had crawled off Faith's horse and been escorted to their bedrolls by the horse.

Joskin pulled his note out of Airria's torn saddlebag and asked Faith to read it to them.

"Joskin,

I thought you may want to know a little about the ax you found. It was forged by a master Dwarven blacksmith before the Rarstocks were Rarstocks, before the Great War. It was enchanted at the time of the greatest magic by the three most powerful Elven enchantresses. It was crafted to look plain and practical. From the beginning it was created for he who was determined to banish those who attempted to oppress the weak. He was tired of the bickering between humans and non-human, males and females.

He led a group who forced many of the Matradom into the Deep Earth and it was his army who drove the bloodthirsty matrataurs into the Black Forest and brought a sense of order to the northern plains. When he felt his task was finished, he hid the ax.

At the time of the rising of the Rarstocks, he was called back from death and appointed as a Guardian to several items of phenomenal power. Your weapon was a gift to you from him. He has decided it is time for the ax to reaffirm peace in the world and you are the being he has chosen to wield it."

Joskin stopped Faith at this point, "You realize I understand only about half of what you're saying?"

Airria knew Joskin understood each word and he wondered why his cousin would say such a thing.

The group stared for some time at Joskin's ax. Joskin broke the silence, "That explains why the mage couldn't stop it. And why the guards fought so desperately to keep it from me." He looked around the group for a moment with a troubled look on his face then said, "None of you are in any shape to stand watch. You all rest and I'll watch the night."

Airria was not about to argue. He rolled over and gave in to his urge to pass out.

Chapter 29 –Home

The sky was bright and blue when Faith opened her eyes. Her shoulder was sore and her heart was heavy. She had not accepted any of those she killed the day before as being human, though she was grateful her horse had gone to such extreme lengths to keep the blood off her. The fact that most of the splatter was caused by her explosions sending the enemy away from her helped as well.

Joskin was in the stream washing his own horse. She wondered why he had prevented her from finishing Jammar's letter. He had been given a very powerful and important gift. Yet his eyes were wrenched in thought and his shoulders were uncharacteristically rounded.

Faith glanced at Carrita, who was meditating. "Why did you not sleep?" Faith asked.

Carrita opened her eyes. She was looking much stronger, though still very weak in comparison to her usual self. "If I had allowed myself to sleep I would not have awakened for days."

"Why?" Faith asked.

"For you, it takes an evening's rest to recover your magical energy," Carrita explained. "Because of who I am and how long and intensely I have been training, it takes me much longer. I simply have too

236

much magical energy to recover."

Airria squatted next to them. He was wet but clean. "How are you both doing?" he asked. His tone let Faith know he wanted more than a one-word answer.

"I am a little sore," Faith answered, "but I should be all right."

"I am still a little worn out," Carrita responded, "but I dare not rest."

Airria smiled, "According to Joskin, we should be able to have a few safe days at home before heading off."

Carrita did not look convinced, but she began rolling up her bedroll. Faith followed suit.

Faith's horse, which she now called Persephone, nudged her as she finished rolling her bedroll. The mare was clean and dry. She turned to thank Joskin.

Before she could, he said, "Your horse cleaned herself. She wouldn't let me touch her."

It did not take long to get ready and back on the move. The group traveled most of the day through the forest away from Tark-Ancia until the forest came to an abrupt end. The trail opened into a huge clearing. In the center of the clearing was as sturdy, three-story, patchwork house as wide as a livery stable with dozens of children running around.

Carrita climbed off her pony and began helping children on it.

At first Faith was hesitant. She knew Persephone was a special horse and would not let just anyone touch her. Then she could feel the horse's desire to participate, so Faith hopped off and helped some children on. She watched closely as Persephone gently allowed the children to play.

Before she knew it, Faith was standing alone with Carrita. Airria and Joskin were already up on the porch hugging two women. Faith could guess one was Airria's mother, the other his aunt.

"Come!" Airria shouted to the girls when he had let the women go, "Come meet the masters of this carnival!"

Faith and Carrita jogged up to the house. Joskin, Airria and their mothers came down the short steps to greet the girls.

The younger woman, around forty years of age, looked down at Carrita, "Airria, are you bringing orphans home now?"

Before anyone could answer, the elder woman, not much older than the first, looked to Faith, "You were right Joskin, she is very beautiful." The woman's words caused Joskin to blush.

Airria spoke up, "Mother, this is Carrita and this is Faith," he pointed to each in turn, "and this is my mom, Sara and my aunt, Desa. Though sometimes I'm not sure why I don't call them both Mom."

Faith addressed the elder woman first, as was proper, "I am very pleased to meet you, Desa." Then she bowed slightly. She repeated the greeting with Sara, then added, "Your sons are exceptionally good men. You should be very proud of them."

"We are quite proud of both of them," Desa said smiling brightly.

Sara smiled at Faith and said, "We are very pleased to meet you as well." She then turned to Carrita with motherly affection, "Are you an orphan?"

Carrita smiled shyly back. "Yes, I am an orphan, but I am not here to join your clan."

Sara bent over and hugged Carrita, "You are welcome here as long as you would like to stay."

Desa and Sara ushered the group into the house. "You look like you can use a real meal," Sara said to them as she sat them around along a rough table. Desa began setting out hand-carved bowls and spoons for the travelers. Then went over to the stove and grabbed a pot of simple rabbit stew.

As the women began dishing the stew, Joskin and Airria looked more excited than when surrounded with elegance and the exquisite entrées Jammar had served. Faith was drawn back to the last meal she had shared with her family. It was the simple feeling of home. She knew it. To the men, this stew was simply a taste of home.

Faith looked out the window at the children playing. "Why do you have so many children?" she asked. "Do people leave them with you?"

Desa handed Faith some bread as she said, "In Tark-Ancia

238

children are often abandoned early in life. The few we find, we try to help." She glanced out the window as well, "Have you ever seen such a beautiful sight?"

Sara, who was now also staring out the window said, "We didn't need to give birth to them to love them."

"How do you keep up with all of them?" Carrita asked. "I mean, there are so many."

"After trying to keep up with these two, the rest have been easy!" Sara jested pointing to the men.

They laughed and talked about all the trouble Joskin and Airria used to get in. Faith listened intently to the stories. It was interesting to hear how Joskin had such an impact on Airria, even more than Airria's father.

In course of time the children began flocking into the kitchen, stopping to greet Faith and Carrita. Several of the older ones offered to show Carrita to a room. Carrita hesitated, then politely declined and sat on the bench. Faith sat on the long bench as the children filed around the table until it was full.

Two of the oldest began passing out bowls and spoons for the children. Desa and Sara began filling them.

The children all looked to Faith and began begging her to tell them a story. She had already told all the stories she dared to the men, but after a moment she began telling them about where she grew up. When they would gasp at simple and basic things such as her wearing a dress through her childhood she realized how extremely differently they had been raised.

When she would finish one story, the children would plead for another. It was dark before Desa and Sara finally offered relief.

"Time for bed," they said. A chorus of tired complaining followed. Soon though, the older children began ushering the younger children up the stairs. One of the older boys fetched some water then headed behind the others.

Desa and Sara began washing the bowls. Though Faith and Carrita offered to help, the two women refused and washed all the dishes, asking Faith questions the whole time.

Airria, whom Faith had not noticed leaving, entered the room and offered a note to his mother. "Jammar, the man whose house we trained at, told me I should give you this."

Sara casually opened the note and began to silently read it. As she read her demeanor quickly shifted. Her forehead furrowed and her eyes scowled. Then she looked up at Carrita and asked in a panicked tone, "You are joining my son on his quest?"

Airria looked sternly at his mother, but it was Carrita who spoke. "Until you have witnessed what I have witnessed, be careful judging this task. The errand which calls to Airria and me is requisite. You can no more prevent me from following your son then you can prevent him from going," she spoke with such passion and elegance, Sara and Desa looked at the ground.

After a moment Sara said, "If there is a dragon and if it is so powerful, isn't this quest certain death?"

"Of the future I cannot assure you. Of your son's safety, I cannot guarantee. Of the dragon, she is real and far more dangerous than Airria knows. Even knowing what I know about her, only death or success will free my soul from the bonds of this endeavor," again the command in Carrita's voice made the child disappear to be replaced by an educated, powerful woman.

"Joskin," Desa said softly, "will you watch over your cousin?"

Joskin hesitated, "If Airria goes, who will protect the family?"

"I know, at best, this quest is crazy," Sara piped in, "and, at worst, it is certain death. I know if Airria has any chance of returning to us, it is with you." She held up the note then added, "We will be fine."

Desa spoke again, "You know how much I care for each of my children. You know how much it hurts me when I lose one. His best chance at returning is if you will watch over him. You know very well the world he'll be going into. You must guide Airria. So, I ask again, will you watch over your cousin?"

Joskin looked torn but there was no hesitation in his voice, "I will, Mother."

In an attempt to lighten the mood, Faith asked, "May we rest here for a few days?"

Desa and Sara answered in happy unison, "You may stay and rest as long as you would like," then they escorted the girls to a small room with a single large straw bed.

"This will be your room as long as you stay," Desa said while Sara lit a candle, "may you find the rest you need." Then, without another word, both women left.

Carrita picked a corner near the foot of the bed and began meditating. Faith knew Carrita was still severely drained of her magic but would not allow herself to sleep.

Though she didn't need to sleep, Faith crawled into bed. It was lumpy and pokey, but for the first time since she had been taken as a slave, she felt honestly at peace. There was no magic, no trickeries. She felt the comfort of an honest home.

Her mind drifted over the course of the last few months. She had been taken from her family, rescued by a stranger, had her beliefs rewritten and learned her lifelong mentor was a lesser deity. Her sister, the only surviving family she had, had demanded she accompany Airria on his insane quest. She had been learning magic and had seen places a few short months ago she never would have imagined existed.

Now she had been taken in by two of the most kind-hearted women she had ever met. Even with the knowledge of the loss of her family, she did not feel alone. She had gained a new family, not one of blood, but a family bonded by need and common goals. Though the thought of their quest was terrifying and overwhelming, it felt right. For tonight, she felt safe.

She offered to allow Carrita to take her magical energy. As Carrita did so, Faith clutched onto the feeling of comfort and drifted off to sleep.

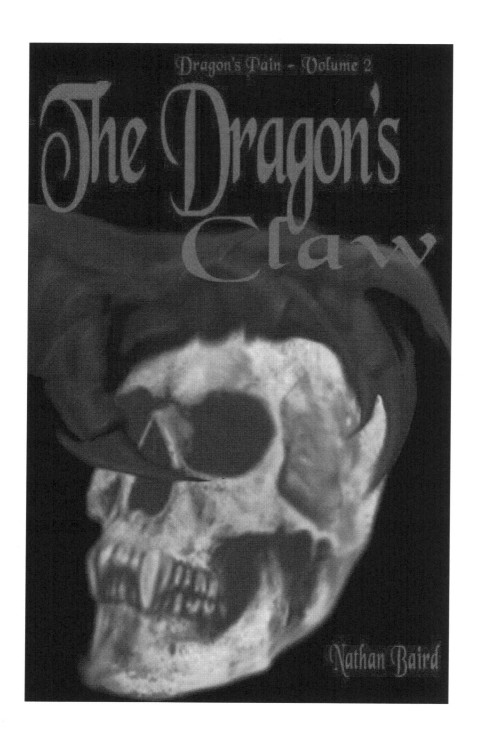

Chapter 1 - Storms

Faith sat on the front porch, the large curls of her auburn hair fluttering in the early evening breeze. She was watching the children play as the sun set. It had been such a peaceful week with the family Airria and Joskin had been raised with, she had almost forgotten the tragedy of the last several months. She had been sold into slavery, tortured, almost raped and rescued by two strangers who had become very dear to her. All of this was just the beginning to a monstrous shift in her life.

She glanced down at her right hand, to the small wooden ring one of the older boys had made for her. It had become a reminder of simple things and simple days.

"It's quite a sight to watch," Sara, Airria's mother came from behind, "I do love watching them play."

"Yes. It is quite enjoyable to watch," Faith's attention was not so much on the children, as it was on who they were playing with.

Several of the children were tackling Airria and Joskin in a futile attempt to pen them down. Airria was agile and slender, hard for the children to hold on to. Joskin was muscular and quick, powerfully dragging several children everywhere he went. The children would pile on them both; then another small group would run into them laughing and they would all fall in a large pile on the ground. Eventually both men would squirm and push their way free, get up and let the children chase them again.

As Faith watched the men she thought of how much she trusted them. How odd, she thought. It had only been a few months since Airria had poked his rusty blonde head into her slave wagon. She was so afraid of him then. A few hours later Airria and his cousin Joskin had saved her from a sadistic group of ruffians.

Absolute trust was not earned until both men rejected a small fortune and risked their own lives to keep her from yet another hostile group, the Order of the Black Claw. The slaver had talked regularly of his Black Claw clients. They were legendary in both cruelty and tenacity. She later learned that Order was Jarmack'Trastibbik's personally picked warriors and mages.

"That Carrita girl," Sara continued, "it's good to see her playing like a child."

Faith looked at Carrita teaching a few of the older children a new game. "It is so rare to get to see her as a thirteen-year-old girl."

"I talked to her yesterday," Sara said, "she speaks like an old sage. How did she grow up so fast?"

There was no doubt Carrita was different. When Faith had met her, Carrita was a scared, abused child. Within a short while Faith had learned Carrita was wise far beyond her years and had a tremendous command of magic; a command which rivaled even the powerful mages they had encountered from the Order of the Black Claw.

"Yes," Faith replied, "Carrita is an unusual girl. One moment I will see the thirteen-year-old she is, the next moment I will be intimidated by how much she understands." Seeing her corn-silk blonde hair, it was difficult to believe it had been a musty raven color when they had met.

Sara asked, "Do you know why?"

Faith responded, "I am aware of only a small part of why she is so mentally advanced. Most of what I do know, you will not want to know."

Sara said, "I know she has her secrets. She likes to keep them close, but is there anything you can tell me?"

Faith almost laughed. She understood Sara was looking for a way to keep Carrita from going on the quest Airria had started. Airria's quest had started when he had witnessed Jarmack'Trastibbik, the oldest and most powerful of all Black Dragons torture and kill his father and uncle. "I can tell you, your son is not the only one who has lost a parent to the dragon."

"So you believe dragons really exist? You believe Airria really saw one?" Sara said, lowering the corners of her eyes.

"I have no doubt," Faith said confidently. "There is no force in the world, aside from death, which could stop those two from facing this particular dragon."

Sara looked at the ground, "That's what I'm afraid of. If this dragon is as large and powerful as Airria told us, they have no chance!"

With what little Faith knew about Jarmack'Trastibbik, she believed Sara was correct. Their chances of surviving were so minuscule they could be considered non-existent. Still, she knew Jammar, the Guardian or lesser deity of this island, had taken time and used his resources to tutor and train them. Though she could not put much confidence in her statement, she said, "Though our chances are low, there is a chance. Carrita knows better than any of us exactly what we will be facing. If she is willing to see this through, so will I."

Sara looked deep into Faith's eyes, searching, "But why take the chance? Why not stay here and live in peace?"

Faith wished she had a better answer, "Neither Airria nor Carrita can find peace until they have completed this quest." She thought back to what her sister had said and to being trained by Jammar and Salle'allak, another Guardian. "There is more at stake here then just us."

Sara asked, "What do you mean?"

Faith smiled nervously, "I honestly don't know. I just understand we need to push forward as far as we can. If it means death, then we will have to accept it."

Sara let out a frustrated sigh and walked back into the house.

248

It was starting to get dark. The children began their nightly journey into the house for dinner. Faith watched the procession to what she thought was the end. She then stood to follow. She, Airria and Carrita no longer needed food or sleep, but it felt good to sit and eat with Airria's family.

Faith felt a small hand slip into hers and start playing with the small wooden ring on her pinky finger. She glanced down to see Molia, one of the children Airria and Joskin's mothers had taken in. The ring had been a silly gift from one of the older boys, but Molia had grown quite attached to it. Maybe it was just a way for the child to feel connected to Faith. Either way, Faith did not mind. Molia was nearly the same age of her own little sister, Natalya, Faith's only living relative.

Faith allowed the child to lead her into the house for supper, but stopped when she heard a loud "crack." Another boom of thunder spun her around though the thunder was not as loud as it had been when she witnessed the storm from the top of the distant range a few months earlier.

Molia gripped Faith's hand tightly with one hand and twisted her wooded ring with her other. The child seemed to be pleading with Faith to stay. It felt similar to Natalya's pleading. In the end, it was Natalya who had convinced Faith to leave.

Carrita caught Faith's attention, "The storm is getting stronger."

Faith glanced down at Carrita who was staring at the storm. "How?" Faith asked, "How can it grow stronger? Will the magic of this island not oppress it?"

"Do you remember the lessons of balance from the shrines?" Carrita asked in response.

Faith nodded.

Carrita shifted her gaze to Faith. Jammar disrupted the balance of magic on this island by training us, by helping us prepare for our journey. The longer we delay our departure from this place, the weaker the island will become.

Desa, Joskin's mother, spoke behind them, "As much as we don't want you to go, if what you say is true, you will need to be leaving soon."

249

Joskin slowly backed up the stairs, fixated on the storm, "Who will protect the family?"

Desa asked in response, "Do you remember the note? The one Airria brought back?"

"Yes." Joskin had received his own note, one he had not shared with his mother. He had not even let Faith finish reading it. It talked of his ax as a gift from the Guardian of Weapons, but the weapon came with a responsibility to fight those who would oppress the weak.

Faith knew this was not the note Desa was talking about. She believed Joskin understood. The note in question was one Airria had given his mother when the group had arrived at the house. Though Faith had been curious as to its contents, she had not asked about it.

Desa continued, "Jammar promised to keep us safe while you're gone. According to Airria he could put you in your place."

Joskin turned around with mock offense, "Mom! You put me in my place all the time."

Faith considered how intimidated she used to be by Joskin's size. He was a little shorter than Airria, but had far more muscle. Even in the light leather armor he always wore and without a weapon, it was obvious he was a fierce warrior.

Airria stepped on the porch, his thin, solid, athletic build showing nicely though his deerskin trousers and dirty white shirt. "Does this mean it's time to move on?" His concerned grin was directed at Faith.

Molia squeezed Faith's hand again. She then attached herself to Faith's leg.

Faith put her hand comfortingly on the child's back, "It will be over by morning."

Molia looked up at Faith with deep set fear, "You sure?"

Faith dropped to one knee, "Yes, Molia, I am sure." Faith then gave the child a hug.

"Will you stay with me until it's over?" Molia asked.

Faith could see the child was asking for more than just the night. "I will stay with you though the night. When the sun comes up the storm will be gone."

The child held Faith longingly. Faith held her back and picked her up. She carried the child in and sat her on the bench. Faith then sat beside her; the child always keeping one hand on Faith's ring.

The group ate without a word. The children jumped with each crack of lightning. The devastating energy from the storm shone through the fear in the eyes of everyone at the table.

Even after the uncomfortable meal the feeling did not cease. Faith escorted the child to her bed. She sat on the bed next to Molia and caressed her hair. Faith did her best to comfort the child, but Molia did not rest until the storm had run its course and the sun peaked over the distant range.

After Molia drifted into a restless sleep, Faith glanced to the doorway. Airria was there, watching her. She felt her face flush slightly. "It is strange to see the children sleeping when the sun is up," Faith said to ease her discomfort.

"Yes," Airria replied. "It's good to see them resting after last night."

Carrita poked her head into the room, "Sadly it is only growing worse."

Some of the children in the room shifted restlessly. Faith came to the doorway so the group could converse with ease and speak more quietly. "We killed the mage. Why is the storm still an issue?"

"The storm is fueled by the magic of Jarmack'Trastibbik." Carrita sounded like an instructor, "Only when she has been dispatched will the storm desist."

Faith looked first to Carrita, then to Airria. They were both looking at her with a question in their eyes. She was not sure why they would question her.

Joskin's deep, soft voice came from close by, "Is it time to move on?"

As Airria and Carrita continued their gazes, Faith understood. The group had been waiting on her to decide it was time to go. Airria and Carrita were still waiting.

Joskin continued, "If we stay any longer, Molia will never let us leave."

Faith glanced again over the room of sleeping children. She had enjoyed spending time with them, but it was time to progress in the journey. "Yes," she said after a while, "we should leave before the children are awake."

Airria glanced into the room, "Do you think Molia will forgive you for not saying good-bye?"

Faith walked back to Molia's bed. She brushed the child's hair away from her face and stared for a moment. She pulled the simple wood ring off her finger and placed it in the girl's small hand.

Molia rustled in her bed for a moment. Faith bent down to kiss the girl's cheek. She whispered into the child's ear, "I hope you will someday understand. What I do is for all those I care about." She stood up, feeling small and shallow for not wanting to give a proper good-bye to the child. She looked to the doorway, then back to the child.

Though Molia's eyes were still shut, Molia had a small tear running down her nose. Her fist was clenched tightly around the ring.

Faith turned and quietly left before she broke down. As a group, they silently walked down the stairs, past the rustic table and out the front door.

"You never did like to leave when we were awake," Sara said to Joskin as he stepped on the porch.

Desa added, "Normally we've been grateful to skip the discomfort of good-bye, but this time we want another look at you before you go."

Airria asked, "How did you know we would be leaving this morning?"

Sara laughed softly. "Why else would Joskin get your horses ready?"

Faith glanced at Joskin. He was blushing lightly. It hit her; she was the last one to know. She thought through the day and realized the rest of the group had been saying their good-byes in their own ways. Even Molia had been more attentive, almost clingy all day.

Carrita reached up and grabbed Faith's hand. "Somewhere deep inside, you realized today we would be leaving," Carrita said as if she could read Faith's thoughts.

252

Faith opened her mouth to argue, but she could find no words. Thankfully Airria spoke up.

"This is the first time I am leaving with him," he uncharacteristically choked on his words. "I thought it would be easier on both of you if you woke up and we were already gone."

"Not this time," his mother responded. "If Carrita is right about what you are getting into, you will be very different when you get back."

"You know…" Carrita began, but was cut off.

"We will hold to the best thoughts," Desa said, "anything else is unthinkable."

Joskin fell into his mother's arms. "I will return." His deep, rich voice had an unusual softness to it. His heavily muscled arms wrapped gently around his mother's strong slender frame.

"I will be waiting," Desa whispered back, "more than ever, I will be waiting."

Airria had a similar encounter with his own mother. As much as both mothers tried to hold to hope, they were hugging as if they would never see their sons again.

After a long moment Airria and Joskin switched to embrace each other's mother. Finally, Desa and Sara took turns hugging Faith and Carrita.

As Sara pulled away from Carrita she whispered, "I can't imagine what skills you have that make it so important for you to join this quest. I do know you have the respect of my son and nephew. Not an easy task. I know I can't change your mind. I just want you to know you are welcome in our home any time."

Carrita whispered back, "You are wonderful parents to many. There are few who would accept such a task. I am both grateful and honored to be counted among those you have cared for. I will do all in my ability to return your sons to you." She then bowed regally and descended the stairs.

The rest of the group followed close behind. It was not long before they were on their way, the feel of the morning breeze in their hair.

Faith had a burning desire to look back, but was afraid she would cry. Each of the others carried the same firm focus. It helped her to know she was not alone.

Chapter 2 – The Silver City

The bustling, smooth, stone streets of O'queen were a drastic change from the laid back time the group had experienced for the last week. Airria had really not wanted to leave home, but the storm had reminded him of why he'd started the quest.

It had been much easier to deal with his father's death since Jammer's potion made it so he didn't have to sleep. Without sleep, he didn't have to dream. Without dreams Airria didn't have to relive his father's death. That is, until the storm started. He could feel the energy from the storm. It brought all the memories crashing back. He didn't even have to shut his eyes to relive each moment.

That was a few days ago. Now he was passing the three-level buildings of O'queen, smooth ditches gently returning the tide water back to the ocean filled with colorful fish. The stones in the street were smooth and brown; the buildings shimmered like fish scales and had no corners. The city was not as big as Gentrail, the Life City had been, but it was far larger than Tark-Ancia, the Chaos City where he grew up. Between the shine and the distracting running trenches on either side of the street, Airria was lost.

Fortunately Joskin knew his way around the city. People ducked out of his way as he barreled past fisheries towards the dock. Of course he was wearing his hard leather armor and brandishing his massive ax. The whole show would discourage basic thugs and robbers from jumping the group.

Before they could even see the water they stopped to gaze at the monstrous silver wall which reached out into the ocean. After opening and closing her mouth in disbelief for some time Faith asked, "Is the wall made entirely of silver?"

Joskin smiled as he answered, "They say it was created by the Mistress of Water herself. From the other side you can see the representation of several swimming creatures. It truly is amazing; you'll see that for yourself when we leave port."

Joskin began turning his head to either side. After a moment he said, "We need to find passage to Credonia," then he pointed to a tavern near the docks called The Drunken Sailor, "You wait here. I'll go and book us passage."

The odors wafting from the rickety wooden doorway reminded Airria of his favorite tavern. Though the doors were crooked they were still far straighter than the tavern of his hometown. "Is there a more relaxing smell than this?" Airria asked, tying his horse to the rail.

Both Carrita and Faith covered their noses. Faith replied, "I can think of a few more enjoyable smells, like the stench of the Dead Swamp."

All three of them laughed as they went through the doors. The walls were covered with old paintings of sea monsters and ships. In most of them the sea monsters were attacking the ships, oftentimes dragging them into the sea. Patrons looked scrappy and were dressed in rags. Airria assumed from the artistry on the wall and on the table that this was a sailor's tavern. The basic conversation was very loud until they walked in.

Airria realized that the sailors, even the female sailors, were not looking at him. It took him a moment to realize they were all looking at the girls. He'd grown so accustomed to having the girls around he'd forgotten the attention Faith could grab with her hourglass figure and rich green eyes.

Both girls were clean and neatly dressed, but so was Airria. He'd noticed a division in stares; most of sailors were admiring Faith, the rest Carrita. One man disgustingly stood out as he was ogling the girl.

257

Airria knew Carrita could level the tavern, provided there wasn't a comparable mage in it, but he still felt protective. He put a hand on Carrita's shoulder and began backing out. The large man with a scraggly blond beard, salt-covered, leathery skin and the pungent aroma of fish blocked their exit. "I remember this one is worth a bunch of money," the big man said looking greedily of Faith.

"The bounty has been repealed," Airria responded, pulling Faith behind him. He'd thought the slaver's bounty had been forgotten. It had been months since the slaver had used a magic potion to teleport off the island, surely he'd not returned.

"And him too!" someone from the back of the tavern yelled.

Joskin's reputation had kept all the bounties and bounty hunters at bay. Now someone had offered enough money to overcome any fear they had of Airria's cousin.

"Five hundred silver for each of them," another voice shouted from an unseen place.

The large man reached to grab Airria. The man was well muscled and reasonably quick, but Airria had been trained by a Guardian, the Guardian of Weapons. He had been training to fight a dragon. Fighting a mortal wasn't even a challenge.

Then again he was now trying to defend both girls against a whole tavern. Not that either girl really needed defending, but he had been helping Joskin defend his family for so many years it was instinct now. This fight could be a real challenge.

As Airria circled the girls he watched the shifting, gathering ring of ratty looking men and women. He could feel a smile cross his face. It had been years since he had an honest brawl. He wasn't going to take out his sword.

After a moment Faith stopped him and backed against his back. It was good to know he had some he trusted there. A streak of panic went through him as he realized he had no idea where Carrita was, but there was no time to think about it. The fishy smelling man swung. Airria ducked below the swinging arm. He caught the arm and threw his back into the man's thigh. Airria was going to throw his opponent over him, but noticed Faith fending off her own attack, right where he would need

258

to throw the beastly man. Instead he grabbed the muscled forearm and pulled down while he threw his shoulder up. Though it took most of Airria's might, after a moment he heard the satisfying pop as the elbow disjointed.

In front of Faith there were two men rolling on the ground in pain, blood gushing out of their noses. A third, a woman, was pulling a dagger. Faith's posture was still confident and she looked ready for anything.

Airria spent too much time admiring Faith's flawless curves and movement. A sharp blow landed hard a little below his ribs, sending him sprawling forward, almost hitting Faith and distracting her. He had to quickly step left to avoid the dagger. Airria tumbled off balance, crashing to the ground.

A loud crash from near the doorway caused the whole tavern to freeze. The pathway slowly opened up from Airria to the door. Joskin was there, his ax haft resting in a pulverized stone tile. Cracks emanated out through the other stones on the floor.

"Joskin," Airria said, "that was quick."

"I was told the ship's captain was here," Joskin's voice boomed through the room.

The corridor widened to reveal Carrita standing quietly near the wall. She was calmly and curiously admiring a man in all black. He seemed be frozen in midstride. The other three slowly approached.

In one hand the man held a very distinctive dagger made of Black Wood. It had no grooves for poison, no scratches on the blade. The hilt was a finely sculpted dragon's claw holding a vampiric skull. Carrita tilted her head back and forth several times before speaking, "The Order of the Black Claw."

"He seems a little ill-equipped," Faith observed.

"He's a grunt," Airria said with a snort.

"No. He's a runner," Joskin said, pointing to a black glass sphere in the other hand. Then he turned around and faced the crowd. "The bounties on these people have officially been revoked!" he called out.

259

Carrita kept tilting her head from one side to the other. "He was to remain unobserved. When we came he was to kill us if he could. The sphere was his escape if he had failed."

"How do you know?" Faith asked.

Carrita stopped for a moment then craned to look at Faith, "It is the only explanation which makes any sense," her face was filled with absolute confidence.

There was a quick flash as Joskin's ax flew through the magic shield holding the man in place.

Airria glanced at his cousin, surprised at the bloodthirsty strike. Joskin's eyes were slanted together tightly in anger. "No one that's associated with the Order of the Black Claw deserves to live!" he said, glaring around the room.

Carrita carefully picked up the dagger and the black sphere. "This weapon is made of wood from the Black Forest. One scratch would prove worse than fatal."

Faith relaxed slightly at Carrita's words, "Is this dagger not as dangerous as the other weapons used by the warrior's of the Black Claw?"

Carrita responded, "In its own way this dagger is far more dangerous than the other weapons."

Joskin opened his mouth as if to protest, but Carrita continued, "This wooden dagger is as strong as iron and caries torturous poison for the souls of any who are marked by its irreversible touch."

Joskin finally spoke, "In all fairness, the warrior's weapons just torturously kill their victims. This dagger turns them into zombies."

Carrita placed her arms across her chest, "If you look at it from the basest level, you are correct, but if you take into account the complexities which make us alive, you are not."

Airria had to be impressed. It was the first time Carrita had challenged Joskin in anything. By the look on Joskin's face he knew Joskin was not happy with Carrita.

In an attempt to change the subject Airria asked, "Did you gain us passage?"

Joskin looked at Airria, "The only ship for Credonia leaves tonight for the port of Cambria. I was told the captain was here."

A tall thin man with a long gray beard pulled into a ponytail and bushy eyebrows stepped out of the crowd. His clothes were relatively neat and comely. A tattered golden insignia was worn proudly on his shoulders. "My name is Earito; I am captain of the merchant and passenger ship to Cambria. Are you looking for employment, Joskin DeAveron?"

Joskin responded mechanically, "I seek only quiet passage."

Then Earito looked at the ground, "What business do you have in Credonia, there are no wars, nor conflicts?"

Joskin smiled courteously, "My business is my own. My travels are not always for war."

Airria was amazed. He had never seen Joskin act so formal. He guessed there was some formality to getting passage on a ship. From the frown on the captain's face, Airria decided the he was disappointed Joskin had turned him down.

After a short time the captain smiled graciously and said, "You know the price of passage."

"The fee has been paid," Joskin replied mechanically.

The captain looked down at Joskin's ax then back to his face. Joskin ducked his head and raised his eyes. Airria almost laughed as the captain hung his own head again.

"Anything else?" the captain said, all formality gone from his voice.

"Yes," Joskin replied sounding more like himself, "we require four rooms at the back of the ship. No less will do." He stuck his hand out, a gold coin palmed in it.

The captain's eyes lit up as he reached out to shake Joskin's hand. The coin was worth almost as much the whole ship. "I will have your rooms read," he nodded behind him to his men.

At the captain's nod, they snapped in line and shuffled out of the tavern. A tall stocky man with thick, sun-streaked hair shuffled slower than the others, his eyes never left Faith's body. "It will be a pleasure to have you aboard," he said as he passed by, leering.

261

Airria looked at Joskin, "Do you think there will be trouble aboard?"

Joskin shrugged, "Never traveled with a woman before, but never had problems."

Airria asked, "How long is the trip?"

Joskin got a half grin, "Four months."

Airria frowned, "That's a long time for the girls to be around guys like these."

Joskin chuckled, "They made it three months with you."

Airria casually swung for Joskin's shoulder. To his surprise he actually connected, both men looked startled and stepped back. In all the years the two of them had been together, not once had Airria solidly connected.

Joskin glanced from his shoulder to his cousin. After a few moments Joskin halfheartedly laughed. "I guess your training has really paid off," he shook his head in disbelief and then looked thoughtfully at the ground, "maybe it's time you started training me."

"That'll be the day," Airria responded, still in shock.

"I'll make arrangements for us to train on the ship," Joskin's tone was sharp and almost pleading.

Airria was again surprised at Joskin. His cousin had never made such a request of him and Airria had never heard Joskin use such a tone. "If you think it will help, I'll be glad to teach you."

"Then head to the ship with the horses. Everything should be taken care of," Joskin said. He slipped back into his traditional tone, "Try not to start any more fights on the way."

Faith asked, "Where are you going?"

"I'm going to get some practice weapons," Joskin replied. "We won't want to be using these on board," he shook his ax. Before anyone else could say anything he headed out the door.

"I only borrowed so many books from Jammar," Carrita said more to Faith than the group, "it would appear there will be ample time for research and study."

Airria asked, "Did you ever do anything just for fun?" He had seen her play with the other children at his mother's, but she always seemed a little out of place.

"What you define as fun I would deem as tedious tasks," Carrita looked a little frustrated. "For me the greatest entertainment is to learn and expand my mental capacity."

"Then perhaps it is time for us to leave," Faith said and she headed out the door. Carrita quickly followed.

Airria held back a moment and thought about what Carrita had said and then followed the girls.

Chapter 3 – The Ship

After events at The Drunken Sailor, Faith's horse, Persephone, was far more protective of Faith. As the group traveled the short distance to the ship, Persephone squealed and bit at anyone who came close. Even Airria and the other horses were not permitted near Faith. Fortunately no one got hurt.

When they arrived at the ship there was a young stable boy waiting at the base of the plank. He looked nervous, especially when Persephone threw a hoof at him.

Faith was embarrassed. She had no idea what would make her horse behave so coarsely. From the time Faith had been introduced to the horse, Persephone had shown an unusually strong attachment to her and an exceptional level of intelligence. In the few months Faith had been riding the horse, she had learned to trust it, but she could not imagine why Persephone would be so adamant to keep everyone away.

"Perhaps I should tend to my horse myself," Faith finally said.

"How about you just lead the way," Airria suggested to the boy.

The boy bowed roughly, "If you want," then led them up on the deck.

"Welcome!" The first mate said, his eyes still fixed below Faith shoulders. "I'm Jericon, the first mate. If you need anything let me know."

"Thank you," Airria said his voice louder than usual.

"Why didn't you take the horses?" Jericon yelled. He then backhanded the boy across the face.

The boy cowered back, "They wouldn't let me."

"Do not hit him again!" Carrita's teeth were clenched tight. Her eyes began frosting over.

Jericon half shifted his gaze to Carrita, "If you fancy the boy, I could have him sent to your quarters tonight. I can arrange for him to be your toy for the trip."

Faith could feel the temperature dropping around her. She quickly placed a hand on Carrita's shoulder, but spoke to Jericon, "If you are an example of the courtesy we can expect on this vessel, we will pass on your hospitality." She placed as much venom in her words as she could.

Jericon took a step back and for a brief moment his eyes met Faith's. "I'll try to be better," he bowed slowly, really raking his eyes down Faith.

"Well boy," Airria said softly, "where do we stable our horses?"

The boy looked to Jericon, who didn't respond, so the boy quickly strode to a large hatch with a ramp heading down to a small stable.

It looked reasonably comfortable, there was fresh dry feed. Unless more animals were to be transported, the group's horses would be the only animals there. There was not much room for anything else.

The boy grabbed an armload of hay and brought it over to the manger. As he cautiously set it down Carrita asked, "How regularly does he strike you as he did this day?"

"Only when I do something to make him mad or when I don't do something I am 'posed to do," he replied standing as straight as he could.

"How did you come to be on the ship?" Faith asked.

"My mama left me here," the boy said with fear. "Jericon took me in."

265

Airria sighed, "There may be something we can do about this, but for now we should settle in."

Carrita hesitated with a scowl.

"We've a long trip," Airria said to Carrita. "Jericon has offered the boy to you for the trip. Maybe you can prevent a few beatings."

"I may take care of the issue permanently," Carrita muttered under her breath.

Faith could not blame Carrita for her distaste of the young boy being beaten. She had spent months being abused in the most hideous ways imaginable. "We will find a way."

A shadow fell across them, "His name is Rosen and if the payment is right anything can be arranged." A scratchy voice ripped into the room. The hatchway darkened with a lanky, slightly hunched silhouette.

Persephone squealed. Airria's warhorse stomped heavily. The boy ducked behind the haystack.

"And what would be the price?" Airria asked.

The silhouette melted into a rundown, gray-haired old man with a toothless smile. "I'm Tarstan, quartermaster for the ship. We can discuss the price later. For tonight, the boy is yours."

Persephone spun around and took two rapid steps forward, then stomped her hooves angrily.

The old man retreated back up the ramp.

Faith could feel the temperature dropping again, Carrita was understandably sensitive to the subject. The abuse she had faced during her time as a slave was extreme. Faith could feel more than just temperature change; she could feel what Carrita intended.

Faith looked back to Carrita, "We will discuss this with Captain Earito. I believe Joskin has an appropriate rapport to resolve the situation." She breathed a sigh of relief as the temperature return to normal.

Carrita shook her head, "I have learned to control a force which could tear the life from his chest, yet I struggle to rein in my rage. Now I have announced my abilities to all who understand and use magic, great and small, on this vessel."

Airria looked from Faith to Carrita to Rosen. His feet shuffled for a moment then he said, "We should take a walk on deck." Without waiting for a response he motioned for the boy, together they walked up the ramp.

Carrita shook her head again, "Now I have revealed myself in the presence of a strange boy."

Faith smiled at her young friend. "The boy we may not know, but I do not believe he will reveal your secrets. As to the magic users on the ship, given what we understand of the robe your mother gave you they will believe it to be the threat. Few would believe such a young person could command such magic.

"Such a belief may place you in danger," Carrita said wrinkling her forehead.

"Joskin has a petrifying reputation among the sailors," Faith replied. "He paid the captain very well. Regardless of how the quartermaster or the first mate may feel, think or desire, between Joskin's reputation and the amount he paid the captain, we should be safe."

"What if Joskin is often required elsewhere?" Carrita asked with childish pleading in her eyes.

"I believe we could maneuver our way out of any situation these men could put us in," Faith responded.

"I really should not expose my skill with magic, not while we are confined to this vessel," Carrita said. "Joskin would not be pleased if we were to diminish any of the staff's existence."

Faith laughed, "We have more than magic and violence to our credit."

Carrita frowned, "To what would you be referencing?"

Faith laughed again, "We have intellect." She knelt so that she was eye to eye with Carrita. "Were you not the one who tried to teach me women cannot always count on men?"

Carrita looked at the ground a moment. "I'm not implying we need to depend on the men. What I am attempting to convey is, the men have a way of accomplishing their goals and may take exception if we employ a different route to accomplish the same goals."

"So long as no one dies, I believe the men will be well with whatever we do."

Carrita looked at the floor again and began brushing her pony. "Joskin and Airria are good men."

"Yes, they are," Faith responded. It looked as though she were deep in thought. Faith was concerned. Carrita had a far greater understanding of magic, the universe and society than she did, even though she was only thirteen. Sometimes Faith wished she could see inside the girl's mind. Other times she was glad she could not.

"We should appear as normal as we are able," Carrita finally said. "We will need to eat and retire to our rooms regularly."

Faith whispered in Carrita's ear, "I believe your display earlier made it clear, at the very least to magic users, we are not average."

Carrita pouted, "I did not intend to get upset."

"If you are careful for the remainder of the journey, those who felt the magic will likely blame on it on me," Faith whispered.

Carrita put her hand on her chin and began tapping it with her finger. "I do not want them to assume you are a mage either."

"I am hoping we will be able to use their assumption to our advantage," Faith said smiling.

Heavy hoofbeats pounding on the deck above silenced the girls as Joskin's deep voice came down the ramp, "Are the rooms ready?"

The captain sounded out of breath, "Yes. Your requests have been met."

Faith quickly made her way on deck. She walked straight to Joskin.

Joskin cocked his head slightly and raised one eye. He watched her walk the whole way.

She walked up to him and whispered in his ear, "We may have a problem."

"What?" He asked far less discreetly.

"There is a slave boy aboard which is being abused," Faith whispered, hoping Joskin would take the hint.

Fortunately he did. He whispered back, "As much as I hate slavery, there is little I can do. Either I have to buy every slave or kill every slave owner."

Faith could feel her heart drop, "I know you have already spent far more than anyone should, but if we do not find a way to help this child, Carrita may find her own way. She has no money and one of the owners has already shown a disturbing interest in her."

Joskin looked ponderously at the deck for a moment, then walked over to the captain and whispered something in his ear.

"Jericon!" the captain yelled.

The crew created an opening to the first mate. His weather-beaten face had a bitter scowl on it. "Yes sir!" He called out.

"Grab Tarstan and meet me in my temporary quarters!" the captain commanded.

"Right away!" Jericon dashed off.

What did you say to him in order to elicit such a response?" Faith whispered in Joskin's ear.

"Carrita shouldn't need to show her magic," Joskin whispered back.

The captain leaned into Joskin and spoke softly, "For this, I will be expecting your help if we are attacked."

"Without question," Joskin replied.

Satisfied, the captain nodded. He spun around and hastily walked for the doorway which led below.

Before the captain reached the doorway, Airria emerged with Rosen. The boy ducked behind Airria as the captain approached.

"Boy!" the captain called out. He stopped near Airria and waited until Rosen poked his head out. "You'll make sure these, our special guests, have whatever they want."

"Y-yes sir," the boy chirped.

Without another word the captain ducked through the doorway.

Airria looked down at the boy and smiled, "Well you have your orders. Better make sure Carrita has what she needs."

Rosen almost skipped as he went to check what Carrita would have him do.

269

For the next few weeks the boy was always with one of the four group members. He held Faith's head while she adjusted to the rocking motion of the ship. He carried books and scrolls around for Carrita. He held Airria and Joskin's weapons when they finished sparring. Occasionally he could even be heard humming happily.

Chapter 4 – Troubled Seas

The next few weeks meshed together. Between hanging over the edge of the ship with seasickness and avoiding Jericon, the first mate, Faith lost track of time. When she and Airria adjusted to the rocking motion of the ship they began training together. From time to time Joskin would train with them.

In the evening while Airria would train, running through a regimen on the mast, Faith would sit with Carrita learning about magic. She found it odd when Carrita allowed Rosen to sit in on their training sessions.

The boy had proven invaluable. He would catch and bring live rats for Carrita's lessons and experiments. He helped Carrita maintain her image of normalcy without making her leave her room. In the evening he would donate his magical energies to Carrita for further experimentation. Using the boy, Carrita had convinced Airria and Joskin also to contribute some of their magical energies.

One late afternoon when Faith was enjoying her daily ritual of watching the dolphins before retiring to Carrita's room for her magic lessons, she was surprised by the young male throat clearing behind her. She slowly turned around, Rosen was at a nervous parade rest.

"I don't think it's time," he said softly, "but Lady has asked me to come get you."

It made Faith laugh inside every time the boy called Carrita "Lady." Of the group, Carrita's name was the only one he had not said the entire trip. Even more entertaining was the way he would blush and look away when Carrita would talk to him. Oddly Carrita did not seem to even notice.

"Lead on," Faith said smiling as she laughed inside. She followed the boy as he ducked and weaved between both crew and passengers with the agile skill of a ship mouse.

Before they entered the doorway leading below, Faith's path was blocked. Jericon put his arm across the doorway. "The boy's served you well?" Even after all this time his stare was unnerving.

Faith ducked under the arm and continued. "Yes. He has done excellently!" she said as she passed the first mate.

A sharp blow to her buttocks spun her around. Without thinking she swung her fist. It met its mark squarely on his nose. Blood erupted, gushing out.

Jericon stood there, his blood running freely. A wicked grin crossed his face. For only the second time his eyes met hers. "The rules've changed. Not even the Cap'n will protect you now. You're mine." His teeth were clenched and his voice was low, "Your boys aren't always around and I'm too important to hurt. They don't scare me," he wiped the blood from his nose and flung it at her.

"Lady waits!" Rosen insisted behind her.

Faith could feel the adrenaline pumping through her veins. A part of her wanted to finish this fight. It would be better to fight while she could see it coming. This brigand had no honor and they were far from their destination. She did not want to spend the rest of the trip with her back against the wall.

"Lady is waiting!" Rosen shouted.

Reluctantly Faith turned to walk down the stairs.

"We'll have them soon enough." Tarstan's voice could be heard behind her as she followed the boy to Carrita's room.

Faith breathed a sigh of relief when they reached Carrita's door. She stood with her back to the wall while Rosen knocked.

"Lady," Rosen said through the door, "I did what you wanted." He stood as straight as he could and brushed off his tattered clothes.

As the door opened his shoulders slumped and his gaze fell to the floor. "Can I do something else?"

"Thank you for being so swift," Carrita's voice was kind and full of excitement. "Will you retrieve our evening meals, please?"

"As you want," the boy said and scurried off.

"You did not need to send Rosen to summon me," Faith said, "I would have been on my way soon."

Carrita grabbed Faith's hand and pulled her in the room, "I needed to talk to somebody before your lesson." She then sprinted around Faith and shut the door. Her lips were slightly turned up at the ends, but her eyes carried deep and ponderous thoughts.

"Are not all our conversations about magic?" Faith asked.

"Most of our conversations still weigh heavily in magic," Carrita responded quickly.

"Then would not a conversation be my lesson?" Faith asked. Carrita had not shown this much excitement since the shrines on the island. "Is this about magic?"

"Without question," Carrita smiled so big Faith could see her teeth, "what else have I had access to?"

"Then why will this not be saved for my lesson?" Faith was having fun delaying Carrita's excited conversation.

"What I have to discuss is far too advanced to teach you," Carrita's hands were flailing excitedly.

"What good does it do to talk about what I will not understand?" now Faith was honestly curious.

"I came across something in my reading and was overwhelmed with a desire to discuss it." Carrita pulled Faith over to the bed and pushed her down.

"Why not talk about it with Rosen?" Faith asked. "He would listen."

"He will not let go of his slave attitude." Carrita frowned and sat hard on the bed. After a moment she stood back up and asked, "Now, can we talk?"

"I felt we were," Faith jested.

274

"Very well," Carrita took a deep breath. "Look at this!" she demanded as she held out an open book.

The writing was in High Elven, far beyond Faith's reading ability. She laughed, "You know I am unable to read your magic books."

"The book tells me of the possibility to permanently attach magic to an object without symbols." Carrita put her hand on her chin, looked at the floor and began pacing. "This sounds as if it were a ward without any symbols. How is it possible? Even Joskin's ax and Airria's sword have a type of writing, though the wording and symbology is far beyond my understanding. Why would the course of magic first demand components, then magic and a combination, then only magic again?"

Faith was at a loss. She understood Carrita was talking of alchemy, spells, and then simple magic. After the latter, she had no understanding. Though she understood the basic concepts behind them, the practice of symbols they were far beyond her.

Carrita paused in her rant. She was staring wide-eyed at Faith, as if expecting answers. Faith thought over what little she understood of symbol magic. "What holds the magic in a symbol?"

"In time a symbol will fade and pass away," Carrita explained. "This," Carrita said shaking the book, "says the magic will never dissipate! For this to be possible the object would need to have its own ability to regenerate the magical energy lost."

"Why is the magic lost?" Faith asked.

"Do you remember the magic suppression crystal I had when you found me? Do you remember feeling it?" Carrita had almost shifted into teacher mode.

"Yes." Faith could easily remember the cold feeling she got from the crystal which bound Carrita's magic when they first met.

"What you felt was the magic escaping. It does not matter how skilled a mage is, magic always escapes." Carrita stopped and looked at the book. She cocked her head side to side. After a moment she simply said, "Interesting."

Faith looked at the book and back to Carrita, "What?" She slowly began turning the book.

"Mages will often code their research," Carrita said thoughtfully. "They write what they can, do some simple script, but will disguise the key elements within the writing," Carrita shifted the book back.

Faith could tell Carrita had discovered something in the writing. She wanted to turn the book and see what it was, but did not want to disrupt Carrita's epiphany.

Carrita dashed over to a book covered desk and began digging through the books. After a moment she pulled one out of the stack and began thumbing through. Some time passed as she read and then she threw the book back on the stack. She grabbed a piece of parchment, ink and a quill. She raced over to the book on Faith's lap and began writing. She began copying each letter, recreating the page. In time she began drawing lines and circles on her recreated parchment.

A knock at the door pulled Faith's attention, but Carrita was engrossed in her work. Faith carefully slipped the book off her lap and gently placed it on the bed.

"I have brought your dinner," Rosen said from the other side of the door.

Faith opened the door. "Please come in," she said as she stepped aside.

"Did you find somethin' else important?" Rosen's eyes fixed firmly on Carrita.

"Yes, she did." Faith glanced down at the boy. He was more interested in the girl than and what she was doing.

"Do you know what?" Rosen blushed when he noticed Faith looking at him.

"No." Faith glanced at Carrita who was still oblivious to anyone in the room.

"Do you understand any of this magic stuff?" Rosen's eyes shifted to Faith.

"Only a little," Faith replied.

"I wish I could; then no one would be mean to me again," the boy said.

276

"No matter how much you know, someone always knows more." In her time with Joskin, Airria and Carrita, Faith had found this to be an immutable fact.

Rosen shifted his gaze back to Carrita. "When you leave the ship, can I come with?"

"I believe such can be arranged." After all this boy had done for them, Faith would do everything in her power to free him from his slavery.

The boy smiled up at her.

Faith smiled back down at him. "Before such arrangements can be made, you need to eat."

Rosen frowned, his forehead furrowed, "I brought this food for Lady."

"Lady would want you to eat some of it," Faith explained. "She is not hungry, but she would be very sad to see such food go to waste."

Rosen looked longingly at the food, "Did she tell you she wanted me to eat this food."

"Yes," Faith lied. She knew Carrita was not hungry and she would appreciate the boy eating.

The boy set the tray on the floor and sat next to it and slowly began eating, glancing regularly to Carrita. In time he had finished everything except the desert. He kept looking from the small pie to Carrita and back.

"Why have you not eaten the desert?" Faith asked.

"It is Lady's favorite." Rosen looked nervous, "I brought it for her to eat."

Carrita was looking at her parchment and rotating it around. She set it on the bed, looked out the window for a moment, then at the floor. She turned around and looked at Rosen, then the tray.

"She said you wanted me to eat the food," Rosen said defensively pointing to Faith, "but I brought the little pie for you. I couldn't eat it."

Carrita crouched so she could see the boy eye to eye. "Thank you. You have done well."

The boy smiled brightly.

"I have much to think on and more experiments," Carrita said placing a hand gently on his cheek.

Maybe she had noticed and was reciprocating the boy's affection. Faith was surprised to see such a show of affection from Carrita.

"Can you find us some fat rats for our lessons tonight?" Carrita asked.

"Yes Lady," the boy responded. He hopped up and glanced down at the small pie. He waited for Carrita to pick it up before he left. Carrita watched him leave, the corners of her mouth turned up.

Carrita blushed when she noticed Faith watching her. "The boy will not be left on this vessel to be tormented by those thugs."

Faith smiled and wondered if Carrita even realized she had a crush on the boy. "We will not let him be left on the ship."

Carrita composed herself, "I believe I have found the key."

"You can have your magic stay permanently in an object without a symbol?" Faith asked.

"I said I have found the key, not how to use it," Carrita said in a childish mocking.

"How will you find how to use it?" Faith asked.

"The same way I do everything else; research and testing," Carrita explained. "This is why I have requested the rats."

"Though I am sure I will not understand, I will ask," Faith was enjoying Carrita not knowing something. "What is the key?"

I have to place a part of my own ability to recover magic into the object," Carrita looked a little frustrated, but was still giddy.

"First of all, it seems to be a very high price," Faith said, now concerned. She knew Carrita was going to attempt to accomplish her experiment. Not to mention the girl said she would sleep for weeks if she depleted her manna. How much longer would it take if she gave up a part of her own ability? "Second, does it not already take far too long for you to recuperate your magic?"

"The price is small when compared to the potential benefit," Carrita said almost dreamily. "Imagine having a cloak which would keep you warm in the coldest of circumstances. What about a door which only admits those you desire."

"Is there a way to take it from someone who will not need it?"

"Everyone needs their ability to recover magic. As with any object, magic escapes and is constantly replenished, if we lost our ability to regenerate our magic, we would die," Carrita explained as she glanced back to her paper. "The question I have now is how do I donate a piece of me to an object?"

Chapter 5 – Dark Water

GONG!

The sound of the warning bell pulled Carrita from her experiments. She had been unsuccessful in finding any ability, much less extracting it. Now she had the key, she was determined to learn to use it.

GONG!

Faith set a soft hand on Carrita's shoulder, "We should see what is happening on deck."

Carrita frowned, she did not want to desist her experiments. She could feel she was close to unlocking this magical treasure of knowledge.

GONG!

The eerie sound reminded Carrita there was trouble coming. She looked out her rear facing window. It was dark, except for several bright white torches coming up swiftly from behind.

"Do those flames look strange?" Faith asked.

Carrita recognized those flames. They were deceptive black fire, a fire which burns so dark it robs any light, creating the illusion of light but inverting all colors. This was the light Jarmack'Trastibbik preferred. It was also the light preferred by all dark blood.

"Orc pirates!" the cry could be heard all the way down the ship.

Carrita sighed, "See the color of the ship?"

Faith squinted, "It looks like blue, almost white around the flames."

"If we factor in the deception of those bitter flames, this ship is likely constructed of Smiff wood," Carrita looked to Faith for some sort of reaction. When she saw none she continued, "It is a rare jungle wood. These are no ordinary pirates."

"You say this using the ship's wood as an indicator?" Faith questioned.

"This wood is exceptionally difficult to find and nearly impossible to harvest and lumber," Carrita explained.

Faith, who was still looking out the window, gasped. Her reaction was far more than Carrita had expected, so she looked out the window as well.

The Pirates had lit a torch near their banner which had slipped into view. The unmistakable image of a dragon's claw crushing a vampiric skull. "The Order of the Black Claw," Carrita gasped.

"What's the Order of the Black Claw?" Rosen had been sleeping in the corner.

Before Carrita could open her mouth Faith said, "The most ruthless and bloodthirsty organization in existence."

"Really?" the boy looked out the window. "I've seen a symbol like that before."

"Where?" Carrita asked gazing at the boy. She was amazed she had spent so much time with him and was unaware he had seen this symbol.

The sound of the door flying open made all three jump. Before they could see who had kicked in the door a very heavy fish net flew over them. A gravelly, toothless voice said, "I'll show you!"

Rosen pleaded, "Please don't hurt Lady! Please!"

"Silence boy!" Tarstan was strutting around the net. He had lightning dancing between his fingers. "I'll do what I want!"

"Why?" Faith asked, shock dripping from her voice. "We paid the agreed sum. Why have you turned on us?"

"Do you know who's out there?" Tarstan did not wait for an answer. "That ship belongs to Bulrock. Not only does he captain the most successful pirate ship ever, but he's also in the Order of the Black Claw."

"He will not be the first of his order we have dispatched," Carrita snapped. She was struggling to access her magic.

"Don't bother struggling against the net. I am well aware of who you are, Tarsella's daughter. This net was created especially for you! It was created by Morzak, a minotaur and master mage." Tarstan laughed, "Oh, by the way, he's on the pirate ship, too. This capture will ensure my admission into the glorious order."

Carrita could not move. Her mind was becoming hazy. Faintly she could hear the thundering of hooves booming down the hallway, almost drowning out the sound of war drums and warning bells.

She focused her eyes on Tarstan and began to feel around for her magic. Slowly she began to gather her wits and her power. Her mind began to clear and she could now see the panic on Tarstan's face. A loud squeal spun Tarstan far too late. Persephone's mouth closed around Tarstan's shoulder. The powerful horse's neck easily threw the haggard figure into the wall. Bones crunched and blood flowed as the horse continued her assault.

In the excitement Carrita had not noticed Rosen slip out from underneath the net. He was now helping pull the net off, keeping Faith between him and the raging horse.

When the net was cleared Faith went to calm her horse. Carrita looked out the window. The pirate vessel was closing quickly. "If Tarstan was telling the truth, as I suspect, we have no time to waste."

Faith had a puzzled look on her face.

"Grab your bow. The troops of this vessel are ill-equipped to manage such a threat. We will need to assist."

Without questioning, Faith grabbed her bow and the girls ran for the deck. Most of the passengers were hiding in their cabins, a few were scurrying to assist with defenses and put out fires.

On deck Joskin and Airria were standing between a row of shield bearing defenders and a row of archers. Three robed figures were curled up in a corner of the elevated deck.

Carrita could feel the daunting struggle. A very powerful and dark magic was being used to corrupt the intellect of inferior mages now cowering in mental pain. There was no subtlety in the magic. Carrita could trace it back to the caster without difficulty. The massive horned figure had his staff held casually at his side. This being carried enough power to terrify Carrita.

Carrita pointed Faith to the beastly figure, "Focus everything you can on him!"

Without questioning Faith began pulling arrows at random and firing at the minotaur. The first one exploded, engulfing his bodyguards and scorching the deck, but the creature stood untouched, a second arrow sent shards shredding the nearby deck. This time the minotaur raised his staff and shouted, "I am Morzak, master mage and destroyer of cities. Bow before me!"

Carrita could feel a huge buildup of dark power, just what she had been waiting for. She had been counting on this mage's overconfidence. As carefully as she could she altered the outer edges of the magic to a shield, doing her best not to change the feeling of the magic.

Almost as quickly as she began her endeavor, she found resistance. Rapidly the resistance grew until she became overwhelmed. Her mind began twisting to an abyssal darkness. The pain drove her to her own knees.

"Lady? Are you all right?" Rosen put his small hand on her shoulder.

Carrita opened her eyes, straining to focus. She pressed back harder. "Keep...Shoot..." was all she could say before the darkness began closing again.

Without warning the ship rocked. The distraction freed her mind enough to put a hand on Rosen's. "Get them!" she demanded breathlessly, pointing to the three robed figures now sitting bewildered in their spots.

As the darkness began closing in she could hear the boy, "Lady wants you there! Help her!"

After far too long she felt an aged, oily hand grasp hers. "Bis'ree tan'ya" the elderly male voice brought the Elven plea to take his strength. More important it helped Carrita remember the basics of magic.

"Grys'ya bondisia dis'con boldortya," she began chanting.

Immediately she could hear the old mage chat next to her, "Bis'ree tan'ya dis'con boldontya."

As the chant began Carrita could feel the magical tide changing. She was pushing back her opponent. She could now hear the sounds of battle. How she could have missed the deafening squeal of Faith's horse defending Faith as she continued to assault the minotaur was beyond reasoning. Pain still racked her body, but she knew she was the only one strong enough to keep going.

Shortly the other two mages joined her, chanting with the old one. Soon she could shape the magic to her will. When she opened her eyes she could see the beast sweating, his massive muscles tearing his robes.

The sight brought her courage. She drove the energy into the beast staff. She pushed, driving it deep. She could feel the Black Wood fibers straining. Finally she felt the satisfying release as the staff shattered.

An orc in black scaly leather armor with a patch on his eye pointed to Carrita. "Dok chek'rat!" he yelled.

"No!" Rosen's voice yelled from behind her, "Don't hurt Lady."

Carrita turned around in time to watch the boy throw himself in front of a dagger meant for her. Her heart ripped open as his blood drained onto the deck.

Jericon easily tossed the boy overboard. In one smooth motion he brought the dagger back toward her throat.

Without breaking her chant she forced her magic into the man, turning all of his blood into ice. She looked around for something to hit him with, but she did not get a chance. Faith had already drawn her sword and stabbed his heart, knocking him over and shattering his body.

Filled with such rage she could not feel her pain any longer. She turned her focus back to Morzak. She focused on twisting his mind as he had tried to twist hers. Every path she tried was blocked.

The oldest mage stopped chanting. Carrita could feel the minotaur pushing into her mind. She dared not look anywhere else.

"There is more than the mage; we need to help our people." The old mage finally said.

"You concentrate on the mage," said Faith.

The old mage frowned, "Our men are dying."

"If you do not focus on their mage, none of us will survive," Faith insisted.

Carrita could see the orc in scaled leather step next to the minotaur. As they talked Carrita could feel an opening. She jabbed her magic sharply into the minotaur's mind. The minotaur bellowed in rage and pain. "I will dine on your flesh as I watch your soul tormented in my master's crystal!" he yelled, causing the battle to hesitate. He then began chanting in a bitter language Carrita did not understand, the orc captain joining him.

As Carrita looked up and started concentrating again, the chanting stopped. Each of the eight assisting mages near her had collapsed again, blood dripping from their noses and ears. Soon she could feel the magical pressure on her own mind. Quickly she built a wall around her mind, similar to the one she had found around the minotaur's mind. In spite of her efforts the pain was raging through.

"You learn quickly child," the minotaur yelled, "but you are not your mother. You cannot hold out forever."

At the mention of her mother Carrita found a little more strength. She pushed the magic back. For a long time she held the magic at bay, though soon she could feel her wall crumbling. The pain slammed in again. She crashed to the deck; sure this would be the end. Vaguely she heard Joskin yell and the magical pressure stopped.

Though the remaining pain was excruciating, Carrita opened her eyes. Joskin's ax was buried deep in Morzak's skull, the beast collapsed heavily on the enemy deck.

Faith was releasing arrows as rapidly as she could. Before the enemy orcs had finished reacting to an ice explosion, there was a nearby fiery explosion. While the orcs were still fleeing from the explosions the

285

one in the lead was turned to a marble statue, tripping up those following.

Joskin was surrounded at the end of a shiny black path of orcs' blood leading from the merchant ship across the pirate deck. His body and armor were covered in the black blood. As the orcs would rush, in Joskin would sidestep the blade and fling it into his companions.

Airria was locked it in a battle with the captain. This fight was so fast and furious no one dared interfere. All of the other orcs and humans gave them a wide berth.

Carrita tried to stand, but her body hurt too much. She rose slightly and then fell back down. Her hand hit something solid and circular.

Slowly she brought the object into view. It was a ring with the insignia of the dragon claw crushing a vampiric skull. There was no doubt Jericon had been associated with the order. There was no telling if he had been a full-fledged member of the order or if he were simply a recruit, like Tarstan, but she still could guess he was the one who alerted the pirate ship.

She glanced around again. Airria and Joskin were the only surviving boarders from either side. Only half a dozen soldiers remained in defense of the merchant vessel. Faith, Airria and Joskin had dispatched almost all of the orc crew. Neither Faith nor Joskin seemed willing to interfere with Airria's fight.

"Help me to the other ship," Carrita asked Faith.

Carrita's voice must have sounded as bad as she felt because Faith looked down and panicked, "Will you be all right?" Faith asked.

"If you will assist me to the other ship I will be all right." Carrita had a plan forming in her mind. She wanted to interrogate the captain to discover how many other groups they may have to face. Also, she wanted to experiment on the captain as she had on the rats. She blamed him for the death of her new friend.

"If you believe it best, I will take you there." Carefully Faith picked up Carrita and gently carried her through the soldiers and over the boarding plank.

Joskin met her on the edge of the ship, helped her across and took Carrita.

Carrita could feel herself on the edge of blacking out. The darkness was closing in; she knew she could not let it take her yet. "Can you ask Airria to stop fighting the orc."

Joskin looked confused, "We definitely want him dead."

As Carrita thought about the captain, anger welled up inside of her giving her the strength she needed. "Death is too good for it!" she took a deep breath.

"I don't want to take any chances," Joskin replied.

Carrita looked to Faith and back to Joskin. Neither one seemed to be relenting. "Please," she begged, "I can use it to help us."

"How?" Joskin asked.

"Do you really believe we have the time to teach you all I know about magic?" Carrita responded impatiently. "Please just ask him to stop attacking."

"Carrita wants this one alive!" Joskin yelled to his cousin.

Airria immediately took a defensive posture, his magical shield fending off the orc's blows.

Carrita looked up at Faith, "Get the net from my quarters and throw it on the orc."

"All right," Faith replied, sounding unsure, but she left at a sprint.

"When he falls, disarm him and bind him. Faith will do the rest," Carrita said to Joskin. Then she reached down deep in her heart to find the strength and began reaching for the orc's magic.

Carrita could feel the mental wall the captain had created. She could tell he was experienced with magic, though not a full-fledged mage. Even in her weakened and pain filled condition it was simple to forcibly extract his magical energy. She collected it all and allowed it to refill her own and heal her.

As the last of the captain's manna left his body he collapsed on the deck. Two men from the merchant's vessel leapt onto the pirate vessel and sprinted for the door to the below decks.

Joskin yelled, "I claim this ship and all of its spoils!"

One man stopped, almost frozen. The other greedily continued on. When his hand hit the door, he began to shake. His sword crashed to the ground only moments before he did. His hand which had touched the door was withered and black.

"Do not go below," Carrita said as fatigue took its course. The vague light and distorted colors faded. The sound of Joskin's voice was first distorted and then it too faded.

Chapter 6 – Dark Ship

The fighting had been intense. Airria's heart was pounding. It took all his restraint to stop his attack on the orc captain when Joskin had yelled for him, on behalf of Carrita, to stop. He hadn't questioned why. Carrita had more reason to hate the Order of the Black Claw than anyone, much of the abuse she had suffered was at their hands, they sold her to a beastly man who almost tortured her to death and worst of all she had been forced to watch as the Order leader Jarmack'Trastibbik had ripped her mother's soul from her body and placed it into a torturous crystal.

Airria knew that if Carrita were asking for this orc to be left alive, she had a plan. He couldn't even guess what she might do, but was grateful to see the captain collapse.

Immediately after the orc captain fell, two of the fighters from the merchant ship jumped the rail and darted for the door.

Joskin yelled, "I claim this ship and all its spoils!"

One man stopped immediately, the other continued on. The one who kept running hit the door hard and began to shake, his hand clutching the latch. After a short while he fell to the deck his hand black and withered. Carrita, who looked very pale and weak, said softly, "Do not go below," she then teetered and collapsed.

Captain Earito yelled for his men to return. The one that was still standing reluctantly returned to his ship. While Joskin went to check the fallen soldier Airria ran to check Carrita. She was still breathing and for the first time he was aware of since he had met her she was resting peacefully.

The man Joskin was checking on was still shaking but holding his withered arm. Tears streamed out of his eyes, but no sound came out of his mouth.

Faith emerged with a fishnet in her hand, her horse protectively behind her. She quickly dashed to the rail and leapt over. She crossed the plank with the grace of an eagle and dashed over to the orc captain. She didn't even flinch when her horse crashed onto the deck after her.

Behind Faith, Persephone raced over the deck and began reaching and biting toward the orc. Faith turned to calm her horse, but stopped, staring at the man lying nearby. Slowly she approached and set a hand on his shoulder. She began muttering.

After a short time the man stopped shaking and his blackened hand began to lighten slightly. He stood up, looked at Faith and ran back to the merchant ship. Faith stood up, her skin slightly paled. "He will be all right," she said.

Joskin said to Airria, "Better get our stuff over here."

"If we can't get below, how will we bring the horses over?" Airria asked.

"It would be extremely hard to get them across," Joskin replied.

Airria looked at Faith's horse a moment, then back to Joskin, "Persephone made it fine."

Joskin chuckled, "I don't think any of us could have stopped her from following Faith."

Persephone moved to nip at the orc lying on the ground. Now Faith had a clear view of Carrita passed out on the deck. She dashed over and put a hand on Carrita's shoulder.

"Will she be all right?" Airria asked.

Faith took her time answering. Her hands wiped the blood from Carrita's nose. She ran her eyes across Carrita's perfectly clean robes. She finally said, "It may take some time before she wakes up. Eventually she will. We should get her to bed."

"She told us not to go below and I'll not leave her on the other ship," Joskin said emphatically.

Airria looked around for possible solutions. He saw Captain Earito, staring at them with pleading eyes. Airria went to the edge of the ship. The captain looked deep into Airria's eyes, "So many of my crew have been seriously wounded. My healer is breathing weakly and unable to even speak."

"I will help where I am able," Faith said from behind Airria, "unfortunately our own healer is incapacitated. Please understand, as I am willing to assist you, we also will need assistance from you."

"If you can help my healer, you can name your price," the captain said rashly.

Faith turned to her horse, "Please keep her safe," then she headed back to the merchant ship.

Airria went with; the few remaining fighters gave them both a wide berth. The crew followed at a distance. As Faith knelt down next to the old man in the tattered brown robes, the crew began curiously circling them.

Faith kept looking up nervously, watching the people circling. Airria realized that the crowd was making her nervous. He began scanning for Tarstan and Jericon. Neither were in the crowd, still Faith was nervous about something.

After a moment he yelled to the crowd, "Get the wounded below!"

The circle of people quickly dispersed, leaving Airria and Faith alone with the robed figure. Faith's shoulders relaxed and her eyes focused on the old healer. She grabbed the wrinkled old hand and placed a gentle hand on the side of his cheek. She began chanting something Airria didn't understand. Her skin paled significantly. Her normally immaculate posture slouched, her shoulders hunched, her left hand dropped to the deck, she teetered as she leaned on him heavily.

"It's quite an accomplishment to heal such hurting on the spot," the old man spoke weakly, the color had returned to his cheeks. "I've been a healer since I was a child, trained in the Temple of Mellinatia, Mistress of Life. From the first time I felt your presence, I knew you had great power." He sat up, leaning on his elbows, "In the forty years since I left the temple, I have met no one who could heal such deep Death magic."

"I'm afraid you will have see to the other wounded," Faith said weakly. She tried to stand, but collapsed back to the deck.

"Will you be all right?" the old mage asked.

"In time," Faith replied. "I will feel better after a long rest."

The old mage bowed slightly and then went to check on the other two robed figures. In turn, he grabbed each by a limp hand and said, "I failed you. I am so sorry." When he had mourned a moment, he dragged himself off to the battlefield to tend to the wounded.

"Have you seen Jericon or Tarstan?" the captain asked from behind Airria.

As Airria turned around he heard Faith respond, "Jericon is no longer here," she said softly.

Airria wanted to turn back. He'd not trusted the first mate, he placed himself between Faith and the captain and he saw anger growing in the captain's eyes.

"What do you mean!" Captain Earito demanded as he began drawing his sword.

"He tried to kill Carrita," Faith responded. "He killed Rosen and tried to kill Carrita," her voice was slightly stronger.

"No!" Earito's teeth were grinding. "Why would he do that? He had no reason!" his sword was slowly slipping from its sheath.

Airria bought his shield up and locked a challenging look on the captain. "If Faith says your first mate betrayed us then he betrayed us," his teeth were clenched and his hand was on the hilt of his own sword.

"This man is grieved," Airria heard a voice in his head. It had been many months since his sword had spoken to him. He almost jumped. *"To kill him would be unneeded."*

Slowly Airria pulled his hand off his sword.

"He and Tarstan are the reason for the attack," Faith said from behind Airria, "they were in league with the Order of the Black Claw. They have been in communication with these pirates."

"That Order is a myth!" Captain Earito began circling Airria, "An Order entirely hand-picked by an ancient dragon? Even children are not so foolish." He stopped and looked deep, studying Airria's eyes. His sword slid back into it sheath. "How would he have communicated with these pirates? How would you know he had?" his voice was still on edge with anger, but much more reasonable.

"Tarstan told us, when he broke into Carrita's room," Faith replied. "You have no need to take my word for it."

A heavy ring tumbled past Airria. When it stopped he could see the symbol. Only then did he notice the irate's banner. His shield began to involuntarily drop. The captain picked up the ring and looked closely between the pirate banner and the ring. After a moment he asked, "How do I know you didn't plant this? It's no secret you hated him."

"What would he be doing up here, when the battle was down there," Faith pointed out.

"We saved your healer and your ship," Airria spoke up, "you owe us the benefit of the doubt."

"Where is Tarstan now?" Earito asked fuming.

Faith responded defensively, "He broke into our room."

"You killed him too?" The captain yelled.

"We did not kill him," Faith's voice was growing weaker again. "He captured us in the net."

"Then he's not dead?" the captain asked suspiciously.

"We were rescued by Persephone," Faith replied. "She does not take kindly to anyone touching me."

Earito took a step back as there was a loud crash on deck. Persephone's ear piercing squeal cleared a path to Faith.

Airria knew better than to stand between Faith and her horse. He moved toward the captain, keeping a defensive eye on this suspicious man.

Faith reached up and touched Persephone's nose. They stared into each other's eyes for a long moment, then Faith asked, "Will you carry me to the other ship?"

294

Airria hesitated. He wasn't sure if Faith was talking to him or her horse. He decided to approach Faith. He kept a cautious eye on the horse as he stuck his shield to his back.

Persephone put herself between Faith and the captain.

Gently as he could, Airria picked Faith up. The surviving crew bowed slightly as they passed, soft phrases of gratitude could be heard in reverent tones.

Once on the pirate ship, Faith's horse close behind, Airria placed Faith near Carrita. He turned around to see the captain rapidly approaching the railing, sword in hand.

"Cut'em loose!" the captain yelled.

A few paces from the rail Captain Earito was tackled by one of the soldiers. "No you don't!" the man yelled.

"I'll have your hide for this!" Earito yelled. "Get off me now and I may show you leniency!"

Two other concerned looking soldiers held the captain while three others bound and gagged him. When they finished, they dragged him to the mast.

The fighter that started the mutiny walked over to the rail and bowed low. "We owe you our lives. You may take what provisions you need. We will help you load your stuff, as you want. We'll make sure everything else makes it safe to port."

"Will you be all right?" Joskin asked.

"Capt'n is grieved, but he'll come 'round," another soldier said.

"You know better than we do what we will need," Joskin said, bowing slightly. "It may be several days or even weeks before we can get below. What do you suggest?"

"We can bring skins and furs to help keep you warm," one sailor suggested.

"If you have books'n stuff, we have a few casks and one watertight crate." The cook suggested coming on deck.

Joskin jumped to the merchant ship. "I'll make sure we secure as much of our stuff as I can," he said walking to the door that led below. "Keep the girls safe," he yelled as he ducked through the doorway.

Chapter 7 – The Key

The soft waves crashing against the hardwood sides of the ship and the salty, cool, early morning breeze rustling against the sails let Carrita know she was not only alive, she remained on the ocean. Slowly she opened her eyes.

"She is awake!" Faith called out. "It only took a little over a week, but she is awake!"

Carrita tried to sit up, but found her pain forced her back down. She knew her body was well. The pain was remnants of the dark magical combat she had participated in. It was all in her mind which had been touched by the bitter magic of Death and now conjured pains which few had the understanding to heal. Even with her vast array of knowledge and her exceptional understanding of magic, it would take her some time to heal the scars the minotaur had left behind.

Before she knew it Joskin was by her side. "Which water vessel are we residing on at this point in time?" she asked, trying to sit up again.

"We claimed the pirate ship as our own," Joskin said. "We're following the other ship to port."

"Is she all right," Airria's voice carried down from the upper landing.

"She's awake, but looks to be a little stiff," Joskin yelled back.

Carrita looked around. She was in a small area near the stairs leading to the upper landing. Persephone was lying nearby, teetering in the rocking motion of the vessel. Several crates and barrels, a few which she recognized as the group's belongings, were lashed neatly to the deck, mast and railing. The orc statues Faith had made with her magic arrows were tied together in the center of the deck.

"It is time to see what is below," Carrita said as confidently as she could. "It is time to see what treasures and traps lie beneath."

The edges of Faith's eyes dropped, "Are you sure you're ready."

"We need to know." Carrita was not sure she could manage the task at hand, but she knew she had to do it. Faith had been an excellent student and was extremely gifted, but she lacked sufficient understanding of the workings of magic to have any conceivable chance of dispelling any magical traps there might be.

From what she knew of Joskin's ax, it may be able to dispatch the magic in the door. It had shown a propensity for dismantling magical defenses. Deep inside Carrita was tempted to ask Joskin to try it on the door, but jealously she wanted to learn the secrets of the enchantments. Also, she was afraid the barbarian elegance of a melee weapon could destroy other valuables, such as magical books or staves, on the other side of the door.

"Help me up and I will see if I can get us past the doorway," Carrita said.

Reluctantly Joskin helped Carrita to her feet. He stayed by her, carrying most of her weight with a single arm.

Through the pain, she reached with her magic into the door, touching the harsh magic contained within. Slowly she studied how the magic was woven into the door, where it drew its power and what bound it there. As she probed, she could feel the magic resisting, tightly wound into each fiber of the wood.

Slowly she began picking at the magic. Each fiber reluctantly relinquished its resentful grip on the enchantment. Each piece of magic

297

she obtained, she converted and used to help alleviate the pain in her own body.

The sun was beginning to set when she had completed her task. Her mind was now filled with understanding on the subject she had queried Faith about a short time before the pirates had attacked.

As the door opened, Carrita's nose was filled with a blast of pungent aromas. She knew most orcs had no concept of hygiene, but the bitter smell of urine and feces almost knocked her over. Even worse, was the stench of rotting flesh, a staple for the dark blooded orcs.

Cautiously Carrita settled her foot on the first step. With all her might she mustered the courage to press on, but the detestable odor was too much for her. She quickly stumbled backward out of the doorway.

"What's wrong?" Joskin asked.

Carrita returned the question, "Can you not smell it? Can you not smell what lies below?"

Joskin poked his head into the doorway and jerked back. Faith began backpedaling. Even Airria could be heard complaining about the stench.

"Would it help if we opened the doors?" Faith asked pointing to the cargo doors in the deck.

"Can we open them?" Joskin asked Carrita.

Carrita reached out with her magic. She could feel an enchantment. To her surprise, it was not dark, nor did it promise pain. It was protective and built with water magic. It was, in effect, triggered only by fire. She probed around and realized it was woven into the entire vessel. After some time she decided to leave this enchantment in place. It would cause no harm and would likely protect them from fire.

"Opening the door should do no harm, save it be to our noses," Carrita said when her magical inspection was completed.

Slowly Joskin and Faith pulled open the huge panels and revealed piles of rotting corpses of varying races. Random paths led between the mountains.

Carrita stood up, went upwind and began reaching out with her magic. Near the stern she felt copious amounts of varied magic. This was fully expected. She had been on enough ships to know the captain lodged in that direction. The most valuable items were likely stored aft as well.

Deep in the ship, toward the bow, she could feel something which made her shake with bitter remembrance.

"Are you all right?" Faith's voice surprised her.

"Something is not right here," Carrita responded.

Joskin laughed uneasily. "There are piles of bodies. Something is very wrong here."

Carrita sighed in exasperation. "The visual display of these orc's cruelty is very disturbing, yes, although, there is an abominable incantation aboard this vessel."

Both Joskin and Faith looked confused. Carrita put up a hand to silence her friends and then reached out again concentrating on the disturbing magic. It took some time, but eventually she found it. A ring had been enchanted to enslave a living creature on board. A ring of such design would have a parent ring to allow the master to control his slave.

She began poking for magic on deck. The net, now binding the captain to the mast, she expected. It was the chilling enslavement magic; the master ring Joskin was carrying which surprised her. "Did you relieve the captain of its rings?" she asked her muscular friend.

Joskin smiled brightly, "I may not understand much of magic, but I do understand enough to take anything from an orc that could help it.

As Joskin reached to retrieve his pouch, Carrita noticed he was carrying a golden dagger and a silvery sword. "It is not typical of you to carry flashy equipment," she said pointing to the new weapons.

Joskin handed his coin pouch to Carrita. "Don't you know what orcs can do with gold and silver?"

Carrita took the pouch carefully. The captain's rings had their magic well hidden. If she had not trained with a Guardian, she likely would have never been able to feel the ring at all.

She looked in the bag. There was a plain gold ring with six brown crystals buried in it, a blue crystal ring and the expected Claw insignia ring. For now it was the gold ring which intrigued her. It was covered in micro etchings characteristically depicting an entire battle scene. The artistry was perfect. With the help of a crystal to magnify it she could distinguish the depiction of the orc captain holding a head of a centaur. Without thinking of the magic, she asked, "What kind of master created this?"

Joskin pulled out the golden dagger and held it for Carrita to examine. It unexpectedly felt to be the same weight as a normal dagger. The handgrip at first resembled tightly wound rope. Closer inspection revealed the depiction of a different battle on each twist so perfectly etched it almost seemed alive.

"It's been said the dwarves are the masters of the craft," Joskin said in a reverent tone. "Though they would never admit it, a good orc smith can put a dwarf to shame."

In all her studies and all her mother had taught her, she had never heard such a thing. All her books proclaimed dwarves to be the masters. She had heard of elves forging silver to be a strong as steel, but half the weight; the dwarves could make silver stronger than steel.

"Show her what it does to other daggers," Faith said, far too excited.

Joskin pulled out a common dagger and hit them blade to blade. Then he held them out for Carrita to inspect. The common dagger had a deep notch in the blade. The golden dagger was unscratched.

"Gold is soft. This cannot be gold," Carrita said, her mind swimming.

Joskin smiled broadly, "I assure you it is gold."

Carrita touched it with her magic. She could only feel the element of gold touched by the bitterness of wood from the Black Forest. She could find no magic on it. "Can it be?" she found herself asking out loud.

"A few years ago," Joskin started into a story, "I was hired by a clan of dwarves to help defend against a small army of orcs. As payment, and to help the cause, they gave me an ax made of their finest steel."

"It must have been a terrible fight to warrant such a payment," Faith said.

"Oh it was," Joskin assured her. "The orc weapons, armor and skill matched that of the dwarves, but there were far more orcs, perhaps four or five to one."

"How did you defend against such odds?" Faith asked.

Joskin's lips widened and a furrow crossed his brow. "It's much easier to defend than attack, especially a Dwarven stronghold."

Though Joskin's stories were entertaining, Carrita wanted to know about the gold, or the reason Joskin had chosen to mention this tale. "I am sure your story has some significance to this dagger?"

Joskin was standing and shifting his weight from one leg to another. "The leader was wearing golden armor," he said swinging his arms. "I thought the gold was just for show. I mean, who would wear something so heavy into battle?"

"It was not just for show?" Faith asked.

"I was able to fight my way to him," Joskin was swinging his arms, acting the story out. "It took some doing, but eventually I knocked him down. In an attempt to win the battle I brought my ax down hard on the golden chest piece." Joskin's hand swung down as if he were reliving the experience.

Faith covered her eyes as though she were watching.

Joskin's shoulders slumped, "My ax, my beautiful ax, shattered. Not only that, but the orc's breastplate was virtually unscathed."

Faith opened her mouth to say something, but Carrita cut her off. "How do they refine such a soft metal into one more solid than fine Dwarven steel?"

"That I don't know," Joskin said. "The dwarves said nothing of the gold and complained that I broke the ax."

"Did they construct you another?" Faith asked.

"No," Joskin replied, "but since that day I have dreamed of having armor like that."

"Armor of such quality would be of the utmost value in battle," Faith said.

Carrita turned her attention back to the ring. The magic was tightly woven deep into each fiber. She poked and prodded at the magic, but could find no way to unravel it. She did however discover this to be the master ring to the slave ring she had felt below. She pondered putting it on and seeing what would happen, then she thought again.

"Faith," Carrita asked, "would you place this ring on your finger?"

Though Joskin had proven a skilled warrior, Carrita did not want him distracted by the attention it would take to control the slave. This ring was small enough it only could be worn on the orc's small finger. Carrita hoped it would fit on Faith's middle finger.

Faith reluctantly retrieved the ring from Carrita's hand. Slowly she placed it on her middle finger.

"This may be somewhat confusing and even a little painful," Carrita said to Faith. "In the end it should help us."

As the ring slipped into place, Faith placed both hands on her forehead and collapsed to the ground.

Carrita could feel a touch of panic run through her. This was a far more severe reaction than she had expected. Instinctively she reached out magically to understand.

She had expected a single magical trail leading to a slave below. Instead she could feel a half-dozen links.

Chapter 8 – Many Minds

Carrita had asked Faith to put on a gold ring the captain had been wearing. Faith deemed it an odd request. In her heart Faith knew Carrita would ask nothing of her which would be dangerous. On the other hand, the gold ring had been worn by a servant of Jarmack'Trastibbik.

After a small hesitation, Faith took the ring and placed it on her middle finger. It slipped easily over her petite knuckle and should have been very loose on her hand. When it reached the center between the bottom joints it became comfortably firm on her finger.

Before she could surmise the ramifications of the new magic ring, she found her head swimming with visions, thoughts and feelings which did not belong to her. In her mind she could see several different ceilings and a hammock. As if she were looking through a dozen eyes. Fortunately the thoughts and feelings were very similar, in that they were all focused on food and freedom. Almost as torturous as the visions were the hunger pains and fatigue.

Overwhelmed Faith closed her eyes, trying to reduce the visual confusion. "Eat!" she said, though not sure if it were with her lips or in her mind. All of the visions began moving. She became very dizzy. Without thinking she pulled the ring off. Immediately the visions, thoughts and feelings vanished from her mind, though she still felt dizzy and disoriented. When she had regained her equilibrium she said, "Such an experience will take some getting used to."

Persephone was running her head across Faith's back.

"What did you experience?" Carrita asked.

"I felt as if I were in several minds and bodies." Faith noticed she had fallen to the deck. She still had her eyes closed. "I felt more than just in control of all of them."

"Something's coming," Joskin warned. Faith dared to open her eyes and peered down into the disturbing hold. A scarred orc in blacksmith-leathers appeared through the doorway. It did not seem to care or notice the three watching it.

"That's a little unnerving," Joskin said as the group watched the orc bite into a slightly green human arm.

"It needs to eat," Faith said.

"It is an orc," Carrita pointed out. "It is a member of the pirate crew we defeated several days ago."

Faith asked, "If it were of a mind to do us harm, do you not think it would have?"

Carrita returned the question, "Why would you defend this creature?"

"I believe it is one of the slaves this ring links me to," Faith responded holding up the ring. She was sure of it. This poor creature had been enslaved by those of its own race.

Faith watched the creature eat; she could not help but feel sorry for it. Even now it was appeasing its hunger, not because it desired it, but because it had been commanded.

Carrita's eyes narrowed, "As you have shown an interest this creature, you shall decide its fate."

"Wait a moment," Joskin said. "We can't let this creature live. If we do, it will kill us in our sleep."

"It will not as long as it wears the ring," Carrita said, her eyes were still locked on Faith's.

"How do you know the ring will keep it from hurting us?" Joskin looked at Carrita, then he shifted his gaze to Faith. The tone in his voice lowered, "Someday you'll have to teach me that."

Faith laughed uneasily. She knew exactly what Carrita was implying. Faith would have to become the slave master until such time as

305

they could free this orc. In an attempt to break Carrita's stare Faith looked at Joskin. "I have been working now for months and still do not understand how she understands nor how she does what she does. Are you sure you want to know?"

Joskin said nothing. He began watching the orc suspiciously and pacing around the opening. "What fate will you choose for this creature?" Carrita insisted.

"He will live!" Faith exclaimed more forcefully than she had wanted. "In time he will be free. For now I will learn to use the ring."

Carrita sighed deeply and looked at the orc still eating. "Then it is decided. The orc stays."

Faith watched the orc until it seemed to be uncomfortable. She realized the creature and likely all the other slaves tied to the ring, would eat themselves to death. She was not looking forward to putting the ring back on her finger. Her head was still reeling from the last encounter, but if she did not put it on soon some of the slaves could die.

She swallowed deep and placed the ring on her finger a rush of images flooded into her mind. Pains not her own, crashed into her. She tried to sort through the thoughts rushing in on her. Focusing her energy she yelled, "Go to bed, then sleep!" As quickly as she could, she yanked the ring off her finger again.

Joskin rushed to her side, "Are you all right?"

Carrita had a knowing smile. "Are you positive this is what you prefer?"

"This is most definitely not what I prefer," Faith said, trying to shake the images from her mind. "This is the right thing to do."

Faith looked through the hole. The orc was making his way back through the maze of rotting meat and through the door.

Faith was filled with dread as she watched the orc's absolute obedience, but she did not know what else to do. She had never met a kind slave master and wanted to avoid becoming a slave master at all. With the power to control came a feeling of authority. The thought of allowing the feeling to take control was more difficult to deal with than the multitude of visions. She resolved to free each of the slaves as quickly as she could discover whether it would be safe for both the group and the individual. Right now Faith did not want to ponder the possibilities and ramifications of her decision. She glanced around, looking for a release. Her eyes crossed the crates and bundles of equipment and books tied to the railing. "Has it been long enough for the odors to dispel sufficiently to make it tolerable to go below?"

Joskin's shoulders visibly relaxed. "The first door was magically trapped. It's likely there are other traps down there. Airria is better than me at spotting and disarming those." Without waiting for a reaction he darted up the stairs to take the wheel.

A few moments later Airria descended the stairs. "Guess he doesn't like the smell either."

"You only smelled some of what has been released," Carrita said with a giggle. "What lies below is far worse."

"Then we best get this over with," Airria said walking toward the door.

"Are you sure it would be best for you to go first?" Carrita asked. "There may be more magical traps."

"We know my shield absorbs magic. If I keep it in front of me it should block any lightning bolts. Right?" Airria did not sound sure of himself.

Faith put a hand on Carrita's shoulder. "We cannot afford to lose you to a non-magic trap."

Airria picked up his shield, "Then I'll go first and hope for the best."

Shield firs,t Airria carefully descended the stairs. Carrita was close behind, both hands out. Faith followed Carrita while trying to simultaneously reach out with her magic and keep her eyes searching.

At the base of the stairs was a solid wooden door. By the position in the ship Faith guessed this was the captain's quarters. There were copious amounts of magical energy coming from behind the door. Oddly the door itself had very small amounts of magic emanating from it. Stranger still was the lack of fastening or latching mechanisms.

Airria pressed on it with his shield, but the door did not budge. He stepped back and prepared to kick it.

Carrita stepped into his path and placed a hand on the door. In a moment she turned back with a smile. You know it is locked. You would break your foot before kicking this door open."

"There's nothing to open it. How can you get in?" Airria asked.

Carrita giggled, "We can use the key."

"There is no keyhole." Faith interjected.

"Can you not feel what is used?" Carrita's smiled drooped.

"The magic is the lock?" Faith questioned. "Why not dispel it?"

"No, the lock is mechanical." Carrita's bottom lip extruded slightly, "The magic works the lock. If I dispel the magic the door will be locked forever." She pulled out one of the captain's silver rings and added, "Why go to the trouble of dispelling when we have the key," her smile returned as bright as ever.

"I'm not placing this ring on my finger," Faith said, emphatically crossing her arms across her chest. "I have enough to deal with."

A boyish look crossed Airria's face, "What you mean?"

"The last ring Carrita had me put on forced me to become slave master to several slaves." Faith had said more than she had intended, but she felt Airria should know. "When I put on the ring, I am mentally linked to about five or six different minds. I have to see through their eyes and feel what they're feeling. As near as I can tell I need not even speak to them to command."

Carrita placed the ring against the door and twisted slightly. There was a soft click and the door swung open. She stepped aside to allow Airria to enter.

As he stepped past her, her eyes became focused on the next doorway. Her jaw dropped open. Mindlessly she began walking toward the door.

Faith could feel magic coming from the room, though she couldn't tell what type. "What is it?" she asked the girl.

"Magical knowledge," Carrita replied.

Faith asked, "How do you know?"

"I can feel it," Carrita said. "All of the minotaur's books are in there."

308

"You know he understood some very deep Death magic." Faith was very worried about her young friend. "Are you sure you want to learn this magic?"

"Such a powerful mage will have insights to realms of magic I can only acknowledge in my deepest subconscious," Carrita's eyes were still solidly fixed on the door.

"Please be careful," Faith pleaded. Such a creature would not leave its knowledge lying about unguarded.

Carrita continued forward, opened the door and disappeared inside. They tried to follow, but Carrita closed the door behind her. Such behavior concerned Faith even more. She stood at the door wanting to follow. After a moment, she decided to let Carrita alone. *She closed the door for a reason. It is not my place to challenge her*, Faith thought.

All of this exploring made Faith uneasy. Airria was rummaging in a room where the captain stayed. To top it all off, she was responsible for at least one orc.

She decided she would find this orc and see why it had been enslaved. The ship was not as extensive as the large merchant ship had been, but it was quite large. With the atrocious aromas, Faith did not want to wander around aimlessly. Slowly she slipped the ring on her finger.

This time there was only peaceful rest from the slave. If she focused she could see each of their dreams. She could feel them one at a time. She could feel where they each were.

There were a total of five living souls bound to the ring. One ring was tied to a slave who had died before Faith put the ring on. She could feel the death, the soul hovering around the body waiting for orders. "Go to your eternal reward, it is time you moved on and left your body and slavery behind." She felt the ghost pull free of the bond and left the ring blank.

She passed two more rooms and through the doorway into the piles of mangled and rotting corpses. On the far side she could see the doorway the orc had disappeared into. Carefully she traversed the maze of bodies and found another set of stairs next to another large door emanating Fire magic. Faith wanted to find the orc so she left the room alone and descended the stairs.

The stairs led to an extensive room packed tightly with hammocks. The one closest to the stair was occupied by a green, deceased, lizard-like humanoid with a large golden ring on its finger.

Faith only took a moment to examine the creature. It had widespread, bulging eyes and no claws. It had small teeth and rough pads on its hands and feet. Both hands and feet were designed with three fingers and two thumbs, one on each side.

On the center finger of one of its hands was the golden ring. Carefully she removed it and placed it in her money pouch for Carrita to destroy and she continued through the room. On the last hammock the orc lay sleeping. On his left little finger was a small golden ring. Carefully she removed it.

The orc bolted from its bed and down into a corner.

Faith tried to smile reassuringly, "I will not hurt you."

The orc was mumbling something in a language Faith had never heard before. It reached out his hand pointing to the ring, then fell back. He did this for some time, finally he said in rough Trade, "My ring! My ring! Give my ring!"

Faith tossed the ring back to the orc. It suspiciously crept forward, snatched the ring and placed it on its finger. Suddenly Faith could see herself through the creature's eyes; she closed her eyes so she could sort the creature's mind from her own. She knew she was looking though the creature's eyes. She could feel its anxiety. Still, the feelings all felt as if they belonged to her. Her head began to swim as her thoughts swirled round mental images she did not recognize.

Slowly she reached back and touched one of the hammocks. She felt her mind beginning to twist and turn with questions from the creature she had no answers for. Even worse was her failed attempt to deduce which questions were her own and which were from the creature.

In an attempt to stop her stomach from convulsing, she lay down and began picking the thoughts apart. The task would not be easy, but deep inside she knew she had to complete it, not only for this creature, but for all the slaves linked to the ring.

Chapter 9 - Secrets

Airria entered the captain's chambers. The room was cluttered
with old bones and rags. Rats were scurrying about seemingly unaware
of Airria's existence. The ceiling had chains dangling and shackles on
the floor. On the table was a corpse and two cat-o-nine tails covered in
dried blood.

On a shelf was a black cubical frame with a sphere in the middle.
The sphere was hazy blue with dark blue waves twisting randomly
inside. The calming motion was such a stark contrast to the rest of the
room that Airria just stared into it. He let his mind wander the oceans
inside till he almost didn't notice the light from the back window fade
into night.

"Master wanted me bring you here." The graveled voice jolted
Airria out of his daze.

He glanced down at the hideous orc in its scorched leather.
Instinctually he reached for his sword. Airria hesitated when he saw that
the creature had no weapon.

"No hurt," the creature said. "Master asked me get you."

The broken Trade tongue was almost like the creature had
learned from drunks, but his posture was that of a dedicated servant. By
the ring on his hand he guessed it was linked to Faith's.

"Come, come," the orc insisted as it backed down the hall.

Apprehensive, Airria cautiously followed. He didn't know where the others had run off to, but he was nervous this creature was leading him into a trap. Still he followed.

The orc led Airria through the cargo hold filled with piles of rotting corpses, down another flight of stairs and into a long, tight room filled with hammocks. There was a dead human-sized lizard creature on the first one. On another one Faith was lying, her eyes closed, her hands clasped over her chest.

Airria rushed over to her fearing the worst. "What have you done!" Airria accused the orc. He began to draw his sword again.

"It is all right," Faith's angelic voice was sweet to his ears. "I am having a difficult time seeing through two sets of eyes. I wish Carrita had accepted this burden, although she does get somewhat vengeful and bloodthirsty when it comes to slavery, so perhaps it is best I carry it."

"You see through its eyes?" Airria asked looking hard at the orc.

"His name is Taksek," Faith said sitting up, her eyes still closed. "I believe he will soon be Joskin's dearest companion."

"Why?" Airria couldn't imagine why Joskin would care for an orc. For years Joskin had told Airria stories of wars with orcs. Most often they came to battle ruthless and blood drunk.

The orc closed its eyes and Faith opened hers. "Two reasons," Faith was smiling and it made Airria nervous again, "first, this orc is a master craftsman, specifically a blacksmith. He was the talent which made Joskin's golden dagger. He can make anything out of almost any metal," Faith paused, examining Airria, she frowned slightly when he didn't react.

"And second?" he asked to ease her discomfort.

Faith walked over to the wall at the end and closed her eyes. The orc opened its eyes and stood beside her. He put his hand on the wall and said something Airria couldn't understand. The doorway opened up.

The orc closed its eyes and then Faith opened hers. "After you," she said.

Airria carefully poked his head through the door. It was a room with walls lined with swords, shields, bows and arrows. Airria couldn't help himself. He was drawn into the room. Immediately he picked up a sword. It was made of the highest grade steel and perfectly balanced. Arrow shafts were Black Wood and the tips were designed specifically for maximum damage. "These were definitely not the comparatively shoddy weapons we fought against when we boarded," Airria was in amazement. "These are exquisite. Are any of the magical?"

Faith smiled uncertainly, "As far as I can tell, these weapons are just well made."

"Junk!" The gravelly deep voice of the orc startled Airria. "Sad I weren't given to forge'em well."

"Where are the good weapons?" Airria asked.

The orc smiled with pride and excitement. He looked at Faith, who nodded. Then it did a strange little dance, went to the center of the floor mumbling something Airria didn't understand and put its hand on the floor. Its muscular, scarred hands began stroking the floor in an elegant pattern. After a moment a section of the floor slipped away.

Airria jumped. He'd seen no indication of any trapdoors. He had spent much of his life dedicated to unraveling hidden secrets. There was not a trapdoor he couldn't easily see and open, or so he had thought. To rescue Faith, he picked a legendary Dwarven lock. Now, here, these crude orcs had created not only one, but two trapdoors he not only couldn't find without help, but was clueless as to how to open.

Airria glanced at Faith who was staring at the hole with eyes wide open.

"Master," the orc said, "you say'd I can show. Why you not speak?"

"How did you hide the secret from me?" Faith asked.

"Master never asks about it," the orc said, rubbing his knuckles nervously. "I do and tell all master asks. Please no hurt."

Airria noticed both Faith's and the orc's eyes were open and they were communicating verbally. Airria had assumed the two communicated somehow through the rings. The evidence of Faith not verbally commanding the orc weighed in favor of that. "Are you sure you have complete control of it?" he asked.

Faith and the orc looked deep into each other's eyes for a long while. "Yes, I am still in control," Faith finally said. "I am only now beginning to realize how to use the ring and keep my mental faculties intact," she spoke as she shifted her gaze to the hole. "Look, it is time we let Joskin see the riches he has earned. After all, I believe it was you who promised he could have all the treasure we find."

Slowly Airria lowered his head into the hole. He couldn't believe his eyes. The entire room was filled with piles of gold, silver and a large variety of precious gems. Most of the treasure was in coin, but there were a few piles of assorted jewelry.

"He says the weapons are near the edge," Faith said, pulling Airria out of his daze. "He says they are much better than the ones in this room."

It was no lie. On a small rock near the opening, within easy reach, were two beautiful broadswords and a brutal looking battle ax. Airria reached in and grabbed the first sword. The balance was perfect. The blade was sharp and had weaving blood grooves. The sword was as functional as it was beautiful.

"Cap'n not care so much for good makes," the orc said proudly. "Wish he letting me work good metal."

Airria was astounded. The only weapons he had seen of any better quality were the artifacts he and Joskin were carrying. "Good metal?" Airria finally squeaked out.

"Gold and silver," Faith said. "He is the blacksmith who forged the dagger Joskin was so excited to see."

Airria couldn't speak. He was in the presence of a craftsman whose skill even Joskin had believed to be only legend.

Faith placed a hand on Airria's shoulder. "We need less conspicuous weapons for our travels. This orc can construct such weapons as we need."

"Then we'll have to get it to a forge," Airria said struggling to breathe.

Faith responded, "He says there is a special forge on the ship."

Airria's mind was swimming, "Special?"

"I show you!" The orc said excitedly. It looked up to Faith.

Faith motioned and the orc took off at a sprint. "Come, come!" he yelled over his shoulder, "I show!"

Quickly Faith and Airria followed the orc through the barracks and up the stairs. The orc quickly opened the door at the top of the stairs. "Cap'n had made just for me."

The room was clean. It had four anvils of different sizes and shapes radiating around a fair sized hole in the wall. Hammers of varying size were firmly fixed to one wall. On the opposing wall there were well-secured stacks of iron ingots and Black Wood. In one corner there were stacks of molds and cauldrons.

"Watch! Watch!" the orc said jumping to grab an iron bar, then darting to grab some tongs and a hammer.

The rapid movement of the suspicious creature made Airria instinctively pull his weapon.

The muscular orc didn't even seem to notice. It walked over to the hole in the wall. It took the iron ingot with the tongs and placed it in the forge. The metal slowly began to glow. The orc pulled the hot iron out and began pounding on it, "The heat always perfect," it said almost to itself.

Airria had seen no flames and was curious, so he slowly placed his own hand in the hole. There was no heat. No ash. Nothing to indicate how the metal had been heated.

"Yes," Airria said after a long, ponderous while, "Joskin would definitely want to know about this."

After the orc had put his hammer away the three headed up on deck. Airria excitedly began to climb the stairs leading toward where Joskin was. He stopped when he noticed Faith making her way slowly towards the orc captain.

"He has not eaten in over a week," Faith said. "He should be weak."

"I'm not sure how he's survived this long," Airria replied.

"Orc go very long time with no eats or drinks," the blacksmith informed them.

Faith pulled the ring out of her money pouch and handed it to the smith. Excitedly the creature ran to the captain and jammed the ring on its finger.

Shaking, Faith fell to the deck. Airria raced over to assist.

When he arrived Faith held up a hand. "I am well. It takes time to adjust to being in another mind. Gratefully the lessons I have learned from dealing with Taksek will help."

Airria asked, "Is this one under your control as well now?"

Faith responded, "Yes."

"Are you sure you want to enslave another?" Airria was surprised Faith would want to make any creature her unwilling slave.

"This one deserves far worse," Faith's response was sharp and had a touch of venom. She slowly stood back up, blinking her eyes.

The smith slowly began untying the net. When the net dropped away the captain stood with slumped shoulders. Its eyes were closed. After a moment it walked over and jumped into the cargo hold.

"It will eat its fill," Faith explained. "When finished, it will begin to clean the ship."

Airria was more than a little nervous about the captain being below, but he trusted Faith. "Shall we introduce Joskin to your smith?"

Faith nodded and the three ascended the stairs. Joskin leaned over the wheel smiling. "I take it this is one of those tied to that ring?"

"Taksek will be your favorite orc ever," Faith replied.

Joskin laughed, "It already is. It's not trying to kill me."

"Let it explain about your dagger," Airria said.

Joskin's smiled disappeared. His mouth opened slightly and his eyes grew wide. After some time he said, "This is the smith?" He gradually pulled the dagger.

The orc slowly moved forward. He gently touched the dagger. "When I made knife, Cap'n give to me ring."

"And you can make armor like this?" Joskin asked leaning hard toward them.

"The creature asked, "You wish armor to looks like knives or armor made of knives?"

"The metal!" Joskin exclaimed.

The orc looked to Faith, then back to Joskin. "I can make armor, weapons, anything master wants from Taulkrick gold. Only need gold. Also can make Taulkrick silver."

Joskin eased back, "Now where can I get that much gold?" This question was soft and almost unheard. "I don't know how much gold that would be. Do I have enough? I guess I never thought I would have this chance."

Airria interrupted his cousin's ramblings. "Before you go completely crazy with not having enough gold, Faith has something to show you."

Joskin's eyes shot sharply to Faith. They smiled brightly, "This was a pirate ship you know."

Joskin left the wheel in a daze. "Show me, please."

Airria dove to catch the wheel. He watched as Faith and the orc led Joskin below.

Chapter 10 – The Key

Carrita could feel the magic energy flowing through the room. Much of it was disturbingly dark, but the knowledge she could feel in the magic was rare. Being in this room she could feel the connection the minotaur had to the enchantment she had dispelled. Somewhere in this room there were answers she had been looking for.

She could feel the creature's influence on every volume. It had spent countless time searching, studying and comparing from book to book. There were so many to go through. Decades of journals and collected magic books were tied onto the shelves.

Somewhere in this collection must be the final master journal, one which contained an explanation as to how the minotaur had bound magic into the door, one to help Carrita understand.

She needed peace. She needed to know. Almost without thinking she stepped into the room and locked the door behind her. She perused the room, searching for the book with the strongest magical essence.

Her search concluded when her eyes crossed a thick book in oilskins next to an oversized hammock on a desk. She carefully approached, reaching out with her magic to feel for any traps. As expected she found one ward placed on the book. It was simple but deadly. She carefully began unraveling the incantation. The dark spell proved more difficult than she anticipated. Beads of sweat formed on her brow as the simple ward turned into a complex spell and she could feel the pull of a creature far beyond her ability.

She struggled to keep the creature from manifesting while unleashing the summoning magic. Finally it broke. The creature began to form, then faded back into nothingness.

Carrita breathed a sigh of relief and sat on the huge skins lying on the oversize hammock. After a moment she retrieved the book and began looking through the pages. It was written in Draconian, a language very few knew existed and very few of those who knew about it could read it. Fortunately, her mother had insisted she learn it.

This language was complex enough to explain in real detail what she desired to know. She dove into the book. Time flew past. Periodically she could almost hear a knocking or Faith's voice in the distance. Nothing truly registered. Her mind was engaged by the words and enveloped in the meanings.

Finally, most of the way through the book, she felt the pieces all fall into place. It all made sense. There was even an in-depth and very disturbing description on how to extract intelligence and magical essence from another to make magic permanent.

The journal described using an Arbnot, an intelligent, lizard-like humanoid referred to as "the barnacle scrubber" as a test subject. Its ability to reason without the captain's help diminished slightly. It recuperated from magical drain slower although it retained all of its knowledge and understanding.

A loud knock at the door finally penetrated to Carrita's cognition. Slowly she approached the door. She tiredly pulled back the securing latch and peaked out the door.

Faith looked down at her relieved, "So, you are alive!"

By Carrita's recollection she had been in the room for a short while, though she was sufficiently mentally fatigued to have studied for weeks. "Of course I am alive. Why would I not be?"

"You locked yourself in this room over three weeks ago," Faith said with almost motherly concern. "None of us dared to break the door down to check on you."

"Three weeks?" Carrita asked. "How could it have been so long?" She looked at the book, then around at the other books strewn about which she had not even noticed herself pulling as references from the shelves. Faith asked, "Are you well?"

Carrita replied, "Just fatigued."

"Do you need rest?" Faith asked. Then she added in jest, "Perhaps you should rest somewhere with fewer books."

"Though I am fatigued, I am desirous to try what I now understand." Her mind would not leave what she had learned. "I could not sleep if I had nothing else to do."

Faith laughed softly. "We have no rats for you to experiment on."

"Rats would be insufficient for my needs." Carrita explained trying to consider how she could accomplish her goals without diminishing her own companions. "Of the slaves you control with your ring, are any of them worthy of mental reduction?"

Faith bit her bottom lip hesitantly.

Carrita continued, "I will perform experiments and lessen my own abilities if necessary."

"The pirate captain," Faith finally said, "he is now under my control. If you must reduce anyone's intellect, the captain is the most deserving."

Carrita felt the excitement rush through her. Though the thought of destroying another being's ability to reason, especially a magic user, did make her a little sick, if her experiment worked she would be able to help the party even more. She would need all the help she could get to retrieve her mother from Jarmack'Trastibbik. "Please send for the captain."

"If you insist," Faith said sadly.

"While we wait, what have I missed?" Three weeks was quite a sum of time and the ship was a large vessel, Carrita was sure she had missed much.

"Well," Faith began, "the first orc slave we saw was the blacksmith who made the golden dagger."

Carrita giggled, "I would daresay Joskin started complaining he did not have enough gold."

Faith laughed as well, "He did. Though this was a successful pirate ship and the blacksmith knew where the trove was stored so the complaining did not last long."

"Is it working on Joskin's armor now?" Carrita asked.

Yes. Taksek is enjoying his time in the forge," Faith said with a smile dipping slightly.

"When did you learn his name?" Carrita was concerned Faith was talking of this orc as though it were a person.

"I not only see through his eyes, I see through into his heart. He is no longer a monster to me. He is a person in another skin," Faith said gently.

For the first time in her life Carrita began thinking about orcs as something besides raging beasts. Maybe they had families too. Perhaps some of them had little ones they cared for. For the most part of her life she had been near her mother casting spells to protect their own town from the beasts of dark bloods. Orcs, goblins, hobgoblins and kobolds had been relentless in their attacks. Carrita could not believe she had not considered where the creatures had come from.

"Has your concern for the orcs extended even to the captain?" Carrita asked.

Faith laughed uncomfortably, "The captain is still a beast in my eyes. It is even more so since I have been inside its mind."

Carrita asked, "Then why hesitate to use them as we have the rats?"

"The fear of taint," Faith replied. "If you are successful, as I assume you will be, examining the same track you were when we left the other ship, the taint will be in anything you create."

"Tank juice," a rough voice boomed from behind Faith. "I's work hard to develop monster taint."

Carrita jumped, "How much conversation did it hear?"

Faith laughed, "Now who is concerned about what the captain thinks?" As she let the creature by she added, "It heard most of the conversation and is pleased."

Now that the orc was towering over Carrita it looked much larger than it had before. Carrita searched to make sure he was sufficiently tied to the ring. After a moment of prodding she determined its tether was sufficiently strong.

"What should we try?" she finally asked.

Faith returned, "What would be the most likely to succeed?"

"Perhaps a simple color change," Carrita said unsure. "Do we have something which could use a different look?"

Faith's thoughtful look and ponderous face told Carrita Faith was serious. "What about Airria's sword and shield. They are obviously unnatural and we need to hide our possession of them."

"Those weapons, as well as your bow, Joskin's ax and my robes, are far beyond my understanding," Carrita said after some thought. "Although Joskin's dagger would work nicely here."

Faith closed her eyes for a moment. When she opened them she said, "Joskin will be here shortly."

Carrita was surprised Faith could communicate so easily with Joskin. "You have not enslaved Joskin, have you?"

Faith laughed, "No, he was watching his armor being forged. I had the blacksmith send him."

Carrita let out a sigh of relief.

Shortly Joskin could be heard, "Is she alive?"

Faith chuckled again, "Yes, she is well. Apparently she was studying this entire time."

"Do I want to know?" Joskin asked more seriously than Carrita would have liked.

Faith replied, "Not likely. It is beyond my understanding."

Joskin leaned into the room, "I'm glad you're well. How can we help?"

Carrita blushed slightly at his chivalry and concern. "May we use your golden dagger?"

Joskin jested, "Will I get back?"

"If you do," Carrita replied, "it will either be less conspicuous or unchanged."

"Less conspicuous would be nice." Joskin stopped talking as his eyes fell on the captain.

"This one still gets to you?" Faith asked with real question in her voice.

"I really don't think I'll ever get used to it." he said almost spitting. "After what you told me about it, I wish you would let me kill it."

Carrita reached a hand to touch Joskin's, "If this works he will slowly suffer a fate worse than death."

Joskin reluctantly handed Faith his dagger, "I know you trust your control of it, but I ask you don't let it touch the dagger."

"Thank you," Faith replied. After Joskin left she turned to Carrita. "Would you like me to stay or leave?"

"I believe you can assist," Carrita said, examining the room for the best arrangement for all of them. "Have the orc sit here," she said after a moment pointing to a spot on the floor. "Will you watch from the hammock in case something goes awry?" she asked Faith.

After Faith had taken position, Carrita sat so she could stare into the dark eyes of the orc and placed the dagger between them. Slowly she started weaving her magic into each part of the dagger to form the magic into an illusion she wished people to see.

Now the easy part was finished. While sustaining the illusion, she reached out with her magic. She could feel the orc fighting Faith's will. She still could not find a way to reach into the orc to remove the mental part of it. She focused deep into the orc's eyes. She began to release her own soul, allowing it to reach deep into the abyss she now saw before her. She could feel the creature's entire past, feel the abuse as a child and the pleasure of each kill. She could feel ecstasy as its claws had ripped off the heads of small children in front of their mothers. She could feel the chill as it accepted its calling from Jarmack'Trastibbik.

When she could feel the abuse of his childhood Carrita almost pitied the creature, but it had chosen to hold onto the bitterness and turn its pain to pleasure. This being chose to be a monster and relished every second of its existence.

Reaching with both soul and magic she was relieved to feel and know she was feeling the captain's ability to recover magic. As she had read, she carefully extracted a small portion and placed it into the center of the dagger's particles where she had interlaced the threads of her spell. Finally she bound them all together.

When she was finished she allowed her soul back into her own body, enjoying the warmth she had taken for granted. Her mind, now linked to her soul, began processing the information she had encountered. Her own painful memories came to mind. As a tear rolled down her cheek she noticed the glint in the orc's eyes.

"I will take it all from you," she said through her teeth in the captain's ear. "I will take your magic and eventually I will take your mind a piece at a time until you will feel nothing. Only then will I release you."

Faith said from behind Carrita, "You know I can hear everything he hears, right?"

"Now you know my plans," Carrita said. "Do you intend to stop me?"

Faith shook her head. "I know everything this beast has done and how it felt as it did them. This creature deserves far worse than you promise. I, through my ring, am forced to participate. Just know what you are doing makes me ill. Sometimes, what must be done is horrible beyond comprehension. Please, make sure you do this for justice, not revenge. Do not become what you are fighting."

Chapter 11 – True Pleasure

Master said he could. The one called Faith had told him to do it. He needed no incentive. He was a master of the forge. He had been instructed to use the gold to make her big guard, Joskin, his highest quality of Taulkrick Gold. When finished with the big guard's armor, Taksek would make Taulkrick Silver armor for Master and her small guard, Airria. Only Master's mount was on the ship to be fitted for barding. Taksek was skilled at many crafts, but he was a master of the forge.

While the big guard watched, Taksek emptied bag after bag of gold coins into his special caldron, filling it to its mark. Small golden chains, rings, bracelets and necklaces recently freed of valuable stones were added to the mix.

This gold was not good enough yet. Only the most pure of gold could be used. He had to clean it, to burn off the impurities. Slowly the gold melted. The contaminants floated to the top and burned away. When he could clearly see his reflection the metal was ready to start conversion to Taulkrick Gold.

Only orc blood carried the proper strength to start the process. He had contemplated using his own blood, but Master told him to use to use Cap'n's blood.

When Cap'n arrived, Taksek chose the dullest knife he had. After months of torture for Cap'n's pleasure, Taksek found his own enjoyment in Cap'n's pain. Even when Master scolded him, Taksek was filled with happiness.

Now that the blood had given strength to the gold it was time for the hard part. For this he asked Master and her guards to stay away. He placed two of the Black Wood sticks into the mixture. Slowly the smoke began to swirl in the cauldron. It twisted and taunted to him. It beckoned with promises of sweet pain. Laughing and swirling in a seductive promise. Even after all these years and as many times as he had fallen prey to the torturous smoke he still found himself reaching towards it.

Before he injured himself again, he pulled away from the bitterly enchanting smoke and grabbed his stir stick made from the bone of a giant wolf. As he mixed, the sultry tendrils swirled downward, becoming trapped in the gold.

He could feel the sweat pouring down his body and the dark torment in his heart. Though many would call such an ordeal torture, to him it was a small price to pay for his craft. This was the foundation of his passion.

He carefully poured the precious metal into the ingot molds to let them cool. The nearly overpowering urge to scorch his hands in the molten ore almost overwhelmed him.

He carefully looked over the cooling stock. This Taulkrick Gold was to armor the big guard as well as a warhorse. It was also needed to create a large, pole arm style axe. He carefully calculated where each bar of stock would be used.

No, he thought, this is not enough. He would need another batch. He would need five batches of silver for all the other armor, barding and weapons he had been instructed to make.

He left the room to retrieve more gold. Master stopped him.

"You should not need to put yourself through such an ordeal," Master said.

"I no be feared," he responded.

She looked him in the eye, "Do no more."

He could feel the pull to obey. His mind began ticking. A cage began closing in around his will. "Please no be like Cap'n," he pleaded with his last free breath.

"You truly wish to continue?" she asked.

He could feel the cage door open slowly. Master asked for his wishes. "Yes, please. I make best equipment for master and guards. Even little girl's pony should have my artistry to guard on journey. I make it perfect for Master.

As Master searched his eyes he felt the cage begin to vanish. After some time she sighed, "If this is your desire, then continue," she stepped aside.

Quickly he slipped past her. She had given him license to build the best he could. Back and forth he ran. For the first time in years, since Cap'n had brought him on board, he would have the chance to test his own abilities.

It took him three days to prepare the metal. It would have taken less time, but Master forced him to stop to eat nasty dry fruits and sleep. He had not wanted to eat or sleep. He only wanted to work the metal.

By the sunset on the third day he had all the measurements and Master's permission to start. His tools were readied. This is what he lived for.

Bang! Bang!

His heavy hammer fell hard and precisely, roughly forming each ingot. One by one, piece by piece, the armor took form. One scale at a time; chest, arms, legs and helm took shape better than he had expected. Each piece looking as if it were one solid piece of metal, but was actually made of many tiny scales. This would stop any blow, but allow for perfect freedom.

Clang! Clang!

The sound his medium hammer made was sweeter than any other music. Carefully he placed the scales together. He knew this craft well. Each joint could move freely without a visible seam. He truly was a master of the forge.

Before he would put the finishing touches on the armor, he wanted to have the big guard try it on. He picked up each piece and carried it to the big guard. "Put on!" he demanded.

Master and both guards seemed upset.

"Did I do something to displease Master?" he asked.

"It has been a week since you have eaten or slept," Master said. "You have ignored my summons."

Taksek hadn't remembered any summons. He had been crafting. Now that Master had mentioned food, he was noticing the pain in his stomach. "Forgive I not come. Making armor as requested. I eat now. Make happy?" He wished for some nice flesh covered in rich green mold, but Master made Cap'n throw it all to the fishes. "Perhaps armor will make happy to give meat?"

The faces staring at him didn't soften, but the large one started placing the armor on himself. Carefully he latched each buckle. When fully donned, he began moving. "I don't know if this is any good."

"Armor not finished. Need to make right," Taksek said.

"Is it finished enough to test?" the small guard asked.

"Little test good now," Taksek responded. "Need make final fixes."

"It's too light. It almost feels as if I'm wearing nothing," the big guard said. "This wouldn't protect me against a child's practice sword."

"Test," Taksek suggested.

The small guard picked up a staff and began poking the armor.

That was no test for his armor, "Hit, see strong."

The small guard said to the big one, "Close your eyes."

The big one closed his eyes and raised his arms. The small one swung with all his might. The staff shattered. The big guard flew to the deck.

Frustrated that the humans refused to test the armor for real, he walked over to some weapons that were on the deck. He picked up the axe, the one the big guard had chosen from the better weapons C'ap'n had hidden.

The humans were happily discussing the armor and didn't notice him come back. While the big one was on the deck, Taksek wound up and hit. "Silly humans. That no test," without waiting he swung with all his strength. The large human skidded across the wooden floor. The other two trained weapons on Taksek, but he didn't care. He was already inspecting the armor dropping the now broken ax on the deck. "Now can see what needs fixes."

The armor had flexed more than it was supposed to. The human's muscles had moved slightly differently than an orc's. He would have to shift some scales.

"Take armor," Taksek said after he had finished his inspection.

"It is already better than I could have hoped," the big guard said. "What more could you do?"

"Not finished," Taksek said. "Need fixes." He stomped a foot. "Take armor!"

"Eat first," Master said handing Taksek some tough dry meat.

He took the food. "Sorry, Master. Just want finish armor. Will eat now. Ask big guard take armor so can finish."

The big one began removing the armor, "I will bring it back to your forge."

Master spoke hesitantly, "You need to sleep, too."

Taksek couldn't sleep now. He was in the middle of crafting a masterpiece. This would be the greatest armor he had ever made. "When armor finished, will rest."

When Master finally nodded, he took his meat to the forge. He wondered why the big guard would be upset about the broken axe. It had amazed the humans, but Taksek had promised to make better. He would show them what true quality was.

He started with the head. He welded the ingots together, then splayed and flattened them out to create four points with crescent webbing between them much like a drake's wing on both sides. Carefully he hollowed out a place for the hilt. He sharpened the blade.

When he was satisfied with the form and functionality of the head, he drew sequences of battles Master has shared that proved the prowess of the big guard. He used a gem to make sure each mark was perfect. When the scene was finished, at a distance it looked dull and plain. Only the best eyes would see the truth of his artistry.

Now that the head was finished he began on the handle. He flattened out several ingots and rolled them together to make a hollow tube so the handle would not be too heavy. For the pommel he carefully placed pure gold encased in some Taulkrick Gold for balance. The top he fitted with a perfect spike.

When finished, he realized he was not alone. The Master and big guard were in the doorway. "I make better," Taksek said in surprise.

Master frowned at him. "You need to rest. Also, you did not finish your food," she pointed to the dried meat on the floor.

Taksek's heart sunk. He had only wanted to do right by Master. Slowly he bent down to pick up the meat. He remembered the ax and stood back up. "I make this to rest. Broke ax testing armor. Made replacement. Now no break. Taksek is refreshed and ready to finish armor. Will eat food first if Master wishes." He slowly handed the big guard the ax and picked up the meat.

Master let out a frustrated breath and spun around. The big one stood staring at the axe.

Taksek was confused. He had expected the human to test the new weapon. Instead the big guard just stared. "Did Taksek make wrong? Why not test ax? You not break. Has well balance. Test, you see."

The human shifted his gaze. "Thank you," his voice was hoarse and broken.

Taksek stood, stunned as the human slowly turned and walked away. He had never been thanked in such a way. Such gratitude made Taksek even more determined to make the best armor.

From that day forth, the big guard brought Taksek fresh fish, raw and wet to eat. Master did not make him sleep and praised his work. Often she would compliment his determination. When they made port, he could finally finish the horse's barding.

In total he made three suits of armor and four sets of barding. The armor for the men was full, battle ready, with helms that left the face open. Only the pony received light chain. The other horses' had barding custom to the owner.

Master's armor was far less protective then Taksek would have liked, but the girl had instructed him to make it different. She said Master must not be covered in too much metal. So he did his best to make it match Master's elegance.

Chapter 12 – Dark Magic

Carrita was elated at her success with the dagger. It now appeared as a common, dull stiletto. She had learned how to use the information she had been collecting. She now knew how to enchant objects with her spells.

The cost of the knowledge was tremendous. Her body and soul had become partially separated for a short while. She had been forced to see, and in part live, the past and present of the orc. Perhaps she had even seen its future. She could not be sure which was which. All of it merged together in a twisted mesh of reality and possibility.

All of this was both exhilarating and infuriating. It reminded her of the day the crystal had been removed from her navel. It was time to learn where her soul had gone and how to use this place to augment her magic.

The whole experience had left her shaken. It was difficult for her to focus on what she knew, or even what she had done. Her past and future had become meshed together. Her soul felt uncomfortable in her own body.

"Are you all right?" Faith asked.

Carrita took a deep breath. "It will take time," she was talking more to herself than to Faith, "all things magical take time to master." She was sure the books would help. When she understood what was happening she would be able to control the way she was feeling.

"Are you positive there is nothing I can do to help?" Faith asked.

Carrita realized, with Faith's question, she was looking as confused as she felt.

"Mages call it the Astral Plane," the rough orc voice sounded almost gleeful. "It is the place free spirits walk." It had a satisfied grin on its face.

Carrita pondered what the orc had said.

Faith spoke in a slightly shaken voice, "It wanted you to know the name. Be careful. Your knowing has made it very happy. It believes it will destroy you."

Carrita tried to straighten her shoulders. "I will be careful. Now I must study more. Return when Joskin's armor is finished." She did not want Faith to stay, but feared she would disappear.

The captain had given Carrita a clue to understanding. She dove back into the minotaur's journal. As confused as she felt, much of what she had not understood earlier began to come clear.

The partial detachment she had experienced was necessary for her to access the orc's ability to regenerate magic. This ability was a combination of body and soul. To take the reasoning ability would require a full detachment.

"Was this not death?" she asked herself. "Will I have to die to accomplish my goals?" With the trauma and confusion she had experienced she wondered if it would. She was not even sure if she would be able to handle any more of the pain. "If I can handle what I see and feel there, would I even be able to find my way back? Maybe this is why the orc wishes me to go there."

The minotaur had been to the Astral Plane. He had returned. So, there must be a way.

The stacks of reference books around her grew. The shelves became bare. Nothing told her how to come back and she had to know!

She began walking around the room. She found herself muttering something even she could not understand. The room began to feel tight and stuffy. She decided to go for a walk.

She left the room and wandered down the hall. The cargo hold had been cleaned and scrubbed. A faint banging from the forge could be heard. Perhaps the enchantments on the forge would hold some answers.

Joskin was not watching. The orc blacksmith was working away, it looked so content. She got lost, almost forgetting her own burdens. It was almost as if she were watching herself study. It was obsessed and driven.

She reached out with her magic and was shocked to realize the creature was crafting of its own free will. The ring's magic had mostly been altered by the orc's full-hearted dedication to his craft and loyalty to Faith. The magic had been altered by his honest devotion.

"Are you making armor for everyone," she finally asked the creature, "or are all your efforts for Joskin?"

The orc did not stop working, "I make armors for Master and guards. The human called Joskin is the only one to gets special gold armor. Just him and horse. When I can get measures of horse. It on other ship they says to me."

"You were not instructed to make armor for me?" Carrita was surprised.

"Master say the girl not want," the orc said, stopping a moment to look at Carrita. "Will make if girl want. New challenge for Taksek."

Carrita smiled about the orc calling her "girl." "Faith…Master is correct. I cannot use metal armor. Will you be making all the armor the same?"

The orc went back to his work. "Master gives me free to make what be best for each. I make armors for many fighters. I make best armors Master and Guards."

"Have you ever made armor for a shaman?"

The orc set down his hammer, "Shaman no like armors. Make bad magics. Is Master a Shaman?"

338

Carrita was startled the orc had relinquished its tool. "She is not purely a shaman. She fights also." She began preparing to defend herself. The rough voice and speech made her nervous.

The orc's eyes were filled with concern. "How make armor to protect and not make magics bad?"

Carrita knew the more heavy armor Faith had on, the more difficult it would be to cast the spells. Faith was very gifted with magic, but had focused as much on archery and swordplay, although lately she had been paying more attention to Airria than anything else.

"She will need a solid support for her chest," Carrita finally said after much thought. "She will definitely need protection for her shins and forearms. A full plate over her thighs would be too much, but her upper legs need protection."

The orc scratched his chin thoughtfully, "Understand. Will make best armor."

For a moment Carrita stood in shock at herself. She, like Faith, now saw the orc as a person. She had been talking and planning with him and she had enjoyed it enough to forget her trauma and focus her mind.

The focus did not last long. Her mind shifted back to the Astral Plane, then to her past and pain. She began wandering; the mindless repetition of her steps reminded her she was real.

She looked down the stairs but decided to go back to her studies. Before she entered the room something she had forgotten caught her attention. It was magic from inside the captain's quarters. She had felt it when she had unlocked the door but had forgotten about it. Now felt like a good time to investigate.

It did not take long for her to find the sphere. It looked like an ocean in the midst of a relentless storm. It was hypnotic and strangely relaxing. She could feel her mind getting lost in the turmoil.

She focused on the sphere, curious about the magic which made it work. It was Order magic, but it was flooded with water essence. The waves were trapped within the pure magic globe.

She focused on the waves. As her magic touched them she was filled with understanding about oceans and storms. She knew where every ocean current was, even regions she had never heard of. Moreover, she knew the best way to steer the ship through the most dangerous storms.

The rush of knowledge did not help her mental state. She quickly let go. The understanding vanished, but reality became even less clear.

She could not be sure of anything. The globe did not seem to have trapped any souls, it seemed to be only understanding. Moreover, it did not feel as if the knowledge had been stolen, but it had to come from somewhere. Or did it, she thought.

As she was attempting to contemplate the ramifications of the sphere she noticed a map on the wall. Her mother had shown her a similar map. Jammar also had one on his wall. This map showed the whole world in great detail. It even showed the magic wall which designated the area dragons could not venture.

The magic in the map was open. It felt as though it was meant to be tied to something, but as for now, it had not been attached. Her mind and perspective were clouded.

"Focus!" she chastised herself. She had focused on the armor and her mind was clear. She had focused on the orb and her mind was sated. Focus was the key, but how could she realign reality with her thoughts? The orc captain had given her the answer. The Astral Plane, she had to return, only there could she clarify this confusion and pain.

The last two times she had received a glimpse her mind had slipped farther from reality. She had seen so much which had made no sense. To top it off, the orc captain had suggested it. She was sure his motivation was for Carrita to lose what was left of her sense.

It did not matter. She had to do this. She had to know. All she had to do was find something real, something to help her stay focused. The captain had used an existence of pain and lies to gain power. Faith, Joskin and Airria were good and honest, but they had too many unknowns in their pasts.

How she wished her mother was with her to guide her through this. She looked at her hands wondering if focusing on herself would be sufficient. Her robe caught her eye. She still had only a vague understanding of the magic it contained, but it was from her mother. She could trust it would not hurt her nor show her pain. The mere thought gave her strength and focus. It seemed to clear her mind.

She quickly re-entered her room. She locked the door and hid all the magic books. She removed her robe and placed it in a corner, then she sat facing it. She focused, concentrating on the concern her mother had for her. Remembering her mother had saved her from the cruelty of Jarmack'Trastibbik. She let the peace of the robe filter into her.

Just like she had with the orc, she allowed her soul to disconnect from her body. As expected she could see the robe being created, at the same time she could see it as raw silk fibers, she could see it as destroyed, owned by another and even dragon scales. None of it made sense. There was no chronology.

She knew what the robe was now. She concentrated on it. Slowly all the confusion and congestion of images slipped into the vision of the robe as it was. As she did so, she was able to do the same with all of the confusing images she had seen the last two times she had visited the Plane.

Slowly she allowed her soul to slip away from her body. She could feel her own heartbeat, but nothing else. For the first time since the crystal had been removed she was losing touch with her magic. Though she was terrified, she continued.

She could see her robe clearly, but could also see so much more. Her eyes could see the magic infused into the garment. It was white and warm with golden swirls. Just looking at it she could see the love and protection her mother had woven into it. It helped her feel secure in what she was doing.

Slowly she began scanning the room. The minotaur's books had a black aura with bronze swirls. Having read them she knew the kind of magic they represented. All her life she had known which colors represented which elements of magic. Now she knew why. Now she also understood why each dragon was the color it was. After all they were made of the pure essence of magic.

Curious she altered her view to her own body. She was covered in a swirl of color. Though gold and white were the most regular, the other colors where fairly well balanced. The brightness of the aura, she guessed was the magnitude of the magic potential or the abundance of magical energy available.

She was interested to see the rest of the group. She slowly walked over to the door, but found she could not open it. Her hand went straight through. It was then she realized she could not feel the floor. Her reality was being challenged again. "How can I walk when my feet are not pushing me forward? If gravity is not holding me down, why do I not leave the floor?"

She looked at her body. She was no longer physical. The physical world no longer had a hold on her. She reached out and touched the vinework of color surrounding her own body. She grabbed a blue thread and held it. She watched it closely. It resembled the blue in the globe. The thread represented a piece of her understanding of water. "Can I give this understanding to another? If so, why did the orc not claim the knowledge himself?"

Thinking of the orc captain made her reach inside herself. She had been able to reason and learn, but as she had gained understanding she could see it track back to her body and join the swirling knowledge already there. The ability to reason was an attribute of the soul. She had not been able to take the orc's ability to think and reason because it is tethered to the soul. Memories and knowledge belonged to the physical realm.

To keep her promise to the captain, she would need to balance between both realms, teetering between the two. She would also have to find a place in the orc's mind and bind it away from him.

As she slipped back into her body she began to giggle. The captain had sent her to the Plane believing it would drive her insane. Though it had come close, the creature had underestimated her. Now she possessed a far greater knowledge. She would use this knowledge to destroy the captain and make the ship into a self-managed water vessel.

Chapter 13 - Trust

Since leaving the merchant ship Airria had been enjoying his journey. The weeks had flown by. Carrita had locked herself in one of the rooms; this meant he got more time with Faith.

They had kept to their daily training regimen, but in the time Joskin slept, Airria and Faith stared at the stars. They never seemed to run out of things to discuss. He never grew tired of listening to her.

The few times Carrita called for Faith, or Faith would make the orcs do something, he would sit at the wheel and talk to his sword, learning enough to get by steering the ship.

It was fortunate the days had been clear with a solid breeze. This ship was too large for one, or even four people to bring through a storm. Bringing the ship into port, his sword had told him, may be too much.

Joskin had been constantly arranging and rearranging everything on deck. He would shift the nets, marble orcs and the few crates left, from one spot to another.

On day Carrita emerged from beneath, "I have a plan! I know what we need to do!"

Airria placed an old staff in one of the spokes of the wheel to lock it in place and came to the edge of the upper deck.

Faith joined him. "What do we need to do?" she asked Carrita.

Carrita walked from one group of marble orcs to another. She was almost skipping, "I will need everyone's help."

Faith smiled big as she asked, "What would you have us do?"

Carrita surveyed the deck, "Call the captain. He can help too."

Joskin grabbed Carrita by the shoulders and held her until she looked him in the eyes. "We can only help if you tell us what you need," he said gently.

"Exactly how many marble orcs do we have?" she asked, almost oblivious to the questions being asked.

"Five," he responded, "I thought they may be worth something in port."

"They will be to us soon," Carrita said. "They will be more valuable than any money."

Joskin took a suspicious step back.

Faith asked, "How will you do this?"

Carrita seemed to ignore Faith's question. "Please move the orcs here," she said pointing to a spot on the deck.

The orc captain stood firm. Joskin tilted his head and placed his arms across his chest.

Carrita scowled at Faith, "I have spent countless days having my reality redefined. It pushed me past the edge of sanity and I have recently clawed my way back. Do you really want to walk such a road to understand what I am doing?"

Joskin dropped his arms. He began slowly heading to untie one of the statues.

Faith spoke up, "I do not need to know how you will be accomplishing your task. I only would like to know what you will be creating using the stone orcs."

Carrita smiled, "I will make them able to walk and fight and lift. They will be able to clean and work. They will be able to walk tirelessly."

Faith asked, "They will be slaves?"

Carrita's smile drooped into a frown. "The creatures I will create will have no feelings or even a soul. The orcs these statues used to be are dead. They have moved on to their final destination. The statues' movement will be purely upon our wills. There will be no removal of free choice. These creatures are created for the purpose of serving. They will be as sentient as a rock. Do not concern yourself with their souls."

Faith replied, "We already have slaves we do not know what to do with."

Carrita pondered for a moment. "Do you enjoy your role as master?"

Faith pursed her lips, "You know how I feel. I thought you felt the same."

Carrita's shoulders relaxed, "Then do not hold onto them. No living being should be forced to serve. No soul should be bound to another against their will."

"Golems?" Joskin blurted out.

Airria asked, "What?"

Joskin responded, "Faithful, mindless guardians. I faced one years ago. It was the only fight I have ever run from." He grabbed Carrita again, "You can do this?"

"Yes," Carrita responded. "Then we would be able to guard the ship while we look for Airria's armor."

Carrita looked solidly at Faith, "If it is all right. I believe they will be worth more than their weight in gold to us."

Faith and Carrita locked eyes. For some time it felt as if they were locked in a battle of wills. Their expressions changed. Brows furrowed and flattened. Eyes squinted and opened. There was something going on that Airria didn't understand.

Finally Carrita broke the silence. "I will create one. Then if you can get your blacksmith to relinquish his ring, you will see. Can you trust me so far?"

Reluctantly Faith waved her hand, "Fine."

The orc narrowed its eyes, but began loosening the largest of the statues.

As quietly as he could Airria asked Faith, "Why don't you trust her? It's not like you."

Faith looked sadly at Airria. "Carrita has spent all these weeks obsessively studying the most cruel of the magics. She has been to a

346

place the orc captain suggested she go. Now she is asking us to help her test what she has learned. She is determined to create a creature which neither you nor Joskin will be able to defeat." She sighed, "I do not know where her mind is."

Airria asked, "How much of your concern comes from something you got from the orc?"

Faith looked hard at the deck. "His argument makes so much sense. Also, lately there have been intense amounts of magical energy coming from her room."

Airria laughed. "How much of what has happened to us in the last year makes any sense?"

Faith laughed softly.

Airria put a hand on Faith's shoulder. "Carrita has one goal in mind. No influence, rational, understanding, or piece of knowledge will change that. Trust me. She is the same girl she was."

Faith leaned her head on Airria's shoulder, "I will trust you."

"There," Joskin said loud enough to get everyone's attention, "will we need to stand it up?"

Airria asked, "What will you need from me?"

"For the first one, I will mostly need you to sit nearby and think of your training." Carrita was looking thoughtful, "If you do not mind, I could use your magical energy."

Airria asked, "Won't I need my energy for the fights ahead?"

Carrita smiled, "You will regain all I use. I promise, you will be missing nothing. You will only feel tired for awhile."

Airria had just tried to convince Faith to trust Carrita. Now Carrita was asking him to trust her. He swallowed hard. "Of course," he finally said. The orc had put thoughts of doubt in Faith's head, now Faith had transferred some of that doubt to Airria.

Carrita pointed to the deck and waved for him to sit down. "When you feel energy leave your body, let it go. I promise you will be all right."

Airria sat. Faith sat next to him and put a hand on his. Joskin sat on the other side. The orc captain was on the other side of the statue.

Carrita asked Faith, "Will you be helping or merely observing?"

347

Faith looked to Airria, then back to Carrita. "I left my sister behind for the unlikely chance this quest could succeed. I cannot allow the thoughts of a bitter creature to taint our chances. If you believe this creation will assist us, then you have all my resources at your disposal."

Carrita's shoulders cocked back. Her voice took a tone of command, "All of you concentrate on your combat abilities."

Airria closed his eyes and began running drills in his mind. Unexpectedly his drills became more complex. He could see himself crossing swords with the orc, Joskin and Faith in a brutal meat-grinding battle. The battle grew more intense then was gone. For a long moment he couldn't remember how to even hold a weapon.

He could feel Faith gripping tighter to his hand. He could feel his energy being pulled out of his body. He was growing more nervous.

When he was about to open his eyes, his weapons ability and understanding returned. He was relieved, though he remained fatigued. He almost collapsed on the deck. Faith relaxed her hand.

"It is finished," Carrita finally said.

Airria looked at the statue. It appeared the same. "It looks the same. What did you do to it?"

"It only follows the orders of its master," Carrita said with her childish grin.

Joskin stood up, looking a little shaken, "Then command it."

Carrita giggled, "I am not the master."

Faith begrudgingly opened her eyes. "What have you done?"

Carrita's grin faded, "The creature is your tool to wield, not mine. You can verbally command or through one of the slave rings you can command with your mind."

"Where do we get another ring?" Faith asked. "Both we have on this ship are in use."

Carrita giggled again, "I think you know one of them is not really in use."

Joskin asked, "What do you mean?"

Faith looked at the water and shrugged.

Carrita dropped one eyebrow. "The blacksmith, Taksek. His loyalty has exceeded the demands of the ring. The ring is only a mental link between Faith and the orc."

Faith eased her gaze back to Carrita, "The mental link has not been working very well lately."

"You gave him freedom to live his passion," Carrita said. "The link is strong. His obsession is stronger. Fortunately his devotion is still more powerful." Carrita looked to the golem, "For now try a simple command. I would like to see if all this has been worth the trouble."

"What should I command?"

Carrita put her hands on her hips. "Try something simple. Tell it to stand up."

Faith hesitated. She looked to Joskin and Airria. Finally she said, "Stand up."

The creature moved. It stood solid and proud. The rocking motion of the ship didn't make it stop.

Carrita grabbed Faith's hand. "You will have to be specific. The creature has little reasoning ability."

Faith frowned thoughtfully. "The orc has lost some of its ability."

Carrita looked at the orc. "Yes. It has," she looked at Faith. "This is for the good of us all, not for my personal vendetta."

Faith took a deep breath and helped Airria to his feet.

Joskin was poking the statuesque orc shape with his ax, "What else can it do?"

Carrita smiled playfully. "This creature can fight as well as all of you. If you would like a test, you will have to ask Faith." She turned to Faith, "When you feel ready and comfortable we will make others."

Airria was leaning heavily on Faith. "Would it be able to help us make port?"

Carrita responded very slowly, "They should." She looked vaguely to both sides. "I may know something which will help even more." Without another word she vanished through the doorway.

Faith helped Airria to the wheel. The ship had drifted slightly off course, so he made corrections. The wheel was heavy and he had little strength. On his own, or even with the rest of the group, it would be impossible to steer into port.

Slowly he could feel his energy returning. The wheel became easier to control, but still he knew they needed more.

While he was pondering this, Carrita poked her head back up over the edge. "I do not know why they never finished, but this ship is prepared to be enchanted to be a golem of sorts. It will take us to and make port anywhere we desire. I need to complete the incantation."

"I am not taking responsibility for this vessel," Faith said quickly.

Carrita stuck out her lip, "Then I will take this responsibility on myself."

"I don't think I can help add anything for awhile," Airria said tiredly.

Carrita grinned, "This is far less complicated. I need only Faith to assist with magic and the binding element from the orc. Is this agreeable?"

Faith took a deep breath, "This is acceptable. Where do you need me?"

Together they sat on the deck. Carrita produced the blue orb and set it on the map from the captain's quarters. She held it between both her and Faith. For some time they sat with their eyes closed, almost half a night later they opened them again.

Carrita put on a silver ring and said to Faith, "Thank you for trusting me."

Faith collapsed on the deck. Airria, now feeling stronger went to her aid.

"I am all right," she said.

Airria realized he had left the wheel unattended. He looked back. It appeared to be controlled by an unseen force. He looked to Carrita for answers.

Carrita said, "The ship will maneuver itself, no need to worry, we will reach our destination safely.'

Over the next several days Carrita followed the same procedure to create four more golems. She made all of the weapons and armor the blacksmith had made to look plain and dull. She even made three cloaks that made the now frigid night air comfortable.

By this time the captain was like the walking dead. They took the orc to the captain's chambers and had it hold the orb securely. Faith then used one of her arrows to turn it to stone.

Chapter 14 – Mountain's Snakes

Faith was sad to leave the ship behind. It had been a break in the
storm of her life. She had been able to enjoy evenings with Airria and
help Carrita learn. The orc had made her a special sword which was
specially designed for her smaller frame. She had felt almost at home.

Now, only the golems and Taksek remained on board. They had
left the orc with all the supplies he would need; including food and iron
ore. The golems were not to let anyone on board.

Before leaving, the blacksmith had completed all of the armor.
Even Carrita's pony had some light chainmail to help protect it. All of
the magical weapons had been bundled and bound to the backs of their
mounts. Jammar had instructed them to hide the weapons until they had
found the armor. Flaunting such artifacts could attract more difficulty
and result in unnecessary deaths.

Both men were very proud of their new armor and weapons.
Joskin would swing his ax around while he rode his horse. Airria held his
new sword and shield far too proudly. In the evenings they would hit

each other and laugh. Only a year ago Faith would have counted such behavior as foolish and barbaric, now she wanted to join in.

Any way she looked at it things were going to change again. The small port had been good to them, but now it was time to move on. Even the trees seemed to be screaming about the change which was coming.

As they rode through the gate Faith saw them. All of the trees were shaped like inverted cones. Their leaves were thin and sharp, like needles. "What is wrong with the trees?" she asked.

Joskin laughed. "That is how trees grow in the area. It is so the snow will slide off them better."

Faith was having a difficult time breathing. She could not believe the speed at which things were changing. She did not even understand what Joskin was explaining. "What is snow?"

He responded, "It is wet and white and you will be tired of it before this trek is finished. You may want to do something foolish before you see it for the last time."

"What do you mean?" Faith asked. She looked to Airria for an explanation, but he looked as confused as she felt.

"You will see in a few days," Joskin yelled over his shoulder as his horse broke into a gallop.

It took several days just to hit the base of the Arstock Mountain Range. The ground became steep and rocky; at times the trees seemed to be growing sideways, lying against the ground. In reality the slope was simply that vertical.

Fortunately they had found a small road twisting back and forth up through the trees. It reminded Faith of the switchbacks she had to transverse to pass the mountains on the island they had left. It seemed so long ago.

For the next week they kept climbing. From time to time they would step to the side of the road to allow travelers, mostly hide and wood collectors, to get by. The higher they climbed the rarer it was to see others.

The nights grew colder and the wind grew stronger. Faith was glad for the cloak Carrita had enchanted. She could see her own breath and the waterskins would freeze solid in the evening.

Around midday, toward the end of the second week of their journey, Airria and Faith noticed a white, cloudlike substance on the ground. They had been in the lead that day and stopped for a moment to admire the glare of sunlight from it.

When they reached it both of them jumped off their horses and had to grab a handful of the white stuff. The chill on their hands made them drop it.

Joskin and Carrita laughed at their friends. Joskin dismounted, grabbed a handful of it and balled it up. He threw it and hit his cousin squarely in the ribs. The white substance shattered against his armor.

Airria stood in place looking from Joskin to the substance. Eventually he asked, "Snow?"

"Yes," Joskin answered.

Airria picked up some more snow and made his own ball and threw it at Joskin. A flurry of snow followed. The two played for some time while the girls watched.

It ended when some hit Faith. She realized this was a good time to get Airria. She pretended to be upset, grabbed a handful of the stuff and forced it down Airria's armor. Then she playfully mounted her horse and took off at a full run.

Airria was slow to react but finally jumped on his horse and began to chase her. The playful chase had only began, when Joskin yelled, reminding them they were looking for a camp site. The two gave up the game and returned to looking for a decent shelter.

Faith spotted a cave as the shadows were sliding down the mountains. Though she could not believe any place around here could be warm, it would be nice to get out of the wind. It looked big enough the horses could come in.

When the group arrived at the entrance, they noticed some tracks of a four-toed, giant humanoid. The human-like track had fluff marks around it, indicating it had hairy feet.

"What is it?" Airria asked.

Joskin replied in jest, "A footprint."

Airria took a quick, lazy swing at his cousin. "I could have guessed that. What is it a print of?"

354

Joskin responded only slightly more seriously, "Do I look like a tracking hound to you? Around here it could belong to any number of creatures." He climbed off his horse and examined the print more closely. "Most likely it is a troll track. It is several days old, so hopefully it's moved on."

Carrita asked, "Do you believe it is safe to stop here for the night?"

Joskin answered, "Yes, I think it should be safe for the night."

Airria jumped off his horse, "Good. My padding is wet." He cast a mock angry-look at Faith, "I need to dry it out."

Airria, as was usual, went first. He took his Orc-forged sword and shield. After twenty paces into the cave the sun's shadow passed its entrance.

Airria thought he could see three pairs of eyes not quite glowing in the back of the cave. Almost as quickly as he stepped into the cave the shadow passed. Shortly there-after there was a loud bang. Airria came tumbling out of the cave in the midst of a cloud of splinters.

Faith did not like the sounds she heard coming from the cave. They were deep growling sounds half-way between a dog and a pig. It was getting dark and she didn't know what to expect.

Airria got to his feet and prepared for a real fight. Joskin hopped off his horse and joined his cousin. Even Carrita slowly dismounted.

Faith was not about to be left out. She armed herself with her new bow and nocked a black arrow. She followed the group in, but stopped when she saw the creatures. They were twice Airria's height, covered in ratted brown hair, had a long, hairy, hog-like snout and ram-like horns curling down to the bottom of their jaws.

"Trolls!" Carrita and Joskin said in unison as they noticed them.

Joskin took a step back.

Carrita yelled, "Cover your eyes!"

Before Faith could react, there was a flash of bright light. The grunting-growl stopped immediately, but Faith could see nothing of what was happening. She drew her bow, listened and reached out with her magic. She could feel Airria, Joskin and Carrita's magic. All she heard was Joskin and Airria backing against the sides of the cave.

After a while she could hear the clattering of sticks. She felt the warmth of Fire magic and then the soft crackle of a fire.

It took some time, but her sight did return. Carrita was sitting on a small stone near a clumsy fire in the middle of stone statues which looked exactly like the trolls.

Faith helped Airria and Joskin to the fire. They were still blinking and rubbing their eyes. Faith turned to Carrita, "What was the light for? It blinded all of us."

"Mother said light was the easiest way to fight trolls," Carrita had a look of childish innocence about her. It had been weeks, maybe even months since she had looked so young.

Joskin responded, "It definitely did the trick, but next time could you give us more warning?"

Carrita giggled, "You should have been faster."

Airria got up and walked to the back of the cave, Faith followed. They found a small trove of treasure, weapons and armor. There were two females' breastplates, one small enough for Carrita, except it was made for a more womanly figure. The other was big enough for Joskin to wear and had enough space between the shoulder and the bottom strap for three arms to fit comfortably. To the side of the armor were three swords which were unusual. Two of them had blades as long as Airria's leg and only as wide as two finger joints. One was smaller, a good size for Carrita. The odd part was, all three were bladed only on one side and only slightly curved. They looked to be light and had unusually long handles made of ornately decorated tusks of trolls. Both the armor and the sword handles were beautifully decorated.

Airria held the smaller sword up to Carrita, "It is a good size for you."

Carrita rolled her eyes, "What would I do with a sword?"

"I could teach you to use it," Airria insisted.

Carrita put a hand on his armor. "Do you believe a sword would assist me in any way?"

Steam began rising out of the cracks in his armor. He grit his teeth and his eyes opened wide.

356

Faith laughed as Airria began dancing around. She said, "I guess your armor is dry now?"

When he finished his dance he patted his armor. "I guess that problem is solved."

Joskin took the small sword. "Carrita, there is no doubt you are great with your magic. There have been times you couldn't use it, though. We would feel more comfortable if you would just carry a physical weapon."

Her lip pouted out, "Very well, but I will not be training with it."

Joskin and Airria seemed satisfied, so Faith began examining the armor. It was solid and reflected as well as silver. It was light, almost half the weight she expected. The decoration was elegant and reminded her of the wind blowing.

After a moment Faith asked Carrita, "Did you not tell me once of elves who could forge silver as strong as steel, but much less weight?"

Joskin grabbed the larger chestplate off the ground. "You think this belonged to an elf?" He went quiet, hefting the plate and inspecting it closer.

Carrita returned to the fire, "I have seen chain of the silver. My mother had several items she received as gifts from the elves. I thought nothing of them at the time I saw them, but you may be right. Perhaps it would be best to return the items to the elves who made them."

Joskin held up the chestplate he was holding, "This was not worn by any elf I've ever heard of. It's not big enough for a giant and far too big for any of the humanoids I have encountered."

Carrita looked into the fire, "There are many creatures to encounter in this world. Mother had a library dedicated only to the many creatures she had encountered. I have not had time to examine the entirety of them."

Faith wanted to alleviate the tension she could feel forming. She held up the smaller plate and said, "If an elf wore this, I am definitely not an elf."

Airria tilted his head and smiled.

Faith had expected more of a laugh and she blushed when Airria stared. Even more uncomfortable, she began tying the armor and two larger weapons to Carrita's horse. When finished she went back to the fire and thought about what else could be out there.

The night in the cave was the last good rest they had for some time. For weeks the group spent their time trudging up and down snow covered mountains, often the snow rose up to the gigantic horses' mid-chests. From time to time the wind would almost blow Carrita off her horse.

About three weeks after the group saw the first of the snow, they found a solid path in the snow. The horses seemed to move much quicker on the solid white trail. As Faith could not walk on the trail, she wondered if the orc had done something special to the horses' shoes.

The group followed the trail for several more days, spending their nights in snow huts they found along the trail. Each hut was large enough for the horses to come in and they were stocked with feed resembling mushroom-grass. By this time the horses were looking ragged and Joskin was living off the same feed as the horses.

One morning Faith, in the lead, saw some giant snake tracks on the icy trail. *What could make tracks like these*, she thought to herself, *is it possible a snake could live this high in the mountains, especially one of such size?* She got off her horse to check it out.

As Faith scanned the area she noticed snow covered rocks erupting through the snow with covered white bushes in military precision, flanking the rocks. As a glint of sunlight found its way through the clouds, she wondered for a moment if she had seen a touch of armor in the bushes.

She shrieked as she noticed the shadows seemed to be moving, as did some of the bushes. Her head shifted around. Her eyes caught hold of a beautiful woman with six arms, white skin and long black hair. She could only see her from the waist up, but all she was wearing was a silver plate similar to the one they had found in the cave. Four of the troll tusk handles stuck out from behind her and two of them were attached to her waist.

Faith's eyes moved to the other shifting bushes and shadows. She was amazed to see how the hair, skin and armor contrast could work as camouflage in the snow. She noticed two others armed as heavily as

358

the first. There were four more with two swords, three with four swords and one with only one staff. The one with a staff had only a furry leather chest support for covering.

As the creatures closed in she noticed the body below the waist resembled the black back and white belly of a snake.

Faith looked back at the rest of the group. The horses were lying down; each rider was trying to get off before the horse lay on them. Only Persephone stood. Faith quickly rode back to Carrita and readied her bow.

Carrita quietly motioned to Faith to put her bow down. "Naga," she whispered, "they are the defenders of the mountains. They won't kill us."

The snake women moved rapidly in the snow, in spite of the drifts they had to crush to move. As Joskin and Airria readied for battle, only the three best armed naga moved in. Their movements were so fast the men had a hard time keeping an eye on them. Two of them drew their swords.

The creatures were obviously only interested in the men and were moving quite aggressively. Faith was worried for her friends. More so, they moved blindingly fast. Even with magic weapons, Faith and the men would struggle defending themselves.

One of the creatures swung at Airria. He was quickly driven onto the crusted snow; luckily he was small and light enough to stay on top. The blows from the naga came so fast and hard all he could do was retreat, the blows to his shield throwing him off balance.

Another naga struck at Joskin with two of her swords, but soon found that she needed four of her weapons to defend herself. A blur of silver ensued. This creature began driving Joskin backwards, the constant blows flying too swiftly for Faith to follow. The fight continued for several moments and ended with one pair of swords holding the ax head, the second set holding the handle, pinning the ax against Joskin's grounded body. The third set of swords was placed at Joskin's throat.

When Joskin went down, Airria seemed to gain courage and strength. Within a few strokes the naga was no longer manipulating his movements. Within a few more strokes he actually drew blood.

The injury, though only a scratch, seemed to ignite a fire in the naga's eyes. She began to fight like she was possessed. The bladed fury began driving Airria back again.

Three of the blades caught the shield directly, forcing Airria to take the full power of the blow. They ground across the front, causing a shower of sparks and a loud screech. As the blade slid by, Faith could see gashes cut through the shield. Another deadly assault grazed across the shield as Airria ducked under the naga's blows, deflecting one of them. This time the sword peeled up a large section of the shield and became lodged in in it.

Faith began to raise her bow, but Carrita brought her arm back down.

Airria's shield ripped from his arm. He rolled back and jammed his sword into the crusty snow. Then he put his hands in the air, palms toward his attacker. The naga began her swing, stopping with a blade at each of Airria's limbs and one at his heart. The fire into her eyes was still raging, "Cheap trick." The fury in her face seemed to directly pass in her words, for she calmed down.

A third naga who had approached them without Faith noticing, apparently the group commander, said with sincerity, "Impressive fighting for men, but more important, intelligent actions."

Joskin, still pinned, blurted out, "That is an opinion not shared by all."

The commander laughed and called the other two back to her. They picked up the men's weapons and placed themselves behind the leader. When they were in position, the commander said to the girls, "I am Bastraya, High commander of her majesty, Queen Santrina's Royal Guard. We are looking for a couple of young members of a patrol. They have been lost for over a month. Could you help us in any way?"

Carrita took a step forward. "These missing individuals, would they happen to be an elf and a naga?"

"Yes," came the simple reply.

Carrita went to the back of her horse and untied the armor, "Did these belong to the elf?" She held them toward Bastraya.

One of the naga from the side rapidly slithered in and gently took it from Carrita. When the commander had inspected the armor she cast a suspicious glance at the men, "Where did you get this?"

Carrita answered quickly, "A troll cave down the mountain."

Bastraya looked at Carrita for a long moment, then, satisfied Carrita was telling the truth, she said, "Come to Carodilice, my home city. Your horses could use the food and rest."

Carrita stopped the nagas before she turned, "I also have this," she pulled out the elf's sword.

Bastraya looked at it for a moment, then said, "You keep it for now." She turned to the other naga and issued orders to bind the men but to leave their armor on. The commander had the girls bring the horses. The men were allowed to ride, but not allowed to hold the reins.

Chapter 15 – City of Ice

The naga city seemed to form out of the mountain. The walls surrounded the mountain top with large bulb-like towers at each of the corners and either side of the gate. The walls were made of brilliant, immense, white marble blocks with almost invisible silver seams. The wall reached more than ten time Airria's height.

When the group got within the city they were allowed, at Carrita's request, to pause their horses long enough to admire the craftsmanship of the gates. The white wood of the Elven island, Buzlin, looked to be made of two large boards. The wood was supported by silver hinges in the shape of a griffin.

Inside the walls the city was even more spectacular. The houses and shops were built of the same marble blocks with silver mortar and graceful artistry. The buildings were larger than the inns they had stayed in.

Carrita said under her breath, "I have heard of the family houses of the Snow Elves, but this is amazing."

The whole group quickly noticed that all of the elves and naga on the street were female, even all of the guards were female.

The group was led directly to the palace. The palace was smooth and rounded, a center spire surrounded by four smaller spires joining together for the first five floors. Two Elven men with hunched shoulders and no eye contact came to escort the horses to the stables.

Persephone pawed at the elf that tried to grab her reins.

Faith spoke directly to the elf, "I am sorry, she is very protective of me."

Bastraya responded, "It is truly rare to find an animal so dedicated to its owner."

Faith looked a little uneasy. She pet her horse's nose. "Sometimes I wonder if I am hers, not the other way around."

"Either way she will be well tended," Bastraya promised.

The walls of the palace halls were covered with ice, light emanated from them. In the frequent alcoves there were exquisite stone statues of naga and Snow Elves.

The group was led down white stairs for what seemed like forever. At the bottom of the stairs was a hall big enough for a frost giant to walk through comfortably. At the end of the hall there were two life sized statues of human men. The group stopped to stare as they noticed the statues' glow. Airria was surprised the naga were not pushing him.

Carrita's eyes were wide and her mouth open slightly. She whispered, "Forged moonlight?"

Faith looked at her, confused, but said nothing.

It sounded as if these creatures could actually transform the light of the moon into tangible objects, Airria would have to ask about it later.

The escorts opened the double doors to the queen's council room. The rooms made the hallway seem small. At the hallway ceiling height there was a terrace surrounding the room. In the center, on the far side of the room, was the throne.

The queen was resting on the throne. She was armored similar to the guards, except that her breastplate was of the same material as the statues. On her right was a naga with a small leather chest support and two large white staves, obviously this was the head mage. On the queen's immediate left was a human man in full armor also made from the forged moonlight. He had a two-handed, forged moonlight sword in his hands, the hilt resting against his chest.

To the head mage's right was a Snow Elf warrior clad like the human male, except with two naga style swords. The sword handles were pure silver inlaid with a golden spiral. The blades were of forged moonlight and readied for a fight.

To the left of the fighter was an elf unlike any the group had seen in town. Her hair was long, silky brown. Her skin was far darker than the elves in town, almost to the tint of a tan human. She had eyes like emeralds and was dressed in a long green robe with white trim. A green, woman looking, marble golem, twice the mage's height, stood behind her. The mage had a green crystal staff in her right hand.

Bastraya, who had headed the party, took a note to the queen, bowing two paces in front of her, then handing her the note.

The queen opened it and took a moment to read it. She motioned to the knight beside her, when he leaned over to her she whispered something in his ear.

"Who's blade was chipped?" the man said to the naga guards.

The naga who had fought Joskin slithered forward and pulled one of her swords.

"Where is the weapon you chipped it on?" the man showed no emotion.

A naga slithered forward from the back of the group carrying the men's weapons and handed them to the knight. The knight examined Joskin's axe, then the naga's sword. "This is gold forged by an orc, enchanted to appear as a common weapon," he said, still showing no emotion.

The mage to the side of the queen examined Airria's sword. After a moment she looked up with a twinge of anger in her eyes, "The enchantment on this sword was created through dark means."

The green mage stepped forward, "A necessary evil," the green mage was looking at Carrita.

Carrita hid behind Faith.

"Untie the men," the queen commanded. The back guards slithered forward and untied them.

Airria's shield was then examined by the knight. As the knight picked up the shield he smiled as he said, "I always wondered what would happen." He showed the queen the shield, running his finger down one of the slits. He continued, "We have always known that the orcs could forge silver harder than the elves."

The queen responded, "Now we know that our sword style is sufficient to compensate for the difference."

"Will you help us?" Faith interrupted in a humble tone.

"Help you with what?" the queen responded.

"We are looking for two sets of armor. They were last known to be in this mountain range, according to Jammar, the Light Bringer," Faith's voice was shaky, she kept looking back to Carrita.

"Jammar sent you to find armor?" The naga queen sounded surprised.

"Yes," Airria said, gaining confidence.

"We are the only creatures, outside of trolls and a few roaming bands of nomads, which live this high in the mountains and we rarely sell our armor," the queen said calmly.

Airria said, "These suits of armor were made centuries ago. They belonged to Theilord and his wife."

"Viehasia and her husband's armor? Either Jammar wanted you dead or you have an impossible task he cannot help you with." The queen began to smile, "We will help you, on condition that your men can prove themselves." The queen spoke to the girls as though they owned the men.

"How can they prove themselves?" Faith asked.

"We will let you know in a couple of days. In the meantime, you two will be tutored by my mages and fighters. The men will be given a place to stay and be provided with room to prepare."

Airria began to protest, but was silenced by a glance from Joskin.

The group was led out, back up the stairs, to some rooms. The rooms presented to the girls were very nice. The walls were covered with elaborate tapestries. The lush bed was surrounded by a thick grey cloth. The naga who had taken them to their rooms showed them how to shut the window and raise the temperature in their rooms.

The men had to share a room with only a wooden box of straw for a bed. The stone walls were uncovered and a forbidding gray. The men had only begun to discuss the pathetic arrangements when there was a knock at the door.

When Airria opened the door, it was the knight from the throne chamber. The knight spoke, "I am Kore Tamarack, the second male in the naga's history who has gained their trust and respect."

Airria asked, "Why are you telling us this?"

"You do not know much about the naga do you?"

"I haven't even heard legends of them," Airria replied.

"They are strong believers that men are little better than work beasts or a comforting pet. The Snow Elves are more tolerant of males but only for dealing with outsiders. You two are fortunate to have these accommodations."

"How did you gain their respect?" Joskin piped in.

"I was a part of a group who defeated two major enemies of the naga, a lich and an enchantress." Kore's eyes carried a glint of pride, though his face showed almost no emotion.

"Were you the only man?" Airria's arrogance and ignorance of other races showed through his sarcasm.

"Yes, I was the only MAN, but I was not the only male. The others never showed enough respect or appreciation for what they received. It was my honor to serve and they have honored me in kind."

"What happened to the others?" Joskin asked with sincerity.

"After we had proven ourselves by destroying the enchantress and lich we were called before the Dragon Council."

The hair on the back of Airria's neck stood up. "Was Jarmack'Trastibbik there?"

"All of the High Dragons were there," Kore's eyes almost seemed to be jesting.

Airria could feel his blood heating up, "Where can I find her?"

366

"Is that why you are looking for Theilord's armor?" a smile crept across Kore's face.

"Will you help us?" Airria asked, trying to rein in his excitement.

"I cannot help you without the permission of the queen," Kore said, the corners of his mouth turned up slightly.

"Are you a slave?" Airria asked.

Kore jerked back, but calmly explained, "I am not her slave; I chose to serve her. The council gave us the option of where to serve, where to be Guardians. It was an easy choice for me. The Snow Elf and green mage you met were two others in the group."

Why did you come here today?" Joskin changed the subject.

"I was sent to find out why you have quested to this place and give a challenge or opportunity to prove yourselves. Both of you have already shown yourselves to be adequate fighters, but you will have to prove that you are exceptional, both physically and mentally. If you do not accept you will live in this room until the women you came with are ready to leave, then you will be escorted back the way you came. If you accept, the naga will help you.

Joskin quickly asked, "What will be the trials?"

"You have just passed the first one," Kore said. "The first test was to see if you would mindlessly take a challenge."

Airria slightly blushed, he had almost accepted. In an attempt to cover his near folly he asked, "What do I need to do?"

"You will have but one trial. You will fight, to the yield, the two best naga fighters," Kore said. "Be warned they may have assistance."

Airria remembered the beating he received at the hands of the last naga he fought. "Two?"

"An easy task, when compared with the purpose of your quest," Kore smiled.

"May I choose my weapons?" Airria hoped he would gain help from his magical sword and shield.

"Your shield has already proven veritably useless against the swords. The swords your opponents will be using are far better than the ones used to slice your shield."

367

"I have a backup on my horse."

"If it will give you confidence, I will have your equipment brought up to you." Kore paused for a moment to allow the smile to return to his face, "Do you accept then?"

"What help could they have?" Joskin asked.

"Each naga will be allowed to choose one to assist them."

"That would be four fighters!" Airria's voice cracked with fear.

"Still an easy task compared to a fight with Jarmack'Trastibbik. It would be a simpler task to fight this entire city than the dragon you have chosen. She is faster than lightning, more magical than all the lords combined and stronger than the hosts of all thirteen hells. If you can't win this fight, the armor you seek cannot help you enough. We will not willingly donate the armor to any Black Dragon's loot pile." Kore's face now showed sincere concern.

"You leave me little choice." Airria was beginning to doubt his abilities.

"You have three days to prepare." Kore then turned to Joskin, "You will have two more trials. The second will depend on how well you do on the first. Your first trial will be a maze with traps and shifting walls. Do you accept?"

Joskin would rather have fought Airria's fight, "I accept."

Kore turned to walk out the door, "Your equipment will be brought up immediately. Your first trial will be tomorrow." When he reached the door he added, "If you pass your first trial, you will gain enough respect to get better accommodations."

When their stuff arrived Airria pulled out his sword and shield and sat in a corner as if to meditate. He began to explain to the sword what had happened to them and the challenges.

Do you have any idea the task you have accepted? said the sword.

Not really, that is why I have come to you, Airria returned.

The naga are one of the most powerful creatures in the known world and I will not be able to help you.

Why not? in his desperation, Airria almost spoke the words out loud.

They are good, they live in these mountains to destroy trolls and protect the helpless.

"I need to pass this test so they will help us get Theilord's armor!" Airria's words came out vocally. Joskin looked at him funny, but said nothing.

This sword and shield are well crafted and you are well skilled for your youth. I will not distract from your skill, but I cannot help with this. It will have to be your skill against theirs. The shield will defend you against magic and projectiles, though.

Airria thought it interesting that the voice from the sword spoke for the first time as though it and the sword were not the same. More to the point, he found little comfort in what the sword had told him. He spent the rest of the evening going through his drills, trying not to keep Joskin up.

Chapter 16 - Help

Faith looked around her room. The lush bed was covered with thick white blankets. One wall was covered with basic books of magic and history. Against the wall between the bed and the bookshelves was a desk supplied with ink, writing parchment, scroll parchment and scroll writing supplies. On the other side of the room was a large tub filled with flowing water with crystals to one side. The wall by the door had similar crystals.

"May we help you with anything?" one of Faith's two escorts asked. "We understand this is your first visit to our city. We have been instructed to help you with anything we have the ability to grant."

Faith was not sure how to process these two. She was not sure if they were sent to keep an eye on her or if they were truly for her assistance. They were both slightly taller than Carrita and moved very elegantly. They both seemed very honest and attentive. "What are your names?" Faith finally asked. She made a conscious choice to trust these two.

One of them stepped forward. "My name is Centris and this is Karen."

It had been several months since Faith had had a bath. The water in the tub looked so refreshing. While she put her hand in it to test the temperature she asked, "How long have you been slaves here?"

Centris laughed, "We are not slaves. We are servants. I personally have served Her Majesty for over three hundred years."

Faith spun around, both Joskin and Carrita had talked about the long lives of elves, but somewhere inside she had not believed it. She tried to hide her surprise, but it was not working.

Though both elves had a glint of amusement in their eyes, neither said anything about Faith's reaction. Karen asked, "Is the water too chilly for you? Shall I show you how to adjust the temperature?"

"Yes, please," Faith answered.

The elves showed her how to warm and cool the water by rubbing the stones on either side of the tub; they then sat on the bed while Faith adjusted the water and climbed in. The three of them started out with light conversation of Faith's history; where she learned her magic, where she came from, why she was traveling with Airria and Joskin.

After a while Faith's curiosity got the better of her, she asked, "Why do your people and the naga look down on men?"

Centris replied, "Men are inferior." The confused look on her face told Faith that these people felt this statement to be self-evident.

"Why do you consider men to be inferior?"

"Among the naga, the men are smaller, weaker and only have two arms. They also carry less ability to learn and use magic. The naga have taught us the power of magic. Women carry a stronger affinity with magic. Magic gives us strength to defend ourselves. Therefore, the women rule." The elf appeared very proud.

"But the Elven men are physically stronger, are they not?" Faith asked.

"The men take care of many of the physical chores and help with much of the child rearing."

"What will happen to the men I came in with?"

"They are lucky to be alive."

371

"Why?"

"Artana, second in command for the naga militia, does not take well to men she cannot control."

Faith wanted to explain how much Airria and Joskin had done for her and how Carrita's magic was not enough alone, but felt this was not the time. She was also enjoying this change of conversation. She was so fascinated with the white skinned elves and the six-armed snake women.

Karen changed the subject. "I understand you were brought before the queen. What did she tell you?"

"She spoke little to me." Faith paused for a moment then asked, "She talked about 'fighting style.' What is different about the way you are taught to fight?"

"I can't explain the difference, because I have only ever known the one style. One thing I understand is that strength is less important than speed. In a strength based physical confrontation, men will almost always win, except for among the naga, of course. I understand that is why outside of the naga culture women are often thought of as second class fighters and often little better than beasts. That is why we train the way we do."

"Could you teach me?"

"I am not much of a teacher, but I will arrange for you to get some lessons from the weapons master. Will you be up for it tomorrow?"

"Yes, I would be glad of it," Faith said, then added, "Thank you." She halfway expected the servants to give some sign of surprise, but it almost seemed as though it was commonplace for them to receive appreciation.

"Do you mind if I ask you a personal question?" Faith asked.

"Please, you are welcome to ask anything you would like," Centris responded.

"How did you come to be a servant to the queen?"

"I was hired when I was very young, perhaps almost sixty-five."

"How old are you?" Faith remembered she had been a servant for a few centuries, but to hear her talk of sixty-five as being young was a little mind boggling.

372

"Four hundred twenty seven years this spring."

"Are you content as a servant?" Faith asked.

"Yes, the queen is very good to us, she has never treated either of us as slaves," Centris said.

Karen added, "Normally she treats us more like friends."

Faith spent the rest of the evening talking casually with the servants. Even when her bath was finished they continued talking about the wonders of the city and offering to show them all.

As the sunlight peeked through her window, Karen said, "I will go ask the weapons master if she can teach you. Perhaps you can stay for some time and learn to be an amazing warrior in your own right." Without waiting for a response she left the room.

Centris bowed low, "I am sorry. We have taken your entire evening. Perhaps you should rest before you begin training. I understand humans need more sleep than elves."

Faith smiled at the courteous servant. "I will be fine. Thank you for an informative and enjoyable evening."

"Is there anything I can get for you to make your stay more comfortable?"

"Thank you for your offer, but for now I would like to see my young friend. I will send for you if I require anything else," Faith bowed respectfully.

As Centris slipped through the door she said, "The offer is true, you are welcome to remain with us for as long as you can. You are very welcome here."

Faith waited a moment for the servant to leave then made her way to Carrita's room. She figured Carrita would have been caught up in all the books in the room. As she opened the door to her room she saw the mage in the green robe leaving. She waited for the mage to disappear around a corner and then ran across the hall.

Carrita was reading when Faith opened the door. "Carrita, what did the mage want with you?"

"To talk," Carrita said very casually.

"About what?" Carrita's evasiveness was beginning to frustrate Faith.

"Magic," a small grin slipped across Carrita's face, her pride showing through.

Faith could see Carrita's pride, but didn't want to push her frustration any further. She did want to know what it was they talked about but figured it was over her head or that she would have to pry harder than she wanted to to get the information. "They said they would teach me to fight their way," Faith let a big grin cross her face.

"What is wrong with what Airria has taught you?" Carrita still felt that Faith's time would be better spent leaning magic, but had no way to convince her.

"He has taught me a lot about fighting with swords, but with his style. Men, with their strength, have the advantage."

"Yes?"

"According to the elves I talked to last night, the naga's style takes this advantage away from them."

"How?"

"I did not understand their explanation."

Carrita's face changed to a more distant look. "Do you trust them?"

"Why should we not? You seemed to trust them when they attacked the group," Faith was surprised by her own question.

"Until I met them I was becoming very confident in my abilities." Carrita stared at the floor, "They know better than I do how powerful I am." She looked into Faith's eyes, "Unlike most people I have met who find out I am a mage, they have no fear of me or what I can do. They even seem to want to help me." Her eyes shifted back to the floor, "I do not understand."

"I am not sure I understand." Faith thought Carrita would be excited at the chance to learn from someone better than she.

"In my experience people do not give without expecting something in return."

"What do you think Airria expected when he freed you from those thugs on the island? What did you think I expected from caring for you? What return do you think Joskin expected for the fortune he spent on healing and protecting you?" After all Joskin and Airria had done

374

without asking anything, Carrita's attitude shocked Faith. "The magic and friendship were bonuses. We all did what we thought was best. Not for reward or compensation, but because it was the thing we felt needed to be done." She got up and turned to leave without another word.

Carrita ducked her head. "I am sorry. You are correct. You have asked nothing of me. I have even tried to force my own enjoyments on you. Neither Airria nor Joskin has asked anything of me. Joskin has spent a fortune."

Faith was happy to see Carrita learning more than just magic. She instinctively gave Carrita a hug.

A knocking across the hall brought Faith to the door to investigate. Karen was there. "The weapons master is ready for you. She has volunteered to teach you personally."

Carrita asked, just loud enough for Faith to hear, "Why are they being so helpful to us, but demand to run the men though some sort of test?"

Karen apparently had exceptional hearing because she answered, "I don't know all of the details, but it is very rare for us to meet a male of any real use, but if I overheard correctly, only the one with red hair will need to pass any test."

"Why only him?" Faith asked.

Karen looked up and down the hall, "It seems Kore, the man the queen trusts discovered something this morning. I do not know what, but they were going to cancel the trials altogether. If Artana had not demanded she have the opportunity to fight him, they would have been given better rooms."

"Why would she demand a fight with him when the queen had deemed him worthy to help?"

Karen laughed lightly. "If he was the one to give her the cut on her face, then he is the first fighter of any race to touch her with a blade in more years then I have been alive. That is more than enough reason for her to want to challenge him."

Carrita asked from behind Faith, "What happens if Airria fails, or loses the combat?"

Karen put a hand on her chin. "He has to accept first. No man is that stupid. Even the trolls run when Artana approaches."

Faith's heart sank. There was no way Airria would turn down such a challenge. "What if he is so foolish?"

"Then he will become her personal slave," Karen's eyebrows were raised. "With Artana, his slavery would mean death. She doesn't like men at all."

Faith did not want to discuss this any further. "Perhaps I should meet with your weapons master."

Karen escorted Faith to the naga's training facility to get some pointers. The room was large enough to put a small town inside. There was a sand track around the outside and miscellaneous posts and other training implements.

In the middle of the training area was a huge rack of assorted combat and training weapons. Karen took her to one of the Elven weapons masters and stood and waited for acknowledgement.

While two of the Elven maidens were sparring, the master turned to Karen and said, "May I help you?"

"Here is the human you asked to train," came the reply.

The master stopped the sparring and had the elves kneel to the side, then she collected the training weapons. As she handed one to Faith she said, "Let's see what I have to work with."

There was almost no pause before the master took a swing. Faith barely got her sword up in time to defend herself. The attacks were far different than any Airria had showed her and she couldn't find a way to go on the offensive. After a short while Faith cast a quick spell to block the master's weapon. She felt her spell taken away from her, it never took physical form.

When Faith's arms began to tire, the master stopped, "Not bad for a human, though by your spell I could tell you have little practical experience."

"What do you mean, 'little experience?'"

"You didn't even try to disguise your spell," the master said, "and you assumed I wouldn't be able to counter it. Outside of these walls a mistake like that could cost you your life." She paused for a moment, then asked, "May I see your personal weapon?"

Faith looked suspiciously at the master, "Why?"

"So I can see what type of weapon you will be using."

Faith began to unsheathe her sword. The master stopped her, "That blade is of Orc make. As long as you use that weapon you are on a lower footing than men. I am surprised you defended yourself so well considering you learned to fight with such a crude weapon."

Faith shot back, "This weapon is of the finest Orc silver. There are few weapons to compare, I assure you."

"I meant no offence. It is of tremendous strength and, I am sure, balance, but it is designed to be in a man's world, used by men. It was not the quality of the weapon, it is the style."

Faith had no idea how to respond to such a comment.

"If you will allow me I will demonstrate." The master stepped back and pointed to one of the students, "You are equally strong to Shessa." She then handed the young elf her own sword and added, "Try to hit her in the head."

Faith questioned the sanity of this test, but the elf confidently stood up and took the sword. Faith swung her blade. The blow felt as though Faith had hit a tree. The vibrations in her hands almost made her drop her sword. The elf on the other hand had already begun her counterstrike.

Faith pivoted toward the oncoming blade and placed her sword in position to block. The Elven blade sparked as it slid across the blade and stopped short of Faith's throat. After she recovered from her shock, she noticed the scratch mark in her blade.

Faith could do nothing but stand in amazement at how easily her opponent had just defeated her. Almost as amazing to her was this iron blade had marked her blade in a way Joskin could not.

The master spoke up, "The extended handle gives the ability to block heavy blows and the slight curve in the blade gives the ability to keep a fluid motion at all times without letting down your defense."

"Can you teach me?"

"That takes time and a change of weapons. To teach you correctly would take years." The master paused and then asked, "How long have you been training with that sword?"

"Almost a year," came Faith's simple reply.

"That is impressive. Have you had any other weapons training?"

"I am good with a bow."

"You must have had an excellent instructor to bring you so far so fast."

"One of the men we have been traveling with taught me."

"A man taught you? What did that cost?" The master's voice was filled with contempt.

Faith didn't like how pointed the question was, "It cost me only hard work!"

"There are not many men like that," the master now looked truly impressed.

Faith's thoughts drifted to all of Airria's good points, "No, there are not many men like him."

"Can you fight with either hand?" the master said to bring her back to the training area.

"I am not very good with my left hand."

"I will show you a few rhythmic patterns to work on with some sticks." The master waved towards the weapon rack, then waited until the other student ran and brought it to her. The master then continued, "If you are up to it I will teach you a few moves within our style of fighting. Use what I teach, experiment with what you have already learned and you will do ok in the men's world."

Faith spent until midday training and only stopped long enough to watch Airria's challenge.

Chapter 17 - Astral

Carrita went straight to the books on her wall. Most of them were books about the understanding of Order, Ice and Air deities and principles. The rest were on highland survival and creatures. She was disappointed not to have something on magic. Sadly, she picked out a book on the element of Ice. It was poorly scripted, or at least far worse than Jammar's books but not as bad or difficult to read as the minotaur's had been.

She didn't even notice the Snow Elf servants come in. They patiently waited by the door, watching her read.

Before Carrita finished her book, one of the servants fell asleep. The sound of the elf hitting the floor almost made Carrita drop her book.

Carrita spun around and prepared to defend herself. "May I help you?" her voice carried a slight shiver.

The elf who was still standing said, "We were sent to assist you with anything we can." The other elf, which had obviously fallen asleep, stood back up.

Carrita reached out with her magic to feel the servants. Sure enough both of them were magically awake and somewhat trained. She didn't like the idea of having possible mages around who might spy on what she was doing, although she trusted the naga more than she had anybody outside of the group for a long time. Faith was the only individual that Carrita trusted completely so she sent the servants away and continued reading.

Carrita was pulled from her reading a second time by one of the Elven servants. It was breakfast, rich sautéed mushrooms and a warm, light and flaky meat she did not recognize. "We do have a magic library, if that would suit you better. The books provided are only meant for light readers."

Carrita felt ashamed for not trusting the naga enough to ask for better reading material. They had done nothing to cause her distrust and everything she had read and heard about them said they should be trusted. She was digging deeper into magic and didn't want people to know. Her mother had warned her about gaining too much knowledge too quickly, she supposed this was where the paranoia came from. She apologized to the elf for her lack of consideration the night before.

The elf smiled and bowed, "Bregette the Green Mage has been waiting for your trust. I will get her now." The elf turned to leave then stopped and said without turning back, "You have nothing to fear from us," then she left.

A short time later there was a knock at the door. "Come in," Carrita answered. None of the servants had knocked, Carrita was curious why the knocking.

Bregette came in, "How was your evening?"

"I was a little disturbed at first, when I saw there were no books on real or deeper magic. After I started reading I realized I have been neglecting my studies of the elements of magic. This has been a very educational experience."

"Would you like to continue reading or would you like to learn more about the Astral Plane?" Bregette asked simply. "It is in your eyes. Only those who have been there carry your understanding and only those with understanding can go," she said as if she could read Carrita's mind.

She paused for a moment, then continued with a hint of pride, "I can teach you magic in ways you cannot yet understand. Through the Astral Plane I can teach you faster than even Jammar."

"How is it possible?" Carrita asked.

Bregette's smile was gentle and welcoming. "The same way your mother did for me."

"You knew my mother?" Carrita asked. She knew she shouldn't be surprised. She had encountered so many in the last year who knew of her mother. This was only the third who had implied she had met her.

"Of course," Bregette took a step closer to Carrita. One cannot travel the roads I have trod for as long as I have and not take the opportunity to meet the being even the high deities speak reverently about.

Bregette reached out. Carrita recoiled on instinct. There was no reason for Carrita not to trust this woman except she didn't know her.

"You will have to trust me or even I can do nothing to help you."

"What do I need to do?" Carrita asked, folding her arms across her chest.

"I cannot tell you. It is something that has to be seen," Bregette said stepping back. "If you decide you want to try I can bring you to the mage dueling area. When you are ready, there will be an elf waiting outside."

"Am I a prisoner to my room?"

"No, far from it. The elf is a guide and a messenger. If you wish to venture on your own, you are welcome. Though I warn you this city is very large and it is easy to get lost. If you do get lost, only mention my name and anyone will help you back to the palace."

"Why have you been so generous to us?" Carrita asked. She wished she could feel more comfortable, but it was obvious this woman knew far more then she was allowing to be heard or seen.

"We always take good care of our female visitors. The extra attention to you and Faith is at my request. I could tell through your enchantments that you are an extraordinary mage, but you are so young. I was curious as to how you became so powerful. I know your mother was the most amazing teacher and I have a feeling my tutelage of you on the Astral Plane will not be your first, only the first you will remember of it."

"Maybe I will accept your offer sometime. For now I need to read more about the workings of Ice."

"When you are ready I will be waiting," Bregette's voice reminded Carrita of her mother's.

Bregette bowed elegantly and left. Carrita decided to examine the city as the green clad mage had suggested, but did not want anyone to see her looking about. On the ship, she had become quite adept and comfortable walking the Plane. In this form, no one had been able to see her. Also she would always be able to find her way back.

As she walked, she paid special attention to the auras of the people. All of them produced auras of honesty. They were very devout in their religion Order, Ice and Life. Even the naga were solid in color patterns.

Slightly before midday she noticed someone walking beside her. She jumped with surprise when she noticed. It was Bregette.

The mage stated, "Fascinating, is it not, every one of the naga look almost the same from this vantage point. There are a few we worry about." She looked exactly the same in her astral form as she did in the flesh.

"How long have you been with me?"

"I have been with you for much of your trek."

"Why did you not let me know? Were you worried I would learn something I was not meant to see?" This was her first time talking to anyone on the Plane. The words transferred without filter. There was no chance of deception here.

"You wanted to see more than could be seen with natural eyes. You wanted to see what you would not have dared if you knew I was here. I will be honored to show you even more than you would know to look for." The mage seemed happy to see Carrita's curiosity and showed no sign of offence. "I have been waiting to see if you would like to learn more about magic."

"Let me get my body," Carrita said starting her way back.

"I can teach you better here, like this." Bregette's face became more serious, "I would ask that you teach me in return."

"What can I teach you?" Carrita asked. "You are already a far better mage than I. I cannot imagine there is much about magic I can teach you."

"You would be surprised what you have to offer." Bregette looked intensely into Carrita's eyes, "What you did in making those enchantments is something I have never been able to do."

Carrita looked at the ground, "As your mage friend said, it took dark magic to accomplish."

"I am lacking in understanding of Death," Bregette said. I have studied enchantments for more millennia then the elves have records. Still the ability has eluded me."

"It is difficult for me to believe you would not know anything I came to understand in a short transport," Carrita responded.

"You were able to use someone else's magic to enchant things. You destroyed lives, wicked lives, to bring comfort and safety to your friends," Bregette said this in a sincere voice. "Your methods may be considered unorthodox, but what you have accomplished is for the greater good."

"Only one orc's life was destroyed for those enchantments."

I had guessed it was orc essence I felt sustaining those enchantments," Bregette said. "The one who died, he must have been a powerful shaman."

"He was a pirate captain."

"You are efficient!" the mage looked honestly impressed.

Carrita's pride crept in, "I also made five golems which are still on the ship."

"Did you use the orc in blood sacrifice to do so?"

"No!" Carrita's had not even considered such a line of reasoning although she could understand from what she had read how one might come to such a conclusion. "Do you consider me to be so cruel?"

"No, but you did use dark magic." Bregette paused for a moment then asked thoughtfully, "How did you do it?"

384

"We will make an agreement," Carrita suggested. "As long as we are in this city, you instruct me as you have promised and I will explain how I created the enchantments."

"I do not believe you fully understand why you were able to learn in a few months what I have been unable to in so long," Bregette said with a knowing smile, "nevertheless; I believe you will be able to help me with what I have not understood. For now we must return. Airria, one of the men you came in with, has accepted a challenge to dual Artana in the arena in a short while."

"I assumed as much. As fair warning, he has a shield and sword which are incredibly powerful," Carrita said in the spirit of full disclosure.

"We have been made aware," Bregette said in response. "He has somehow found favor in the eyes of the Guardian of Weapons."

"The favor has been well earned and at great cost," Carrita said.

Bregette looked over her shoulder. "Perhaps it is time to get back to our bodies."

Carrita began wandering back as she always had, as if she were walking.

Bregette stopped her. "Perhaps we have time for one quick lesson. You are controlled by your mind here. You can travel by thought. You can arm yourself by believing. In this place your quick mind will give you an edge over most."

"Thank you for your assistance," Carrita said as she concentrated on returning to her body. Rapidly she was flung though the halls and to her body. She was elated because of her discovery, but worried for Airria.

When she made her way out of her room she was met by a servant who guided her to the arena. Carrita was greeted at the arena by a young naga woman with a small silver crown. "Mother told me to escort you to her side."

When they arrived Faith was already sitting with an empty chair between her and the queen. Joskin was standing, talking to the male knight. Carrita supposed Airria was getting ready for his fight.

The competitors entered the arena. Carrita was expecting a loud cheer, but the only noise she heard were Airria's footsteps in the snow. She quickly slipped into the Astral Plane to see what discipline of thought was dominating Artana's mental state. The snake woman's aura was a thick golden cloud with black and white streaks, like lightning, across it. *She will fight honorably. She is out for Airria's death, but will submit if she loses,* Carrita thought to herself.

When Airria stepped into the arena it fell silent. Hundreds had come to see the "man who struck Artana." Airria appeared nervous, not his usual overconfident self. He was swinging his sword around and rolling his shoulders.

The naga was circling her victim, watching him closely. She'd jerk inward then weave back out.

Airria kept his sword sheathed for quite awhile. His eyes were fixed on his opponent. When she would weave in, he would brace, but always kept his eyes focused.

The queen put a finger on her ear. She kept tilting her head. Finally she said, "Your man has not attacked. The account Artana gave made him sound far more aggressive."

After this dance had continued for some time, Artana drew all six of her swords. Each blade was forged in the classical Naga style, except that they were forged of pure moonlight. She wielded them in perfect harmony and rhythm.

In turn, Airria pulled his sword. The blade erupted into a white flame. Unexpectedly he almost dropped it. He glanced at it for a moment, the naga used the opportunity to send two small lightning bolts, she seemed undeterred by the flaming sword.

His shield absorbed the energy of the bolts with ease. The naga then started again circling him while he maintained his defensive posture.

Without any more warning the naga coiled her tail and seemed to fly in. A blur of white fire and translucent blue swirled together in a magical dance. Each blow knocked Airria a different direction. Only his shield kept him from being hit. Blue sparks flew into the air.

With all the naga's training Airria found a weakness, if he stayed low he could deflect her swords' upward. Soon he was standing his ground, circling to keep the massive snake woman from driving him.

The naga retaliated by swinging lower. When she did he leapt her sword and swung with his, there was an explosion of blue sparks, the entire crowd gasped.

The queen put her hand on her chest. "I have never seen a weapon with the strength to break one of our moonlight weapons. This is devastating."

Kore and Bregette were standing, more interested than surprised.

The large snake woman backed off, her eyes fixed on her broken weapon. After a moment she screamed. She quickly dashed around the arena. Suddenly she stopped in front of Airria, her eyes fill with fear, the remaining five swords fell to the ground.

Airria put his sword away.

"What was once mine is now yours," the naga said with a respectful bow.

Airria dropped his shield on the ground and knelt. He was shaking. He said, "I ask only for training for my friend, two of your blades and help obtaining the armor I seek." He jumped as the crowd cheered.

The queen said in a reverent tone, "He played that well. He asked only for what you all would have received anyway. Today he earned the respect of my people.

Chapter 18 - Decisions

Two months after the fight in the arena the group was still living in the naga city. Faith had begun training in the naga style of swordplay, trained by Artana. Airria had an all day, all night training regimen using a wooden shield and sword. He was constantly sparring with the naga trainees, teaching and learning as much as possible. Joskin also took on a rigorous training schedule, sparring for a few hours a day using a mock-axe and sparring with naga trainees.

Carrita would shut herself in her room for weeks at a time. The few times Faith had checked the girl, she was sitting in her chair as if meditating, except her magic energy was uncharacteristically blaring. Carrita did not even seem to have time to teach Faith magic.

In order to be fast and accurate with her magic, Faith was required to use less armor then Airria or Joskin. Fortunately, Artana had taught her how to better use her magic in a fight. Now Faith knew better how to use her magic to protect her exposed limbs, as well as when to attack her opponent. She learned how to balance between her physical fighting and her magic.

She missed her archery practice, but found this new style of swordplay very interesting. It was more like a dance. It was elegant and precise. Unlike what she had learned from Airria, she had to balance and move. She depended more upon her movement then her weapon to defend herself.

Even the way she used her sword to attack was different. She was taught to use the whole length of the blade, to keep the blade in motion and dance around her opponent.

Airria was still far faster and more precise with his strikes, although his powerful hits no longer knocked her around. With her wooden practice blade she cut a slit in his mock shield. She would now be able to challenge him a small amount and help him when they sparred.

The next day Airria stopped his own training schedule to watch Faith for awhile. "It's time," he said, after Faith touched her sword to Artana's shoulder.

Artana distanced herself, breaking the conflict. "How do you learn so quickly?" she asked Faith. "You have mastered in a few months what should have taken years."

"Have you ever had a student as determined to learn as I have been?" Faith responded. She suspected the potion she had taken allowed her to advance her education at a rapid pace, though she hoped her dedication was helping.

"Airria has trained with them more extensively," Artana still struggled to say the name. Her teeth were clenched as she spoke it. "He has been relentless in his sparring. He has fought a wide variety of partners, including you. Yet you have progressed much quicker. You have even become proficient with two blades and the kata associated with them."

Faith smiled, hoping she looked more sure of herself then she felt. "Airria has practiced what he already knows. He has fought the same way he learned as a child. I have been learning. I have been working to bring my own talents into a new paradigm of fighting. I have been learning philosophy related to this style of fighting. Everything I have done has been to understand. Equally as important is I have had an incredible instructor."

Airria kicked the dirt on the ground. "It's more than that; your dedication has been greater than mine. This quest is very personal to me and Carrita, yet you are the one who learns so fast."

Faith pondered as she looked at the ground. She really had learned a tremendous amount. Even Kore had complimented her on her dedication. "You know, I left my sister behind. It is very personal to me as well."

Airria looked at Faith. He placed a hand on her shoulder. "Then, perhaps it's time for us to move on."

It was not fair. Airria was asking her if she was ready to move on. She had come on this quest to help, not lead. It was not her place to make decisions. This quest was more for Airria and Carrita. "Why do you leave it up to me to decide when we move on? I do tire of it."

Airria only smiled and looked at her for a moment. "Then perhaps you should get Carrita," he said, not really answering her question. He turned and walked away.

"You will not be able to rouse the young mage. She is walking the Astral Plane with Bregette. I will send for her. Perhaps you should gather your things."

Slowly Faith wandered the endless hallways leading from the training grounds. She was pondering her motives. Her sister had expected Faith to join the quest. Carrita had an incredible command of magic. Airria and Joskin could both fight with unbelievable skill. Much of the time she felt as though she was holding them back. They had stopped here, in this city, to allow her the opportunity to train.

She walked into her room and began preparing for travel. She picked up the swords Airria had received from Artana after his fight. The weapons were long and very difficult for her to control, yet she had kept them.

When she had begun this quest, she had understood her contributions would distance the group from their chance of failure. She had trained with the hope of returning to her sister in safety. Now she found her motive was to help Airria and Carrita return, even if she did not.

"They are nice weapons," Carrita startled Faith. "I wonder what you will do with all five of them and the silver one you brought with you. If you carry them all, with both your bows and all your arrows you would look like a seamstress' pin cushion," Carrita laughed at her small joke.

Faith had been a little sentimental with her weapons. The bow and arrows she had retrieved from the ship were the only weapons she was carrying with purpose and even the reason to carry them was becoming murky. "Perhaps it is time I let some of my weapons go. What would you suggest?"

Carrita smiled brightly, "As long as we are in this region you should keep your magic bow hidden. The silver sword no longer caters to you style of fighting. These weapons," Carrita pointed to the naga swords forged of pure moonlight, "are far too large to be practical for you. Perhaps you could convince the naga to make you something a little less extravagant."

A light knock at the door made Faith jump, she had not been expecting anyone and was still considering her options.

Without waiting for an answer Artana cracked the door. "Her majesty would like to talk with you before you continue on your journey."

When the girls arrived in the throne room, Airria and Joskin were already talking to Kore. Kore and Bregette were by the queen's side. Kore asked the men to come with him. Bregette asked Carrita to go with her. Faith turned to leave with Carrita, but was asked by the queen to stay.

Once they were alone, the queen asked, "Are you ready for your expedition?"

"I guess so," Faith responded, unsure of why the queen would be asking. "Airria seems ready, so I guess I need to be."

"Has your training gone well?"

"Yes. I have learned so much about your style of fighting. Some of the elves have even taught me a little about moving quietly and using my surroundings to hide."

"You have learned much in the time you have been here." The queen rose from her throne and descended the ramp.

"I have been well instructed," Faith said. She was becoming nervous as the queen approached.

"Airria, he gave you five swords, his 'trophies' from the arena fight?" The queen's voice was almost melodic.

"Yes," Faith responded. "I have them with me, though I don't know what I would do with such large, uncommon weapons."

The queen smiled slightly, "Perhaps we could come to an arrangement?"

"I would be happy to, but may I ask why?" Faith asked.

"I would prefer not to let those swords leave my queendom. The material they are made of, pure moonlight, has become only myth to most of the rest of the world. I would like to keep it that way. Besides, I think the swords we have made as replacements will serve you better."

Faith unbuckled the swords from her back and reluctantly approached the queen. When she was only two paces from the queen, the queen waved two of her hands, a sword formed in each. The sheaths and handles were almost identical to the swords she was trading for them, except of a manageable length.

"These swords are lighter and will draw far less attention to you than will the moonlight. The magic in them makes them almost as strong."

Faith responded under her breath, more for her own thoughts than to be sarcastic as she handed the swords to the queen, "I had heard the elves could make silver to be as strong as iron yet weigh far less."

The queen spoke with respect to Faith, "It will take some time to adjust to the weight difference, but once you do, you will be faster and better than you can imagine."

Faith gave the swords to the queen and received the new swords. She left her arms outstretched for a moment in surprise, "They weigh as much as my daggers." Her excitement mounted as she put the belts around her waist. She buckled on her new swords and, looking at the sword Taksek had given her and giggling lightly she said, "I look as though I am a swordswoman, not an archer."

"Though many times in your journey you will have chances to use you swords, your bow is still you most important weapon."

Faith pulled the sword. "I am not sure I have a use for this anymore. Perhaps your blacksmiths could rework it for your own purposes. Would I be able to trade it for a better bow than I currently have?"

"I believe the one Jammar gave you has no equal," the queen replied. "When you find Viehasia's armor, it will only become more powerful."

"Jammar suggested we hide the weapons for the time being," Faith responded.

"It will likely save you some fights, but it will also divert bandits from their course," the queen suggested. "The choice is yours. You may not want to use your magic arrows as they are far more destructive than necessary. Perhaps if you are careful the Black Wood arrows will work for you. Yes, I would say the time for such discretion has passed. Your enemy searches even now for you."

The queen clapped one set of hands. A few moments later the others returned. Several of the queen's personal servants and advisers, including Artana, came as well.

Airria looked as though a huge burden had been lifted from his shoulders. Both he and Joskin were wearing amulets with the queen's symbol on them. Airria strode directly over to Artana and whispered in her ear.

She bowed to him then to the queen. With a wave of the queen's hand Artana went to the back of the room to wait.

"She is officially released from her bond," Airria said with a smile.

Carrita and Bregette stood quietly by the door and waited until called forward. It was then Faith noticed Carrita's new staff. It was slender and silver with a clear crystal on top. Inside the crystal seemed to be a green energy ball swirling in random directions.

"May the blessings of the Rarstocks go with you in your journey," the queen said to the group.

Each member of the group thanked the queen, bowed and went to the back of the chamber to wait for the others.

When they were all together again Artana said, "Follow me," then she left the room.

"Why are you carrying your old sword in your hand?" Airria asked. "Where are the swords I gave you?"

"This sword is a donation," Faith said. This earned her a confused look from everyone else. In her defense she said, "We have a truly amazing craftsmen on our ship and the naga can make better use of this silver than I can."

"And the swords I gave you?" he asked again.

Faith patted the swords at her sides, "These will serve me better." She stopped at the armory and placed the silver sword on the rack.

"Do you know what that is worth?" Joskin asked.

"We have all received much more in food, lodging, gifts and training."

The protest stayed on Joskin's face, but quickly melted on the others.

Faith began to feel uncomfortable so she asked, "Shall we go?"

When they arrived at the stalls, the horses were saddled and Joskin's food supplies were restocked. Carrita was the first to notice a new blanket under her horse's armor. She asked one of the stable hands about it.

"They are blankets of nourishment," she responded casually.

"Why?"

"There isn't much your horses can eat up here. They were made to keep your horses alive while traveling the frozen lands."

The others, overhearing Carrita, checked their own animals.

Faith found hers then became curious, "How do they work?"

"I don't know, I was just told to give them to you," the servant bowed respectfully. "Before I forget, here is something I was asked to give you," she handed a note to Carrita.

Carrita looked at the parchment for a moment then handed it to Joskin, "I believe this will help us."

394

Joskin looked it over for a short while. "Yes, this map will be most helpful. It seems to have a detailed map of the area; it should lead us straight to the armor. It also suggests a route through the mountains."

Chapter 19 - Runes

As the group rode through the streets Carrita noticed the people silently watching. Elves and naga alike stood, watching with an eager sadness. The young elves held tightly to their parents' hands. The young naga stood with a hand over their heart, eyes cast down.

She had spent the last couple of months learning about the base elements from a Guardian. She had learned things which could not be written, not even in Draconian. Bregette had become more than a teacher, she had become a friend. Carrita had been treated as an equal.

It was overwhelming to think of herself as an equal to one of the lesser deities. Still she felt alone so often in her magic. Part of why she had worked so hard with Faith was to develop a partner. Sadly, she had been paying more attention to Airria and her physical fighting studies. Now, more than when she had arrived at the city, she felt alone.

A glance at the swirling green energy in her staff let her know she would never have to be alone again. As she rode she watched the green waves pass in the crystal at the top of the staff Bregette had given her.

When the city gates were far behind the group Faith broke the silence, "Did you get the feeling they know more about our journey than even we do?"

Carrita chimed in, "Jammar had let us know Airria's quest was noted by the deities and Guardians. As a Guardian, he trained us. Salle'allak provided us with weapons. Now, a few more Guardians have lent their help. "

Joskin said ponderously, "There is no way we are caught in the middle of a deific battle. We haven't fought anything tough enough. I know there are far more powerful creatures the deities could send after us. There have been no elementals of any kind. I mean, the most impressive thing we have had to fight has been a minotaur mage that Carrita could handle without her staff."

Carrita wished Joskin had not brought up such a painful memory. "It was you and your ax, not I which defeated the minotaur. Still, I am surprised The Order has sent so little to face us. It is as though much of their forces are engaged elsewhere."

Faith said thoughtfully, "The naga, elves and Guardians have given us so much and asked for nothing in return."

Airria said, "I just thought they were like that."

Faith asked, "Did it not make you wonder why Artana gave up so easily when she had made such a big deal about your earlier attack?"

Pride beamed form Airria's face as he replied, "She realized she was no match for me and my weaponry."

Faith opened her mouth to speak, but Carrita held her hand up to silence her. Silence continued until camp that night.

After the fire was built Joskin asked Carrita, "When do you think the dark deities will begin to interfere?"

Carrita focused on the fire, "They may send small things our way, little distractions, but they likely won't try to kill us until we are in the Black Forest. Only the dark deities are allowed in there. The light deities will not be able to help us."

Faith added, "They may send something to try to stop us from getting the armor."

Joskin thought for a moment, "Do you suppose that was the purpose of the pirate ship? I mean, if we had not beaten them, we would have been dead for sure."

"It is very possible Jarmack'Trastibbik has severely underestimated our current abilities," Carrita replied.

Airria frowned, "I am here for the armor. I still have a dragon to kill." He got up to leave, then added, "I made my choice on my own. If the deities can use my quest to their advantage good for them, but I act on my own." He left slowly, glancing back to the fire.

Faith looked at the ground for some time. Slowly she pulled her swords from her side. She gradually dragged her eyes across the shiny blades. The blades were definitely of naga design. Smooth and shiny, each blade was as long as her leg and only slightly curved. With the handles, the swords came up to her lower chest.

"Where did you get you get those swords?" Joskin made Faith jump.

Faith replied, "I traded the larger swords for these," then added, "they are less noticeable."

"Less noticeable?" Carrita asked in surprise. "Look!" Carrita pointed to the swords; the blades were glowing in a strange knotted, vine type pattern, similar to the patterns she had seen on the moonlight swords. It also resembled Draconian, except is had patterns and symbols she did not recognize.

Joskin stepped back.

Carrita looked up at the moon, which had just come out from behind some clouds, "It is full tonight," she turned to Faith and asked, "May I see the swords?" Faith handed the swords to Carrita without reservation.

Carrita reached out with her magic and touched the vinework. She could not feel any magic, but she knew there had to be some. Like the robe her mother had Jammar give her, she could not tell the purpose of the magic. Years ago, her mother had told her of a type of writing which was the language of magic. This writing, called Runes, was an unspoken language so powerful few could master it. Now she realized she was in the presence of Runes which only appeared in the moonlight. "Moon Runes!" she exclaimed, excitement rushing though her body.

Recognizing it was the first step. Her mother had told her not to pursue understanding Runes because as she learned more of magic the understanding would come. She would be able to read it without being taught.

"What?" Joskin asked.

Carrita smiled, "These are special Runes, harder to identify. They can only be seen in the light of the full moon and only magically felt with a new moon." She had only heard her mother discuss such magic with visitors in their basement when she thought Carrita was asleep. Carrita had thought them only theory.

"Where did you learn about them?" Faith asked.

"I have learned a lot in the last few weeks," Carrita said cryptically. She had not learned about them from Bregette, but did not want to let the others know her mother was the Fairen they had learned about at the shrines on the island. Joskin looked as if he had more questions than she wanted to answer. She handed the swords carefully back to Faith.

Joskin asked to see the swords. He began to compare the marks on his ax with the brighter parts of those on Faith's swords. He ran to get Airria's sword and shield. They had some similar makings too. He ran to where Carrita was seated and asked with a shiver in his voice, "What are Runes?"

Carrita replied the best she thought she could, "You wouldn't understand."

"I may not understand how they are made or how to tell what they are for, but I can understand what they are!" Joskin's voice was gaining confidence.

Carrita thought for a moment and said, "Runes are the writing of pure magic." She giggled, "Do the Runes make you nervous?"

Joskin took a deep breath, "I have learned you know more about magic then I ever will be able to imagine. You are being very vague, as if even you don't understand. I depend on your confidence in your magic and knowledge to let me know if there is danger. When you don't seem to understand, it makes me leery. I have listened to some of your lessons with Faith. You have talked about Wards and Symbols. Is it a writing like that, or is it more like Elven or Dwarven?"

Carrita was still very cryptic, "No and yes."

Joskin shook his head, "You're not helping me feel better about this." He held the swords up, "Please explain."

"The Elven script is the mortal writings of relatively weak magic. Symbols are the writings to influence magic. Runes are the language spoken by magic alone, the most powerful magics. It is written, like Elven or Dwarven, but the written words can be magical all by themselves. They have to be written by the purest essence of magic." Carrita was having fun teasing Joskin. He was trying so hard to understand, but it was beyond Carrita to understand how it all worked. She had realized by her mother's tone when she had talked to others, that the study of Runes was a very advanced aspect of magic. Carrita had always felt it was far too dangerous to learn and had never pursued it. "If you learn the patterns you can read it like a book. Unfortunately this is more difficult than it seems."

"Can you teach me?" Joskin asked. His eyes were pleading with a nervousness she was not used to seeing in them. "I would like to be able to read my ax."

"I dare not learn about them. I know this does not help you feel comfortable about the Runes, but I do not have sufficient understanding to even pursue the knowledge of this language," came Carrita's gentle reply.

Joskin got a confused look on his face, "You don't know how to read them?"

Carrita shook her head. "I don't know enough about magic to read the Runes." Talking to Joskin filled her with the desire to start learning. Perhaps she would wait until she had her mother back before she pursued it any further.

Joskin stepped back, "'Understand about magic'? Isn't it like a regular written language?"

"The more you understand about magic the more clearly you see the Runes for what they are," she still carried her sad smile.

Joskin looked confused.

Carrita became more thoughtful, "When you first received your axe.you thought it was just decorated, perhaps even just scratched."

Joskin gave a nod.

"I can tell from your face, you now see the patterns which imply a written language." Carrita was thinking hard of how to explain. She knew she would fall short, but had enough respect for Joskin to try. As you learn more about magic, you also learn how magic works, how it speaks, how it writes." She paused for a moment to examine Joskin's face, "Is my explanation sufficient?"

Joskin nodded, but looked more confused than before, "I guess it will have to do." He handed the swords back to Faith and went to set out his bedroll.

Carrita looked up at Faith, "How much of what I said to Joskin did you understand?"

Faith smiled, "I would guess I understood more than Joskin, but not enough for it to make much sense."

Airria had returned and was looking at his sword now. "Do I have these Runes on my sword? I see no scratches or marks."

Carrita laughed and took his sword. She looked closely at it. Now she knew better what to look for she could see the markings. They were much more difficult to recognize with the swirling light behind, or possibly around them, but they were there. She looked at Joskin and back to the sword. After a moment she handed it to Faith. "Do you see them?"

Faith squinted at the blade. After her inspection she gasped, "Yes, I do see them. They talk of the sun's fire."

Nothing about Faith made sense. She learned magic as if she had been reminded of it. When they had stopped at the Life Temple the High Priestess's son had mistaken Faith for a priestess. Carrita had felt a power in her, one far beyond what should be, even in an advanced mage, yet she had started with little to no understanding of magic and now was implying she could understand Runes.

Carrita asked, "You can read this?"

Faith blushed. She began shifting uneasily on her seat, "It wasn't exactly me who read it."

"What do you mean?" Airria asked.

"Persephone read it," she responded.

Airria looked at the horses then back to Faith. "Your horse is too smart." He put his hand out for Faith to return his sword.

Faith handed it back and said, "She truly is." She looked to her horse then to Carrita, "She says it is the only word she knows."

Carrita looked at the horse then back to Faith. "How do you two communicate?"

Faith shook her head, "Mostly she sends me images or feelings of what she wants to communicate. I can only guess how she receives my thoughts."

Carrita looked into the fire as she pondered how a horse could know something so advanced. It was unnerving in the least. Faith's horse understood something of magic Carrita had not yet understood. She took a closer look at Faith's weapons. She stopped looking at the patterns and began looking at the motion the images created. She thought back to her lessons with Bregette. She allowed herself to slip into the Astral Plane and examine the weapons and then came back into her body.

She began looking for the elements themselves. There it was, still incomprehensible, but there. The patterns seemed to shift and she could see pieces of all the elements. Wind and Water were the strongest. She could not understand what she was seeing, but she could see as much as Persephone.

Carrita looked up excitedly at Faith. Surprisingly her brow was furrowed and her eyes were wide.

Faith asked in a shocked voice, "What happened there? What was it you did?"

Carrita had not done anything special. She knew Faith had seen her body when she had slipped into the Astral Plane. "I slipped into the Astral Plane for a short while to see if I could better understand the magic of your sword. I do not understand your acrimonious reaction."

Faith pointed at Carrita's eyes, "Your eyes, they changed to cold silver for a moment. How did you do you accomplish this? Why did they change?"

402

Carrita responded, "What do you mean? I honestly do not know."

Faith took a deep breath, "I have seen you when you walk the Astral Plane. This was different. I have felt your presence since you got the crystal out, sometimes stronger than others. This time you felt like the wind flowing by and then you felt as if you were a pure mountain stream. How did you do it?"

"I truly do not understand what you are asking," Carrita said handing back the swords. Uncomfortable with the look Faith was giving her, Carrita suggested, "The wind is growing stronger; perhaps what you saw was a glint of snow reflecting the firelight or the moonlight."

Faith still did not look convinced. After a moment she said, "Perhaps I should go train with Airria tonight." She got up and left Carrita to her thoughts.

Chapter 20 - Ice

Faith joined Airria early that night. She appeared shaken, looking back to Carrita. She was dragging her swords in the snow.

"What happened?" he asked.

Faith looked down at her swords and took a deep breath. She paused a moment but she squared up her shoulders, "It's time to practice," she said.

Airria was not convinced, "I thought tonight Carrita would want to share all she's been learning."

Faith glanced back to Carrita, "It may take some time for her to realize how much she has learned." She pulled her swords to a ready position, "You may want your good shield tonight."

Airria almost didn't get his shield on in time. Faith dove in, both blades swinging in a beautiful rhythm of light and metal. Her steps were a deadly dance of elegance. For much of the night she kept the attack up and kept control of the fight.

Whatever was bothering her seemed to drive her. Normally she was much easier to control in the fight, Airria had always set the tempo. Tonight as quickly as he adjusted to her attacks she would change her style and begin driving again.

It was good for him to practice with someone far less predictable than she had been. Airria was sure this night's unexpected training was caused by something between Carrita and Faith. There was no indication as to what.

The uncomfortable silence between the two girls made travel seem slow. The winds blew constantly, making it impossible to talk. Without talk Faith and Carrita couldn't mend the rift.

The days meshed into weeks. Still the group kept climbing. By this time there was no wood for fire. There was only snow and ice. The trail had faded to barely noticeable. Even the magic in the cloaks was not enough to keep the chill out.

One day the group found a canyon of ice to cut through. They were not sure where it led, but Airria didn't care. He wanted out of the wind and a place for the girls to talk.

They had only started into the crevice when they heard a group of cries, silenced short. There was a loud shatter and a cruel, deep laugh. Without a thought, Airria raced ahead.

There was an entire nomadic village encased in a sheet of ice. The villagers were frozen in mid scream. Near the center, one of the tents had been smashed, pieces of frozen hides and body parts were scattered about.

Airria quickly dismounted and began exploring, his magic shield held to the front. The walls of the twisted canyon made it difficult to see past the village, still he could hear the thump of heavy footsteps and even the earth seemed to shake as he walked.

He pulled his sword, the blade burned white and hot, *Your first real challenge!* the voice echoed in Airria's head. Airria wanted to stop and ask what his sword knew, but there was no time.

A loud human shriek came from around a bend, followed by another loud crash. A chilling wind blew up the canyon. Moments later a tall, muscular woman in heavy animal skins came sprinting by in a panic.

Shortly after the woman ran past, a thick frost hanging from her back, a large human-like creature came around the corner. The humanoid was almost three times Airria's height with a long white beard, almost silver hair and frosty white skin. In his right hand he carried a frost coated ax and his body was covered in what looked to be armor made of ice.

405

Suddenly Airria wished he was back in the arena fighting Artana. The extraordinary height of this frost giant was enough to make Airria wish he could run. Even as menacing as this was he knew this creature would be easy compared to the dragon he was pursuing, he also knew he was not alone.

Before Airria could react, Faith readied and fired one of Jammar's arrows. The red tipped arrow flew like a streak of flame. Its path was interrupted between Airria and Faith by a large sphere of ice. Airria got his shield around to block most of the falling shards. The shards of ice which flew at the giant seemed to melt into his skin like water on a sponge.

A gust of icy wind erupted from the giant's mouth, a wall of ice formed in front of Airria's shield curving over his head.

The giant's voice boomed, "This little bite is not playing fair. It has brought friends." His ax, longer than Joskin's, had a handle thicker than Airria's arm. He swung it with ease.

Airria easily sidestepped the heavy blow. Ice flew in all directions.

The giant swung again with a sweeping blow. Airria tried to deflect it up as he twisted to move into striking distance. There was a loud eruption as the giant ax shattered. The impact sent a loud shock wave through the canyon. The substantial blow sent Airria tumbling. Shards of frosted metal showered around him.

It was then that he noticed an ice wall filling the entire canyon width. Flashes of colored light could be seen, as well as the muffled blasts of Faith's magic arrows.

The giant screamed in rage, "You broke my axe!" then the giant plunged his monstrous hand toward Airria.

Airria got a good swing in and sliced a nice gash across the giant's palm. He didn't notice the second hand which grabbed him, pressing his shield against his chest. The giant let out another scream as his hand, holding the shield, began smoking. The giant threw Airria at the magical ice wall yelling, "This isn't finished!"

Airria braced himself for the impact, but quickly opened his eyes when he heard Carrita's voice, like a raging fire yell, "Yes, it is!" Her

406

words shook the icy walls of the canyon. "This is your end!" she pointed her staff at the giant.

The giant put out his burnt hand and began to form a shielding globe of ice. His shield barely grew a pace in diameter before the giant exploded in a huge ball of fire. The flames were held away from the group by an unseen barrier. The walls of the canyon began to melt, sending a river of water down the path the group would have traveled, washing away the evidence of the village.

Carrita's hair and arms were on fire. Her eyes were glowing bright red. Airria panicked and jumped to his feet. He figured it was only some magic intimidation spell until he noticed Faith.

Faith had turned her face from Carrita. She had thrown up a golden magical shield. That is when it hit Airria, Faith was afraid Carrita was losing control of her magic. He wondered if Carrita knew what was happening.

It took a moment for Carrita's pony to react. It jerked right then left. It spun around and bolted, throwing Carrita to the ground.

Joskin leapt from his horse and ran over to make sure Carrita was all right. By the time he arrived at her side the flames were gone without a trace and only the faintest bit of red was left in her eyes. "Are you all right?" Joskin asked.

He stopped as the girl got up stiffly. "I will be fine. What spooked my pony?"

Airria slowly approached, "Maybe it was the fact you burst into fire."

Carrita looked at herself, confused, "I believe I would have noticed such a painful display."

Faith finally entered the conversation, "One might think you should notice such a display of power."

Carrita looked reflectively down the already iced over trail for a long time. Finally she said, "I sincerely do not know whether I should be excited or terrified."

Faith let out a sigh of relief, "I have been waiting for you to decide as well."

Airria, now close enough to, placed a hand on the girl's shoulder. "The flames didn't seem to hurt you, why would it scare you?"

Carrita put her hand on Airria's, "Do you remember the day you first struck Joskin, even though you were not meaning too?"

He did remember it well. That day was when he realized how far he had come. His understanding of his part in the world shifted. He was now the protector and Joskin was the lesser fighter. While he pondered that day his eyes drifted.

Carrita continued, "Today I have crossed a boundary I never witnessed my mother crossing."

Faith chimed in, "Today? What about the other night."

Carrita looked at Faith, her eyes filled with longing. "What happened the other evening, I cannot tell as I did not see. However I will trust it happened then as well."

Faith still kept her distance, "Does this not mean you are losing control?"

The corners of Carrita's mouth turned up. "This means I am attuning to the elements."

Airria pulled his hand away, "You are what to the elements?"

Carrita collapsed where she was.

Joskin knelt by her side, "Are you sure you're all right?"

Faith dismounted and stood beside Airria. "Perhaps it would be a preferred idea to rest here for the night. Your fall did look painful," she said.

It was good to see the girls talking again. It had been far too long. Airria smiled at the prospect of the girls getting along. Not to mention it would be nice to have some casual time with Faith, rather than her taking out her frustrations on his shield.

He remembered the wood from the village, but it had washed down the canyon. It would still be light for some time and he would love to have a small fire to warm himself next to. He looked down the canyon and could see no trace of the village, but he was determined. If there was wood within reach he was going to find it.

Before he could announce his intentions, Joskin said, "This is a good place to rest. There are only two directions trouble can come from and the wind is slowed. I am sure the chances of something attacking tonight are small."

Airria saw a chance to make the girls talk out their issues. "There is some wood down the trail. Will you help me get some?" he said to Joskin.

Joskin leapt up, "Great idea!" He sounded far more excited than he should have. Perhaps the girls not talking had bothered him, too.

Together they hastily began walking, as soon as their feet hit the new ice they went out from under them, causing them to toss their weapons behind them towards Faith and Carrita while they went sliding down the ravine and crashed into the far wall.

Faith yelled behind them, "Are you both all right? Do you need us to rescue you?"

Their armor had protected them from the pain of all but their wounded pride. Ax, sword, shield had all slid back to the girls. They did not want to risk having the girls try to slide their weapons back to them for fear they would slide past or badly injure one of them. They would just have to be careful.

Using their daggers, they stabbed them into the ice to provide handholds as they inched their way around the corners and controlled their slide down the next part of the trail. Finally they hit where the logs were.

Before they began digging Joskin asked, "Do you think today's display from Carrita will be enough for them to start talking again?"

Airria began chipping away the thin layer of ice, "I certainly hope so, for all of our sakes." He had seen on the ship what a powerful combination they had made, not to mention he wanted to see Faith smile again.

Joskin joined in, digging though the ice on the other end of the log. "That girl is more fragile than we like to think. As much as I try to be there for her, she really needs Faith."

Airria thought for a moment. "I think Faith needs Carrita as well. Maybe it has something to do with her leaving her sister. Though Carrita is older it makes Faith miss her sister less."

Joskin laughed, "You may be right; I did help several young, squirrely types when I started fighting. Guess they reminded me of you."

Airria threw a chunk of ice at his cousin. Unexpectedly, the force of throwing the ice caused him to shift. He was not slipping fast, as his armor was gripping and the slope was mild, but it still surprised him. Before he knew it his knife was out of reach and he was gaining speed.

Joskin started laughing, "Can't you handle the ice?"

Airria began to panic. He had nothing to stop him. His dagger was getting farther away and his cousin was offering no suggestions. All he could do was look bewildered at Joskin.

A dull thump and Airria stopped against another log. There was a loud crack as the small log broke free, but Airria spotted his escape. He reached for the hole the log had made and gripped tight.

The small handhold was enough to stop him. The thought occurred to him, "We figured out how to get this far, but how were we going to get back with the wood?"

Joskin laughed again, "I wanted to see how you would handle the slick ice." He gripped his dagger tight and rolled over to his knees. The spikes on the end of his shin guards dug deep into the ice. Slowly he crawled over to his cousin and grabbed the log now lodged under Airria's thigh. He pulled a leather cord out from beneath his armor and tied it to the log, "I hate to waste all your hard work."

Airria thought about hitting Joskin. Then he thought again. Slowly he rolled over and dug his knee-spikes into the ice as Joskin had done. Carefully he made his way back and retrieved his dagger. He chuckled as he picked it up, "It is a good thing that Taksek knows his trade. Can you imagine the damage we would have done to both our armor and our daggers if they had not been made by such a great craftsman?"

The corners of Joskin's eyes dropped, he looked at Airria and said, "You have no idea how horrible it is to have your armor fail or your sword lose integrity when you need it most."

"That is one lesson I hope never to learn." Airria finished chipping the original log out, then used another cord Joskin had with him to tie it up. Slowly they made their way back to the girls.

410

Chapter 21 - Gailexa

Faith laughed to see the men slowly crawling up the ice with the small logs behind them. It had been a very difficult day and she needed the amusement. She was sure the men had not created this situation for her enjoyment, nevertheless; she was grateful to laugh.

Carrita was giggling, too. For the first time in weeks she looked like the little girl she was. Seeing her in such a light eased the mood even more.

Since the men left, Faith and Carrita had been talking. Carrita had frightened Faith with all the power. It seemed the magic was taking over Carrita. The girl claimed this was not the case. Persephone had concurred with Carrita, but Faith still was not sure Carrita was not out of control.

Airria had a big smile on his face when he said, "If you want fire in the morning you will have to get the wood. This is too much work."

Carrita giggled again and leaned into Faith, "We will enjoy the fire for tonight."

It felt good to have the girl lean into her. Almost on instinct she placed an arm around her friend. It had been too long.

Faith held onto Carrita while the men built a small fire pit and started the fire. It felt good to have heat. The flames were warm and inviting. The smoke was minimized by the expert fire skills of Joskin.

Faith was getting lost in the flames when she heard the clop of small hooves. The muscular woman who had run away earlier was leading Carrita's pony, holding her still frosted skins tightly around her body. She was shivering. Her skin was almost blue. She asked, "I share fire? I very cold. Your horse I return. Please share fire?"

Both men stood up, but it was Carrita who spoke. "You are most welcome to share our fire. Please, come, warm yourself. You have had a very trying day and should relax and allow yourself to heal."

The woman glanced at Carrita and hesitated. She stepped forward, then back. She began wringing her hands. Her eyes shifted from the girl to the fire and back.

Carrita giggled, "You have nothing to fear. I will use no magic on you, nor will I force you to witness any. You are safe to share our fire and our company."

The woman approached the fire, positioning herself across from Carrita. She leaned forward as if she were trying to catch the heat in her hood. Stiff locks of white hair fell out. The ice covering her reflected the firelight. She looked at Joskin, "Gratitude I share fire with you."

Joskin responded, "Thank you for the return of our pony. I know food is scarce up here. The pony could have fed your clan for a full day."

"I clan no have," the woman said reaching out for the flames. The blue was leaving her face and the ice was starting to melt off her clothes. "Destroyed by big ice clan has. I alone now," her voice began to shake.

Faith could not help herself. She let go of Carrita and walked over to the woman and wrapped her cloak around her. "You must be freezing. Is there anything we can do to help?" Slowly she put a hand on the woman's face.

Shivering the woman only pulled away slightly, then gave in and let Faith touch her.

Faith began a silent healing spell mixed with a touch of warmth. Fully unexpectedly the magic would not freely flow into the woman. She had never experienced anyone resisting a healing spell.

She concentrated harder and finally her magic made its way into the woman who turned sharply.

"What doing are you?" the woman said still shaking, though far less then she had been.

Faith pulled her hand away slowly, "I am simply trying to help."

Across the fire Carrita giggled again. "This woman distrusts magic to her very core. Any magical energy intruding on hers will be felt and repelled to her best. It is indicative of the Mountain people of the north, but not them alone."

The fur-skinned woman leaned away from Faith. "Plenty help to share fire. No need I other help."

Faith made her way back to Carrita and asked the new woman, "Our food supplies are running very low. Would you teach us how to acquire food in these high mountains?"

The woman stiffly looked to Joskin, "What trade can offer?"

Joskin replied, "We can offer safety, warmth and companionship. This is all we have we can part with."

"You'll not be using your Orc ax anymore," Airria interjected, "my silver sword will be going to waste."

Faith nodded, "The time for discreet weapons is over. We will need to stay at the top of our game now."

Carrita leaned back into Faith, but kept looking at the large woman. "I have no desire to make an exchange with someone with whom I have not become acquainted. May I ask what you are called?"

"Gailexa to be called," the woman said as proudly as she could while hunched over the fire.

Faith did not want to bring up the painful subject of the woman's tribe, but she wanted to know, "What will you do now your tribe is gone?"

Gailexa's eyes drooped, "I find new tribe."

"How difficult will it be for you to find a new tribe?" Faith asked.

"Will need make new bow," Gailexa responded slowly. "Also need new ax. Am good fighter and know good plants. Will find new tribe and prove worth."

Faith asked, "Would you like some company while you search for your new tribe?"

414

"Yes, would like to accompany until find new tribe," Gailexa kept shifting her eyes to Carrita.

Joskin got up and went to his horse. He reached in his bag and produced one of the naga ration packages they had given him. "For tonight you need to be warmed. You need some food. You need some rest. Tomorrow we will talk about trade." He handed the ration to the barbarian woman and went back to his place.

Gailexa took the ration carefully and opened the chilled cloth. She rotated the package in her hands for a short while. Then she placed it almost in the fire. "Such food rare. Best eat when hot. Will help warm body. Gratefulness to you."

Airria asked, "What did you do in your old tribe?"

Gailexa turned to Airria, "Help find and make food for family."

Carrita sat up, "I know some little about cooking. Perhaps you would be kind enough to teach me where to find good plants for cooking and I will teach you some about how I use them to help in healing and such."

"You teach me medicine?" Gailexa asked. "You know to be shaman?"

I have long studied the art of alch…being a shaman," Carrita was sitting a little straighter.

Faith felt a touch of jealousy creep in. She had only started to get her friend back. Though it was her own mistrust working between them, she still wanted a night for just the two of them. Finally she suggested, "Tomorrow we can discuss alchemy and food. For now, we should allow Gailexa to eat some food and get some rest."

The woman pulled the now steaming food out of the fire and began eating. Her shivering slowed and her eyes began shifting uneasily, but she said nothing.

Joskin went to Airria's horse and retrieved his bedroll. "You can use this for the night. He won't be using it and it should keep you warm," Joskin said as he handed her the stack of hides and blankets.

The woman took the coverings and rolled them out next to the fire, "Where others sleep?"

415

Joskin began setting his own bed out, "They will keep watch for the night."

"When they sleep?" the woman asked.

Faith stood up and assisted Carrita to do the same. "We do not sleep much."

Airria also got up. He grabbed his practice sword and magic shield. "Get some rest. We will be moving in the morning." He threw a playful glance at his cousin.

Joskin rolled his eyes and climbed into his bed.

Gailexa carefully climbed into bed. She had to curl her legs to fit under the blankets. She lay there, staring wide-eyed at the fire.

Faith expected more mourning from the woman. Perhaps the woman was in shock or maybe her people mourned differently than Faith was used to. Carrita seemed unshaken, so Faith opted to trust.

She grabbed her swords and went to where Airria was beginning his practice. She pulled her swords and asked, "How would you like to practice tonight?"

Airria glanced behind Faith, "Your swords have got to be getting dull. Let me sharpen them for you tonight."

Faith looked closely at her blades. The beautiful designs had faded several nights ago. Her blades remained unchipped and completely sharp. "They are unmarred and ready for anything. I think the magic in them keeps them from getting dull."

Airria leaned his head, making it more obvious he was looking behind Faith, "The barbarian woman has had a tough day. I think we should skip the melee training for the night."

Faith looked behind her. Joskin was already asleep. Gailexa was still focused on the fire. Carrita was standing looking at Faith, her hands crossed low across her body.

Faith could now see what Airria was hinting at. She turned to him and said, "It would be a good idea for me to train with Carrita tonight. After all, she has learned so much and could help me be a better mage. I think it will be best if I train with her." She was trying to convince herself, "Yes it is time we discuss what she has learned."

416

Airria chuckled softly, "Yes it would be good for you two to talk."

Faith sheltered her swords. She walked over to Carrita and put a hand on her shoulder. "I know I cannot learn everything you have. I dare not walk the Astral Plane, but I know you have much you can teach me."

Carrita fell into Faith, wrapping her arms around her. "I will be pleased to share what knowledge I can with you."

Faith led Carrita to a small alcove in the canyon wall. "What were you learning about for so many weeks?" Faith asked.

Carrita giggled, "I would have to show you in the same way I was shown. There is no way to instruct you in what I learned. Fortunately there is no reason for you to walk the path I have to learn what I have. You are far from exhausting my understanding of what I have to share."

Faith was excited to talk to Carrita again, but she wanted to know what had happened to her over the time she had spent away. "On the ship you spent almost the entire trip hiding in a room, obsessively learning about deep and dark magic. I worried then. At least you kept me informed, or at least as much as you could, about what you were learning."

Carrita sat on the ice trail, "I did attempt to talk to you on the ship, but you were more fascinated with Airria and your physical training. I believed you would appreciate the break from your magical studies."

Faith sat next to her young friend, "I did enjoy the time learning about sword-play. Believe it or not, training with Airria helped me immensely to understand and learn from the naga."

Carrita put a hand on Faith's, "I was able to watch your training. You were able to learn from the naga as well as you did from me at Jammar's. Even without the magic of Jammar's house you have been able to learn exceptionally quickly."

"A long time before you met Jammar you were learning magic," Faith rebutted. "You learned more about magic in your short life then most mages ever do in a lifetime of study."

Carrita looked down and stroked her dress. "My mother was a tremendous instructor."

Faith lifted the girl's chin, "I believe she was as you have said. Her ability to instruct has been reflected in the way you instruct me. You have told me many times I have learned very quickly. However there is more learning taking place in both of us than even the instructing should allow."

Carrita looked deep into Faith's eyes, "There was something familiar with how Bregette taught me. More than ever her instruction felt more like a reminder than something new. Perhaps my mother instructed Bregette as well."

Faith replied, "Perhaps you have learned things before, I cannot tell. Still you learn magic very quickly. Your mind absorbs knowledge you deem important. You focus and drive yourself to understand."

Carrita asked, "Is this why you feel you have learned an entirely new style of swordplay in so few days?"

Faith replied, "I believe such determination gives much of the explanation. Airria did little by way of instruction. All I learned from him was simply watching what he did and defending myself. When in training with the naga's what they told me and how they instructed me to change only seemed natural. I was not learning something new. I was only adjusting what I already knew." As she brought up the naga training, something clicked in her head, "Wait, you saw me training? How is it possible? You were constantly in the Astral Plane."

Carrita explained, "One of the things I did learn and can share with you is the Astral Plane is not another place. It is the world souls walk before they reach their final destination. Being there allows me to view our world with a different perspective. Yes, I was able to watch you train."

"All life taught fear magic," Gailexa's voice startled Faith. "I always told magic bad. Today I see magic do helpful. Inside I conflict. I eat food and feel conflict. You teach me use?"

The barbarian was talking directly to Carrita for the first time.

Carrita responded in kind, "I will teach you to be a shaman; I will teach you what I can so you can use magic in the form your people

418

know and do not reject. I will teach you enough to help your people in a way they will not reject you."

"What trade you make?" Gailexa asked. "You offer much. What you want given?"

Carrita held tightly to Faith's hand. "My friend and I have already told you what we desire of you. I will instruct you. In return I will need you to show me how to gather and how to survive in this frigid environment. Teach me how you live without fire."

Gailexa frowned, "What you ask, small thing. Ask more to make fair trade."

Faith answered, "What we ask may seem trivial to you. Such is common knowledge among your people. For us such knowledge is worth very much."

Gailexa uncrossed her arms, "Trade is agreed. We will start when sun climbs." Without another word the woman turned and returned to the bedroll.

Faith was glad to have someone along who knew about the mountains. "Will you have time to teach us both?"

Carrita leaned into Faith again and embraced her. "She, like Joskin needs to sleep. Besides, you know a great amount of magic. You are training to help and support. You know enough for such. Now you need to better yourself on when and where to use magic in battle. The naga have given you an excellent beginning. As to my training you, I will be glad to answer any questions you have. I will, however; need some time with you each day to talk. I do miss having such time with you."

Faith hugged Carrita back, "We have an agreement, each day we will take some time to talk." Faith felt relieved to have the child trusting in her again. She still felt like she had no real place in the group, but now she could enjoy the journey.

Chapter 22 - Armor

A few weeks after the group's encounter with the giant they had set up camp in the area Airria believed was near to where they were to find the armor. The barbarian woman helped them set up a small camp by digging into the deep snow under the sheets of ice to provide a shelter for them.

While Joskin, Airria and Faith went to look for a cave the armor could be hidden in, Gailexa and Carrita did experiments on the strange herbs and lizards Gailexa had found in the snow. It was nice to come back to something warm to drink, but without wood, there was no fire.

Faith had been using her gray arrow, the one Tarsa, Jammar's wife, had said would point them in the direction they should go. It would lead them one direction for a time, then shift for a while.

One night, after over a week of searching, Airria started venting his frustration, "Why can we not find it?"

Joskin put a hand on his cousin's shoulder, "Do you remember the cave we found our weapons in?"

Airria rolled his eyes, "Of course I do. How could I forget?"

Joskin responded casually, "Do you think there is any way we could have found it without Salle'allak's help?"

"You have a point," Airria conceded, "but this time we are searching for what he sent us to find."

"You look for what?" Gailexa asked.

"Have we not told you?" Carrita's responded. "We are looking for a set of armor."

By the look on Gailexa's face Airria could tell she knew something so he asked, "Do you know where it is?"

"You have good heavy armor. Why you want other?" Gailexa asked in return.

"This is a special suit of armor, protected by magic," Airria replied.

"Is possible to know where is, but you no want go there. It certain death!" Gailexa's voice had a slight shake in it.

Airria's eyes brightened, "We're aware of the danger. Will you show us where the armor is?"

Gailexa hesitated, "You be so good to me. I no want see you to get hurt. Bad always happens when go there."

Faith looked from Airria to Carrita for some time. Finally she suggested, "We have been sent here by higher powers."

Gailexa stood up and took a step back. She was silent for a moment, after which she fell to her knees, suddenly afraid to look up at the group.

Carrita said, "If we were Treasents, would we need your help to find what we are seeking?"

Gailexa peeked past her white hair, "If you no Treasents, then how you make giant explode? Why do I never see you eat?"

"We are not deities, we are only sent by them," Carrita could not believe what she was saying, but it seemed the best way to get the woman's help. "They help us from time to time."

"Why they no help find the armor?" Gailexa's voice changed from fear to suspicion.

Airria chimed in, "They wanted to see if you would be willing to help."

Gailexa questioned, "So this a test?"

Airria blurted out, "Yes."

"What happens if I pass, what happens if I fail?" Gailexa asked.

"You get to understand things most of the world has forgotten," Carrita said.

"I show you," Gailexa hunched her shoulders and looked closely at each member of the party. She walked about a hundred paces from her seat and began digging into a small drift.

Airria hoped her digging was more than her setting up a new place to sleep or trying to find more lizards.

It took most of the night, but Gailexa finally stepped back, "My people guard this secret for thousand years." She pointed into the small cave she had just uncovered, "I hope for all sakes you tell me truth. Very powerful magic guard here."

Carrita stood there, eyes wide, looking from the barbarian to Faith and back. Finally she said, "I am standing this close to the entrance and I still cannot feel any magic."

Faith said, "We tried the magic arrow and it did not guide us here."

Carrita shook her head, "I can understand why the arrow would not lead you to the cave. It would make sense the cave existed in a dimension outside of our physically known, much like the rooms in Jammar's house. I could feel magic in Jammar's rooms, I cannot feel magic here."

Airria was halfway between furious and ready to laugh. He had become so frustrated looking for the armor and it had been this close all this time.

Joskin's laugh lightened the mood, "All this looking and all we had to do was ask."

Gailexa's eyes widened and she stepped back, "I show place to go. I not go too."

Airria had come a long way to see this armor. Salle'allak and Jammar had warned him of the danger. He had faced a giant, naga and

422

the bitter cold of this range. He would not let a little thing like threats of magic stop him.

Shortly after entering the cave he came upon something he didn't expect. It was an enormous room, far larger than the distance he had traveled would indicate. The walls of the room were strung with silvery vines, whether they were real or not he could only guess. The floor was covered with neat piles of gold, silver, gems, weapons, armor and other valuable items. On the far side of the cavern were two suits of armor, one obviously for a man, the other for a woman.

"Now we will see if Jammar was right," the deep, educated voice came from behind the armor. The group's focus shifted to the minotaur as he walked out. "Only Theilord's heir can touch this armor. Jammar thinks you are that heir."

Airria's heart raced as he approached the armor. The symbols on the base of the pedestal lit as he approached. Hypnotically his hand reached up to touch it.

"Wait," his cousin yelled from behind him.

Airria carefully lifted each piece of armor from its place. The armor was amazingly Airria's exact size and build. It consisted of a full chestplate, thigh guards, shin guards, shoulderguards, gauntlets and a helm. There was a golden silk shirt and matching trousers under it all. Each piece was forged of a white metal. The chestplate looked like an ideal man's chest. The shin guards spiked above the knee as his old ones did. Both shoulderguards and shin guards were decorated in a golden weaving rope. The helm covered everything but his face. His gauntlets reached almost to the elbow.

Without thought of anybody else or the temperature of the cave, Airria removed his own armor and gently pulled on the silk top and bottoms. They seemed to form to his body. Then with the same care he placed each piece of armor in its correct place.

Once the armor was in place, he began moving and twisting. His movements were as free as though he were naked. Even the amazing craftsmanship of the orc crafted armor seemed crude by comparison.

He could now feel magic flowing through him. He could feel the speed, the power and the strength the armor could lend him. He could feel the armor bonding to his very being as if it were joining with him. He could feel the presence of each person in the cave, even the essence of Carrita and Gailexa, who had apparently decided to enter after all.

Airria was pulled out of his admiration by Salle'allak's voice who said to Faith, "We shall see if you are worthy for the other suit of armor."

Airria asked, "What determines if she is worthy?"

Salle'allak answered evenly, "I am not allowed to say."

As Faith approached the armor, Airria froze with fear. It seemed like an eternity as she reached up with hesitation to touch the armor. As she began to pull down the separate pieces, Airria let out a loud sigh. Of all the people in the cave, she was the one he least wanted to see hurt.

She was not as reckless as Airria, she called Carrita over. Carrita approached the armor slowly. She had her arms out and her lips were pursed. When she got close to where the armor was, she magically held Faith's cloak as a shield to dress behind.

When the cloak dropped Airria couldn't believe his eyes. The silk top and bottoms sucked in comfortably to her skin, leaving nothing to snag, but allowing good protection. The breastplate covered from her shoulders to the ribs with a small white chain mail hanging over her stomach. She was running her fingers over the artwork on the breastplate. It had a beautiful design of green crystal vines, starting at her sternum and spiraling out to six white crystal flowers.

There was only one shoulder guard, but it, the shin guards and the thigh guards each matched Airria's new armor. Her bracers matched her breastplate. Her armor also came with a white silk cloak trimmed in gold.

She began moving around, running through some katas. As she moved, even the cloak seemed to dance out of her way.

"Impressive," Salle'allak said. "I guess it is time to give you her bow," Salle'allak added.

Faith asked, "What of the bow you gave me at Jammar's, is it not good enough?"

Airria stood in absolute amazement as Salle'allak formed a hole in the air, reached in and pulled out the bow. "The bow Tarsa gave you was her bow. I will be returning it to her when we are finished."

The bow was a white metal with green and white crystal vines and golden flowers weaving up it. The basic shape was Elven in design. The string looked to be made of pure gold.

Faith asked, as she handed her old bow to Salle'allak, "Why did I not receive this bow when I received the arrows?"

"This bow," the deep voice resounded gently, "is tied to the armor. It will now only function for you. It would have done you no good before now."

Faith accepted the gift with a bow. She began running her finger up and down the vinework. "It is beautiful," she said after awhile.

"May it serve you well," Salle'allak said as he strode past most of the group. He walked up to Gailexa, "You and your people have served me well. It grieved me to learn your clan was destroyed. I will assist you in finding a new clan."

Gailexa was already kneeling flat on the ground; her eyes were glued to the floor.

The minotaur reached down and helped the barbarian woman to her feet. "I will make sure you have whatever position you will request."

Hesitantly Gailexa raised her eyes. In a quivery voice she said, "Small one taught me to make small magic. I know it hard make me shaman. This is only request."

"I have great ability to influence the peoples of the mountains," Salle'allak said glancing at Carrita. "I have a feeling you will be the greatest shaman your people have ever known."

Before another word could be spoken he waved his hand and the cave was left dark and cold. When Carrita made a small globe of light, Gailexa and Salle'allak were gone.

Airria was also left feeling a little hollow. For weeks now Gailexa had been a guide, help and extra pair of eyes. She had taught the group so much. Now she was gone and that part of Airria was gone with her.

Carrita was the first to say anything, "I will miss her. I am not sure if we would have come so far without her."

Faith spoke next, "We will have to hope what she taught us will be enough to carry us the rest of the way. If I read the map correctly, we are months of travel either direction to a port."

Joskin pulled out the map, "Sure enough it is a long way to a port. It looks like the one to the northeast is the closest, but our ship is back the other way."

"The ship will not be a problem," Carrita said. "If you would like it to be in the north port, then I will make it accordingly." She paused for a moment, "Will we be able to travel safely either direction without Gailexa?"

Airria stated, "It doesn't matter, with or without her, nothing we do will be safe. She is safer away from us. I will miss her too, but we need to be going."

Chapter 23 – Black Armor

Faith sighed as she watched the clouds move wildly below her. They seemed to twist from one side to the other between the sharp ridges. It almost made her sad to watch the futility; it reminded her of her own seemingly never-ending journey. It had been over a month since they had left the last naga city. Nothing but mountains, snow and the occasional snow herd.

At first Faith had found it interesting how the large, soft pawed creatures with their pointed noses lived on nothing but the strange plants which grew deep in the snow. Even they had become boring. *What I would not give to see some grass, a meadow, a valley floor. Along such thoughts, what I would not give to see something besides horses with color in it,* she thought to herself. "Do you think we will ever see the end of these ridges?" she said as she began running a finger over the leaf pattern on her armor out of boredom.

"It has to end sometime," Airria said, trying to make his voice carry over the wind.

Faith appreciated Airria's attempt to keep his horse in position to keep the wind off her. The wind was far too strong on the ridges to ride the horses, so her legs were tired. She had even noticed Carrita shivering.

Joskin had not slept for three days. The shelters, like the ones they had used coming up the mountains had been three days' journey apart. It was now day three, almost evening and still no sign of shelter.

"We will spend the night here!" Joskin yelled over the wind. He had been trying to block the wind for Carrita.

Carrita collapsed on the side of the trail with her back to the wind. She looked at the sky as if she were pleading for relief. She had not been doing well for the last week. Faith had tried to help where she could, neither her magic nor her strength were enough to make any real difference. The girl was a very powerful mage, but she was still just a girl.

Even Airria and Joskin were looking very tired. Joskin looked especially exhausted, but had kept going.

Joskin and Airria pulled their horses off the trail and used them to trample down the snow, creating a hole, a shelter from the wind. The hole did not provide much protection, but with the wind and cold every bit of protection counted.

Faith sat down next to her friend and put a comforting arm around her.

"I know it has to end sometime, but I cannot handle any more of this," Carrita's voice was soft and shaky. "We need some heat, some fire. There is no way I could have known it would be this cold."

Faith could feel Carrita shivering; somehow it made her feel colder. She had to help! The trees were well below the cloud line. The only wood they had was the arrows in her quiver. "I know what to do!" she caught herself saying out loud as she reached back and grabbed some arrows. "It may not be much, but it will keep you warm for a little while," she said to Carrita's questioning eyes as she began straining to break them.

She could feel the blood rushing to her face as she struggled. She could feel Carrita, weakly helping with her magic. Finally, one at a time they broke.

"They will burn long and hot, but the smoke will be very dangerous," Carrita hesitated as she spoke.

"This will work," Faith said as she quickly handed her pile of broken shafts to Carrita.

Carrita winced as she took the wood, "This should be interesting."

Faith excitedly ran off to instruct Joskin and Airria on how she wanted the shelter to be designed. "Can we dig a little under the crust?" Faith asked as Joskin and Airria were pulling the horses into position to put them down for the night. Without waiting for an answer she walked over to the wall farthest from the trail, the side the wind hit first and began digging. She quickly found it was divided into layers. Some of the layers were almost as hard as ice, some were softer than cotton. She dug, chipped and pushed the snow until she had made a small spherical cave just large enough for the four of them. She then went over to her horse and pulled out one of the hides she had been carrying and placed it a few paces away from cave.

"What is she doing?" Faith could hear Joskin asking. Both Joskin and Airria had sat and were watching the whole thing in wonderment.

She only gave them a mild glance, pulled some glowing ash out of a pouch and carefully placed it on the skin in a small circle. "Elen she taran tic," she began to chant over and over again, magically binding the brighter glowing ash to the hide and infusing her magic into the mix. *This should do it*, she thought to herself and ran over and grabbed the broken shafts from Carrita, then she ran back and carefully placed them on the hide.

With the sticks in place she formed a small sphere of fire in the center of the pile. Hotter and hotter she made it. She watched carefully and backed away as it got too hot for her to handle. She put more manna into heating the sphere. "This is taking more than I thought," she kept telling herself.

After what seemed like way to long, smoke began to rise from the broken arrow shafts. Shortly after that, a swirl of black flame began to flicker with cruel glee. It grew darker and bigger. It seemed to pull any light and happiness out of the air.

430

As the flame grew, Airria paced back and forth outside of the reach of the fire. He would stop, look at the flames for awhile, then would look at Faith, then Carrita, then back to the fire; finally he would begin pacing again.

Faith watched the cycle a few times and then turned to Carrita. She was reaching for the warmth of the fire, but her eyes were twitching uncomfortably.

The waxing moon was rising slowly in the sky.

Joskin bedded down near the horses which were growing uneasy. Joskin set his bed and lay with his back to the fire.

Inside Faith had been proud of her ingenuity, but it seemed as if her actions had made the entire group very uncomfortable. Even Airria seemed unwilling to be around her. She looked at the fire while she contemplated everybody's reactions.

She was soon pulled away by the vicious dance of the dark flames. In them she could see her father selling her to the slaver with a malicious grin on his face, as if he was glad to get rid of her. She could see every bad thing that had ever happened to her. As she watched, the inviting cruelty beckoned her closer, as if touching the bitter flames would make the pain go away. The closer she got, the more her anger and depression grew. She felt herself reaching out, knowing deep in her heart of the fire's lies, but the hope of relief kept her reaching.

"No!" Airria screamed, only vaguely registering to Faith. He grabbed the corners of the hide and flung the flames deep into the snow out of the protective hole. Then he threw the hide as far away as he could.

Both Faith and Carrita let out a shriek of painful protest. In her heart Faith was glad to be rid of the pain, lies, and all else the fire had brought, except for the warmth it brought to her friend.

Carrita had a look of horrified relief on her face. Her hand was stretched out, reaching after the now gone flame. Then she noticed webbed veins of black running from the tip of her finger to her wrist. Her eyes were distant, much like they were the first time Faith had seen the girl.

431

"What is this!" Faith yelled to no one in particular as she grabbed Carrita's hand. "What happened to your hand?" Her eyes watered up as she looked at Carrita.

Carrita stared with a blank longing after the flames and did not respond.

Airria ran over next to the two of them and yanked Carrita's hand away from Faith. "What have you done?" His face showed anger and then immediate regret for yelling at Faith.

"What is going on?" Joskin was standing, ax at the ready.

"Faith cursed Carrita!" Airria seemed surprised at his own words.

Joskin carefully laid his ax down and came toward them. "What happened?" he pointedly, yet calmly asked Faith.

A tear rolled down Faith's cheek, "I just wanted to let her have some warmth. I didn't mean…" She really was beginning to believe it was something she had done.

Joskin cut her off, "What happened?" This time he asked with more concern and less accusation. "What is going on?"

Airria held up Carrita's hand. Joskin grasped it, looked at it for a second and then looked at the snow.

"Is there nothing we can do?" Faith asked, more to Carrita then to Joskin.

"I have never seen anyone come back from this," Joskin said sadly.

Carrita began staring at her hand with a dazed fascination and began blankly humming childish songs.

"There is a way to help her," a weak melodic voice chimed in.

Carrita didn't even seem to notice. Joskin stepped toward his axe. Airria and Faith stood up to see where the voice came from.

On the edge of the hole knelt an Elven woman with waist length brown, naturally curly hair dragging on the ground. Her emerald green eyes glistened in the faint moonlight. Her frost covered, firm body easily showed through her tattered cloth covering. "I can help her if you will allow me," the voice chimed again.

Faith began to remove her cloak, but she noticed Joskin with a hypnotized look walking by her with his cloak outstretched.

"Please, how can you help?" the gentleness in his voice surprised Faith.

"I have never seen him look or speak to anyone like he is looking and speaking to her," Airria said with soft suspicion.

"If she can help…" Faith said putting a soft hand on Airria's back. "We will keep an extra eye on her." She was trying to convince herself as much as Airria. "We have no choice."

The elf seemed grateful for the cloak. She wrapped it around herself and smiled gently at Joskin, "Your kindness is most welcome." She cautiously approached Carrita. Carrita was still calmly examining her hand, watching the black veins creep up her arm.

The elf examined the girl for a short while at a distance and then she came closer to her. She gently grabbed Carrita's hand with her left hand and began tracing five veins at a time with her right hand. She followed the veins, one finger on each, all the way to Carrita's fingertip. When she was finished she started on another five veins.

After the third sweep, a small amount of black fluid began oozing out of a tiny hole in Carrita's finger. "This is not enough!" the elf gasped, looking around frantically. When she spotted the dagger handle on Joskin's hip, she asked him, "May I borrow your knife?" Without thinking, Joskin handed it to her, concern in his eyes.

It was difficult to see what the elf was doing through her elegantly wild hair, but it became obvious that the black veins had stopped climbing up Carrita's arm. They even started retreating slightly.

"The sliver will have to come out," Joskin offered.

"Sliver?" Faith asked.

"This is what happens when you get a Black Sliver," the elf explained gently. There is a reason this wood is the favored weapon of assassins, undead and is favored for arrow shafts near the Black Forest."

"So this IS my fault!"

"Yes, but…" Airria caught himself before he said any more.

"It is very cold up here," the elf comforted, "this is a hard lesson for someone this young to learn, but I think she needed the warmth. I imagine this is a hard lesson for you, too," the elf's words brought little comfort.

"Carrita must have known what would happen," Faith heard herself trying to justify.

"I don't know how a young human from outside of this area has survived to reach this place," the elf said. "Even with such obviously adventuresome companions I am surprised you recognized what was happening, much less so quickly," she added with a touch of suspicion in her voice.

"I have traveled a bit," Joskin almost smiled.

"It does not matter now. There is a fungus around here. It grows in the snow, near branches of the top-line brush." The elf looked at Faith. "It is very difficult to find without magic. If you can feel the magic, you can find them." With her right hand the elf reached out and grabbed Faith's hand.

Faith felt a frosty, cold feeling rush through her and the elf said, "That is what you are looking for," she then went back to work on Carrita's finger.

Faith began to protest, but Airria stood up and said, "If it is the only way we can help, then we will try."

Chapter 24 - Healing

Faith closed her eyes and held Airria's hand as they headed down the slope; the sky was filling with stars. She reached out, trying to feel the magic. For quite a while all she could feel was Airria. Then, still well above the tree line, she began feeling what Joskin had called pseudo-plant life, plants that grow in the thick layers of snow, never touching the earth.

The moon was high in the sky when she finally began feeling the first earth-based plants, the top-line brush. For some time Faith ran along the edge of where she understood the fungus should be. Finally she felt one, but it was very deep in the snow. She could feel they grew in groups and were at varying depths.

When they found one not far from the surface, Airria used his sword to break though the icy crust around the top of the plant, then used his shield to dig in the softer snow until he had cleared out and smashed down enough snow that the plant was uncovered to his height.

There were only patches of the fungus on a plant which more closely resembled a root than a bush. Steam rose from the fungus as if it were hot and the snow melted off the branches as if they were warming up.

Airria cut the whole bush, as much as was now above the snow. He pushed it up to Faith then broke a path, a ramp, out of the hole.

The plant was very warm to the touch when felt through the glowing spongy looking fungus. When Faith started peeling off the fungus, she noticed the woody plant became too hot to touch.

Airria said, "We don't know how much we will need, so why don't we take the whole thing back," he paused for only a moment and then began dragging the bush up the mountain.

When they arrived back at camp the elf was still trying to extract the poison from Carrita's hand. The dark veins on her arm had receded very little and a grey-green hue had overtaken the pigment of her skin. Joskin looked extremely concerned.

"Here it is," Airria said with apprehension and then he asked, "is there anything else we can do?"

"I could use a copper kettle and a mortar and pestle, if you have one handy," the elf said as she looked up for a moment.

"How is she?" Faith asked.

"Her mind is slipping away," now even the elf had concern in her voice. "On the bright side, her mind is slipping away much slower than expected," the elf said trying to muster some courage. "She is very strong."

"You obviously know about magic, why will you not heal her?" Airria asked as he returned with the requested items.

"Herbal magic works very differently than spells. The sliver was Black Wood, the most powerful of raw herbal magics," the elf said as she took the mortar and pestle then used the knife Joskin had handed her earlier to scrape a little fungus into it. She then chopped off several other branches with the fungus on them and placed them in a very specific pattern, fungus toward the center. Finally she filled the kettle with snow and placed it on the sticks.

"Can you not simply magically pull the poison out of her?" Faith asked.

"I have been trying," the elf replied as she crushed the fungus. She would stop for a moment and rub her hands over the kettle and she leaned in slightly. She glanced up at Faith and added, "You are welcome to try, but it is far beyond me," then went back to her work.

As the men watched, Faith placed her fingertips on some of the black veins and reached out with her magic to touch the poison. It was not hard to find the toxins; they felt like the same merciless temptations she felt with the black flames. She began trying to pull them, as the elf had done, but not only found resistance, she found she wanted to be a part of it, to join the blackness. She began running her hands down the streaks, longing to get enough of the bitter poison for herself.

About halfway down Carrita's arm Faith was blasted with a rush of free magic. She could hear Airria and even Joskin gasp. The elf screamed, "What is she!" The blasts of energy were like standing in a forest blaze for Faith. It was all she could do to keep it from overwhelming her.

Airria dove on Faith pulling her grip off Carrita. The heat subsided; the overwhelming magic lessened to tolerable, but was still very strong.

Again the elf asked, a little more in control of herself, "What is she?"

Faith looked up, "A very special girl."

The elf's brow furrowed and her eyes lowered. "This can't be allowed to happen," she said under her breath and began crushing more purposefully. When she was done she added the powder she had just created to the now boiling water and went to the saddlebags where Airria had pulled out the copper kettle. In frustration she checked the other side. Finally in disgust she said, "I do not know if I can refine it enough!" as she handed the cloak back to Joskin.

Faith put a hand on her shoulder, "She is just a girl. Whatever you do it should help."

"She is not just a girl! She is obviously not even 'just' human," the elf said sadly. "That level of magic is only heard of in legends of the ancient days of power. She is not turning into a zombie; she is turning into a lich, an undead mage of pure death!"

438

Both Airria and Joskin took a step back. Faith persisted, "She is a very powerful mage, this is true. She has power and knowledge far beyond her years. Sometimes it is hard, even for me, to remember, but in truth she is just a girl. I do not know the dangers of trying to help her. I don't know what could happen. I do know you had an idea, a chance of a method for helping. If you have not the courage to continue then please instruct me and I will take the risk.

"The risk is; if we fail she will finish the transformation," the elf said in frustration. "The poison is feeding on her magic, defending itself. Normally the process leaves the victim completely drained, devoid of any real life force. She is so powerful…" her voice trailed off as her eyes dropped to the ground.

Faith lifted the elf's gaze to meet her own, "If we do not try, we will fail. Failure is not a possibility to me. I have given up too much to stop trying. So, what shall I do to finish what you started?"

The elf worked side by side with Faith deep into the night. The bitter cold seemed to melt away in the strain and worry of preparing the potion. They used almost the entire bush to heat the kettle, first by using some of the fungus covered branches, then they burned the uncovered part, finally they used heat from the branches to simmer the mixture.

Airria and Joskin stood and watched. When Airria suggested Joskin get some sleep, he replied, "There is nothing I can do to help Carrita." Then he looked at the elf and added, "This elf did not choose those clothes for her travels. She escaped from somewhere; they will likely be coming for her. There is nothing I can do to help Carrita, but I can help protect the one who can." His eyes scanned the moonlit snow as if he were looking for a fight.

As the simmering liquid began to gel, there was a sharp horn blow in the distance. The elf looked up, "I wish they had been a little slower," she said under her breath. She looked at Faith, "The orcs are coming now," then she continued by giving a rushed explanation of how to administer the potion.

Before she could finish Joskin said almost excitedly, "This is a job for the grunt labor," slapped Airria on the back and jumped up on the now solid, frozen snow bank and readied for a fight. Airria stood next to Joskin his sword and shield readied.

Faith turned to the elf, "Finish what you started, we will keep them at bay," she said as she grabbed her bow and arrows.

"This is my fight," the elf said sadly, "I can at least lead them away."

"Carrita was our fight, one we would have lost already without you," Faith said with a smile. "Besides, I don't think we could talk the boys out of this fight." With a wink she took up position behind Joskin and Airria.

The first thing they saw was a worg, a thick haired wolf the size of a healthy pony, with a rider in silvery mail and a long spear in hand. He was closely followed by several others, though not so well armored. The last rider to be recognized in the dim moonlight was in a long flowing robe with feathers flailing in the wind.

"There is my target!" Faith said as the magic user came into view.

"Which one?" Airria asked, but there was not time to answer. Faith stepped sideways and let her first arrow fly.

A bronze colored shield began to form in front of the mage, but exploded, the arrow was undeterred. The orc turned to stone and tumbled off his mount, disappearing into the deep snow. The worg's body fell limp, sliding across the snow.

The lead orc slowed his pace, but motioned and screamed to the others in something Faith recognized as the Orc Tongue.

Joskin and Airria charged in, with movements so quick they dropped the worgs, sending them crashing into the snow and quickly dispatched the grunting orcs.

A loud crash sent Airria tumbling face down into the snow. Splinters rained back as far as Faith. The lead orc, who had never made it to the boys, had thrown his spear with such force it had shattered on Airria's back. Without thinking Faith lined up and released an arrow, directly over where Airria had fallen.

Airria, who was trying to recover his feet, was yanked up by his shield to block the arrow. The force of the arrow knocked Airria over the other way. Faith ran to his aid as the orc turned and disappeared into the darkness. Airria was sitting in the snow and had already removed his helm. He had a disgusted look on his face. Faith began to apologize but was interrupted.

"I can't believe I turned my back on a live target!" Airria and Joskin said in unison.

Faith was relieved to know they were all right and not upset with her, though she chided herself for not remembering about Airria's shield. "Now we see what happens when we get overconfident," she said it as much to herself as to the boys.

Airria took his time getting up. Though it really did not take long, Joskin was already back, checking on Carrita. By the time Faith and Airria arrived, Carrita was in convulsions and had begun screaming. Magic lashed out in guided waves, like a whip of pure violet. Joskin was trying to hold down Carrita while the elf tried to fend off the powerful attacks. The elf was quickly wearing out; sweat was running down her slender body and her knees and arms were shaking.

Faith began creating a protection globe for the elf, but she quickly found herself on the defensive. She had seen Carrita do some extremely powerful things, but now she had the opportunity to feel the actual power. It amazed her how much magic the girl possessed. The lashes split every shield Faith put up.

When the lashes knocked her to her knees, Airria jumped in and began using his shield to fend off the attacks. He was trying to stand tall, but the power of the buffeting knocked him to his knees.

Why is she not attacking Joskin? Faith wondered. *What is different about what he is doing?* In desperation she darted out from under Airria's shield, ran over, dodging the lashes and grabbed Carrita's hand. "I am here!" she shouted. Then, as calmly as she could, added almost under her breath, "I will help you where I can until you are better," more as a resolve then to reassure Carrita.

The rage filled magic waves stopped and the only sound that could be heard was the gasping of air and the unrelenting wind over their heads. After she caught her breath, the elf said, "Now it is up to her."

Faith replied, "We will stay and watch."

441

"Thank you for the warmth you have shared and for reminding me why I came to this place. I am sorry I can do no more for your friend. The orcs will continue looking for me. I am not sure how you staved them off, but they will send more. I cannot put you in any more danger," she handed Joskin back his cloak.

Faith was about to ask her to stay but was cut off by Joskin. "Carrita is still ill and you are cold," he said as he waved off the cloak. "You have spent much of your energy to help us. The least we can do is offer you some warmth and protection for the night." He received an almost playful smile from the elf for which he added, "Besides you are not the only one they will be looking for now."

"Why would a band of orcs be so concerned about a simple elf?" Airria asked. His question earned him a sour look from Joskin.

"It is quite silly, I think, but their head shaman believes my hair will help him create a fertility potion. Apparently the queen is having trouble in conceiving," the elf said, a little embarrassed, still holding out the cloak.

"Why your hair?" Airria continued the questioning.

My hair is very dark for an elf in this region," she smiled. "Orcs have their own ideas on magic. Everything I have studied indicates they are wrong."

"Not to mention slave trade and the fact that, to an orc, there is no better meat than elf," Joskin added.

"That still doesn't explain why they would pursue you with the vigor you are claiming," Airria insisted.

"Revenge," Faith interjected, "she obviously escaped. If I am guessing correctly, they wanted some information from her." Faith looked up and examined the elf. "An orc interrogator," Faith shuddered as she said it, "thankfully, I can only imagine."

By the look on the elf's face she knew she was closer than the elf would have liked to admit. "Escapes, as you well know," she continued, looking at Airria, "are often bloody. If the wrong orc tried to stop her, the whole escape would become personal to the king." Faith sympathetically glanced at the elf again.

442

The elf looked at the ground, "The torture master was the king's brother. The inquisitor was the queen herself." She collapsed in the snow, "The spell was not supposed to kill them. It was just a defense. I panicked and there was an explosion," a small tear fell down her cheek.

"They are orcs!" Airria exclaimed. "Why feel bad?"

The elf looked up at Airria but didn't get a chance to say anything. Joskin spoke up, "They are a part of life." He picked up his cloak and placed it around the elf's shoulders and looked deeply into her eyes, "We have been dealing death and seeing the effects of several who have an orc-like mentality for so long, sometimes we forget how valuable life can be. Sometimes we need a reminder."

The elf grinned pleasantly at Joskin's attempt to placate her. "Sometimes I forget there are people who view life in varying degrees of value," she said with only a hint of chastisement.

"Without people like these," a weak voice chimed in, "you would not have had the chance to learn what you have." Carrita's voice was like music to their ears.

Faith, without thinking, pulled Carrita up into a hug. Her body was still limp. Faith released her grip to make sure Carrita was still breathing.

Carrita gave a weak smile. Faith gently laid her back, not knowing what to say.

"That was much quicker than I thought it would be," the elf said.

"Your skill with potion making is better than you know. The potion was a very difficult one. Not many could have done so well with such crude instruments," Carrita looked gratefully at the elf.

"I think you are stronger than you would like for anyone to know," the elf smiled. "Nonetheless, thank you for your compliment. From one such as you, so well mastered in the magical arts, it is a true compliment."

A weak look of concern crossed Carrita's face as she glanced at Faith. Faith responded to the look with a smile, "Somewhere along the way you let go of your magical restraints and even lashed out a little."

A sad look crossed Carrita's face as she noticed the magic burns on all of them. The elf spoke up, "All will be well before I leave." With a sparkle in her eye she looked around the group and added, "I have witnessed their courage and caring for you. They would do it all again and more to see you well again. Such compassion and dedication I have rarely seen among humans."

"You have seen only a small portion of the dedication and compassion from them," Carrita said with pride, still very weak.

"It appears I am no longer needed here," the elf said. "You are healing quickly." She got up and hesitantly removed the cloak.

Joskin began to protest, but Carrita's weak voice took control of the conversation, "I will give you three good reasons not to leave. Please listen to what I have to offer, if afterwards you still desire to leave we will provide you with warm clothes, directions and our blessing to help you along your journey." When the elf nodded and replaced the cloak around her, Carrita continued, "This mountain range is vast and harsh. It takes several months to cross it. On your own, the chances of surviving are very low. If you leave, it would hurt us as much as it hurt you to take the lives of the orcs."

"Reason two, if you stay to see me fully well we can exchange knowledge."

The elf made a quick protest, but was cut short. "I do have a reasonable understanding of magic, but there is always more to learn. Even the newest apprentice mage has knowledge the greatest mages do not. I believe you are not a beginner, so I believe there is much we can give each other."

"Third, you promised to help clean up my mess," Carrita smiled still weak, yet nonetheless playful.

"Your words and wisdom are far beyond your years. I can appreciate your concern for me and I do not long to feel the chill of these high peaks. As I am sure you have guessed I am not from this region. I was sent to deliver a message from my people to the Snow Elves. I was severely delayed by the orcs already."

"Yet you stopped to help us," Faith said.

"Which has cost me precious time."

Carrita got another big smile across her face as a glitter crossed her eyes. "What if I said your message could be delivered within two days if you will but trust me?"

"How can I trust you with something so important when I cannot even receive a straight answer as to who or what you are?" the elf said.

"Fair enough. They call me Carrita, I am daughter of Tarsella. I have trained under many, including Jammar, the Light Bringer, and Bregette, Guardian mage of these peaks," Carrita paused for a moment.

The elf had turned ghostly white, "Your mother is…"

Carrita tried to sit up and interrupted the elf, "Yes. She was governor of Darian, among other titles." Carrita lowered her head but kept her eyes on the elf.

The elf began to bow, but Carrita held out a hand, putting her other softly on her mouth, "I have shared more about myself than I have with any outside of this circle. Now will you trust me?"

"Few even know those names," the elf gasped, "If I had not been sent on this errand I would know your mother's name and that only by legend."

"Will you stay?" Joskin asked.

"I would consider myself the greatest of fools not to take such an opportunity." She bowed to both Carrita and Faith.

Carrita smiled, again showing her fatigue, "Then it is settled, when I am rested I will make sure your message is delivered. For now, I need the rest." The sun broke free of the peaks as she shut her eyes.

Joskin asked, "Since you will be with us for awhile, what should we call you?"

"I am Niesla, from across the sea," the elf said, keeping her eyes on the snow.

They smiled and introduced themselves formally and began cleaning up camp. Joskin made a large pack out of his blanket and Faith helped him put Carrita in it. Airria helped him put it on. When Niesla began to protest, a kind yet resolute glance from Faith silenced her.

Joskin said, "The orcs will be back here tonight. We will want some distance and I think Faith can cover our tracks well enough that we won't have to fight any time soon."

Chapter 25 – The Long Walk

Carrita awoke to the sound of the wind in the trees. It had been a long time since she had heard such a calm melody. The light bounce and sounds of laughter let her know the group was traveling and in much better spirits. She opened her eyes and saw trees. It was still bitter cold but the wind was far less intense.

"Hey there little girl!" Faith said when she noticed Carrita's eyes open. "Good to see you awake. How are you feeling?" The entire group stopped at Faith's words.

"I feel warmer than I have in a long time, but I feel a little restricted," Carrita responded. Though it was still bitter cold, the magic in her robes was now enough to keep her warm. To see everybody happy again warmed her heart even more.

"It's about time," Joskin said with a chuckle. "You are getting too big to be carried around." He set Carrita down gently and helped her out of the pack.

Her legs were stiff, her whole body hurt, but it felt good to move around. She threw some snow in the air just to watch it hit the branches.

She looked down at her hand. There was a hint of webbing still running up her arm, like a faded tattoo. She had not noticed the frown which crossed her face until she heard the elf, "I have only heard of two people in the elves' long history who could get rid of those marks, Mellinatia and your mother." Her voice was much stronger than it had been and still sounded more like music than speech.

"She was an exceptional mage," Carrita said with sad pride.

The elf was now wearing a caribou hide jerkin, trousers and boots. Carrita took a moment to admire the craftsmanship. "Did you do this?" Carrita asked as she touched the elf's sleeves. Faith's old cloak was partially wrapped around the elf.

"I have a little practice with making clothes. Besides, Faith's armor was a little big for me," Niesla said, waving her hands in front of her to indicate the obvious chest and hip difference between her and Faith.

"Are you wearing products of death?" Carrita asked.

The elf blushed slightly, "It is surprising how your views on life can change when faced with death. This whole trip has taught me much about this world," she smiled at Joskin.

"It is good to have high ideals, but there comes a time when you realize one life lost may save many others from death or worse," Carrita added.

"If I had not killed those orcs, my message would never have had a chance to get to the Snow Elves. Without this caribou we would have died," Niesla continued.

"How long was I asleep?" Carrita asked, amazed at the change in the elf.

Airria answered, "A week."

The look on her face must have matched the shock she felt inside, because the elf chimed back in, "You used a lot of magic while you were sick. Also you had a lot to physically recover from."

Not wanting to go into her ordeal with the sliver, Carrita changed the subject. "I am sorry; I did not mean to delay you so long. If you would like I will deliver your message for you now."

Niesla smiled, still avoiding eye contact, "Very well. If you could get word to Bregette; Marren, the Governor of Sulitamis sends word…" she paused, a look of sadness crossed her face, "her free port city is under siege by Zerith."

"You made this trip to deliver that message?" Joskin asked in confused curiosity. "Zerith has been trying to take that port longer than even the elves can remember."

"This time is very different. As you know, Zerith has always been a slave-based country. Any non-humans are considered less than the dogs. This time the siege has been joined by orcs, goblins and even creatures too evil and powerful to describe." Niesla's voice began to shake, "The siege engines and magic attacks continue both night and day."

"By your description… are you sure the city still stands?" Joskin paused to think, "I mean, it would have taken you months to get this far."

A small tear ran down her face, "No, I do not know if they are all right, but I had to try."

"We will get your message to Bregette," Faith reassured her.

"Why her?" Airria asked. "Are there no Guardians closer who can help?"

Niesla glanced at Faith, and then to Carrita, "The land is cut off by the siege. Marren said the Guardians were already busy," Niesla replied.

Carrita interjected, "It does not matter why the message is for Bregette. What does matter is I promised to deliver it to her." Without another word Carrita sat down in the snow, back against a tree and passed into the Astral Plane. She looked back at her body; she wished in herself she could control her manna. She was growing brighter each time she saw her body and still did not want anyone to know.

This was not important now. Now it is time to deliver this message. She retraced the steps back up the slope at the speed of thought. She slowed to see a mess of orc souls around what were cleaver traps.

The blur of magic around them let Carrita know Niesla set a few magical ones as well. She had to admire the craftiness, but was disturbed to see this many other orcs traveling down the trail. Thirty to forty with auras like pitch. One with enough power Carrita could not even see its form, just a huge sphere of black.

I had better go back and warn them, was her first thought. *No. I have a duty of my own. Besides, they likely have many more such traps. This set killed most of them. Another set should finish them off...* Her thoughts were cut short by the huge number of orc spirits advancing menacingly toward her. She began to form a spell out of instinct, but quickly found she did not have access to her manna. In panic she began to run, hoping she could outrun them.

It didn't take her long to realize she was much faster and she changed her course to circle them, then wisped up the trail, diverting around six more such groups of orc spirits. Each joined the chase. The faster she went, the more tired she became. It was as if she was using magic. When she had a comfortable lead she slowed to save energy.

It took her most of the day to reach the naga city, now on the far side of the range. Relief rushed over her when she saw Bregette was waiting for her at the gate.

"You bring quite a crowd with you," Bregette said with a smile as Carrita rushed up.

"There were too many for me. I am sorry," Carrita said childishly.

"Yet another danger of traveling this plane," Bregette said as a gentle warning. "They will have to be dealt with before we talk." She raised her arms straight in the air, the palms of her hands facing up. Then she began chanting in a tongue Carrita did not recognize. When the orcs were easily in view, she violently brought her hands down and pushed out. A hole formed out of nothing, opening what seemed to be a portal into what appeared to be a judgment chamber. At one end of the chamber sat a council of eight; a minotaur, an elf, a vampire in full demonic form, a human, an ogre, a merman, a dwarf and an eagle-man. Across a large bench from the council seemed to be countless souls waiting.

The council looked at Carrita and Bregette. The human spoke, calmly he asked, "Why have you opened this door?"

Bregette simply pointed to the oncoming orcs. Without another word, the entire council waved their hands and a black portal opened up and swallowed the entire army. The vampire and minotaur looked especially pleased.

Bregette nodded and the doorway closed. When it was closed, she said, "They usually protest more when I do that, but with these orcs their fates had already been sealed." She smiled down at Carrita, "Now to answer your message..."

Carrita cut her off, "How do you know what the message is and how did you know I was coming?"

Bregette smiled, "I have known she was coming since before you left this city. The unrest which has led Airria on his quest has consumed the known world. Not long after you arrived, the Naga Council, Elven council and I got together and scryed to check on Sulitamis. In the past it has been one of the first places to be attacked when trouble erupts. It just so happened it was on the day your new elf friend set sail. I have been trying to keep an eye out for her, but I lost her a few weeks ago. I found her again as the whole group was descending the northern slope. The rest I figured based on a history I will not go into right now. The naga on the other side of the range sent word though this same method that there was an army of orcs on the move and a large number had been killed by some very well designed traps. I have been waiting here for two days now, in hopes you would be coming. That part I did not know. I only hoped you would come. I thank you for helping the elf; she would have died without you."

"And I would have died without her," Carrita looked at her hand for a second. She knew she could make the webbing go away in this place with a mere thought, but oddly it was now a part of her and a reminder she wanted to hold on to. "She saved me first..." she caught herself and changed the subject back to the task at hand."What will you do about the siege?" she asked.

"I have already done it," Bregette said with a proud smile. "Did you not find it odd that a society so steeped in matriarchal tradition

450

would stop what they were working on and dedicate so much time and resources to a group obviously led by two men?" Then with a little more serious look she added, "There are three Guardians who live here when we get the chance. We are bound to our sphere of Guardianship. Usually we are far too busy to stop and train. Yet each of us helped teach each of you beyond what we have ever taught any mortal or demi-mortal."

"I had not thought of it," Carrita replied sheepishly. "Would it not have been easier to send some naga and elves to help?

"Easier, maybe," Bregette said with the patience of age showing on her face. "We, as Guardians, are not here to force our wills on others, only to advise and protect them. The naga were not ready to let the world know of their existence much less their abilities." She smiled and added, "Besides, they have their own troubles to deal with here. The orcs and giants are on the move and the trolls are multiplying." She paused and thought for a moment then continued, "From everything I have discovered, every bastion of hope or freedom is under siege and every major tyrant has been fortified with dark forces or has joined forces with other tyrants. The naga have, only just this month, staved off a siege of giants and trolls. Only the kingdom of Athlstan, south and west of Zerith has had no major trouble yet, but they have sent many troops to defend Freeholm, a free port on their borders. There are no extra resources." With a rueful smile she continued, "I believe it will not be long before the Guardians will have to intervene, as will the entire pantheon of deities to restore any semblance of good back to this world."

"So, you expect us to break this siege?" Carrita asked sincerely.

"We expect nothing of you," Bregette smiled. "We have given as much as we could. We only hope it is enough. This port is the port Airria will need to go through to reach his destination. From what we have seen of you four, you will not have the heart to walk away. I can also tell you, you will not be able to break this siege on your own. We only hope what we have given you will be enough to tip the scales.

"Then I guess we had better be on our way," Carrita said, her voice full of resolve. "If the port is still free we will do what we can."

"The port is still free. It has high, magically protected walls, many powerful mages, strong warriors and a wise leader." For the first time Bregette showed true worry, "Even with all of that, I don't know how much longer they will be able to maintain the defense."

"Then I best not delay," Carrita said with regret, "I know the others will be glad to help where they can, though I would have liked to have more time to talk on pleasant things."

"I do not believe this will be out last encounter," Bregette said with a comforting smile. Then she added a word of caution, "Remember that when you are on the Astral Plane it is the speed of your mind which is your power. The quickness of your mind is all the physical attributes you are used to on the solid plane. If you encounter those who have died and you run, you will be plagued with them for the rest of your existence. You will need to weaken their hold on this dimension so they can be sent to their judgment, to stand before the council of souls."

"How?" Carrita asked, "I do not have access to my magic."

"As you know, your speed, agility, strength and all other physical attributes are governed in this plane by your mind," Bregette explained, a sword forming in her hand. "Holding it toward Carrita she added, "this is no more real than are your clothes, but to a spirit this is a sword and when they are struck, just like a real sword on the Physical Plane, this will weaken a spirit's hold on the Astral Plane."

"Thank you again for all you have done," Carrita said with a bow. "It is time to be getting back to the others," she added as she turned to leave.

Carrita wished she had spent more time learning to fight with a sword. As she rushed back to the group she began to think about what Bregette had told her. *If I have to fight a physical battle, I should dress for it.* She began imagining the armor Faith wore. She looked down and admired how perfect the armor looked. Then imagined herself armed with Faith's bow and arrows and Airria's sword and shield. Everything was scaled down to her size and was exactly how she remembered them.

Chapter 26 – War Stories

"She's been like this most of the day," Airria said, looking at the dark looming cloud climbing down the mountain trail. The cloud had been in view for a couple of days now. Niesla had said it would allow the orcs to travel and fight during the day. This also meant it would be more difficult to fight the orcs.

Faith reminded him, "You know she was like this for weeks at a time while we were being trained in the naga city."

Niesla was shaking her head as they sat in a circle around Carrita. "I am still having a difficult time believing you actually talked to naga. They really exist?"

Joskin put a muscular hand over the petite elf's hand and said, "They live with the Snow Elves in the tops of the mountains."

Niesla's eyes were wide as she gazed at Joskin. "You trained with them? You actually trained with them?"

Joskin smiled as he let out a soft sigh, "Airria and Faith trained with them. I was trained by a fierce elf named Aktu and a talented human fighter named Kore. They said I missed out on my training with Jammar, so they were pushing me to catch up."

Niesla put a hand over her mouth. "Aktu? Kore? You met them, too? How was it? What are they like?"

"Why are you so curious about them?" Airria asked.

Faith smiled at Airria sweetly, "They are Guardians. Even I know few people have the opportunity to meet, much less interact with them. Most who have met them are unaware they have met a lesser deity."

Niesla pulled her gaze from Joskin, "It is more than that. I was raised on stories of their adventures while they were still mortal. I thought them only legends." She began her story, "It is written Aktu removed the monstrous leg of a matrataur in one swing of her sword. Kore is rumored to have sliced clear though an orc in full Taulkrick gold armor, shield and all," she winced as she brought up Kore's exploits.

Faith asked, "What is a matrataur?"

"Until lately I thought they were legends as well. Now that I know Aktu and Kore are real, perhaps the beasts are real as well."

"At the rate we are going, we will have to face one someday, I am sure," Faith insisted. "What are they like?"

"According to my books they are ruthless, blood thirsty and cruel; the pride of Rantail's existence. By all description they are larger and stronger in both physical strength and magic than minotaurs. They have horns as black as a starless sky and sharp teeth meant for ripping the flesh from their still struggling victims."

Airria thought back to the shrines on the island. The description Niesla had given brought to mind the final creatures Rantail had made for the Great War. Through the shrine he had witnessed how cruel and powerful they could be. He hoped he would not have to face one.

Niesla continued, "I hope they are legend."

Faith sighed, "Only a year ago I believed magic and elves were only myth." Faith summoned a small globe of fire, "now I am talking to an elf and casting a spell."

Airria's jaw clenched and unclenched as he thought about the day he learned that dragons were real. "It was a hard day when I learned some legends are real."

Thankfully Joskin took the conversation back to a less disturbing topic. "The captain of the ship we started our trip here counted the Order of the Black Claw as a story meant to scare children. His first mate was a member."

With the mention of the Order, Airria looked up the slope. The cloud was still moving. "Do you think our traps have eliminated many of them?"

Joskin stood up and readied his ax, "They are coming down the trail very fast. Perhaps we should set a few more traps and ambush them."

Faith stood up as well and began looking around. "I had hoped Carrita would be back before we faced these orcs."

Niesla was also looking around, but she was looking farther down the trail. "Do you suppose we will disrupt what Carrita is doing if we move her? Will we be all right to shift her to a safer location?"

Faith answered, "I don't believe it will disturb anything."

Together Faith, Airria and Niesla moved the girl into a nearby thicket behind a large evergreen. They threw a few branches over her.

When they felt Carrita was safely stashed Niesla said, "I don't know what good I will be for a fight. All my magic is good for is healing. I know nothing of death and killing. I also do not think I have the stomach for it. I still struggle to wear these animal skins."

Faith smiled gently, "Can you keep Carrita safe and hidden. If they have a magic user, she could be in real danger. When she relinquishes control of her magic she blares like the noonday sun."

Niesla laughed uneasily, "I think it would be easier to hide the sun, but there is something I can try. I will stay with her and help keep her safe."

Joskin walked up from behind. "We will try to keep them at bay long enough for Carrita to come back. You shouldn't have to worry," he said to Niesla. He turned to Airria and said, "We are out of twine. I have nothing to set the tripwire with."

Niesla put a hand on Joskin's shoulder, "I have set magical traps to help you. I can set one more to spring the traps."

"Thank you," Joskin responded.

456

As a group they used the trees and snow to create traps of varying sorts and styles. As Airria was placing the tripping mechanism on the last one he said, "If these traps haven't helped before, I don't know what good they will do now. If they have learned to spot and avoid them before now, why would they not see them this time?"

Joskin back-hand slapped Airria's arm, "This time we will be waiting to drive them into the traps."

Long before the darkness overshadowed them, Airria could feel it. "Something tells me this fight will not be as easy as the last one was."

Joskin chuckled and slapped Airria on the back, "As if the magical darkness approaching wasn't a dead giveaway."

Airria could feel something more than the darkness. It was a presence void of life. It made no sense to him. He wondered if the minotaur mage would have felt like this if Airria could have felt him then. He returned Joskin's laugh the best he could, "It is too late to do anything else. Guess it's time to take our positions."

Airria took up position in the middle of the trail. Joskin was on his horse right next to him. Faith was behind a tree on the other side with Persephone lying in the snow nearby.

Airria could feel his pulse race. He had faced the pirates without fear. This time, he was struggling to stand in his place. As the darkness crept over him, his sword erupted.

This fight I will relish. This coward escaped my wrath a millennium ago. Together we will end him, the sword whispered in his mind. The flames seemed to be dancing.

It brought Airria some comfort to know his weapon had such confidence. He looked down at his armor. This would be his first real fight in it. It was meant to help defeat dragons, an orc army should be no challenge.

Still he could feel the dark, as if it carried a fear of its own. Suddenly he was reminded of one of the rooms Jammar had required he train in. It was white and empty. It filled him with fear and doubt. It was far more overwhelming than this was. Recognizing the similarities helped him to again find courage.

457

Thirty-seven worgs came into view, though several of them had no riders. They began circling around Airria.

The group was led by a burly creature with blood-red eyes and covered in golden armor. He was barking orders and looking around. He had a black shield and sword in his hand.

To the leader's right was a creature Airria could feel magical fear coming from. It looked like a pile of old black rags hung haphazardly on a humanesque form of sticks. Its eyes blazed from beneath its hood like Jarmack'Trastibbik's crystal.

There was a loud clang and three trees crashed to the ground. The screams of crushed and yelping wolves could be heard.

Joskin reached deep within to find the courage to say anything. "It looks like you have already lost most of your force and we haven't even started fighting. Do you think you have any chance against us?" He hoped his words would show confidence.

The leader responded in a voice that did not sound like an orc. It was well spoken and smooth, almost hypnotic. "I have waited long for a chance to disgrace that sword again. You are not Theilord and even he was unable to slay me. I am now far stronger. My minions came to avenge their queen. I have come to claim what should have been mine."

Joskin broke the charm of the leader's voice, "He's not fighting alone," Joskin kicked his horse into rearing up.

The leader didn't flinch. "I can see your armor as it truly is. Only an orc can craft with such skill. You could only have such armor if you had been honored by a king of the highest order. I will make you this offer. To respect the orc king who gave you your armor, I will give all four of you eternal life to serve me, if you will relinquish your weapons."

Airria could feel the confidence returning to his heart, "An offer you should have kept to yourself. I am already immortal. I don't need you to give it to me."

A soft twang was quickly followed by an explosion near the rag clad creature. Though the half-dozen orcs left behind the leader were shifting back and forth looking for an escape, the two in the lead stood unyielding.

A hollow voice slithered out of the robes, "Do you know the reach of the Dragon's Claw? We are the arm of Jarmack'Trastibbik and will not be defeated. You will perish here today. You will know the pain of a thousand deaths, yet you will never know peace. Your trinkets will not save you from my master's wrath. Any more than it saved the previous owners."

Airria could feel a spell growing in between the thin gloves of the ragged creature. It was dark and painful. He was not waiting any longer. He charged his horse.

Another arrow came flying in. This time it was targeted on the orc in gold armor. Without even shifting in his saddle he grabbed the arrow out of the air. "I missed the day Viehasia entered the camp. I will enjoy claiming her weapons as well!"

Airria's horse stopped and spun hard, throwing him to the ground. His armor protected him from the impact so he was able to roll to his feet.

"You do not even realize what you are trying to fight. No creature approaches me without my permission."

Faith stepped away from her tree, "You will have to rip this bow from my dead hand!"

Airria could hear the beginning of a continuation of the banter, but didn't care, he charged in on foot. The worg snapped at him, but Airria brought his shield sharply into the animal's lower jaw. He rolled under the head and thrust his sword deep into the creature's heart. The smell of burning flesh and hair filled his nostrils, but he didn't have time to care. He pivoted again into the knee of the worg under the robed figure.

His sword crashed into the armor over the joint. There was a hollow ring. It was then that Airria noticed the flesh peeling off. The creature was as dead as its master.

The first worg fell. The orc in golden armor dove and rolled free of its mount. With inhuman speed it charged Airria, drawing two golden axes as it approached. The force of its impact on Airria's shield knocked him tumbling to the ground.

Before Airria could get his shield around, the creature brought its swords down on him. A large ax made a sweeping blow. Joskin caught both swords and knocked the leader back. Airria leapt to his feet. Between the cousins, the orc was driven back.

There were several loud crashes that sounded like thunder, but Airria didn't have time to look at what was happening. He and Joskin had to finish this creature quickly. Faith would be facing the rest of the army and the undead mage. No matter how he tried he could not get a blow in. As quick and powerful as his shield was, the opponent still struck his armor from time to time. Even with the strength and speed his armor gave him, he couldn't hit the being. It was even smiling. Twice it deflected arrows with its sword.

Airria was feeling fatigue taking its toll. His strength was depleting. It didn't matter if he attacked high or low, whether he and Joskin were on opposite sides or on the same. Either way, the creature was too fast for them and had the strength to defend against both their blows.

The orc began laughing, "I gave you a chance to serve me." Its fangs shone in the drastically diminished light. "You have no idea what you are fighting."

Airria remembered what his sword had said before the fight. "You ran from this sword last time you faced it, like a child from a monster. You should have stayed away!"

"I run from nothing!" it spat. "I will drink you dry for that!"

Airria swung in with his shield, exposing himself, counting on his armor to save him. The creature swung. Airria stepped sideways, hoping his movement would cause the axe's blow to glance. With his sword he continued the forward motion.

Airria's sword sunk deep into the orc's flesh. Flames erupted from the hole, quickly consuming the creature. It screamed in rage and pain. After a moment only the armor could be seen steaming on the ice.

Airria turned to see how Faith was faring. She was surrounded with corpses. Some of the worgs had holes big enough a child could crawl though them. Many of the orcs were ripped in half. Black blood was scattered across the snow and high into the trees.

Faith was standing with a sword in one hand and her bow in the other. She was looking down at herself with wide eyes and open mouth.

Airria turned to the only target he could find, the lich. It was sitting on its mount peacefully, turning its hooded head from side to side slowly. A hollow laugh could be heard.

"It is time for my revenge! The daughter of Tarsella will pay!" the pile of rags yelled and released its energy.

The rags fell to the ground. The mount collapsed. A bitter white dust flew up.

The nervous voice of Niesla could be heard, "I thought the dark would be gone when the lich was gone."

Airria could still feel the presence of the creature. He could also still feel the orc. "They may not have their bodies, but they are not gone," he finally said. "I only hope Carrita is ready to deal with them."

Chapter 27 - Return

Her pace was so quick no detail could be seen except the bright blare of the naga cities walls as she passed them. *I wish I could have passed this quickly the first time traveling this path,* she thought to herself.

She slowed down as she passed each point she had seen the orc spirits at on the way up the hill, but saw nothing out of place.

When she arrived at the group there was a barricade of orcs. There were about forty well armored soldiers, an obvious mage with a raging black aura and their leader, covered from head to toe in Taulkrick Gold.

"I know who you are," the leader grunted with a malicious grin. "Rantail will reward me well for bringing her your soul!" he added as he stepped forward.

"How do you know me?" Carrita asked as she maneuvered to the side.

The mage laughed with a hollow sound. "I was there the day your mother traded her soul for yours, foolish child. Do you not understand that it is your lust of knowledge which has brought you to this fate? It was your curiosity that opened the door for me to take you from your home. It was your mother's weakness that allowed her to be trapped. You were to be my bait for my revenge, but my master had other plans."

Carrita could feel the anger boiling inside her. Instinctively she reached for her magic, but realized it was too far away. Knowing that rage was what her opponents' wanted her to feel so she would lose her focus, she took a moment to gather her emotions. "With an aura like yours I can imagine my mother would do her best to dismantle any plan you might attempt." As the thought of her mother entered her mind she found a new focus. She almost felt as she had as a child when she stood on the battlements and joined her mother defending Darian, her home.

The best defense she could think of was to show her tormentor it had failed. As casually as she could she asked the leader, "Is it your antagonism toward my mother or is it directed toward me directly?"

"I am a blessed of Rantail!" The orc's cruel grin now showed his vampiric fangs. "Few know as much as I do, few have lived as long as I have. I celebrated when I heard news of your mother's capture. What I do now, I do for her!"

Carrita summoned a shield which resembled Airria's and a sword like Faith's. She had watched them spar many times and figured it would be a safe combination. She hoped she could mimic the movements she had seen them make. "You masters fear me and send their foolish minions to contend for them. If they are afraid of me, do you believe you will fare any better?"

Now close to Carrita he leaped directly at her, two golden blades out. The blades swung so close to Carrita's face she wondered if she had been struck. She had no time to think, another attack came at her.

I let him get too close, she chided herself as she side stepped to deflect another attack. Her strategy had worked. The vampire was swinging wildly. If he had been alone, she would have been able to strike him at will; unfortunately it did not take long for the mage to join in. He swung his staff faster than even the vampire. It was not unexpected, this was a magic user and if her memory served correctly this was likely a lich.

Quickly she danced around the vampire using the shield to block its attacks. She could easily duck the mage's attacks as well. However, she could not get a strike in. Between her two major opponents she was too caught up in defending herself.

While she was fending off the other two, one of the other spirits timidly joined the fight. The rhythm she had gotten into was disrupted and she was forced to retreat. Her retreat gave confidence to the other soldiers' souls. They began circling her, reducing her ability to retreat.

The soldiers were far slower. She ducked behind them, using them as shields from the onslaught. She eluded the dawdling blows and weaved deliberately between them, thrusting with her sword toward her attackers from time to time.

In her attempt to use the soldiers to defend herself, she inadvertently eliminated them. The rage filled swings of the vampire were far less precise than those of the lich. Often the vampire would swing at Carrita only to hit one of the soldiers.

As each soul was hit, it faded and wisped away. One by one the soldier spirits were eliminated as she carefully wove herself between them. As each soul disappeared the vampire grew more feral, allowing his control to dissipate.

She could feel the mental fatigue taking effect. Her movements had slowed significantly and her opponents were still moving quickly though she had struck them both several times.

"This time we are free!" the vampire said. "I see you are wearing down already. Soon you will lose your ties to your body. Then I will claim it and all your power for my own."

Carrita's mind was racing. She would need magic, magic she could only access from the Physical Plane. But she would have to hold her access to the Astral Plane to use it on them. Both of them had existed between life and death and defied them both. It would take someone in an equal state, someone who could walk both planes.

In an attempt to delay her opponents she asked, "Before I send you to your eternal reward I would like to know, what was it which requisitioned such an enamored hatred of such a failed mage?"

Her comment caused the lich to take a step back, "She stole my right of rule and decimated my army!"

Carrita laughed as confidently as she could. Her reaction earned a diving thrust from the vampire. Without the lich's added attack, she had enough time to slap the vampire on the back with her sword, a tactic she had seen Airria use to great effect on Faith.

From her vantage point she noticed her body. Her magic was glowing brightly and strong. How she longed to reach out and touch the magi...*Is it so different than what I have done on the ship?* she thought. "I know what to do!" she heard herself say out loud and began smiling.

The orcs seemed to notice her newfound confidence; the attacks became slower and more cautious. They began circling. When she saw an opening she pushed herself with all the mental power she had left and rushed for her body. She could feel her magic warm and comforting around her. Before she allowed her soul to combine to her body, she spun around and reached for all her knowledge of life and death. She could now see the life or unlife, she could see how life and death cycled, keeping the souls of the orcs from moving on. As she commanded it, her magic reached out and grabbed the leader, ripping the life from the death. It split the orc into two beings. One was solid and black, the other was frosty white. "You just lost your advantage!" she yelled at them as the black and white tendrils reached for the mage. Golden tendrils of magic viciously attacked both halves. With the help of her magic, it only took a few moments to dispatch them. As they vanished into the ether Carrita sank exhausted into her body.

She opened her eyes and tried to smile as she looked as Niesla, "She has been informed." She looked around at the corpses lying on the ground including worgs with holes big enough she could crawl through them. "It would appear you had a struggle of your own. Did you enjoy yourselves?"

Niesla looked at the ground, "I am never glad to see death, but I am very happy to know you are well."

"You should be happy. A lich and vampire have been sent to their eternal judgment," Carrita said weakly.

"I am sorry you had to deal with such a task on your return," Niesla added. "I don't know how you traveled, nor do I wish to keep you from your rest, but I would like to know what Bregette told you, what help she can send."

Carrita took a deep breath, trying to gather her strength. "She was already aware of the plight. This port is the very one we are to pass through in our journey. We are the help the Guardians have sent."

Joskin choked on the water he had been drinking. "We are what? Nobody asked us to do anything."

Niesla turned to him, "I am asking now. Will you help us? I have little left to offer as my village has been destroyed. Anything within my power I offer to you."

The corners of Joskin's mouth rose playfully. "Anything within your power? That is quite an offer from my vantage point. First I have a question for you. Do you remember what you asked for when you helped Carrita only a few days ago?"

Niesla blinked rapidly, "I asked for nothing."

Faith laughed as if she could see what Joskin was hinting at. "Such is not quite true. You did ask for something. You asked us to let you run. You asked for the opportunity do all in your power to keep us safe."

Even Airria was chuckling now. He stood up and walked quickly away.

After the many months of traveling with Joskin, Carrita knew what he would ask. She was not going to reveal it. She would let Joskin play his little game.

Niesla began looking to each member of the group for more information.

Joskin stood for a moment rubbing his chin, "You asked us to allow you the opportunity to do all in your power to protect us. If we are to help in this fight we will need you to promise to trust us and allow us to do our best to keep you safe."

Niesla's mouth opened slightly and her eyes widened. Carrita could not help but start giggling. Of the entire array of things Joskin could ask for, he wanted only to protect his friends and, it appeared,

Niesla had not only been accepted as such, but she had been escalated to the position of highly revered.

Joskin waited several moments and then asked, "Do we have an accord? Will you trust us?"

Niesla looked around again. She looked extra hard at Carrita. "Is this what you all require? If I agree to trust you, will all of you promise to help defend Sulitamis?"

Carrita giggled again, "Will you not accept if only one of us will assist?"

Niesla looked at the ground again. Her brows began twitching thoughtfully. "It does not matter who of you commits. I would ask you all to join." She focused on Joskin, "We have an accord. I will trust you to protect me."

Joskin chuckled loudly, "It will be good to fight at Marren's side again.

Carrita was surprised, "All this time traveling together, how is it I did not know you had met Marren?"

Joskin looked at Carrita and said, "You never asked. How do you know Marren?"

Carrita knew far more of Marren then she was willing to say right now. She pondered what to reveal, "She was governor of the city and orphanage I was sent to after my mother was taken."

Niesla asked, "Have you defended Sulitamis before?"

"Once, a few years ago," Joskin responded. "Marren caught wind the generals were going to hire me. She sent her own offer, one I couldn't refuse."

"What was worth so much you would refuse the Zerith's gold?" Niesla asked.

"It was not the first I had heard of Marren. It was said she always honored her bargains. She offered me a favor of my choosing, without question. Like you, she expected me to ask for gold or pleasures," he stopped talking, smiling playfully.

Niesla had shifted her body forward and placed her hand on his arm. "What did you ask for?"

Faith said, "I would dare to guess you have yet to name your price. You fought the battle and have yet to ask your reward. Am I right?"

Niesla asked, "Why would you not name your price?"

Airria came back into the circle group, "He said he may need a safe place to retire. Pfff, as if he would retire away from the family."

Joskin blushed, "In truth you never know when you will need the favor of a governor, especially one as honorable and powerful as Marren."

Carrita giggled. It made her realize again how fatigued she was. "I apologize for requesting this of you, but would you mind terribly to continue to carry me? I am exhausted and could use more rest."

Joskin began preparing the bag. "It works out nicely. This way Niesla has her own horse to ride and I get a better workout." He helped Carrita into the pack. Before he had put her on his back she was asleep.

Chapter 28 - Port

There was no doubt the attack had been orchestrated by the Order of the Black Claw. Though the vampire leader had no indication of affiliation to the Order, the lich carried a ring with the all too familiar insignia on it. It was intimidating to realize the group was as far from the dragon as they were going to be and her servants were still able to find them.

Faith did feel more protected in her armor. Though she supposed she was not as skilled as Viehasia had been, the armor struck anyone who got near to her. Several of the orcs had been sneaking around and attacked her while she was not watching. She had not seen what happened; she had only heard a series of loud thunderings. When she had turned to see, there were a few orcs and worgs lying dead on the ground with large smoking holes in them. She was not sure how many assaults the armor would strike with at a time, but she did not want to test it. It was certain now, as the group would be traveling closer to the dragon's residence, she would have no choice except to test it in another fight.

470

Surely there would be an even bigger army besieging Sulitamis. Somehow the group would have to end the siege to continue on their quest. This was not something she cared to ponder on at this time.

For now she was dwelling on the weather warming as they descended the frozen switchbacks. A few fluffy white birds were singing in the trees. The sun was shining on the ice on the trees like a crystal chandelier. She was going to do everything she could to enjoy her time away from the fighting.

It took only a week to descend the range to a wind-swept wasteland. Carrita woke up shortly thereafter. Once she was awake, Niesla began riding with Joskin and Carrita rode her pony.

It felt good to ride Persephone again. Though they had not been apart long, the descent had made them both anxious. They felt most secure when they were together as a team. Even on the few days when the wind was severe she stayed on her horse.

The most exciting evening was the one when they saw the distant lights of civilization. The conversation had been entertaining when they could talk over the wind, but they all wanted to sleep in a real bed and the girls all wished to take baths. The only remotely intelligent encounter they had experienced in the past few months was the battle with the orcs.

For the whole night all Airria could talk about was eating some good stew and fresh bread. Although he had no real need to eat, he just wanted to feel the heat of it running down his throat, or at least it is how he described it. Faith thought maybe he just wanted to remember home.

Two days later as they entered the gate, Airria leapt off his horse and thanked the gateman for being kind enough to allow them through. He even gave the unsuspecting dwarf an uncomfortable hug.

While Faith and Carrita waited for Airria to greet everyone who would allow him to approach, Joskin and Niesla went to make arrangements for the evening. Fortunately it was a small port town with few people for Airria to greet. Even though it seemed to take forever to get to the stables, Faith enjoyed watching Airria make a fool out of himself.

When they finally did arrive at the boarding stable they were welcomed in by a boy around Carrita's age. "Your friend already paid for your horses," he said as he struggled to open the large barn door.

He showed each to a stable near the back with clean straw on the floor and well preserved hay in a manger. As Faith removed the barding from her horse she could not help but feel sorry for the animal. She could see the horse's ribs and the fur had worn off in a few places.

"As I told your friend, no animal should be forced to wear tack for an extended time!" the boy lectured.

"Uh-um," a lovely, healthy looking woman came through the door and silenced the boy. "We will tend to your animals. Don't worry. This may be a small port, but we do have quite a bit of trade come through, especially from the elves and dwarves."

The tack was carefully placed on the rack and the group found their way into the nearby inn. The entrance room was comfortable with several tables and a raging fire. A table had three steaming leather flagons and a flour-covered, well-set woman with a pleasant smile.

"I'm Ria," she said. "I have been asked to wait here for you and provide you with these drinks," she stopped as her eyes fell on Carrita. "How did you survive such a harsh trek?" She stood and walked over and wrapped her arms around the girl, "You poor thing."

Slowly Faith came over to the table and reached out with her magic. She had no reason to mistrust the woman, but she now had an idea of the reach of the Dragon's Claw, or the reach of the Order of the Black Claw.

She felt nothing amiss in the drinks, so she picked one up as sipped it. It was not only warming to the touch, but was well spiced and enjoyable to the taste. It warmed her from the inside, a sensation she had never felt so pleasantly. After the long cold ride, it was nice to feel a little like home.

Airria asked, "Did our friends order some stew?"

The woman let Carrita go and looked down at her, but answered the question. "Yes, but I am to usher you into the bath chambers first." She paused for a moment to look a little deeper at Carrita. She then looked at the others. "Drink your cider first. It will help warm you and prepare you for your baths."

"I don't need a bath," Airria protested.

Faith giggled. He smelled worse than the horses. "Yes, you most assuredly do!"

His eyes began shifting and his mouth opened and closed. Faith recognized this gesture well now. It meant he wanted to protest but could find no argument to justify his attempt.

Faith picked up another flagon and handed it to Airria. He took is slowly and began to sip. He shivered as the liquid made its way into him. He began drinking faster. When he was finished he asked, "Can I get some more?"

Ria laughed, "You can have some more after your bath. Your elf friend was very insistent."

"The elf?" Airria questioned. "Not the man who is paying?"

She laughed, again stroking Carrita's hair, "He didn't argue."

Airria's eyes drooped and his lower lip stuck out slightly. "Fine, where is the bath."

Faith snickered as well. It was adorable to watch Airria protest taking a bath. She had never found anyone who seemed to dislike being clean so much. Carrita seemed to be enjoying the protest as well. She had picked up the flagon, but had yet to touch it to her lips, but she was smiling.

Ria offered, "May I show you to the bath so you can finish up and have some stew? It will be a little while before it is ready, so take your time and clean yourself well."

Airria made his cute little frown again. "Fine," he said as he followed her.

Carrita took a sip. She closed her eyes and calmly smiled. "It is undeniable; these people know how to stay warm with only fruit juice and spice. I am sure they pay dearly for such a luxury, but there is no doubt it is worth every tin piece." She began rolling her head and shoulders. "This feels better than the fire."

Ria was gone only a short while. When she returned she watched Carrita drink. "It helps with the cold, does it not?"

473

"This drink is marvelous," Carrita said after she finished the last of hers. "What brilliance devised such a concoction?"

The woman looked slightly perplexed by Carrita's words. She spoke hesitantly, "When one lives in the cold one learns what spices only warm the mouth and which spices warm the body." She motioned to the back room, "Are you ready for your baths?"

"Are the men done?" Faith asked.

"We have a separate bath for the women," Ria responded.

Without another word the girls followed Ria to a room filled with steam. In the middle there were four large tubs filled with hot water.

Niesla had one of them occupied. "It feels so good to finally be able to wash the orc off of me."

Faith began unbuckling her armor. It almost felt like she was removing her own skin, she had been wearing the armor for so long she had forgotten what it felt like to be without it. Even with the beautiful padding she found herself covering up. She felt so exposed. But piece by piece, she removed it.

When she was ready she looked to find Carrita already in one of the tubs.

Carrita smiled at Faith, "Our hosts have placed pleasant smelling aromas and salts in the water. I do not believe I will be leaving this bath."

Niesla asked, "What of when the water cools?"

Carrita's chin dropped and her eyes rolled to the top of their sockets. "Do you really believe I would allow such to happen?"

Faith laughed. She did not want to think of what was to come, but when Niesla mentioned the orcs Faith's mind was forced to remember the lengths the dragon had already gone to to stop them. "Do you really believe we will survive even to stand face to face with the dragon?"

Niesla interrupted, "Why would anyone pursue any dragon? I mean if dragons are even real, why would anyone attempt such a quest?"

Carrita answered her. "You know of my mother. I assure you dragons are real and the most ancient and cruel of all Black Dragons has my mother's soul trapped in a crystal meant to torment those trapped within."

"Why do you believe so animatedly?"

Carrita dunked herself in her tub and came up again. "Much like Airria, I witnessed the cruelty. I very well understand the pain she is causing."

Faith asked again, "Do you really believe we will face the dragon?"

"I will not stop until I have the opportunity to face the dragon. With what I now know, even death will not stop me," Carrita said as she waved her hands in the tub.

The loud clang of the town warning bell sounded, causing all three to leap from their tubs and dress as quickly as they could.

As Faith was buckling the last latch on her armor Ria came rushing through the door, "Bulrock the orc pirate is coming! We must find a safe place."

She grabbed her bow and stopped. The name seemed so familiar. She looked to Carrita for an explanation.

Carrita asked Ria, "Do you know only one orc pirate captain?"

"Of course," Ria responded. "All other pirates flee from his banner. No one dares face him. His ship is the fastest thing on water. We have found over the years to send the women away and set out supplies for him to loot. He still kills four or five of our men every time he comes to raid."

Faith started laughing, "Yes, he was exceptionally cruel and ruthless, but I promise he has not come to raid your town at this time." Anyone raiding this struggling town was not something to laugh at. She found it amusing it took so long for her to recognize the name. She had spent weeks in his head and dealing with his thoughts.

"My husband saw the ship entering the bay. It will only be moments before his landing party begins its savagery."

Carrita placed a hand on the woman's side, "Would it help you to know Bulrock has been exterminated?"

"But his ship!" the woman insisted.

Niesla joined the conversation, "What do you mean the orc pirate has been exterminated?" She had one hand across her body and the other on her chin. "You have taken his ship and made it yours?"

Faith tried to be sympathetic to the panicked bar maid. "Yes, the ship is ours now, though I am not sure why or how it is coming into your port." She looked at Carrita for the answers.

Carrita looked at the ground shifting her eyes back and forth. "You did not want to control any more of my experiments. You said the golems were more than you wanted. So I kept the control of the ship."

"This I remember," Faith responded. "How did you control the ship from such a distance?"

Carrita smiled big and tucked her hands behind her back. She began rocking slightly, "The ship maintains and steers itself; I only suggest a destination for it. Much like the link you have to your golems, distance is irrelevant."

Niesla dropped her arms, "You can call your ship, which you took from an invincible pirate, to any port you would like?"

Carrita replied, "The captain was not so invincible. The minotaur mage was far more difficult for me to fight."

Ria was standing against the doorway with her mouth open. From time to time it would half close, then drop open again.

Faith walked over and grabbed the stunned woman's hand. "Perhaps we should inform the town about the ship. I believe we should stop the panic."

When they arrived on the street there were two dwarfs pushing a wagon loaded with caribou carcasses and iron ore. "I don't see why we always have to use our goods to get this raider to go away," one of the dwarves could be heard complaining.

Joskin and Airria were already in the street preparing for the fight. Faith and Carrita walked up to them.

"By what the villagers are saying, this is going to be a difficult fight," Airria said with his hand on his hilt.

Carrita giggled, "These ruthless pirates may even have a master mage with them one with long hard horns and a bloodthirsty attitude."

Faith rolled her eyes. It was a silly game Carrita was playing. Though Faith was not sure it was the best timed, she decided to join in, "The orc captain sounds ruthless."

"The innkeeper said he is early this year," Joskin added. "They aren't sure if he will leave with this tribute. I think it is time we try to end him."

Niesla slowly approached the group. He voice was shaky, "Haven't you already disposed of him?"

Carrita frowned as Joskin shot Faith a look of surprise and curiosity.

Faith shrugged, "How bad can this pirate be, he helped keep us warm through the journey?"

Joskin grabbed a handful of his cloak and looked from it to Carrita.

Reluctantly she said, "The vessel coming into port is ours. The captain the townsfolk are speaking of is the very one I used to create the enchantments on our cloaks and weapons. There is nothing to panic about."

Though the dwarves were a considerable distance away they stopped. "There be no pirate coming?" one of them asked.

The other started grumbling, "We work to prepare all this and push it out. This be loads of work. Someone else gets to push it back and unload it."

"Master dwarves," Joskin stepped toward them and bowed slightly, "would you prefer to sell these wares?"

That's why we bring them to this icy waste of a town," one dwarf said with a scowl.

"Then when the ship makes port we will help you load the ore and drag the caribou to the butcher to be smoked. You won't need to move your wagons on your own."

Slowly the people filtered out to the street. "Is it true?" the innkeeper asked. "Is Bulrock really dead? He will not be returning to this port ever again?"

"You cannot imagine the relief this is," said a man in a bloody, white apron.

A man in fine linen stuck his head out of the inn door, "We all owe you a great debt, but can you leave on your ship soon."

Airria turned to the man in a bloody apron, "If you will purchase the animal on the wagon, we will buy all of your smoked meat and be on our way."

The innkeeper looked crossly at the well-dressed man, "There is no rush. You may stay as long as you would like."

The group turned and looked at Niesla, but it was only Joskin who spoke. "Sadly there is a rush. We need to be moving on. We have somewhere we need to be."

When the ship slid next to the dock Faith had one of the golems set out the gangplank. She told two of the orc golems to walk to the two carts. She knew they were very strong and heavy and would have no trouble pulling the wagons.

The dwarf in front of it stood with his arms across his chest, looking nervously from the golems to Joskin. "There is the matter of payment."

"As a town we will pay you, just like if Bulrock had taken it," The well-dressed man said stepping through the doorway.

"No," Joskin said, "I will pay my own debts. I refuse to become what Bulrock was on any level." He jogged to the ship.

"And my meat?" the other dwarf asked. "Does it go to the butcher or the ship? And who is paying for it?"

"I will pay you the price I always do," the man in the bloody apron said.

The dwarf scowled, "Then I aren't gonna pull it."

Faith had the golems pull the wagons to where they needed to go and unload them. Each dwarf followed their wagon closely. When the one at the butcher shop was finished unloading, she had the golem load all the smoked meat she could. And had it drag the wagon to the ship.

By the time she arrived at the ship, the ore wagon was unloaded and the dwarf was watching the ship with a satisfied grin on his face.

Niesla was on board already. "I am sorry to ask you to leave so soon and interrupt your rest, but it is imperative we be leaving as soon as possible.

As quickly as they could the group loaded the supplies and horses. Once loaded, while Joskin was still pulling up the plank, the ship began moving. Although the rest on the ship would not be as nice as staying in the inn, time was short and they needed to keep their promise to Niesla. To Faith it was all just a part of keeping her promise to her sister.

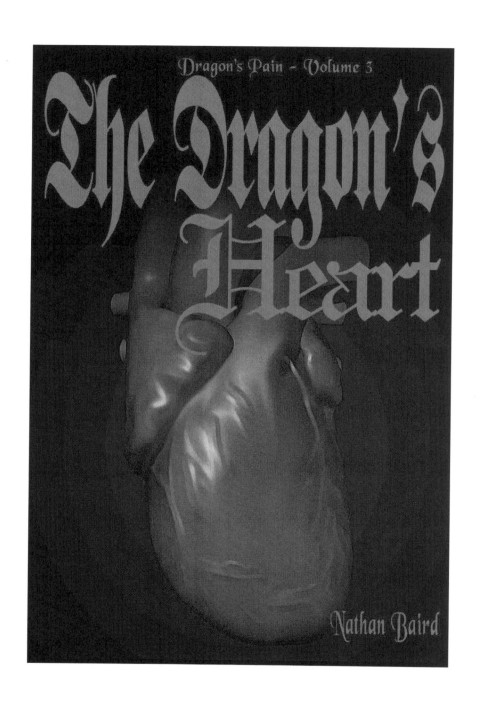

Dragon's Pain – Volume 3

The Dragon's Heart

Nathan Baird

Chapter 1- Long Voyage

The stale aroma of musty books was nauseating. Carrita had no idea how long she had been alone in her room studying the minotaur's books and magic journals. The ship had been enchanted with many incantations of protection including a guard from rot and mold. Unfortunately the books did not share the safeguard.

What added to her disgusted disposition was rereading over the minotaur's depraved experiments. She felt no sorrow for her part in dispatching the creature. It had been a monster which took the greatest of pleasure in the suffering of others.

As she sat on the hammock pondering what she had read, she realized how close she had come to allowing her own hatred to twist her into such a creature. It had been only the gentle words of her dear friend, Faith, which had prevented her transition. For those same words, Carrita had sent Faith away.

Carrita threw her own journal against the wall. For the first time she could remember she was tired of studying magic. She slipped off her hammock and straightened her grey robe without a thought. After a moment of standing, wondering what she should do with herself, she began mulling around her room. It seemed like weeks since she had sent Faith away. Even Joskin had stopped checking in on her.

Faith had kept insisting Carrita was too bitter and vengeful. She had recommended Carrita put the books away and enjoy the fresh air. At the time, her friend's advice seemed to be the greatest of foolishness. As Carrita looked over the shelves and pondered the hollow feeling in her heart, she decided the recommendation was very wise.

Slowly she slid the latch on the door aside and peered out into the hallway. The orc, Taksek, was in his magical forge. It contained the sound; however, Carrita could see him clearly. He was happily swinging his hammer on one of his projects.

She watched him quietly for a short while, drinking in the freedom she felt, no longer tied to her books. He looked so content, so at peace, yet so focused. It had now been years since she had felt that way. Only magic had brought her close to it and now even it was no solace.

Slowly she walked back up the hall, feeling a need for interaction. She glanced into each room as she passed. When she approached the stairs her pace quickened as the air became less musty.

The cool morning breeze felt good on her face. Even the smell of salt and fish was relaxing. The sound of water being pushed aside as the vessel passed was a welcome, yet frustrating, reminder they were still at sea.

Faith had often spoken of the dolphins and merfolk playing alongside the ship. As no one was at the rail, Carrita guessed there would be no such pleasure.

"In truth, she does live!" Airria shouted from the upper deck. It was nice to hear him so jovial; however, his voice made her jump.

"Even I was beginning to wonder," Faith came into view next to Airria. Both of them were covered in sweat and dried salt.

Carrita laughed, "How long has it been since I sent you away?"

Faith replied, "It has been more than three weeks since you told me you did not want to be disturbed." She began descending the stairs to the lower deck.

Carrita looked at the deck, then back to Faith. "I apologize for neglecting your magic lessons." Really she was not sorry about the lessons, they had developed into Faith educating Carrita on the prowess and agility of Airria. Magic had not been much of the conversation for some time. Carrita had witnessed Airria's speed and skill each time the group had encountered opposition by elite soldiers and mages belonging to the Order of the Black Claw. What Carrita was regretful of was the lack of company.

The soothing deep voice of Airria's cousin, Joskin, grabbed Carrita's attention. "Be careful. After so long below, you might burst into flame if the sun hits your skin." He had attempted to bring her food for some time, even after Faith had stopped trying to make contact. She did not need the nourishment and she was growing irritated at the rats accumulating around her room.

Carrita curtsied elegantly. "My lovely robe will protect me," her hand reluctantly released the soft silk fabric, "my mother only knew how to create quality."

It had been some time since Carrita had remembered or felt the pain of her mother's loss. Only Airria had any idea of her pain, although his understanding was only through observation. Not only did she have to carry the weight of her loss, she had to remember the months of abuse she now knew were at the instruction of Jarmack'Trastibbik, the great Black Dragon who had taken her mother's soul. Touching the magnificent grey silk surrounding her was a welcome and painful reminder of her mother's sacrifice.

As the thought of the dragon crossed her mind she could feel her face harden. "How far are we from port?" She was feeling a drastic need to continue the quest they had started over a year ago.

Joskin chuckled loudly, his massive solid form quaking. "By my reckoning we are a little over half way."

The gentle, melodic voice of Niesla chimed in, "The magic of this ship is astounding. I believe we have traveled much more rapidly than most ships that pass this way. It is difficult to judge how far we have actually gone." Niesla was a Forest Elf the group had helped in the most unlikely of places. She had become a most welcome member of the group, not only for the sake of saving Carrita from a fate worse than death but also for her soft smile and the gentleness she brought to Joskin. "I, also, am anxious to walk on solid ground again." She smiled brightly and set a hand on Joskin's arm.

Faith put a wet arm around Carrita's shoulders. Carrita leaned her fourteen year old body into Faith's curvy figure. She rested her head on Faith's chest, allowing her strait blond hair to fall over her face. Though she loved the show of affection it was also a reminder of her mother.

"Does this mean we will begin our magic lessons again?" Faith asked.

Carrita smiled broadly, but could feel the heaviness in her heart. "Though we both know I have much I could teach you, I believe you have sufficient understanding for the task at hand."

Airria wrinkled his forehead. "Do you know something I don't? Have you seen what we will be fighting?"

Carrita giggled, "We have both seen the worst of all creatures we could face and yes I do know much which you do not. Sadly I have not divined the future. I could only fantasize of having such ability." She looked up at Faith, the large loose curls of her auburn hair fluttered reluctantly in the breeze. "She is to be our archer. She has tremendous potential as a healer or even a mage, possibly more than Niesla. However, when we received our gifts at Jammar's place, her gift was a bow with a quiver of arrows. It was not a staff or robe. The Guardians who have assisted us know better than any of us what difficulties lay ahead. This thought process has led me to conclude Faith has sufficient understanding of magic for what we will face."

Carrita perused over the endless water hoping to see land. She knew the port city, Sulitamis, was governed by Marren, a long time dear friend of both hers and her mother's. Sadly, only a small dark speck could be seen on the horizon. "At least we are close enough to port to see another vessel," she said as she watched the speck grow slightly.

Joskin turned to look. He squinted tightly and put his hand up to block the morning sun. "That's odd. Every other ship we've seen has given us a wide birth. This one seems to be intentionally staying in our course."

Niesla also put a hand up to block the sun and looked to the now recognizable ship. "It is not alone."

Airria sprinted over to the center mast and quickly made his way to the lookout cage. "Land ho!" he yelled down after a short gaze.

Soon the high city walls of the port could be seen on the horizon. A chill of excitement flowed down Carrita's back and she pulled away from Faith to get a better view.

Niesla pursed her lips. She hissed, "War ships."

Airria called down from the cage, "The port gates are closed."

Carrita looked at Niesla, "It would appear we have arrived in time to help. The siege seems to be ongoing."

Niesla grabbed Joskin's hand and looked at what appeared to be a picket line of ships. "We have but one small ship. Will we be able to get through?"

Carrita laughed softly. "A more perplexing question is: will the city watch know to open the gates for us? We are being transported aboard the most feared of pirate vessels."

Joskin's shoulders squared up, his jaw clenched and his face went cold. He looked intently from Carrita to Faith and back. After some time he glanced at Niesla. "We have to get through."

The lovely elf took a step away from Joskin, sending a wave down her waist-length brown hair. She really did not look much older than Carrita, though there were centuries difference in their ages.

Joskin's face seemed to turn to stone. This was the man Carrita remembered from earlier in their quest. This was the warrior who decided battles simply by the side he would fight on. Without another word he ran below.

Airria made his way back down to the deck. "I've never seen him run from a fight before."

Faith said sadly, "We will need all the help we can get." The ship began to shift as the golems Carrita had made began to move and ready for battle.

Joskin reemerged with a roll of green cloth. "Prepare for battle!" he yelled as he began making his way up the mast.

Before any of them could turn to go below Niesla gasped, "The banners are those of Zerith. It is still Zerith."

Carrita watched as the banner of a thorn laden bear on a brown field came into view. "None of our challenges have been as they appear.

487

The slaver was a servant of the Black Claw. The pirates we claimed this ship from were not just basic pirates. Why would this be just a navy?"

A soft thud on the deck behind Carrita pulled her around. It was Faith standing with the staff Brigitte had given Carrita and her bow. She was dressed in the armor she had received in the frozen mountains.

Airria came up behind her in his armor. His shield and sword were both in hand.

Carrita received the staff, "Thank you."

Faith looked at the upcoming ships. "This ship has many advantages over the larger war vessels. They will not get their hands on you again." She looked down at Carrita, "I promise."

There was a loud thud as Joskin landed on the deck. "She's right. They will not have you, nor the city." He glanced up at his banner he had placed. It was a lone, inverted, golden ax on a field of green. "Now they will know to let us in."

"When did you get your own banner?" Airria said, surprised.

Joskin showed no emotion, "It's a long story and now is not the time."

Niesla, who had slipped away without Carrita even knowing, appeared, "I know I should not be surprised. Zerith has been striving to overtake this city for longer than the Elven records have been kept." She had a bow in hand and two quivers of arrows.

"They have been endeavoring to take the city since the dragons were banished, according to my mother," Carrita said.

Taksek emerged with a golden bow and a quiver full of silver arrows for each golem. Cautiously he placed the quivers over the golems' shoulders. It was then that Carrita noticed the orc had a sword at his waist.

In the time Carrita had been aboard she had grown to recognize Taksek as a person, but still she could see he was an orc. She did not trust him. She thought for a moment about what to say and to whom she should say it.

The orc stopped what he was doing and returned Carrita's glare. He crinkled his forehand, crossed his arms and said, "If master fights so do Taksek."

Carrita glared back at him.

Shortly after the group had reassembled on the deck, the first of the warships approached. Before it was close enough to hail them, Niesla let an arrow fly at the first officer she saw on deck. When the arrow hit and ripped through the commander, a bell sounded and a barrage of flaming rags launched at them from the other ship.

The flames extinguished on contact with the ship and sails. Arrows shattered on impact. Carrita used a simple shielding spell to block the few flames which would have hit the group.

Faith released a red tipped arrow. As expected, the arrow exploded, clearing a large section of sailors from the seemingly neverending stream.

Joskin yelled to Faith, "We only need to slow them to get into the city! Can you damage the ships?"

Faith unleashed a rapid barrage of red and blue arrows at the water line, alternating fire and ice attacks. The golems also turned and each released a silver arrow at the same point on the ship.

The wood shattered under the stressful impacts and a large hole formed in the side. The vessel slowed in its movement. It was then Faith began firing the marble tipped arrows. Each one changed a plank of wood to stone and the ship began sinking and slowed the vessel sufficiently to prevent boarding.

Carrita had to admire the soldiers' dedication; even with their safe transport descending toward doom they kept firing rags, stones and arrows.

When the next warship was in range Carrita was kept busy defending the group. This ship was better organized. They were standing in ranks, with shielded warriors standing before the archers. The bowmen were specifically aiming at the party.

The magic navigation in the ship guided them smoothly, weaving and dodging in a sporadic serpentine pattern. One by one, the group slowed each warship and slipped by. As they drew closer to the gate it began to open.

The two remaining warships left their course toward the group and began heading straight for the opening gates.

Faith aimed at the center mast of the each of the ships as they came close enough. It took three of her exploding arrows to destroy each mast enough to bring it crashing to the deck.

The crews were more persistent than anticipated; ores were brought out as was a barrage of flaming stones and rags.

Once inside the harbor the ship jerked almost as if it had hit something, but really it had only quickly slowed to a manageable speed. As the walls crashed closed behind them Niesla breathed a sigh of relief. Carrita got a weak yet satisfied grin across her face, when they heard the loud crash of the ships hitting into the walls.

Chapter 2 - New Adventures

Airria's heart was pounding in his ears. Even with his helm on he could see and hear everything around him. He and Joskin had readied for battle. Between the girls and the golems none of the war ships had gotten close enough to board. One had gotten close, but Faith had destroyed its mast. Now he was left with the rush of battle and nowhere to vent it. Even the crashing sound of the ships on the outside of the wall did not bring satisfaction.

"The shipyard is so empty," Joskin said in a tone that reminded Airria of stone grinding.

Niesla walked over to Joskin and put a hand on his arm. She smiled hesitantly, "They risked the last of their fleet in hopes I and my party could make it through the line to get help."

Airria watched as Niesla's touch calmed Joskin. The stone melted off his face, his shoulders relaxed. Even a small tear formed in his eye. As he observed Joskin's change, the pounding in his own ears slowed until it was almost gone.

Joskin spoke softly and slowly, "How many died to bring us here?"

Airria could only half hear what was being said. He was busy staring at the huge port and even bigger city. The entire naga city could fit in the water of the port. The dark grey stone wall made the tall buildings look small.

Even with this distraction he was filled with a need to repay the efforts of the people who had died. "We shouldn't waste the offering of those who sacrificed to bring us here."

Joskin's face hardened slightly, "Too many have already died."

Carrita slowly approached, "Marren is no fool; she values life more than even Niesla. What she and her soldiers did was for a greater purpose. They needed us here. It will be up to us to break this siege."

Faith began shifting her weight back and forth, "Four of us will make a difference where an army could not? Such is a long stretch of hope."

"This is not the first siege this city has endured while waiting for me," Joskin said with a weak smile. "Marren rarely goes on the offensive. In the past she has left it to me to lead her armies into battle."

Niesla giggled uncomfortably, "Most sieges here are broken by the attacking armies' cost. The city walls are high and impenetrable. You have witnessed the security of the fortification extended even into the depths of the ocean."

"How was such a wall constructed so far into the sea?" Faith asked.

Joskin shrugged and Carrita smiled. It was Niesla who answered, "Legend has it that this city used to be on the edge of an ocean cliff. The walls were created long before history was written. As the story goes, a very powerful mage lowered the whole city to the ocean so that escaped slaves from Zerith could have a getaway if they wanted."

Carrita snickered, "A powerful mage?"

Niesla responded politically, "Have you heard the story differently?"

"My mother said your 'mage' was a vampire and she was not alone, she convinced several lichs to help her do it."

Niesla looked shocked, "One of the elders told me that is what the scrolls said, but nobody would believe it. Why would a vampire go to

492

that kind of effort to help slaves?" She sounded half as though she wanted to teach Carrita a lesson and half as though she wanted to fill in the missing pieces of the story.

"She was a slave of sorts when she was human, from her childhood, an exceptional beauty as a young girl." Carrita's face showed the pain of her own history. "She was treated very horribly." A little peace came into her eyes as she continued, "One day when she was in her early twenties, a vampire came to the mansion she had been sold to. The vampire gathered together everybody in the house, literally throwing them all in the basement, all except the woman." Carrita's voice was solid, but her hands shook. She sounded as if she has heard this story from the one who had lived it. "The vampire saw the torment the woman was already in."

Carrita looked up at the sun now fading behind the walls and bringing out the silhouette of guard towers picketing the top of the high walls. "Vampires, as we know, are usually very sadistic; they like to see people in pain," she continued. "This one knew he could not cause any more pain than the girl was already in. He decided to make her pain eternal by making her a creature of the night. She did not choose her fate, nor did she make any promises to Rantail, so she was able to keep her soul. Her spirit and her will are still her own."

"Still?" Niesla's surprise came out through her raised voice. "No hunters have killed her yet?"

Joskin asked, "How do you know all this? How do you know your books are more accurate than Niesla's?"

Carrita smiled, "How well do you know Marren? Have you ever asked her about the creation of the city?"

Joskin looked uneasily at the deck, "She is only a few years older than I am. How are her sources more reliable than Niesla's. The Elven elders are well-known for keeping track of distant histories."

Carrita shifted her gaze to the pier. "There is much of history not kept in the books and scrolls. I am sure the naga were not mentioned in the Elven scrolls. Yet Marren knew to send Niesla to them." With a wink she added, "Trust me as you did with the naga. There is more to Marren than you know."

"I've fought for Marren and this city a few times," Joskin was now looking to the guards approaching the ship.

"When I was young I was fascinated with stories of dragons, brave warriors and beautiful maidens," Niesla said with a slight hesitation. "When I was considered an adult, I discussed the stories I had heard with the elders. They immutably confirmed that dragons were only in legend. I know not if the ancient scrolls talked of naga. One thing I now understand is that Carrita is right, much of history is unwritten and much of what is written is what someone wanted us to believe."

Faith added, "I would have put naga, dragons, elves and vampires in the same degree of truth; myth. Each has been made known to me, except dragons and vampires, but I know Carrita's information to be real and extensive. If she says dragons and vampires exist, I have little doubt of their reality. I no longer doubt simply because I have not seen."

"Hail!" a deep voice barked from the pier.

Airria looked overboard. There were four human guards led by a tall, muscular, wolf-like humanoid in well-crafted plate armor. His flowing brown cape was embroidered with the sigil of a yellow broken chain.

"Who are you and where did you get that banner?" the wolf-man growled deep in his throat as he began raising his battle-scarred halberd. His teeth were bared and chipped. His scarred arms held his weapon tightly.

Joskin stepped to the rail, "Captain Garfrun, It is good to see you still ready for what might come." He slid out the gangplank and stood at the head.

The captain's growl grew louder, "Nobody is ever ready for you!" He dropped his weapon and charged up the plank.

The guards behind the captain reached for their weapons, but didn't move forward.

Airria reached for his sword but found it hesitating in its sheath. He knew his cousin could take care of himself, but it was automatic now to prepare for battle.

Joskin dropped his ax on the deck and bared his own teeth. He set one foot back.

Though the wolf-man was more than a head taller than Joskin, they met shoulder to shoulder. The clang of armor rang out, Joskin slid back more than a pace.

Without warning the wolf-man took a stiff step back with his hands in the air. His eyes were wide and filled with fear, "Do you not remember me child?"

Joskin caught himself and stepped back to follow the captain's gaze.

Airria spun to look as well. Both Niesla and Faith had bows drawn, but that is not where the captain had his eyes fixed.

Carrita was standing on the upper deck with her staff raised. Lightning was crackling around her staff and through her eyes. Her skin had paled and her robes were fluttering even though there was no breeze.

Joskin stepped in front of Captain Garfrun, keeping his eyes on Carrita.

Carrita's staff let off a soft humming. "I am not the same girl you failed to guard!" She slowly hovered down to the main deck.

"I don't know what more I could have done," Garfrun whimpered. "When I found you were missing I tore this city apart looking for you." A puddle formed at his feet.

Step by step she came closer to the captain. "I learned a new definition for suffering after I was taken. Do you want me to show you?"

"Please do not!" Faith pleaded.

"I did everything I knew to do," the captain whined.

Without warning Carrita sprinted at the wolf-man and threw her arms around him. "I believe you did. Several times your spies almost freed me. If it were not the Order of the Black Claw who had taken me, you would have brought me back safe."

"Why?" was the only sound Garfrun could make.

Carrita smiled up at him. Her skin and eyes were back to normal. "You are no longer the only one who knows how to intimidate. If I meant to hurt you, you would not have a warning."

"You really are a different girl than left here," Captain Garfrun put a clawed hand on the girl's head and began stroking her hair. "As

495

much as I hate to see the little girl gone, we could really use the terrifying mage I see before me."

Faith and Niesla were still standing, bows drawn and mouths open.

Joskin's shoulders dropped slightly. "Speaking of people who can terrify you and charm you with a smile," he looked at Carrita as he spoke, but looked up to the captain as he continued, "where is Marren Bloodstone?"

The captain looked up to Niesla, "Do you have a message or reply for her?"

Joskin smiled, "I thought my presence at these dire times would be message enough."

Captain Garfrun scanned the group. "You have brought a few others with you and returned with our messenger." His scan stopped at Niesla. His head began shifting side to side, after a moment he stopped and said, "I have never seen an elf hold a bow for so long. Do you mean to shoot me?"

Slowly both archers lowered their bows. Niesla looked at the deck, her face more red than usual. "I also am very much changed."

"I can see that," Captain Garfrun said with a smile. "When you left, you would never have pointed an arrow at another living thing." He turned his attention to Taksek who had taken up position between the wolf-man and Faith. "You are traveling with an orc? How can you trust an orc?"

"It is small thing if learn to trust a dog!" Taksek blurted out.

Faith stepped forward and placed a hand on Taksek's shoulder. "He has been a dear friend and valued ally from the time we freed him from the dispatched captain of this vessel. He is a true craftsman. Observe the quality of his work in the armor Joskin now wears."

"I makes good armors, not like silly stuffs you wears," the orc said proudly.

The wolf-man glared at the orc, "This armor was made by the best smith in this area."

Taksek laughed,"You no know quality. You people think any metal cover will work. Pfffttt," he spat on the deck.

Airria stepped closer to the wolf-man. "He truly is amazing."

"What does an orc know of quality!" The captain proudly put his arms across his chest as Carrita took a step back and looked at Faith.

Faith nodded. She looked at the captain and said to Taksek, "I do not think our new friend believes you can make better armor. Do you have the courage to show him?"

Taksek looked suspiciously at Faith, "You want for me to make armor for this dog?"

Faith leaned up and whispered in the orc's ear. He scowled, but walked over to the captain.

The captain stepped away. He crouched defensively, bringing both clawed hands to bare. "That creature will not touch me."

Taksek folded his arms high in his chest and bared his lower teeth. "Stupid chicken-dog. Master say no hurt, I no hurt. Master say prove I make better armor, I show you so. Now give armor so I can make better."

Garfrun glanced to Joskin.

Joskin smiled back. "You know I've tested the best armor dwarves could make me," he waited for the wolf to nod. "You'll not regret allowing this orc the opportunity to prove his skill on your armor. Look closely at mine and you'll see."

Carefully the wolf-man stood and examined Joskin's armor. At first he kept one eye on Taksek. Slowly his focus shifted more strongly to the armor. His hand reached up and felt his shoulder guard, where the two had collided. His finger blindly circled the dent from the impact. Finally he spoke, "This is gold. How's it possible?" He shifted his gaze to Joskin's eyes. "This creature really made this for you?"

Joskin smiled and looked to Taksek, "He's a true master."

Slowly the captain unbuckled his armor and placed it on the deck. Taksek stood by and waited, tapping his foot.

When Garfrun was finished, the orc swept it all together, picked it up and turned to Faith. "Gold, silver, or steel?"

Faith looked at Joskin, "What do you think?"

Joskin laughed, "We don't want to overwhelm the poor captain, steel should be good enough."

Faith nodded.

"I make armor better, not good as for you, but better, so it is good. I not make padding. I not use what he have it..." Taksek place a finger in each nostril and headed below.

Once the orc had disappeared the captain asked Joskin, "Who have you brought with you?" Airria stepped forward, relieved the tension had left the air, "I am Airria DeAveron, Joskin's cousin."

Garfrun laughed, "Joskin, this is the runt you told me about? The one you said would never wear armor no matter how many times you hit him?"

Airria scowled at his cousin, "You'll pay for that."

Joskin looked to the darkening sky. "You know we've stepped into the middle of a siege. This is not the time to get upset over things said years ago."

Faith stepped forward putting a hand on Airria's shoulder. "I am Faith Marsady. I am here to help where I can."

The captain bowed crudely, "We'll need all the help we can get." He looked at the sky. "It's time we get you to Marren." Without another word he led the group off the ship.

Chapter 3 - Monsters

The air of the cobblestone streets was choked with despair. The way Carrita and Joskin had spoken of this city and its defenses Faith had expected a different atmosphere. The few people they saw had been bandaged and often had burns. Even many of the children had splints and crutches.

When they arrived at a mansion on a now torch-lit street, the most elegantly poised woman Faith had ever seen was waiting at the gate. She had long black hair braided into a bun with one braid running down to her knees. The pale of her face and ice-blue of her eyes contrasted sharply with her long black dress which covered her from neck to ankle. Covering her torso she had an elegantly decorated leather corset which accentuated her hourglass figure. She curtsied regally before the group. As she straightened back up she said, "Joskin, you came, but I only sent word to you a month ago. Also, you have come in the most dreaded pirate ship on the seas. How have you come so quickly? I already owe you more than I could ever pay in gold or weapons, but will you help me now in this solemn hour?"

"I received no word from you, m'lady. I am here on other business," Joskin bowed with extreme courtesy and respect. "We did come across one of your messengers by a stroke of luck. Niesla has proven to be a valued friend and companion." Joskin stood straight again, "Though, as always, I will do what I can to help here."

She smiled softly, "You have always been true to your word. Your presence will give my dear defenders hope. Though sadly I have little hope we will survive this siege." She placed a hand on Joskin's shoulder. "As always, you have full access to all my resources: my armory, my alchemy stashes and even my mages, the few who are left."

"You are too kind m'lady," Joskin turned his head to look at the group. "We have already been given better than I have ever seen.

The woman looked over the group admiring the armor. "I know these weapons only through legend. Of all the elves and Guardians I have met only a handful could remember seeing this armor." Her finger traced the intricate vinework on Faith's armor. After a moment she touched Joskin's ax. "Only my dear friend Tarsella has told..." Her words stopped and her eyes opened widely as they fell on Carrita, "My dear! You have changed so much since you were taken from here I almost did not recognize you. I thought I would never see you again."

Carrita ran to the woman, buried her face in her corset and began to cry. The woman in turn wrapped her arms around Carrita, her long drooping sleeves almost completely hiding the girl.

"I know that cry, it holds two parts. I only wish I could help on both accounts." Blood ran to the woman's eyes turning them red and for a moment her pale skin went almost white.

The woman was so similar to Faith in height, build and manner of holding Carrita, it felt to Faith as though she were looking into a darkened mirror.

After a short while of Carrita's crying, the girl looked up at the woman's face, "Maybe I can help you. I have learned a tremendous amount in my captivity and freedom. I have been tutored by two Guardians. Marren, please do not hide me for my age. I have competed against the most powerful mages the Order of the Dark Claw has sent."

Faith and Airria both stepped forward to support Carrita's claims. Before they could get a word out Marren spoke again, this time her voice was stern, "You may have bested the best sent, but what we face tonight is more devastating than a horde of drakes." Her tone softened again. "By your mother's love I believe you can help." She looked over the group, "I only hope it will be enough.

Joskin fell to one knee, "I'm sure we will soon see the battle. It sounds dire, but as always you have my ax, my armor and, if necessary, my life at your command."

Marren gently set Carrita to her side, knelt down before Joskin and leaned in on a bent arm. "You know I owe you more than my life. It is not appropriate for you to kneel to me. We are friends, are we not?"

Joskin nodded and let his eyes meet Marren's, "I failed you, I lost your man. For that I'll always feel guilty."

"He chose his path and his sacrifice helped you win the battle." She lifted Joskin's chin, "Don't take his sacrifice away from him. It was his choice."

Marren helped Joskin to his feet and then softly grabbed Niesla's hands, "What word from the frozen mountains across the ocean?"

Niesla ducked her head, "I have failed you."

Carrita stepped to Marren's side, "Your words are not truth."

Both Marren and Niesla looked to Carrita quizzically.

Carrita continued, "Though the salvation of this city is not our primary reason for coming, we have been armed, trained and dispatched to your aid. You have already made note of our legendary arms. You have noted my difference. We are all the assistance any city can muster at this dire time."

"Between the four of you I have no doubt an army would fall in less than a day," Marren said, running a hand around Carrita's ear, "but, we are not facing a mere army. We are facing creatures with hearts so dark even the Mistress of Death seems kind. These are creatures so powerful they hunt ancient dragons for sport."

Airria bowed slightly, "If they stand in my way, I will cut through them. I have trained under..." His voice trailed off as Marren's kind gaze met his own.

She stared deeply into his eyes for some time. "You are the cousin Joskin has told me so much about. I can see you are determined. I can see what you have lost. You are so young to have paid such a price. I only hope it will be enough."

Marren turned her attention to Faith. Looking in the icy eyes Faith now understood Airria's silence and Joskin's devotion. The eyes seemed to pierce her soul, see through her life. There was no judgment, only understanding. This was no ordinary woman.

Faith wanted to look away, but was trapped, entranced by this woman's gaze. It was not unlike looking into the Black Fire. Faith was enchanted and terrified all at the same time. She dare not speak. She wanted to leave, to go back to being anonymous, yet wanted to gaze into these eyes forever.

Marren broke the silence, "Who is this lovely creature?"

Carrita answered, "This is Faith. She is another who has been trained and come to assist."

Faith wondered how Carrita seemed so unaffected by Marren's presence. She knew Carrita's mother was a very powerful mage. She knew Carrita had met other powerful beings as a part of her growing up. But it was still bewildering how anyone could get used to Marren's stare.

"My friends," Marren said, addressing the whole group, "I am afraid you have come in the midst of dire times. Even with all the magic and strength I command, I am not any closer to ending this siege than when it began." Her head sagged slightly and her shoulders drooped. "The most dangerous part of this siege is about to continue. To the wall if you desire to see the challenge." They all followed her as fast as they could. Marren swept Carrita up in her arms and carried her with absolute ease.

Taksek's rough voice ground out from behind the horses, "If master fight, Taksek fight!"

Marren laughed, "I never thought I would see the day Joskin DeAveron would be traveling with an orc."

Joskin chuckled uneasily, "Neither did I, but he's an amazing craftsman. He forged my armor and all our barding."

Marren took a moment to examine Joskin's armor more closely. "Truly he is a master of masters. Would it be possible to have him assist in the armory? It would be a tremendous loss to have such a craftsman injured."

Faith turned to the orc, "Will you see to the armory? Will you make better weapons and armor so the soldiers here can guard me better?"

Taksek scowled, "Master want me leave her to these? Master want me take orders from dirty humans or dwarfs?"

Marren placed a hand on the orc's shoulder. "Taksek will take no order from the humans or dwarves. He will give the orders to the humans and dwarves," she gave a quick glace to Garfrun.

Faith added, "Will you teach them. This city is large and will need many blacksmiths. Even you cannot create sufficient armor in time. Will you do this for me?"

Taksek scratched his nose for a moment. "Taksek no teach gold or silver, but will teach iron and steel."

Faith wrapped her arms around her friend's neck. "Thank you," she whispered into his ear. She could feel his body stiffen, so she backed away.

His skin had paled to a sickly green. His eyes were bright and wide. He stared for some time shifting his weight. Suddenly he dropped to one knee, exactly as Joskin had done to Marren. "Taksek make Master proud," a small cloudy tear rolled off his nose.

Faith reached down to help the orc up, but he spun to stand facing Garfrun. He demanded, "Where forge? Take me!"

Faith watched Taksek walk next to the wolf-man. He seemed taller. His shoulders more square. She could almost forget he was not human.

"In all my time I have never seen an orc surrender so much respect for anyone, much less a human woman." Marren's voice reminded Faith of the siege. "He will do well. He will make you proud."

Faith reached to grab her horse.

Marren said, "The wall is no place for a horse."

Joskin laughed, "If Faith is going anywhere remotely dangerous, the rest of us may get killed trying to stop Persephone. Faith's horse is more dedicated than her orc."

Marren conceded, "Persephone can come as far as the wall, but on top she would be dangerous to those who need to be there."

Faith nodded, "She will wait at the base of the wall if I ask her to."

Marren again swept Carrita into her arms like a small child. "Good, then I will take you to see the challenge we face."

As Marren led the way, she asked Faith, "Would you walk beside me?"

Faith reluctantly came to Marren's side. She reached out with her magic to feel the aura Marren was carrying with her. It was dark, darker than any she had come across since the group had dispatched the lich and vampire on their way down the frozen slopes of the Arstock Range a few months ago. This aura was not unexpected. After all, Carrita had warned Faith, Marren was a vampire. If Faith understood Carrita correctly, Marren was the vampire who orchestrated the conversion of this city from cliffside to port.

Faith looked to Marren and how she carried Carrita like a small child. "How long have you been Governor of this city?" she finally asked.

Marren laughed softly, "I have protected this city much longer than I would care to remember. The years have run together. Why do you ask?"

Faith felt a little uneasy. She did not know how to ask what she wanted to.

Carrita giggled, "Mother said Marren could measure her governorship in millennia."

Marren reached her free hand up and stoked Carrita's hair. "Don't say it that way child. You make me feel so aged."

Carrita rolled her eyes, "I believe it has been some time since you worried about your age."

"Young one," Marren said with a mocking scowl, "I will have you know I celebrate every year of my existence."

504

"How have you kept your nature a secret?" Faith queried.

"For the most part, the citizens don't care who leads them, so long as there is food, low crime and good commerce." Marren looked up at the edge of the wall and accelerated her pace. "Few have seen me and none by the light of day. The humans assume me an elf, the elves who don't know the truth, assume me an old mage. The few who do know the truth, already know who I am and are willing to help me maintain my position."

Marren looked to the wall again. "Forgive me for preventing your questions. I am sure you have many more. You wear the armor of Viehasia so I am not able to tell if I feel correctly from you. It would seem you are a High Priestess of Mellinatia, Mistress of Life. If it is so, why have we not met before this day?"

Faith could feel her face flush. This was not the first time someone had assumed she was a high ranking Life follower. "I am but a humble farmer's daughter, trained in bow by Jammar. Carrita has introduced me to magic, but I have not been so valiant in learning."

Marren frowned slightly, "This is not what I expected the armor to feel like."

Carrita chimed in, "It is not the armor you feel. High Priestess Valnicia felt the same thing. Even her boy could feel the potential."

Marren's porcelain-like face relaxed, "The blood is strong in her. Her potential is almost as limitless as yours," Marren ran her hand down Carrita's face.

The long stairs running up to the top of the wall could now be seen in the dim torchlight. Marren took a deep breath, "Are you sure you all want to know what we contend with this night?"

Joskin inhaled deeply, "We need to know. We have to break this siege to continue on our quest. Whatever it is, we will need to get past it and I will not leave this city to the mercy of anything that makes you nervous."

Faith looked up the long staircase. "You know we cannot see in the dark. I do not believe this torchlight will be sufficient to perceive anything on the field except torches and fire."

"See you must," Marren reached into a small pouch at her side and produced five vials of milky liquid. "This will allow you to see."

Carrita looked at them for a moment. "You know I could use my magic to see."

Marren smiled slightly, "Young one, you will need your powers for other purposes tonight."

Carrita took a vial and drank it quickly. Faith did not know Marren and was uneasy about drinking something she did not know, but she trusted Carrita so she drank one and passed the rest to the others. The darkness began to melt away. Within moments it seemed as though it were midday.

Marren did not wait for the group. "I will see if they are prepared yet," before anyone could ask any questions she was climbing the stairs. The others followed, struggling to keep up.

Faith turned to her horse, "Please wait here. Marren says you may get people hurt up there. "

Persephone shook her head in protest, but only for a moment. Eventually she walked over to a wagon of hay and started eating.

Relieved, Faith made her way to the battlements. When she got there, Joskin, Airria and Niesla were still breathing very heavily. She looked over the field of broken towers and catapults. The entire base of the wall was covered in bones and gore. At a safe distance she could see a camp of men. They had oxen dragging the remaining catapults back.

"Marren," Faith asked, "how long will I be able to see like this in the dark? Is this permanent?"

The corners of Marren's lips curled slightly. "I am sad to say, it is only temporary. I am not sure if it will last a month or a week."

A loud commotion brought Faith's attention back to the enemy army. Men were scurrying quickly to get out of the path of three large figures. The few too slow in getting out of the way were ripped in half by the creatures.

The creatures were very tall, three times the height of the soldiers. Their horns shaped like a demonic bull and dark enough they seemed to make the starless night seem comparatively bright. What could be seen of their bodies were like giant, well-muscled humans

506

above the waist that faded in to bovine legs. A wave of power and fear swept the wall as the creatures approached.

Both Carrita and Joskin gasped. For the first time since she had known him, Joskin had a look of pure terror on his face. When Carrita regained her composure, she gasped, "Matrataurs!"

Joskin looked at Airria, "The only other time I have ever seen these I was helping an army in Athelstan. There was only one of them and I was a part of an army of over a thousand. I was one of thirteen who survived! As it died, it was laughing! This night may be the end of my adventure in this world."

Marren looked at them and said, "The new Zerith king has made some sort of pact with these creatures to bring this city to its knees. I would guess I am the prize for them."

Two of the matrataurs, dressed more like barbarian warriors than mages, began a magical attack on the gate. Each hit made the whole wall shudder. The third was female and dressed in long, black, flowing robes. She put up a magical, semi-transparent barrier as black as their horns.

The archers stood and watched in terror. Carrita began a spell, but she was stopped by Marren, "Even with your staff, you alone are no match for these creatures. I have lost six of my best magic users to them already."

"I have improved since last we met," Carrita pleaded.

"I am aware of your improvement," Marren said setting the girl down.

Carrita continued her protest, "We cannot stand here and do nothing. They will eventually make it through the gate."

Marren looked at Carrita with understanding, "They have been at this for two months; the magic protecting this place is wearing thin. Tonight they will break through. We will need all of our strength for that time."

Joskin interrupted, "We cannot let them enter this city on their terms. Give us a little time and we may be able to do something." He put his arm on Airria's shoulder and forced an uncertain smile, "Trust me."

"How much time will you need," Marren asked.

"When you hear us charging toward the gate, open it," Joskin's voice was shaky. He then looked at Carrita, "When the gate starts to open, they will back up to see why. When they do, use what magic you can to distract them. Destroy them if you can. I know I've been a little critical of your power, but please don't hold back…if you do, they'll destroy us all, not just our bodies, but our whole souls and laugh while doing it." He paused for a moment to look at Faith, "Use every mage you can, except Faith, we will need her arrows and skill."

He looked at Niesla with eyes that seemed to say good-bye. "I know killing is against your nature, but these creatures are worse than the cruelest lich. Help where you can." He placed a hand on her shoulder then slowly ran it down her arm, prolonging the touch.

Joskin grabbed Airria and they ran down the stairs.

Marren sent word to her remaining mages to come to the wall, and then set Carrita down. "You have Joskin's respect, I have underestimated you."

Carrita smiled with less fear, "They will bring my staff." She looked at the matrataurs for a moment then looked up at Marren, "We will need all the help we can get. Do any of your alchemy shops nearby have crushed violet crystals and perhaps some angel feathers?"

Marren looked confused but sent a runner for the ingredients. When the runner arrived with the requested items Marren's black-robed mages were showing up.

Faith had only a remote idea what the girl was planning, but knew her own role. She dashed down the stairs and grabbed her bow and arrows from her horse.

Persephone pawed at the ground.

Faith stroked her mane, "I wish you could help me, but all the fighting will be at range. If anyone is to try to hurt me they will have to ascend these stairs first. "

The horse began moving around Faith.

Faith waited for an opening, then slipped around Persephone and darted to the top of the wall. There were already twelve robed figures there. Carrita had them sit in a semi-circle next to the edge of the wall. Niesla, Carrita and Marren stood in the center.

Not long after the group was settled the runner returned with the requested items. Carrita began making a life symbol with the crystal dust. When the leaf-shaped symbol was complete, she put the feathers top to tip in a circle around the crystal.

Marren began to back away and the mages began to stand up.

Looking up, giggling, Carrita said, "I do know with whom I am working. I have learned from each of you. I would not intentionally do anything which would endanger any of you."

For the first time that evening, Niesla began to shift away from Marren.

Marren saw the panic on Niesla's face and said, "I did not hurt you before. I even helped you to leave this land. I will not let anything happen to you now."

Niesla relaxed a little, but kept one eye on Marren.

Carrita giggled, "I told you truth. Marren is the protector of this city. She will do all in her power to keep us all safe." He tone grew more serious. "I need you to concentrate."

Niesla shifted uneasily and looked around her. She uttered no word, but nodded slowly.

Chapter 4 - Dark Battles

The clatter of warhorses running on the cobblestone streets brought a breath of relief then the horrible realization that it was time. Most of those participating had little knowledge of the whole plan, but knew enough to fulfill their parts.

"Open the gates!" went Marren's cry.

The robed figures joined their boney hands and began chanting; Marren and Niesla joined hands around Carrita and joined the lichs in chanting. The sounds of their words made Faith shudder.

The men raced their horses through the open gate. As Airria tossed Carrita's staff in the air like a javelin, Faith tried to use magic to help her catch it, but she could feel another, familiar force catch it, directing it into Carrita's waiting hand.

With staff in hand, Carrita joined in the chanting. Faith could feel dark magic being changed to raw power. It swirled around the group on the wall like an isolated windstorm. The crushed crystal began to levitate and glow. The feathers began twirling up, rotating around the crystal and making Faith feel dizzy.

As Joskin predicted, the matrataurs backed up several paces sending the army behind them scattering into the woods. A semi-transparent dark wall appeared between the monsters and the oncoming charge.

Joskin was in the lead. His ax was held as though it were a lance, its blade only slightly in front of his horse's face. His horse was fully barded in the golden armor Taksek had made.

Airria was a half length behind. His sword was raised high above his head, blazing like a small sun. With his white and gold armor he was like a burning beacon in the bare field.

A huge ripple went through the matrataur's shield as the ax ripped through it. Faith could feel the magical wave of energy released from the collision.

Joskin veered his horse slightly to the left and began swinging his ax in a well-practiced rotation, only to have it blocked by an ax even darker than the matrataur's horns. The horse sidestepped into the creature, only to bounce off it and the force of the rush almost caused it to lose its footing.

The matrataur shifted his weight only slightly from the impact causing the deadly arc of his ax to lift slightly. Joskin used the motion of his ax to help him regain his seating. It swung hard into the monster's black weapon. Between ax collision and the shifted arc, the brutal swing slipped over Joskin's shoulder.

Joskin did not slow. He shifted his path toward the female. His ax was again positioned as a lance.

Airria directed his horse toward the other male matrataur. He ducked and used his shield to redirect the incoming blow then dove off his horse into the massive creature. The beast brought its handle down into Airria's path and spun him off.

His shield blocked another massive ax swing while he was still in the air, slamming him to the ground. When the ax struck the shield it splintered and caused an explosion of black energy which sent the matrataur flying back over a hundred paces. Airria struggled to his feet, fighting to keep hold of his sword. His horse lay softly squealing only slightly lifting its head. The matrataur was lying motionless on the ground, its muscular chest ripped open.

At this point Faith realized she was getting sick from the extreme amount of magic the group of mages was trying to control. *A distraction… this would be a good time to help distract the beasts!* she thought to herself and began releasing arrows as fast as she could only to watch each one explode on an unseen shield in front of the one in robes. Faith could tell her efforts were helping as the group on top of the wall was pushing the magic away.

The creature Joskin had passed roared so loudly the wall shook. It spun itself once and threw its ax at Joskin.

Joskin swung his ax back, over his head to divert the oncoming projectile. He hit the ax forcing it to twist, but it was so massive it did not change direction much. A loud screech could be heard as the black ax ripped through the horse's barding and lodged deep in the horse's flank. Both horse and rider came crashing to the ground.

Even at a distance Faith could hear Joskin's armor scraping on the rocks as he and his horse slid across the ground. The animal was pawing and twisting, but had lost the use of its hind legs.

The male matrataur was pulling out a whip and began cracking it toward Joskin.

With the creature's back to him Airria slowly made his way to it. He gained strength with each step, lifting his sword more strongly from the ground.

Without warning the long whip cracked back. Airria deflected the blow with his shield, but was knocked over backward. He rolled to his knees and tried to stand, but another pop sent him tumbling back again.

Airria struggled to gain some footing, but yet another crack sprawled him out on his back. He rolled to his side to avoid the next blow. Finally he pulled his legs under his shield, curling into the fetal position.

With its back now to him, Joskin threw his ax at the matrataur. It drove deep into the creature's head slamming it to the ground.

The mage raised her staff and rammed it into the ground. A blast of energy threw rocks and rubble through the air. The force of the blast knocked Joskin's horse over him and pinned him in an even more painful

513

position. Then the monster let out an earth-shattering bellow and charged Airria.

Airria seemed to gain strength from the blast. Though still shaky he found his feet and began approaching the robed creature. Its staff battered Airria back and forth like a cat playing with a mouse.

Even with all the distraction, this matrataur was able to magically keep Carrita and all the magic users at a distance and deflect Faith's arrows. It even seemed to be enjoying the fight, as if it were only playing a game it could win at any time.

Airria ducked low and spun in, his sword swung weak and wild. The creature grabbed Airria's shield and lifted him off the ground. A bloodthirsty yell went out as flames erupted from its hand.

Faith had long since ceased paying attention to the arrow she was using. She knew she would always have access to powerful arrows. In this short battle it had not mattered which she shot. The creature had shattered them with magic. When she saw Airria in his dire circumstances she shot one more arrow then turned to run down the stairs. She was going to join the battle with her own magic and swords.

A cheer rang out across the wall. Faith turned back to see what had happened. There was a perfect replica of the creature in stone standing over a collapsed and un-moving Airria. Though she was not sure exactly what had happened she knew both Airria and Joskin needed help.

Quickly she sprinted down the stairs and jumped on her faithful horse. Together they bolted out of the nearby gate, directly to Airria. Before her horse had come to a complete stop she leapt from her saddle. She landed hard forced to run to a stop.

"Are you all right?" Faith asked as she removed Airria's helm.

Airria was breathless, gasping, "Joskin, check Joskin."

She started to stand but noticed Marren single-handedly rolling the horse off Joskin. With the bloody, wriggling animal removed, Joskin rolled to one arm.

Carrita was standing nearby. There was a massive sphere of energy over her head swirling inside a ball of crystal powder and spinning feathers.

Faith yelled to Marren, "Can he be moved? Airria is asking for him."

Airria spoke quietly, still recovering his breath, "Can the horses be saved? Was anyone else hurt?"

Carrita was already tending to Joskin's horse. There were some sickening pops followed closely by the horse's squeal. "I will mend the horses only enough to keep them from passing over. You will need to heal them and the men. I have other uses for this magic."

Marren picked Joskin up like a rag doll. His leg was contorted and his face bruised and bloody.

Faith rushed over and began pouring her healing magic into him, but Marren stopped her. "We need to set the bones before you mend them."

Faith pulled her hand off Joskin, "I am unaware of how to set bones or fix joints."

Marren grimaced, "I know how and will do so, but this is a painful possess. The best we can hope for is that he passes out."

Without waiting for another word, a bone popped back into place. Joskin let out a scream. Fortunately his eyes closed softly. "Now we can work."

It took some time, but each bone was set and joint placed. Faith began her work. Through her magic she could feel the bones mending and the tendons and ligaments reattaching. When she was finished there was only a slight discoloration where the bruising had been.

By the time she was done Persephone had herded the now limping and still bleeding horses to Faith. She took turns pouring some healing magic into each horse until she felt weak.

Carrita was standing near the statue. Her magic cloud was not swirling around the creature. Without even looking Carrita said, "You do not have enough life force to heal everyone who is hurting. The blood from the creatures will make a wonderful base for a powerful healing potion."

Niesla approached on her horse, "What can I do to help?"

Carrita was staring intently at the statue, as if she were studying it, but answered Niesla, "In the mountains you spoke of making a healing potion with troll's blood. Do the same using the matrataurs' blood. Many need healing; you should gather as much blood as you can."

Faith laughed under her breath. Both Niesla and Marren were older then Carrita by centuries, but they both rushed when Carrita gave a command. She pondered this as she helped Airria onto his horse. As she climbed onto Persephone she noticed the black robed figures gathering around the statue and linking hands. She reached out with her magic to see if she could feel what their purpose was.

It did not take long for Faith to realize Carrita was using the magic she had captured from the matrataur and lichs to create a golem out of this massive creature. To her worry, she could feel something different than when the ship golems were created. From time to time she could almost see the slain beasts swirling in the magical cloud.

"It will be all right," Marren's voice startled Faith, "what she does is to help the city. All will be well." Marren's words did not sound sure, but she loaded the waterskins of blood onto Airria's horse. "Joskin is secure on his horse please take him to my house. My day servants will tend to all of you. I will join you when I am finished."

A surprising thought came to Faith, "How did you arrive when I did. I rode my horse and left before you. How did you come so quickly?"

Marren smiled, "I flew with Carrita. I know some will now know the truth of me, but I needed to see if I could help Joskin. He risked his life to save this city again. If there was a chance I could save him, I had to do it." Marren stepped aside as Niesla secured the weapons to the horses.

"Will it be acceptable if I use your alchemy laboratory?" Niesla asked. "I have much to do and little strength left to do so."

Marren bowed to each of them individually. "Please use what you can. This siege is far from over. Joskin will be unconscious for a few days while he finishes recovering. Your horses need rest. All you do puts me further in your debt. Feel free to use my alchemists and servants as you can."

Faith nodded, so tired she was afraid she would pass out on her horse. Slowly, with Airria, Niesla and Joskin in tow, she made her way back into the city to Marren's stables. As she rolled off her horse the straw seemed so soft she decided she would sleep with her horse.

Before she lost awareness she felt an arm wrap around her. She pressed in. Even with both suits of armor between them she felt the comfort and security of human touch. Warm and tired she surrendered to sleep.

Chapter 5 – Big Magic

After the lichs had bound all three matrataur souls into the statue Faith had created with the last arrow she had released, Carrita wove the collected magic into the stone. She had learned well how to weave life into an inanimate object, but this time it was different. The other golems she had made had just a piece of life essence which had been torn from an orc. This object had the entire life essence of three powerful beings, any one of which would best her in a magical battle.

The deed had been done. She would have to trust the lichs and their understanding of the dark binding magics. More difficult was trusting in the lichs' intentions. They had earned their undeath through their incredible understanding of such rituals and exceptional intelligence and cruelty. The lichs surrounding her had allied themselves with Marren and such allegiance would have to be sufficient for Carrita's trust.

"Is it finished?" Marren asked.

Carrita looked up at her friend and one time mentor. "It is almost complete. We are missing a singular component."

"What do you need?" she said looking around.

"You," Carrita could not hide her little smile.

Marren's eyes grew wide and she took a step back, "What?"

Carrita looked at the stone creature then back to Marren. "I need to bind it to you. I will need your cooperation to accomplish this task."

Marren laughed, "How could I forget such a crucial factor?" She sat down, spreading her dress neatly around her, "Very well, let us bind this creature to me."

Carrita was always amazed at how Marren could make even the most revolting task appear elegant. "Your mind will be bound to this creature. Your thoughts will drive it to your will. Such can be disorienting."

Marren lowered and then raised her eyes. "You do know this is not the first creature to be bound to me. I am aware of the cost."

Carrita had grown accustomed to explaining everything she did to people who considered a decade a long time. Being only fourteen, she often forgot there were beings who had lived for centuries. It was a nice feeling to not have to explain.

Carrita knelt down on Marren's dress, "Then shall we begin?"

Carrita closed her eyes and tried to concentrate. She could not settle herself. Her stomach felt as though a plague of moths were residing and fluttering about within. Her mind would not shed the possibility of diminishing her friend.

Marren must have sensed Carrita's discomfort, for Carrita felt Marren's gentle hand on her own. Marren's voice came like a soft breeze, "I will be fine. I have done this before and I can guide you if need be. You can do this. Just know I am here for you."

Carrita took a deep breath and allowed her soul to slip into the Astral Plane. She looked around her. The stone figure was glowing with barely contained magical energy. She could see the bodies of each lich blazing with dark energy. Next to each one stood a figure, some male, some female all either human or elf, dressed in white robes.

Marren's body was bright with a rainbow of color surging and twisting. Her soul stood close, appearing as she did in the Physical Plane. "We have all blurred the line between life and death. It is a part of becoming what we have."

Carrita looked at Marren, then to the others. "You have chosen to appear as you are in the physical world. Why have the others elected to show themselves in white robes?"

An elf stepped forward and bowed low. My creator, the Fairen, Governor of Derain, and your mother saved us from our dark fate. She taught us the error of our ways and to abhor all we were. I speak not for the others, though I know they feel the same, but I will divert as far as I am able from the life I once led. We are not Marren's thralls as has been noised abroad. We serve in a meager attempt to make recompense for our dark deeds."

Carrita asked, "Why do you dress in the black robes of Death?"

The elf stood up and stepped back to his place, "We do not wish to defile any other robes with the depravity of our birth."

"The magic will only contain the matrataurs' souls for so long," Marren's words reminded Carrita of the urgency of her task, "we should finish the binding."

Carrita smiled. When she was a child she was determined to understand everything. The only thing she truly had learned was there was always more to be educated about. The more she understood, the more she realized how little she knew. "Yes, it is time to complete this ritual to imprison these souls and to bind their will to yours."

A black mist began to swirl around the glowing statue. As the mist began to melt into the stone the souls of the matrataurs could be seen struggling to leave. They could be heard screaming in agony. The astral energy closed in. Everything was fading into darkness.

"No!" Carrita cried out. "This is not the way. Even these creatures do not deserve such a fate."

"They must be bound!" the elf exclaimed. "If they are freed they will destroy me and my undead kin. They will take revenge on us for Rantail."

Carrita reached out with her own energy to comfort the beasts. "I will not be party to an act so grievous only Rantail and Jarmack'Trastibbik could be proud of it. My mother's soul is trapped by such magic. There must be another way."

Marren's voice was soft and clear in the Astral winds, "Even your mother could not find a better way to confine or bind such darkness."

Carrita looked around her, desperate for one of those helping her to take her side. Each being there, including herself had been trapped in a dark prison of sorts. Each had been freed in part or in whole by her mother. "You are wrong. My mother did find another way. She bound each of you to a purpose and cause with your own wills, rather than against them."

She paused as she stopped looking and began thinking out loud. "Mellinatia created valnaricks, which are the same yet the opposite of vampires. Why can we not use the same concept to bind these creatures to this object?"

Marren reminded Carrita, "Valnaricks are chosen because their will is already dedicated to the purpose of hunting vampires. Their will is never forced."

Ideas were flying through Carrita's mind, but each had flaws, "When you first met my mother was your will not subverted, did you not originally wish her harm?" She did not need the answer. Slowly it was becoming more clear what she needed to do, "We will bind them with Life magic, we will give them peace."

She reached out with her mind and began converting the dark astral energy to light. She carefully broke every torment with tranquility.

The volume of the beasts' cries increased.

Marren still spoke gently, "Are you sure you are not being more cruel? These are beast who are most happy when in pain."

Carrita struggled to speak as it was becoming more difficult to contain the creatures. She had ventured into magics her companions did not understand. "You were once such a creature. In time and with the proper care you have learned to enjoy serenity."

Carrita reached into her body and grabbed her magic. She shaped and formed it into a prison of compassion. Delicately she wove the magic into every molecule of stone and bound it to touch the magic already being contained in the creature.

Gradually she could feel help. The elf first, then the others joined in. Even Marren wove her own brand of peace into the magic.

While Marren was so open and working with the Astral energies Carrita reached into her mind and bound it to the golem.

Marren backed up shaking her head, "I had almost forgotten our purpose here was to bind me to this creature. Now the deed is done will you seal it? Will you finish the binding? The sun will soon rise and our bodies need to be safely inside when that happens."

Carrita pulled the physical magic tight. Carefully she inspected the work to make sure it held the energy fast. When finished she took a few steps back. "Now you have a defender who can contend in the light as well as the dark."

Now the commotion was gone and quiet had ascended, the elf spoke again, "An existence of over twenty millennia and even today I have learned something."

Carrita felt self-conscious at the compliment. "I am also humbled by what I learned today, but Marren is right. All of you need to quickly make your way to your sanctuaries. The golem should afford us a few days of rest."

Carrita watched as each of the white figures dissolved into their boney, black-robed bodies. Each walked quickly back to the city. Only she and Marren remained.

Marren knelt to match Carrita's gaze, "All the time your mother was carrying you, she could not have imagined her child would accomplish what even the Deific Council and Dragon Council could not have believed. I wish I could see her face when you tell her."

Carrita was speechless. She tried to say something. Before she gained her composure Marren had melded back into her body, transformed into her demonic visage and bolted into the skies.

Carrita brought herself back to the Physical Plane. The golem had picked up the remaining black ax and was striding toward the gate. She surveyed the field. Light was creeping over the horizon. The monstrous black staff lay on the ground. The army was making its way back to their places on the field, slowly approaching Carrita.

In hopes of causing fear in the soldiers she used her magic to throw the staff high in the air and forced her energies into it. With little resistance it soon gave way into a large explosion. Black splinters combusted and rained down upon the army.

As the army fled back into the woods Carrita slid into her saddle. It had been a hard fight, but something in the air said this fight was far from over. There was a feeling of power. Something she did not recognize. There was magic driving this army. Fear and intimidation would not be enough. Hopefully the city would have a full day of rest before they would have to fight again.

Chapter 6 - War is More than a Battle

Joskin woke up to the sound of a boulder crashing against the gate. Instinctively he reached for his ax, but his muscles were not cooperating. His head felt like a hammer was pounding on it and his thighs felt as though they were pinned to the bed by hot pokers. His arms and shoulders felt torn and near immobile.

He closed his eyes and tried to remember what had happened in his last fight. He recalled walking up the long stairs to the top of the wall, after that only images of black horns, darkness and fear. It was deep night then and the sun was shining now.

There was still a siege that needed ending; an army's will that needed breaking. He fought through the webbing of pain shooting through his muscles to sit up. He couldn't open his eyes or unclench his teeth while he dressed. He ran a rough hand over his shaved head and focused on his task.

Whatever had happened in his last battle the war was not over. Marren had saved him so many times and helped him so much he couldn't let her down now. Slowly he rose to his feet leaning heavily on his ax. As quickly as his pain would allow he made his way to the dining hall.

The table was covered with maps and figures and surrounded with well armored warriors. Joskin only knew a few of them. Many of the commanders he had worked with in the past were not there. This siege had taken some great advisors.

Garfrun and a Dwarven commander Joskin recognized by the name of Dizrin were nose to nose. Their hands were recklessly placed on the table with fallen figures next to them.

The dwarf yelled in his gravely, deep voice, "Their strength is broken! We should take the fight to them! They won't know what to do if we stop hiding behind the wall!"

Garfrun growled, baring his teeth, "Those gates have held Zerith out for thousands of years, they will keep them out for thousands more."

Dizrin picked his hand off the table and slammed his fist down. "They have nothing to fight with except the rock lobbers and those won't do no good if we're next to them!"

Joskin looked to Marren to referee the dispute. She looked ragged as she sat slumped in her chair. It was obvious she hadn't slept in some time.

She raised her tired eyes, "Joskin, it is good to see you up. How are you feeling?"

Airria was sitting next to her. His right arm was clutching his slumped left shoulder. He shifted his droopy gaze to the doorway where Joskin was standing. Slowly he stood, grinding his teeth.

Joskin pulled himself as straight as he could. "I'm fine. What's the plan?"

Faith spoke from a corner behind Airria, "Sadly our encounter last evening did not prove as effective as we had hoped. Early this morning the army readied for fighting. Even the golem Carrita made has not deterred the opposition's resolve."

Joskin knew there had been a fight. It must've been a rough one for him not to remember anything about it. He was curious how many he had fought, or what he had fought that would leave such a dark place in his mind. Carrita always did things he didn't understand, but now he wanted to know what had happened. He was doing his best to hide his pain and the fact he had no idea what had happened. "Golem?" he asked.

526

Marren laughed, "The only time I have seen you so perplexed after a battle was the first time you fought for us. That demon hit your ax and threw you off the wall."

Joskin was sad that Marren had seen right through his attempts to hide his confusion. "I still don't remember much about that battle. I don't remember any demons, angels or even the humans you said I killed." His gaze fell to the floor.

Marren sat straight in her chair, life flowing back to her eyes. "You will be glad you don't remember anything about last night's battle as well."

He raised his eyes but kept his head still. "One thing I need to know. Is my horse all right? Did he make it through?"

Marren smiled, "Yes, our healers made sure your horse would live. Though I would guess he is as sore as you are."

"Not anymore," Niesla's voice behind him made Joskin jump.

The pain shooting through his back and legs made him lose control of his muscles and he collapsed to the ground.

Niesla circled around Joskin, finally squatting in front of him. "It appears you will need some of this as well. It will help with the pain." She reached her hand out with a box of salve. Matrataurs are terrifying warriors to face, but their bodies have so many wonderful uses. Their blood is an exceptional base for healing salves and potions. Sadly the potions will not be finished for some time. Until then, this salve will have to do."

A young soldier came running into the room, dashed straight over to Marren and whispered into her ear. Her eyes widened and her mouth dropped. After a moment she spoke, "Dizrin, you shall get your wish. Bring your dwarves to the main gate. It looks like it will not be long before Zerith will be breaking through."

The dwarf grinned with a satisfied scowl. "Just make sure your archers don't hit us." He hopped off his chair and sprinted out of the room.

Niesla was helping Joskin unbuckle his armor.

Garfrun slammed his fist on the table. "Impossible!"

Marren kept her composure, "We knew the magics in the gate were wearing thin. If we do not disrupt this day's assault they will breach it."

Airria dropped the hand from his shoulder and stood almost square. "If you have another gate we can get out of I will lead a small assault from the rear. Maybe we can distract them until evening. Give you another night to magic the gate back up."

While Joskin unbuckled his leg armor, Niesla began rubbing the salve on his back. He could feel the pain dissipating with every touch of the soft Elven hands.

Marren stood and put a hand on Airria's shoulder, "It will take many months, maybe even years for us to repair the damage those matrataurs did to the gates. Even if we distract them today, we will have to keep them busy through tomorrow and the next day and the next. We will have to break their will."

Joskin jumped to his feet, "Matrataurs? As in more than one? We need to deal with this army today and matrataurs tonight?"

Marren laughed, "I guess there are some things about last night you should know. You and Airria killed two matrataur warriors. Faith turned another to stone. Carrita animated the third in hopes its presence would frighten the army."

Joskin collapsed to the floor again, this time he felt completely numb. "That didn't buy us even one day?"

Marren dropped her eyes to the maps on the table. "It didn't even break the routine. It even seems to have raised morale in the Zerith troops."

Joskin rolled his head, stretching his shoulder muscles and clearing his mind. "This golem, can it fight like the ones we have on the ship?"

Marren turned her head and looked sideways at Joskin. "It should fight as well as the matrataurs. Will that do for any of the plots developing in your mind?"

The room was silent for some time while Niesla finished putting the salve on Joskin. His mind was inventorying the group's assets. His eyes were studying the enemy placements on the maps.

He began remembering something, "Years ago, I think it was the first siege I helped with, I recall one of your 'evening advisors' talking of raising some of the fallen to defend by night. I would guess it has been some time, but would that be useful to have some bodies? Maybe some wounded prisoners?"

Niesla stepped back, "What are you suggesting?"

Joskin didn't reply. He knew anything he said would be wrong in Niesla's eyes. He kept his eyes focused on Marren.

Marren frowned, "I hate to resort to such tactics again. It has been several millennia since I did so. Perhaps it is time to start acting my part, in all its brutality."

Niesla began to protest, her eyes locked on Joskin, but was cut off by Marren.

"How many have died because I refused to use what I had," Marren's eyes pulsed. Even Garfrun backed away. She closed her eyes and took a deep breath. "Yes, I will use what you can give me."

Joskin turned his attention to Faith, "Is Carrita still sleeping? Can she be awakened?"

Faith stood to check, but Marren answered, "She will need a few days of rest before we disrupt her slumber. It took much of her power and strength to create that golem."

"Have the golem support the dwarves," Joskin said. "We will use their hard heads as shields."

Marren's eyes dropped, "There is little I can do in the daylight."

"Sleep," Joskin replied. "You will have a long night. You will fight the battle I can't and it will be only you and the dead you take with you."

Niesla put her hand on Joskin's face and forced him to look at her. "What will Marren do with those people, the dead and wounded?"

Joskin could feel the ice and stone forming around his heart, "She will end the port siege when we have broken the land siege."

Niesla shifted her gaze to Marren, "You would damn the souls of those who fall to an existence of tormented slavery?"

529

Marren took a deep breath again, her eyes returning to their icy blue. "The damnation will only be for the night then they will be released and can move on to their eternal reward."

Niesla turned back to Joskin, "How could you even suggest such a thing?" Without waiting for an answer she stormed out of the room.

Joskin was still sore, but able to move. He began replacing his armor. "Faith, go to the ship and get my Elven bow and some of the best arrows Taksek has made. Perhaps three quarrels. Airria, your magic sword won't leave enough body for Marren to work with, but use your magic shield. I will use the golden ax Taksek made me. Meet me at the north gate mounted and ready for battle."

Garfrun barked in, "You're not planning an offence without me are you?"

Joskin could see hope entering the hearts of everyone in the room as his own stature became ridged. He hated to see Niesla disappointed in him, but he had a job to do, one he would have to do with minimal magic as protection. You will need to command the wall. When the army turns, open the gates and let Dizrin have his fun.

Faith asked, "Should I change my armor? It can do damage to exceed even my arrows."

Joskin looked at her innocent face, "You are going into the butcher's house and will need all the protection you can have. Just don't expect to come out the same."

"Perhaps Faith should stay on the wall and support with her bow?" Airria asked.

At this point Joskin counted everyone as expendable. The city was more important than any of the people. He looked at his cousin and choked down the knot. "There is not a soldier in this city who can match her blades. Without her magic quiver, she is limited by the number of arrows she can carry. A single ax wielded well can lay waste to far more than a bow. We will need her at our backs."

Faith ducked her head and walked out of the room.

Airria looked at the table for a moment then looked back to Joskin. "She's not a common soldier. She is worth a whole army..."

Marren cut him off, "And that is why Joskin needs her with you."

Airria turned to protest, but Marren continued, "As a fighter, I value Joskin's life above my own, yet I let him go with you to fight the matrataurs last night. Neither of you are up to full strength. Both of you still hurt. You will need Faith's help. I would join you myself if I thought it would help you at all. You cannot take an army with you through the gate or we won't have enough to defend the city. So those who go must be able to fight as if they are an army. Sometimes you have to lose your strongest warrior to win the war."

By this time most of the room was empty, only Joskin, Airria and Marren remained. Marren was picking up the figures and placing them carefully on the map as she spoke.

Airria watched Marren for awhile. "So you're sending us to our deaths?"

Marren glanced up calmly, "I hope not, but I am allowing Joskin to risk what he feels we, as a city, can. Your group has been trained by Guardians, Your armor and weapons are mostly known from myth and legend. If anyone can return from such a grim task it is you."

Joskin ground his teeth, "I'll not ask you to follow me anywhere. Come if you like, but I am going to hit this army in the flank. The soldiers here have held this siege until they struggle to stand any more. We have to break this siege today!" Focused on the fight ahead, Joskin left the dining hall and went to the stable.

By the time he arrived at the stable he was still focused, but had calmed slightly. He found the horses ready as well as a small contingent of fighters mounted and outfitted in new armor with expertly made weapons in hand.

"If there is hope, it comes from following you," one soldier said. His shield stood as tall as him. His armor was shiny and new, perfectly forged.

"Who told you what I was planning?" Joskin asked.

Niesla's voice came from behind Joskin's horse, "I told Taksek, these are the first to receive his armor."

531

A second soldier stepped forward, his shield as tall as the first, but held in his right hand. "Me and Tabin were sent by the blacksmith to guard the one called Master," he said pointing to the first.

Joskin could feel a chuckle beginning in his heart, but the walls that the siege had formed around his heart held it from coming out.

Tabin bowed his head. "We know 'Master' is the archer woman who helps you. Me and Mailt have been shield-bearers for the last five years now. It was you who freed us from the General Moritan, during the last siege."

Joskin remembered the name well. Moritan had the audacity to challenge Joskin in single combat. When the general showed he had his shield-bearers with him. Joskin thought he had killed them both. Once the Moritan's protection was down, the general tried to run. Joskin had killed him before he could finish turning away.

Mailt bowed slightly, "We owe the orc for our armor and weapons; we owe you for our freedom."

Joskin could feel the hopelessness of his design. He had planned on only the three of them against an army. As well trained as he was and as well armed, he was not sure he would make it back. "Anyone who follows me out the gate is likely to die. I, myself, don't expect to return. But I will kill as many of them as I can before they get me. The choice is yours."

Niesla was checking the buckles on the last piece of barding on Joskin's horse. "You will return. If you fall in battle, I will personally damn your soul and make you one of the walking dead!" Her words and tone both filled him with shame and hope. "I will be on the wall with my bow to make sure of it."

"A choice we all need to make," Faith said, walking into the stable. "I will use your Elven bow to shoot from behind you. When the arrows run out, I will join you with my swords."

Airria walked in and suggested, "You supported us well from the wall last night. Why not today? Your magic arrows can decimate this army. Why not use them?"

Faith put her hand on Airria's shoulder and looked him square in the eye, "There is more to this siege then just one small army. Our

532

victory last evening should have sent this army scurrying away. We have more than one front to this siege. No, Joskin knows battle and war better than us. I will follow him out the gate. Without your help, we may fail, but we will try."

Tabin cut in, "Me and Mailt will keep her safe or die trying."

Airria ducked his head and climbed on his horse. Two newly forged swords were buckled to the barding, with a third hanging from a handle. "Live or die, we will break this siege."

The soldiers all yelled in agreement.

Joskin climbed into his saddle. He hoped he could make good on his and Airria's claim to break this siege. Faith was right, there was more to this siege then any motive he had encountered. He looked over the fighters believing they would all die, but hoping they would all live. He nudged his horse and started for the gate expecting this to be his last battle.

Chapter 7 - Bloody Hands

Faith was very nervous to be headed to the actual battlefield. She was wearing armor noted for decimating an entire army, worn by a skilled archer and accompanied only by a magic bow with devastating arrows. She had used the arrows several times in skirmishes over the last year. She knew the destruction they could cause. Joskin had asked her not to use the magic bow or arrows in order to save bodies.

She also felt a little awkward to have her own personal guards. Two humans sent by her friend Taksek to help keep her safe. She saw herself as no more important than anyone else. There were six others following her.

From the look in Joskin's eye, Faith guessed none of them should plan on returning. From the look in the soldiers' eyes, none of them were planning on it. Oddly, the only fear she could sense was hers and Airria's.

When the gate opened slightly, Faith expected to see an army ahead waiting. Instead she saw an open field of packed dirt and tree stumps. "Why is there no army to oppose us here?"

Tabin laughed softly, "We have been under siege for almost a year. The Zerith army is much depleted, they can only cover two of the gates."

Mailt added, "Their command knows the city won't receive any help from the woods so there is no reason to spread their forces out."

They did not get far before the outlying left wing of the army noticed them. A battalion of foot soldiers were dispatched to deal with them.

Faith held her horse back some and readied an arrow. The six soldiers behind her circled around to her front. They formed a V-shape with Joskin and Airria in the lead.

In her mind Faith reminded herself that she had a limited amount of arrows. She watched as Airria and Joskin waded into the soldiers. She began to understand the value of a good horse and good armor. Countless pike, javelin and sword blows were deflected by the armor. Only two of the horses fell.

The small force was quickly surrounded and the horses speedily lost momentum. The initial pikes had broken on the barding, Takseks' mastery shone in the strength of the armor.

Joskin's horse was kicking and pouncing like an awkward cat, while Joskin was swinging his ax with extreme precision, using the horse's movements to increase his own speed. With each swing of his mighty ax several foes fell.

Airria's fight was far less graceful. As his horse jumped and kicked, his strokes swung comparatively wild, though still more precise than the soldiers who had followed. His horse kept the men at a distance.

The archers, previously focused on the main gate, turned their attention to Faith. Tabin and Mailt executed their responsibilities with perfection. Their shields created a wall which kept the arrows out. When arrows began landing in their legs, neither wavered.

As she scanned the battlefield, she deemed the archers to be the greater threat. She carefully chose a target with a second archer in line. She could feel the release of the bow as the black shaft was driven away from her. It seemed as if time slowed as the arrow flew toward its intended destination.

Even both archers, as the arrow drove into them and threw them to the ground, were moving at a greatly reduced pace. She watched their eyes widen as the arrow approached. She noted the mouths widening as they attempted to scream.

She had killed in the past, mostly orcs, but she had never seen the pain she had caused so clearly on a human face. Her heart tore to see such a sight. She would have dropped her bow, but she had two men doing their best to keep the opposing arrows from raining down on her.

Two, sometimes three archers fell with each release of her arrows. She let them fly as quickly as she could. As each archer fell to the ground, she relived the first. The only way she could carry on in her responsibility was to remember the two men painfully defending her.

A loud cry erupted as a dark cloud emerged from the main city gate. The battering ram was shattered, splinters impaled nearby fighters. Soldiers were thrown back on the spears of their companions. Men began running in all directions. Faith could only guess what the cloud was, but she assumed it was the golem and fighters.

To her right Tabin's horse fell and Mailt reached farther with his shield to protect Faith. Though there were only about fifty archers left, it was too much for her remaining protector and soon he fell to the barrage of arrows.

Now out of arrows and noticing Joskin and Airria's entourage had been depleted, she pressed close to the men she had followed away from her home and sister. For a while she held to the precious bow Joskin had loaned her shortly after they had first met.

Foolish girl, let the bow go. You need to use both of your swords. The voice in her mind was unfamiliar, but in the heat of confusion she let the bow and her horse's reins drop, then drew her second sword.

Persephone drew her to the edge of the fight with a few graceful bounds, using her own armor to deflect any blows.

Faith could feel every move Persephone was going to make. Having never been trained to fight with an equine companion, she expected to be as awkward as Airria, but she could feel her horse stepping for her, allowing her to use the dances the naga had taught her.

537

As wonderful as it felt to be so connected to Persephone, the cracking bone, screeching metal and splashing blood made her sick. Group after group of fighters came within reach of the deadly duo. Man after man fell in a heap, many of them crushed beneath her horse's hooves. In an attempt to block out the sounds and gore, she focused on staying alive. There was no time for grief now. She knew she had to press on.

Her armor seemed to come alive as Persephone broke spears with a single, well placed bite. Streaks of powerful energy struck out at many who stood to approach her. She found her arms driven into precise patterns, deflecting arrows with speed that was not her own. Fueled by her gifts of horse and armor, Faith continued through the ranks. She could now see how a single woman could destroy a powerful army.

As the sun approached the horizon an arrow found its way into Persephone's flesh. Faith's elegant horse crashed to the ground throwing Faith far from her saddle. She did her best to use the momentum to get back to her feet but found her back flat against a soldier's shield.

She did, however; manage to keep hold of her swords. Before she even knew it she was caught up in a frenzied dance, blocking thrusts and lashing out. Spearheads and pieces of shields flew into the air. The men fell before her as she pressed on.

After a short while her foes were no longer pressing in on her. Those who could were running for the tree line. Those who could not were cowering, wounded on the ground. There was no place she could step without the gore of the day touching her.

She looked around to see who had survived. Persephone was hopping toward her on three legs. Joskin was standing with his back to his squealing horse. Airria was on one knee, alone. The dark cloud was by itself in the middle of the steep road the army had fled up.

With no one left to fight, Faith began to notice how tired she was. She was covered with thick, heavy sweat, running like rivers down her body. Her arms and legs were shaking with fatigue, streaks of pain running up and down them. They were also covered in small cuts wherever her armor left her exposed.

538

She looked over the battlefield and began to realize how many people, human beings, she had killed and became queasy. Soon she dropped her sword and collapsed to her knees. She found she had only enough strength left to lean over before her stomach discharged what little was in it, then continued to try and release more. When her heaving subsided she sat on the ground remembering each cry of every fallen soldier her blades had dispatched, every crack of bone as her horse had crushed them. She began to wonder how Joskin had lived with this for so long without becoming too hardened to care about anything.

"Am I going to be all right?" she said out loud to herself.

Airria's voice was a welcome sound, "Yes. In time I think you will." He paused long enough to place a hand on her shoulder. "I think I now understand what happened with Viehasia, Theilord's wife in that high valley."

"You have no idea!" though Faith could feel bitterness welling up insider her, her voice was soft and mournful. She looked up to see how Airria was handling the fight and he too was covered in blood, but his eyes held a stream of tears. She had not expected him to show such emotion because he had killed many before this day.

"The day it becomes easy to kill is the day you die inside," Airria collapsed to a sitting position next to Faith.

It was almost as though he could read her thoughts, "How..?"

"After my first battle a good friend said those same words to me," Airria's eyes diverted to Joskin who was now approaching. He added, "Now I know how he knew."

Joskin approached slowly, his eyes shifting back and forth between Airria and Faith. With a tear in his eye he said, "I think it's time for a bath."

Faith blurted out a laugh, she was glad for Joskin's levity. She knew he really did not care to bathe, but it was a source of jest between them.

Joskin switched his gaze to the gate. "It looks like Niesla is coming to check on us. I will go see if any of them who followed us are alive." Using his ax as a leaning stick he strolled away.

Airria's eyes looked up the road, "What is that dark cloud?"

"Forged darkness sucks the light out of anything, or so Carrita says," Faith responded.

"The matrataur golem?" Airria asked, unable to push out a proper sentence.

"Yes," Faith answered. "It was all a part of Joskin's plan. I only hope the fighters who were to follow it are still alive."

She shifted her eyes back to her gimping horse. Persephone was covered in many deep wounds. Faith could almost see how the horse had spun to keep the heaviest of blows from hitting her.

Faith stood up and ran over to her horse. Without thinking she yanked the arrow from Persephone's strong neck muscle. The horse squealed, but did not flinch. Faith put her hand over the wound and began pouring her magic into the injury. Slowly Faith could feel the tension and pain drain out of the horse.

When Faith became dizzy she took a step back. The horse's gashes were almost closed and the blood had stopped dripping out.

"It's always amazing to me how powerful of a healer you have become," Airria had given her an arm to lean on.

Niesla's voice surprised Faith, "You shouldn't be too amazed. I am still bewildered that she has not had much formal training. When I first met her I thought she was a trained priestess. I spent hundreds of years learning to be a healer and Faith has far surpassed me in only the few months she has been studying."

Joskin called out from where his horse was lying, "Niesla, do you have any more salve? My horse could use it."

Niesla scowled, "One of these days he will kill that horse and wonder why I can't make it better," she said softly enough Faith almost could not hear it. She threw her head and kicked her horse.

After Niesla trotted off, Faith looked back down the trail of dead bodies. Near the head of the trail she had made she saw two figures riddled with arrows, pinned to the ground by their fallen horses. Her mind flashed back to the early part of the battle, to the two men who so faithfully stayed by her side and protected her from the piercing arrows.

She was filled with a sudden rush of energy. She sprinted to the figures, desperately hoping they were alive. When she arrived there was no doubt, even Carrita could not save them. Their bodies were mangled by the fallen mounts. The armor was riddled with arrows broken from the fall.

Faith could feel the remaining strength leave her limbs. Her sight was fading. She vaguely heard herself say, "I did this."

"They chose this," Marren's voice shocked the light back to Faith's eyes. "Don't take their courage from them. They chose to protect you. You did not ask for their help. They would choose the same if they had it to do over again. They believed in you, in your men and in your ability to do what you did. They gave everything to be a part of what you did. To them, their sacrifice was small."

"Small?" Faith said as she crashed to the ground. Her grief was an unbearable weight. "They gave everything!"

Marren stooped down and softly ran her hands down Faith's arms. "No. They only gave their lives for you. They have given much more for me. They were driven from their homes, forced into slavery and regularly beaten. Knowing them as I did, they would count their lives as a small price for what you were able to accomplish today and in turn what I will be able to accomplish tonight."

Joskin had said something about Marren using the bodies of the dead to break the ocean siege. Faith pleaded, "I am not sure what you have planned with all these dead, but I ask you let me bury these two."

Marren smiled as her hands reached Faith's, "To them, the greatest honor they could receive in death would be to have their bodies burned. They and their horses will be burned in a great pyre this night. You may stay and watch. Wood is already being assembled for all who fell today in our cause."

Faith could feel the tears flowing down her cheeks, "Will the fire need to be large?"

"The pyre will burn for days." Marren stood and then helped Faith to her feet. "Thanks to the sacrifice of those who followed Joskin out the gate, there are only a dozen who will be on it. I'll not use our own fallen in what I loathe to do this evening."

Faith looked around, wagons had been brought to the field. Taksek was loading one with old armor and weapons. Marren's black-robed mages were walking from body to body, animating them. The re-animated corpses were unloading wagonloads of wood and loading the fallen soldiers on top.

Airria came running up, "What's going on here?"

Marren's eyes drooped, "This is how I must fight tonight. Nothing I do is in my desire, but must be done. Sadly I should begin so it will be finished by morning." She rushed off, stopping only at survivors of the Zerith forces to drain them.

Faith turned to Airria, "It seems so odd. We kill, then use the death to help us destroy more. It seems so pointless. Can anything good come of war?"

Joskin's voice answered from behind her, making Faith jump, "If you had ever seen what a tyrant can do, you couldn't ask that question. The first contract I ever took was for Zerith. I was only sixteen, but could best any man in single combat. It only took me one day in their camp to realize no money was worth fighting their war. When I tried to break my contract I was placed in a cage and tortured for days in ways I'll not describe. It was then that I realized there are things worth fighting for."

Faith turned to face Joskin, "How did you escape?"

Joskin's countenance fell. "I had help," he turned his gaze to Marren feeding on one of the Zerith soldiers. "She broke my chains and told me where I could go for safety. I found a good horse and rode with all my strength for the city gates." Joskin put his hand on his limping horse's nose, "Yes, good things can come from war. Freedom can only be bought from tyrants at such a price. They will never give up their power willingly and constantly thirst for more."

Faith had her doubts about what Joskin was saying, but could see Joskin's point. She asked, "Do you know who the other four were who died today? Marren said only twelve were killed. I know the eight who followed us are dead."

Joskin looked over to the wood being stacked, "Dizrin got his wish. He and his dwarves refused to allow the golem to leave the gate alone. Dizrin and three of his men were killed. Though many of the other dwarves were severely wounded, they stubbornly pressed on. I believe we have them to thank for our own survival." He turned back to Faith,

542

"From this day until our quest is finished never leave Viehasia's bow behind again." He put a hand on Airria, "And you. Never put your magic sword away. This army should have broken much sooner. I think Zerith is being driven and used. Something more terrifying than the matrataurs is driving them."

Faith felt a chill go down her back. She could not imagine anything more dreadful than the beasts from the night before.

Joskin began leading his horse toward Niesla, who was waiting for him at the city gate. He called over his shoulder, "My horse needs some rest, he's had a rough day."

Faith grabbed Airria's hand and surveyed the field. It was just so overwhelming. This was the path her sister had sent her on. This was the path Airria had rushed toward. This was where Faith knew she should be, but she feared her life would consist of nothing else. Touching Airria reminded her there was some good in her life. Gripping the warmth of his hand she allowed him to lead her back to the city.

Chapter 8 - Bloody Bay

Airria led Faith to watch the evening's battle. It was nice to have Faith hold his hand. It seemed to comfort her and helped him forget the ugliness of the day. He took his time going through the streets and up the long stairs. He was not sure it was the best idea. Faith had seen enough battle for one day, but he really wanted to see what Marren was going to do, how she was going to break that part of the siege.

The ocean had grown dark. Shadows of sunken ships could be seen in deep, clear water dancing to the rhythm of the waves. From his vantage point Airria could see the walking corpses making their way around the city and into the sea. To his surprise they floated, softly making their way into the blackness outside of the bay.

The Zerith fleet was still small, but it was much larger then Airria had expected. Even from this distance he could see the crude repairs that had been made. He had expected that more of the ships the group had damaged on their way into the city would have joined the ghostly figures deep in the dark water.

"You have done both me and my people a great service." Marren's voice was heavy with sadness, "It grieves me so many must die for the sake of keeping this city free."

Though Airria was not sure when Marren had arrived, he was relieved to hear her voice. After a moment, looking over the ocean, he said, "I wish we could help more."

"Perhaps there is a trifle more we can do to help," Carrita's soft voice was a welcome sound. "Perhaps you could use a small, yet well-built vessel with enchanted stone figures."

Marren placed a soft hand on Carrita's head, "What do you think one small ship will do against all these warships?"

Carrita smiled broadly, "True the vessel is small. It also is very fast. The golems on board are reasonably well skilled and have powerful weapons." She paused to look over the water, "It created quite a distraction in the skirmish upon our arrival. Perhaps it can provide another disruption, one sufficient to ensure your victory tonight."

Carrita took off her silver ring and handed it to Marren. "This ring will command the ship. The magic controlling the vessel will obey your every command with expert precision."

"The golems will protect and defend the ship," Faith added. "You will only need to worry about your part of the battle."

Marren looked kindly on the girls. "You realize your ship may never return."

Faith looked over the ocean again. "You realize when Joskin left today, he had no belief in his return. Those who followed us into battle did not return. This is the cost of freedom. We have freedom to choose this because others made this choice before."

"Besides," Airria interjected, "that ship isn't so easy to sink. Stone men aren't so easy to kill. Don't count that ship as gone yet." Though he could feel the weight of the situation, he was attempting to lighten the mood. His efforts were rewarded with a smile and small laugh from Faith.

A hollow voice crept in, "I have come to show what the orc has constructed for us." The lich held out a boney hand holding a black staff with an obsidian crystal solidly bound with a braid of the Black Wood.

Marren gently received the staff and examined it carefully. "Is it in condition to be able to be used as a focus for you?"

"It will take me some days, perhaps weeks to bring this staff to its magical potential," the hollow voice stated. "When completed it will be more powerful than the staff the matrataurs destroyed."

Marren's eyes snapped to the cloaked figure, "Will you be able to help me in my fight tonight?"

The hooded head turned toward the city then to the ships in the ocean. "We will start our work to complete our staves when this siege is finished. You will have our power at your command. I only wanted you to know what the orc has contributed."

Marren ran a finger down the wood, "This truly is the work of a master. Not only one who knows metal and wood, but one who has worked with magic."

Taksek's deep voice came from the stairs, "Me likes when people notice good skills." Slowly he came into view.

Marren smiled at the orc, "It is hard not to notice such skill. You truly are a master craftsman."

Taksek reached a hand up and touched Faith's armor. "My best I try, but better are others still than me." He looked back over the city. "Soldiers tell the gate is broken. Does Master wish me repair?"

Marren laughed, "I have not seen such skill in over a thousand years. To me you are a true and modern master. We can use such skill in this city. As to the gates, they will mend on their own, they are not something you can forge." Her eyes carried less weight now.

Taksek looked to Faith, "Master, I ask forgive for I fail you today."

Faith put a gentle hand on the orc's face, "How did you fail me? Your shields kept me safe for most of the fight. Your armor protected those who fought by my side. How did you fail me?" Tears began streaming down her cheeks.

Taksek brushed Faith's hand away. His eyes dropped to the stone walkway. "Armor failed men to protect you. I fail that you are hurt." His rough, heavy hands hovered just past the cuts on her arms and legs. "Even Master's horse is hurt."

547

Faith looked to Airria, then to Marren.

Airria didn't know what to say. He felt a little guilty he stayed by Joskin's side through the fight rather than protecting Faith. As the orc pointed to each cut, though minor in nature, it sliced into Airria's heart.

Marren spoke up, "Your armor allowed the men you sent to protect her for a long time. If it were not for your skill it is likely none of those who did return would have come back. You have honored your master well. She is proud of your work and I am grateful for all the help you have given us."

Taksek bowed crudely, "I do better." He spun and raced down the wall.

Airria put a hand up and wiped the tears from Faith's eyes. "Do you want to go?"

Faith shook her head slowly, "I have reaped soldiers much of this day. As much as I do not wish to witness any more death I must see my sacrifice and effort are of worth. I must observe the end to this siege."

Airria's heart was breaking to see Faith so distraught.

Faith looked back over the water, back the way they had come. "Before this quest is over I may be required to view many more blood-filled days. I left my sister in Jammar's care to follow this path. I must accept it as a part of my life now."

Carrita hugged Faith tightly and joined her in her tears. "I believe before this quest is ended we will need you for more than an archer, but oh how I wish you to never lose the brightness in your aura. Oh how I wish you did not have to see such gore, much less be a part of it."

Airria shifted uneasily for a moment, then he noticed his opportunity to lighten the mood a little, or so he hoped. "What do you mean 'we will need her as more than an archer'? She has already saved you more than once. She has saved you from yourself more than once." He was rewarded for his effort as the girls started to laugh.

The laughter was broken by the hollow chanting of the lichs. Airria looked at them with their arms held high. There was energy flowing from them thick enough even Airria's untrained eyes could see it.

548

It twisted and tore through the air reaching its dark tendrils deep into the sea.

The ghostly shadows of sunken ships left their swaying dance and began circling their way to the surface. The torn sails fluttered in the water as if a stiff ocean breeze was carrying them forward, even the picked bones readied on board as if living sailors.

Airria looked to Marren for answers, but she was already gone. The slosh of the sea giving way before the gate told Airria Marren was on the little ship the group had come in on.

As the dead ships surfaced, the much smaller ship with golems readied on deck, fell in behind them. A small fleet, they made their way toward the picket line. As the wave of risen ships passed into the tide of floating corpses, the bodies peeled off the water's surface and began creeping up the sides of the boats.

The enemy ships responded to the open port gate and oncoming boats quickly. Each ship in the picket line rapidly shifted its sails. The large warships arced around falling into a rigid formation only two ship widths apart. In this formation they headed for the oncoming ships, undeterred even though they were outnumbered three to one.

The ships of the dead moved far less precisely. Occasionally a random ship lurched to the side and fell slightly behind. Rather than the ships forming a neat line, it appeared more as a wave, fluctuating irregularly.

"I am sorry I was not with you on the field this day," Carrita's young voice broke Airria's attention from the military artistry for a moment. "I do wish someone had retrieved me so I could have helped."

Faith came in tight to Airria's chest. After a long moment she said, "I am glad you were not with us. I know you can defend yourself, but I would not want to add the scars of this day to the scars you already carry."

Carrita looked down at the stone floor, "Now you will have to carry the scars for both of us. This is something I had hoped you would not feel."

Faith pulled away from Airria and knelt in front of Carrita, "I know I am innocent when compared to others in our little band, but I am

549

not without my own wounds. I was forced into slavery, most of my family was butchered and I have been forced into the life of a traveling warrior. Today will only add to the pain of what I have already been through. My heart, though hurting, will mend. I will be better for it."

Carrita looked hard into Faith's eyes. Her bottom lip began to quiver. Before a tear could fall, she turned her attention back to the battle at sea.

Faith hugged her young friend, "It will be all right. We have to believe it will all be well in the end." Slowly she let go and returned to her place at Airria's side.

A storm began swirling around the battle. Black clouds pulled into the center and then swirled outward. Heavy winds started the sea churning. The ships began rocking, their sails twisting and flapping. The scent of salt and death wafted to the top of the wall.

As the fleet lines closed Carrita commented, "I feel as a beginner when compared with the power driving this encounter."

When the gap had closed enough, the Zerith warships began using catapults to fire clay jugs. The jugs shattered, scattering oil across the deck and down the sails.

The undead warriors began making their way to the fronts of their respective ships. Often one would slip and fall, crashing into several others. No matter what happened they kept moving forward until they were all stacked on the bow of the ship in a tight pack.

The Zerith ship began shooting blazing arrows through the storm toward the dead ships. Only a few actually made it through the swirling winds, but it only took a few per ship to ignite the oil. Flames burst up, engulfing all visible surfaces, including the undead warriors. Oddly the flames didn't seem to be consuming anything.

As the smoke billowed up, swirling into the clouds Faith asked, "There is so much fire. Why does it not burn the wood or the dead?"

"Water," Carrita answered. "The heat will take time to burn off all the ocean water. It is for this reason the dead were sent to the ocean to be picked up by the once sunken vessels."

Airria could not speak as he watched the lines close. So many burning ships and bodies, still the Zerith fleet did not change course. They showed no sign of running.

Faith asked the question on his mind, "Why do they not run? They move as though they are driven by a demon. Yet, I see nothing driving them. Is it magic?"

Carrita's eyes widened and she began looking around, mostly at the sky far beyond the storm. "Tell me if you will, in the battle today did you see such devotion to the fighting? Was it so difficult to make the Zerith army run?"

Airria was so used to having Carrita helping in the battles he'd forgotten she hadn't been there. "Yes, we had to kill half their army. Even the golem you made didn't make them run. It wasn't until most of their siege engines had been destroyed and half their army was dead that they finally ran. You can see some of the thousands that died today on those ships."

Black and white energy began crackling around Carrita's eyes, "We leave tomorrow morning. I must prepare to make the journey. Please ask Marren to find me when she returns. I will be researching in her library."

Airria was hoping for a day to rest after such a grueling battle, "What if the army returns in the morning? Will we stay to help again?"

Carrita looked at the ships for a short moment, "Whether they return or not, we will travel to my home tomorrow. My mother is no longer in her place to protect them. I must fill her role. They need us far more now." Before Airria could say another word, Carrita sprinted down the stairs.

Faith tightened her grip on Airria's hand. "I would guess we are leaving tomorrow for another battle, one which Carrita fears more than the matrataurs, perhaps more than anything except the great Black Dragon."

Airria couldn't imagine anything Carrita would fear more than the beast they had faced the night before. He could feel his heart starting to race at the prospect. "I hope we are ready for whatever is coming."

551

In an attempt to take is mind off his part in the terrible battles, he focused on the ships now engaging. The Zerith ships tried to split between the flaming ships, but the ships of dead turned into the warships, crashing with great force. The splintering of wood was deafening even at this distance.

The flaming dead were thrown from their perches onto the ships of the living, igniting everything they touched. The Zerith tactics were actually working against them. Soon the warships were engulfed in fire.

Men were leaping into the rough water. Desperately they swam away from the wreckage of the battle.

Marren began picking up the weaponless survivors. The small ship easily wove in and out of the broken vessels. As Marren pulled the men on board the golems escorted them to the center deck and watched them.

"If you will wait by the dock, I will join Carrita in the library," Faith said as she let go of Airria's hand. She took a deep breath and walked down the stairs.

As rapidly as it began, the storm dissipated. The boney mages began to shake. One by one they departed from the wall until Airria stood alone, watching in amazement of the speed and decisiveness of the battle. He could now see how one person could make all the difference to keeping this city free for thousands of years.

Chapter 9 - New Magic

Carrita arrived in the familiar library. She went to the section she had avoided at Marren's request, journals of mages long since gone. Many of authors of the journals in this section had died experimenting with magics far too powerful for their understanding. Her fear of failing to defend her home city of Derain far exceeded all the warning Marren had given.

As with most of her in-depth studies it seemed she had been examining books for only a moment before understanding came. It was obvious to her how many of the mages were mistaken in their approach. They had tried to open a portal using only one facet. You cannot lift a carpet flatly by only one corner.

She knew such magics could only be accomplished by using opposing forces to rip through time and space, but how could it be done? She had walked the line between life and death. Fire and water only fought each other. None of the books she had been through gave any indication teleportation was even realistically possible.

She knew it was feasible to tear the boundaries between the elements of the Physical Plane to bring an object from one place to another. She had seen Bregette do so on the Astral Plane. Deep inside she knew she could do the same on the Physical Plane.

As she pondered this question, she mindlessly picked up the journal of a philosopher who knew no magic. He talked of the four elements and how they were constantly fighting, struggling to dominate and in this struggle found an uneasy peace.

Carrita's mind was pulled back to Ramsal Island, back to the shrines Jammar had sent Airria to find. The last one she had seen was about the gods and the struggles they faced in keeping the peace. Esnie, the last of the gods, had seen the conflicting elements as necessary to build peace. It took all of the facets of existence to keep the equilibrium.

"Of course!" she shouted out. She now understood what the others were missing. "It takes all eight facets to work!"

"Only you could find lost magics in a philosophy book," Marren's voice was soft and filled with amusement.

Carrita had not expected her old friend to be in the library so soon. Of course she really did not know how long she had been studying. She almost fell out of her chair. After she caught her breath she asked, "Is the battle over so quickly?"

Marren smiled. The remains of a trail of blood ran from the corners of her mouth down to her chin. Even her black dress showed the gore of battle. "As I was the one in the ship, I had hoped you would be more concerned with my well being."

Carrita rolled her eyes, "You had plenty of help and I know exactly how difficult it is to attack someone in the vessel we provided."

Marren rolled her lower lip, "You are far too clever for your age."

Carrita smiled back. "You have not cleaned up. Did you only recently return from the fighting?"

The smile melted from Marren's face. "Airria said you needed me. He said whatever it was looked very urgent. I came as quickly as I could. When I arrived you looked so adorable reading there that I couldn't bring myself to disturb you."

Carrita took a deep breath, "There is little in this world as terrifying as matrataur. Mother used to say even young dragons would run from the beasts. We slew three of them and still the Zerith army continued. When the vessels rose from the depths of the sea the war ships should have run. Something is driving them. Something has placed unbelievable terror in their hearts."

Marren placed one arm across her chest and the other hand on her chin. "I had expected to see a lesser devil."

Carrita continued, "Nothing less would drive them so adamantly. Yet you have said nothing of angels to balance them."

Marren's perfect forehead furrowed. "None were sent. In all my days Zerith has never tried such an offensive without supernatural help."

Carrita could see Marren was ready for her main point. "My mother is not in her place to protect Derain, the main gateway to the Black Forest."

Marren's eyes widened, "I don't even know if the city still stands. If it does, I cannot imagine they will resist much longer."

Carrita thought for a moment, "My mother designed those walls. They are high and strong. Though mortals alone could not defend the walls against an immortal assault, with the help of the angels, the city guard could last some time."

Marren stayed tense. Her eyes began darting rapidly. The hand which had been resting on her chin had become a fist. After some time she finally said, "I must go help, if I can!"

Carrita hopped out of her chair. "Have your men ready three wagons. Mostly we will need food, but include bandages and arrows."

Faith stepped out of a dark corner, "Should I have Taksek prepare to travel with us?"

Carrita blinked twice, surprised she had not noticed Faith, "No, he will serve the cause better by staying in this city."

Faith frowned, "You know he will not be happy if I tell him I am going and he cannot come."

Marren turned slowly to face Faith, "He would be sad to leave his forge."

Faith curled her lip, "He will still protest."

Marren smiled, "His protest will be mitigated by his responsibility as Chief of the Craftsman. The city needs him." Her smile melted away. "Yes, his presence will be even more necessary if I am not here. He will need to oversee all repairs to the city." She put an arm around Faith, "Come, let us go give him the good news."

Carrita remembered something, "Will you have time to get to Derain before the sun is seen in the sky?"

Marren glanced back to Carrita, but said to Faith, "Perhaps you should deliver the news, I must leave now." She half smirked, "You are just too smart for your own good. I am glad you are helping us," she then walked out of the library.

Carrita knew she would not have the power to transport three wagons, all of the golems, horses and the party the whole distance without help. All of the magic users in the city, except Faith and Niesla, had been completely depleted. It would be months before many of them would be able to help. She would have to pull her needed magic from her alchemy and knowledge of powerful symbols.

Quickly she made her way to the nearest alchemy shop. When she arrived, the shop was dark. After all, it was the time most people would be asleep. Without regard, Carrita walked up to the door and knocked as loudly as she could.

After the third time knocking, a candle lit deep inside the shop and was slowly carried to the door. The door opened slightly and a wrinkled old eye peered out. "May I help you?" the voice was rough and tired.

Carrita did not have time to waste. "I need essence, blood or skin of elementals. Do you have any?"

The door opened wide enough to reveal a hunched-over, white haired man in only a night shirt. "I have some, I think. I am not sure what elements I have left. Years ago I got some, but I don't know if it's any good. Do you prefer essence, blood or skin? I may have some angel feathers or a piece of devil wing."

Carrita rushed into the store, almost knocking the poor man over. "I can use anything you can find, please."

The man turned slowly and started shuffling toward the counter. "I suppose this is also for the war effort. You know a merchant could lose his shop helping the war effort around here. I've been here for sixty years. Of course I am the only one who gets to harvest the dead elementals Zerith brings to the wall. So I guess it is helping the war effort that had built this place. Really because I help Marren so often, I am able to keep open when other shops close down."

Carrita was in a very big hurry, but did not want to be rude to the aged man. She began admiring the shelves full of bottles of eyes, bundles of plants and boxes of bones. This shop was far better stocked then she could have imagined.

The man rambled on, "I used to have bins of powdered crystals of all varieties. Last night someone came and got the last of it. I hope it helped. They woke me up to get it for them. I hate it when they wake me up. I guess I would hate it more if Zerith made it in this far. I bet they wouldn't pay for anything. Marren never pays for anything either. Not directly anyway. She trades for other things I can sell."

In an attempt to encourage the man to hasten his search Carrita asked, "Which elements do you have?"

"I will see," the man disappeared behind a curtain. There were several odd noises from the back. Finally the man emerged again, "All I have left is this." He set down a decorative box almost the size of a bread box and a bottle glowing with swirls of magical energy. "Years ago I tried some experiments with elemental essences. Sadly I was disappointed when nothing happened. He slid the box forward, I mixed dried and powdered skins from each of the eight elements. I thought it would make a powerful magic powder, but nobody wanted to buy it. I tried something similar with blood. At least it glowed. I used it for a light for many years."

Carrita examined the magical liquid first. She reached out with her magic and probed inside. It was filled with the essence of an elemental from each facet of existence. She could feel the basis for both creation and destruction. The conflict was perfectly balanced.

The powder in the box was no less disappointing. Although it was not in motion, she could feel each element struggling for dominance and separation it was so well maintained.

Carrita was curious, "Why would you combine such potent elements?"

The man leaned forward on the counter, "Years ago, so many I can't remember the number, I met a charming woman. Pregnant she was. Nonetheless elegant and charming. She was the Governor of Derain at the time. She brought me the portions of elements and told me to mix them. Together they were to do something spectacular. She said it might take some time before I would see what they were for, but in time I would. I waited and watched them for years. Nothing ever happened so these are yours for the playing."

Carrita smiled. In her heart she believed the woman this man was talking of was her mother. Somehow, much like the robe her mother had left with Jammar, her mother knew Carrita would need these mixtures. "If you come to the city square outside the market after sunup you may have the opportunity to witness what the woman promised you."

The old man nodded, "Then I best get back to bed so I can be awake for the show." Without another word he ducked behind the curtain and disappeared.

Carrita grabbed the containers and ran to the square. The wagons of supplies were already arriving pulled by the golems from the ship. The large martataur golem was standing by the fountain. Faith was next to it organizing them as tightly as she could. Her pony was tied to one of the wagons, already packed.

Carrita asked, "How did you know this is where I would perform my experiment?"

Faith laughed softly, "This was the best place to gather the supplies. It is close to Marren's mansion and wide enough to bring the supplies together. I am packing them tightly together because I wondered how much area everything will consume."

Carrita giggled. It was interesting for her to watch Faith prepare even though she really did not know what Carrita's plan was. "We will all be in Derain by midday. Keep closing them in as tightly as you can."

Faith's eyes widened, "I understood it would take a few days to make the trip. How will we arrive by midday?"

Carrita could feel her pride swelling up. "It will happen." She reached into her saddlebag and pulled out a copper pot. She examined it closely. "This will work nicely," she said out loud. She then turned her attention to Faith, "It is time to make sure Joskin and Niesla are prepared. Will you make sure they are awake and their horses are barded?"

She did not wait for Faith to leave before she set the kettle on the ground and began pouring all of the liquid in. Next she slowly added the powder. Using her magic she stirred the mixture meticulously. She could see the conflict between each element. As it swirled and churned it began to thicken into a loose gel.

The kettle lifted off the ground and slowly began rotating around. Carrita could feel the unrefined magic emanating from the kettle. She sat on the ground enjoying the raw power.

"Why do I feel I am not going to like this?" Joskin's voice jolted Carrita back to her task. "She is smiling too big. The last time I saw that smile we had to get a priestess to help her."

Niesla's lip curled into a mocking frown, "I don't think I have ever seen such an excited smile. How could it mean trouble?"

Carrita frowned at the mocking, however she could not hold it for long. She was excited to try something new to her and more excited to be returning home. The assured battle waiting in Derain had passed, for the time, from her mind.

Joskin chuckled.

Carrita shook her head, "If anything goes wrong you should know what to do then." She examined the area and began pouring the gel on the cobblestone, creating a large circle. When the circle was finished, she began drawing the symbols for each facet of existence. They were equally spaced and placed so conflicting elements were written on opposing sides.

When she looked up to admire her work she noticed a small crowd gathered around the group.

Garfrun was commanding his guards to keep the mob back several paces from the circle. The rest of the group was inside the circle watching Carrita carefully. The wagons were loaded and the animals were readied for battle.

Carrita walked around the circle once to make sure everything was in order. Satisfied she stepped into the area. In Elven she called to each of the eight elements and then she commanded them to make peace. She could feel her body shaking to maintain such a feat, but she continued.

"Blith villyontsa," she yelled, commanding the elements to part and open a hole in the Physical Plane. Her insides felt as if they would rip apart, still she continued focusing on the streets she grew up in and the house she missed with all her heart.

The city around her grayed and blurred. Everything started spinning into a cloud of color. Swirls of black and white twisted around the group. She could feel the gel melting way, granting her more energy to keep her magic flowing.

Once the gel was gone she could feel her own supplies of magical energy running out. She had never fully depleted her own stores; she had only depleted the magic of others. She reached out for Faith, knowing her friend would lend her more, but she could not find her. She could feel Airria was missing as well.

Her heart sank as she realized her efforts had failed. She was not sure where they were and two of her friends were missing. With her failure in mind she gave in to the swirling energy surrounding her.

She could feel her legs failing her. Briefly, before the dark consumed her, she saw a vision of a dirty stone street near a small shop. Wounded men were being thrown from her. There was the faint sound of stone cracking. Finally everything went dark and silent.

Chapter 10 - Missed Adventure and Fresh Starts

After Airria told Marren where to meet Carrita he helped Garfrun and the city guard escort the prisoners. Many of the captured men were wounded with broken limbs, some were severely burned and all of them had been bandaged.

Airria had expected that once they were in the city the prisoners would try to escape, but they all shuffled along in their wet clothes. There were no ropes, no chains. Every man walked silently forward following Garfrun.

The guard captain led the group down the street to a great walled area. Inside there was a flat area of sand large enough to put the pirate ship on. It was surrounded by dozens of rows of terraced benches.

Airria looked around the place for a short while. Eventually he asked Garfrun, "Is it regular for you to take so many prisoners?"

The wolf-man laughed, "We have only used this place as a prison one other instance in my time as a guard. It is much nicer to be here when we have plays or performances. Personally I love it when the orphans sing."

Airria was about to ask another question, but noticed a flock of bats leaving the city. They were flying north, very organized. "Do bats around here fly like that?"

Garfrun squinted to the north. He shifted his head back and forth slowly. "I don't see the bats, but I can hear something that could be bats. How are they flying?"

Airria had forgotten about the potion Marren had given him to help him see in the dark. "They are flying in a group, coordinated, flying north."

Garfrun put a clawed hand on his sword, "I better go see what it means."

Airria ran to the mansion to find Faith. Long before he got there, he spied her at the little shop Taksek was using. She was talking to the orc.

Taksek's chest was puffed out. His fists were pressing firmly into his sides. However, his face carried a slight smile. "Me want to make Master safe. Most important. Don't make Master safe when she goes if Taksek stays. Why Master leave?"

Faith began pacing, the way she did when she was trying to think, "If you leave with me, who will rebuild this city? You are the greatest craftsman this city has seen in centuries. Who can lead the repairs of this city as well as you?"

Taksek turned quickly and grabbed a hot iron from the fire and his hammer from the nearby anvil. He began pounding. Not the careful strikes Airria was used to seeing from him, but heavy, careless blows. After a moment he said over his shoulder, "Be me work from forge on ship. Do better for me."

Faith turned to leave but stopped when Taksek spoke again, "Hopes to see Master again soon. Will help city to see returned." The orc's hammer began falling more carefully.

By this time Airria was leaning on a post just outside the shop. "I take it we will be leaving soon?"

Faith flinched slightly, "Carrita says we are leaving in the morning. Taksek will stay to oversee the city and wall repair."

Airria thought back to the battle only a half a day ago. "Is Joskin's horse up to a trip like that? Is your horse up to push on?"

Faith glanced back to the stables, "I am not sure if any of us are truly prepared to travel just yet, but it would seem Derain needs us as soon as we can arrive. Carrita believes whatever is waiting for us there is far worse than the matrataurs."

Airria shuddered as the thought crossed his mind. He couldn't imagine anything as terrifying as those beasts. "I will check the animals."

Faith took a deep breath and furrowed her brow, "Persephone is well enough to travel. I will retrieve her so she can help me organize some relief wagons."

Airria pondered the situation. "Do we need to find some horses or oxen?"

Faith answered quickly, "No. The golems can pull the wagons. It will slow us less if we do not need to harness animals every morning. If I understand right there is an inn half of a day's walk from here. We will arrive at the city of Sarckran on the evening of the next day. Sarckran is the mid-point of our trek."

Airria considered how the group had traveled in the past. None of the animals were in shape to carry more than one rider. He doubted if they could even carry their barding after the battle. "I guess I should see if I can find a pony for Niesla. If she's not on Joskin's horse we can travel faster and we will be in better shape if we have to fight our way into the city."

Faith nodded and ran to the stables the group had been keeping their animals at. Airria went the opposite direction to see if he could find a pony for Niesla.

He darted down the torch-lit streets looking for any indication of another stable, one with animals for sale. It took much of the rest of the night, but near the wall, not far from the gate they had exited the day before, was a small coral with three solid ponies. From a nearby barn he heard a rustle.

Airria ran to the barn and yelled, "Is anyone here?"

A disheveled woman stepped out in dirty clothes. Her face had smudges of green and brown. She had a wooden pitchfork in hand.

"What you want?" When she saw Airria she smiled broadly, revealing all six of her teeth. "I mean, how can I help you today?"

Airria asked the woman, "Are any of your ponies broke to ride?"

The woman frowned and leaned on her fork, "These is not big enough for battle. They is good for pulling little wagons though."

Airria thought for a moment. He guessed she'd seen him ride out the day before. He had lost his horse. Perhaps she knew that. "This is not for me. This would be for an Elven maiden. She just needs to ride as we are on our way to Derain."

The woman scratched the arm holding the fork. "Aye. These can carry you that far. They be good trained for transport riding."

Airria didn't want to find an open leather shop and there wasn't time for custom gear. "Do you also have the tack that I can buy?"

The woman scratched her head, "Course I do. Can't train to work with tack if you has none."

Joskin had given Airria some money when they arrived in the city. He'd not had time to spend any of it. "How much do you want for one of your ponies and some riding tack?"

The woman looked conflicted, "They's no good for fight'n."

Airria did his best to hide the urgency in his voice, "I need it only for transport, I promise. It will be well cared for."

"You know there's not many ride'n beasts left in the city. So, what you say to a gold piece?" She paused only for a moment. Without waiting for an answer she continued, "Aye. One gold piece is a proper price."

The price was far more than the animal would normally cost, but the woman was right, the situation greatly increased the value. Airria reached into his coin purse and pulled out the only gold piece Joskin had given him and placed it in the woman's hand.

Her eyes lit up, "Which you want, I get it ready."

Airria pointed to the one that looked the sturdiest, "The bay there will do nicely."

The woman went to work. In short order the animal was saddled and bridled. Airria thanked the woman and started the trek back to the mansion leading the new pony.

As he passed by the City Square he saw a crowd had gathered. The sun was now low in the morning sky. The tall golem with its dark cloud could easily be seen over everyone's head. He could hear Garfrun barking orders to his men to keep the onlookers out of whatever was going on.

Airria made his way to the front of the throng to see Carrita walking around a glossy circle on the stones. The rest of the group, all of the golems and three wagons of supplies were tightly packed around Faith.

Without being asked Airria made his way into the circle. He tied the new pony to a wagon and made his way to Faith.

He was about to ask Faith what was happening when Carrita began chanting in what he only basically recognized as Elven. His shield began to glow, as did both his and Faith's armor.

Carrita had energy swirling around her. She began to shake. Finally she yelled, "Blith Villyontsa!"

The city went gray. A solid wind rushed in. Airria raised his arm to cover his eyes.

When the wind was gone he lowered his arm, he and Faith were standing in the same place as before, everything else that had been in the circle was gone. Many of the spectators were now lying on the ground as if they had been sucked toward the circle.

One old man who had been thrown to the ground was laughing, "That was worth all the waiting! That was amazing!"

Airria's shield was glowing very brightly and Faith's armor had formed a magic ball around her.

Airria looked at the strange man rolling on the ground and asked, "What happened? Where did they go?"

Faith answered, "Our weapons and armor are made to protect us from Carrita's magic. I can only hope everything else made the trip in good order. I guess we will just have to walk."

Airria could feel his stomach start to churn, "Hope? What has Carrita done this time? Won't she come back when she realizes what happened?"

Faith held a nervous smile on her face. "Did you see the way Carrita was shaking when she cast the spell? It is not likely she will be awake to see what will result from the sudden transport. I am not even sure the group has reached their intended destination."

"What do you mean?" Airria was getting concerned.

"There was a lot of weight to teleport such a long distance, especially for the first time Carrita has ever teleported." Then Faith's smile dropped, "The scary part is, Carrita is trying to transport the group based on memories from her childhood. There is no guarantee the street will be clear. Someone could get very hurt. At the least, Niesla should be able to help heal any injuries."

Airria thought about his cousin mixed with one of the stone figures or having an arm stuck in the side of a building. "Shouldn't we see if they're all right?"

Faith looked at the ground and began walking to the gate, "If we push ourselves very hard, as we need no sleep or food supplies, we could arrive at Derain in two days. They will already be dead or healed by then." She paused and placed the nervous smile back on her face, "No. We will just have to make the trek alone."

Airria followed Faith through the streets. "Will we have to fight another battle when we get to Sarckran?"

Faith glanced as Airria. Her eyes were as full of questions as was his mind. "As it has been with the entirety of our journey, I have no idea what we will have to face. All I know is we must push on and hope we will succeed."

Gently Faith reached over and grabbed Airria's hand. Together they headed off through the gate up the road toward Sarckran, but before they reached the tree line they saw an army coming toward them.

There were no banners, but weapons were brandished. Airria pulled his sword and readied for a fight. Faith pulled one of her magic arrows and readied her bow.

As the army got closer, Airria noticed it was surrounding a large group of women and children crying. Airria could feel his blood starting to warm.

When the army was only about fifty paces away one of the commanders stopped the group. He stepped five paces out and slammed his sword into the dirt road. He then took two small steps back and knelt in the dirt, face down. "My crimes against the city of Sulitamis are great! Me and my men throw ourselves at the mercy of the governor in hopes our families will find sanctuary inside the walls. We will not resist."

Airria slowly approached, but stayed several paces away, "If this is your request offer your weapons at the gate."

The commander stood up, "I fought in the battle yesterday. I remember you as one of those who drove us off. Are you not the governor's ally?"

Airria answered, his sword and shield still at the ready, "I am Marren Bloodstones' ally, but I am on my way to Derain. I don't have time to usher you into the city."

The commander put his arms out straight from his body. "When you killed the beasts two nights ago the siege on Sarckran broke. Those forces were sent to join us in our fight to claim Sulitamis. When you drove us off we ran, colliding with the forces from Sarckran. After a small battle, many of us returned to our homes to bring our families in hopes of finding safety outside of Zerith. Even if we are butchered for our crimes it would be better than what awaits on the far side of Derain. If the siege of Derain is successful I fear the punishment on my family for my failure will be far worse than anything the command of Sulitamis could devise." He glanced up to Airria and looked at him for a moment. "If you do not have time to usher us in or take us captive, may we pass and beg at the gates."

Faith and Airria backed to the side of the road. As the commander retrieved his sword Faith said, "Pass if it pleases you. You will find safety for your women and children. I promise nothing for you."

The man bowed low, "This promise is more than we deserve." Determined he led the group down the dusty road.

Airria and Faith watched them pass then continued on their trek.

Chapter 11 - Walking Terrors

Joskin woke up early to the musical sound of Niesla's voice. How pleasant it was to open his eyes and see her face, to feel her hand touch him. She had been in another room for the night so he was a little surprised she was waking him up.

She smiled down at him, "Faith says we are departing for Derain this morning. She says your horse will be readied and waiting in the town square. Are you up for traveling?"

He sat up. His body hurt all over. The battle had hurt him more than even he had expected. He did his best to hide his pain, but by the frown on Niesla's face he could tell he was not hiding it well. "What must be done, will be done," he said as he stood up. "We do need to get moving."

Niesla smiled uneasily, "If you are sure, I will prepare to leave." She left the room at a hurried pace.

Slowly Joskin put on his armor, wincing at every movement. When he was ready he looked up to see Niesla patiently waiting for him in the doorway with a large pack resting on the floor. Joskin took the pack and together they made their way to the town square.

In the middle of the square he could see Faith, the large golem, some well stocked relief wagons pulled by the ship's golems and the animals. As carefully as he could he made his way to the center area. Once there he saw the other golems and Carrita's pony.

Carrita was sitting on the ground next to her copper kettle slowly pouring a colorful powder into it. When the powder box was empty the kettle floated off the ground and began rotating. The girl's lips parted into a huge smile.

The kettle lifted off the ground and slowly began rotating around. Carrita could feel the unrefined magic emanating from the kettle. She sat on the ground enjoying the raw power.

"Why do I feel I am not going to like this?" Joskin said to break the nerves building up inside him. "She is smiling too big. The last time I saw that smile we had to get a priestess to help her."

Niesla's lip curled into a cute frown. She slowly shook her head, "I don't think I have ever seen such an excited smile. How could it mean trouble?"

Carrita frowned for a moment, but her smile returned quickly.

Joskin chuckled but could feel no mirth. He did get nervous when Carrita performed her experiments.

Carrita shook her head and rolled her shoulders like a typical playful child. "If anything goes wrong you should know what to do then." She grabbed the kettle out of the air and began pouring a gel like substance out into a perfect circle around the supplies. When the circle was finished she began creating symbols inside.

Niesla pulled on his arm, "What is she doing?"

Joskin was surprised to hear such a question from her. "You have a better idea than I do."

Niesla scowled as she examined the symbols Carrita was creating inside the circle. "She is using conflicting magic. By my understanding, what she appears to be doing is very dangerous. Such uses of magic may result in all our deaths."

Joskin tried to control his own worry. He was always concerned when Carrita was trying something new. Thus far Carrita had only been unprepared for the results once, but Niesla also understood some things about magic. He only knew Niesla was worried. "She has studied under two Guardians and read libraries of books. That is just in the last year. I have supreme confidence in her."

"I don't understand what she is doing. There is no question she knows more than I, but what she is doing goes in conflict with everything I understand of magic," Niesla explained.

"If anybody can safely do whatever it is she is doing, she can," Joskin's could feel his hands starting to shake. Even with the confidence he had in Carrita he couldn't help but worry after what Niesla said. Cautiously he led Niesla to the circle and stood by his still cut and bruised horse.

A crowd quickly gathered. One strange old man began walking around the circle scratching his chin. Nervous that someone would mess something up and cause Carrita's experiment to fail he began asking the people to step back.

Garfrun stepped out of the throng and asked, "What is she doing?"

Joskin shook his head, "I don't know, but it would be best to keep the onlookers away. There's a good chance of bad things happening if they don't." He glanced to Niesla who was watching Carrita intently.

Shortly after the town guards had pushed the crowd back, Airria emerged with a stout pony. He tied the pony to one of the wagons and made his way to Faith.

Carrita began chanting in her magic language. Niesla put a hand out as if to stop the chanting. Before the elf could fully raise her arm Carrita had energy swirling around her. She began to shake. Finally she yelled, "Blith Villyontsa!"

Everything outside the circle went blurry, though he could see everybody in the group, the golems, the animals and the wagons. He could see everything that they were bringing, except Faith and Airria. Before he could mount a protest Carrita begin to look weak. He could now see different buildings around them. People were being thrown off the violet stone street. The sky had gone from bright and sunny to dark with black clouds.

Carrita fell to the ground. He tried to lunge to her aid, but found himself so discombobulated that he fell into one of the wagons. The horses were stumbling around and squealing in panic. He could hear dogs barking and people screaming.

571

In his dizzied state he could see armed men rushing towards the group. He reached for his ax and struggled to stand. He glanced around, but he couldn't see Airria or Faith. Faith's horse was awkwardly coming to his side.

He looked to Niesla for an explanation. She had collapsed to the ground, struggling to sit up. "What happened?" she finally asked.

A grizzly deep voice began asking, "Who..." A large muscular man with the head of a lion stepped out. He was fully armored, his teeth bared. His words stopped when his eyes saw Carrita. "M'lady!" gentleness came to his eyes as he ran and picked up Carrita. "What have you done now?"

With the girl in his arms, the gray maned lion-man looked over the stumbling group. His eyes met Joskin's. "You must be Joskin DeAveron. Marren is waiting for you on the north wall."

As he walked away with Carrita, the burly figure yelled to the other soldiers, "The wagons are our relief supplies, unload them with care. Assist these people with whatever they need." He carried Carrita into a nearby, large, white house.

One of the soldiers helped Niesla to her feet and supported her. Shaking her head she asked, "Will you take me with the girl. I wish to know she is all right."

The man nodded and propped her up as she carefully put one foot in front of the other.

Joskin wanted to go with. The young girl's childish face still struck a chord of protective concern and Niesla was in no condition to protect herself. They were in a town of strangers. He was not in any condition to protect anyone either, but Faith's horse was not fighting or biting at any of the men. Joskin decided he had no choice but to trust these people. He allowed one of the soldiers to escort him to the wall. By the time he was at the bottom of the steps he had regained his bearings. The wall was gray-violet granite with seams so tight no mortar was needed. The stairs were solid and wide enough for both his and Faith's horse to follow him up them with ease.

He arrived to see Marren giving orders to a man. Her appearance was that of an old woman, worn and about to break. When she noticed

Joskin she regained some of her youth, "How did you get here so quickly? How did you get past the siege?"

Joskin looked back at the large white house. "Carrita," he said flatly.

Marren gasped, "She…"

"Niesla is looking after her." Then to change the subject he asked, "I'm not sure what Carrita did to get us here, or how long it took. To me, only moments ago it was morning. Now it is night. I am still very confused. What is going on here?" He tried to shake what was left of the disorientation.

Marren smiled slightly, "It is still morning. The unnatural darkness you see is a conjuration to allow the devils and undead of the army to fight continuously." She looked out over the army.

Joskin could see the army's encampment and various broken siege engines. "If there are devils, why aren't there any angels? Isn't that how it's supposed to work? Balance?"

"The angels sent to balance the fight have been recalled. I arrived just in time to fend off the devils. I can't do it any longer." There was desperation and fatigue in Marren's voice.

"Why were the angels recalled? Why were the devils not? Doesn't the balance have to be maintained?"

"The angels were severely wounded. Zerith's forces are too strong and well-organized. They are not being led by a typical mortal as they have been before."

They both surveyed the army; orcs, goblins and kobolds stretched down the road as far as they could see. The lesser devils, males, were growling orders to prepare for the next wave. The greater devil, the female, was carefully surveying the wall. From time to time she would say something in a language that made Joskin's hair stand on end. Then the lesser devils would start yelling in the goblin tongue and the formations would change.

"I'm afraid we will not be able to hold it this time," Marren said disparagingly.

"The defenses will hold," Niesla's voice surprised them, "they have to!"

Joskin could feel the urgency in the elf's voice. "I will do everything I can," he said in an attempt to comfort her.

"That is not enough!" There was a fire in Niesla's eyes Joskin had never seen before. "The defenses **will** hold!"

Joskin surveyed the field again. Without the supernatural help of the devils the black bloods would be too uncoordinated to take the city, but with the devils flying around commanding, Joskin was sure the city would fall.

The steady thumping as the golems climbed the stairs to get to the top of the wall sent a wave of fear through the black bloods.

The female devil, the succubus, noticed Joskin with the golem's close behind. Even across the battlefield the huge creature's smile could be seen. She began yelling at one of the kobolds. After a smack to the little creature's head which sent it tumbling, the kobold got to his feet and ran through the army as fast as he could. Alone he ran the distance from the front of the siege to the gate. The archers on the wall readied their bows, but waited for Marren to give the order to fire. Instead she commanded the huge matrataur golem to jump down and kill the wretched thing.

The golem didn't move. Niesla got a funny smile on her face. Carrita had given Niesla control of this golem and Joskin could remember Faith's final instructions to the other golems was that when she was not around to control them they were to listen to Carrita or Niesla. With neither Faith nor Carrita around Niesla had full control of all of the golems, "I suggest we listen to what he has to say."

"They never have anything good to say," Marren snapped. "All they do is try to set up meetings to negotiate our surrender."

Joskin felt as if he would rather be fighting the devils. At length he said, "Let it in. I will talk to it."

Marren bowed slightly. "That is how we lost the angels," her teeth were gritted together.

"I'm aware of how devious Zerith is," Joskin said in his defense. "I am also aware that the city must not fall. We may be able to turn this to our advantage," he cast a quick glance to Niesla.

"If this city is lost it is on your head," Marren said and then turned to the guard "Let it wait at the gate!"

Joskin ran for the gate, a guard slipping out of his way. He only opened the peep-hole and asked, "What is your message?"

"De mas'or rekes aud'ince wit you?" The kobold was very nervous, his eyes kept shifting to the guards on the wall.

"Tell your masters I will only meet with one from your army, in one week. I will only meet a mortal leader," Joskin said with confidence. "We will meet in the field between our army and the wall. Repeat my words back to me."

"You se'nder one week, on field." The kobold stuttered.

Joskin shook his head, "Wait there!" He yelled for a scribe. When the scribe got there he repeated the conditions. Then he handed the scroll to the kobold and said, "This, to your masters, now!"

The kobold ran back across the field to the succubus and handed her the note. She yelled something in the Goblin tongue and a wave of loud commotion went through the army.

Joskin closed his eyes and tried to imagine a way to win this fight. He had counted two incubi and a succuba, creatures he, like angels or pixies, assumed existed, but never thought he would really see. Just one of the incubi could kill all three of the matrataurs that took the whole group, plus all the help Marren could give, to defeat. For this fight he didn't have Airria or Faith, unless they could find a way to get here.

His fretting was disrupted briefly by the thought of Airria. He turned to Niesla, "Where are Airria and Faith?"

Niesla lowered her chin and looked up at Joskin. "It was Carrita's experiment. How could I know?"

Marren's eyes grew sad and her face became tired again, "They didn't come with?"

Joskin was a little defensive, "They were with us when we left and I have no idea what Carrita did."

Niesla shrugged with a nervous look, "She is asleep, she used all her energy to get here and will likely be unconscious for weeks, as powerful as she is."

Marren looked to the white house for a moment. "There are ways to help her wake up more quickly. We may have to use them all. We need her help and we need to know what happened to the others."

Joskin looked over the soldiers surrounding them. They all looked broken. They needed a rest. After a moment he asked, "There was a man with the face of a lion here earlier. He took Carrita. Can I assume he is a leader here?"

"Tesrik is the captain of the guard here. He was for many years the personal bodyguard to Carrita's mother."

Joskin suggested, "If you would send him to the wall, we can start our plans. Hopefully we can come up with some way to defend against what is out there." He turned to Niesla and asked, "Will you help see to the wounded? They will need assistance." Turning back to Marren he demanded, "You do what you need to. Wake that girl up."

Niesla bowed low, "I will do what I can to heal this army"

Marren bowed with a smile, "I will wake her as quickly as I can. Wait on the wall, Tesrik will be there soon."

Chapter 12 - The Bloody Range

The stars were shining brightly overhead. Both Faith and Airria had slowed to admire the night sky. The moon was high in the firmament and the soft pine breeze almost carried the stench of death from Faith's memory.

Airria grabbed Faith's arm, pulling her to a stop and asked, "What do you think happened here?"

Faith looked down. The dirty road was saturated with blood, but there was not a body to be seen. She could feel her stomach becoming queasy again. "I imagine this is the sight of the battle the Zerith commander told us about."

Airria looked up and down the road, "Where are the bodies? If there was a battle, shouldn't there be bodies?"

Faith reluctantly smelled the breeze coming out of the east. There was no hint of death on it. Slowly she walked to the west side of the road and looked down the steep slope. "Here they are," she stepped back, unnerved by the mangled naked bodies, "it looks as though they have already been scavenged.

"Ahhhh!" A woman screamed from the east side of the road.

Faith was glad of the distraction and found herself running behind Airria to discover who had yelled.

There was a tall, thin man standing behind a much shorter, well curved woman with a knife at her throat. She had her hand behind his and was doing a surprisingly good job of keeping the knife away from its destination.

She was covered in tight black leather pants and boots, a black corset, black gloves which came almost to her shoulders and a dark gray cloak. The mask on her lower face covered her mouth and nose; her eyes spoke no fear, in spite of her predicament.

"Prince Macron sends his regards!" the man grunted. He was dressed in baggy, gray green clothes, including a cloak so patched it looked like a hundred different shades about his shoulders. "You will pay for what you've done!"

"This looks like a fun game," Airria said.

Faith could remember him saying something similar when he had rescued her.

"Stay out of this," the man grunted, "it doesn't concern you."

"You're right!" said the woman who took advantage of the distraction by stepping back and flipping the man over her shoulder. She then pulled a knife and tried to stab him while he was on the ground.

Her thrust was stopped by Faith's blade. "Not today," Faith said.

The man took this opportunity to roll out of the way. He grabbed his dagger and ran into the woods.

The woman in black said with the bitter tone, "He will be back. He won't stop until I'm dead."

"Why?" asked Airria.

"A friend of mine had a valuable heirloom stolen from her by a greedy warlord. I took it back. Now he has hired Macron to kill me," the woman's teeth ground as she talked.

"Macron?" Faith asked. "So you know him?"

The woman's eyes shifted a little, "I know **of** him more than actually knowing him."

"And who are you?" Airria asked. "Why do you know of him?"

578

"My name is of no consequence to you at this time," the woman responded. "I caught wind of him hunting me weeks ago."

"Why is he hunting you?" Faith asked gently.

"I told you, I retrieved an heirloom for a friend..." the woman stopped speaking as she noticed Airria rolling his eyes, "very well, it is more than that, I have upset most of the royalty of Zerith." The woman's eyes began to soften towards Faith.

"And how did you upset the royalty of Zerith?" Airria asked in an accusing tone.

"What I have done is my own business!" the woman growled through her teeth.

Faith spun on Airria, "You will not speak to her in such a manner again until we have cause." She took a slow breath, "You have many pieces to your past which you are reluctant to share with myself or Joskin. What makes you feel you have the right to demand an explanation of this woman?"

Airria took three steps back but kept a sharp eye on the woman. "If it makes you happy," he said as gently as possible, "she may accompany us as far as we go the same direction."

"You speak as though she's yours. Yours to do..." the woman snapped.

"No," Faith interrupted, "he is saying this as a friend. He has been a good and faithful friend for over a year now."

"It looks to me as if he has pretty good control of you," the woman mocked.

Airria snickered and took another step back.

Faith said, "Control? Was it not I who stopped him from questioning you. How is it you see him controlling me?"

"You follow him. Women don't need men to survive!"

"Is that...?" Airria's words were cut off by Faith's glance.

"Your words have a sense of truth to them," Faith replied. "My thoughts are: Why make life harder to prove a point which no one cares about?"

Faith could see the bitterness in the woman's eyes. She had been betrayed by someone she cared about and someone she thought cared for

579

her. Faith remembered the feeling from when Henrik had come to collect her and had told her it was her father that had sold her.

She thought back to the morning she had first seen Airria. "I was a helpless woman in a man's world. I thought I needed a man to make me complete. Then I was sold into slavery. One night a man, or rather an overgrown boy, saved me," she glanced back to Airria.

Airria smiled at the insult.

Faith continued, "He rescued me from the slavers and more importantly from the bitterness growing inside me."

"And I suppose this is the boy?" the woman said pointing to Airria.

"Yes. When I met a race who believed of menfolk what most men in our race do of women, I realized it did not matter the perspective, men can't exist without women and women can't exist without men."

"I am independent from such burdens; I have risen to the top of a man's profession," the woman said proudly.

Faith giggled involuntarily, "A man's profession? Since when are men the only ones who know how to kill? If you are so independent of men why do you use them to measure your ranking within your profession?"

"What I do is almost always done by men so they are the standard of the field." The woman began shifting her weight slightly.

"Do you count yourself as an equal to Macron? Do you feel you are really the same?" Faith was not trying to verbally trap the woman she was only trying to understand.

"No," the woman laughed.

"It seems to me you are both rogues, perhaps assassins?" Faith turned to Airria. "Is this not what you would surmise?"

Airria nodded, but remained silent.

The woman's eyes narrowed, "Yes we are."

"You just implied you are different. Why?" Faith began contemplating the variations she had observed, which were mostly only in dress.

"He sells to the highest bidder," the woman said puffing out her chest.

Faith thought on the woman's answer for a moment. She could not name many willing to risk everything for an occupation which did not pay. Airria and Joskin had been the most giving men she had ever met and even they asked for something. "So the profession you are talking about being the top of is unpaid rogues? I would guess you are one of a very few who belongs to such a profession."

After she said the words she realized Joskin, though he took money for what he did most of the time, fought for a cause. Airria had never asked anything of her even though he had risked his life several times for her. She had asked nothing of anyone when she helped defend the city. Most people she associated with spent their time helping others even at the risk of their own lives.

She felt ashamed to have said what she did, but before she could adjust her question, the woman in black answered, "That's not what I meant. Yes, I am a very good rogue. In that way, Macron and I are the same." This woman was very open...about her career choice.

Faith continued asking questions, "You dress very differently than he does. I would guess you are playing to your womanhood to distract the men you encounter. Would you say Macron does the same?"

The woman laughed for the first time since they met. "No. His baggy clothes help him hide, but he is more likely to get caught on something. My clothes are ample to hide, but better when I have to stand and fight. Not to mention most male guards will hesitate to use a killing blow on a nice figure."

"Then you are of your own profession. You are a woman rogue with a touch of fighter and seductress? You are not in a man's world. You make your own way."

"That's right. I do." The woman dropped her hands to her side and relaxed her eyes.

Faith continued, "You do not need to measure your success by a man's ranking system. You don't need their praise."

The woman bragged, "I'm doing very well on my own."

Faith asked, "So you do not have a man waiting for you?" She was a little surprised.

581

The woman shook her head. "I don't need a man, I am happy where I am."

"And so you will be for some time on your chosen path. Things will change. The day will come when you will need what you only desire now. It does not matter how independent you think you are, you can only be free when you accept the truth, when you compromise who you think you are for who you can become."

"I have become great and will be even greater!" the woman sounded so proud.

"You have become great by whose standards?" Faith questioned.

The woman shifted her head slightly as she responded, "By those who share my profession."

"Who are likely men?" Faith found it funny how this woman would rate herself using men, yet would say she did not need them. It was obvious all the pride she had in herself came from the opinions of the men she claimed she did not need.

"Yes," The woman responded.

"It sounds as if you still measure yourself on a man's scale. In this you have shown your dependence on men." Faith was stunned. She had not realized how much she was learning about how unaware this woman was about her own beliefs.

"Men carry the prestige..." the woman started to say.

Faith cut her off, "They only have it because it is given to them. Joskin, Airria's cousin has gained more esteem than most. By his enemies he is feared above almost any other. By his friends he is revered as great because he has helped and even saved thousands of lives. His mother is honored for the first reason I mentioned, however, she is proud of him for the second. Which do you think he takes note of?"

The woman focused on Faith's eyes, "The first of course. As I understand it, he has well earned his praise."

"He takes note of his mother's pride. He would tell you he is the person he is because his mother taught him to be more than others. Through this I learned a woman has a power greater than any wizard. A woman has the power to shape the future for hundreds of years after her death."

The woman placed her arms across her chest, "It sounds like men have brainwashed you into believing the best you can be is a mother."

Faith's body jolted as she realized what she had been saying. She had not realized she had been saying anything of the sort, but this woman was correct. After a moment she continued, "I have not been brainwashed, I have seen what a good mother can do." Faith could feel a smile come across her face as an idea entered her mind. "If it pleases you, I will be glad to show you I can make it in a man's world as well as you." It had been so long since she had sparred with anyone except Airria.

"How?" the woman asked, half closing one eye.

"I believe you should decide. You are the one who feels your skills are superior. I am the 'brainwashed, subservient' woman."

Airria laughed. Faith understood why. It did not matter what physical challenge the woman in black chose Faith had the advantage, she had been trained by Guardians. There was no "fair" contest.

The woman drew her short sword and a couple of black masks without eyeholes. Faith was confused, she had never seen anything of the sort. She looked at Airria who had been looking proud of her, but who now looked worried.

"I'm only here. It's up to you," he said and shrugged his shoulders.

"My expertise is in the dark. To make sure this contest is fair you'll need to put on the blindfold." The woman smiled and turned to Airria, "Keep your eyes open for Macron."

"Are you depending on me?" Airria said with sarcasm which earned him a killer glance from both women.

Faith put on the mask. Airria had taught her to listen for breathing and footsteps. Carrita had taught her to feel the Magic in everything, to let her magic be her eyes. She had practiced many nights with Airria, but had never expected to use it. Slowly she put on the mask and drew one of her own swords.

Airria sat back against a tree to watch.

At first Faith could only generally feel where the woman was. As she allowed her magic to investigate the environment she started feeling the trees and even some oncoming scavengers. In time she could even feel the presence of the steel in the woman's sword.

Faith could feel the woman walking in a toe-heel fashion, her heel never solidly touching the ground. She was almost perfectly silent. Her breathing was muffled by her mask. Even the leather made no sound.

Being in this state of awareness Faith could see all around her better than if she could use her eyes. She allowed her opponent to ease around to her back, lulling her into a feeling of superiority.

Faith could feel the shift in the woman's black aura when she felt she was in a good position. The woman tried to set her sword to Faith's neck, but Faith had moved her own sword to protect herself. Faith spun around and swung at the woman's sword.

As the swordplay began Faith could feel every move the woman was making. For some time Faith played with the woman, matching strikes. Faith never attempted to strike or cut the woman, only the weapon she wielded.

After some time sparring Faith could feel her breathing becoming labored. The woman in black felt as if she were tiring. It was time to end the match. Faith stepped and ducked a blow. To emphasize her ability to hurt the woman she slapped the woman on the backside. The woman let out a startled squeak.

As Faith's sword returned to a defensive position she felt a metal object flying into the fray, Faith swung her sword, deflecting the dagger out of the air. Magically she followed the dagger's path, but was stopped by a very dark aura. She pulled her mask off, but did not let go of the feeling she was tracking.

The dark aura she had felt was a short but stocky fighter in a full suit of black, spiked armor with bronze trim. The blades in his hand had a cruel black flame which flickered with the strain of tortured souls. Looking into his shield was a view into the blackest hell.

Faith pointed at the fighter with her sword and drew her second.

Airria jumped to his feet and looked at the stranger. He immediately donned his helm and readied for battle.

Faith looked for her bow which was being guarded by Macron. He was smiling, "It's funny who you can run into only slightly off the road. My friend is known as 'The Balance'. I am more interested in the balance I will receive by collecting my bounty on the famous Black Dove. Not to mention the price I can get selling beauty such as yours in Zerith."

"We are fatigued; this is not a fair fight," Dove said calmly.

"I did not intend it to be," Macron said. "Then again it never is when a man fights a woman."

"Then let's see what you can do!" Dove exclaimed.

Macron threw something on the ground and everything seemed to go dark and silent. Faith could feel the assassin reaching out to try to find the women. She remembered Carrita had taught her how to hide her magic, her aura, which would make it much more difficult for an opponent to find her. She could feel both Macron and Dove's movements. Faith waited, holding her breath.

Macron got behind Dove and was sneaking his knife within striking distance. In one smooth motion Faith cut off his right hand and leg at the knee. His screams could soon be heard as the darkness dissipated.

Once again Faith stopped Dove from killing him. She used the flat of her blade to knock him out. Then she bent over and poured enough healing magic into him to stop the bleeding. Neither his leg nor his hands came back. Faith looked at Dove, "There are many fates we can give which are far worse than death."

The dim roar of a vicious combat forced Faith to look in Airria's direction. All she could see was a blur of black and white. Sparks of both black and white were showering into the air. No fire started from the sparks as Faith had expected.

She ran and grabbed her bow and arrows, then looked at Dove for support.

"This is a fight we can only turn for the worst," Dove said almost sadly. "If we tried to join in he'll try to defend us as well as himself. Men are so proud."

585

"So are you!" Faith grunted. She was growing tired of this woman's bitterness. She looked for a target and drew back a blue tipped arrow.

What little skin Dove was showing had turned pale. "If you are lucky enough to hit one of them there is only a slight chance it will be the right one."

Faith did not care, she released the arrow. It hit a tree near the two fighters and exploded. Both Fighters spun to block the flying splinters of wood and ice. Both were thrown to the ground.

The Balance darted down the steep hillside into the dark woods.

Faith shot twice more trying to hit the runner, but only succeeded in turning trees into stone. Then she went over to check on Airria.

His armor had protected him well; there was not a scratch on it nor any visible blood.

Dove's voice, now humble, came from behind, "I have a feeling I've seen a challenge beyond any intended for mortal eyes. I don't really believe in dragons but I would swear I just watched two of them fight."

"You may not be as far off as you think," Faith said.

"I kind of get the feeling I don't want to know anymore," Dove turned her head to look at Airria.

As Faith removed his helm he was gasping for breath like nothing she had seen before. He was not fit to fight any more this night.

Dove suggested humbly, "I would appreciate an escort to Sarckran if you can accept me by my trade.

"You are an assassin," Faith said.

Dove took a step back, "You've heard of me?"

"No," Faith said calmly. "Every move you have made since we met has given you away." She paused for a moment then continued, "Your work name, black is the color of death and dove is a bird of peace. I would guess you specialize in the execution of Zerith royalty, likely hired and paid well by others of the Zerith royalty."

"How did you know?" asked Dove, a little unnerved.

"No matter how fast your blade is, or how sharp your sword, your mind will always be your best weapon," Faith replied. "It is all in

586

your words and written heavy in your eyes." While she spoke she never took her eyes off Airria.

"Not to change the subject, but how did you beat me and still block the dagger?" Dove asked.

"I have learned from the best," Faith replied. "It very much goes back to our earlier conversation. Men and women are good at different things. Part of this is because they think differently. It does not matter who is the dominant, they will be corrupt and foolish. If they work together there is nothing they cannot do."

"What does that have to do with you beating me?" Dove insisted.

"I was able to take what I could use from all of my trainers. I was able to use the strengths of each," Faith said. "You worked so hard on entering the 'man's world' you have lost track of your natural gifts."

"I have not," Dove protested.

"It is up to you to accept or reject what I say. I will challenge your words no more," Faith answered gently. She then turned her face to look into Dove's eyes, "I will challenge you no more."

Airria sat up and gave a weary smile, "I-I think I can travel." He had to take a breath between each word. Together the women helped Airria to Sarckran and left the crippled Macron to his fate.

Chapter 13 - New Friend

The sun was just cresting over the horizon when Black Dove excused herself. "This is where I must depart."

Faith smiled and nodded. "It was a pleasure to have met you. I hope you find what you are looking for."

Dove began walking into the trees. Before she vanished she turned back, "A dear friend often walks this road in the mornings. If you should see her I would take it as a kindness if you would escort her to Sarckran. She's a noble born so she needs all the help she can get."

Faith laughed and watched her disappear into the woods. She turned to Airria, "Why do I have a feeling this friend will be around the same height and build as our new friend."

Airria chuckled tiredly, "I would guess you're right."

"Are you not feeling any better?" Faith asked.

Airria stood a little straighter and replied, "I guess that fight took more out of me than I thought. Don't worry, when we get to Sarckran I can rest." He took a deep breath and glanced around, "That's all I need, just some rest." His eyes were drooping as he stood.

Faith had noticed his aura was weak. "Perhaps the armor uses your life energy to assist you in your fights and perhaps it has depleted your natural supply."

Airria chuckled again, "That would explain a lot. If I've learned anything from Carrita's lessons, the ones I wasn't supposed to be hearing, I will need some rest."

They did not take more than a hundred paces before a woman stumbled out of the woods ahead of them. She wore a long violet and red dress with a fairly loose blue corset around her waist. Her hair was in one long elegant braid running down to her knees. As Faith expected this woman was of the same build and as much taller as elegant shoes would raise her. She had a square face and the same striking brown eyes as Dove.

"Hello!" the woman said as she stepped onto the road. "It is not much farther to my home city, but I would feel much safer if I could finish my travels this morning with such fine warriors as you."

Faith laughed softly, this was obviously Dove, but she did not want to be recognized as the assassin. She could think of several reasons why someone would want to hide such an identity, but even a few moments with either and the character of the other would be compromised. "Welcome, Friend of Dove. What shall we call you?"

The woman curtsied as a true noble, "I am called Tarmancia, daughter to the Governor of Sarckran."

Airria laughed weakly, "Tarmancia that is a long name for a less intelligent brute like me to remember. May I call you Tarm?"

Tarmancia frowned, "It is not proper for brutes to degrade a noble's name."

"As you wish m'lady," Airria said with a slight bow. As he did so his knees started to shake.

Faith curtsied with all the elegance she could muster. "Your company will be most welcome." She heard Airria's gasp. Instinctively she reached for an arrow and glance back to her companion. He was just staring at her, but his breathing was rapid and shallow. She turned back to Tarmancia. "I am afraid we are not much protection, but we offer what we can." Faith looked at the corset on the woman. It looked as if she had tried to dawn it alone. "Before we depart, may I fix your corset?" Without waiting for an answer Faith grabbed the woman and turned her around. She pulled the strings tight, "It would be best if it did not look as if we had done something inappropriate when we arrive in town."

When they arrived at the gates of Sarckran a burly woman with several bandages, a large ax and a scarred shield met them. "You parents have been worried sick about you. There are rumors of a knight in black armor killing everyone he comes across."

A woman in a violet dress with a green corset came rushing out of the gate. "Where have you been? We have been pacing all night." She fell on Tarmancia's neck. She had long brown hair and deep green eyes. Her poise was that of a broken parent.

Tarmancia looked at Faith and rolled her eyes. "These lovely people have escorted me home, mother."

"We thank you," said a tall man with silky black hair and deep set eyes. He was dressed in a perfectly tailored green tunic with matching trousers. Over his right shoulder was a violet cloak. "If there is anything we can do to repay you. It will be done."

"I had business to attend to, Governor," Tarmancia said impersonally addressing the man.

"I received word of a strange man killing all he comes across. I was worried for you," Tarmancia's mother said.

"Mother, you needn't worry about me like you do," Tarmancia sounded happily frustrated. "I'm not a child anymore"

"You'll always be my child." Her mother's eyes shifted from Tarmancia to the other two, "You brought more refugees?"

Airria still looked to be in rough shape and Faith could imagine she was not at her best.

Tarmancia answered before either Faith or Airria could, "They are travelers. They played a large role in dealing with the Zerith assassin who's been after me." Tarmancia looked at Airria and added, "We also met a killer and if I saw what I think I saw these magical gates will be ineffective against him." She turned back to the governor. "Now we are in need of rest. If you'll excuse us."

"Of course." The governor looked a little disappointed.

591

"Oh, before I forget." Tarmancia grabbed her purse and tossed it to her mother. Then with a smile said, "I will tell you all about it when I get up."

The governor looked pleased and confused but nodded his head and told the guards to shut the gate.

As Airria, Faith and Tarmancia were walking away, Faith said, "Have you really become so callous even with your own mother?"

Tarmancia asked in confusion, "How do you mean?"

"She obviously cares and is concerned about you," Faith said. "You talked to her as if she has no business in your life."

Tarmancia scowled. "She's just overly protective. I had an older sister who was supposed to govern when my parents are gone, but years ago she left and we haven't heard from her since. Now my parents only want me to follow in their footsteps. To them I'm someone to carry on when they can't."

"Even I could tell you are more to them than only a legacy," Faith replied. "You are their own flesh and blood, you are their daughter."

Tarmancia frowned, "I have done more to keep this city safe than any other person in this town. They should know by now I can take care of myself. They hate what I do. I stopped telling them about it years ago. When I get up my mother will come to me and ask what happened. I will start to tell her and she will stop me and tell me about my responsibility to the city."

"It may be so, but your parents still want to know," Faith pleaded. "Tarmancia, look in her eyes when you talk to her next. You'll see."

Tarmancia frowned and looked at the ground, "I was never supposed to rule. Both of my brothers were killed defending this place. My sister is likely dead as well. I never wanted a man controlling my life so I learned to fight and sneak. I can't stand to see the disappointment when I don't measure up to what they wanted."

Faith looked up at the late morning sky. "From someone who once felt the way you do and now has no parents to disappoint, I recommend you find a way to make peace with them. I suggest you find a way to compromise. If what you say is correct, they are all the family you have left."

Tarmancia looked at Faith as though she wanted to say something, but nothing left her mouth.

Faith began looking around the town, which was a little larger than the town she had grown up in. All of the buildings were made of gray granite. The streets were paved stone. The air was filled with despair.

Faith looked back at the burly, female guard who had been quietly following. "Are those injuries from the siege?

The woman nodded, but said nothing.

Faith looked at the people wandering the streets. Even the children were bandaged. "Will you show me to your place of treatment? I believe I can help some of these."

The guard looked at Tarmancia who stopped and nodded. Without a word she began walking down a nearby street. She stopped in front of a building with a large open door. People with bloody bandages were strewn in front on make-shift cots.

Faith gasped when she saw all the wounded. There were many different races, human sized lizards, wolf-men, tiger-men, dwarves and elves. The sight which caught Faith's attention was how many of them were bandaged or had a sling. Several of them were missing limbs. Faith wanted to cry.

"Our healer was killed three days ago trying to get some wounded," the guard said sadly.

Faith wandered into the carnage, "I'll help where I can."

"Do you know magic?" the guard asked excitedly.

"Some," Faith replied, entranced by the injured.

A tall, thin woman with only seashells to cover her mild cleavage and groin, limped up to Faith, "Your Grace, I know nothing of the healing arts, but if you will teach me I am willing to learn."

Faith could feel a strong essence of water magic emanating from the woman. "What shall I call you?"

The woman smiled, "It is difficult for humans to say my given name properly. Please call me Ella. How may I assist you?"

Faith looked around. There were far too many wounded to use only her magic to heal them. Even the strong magic she could feel emanating from Ella would be insufficient. She wished she had paid more attention to Niesla and Carrita when they discussed alchemy.

Faith turned to the guard and placed a hand on her shoulder. She began trickling her magic into the wounds and healing them. "Will you go to the slopes outside the wall and gather a few herbs for me?"

The well-muscled woman began rubbing her cuts with her eyes wide. Suddenly she dropped to one knee, "Whatever you request m'lady."

Faith hated when people reacted to her this way, but had no time to correct this behavior. She described various berries, leaves, plants and grasses to the woman and then sent her on her way.

Turning to Ella, she placed a hand on her shoulder and taught her the first healing chant Carrita had taught her. When finished she said, "If I am correct about you, you will understand enough about magic to use this chant to heal. Only use enough magic to stop the bleeding. Later we will make a salve to help the healing. Do not deplete yourself enough to pass out, I will need your assistance."

Chapter 14 True Healing and Bloody Vengeance

Ella walked over to one of the men lying in his armor. Faith stopped her, "You start with the children. When the parents see their children recovering they will find strength to continue and help where they can when they can."

Ella hesitated, "Will we not need the protection?"

Faith thought about the question, "If the children are healing, it won't matter how injured the adults are they will find a way to defend."

Ella nodded and began helping the children.

Faith looked over the others, "Who in here is the best baker?"

A severely wounded man to her side reached out and touched her knee. "My mother makes the best bread in town. I don't know if she survived the last attack. Our shop was destroyed by a flaming stone."

Faith knelt next to the young man and placed her hand on his head. She could feel his energy fading. She let her magic trickle into him and start healing his burns, but only enough so he would stop bleeding and be able to assist her in finding his mother and help her bake. She talked softly to the young man, "I have helped you. Now I need your help. Find your mother and any other good bakers. There is no competition here. We need the food so we can heal as a town."

The young man began going down the rows of cots examining the occupants. From time to time he would yell, "Here," and wait only long enough for Faith to see him, then move on.

Faith would move to the indicated person and heal them enough for them to start working.

As she was walking through the cots an old man sitting with a bandage on his head stopped her. "I have been a guard here for many years. I know what you are doing. My wounds are not fatal, but I do hurt. If you'd borrow my energies you can help more of those who need it and I can get some sleep."

It seemed as if all he could see in her was the ability to help his friends. "I appreciate your sacrifice and so will several others," she took his magic and let him rest.

Before long Ella was looking fatigued. She had had some parents make a similar request as the old guard, but it was not enough. Faith called her over. "You look as though you have used all the magic I would prefer you use. Please rest, I will need you when the guard returns with the herbs."

Ella looked around over the cots. She smiled, "You are an excellent healer. I would never have guessed so much could be accomplished by healing the children and bakers. I am glad a priestess such as you has happened our way."

Faith looked around at the children, though still wounded they were sitting by their parents playing. The smell of fresh baking bread filled the air. Fear and despair had been replaced with hope. She had only done what had made sense to her, but Ella was correct, there was more to healing than just the bodies.

"Where'd you want me to put these?" the guard woman returned with two cloaks folded into bags and they were bulging with plants.

Faith had the guard set the cloaks outside on the ground and spread them. Then she sent the guard to get some pots. She had an older boy build her a small fire. Finally she began sorting the vegetation into groups.

When the guard returned Faith had Ella begin crushing berries in the pot and had the guard pull seeds from the various plants and crush them. As the crushed seeds were handed to her she added them to the berries. When the pot was sufficiently full she placed it over the fire and had the skinny woman stir it. In time it formed a paste.

Feeling drained she asked Ella to apply the salve to those with wounds. After Ella accepted, Faith made her way to a cot and collapsed with the idea she would close her eyes for only a moment or two.

She woke up to Airria's boyish smile staring down at her. "It looks like I wasn't the only one who needed a little rest. You've been asleep for three days."

There was a small crowd behind him. Ella spoke from the side, "Such power to heal. I can only dream of such ability."

Faith sat up and looked around. All of the cots were now empty. Bandages were stacked neatly on shelves around the room. The cots were stacked against one wall. Even the blood had been washed off the stone floor.

Tarmancia was standing between her parents with an arm around each.

"Have you talked to them today?" Faith asked.

"They were happy to hear the whole report, though they had several questions about the two of you. But, that was a few days ago."

"What did you tell them?" Airria asked.

"Only that you helped me and that you fought the murderer who has been terrorizing the people of this area."

Hearing Airria's voice reminded Faith of her question. "Do you know why the fight took so much out of you?" she asked Airria.

Airria looked deep into Faith's eyes, "You were right, the armor had to draw on my magic to drive me fast enough to keep up. Fortunately it did the same to my opponent," Airria explained. "With this knowledge and what little I know of magic, I have consulted your new friends and they seem to think it's time you take a little of my magic every morning."

The Governor sat on a chair near Faith and asked, "Will you do us the honor of joining us for dinner tonight?"

Faith looked at Airria. She was reminded of how much time had passed. She was worried for the others who had been teleported, "I wish we had time. We have an errand we have already delayed far too long. We really must be moving on."

Airria had Faith's bow ready for travel. He was dressed in his armor with his shield on his arm. She stood up and began walking toward the north gate when the cries of a child forced her to start running up the road.

"Help! Help!" the young boy cried. He was only just entering the gates.

Faith ran directly to the child. A guard was already trying to comfort him.

"They have them, they have them!" the boy kept saying.

"Who?" asked the guard, but only got the same response.

Faith picked up the boy softly and gave him a comforting hug. She held him for short while. She softly wiped the tears from his cheek. "Who has been taken?" she asked softly.

"My family!" the child cried between sobs. "They took my family. Jenna, Barra, Nist, mom and dad, all gone."

"Who took them?" she asked.

"A fat man from Zerith and a knight in ugly black armor," he sobbed.

Faith could feel anger boiling up inside her as her memory went back to her own enslavement. "Take care of him," she said to the guard as she handed the child back.

Together they walked as fast as they could. The waxing moon was high in the star-filled sky when Faith realized that she hadn't asked the boy where or when his family had been taken.

Airria grabbed her hand and said, "Don't worry, we'll find them."

"Yes. We will. We have to." Faith was hoping she was right. She knew there were few roads off this one.

Together they walked through the night. A little before the sun's light began to show itself Faith spotted a campfire where there were a few wagons and several grubby guards. The wagons were unmistakably familiar. This was definitely Henrik's group.

Airria stepped back, "I think this is your fight."

Faith handed Airria her bow and drew her swords. She walked quietly to the camp, not sneaking, but with no extra noise.

"Look at what is coming into camp!" one of the guards yelled.

Around the wagon came several more, including one in black armor. Unlike the guards Airria had saved Faith from, these were all sober.

The one in black armor was not the one they had fought earlier, but showed quickly by his every movement that he knew what he was doing. He ran to his horse, jumped on and grabbed the spear, but he stayed near the slave master's wagon.

When the slave master exited the door he yelled, "You've come back to me!" The tone of his voice told Faith that he fully intended to take her alive. When his eyes caught Airria he shouted, "I know a thousand fates worse than death. You shall suffer them all!"

At this point Faith lost all ability to hear or do anything rational. She only said, "This time your career is over," before charging in.

The rhythm of her swords was perfect. She easily danced around the comparatively clumsy, hireling thugs. By herself she cut through the regular guards with ease.

With the gore around her she looked at the Henrik. Out of the corner of her eyes she saw the black knight charging, spear out. She dove to the side of the horse and rolled up to a half sitting position, bringing her sword through the animal's knee.

She did not bother to look back to see what happened. She was focused on Henrik, his deception and abuse of so many. One step at a time she came closer to the slaver.

His once confident eyes were now filled with terror. He tried to move his massive body to the horses but found Faith standing before him.

"You know," Faith said in a spine tingling tone, "there are many fates worse than death. Fortunately for you, I will only apply a few." She brought her swords quickly and delicately across his eyes. As he brought his hands up to cover them, Faith sliced them both off. Next she cut precisely, but with lightning speed, through his clothes. Every scream he made increased her fury, filled her with excitement but relieved none of

599

the tension. She proceeded to cut his skin ever so slightly until she grew bored. Her final blow to the slaver rendered him a eunuch.

Seeing the man in such pain she began to calm down. Only to realize he was bleeding to death. She drove him at sword point to the fire and pushed him in.

He was already off balance and stuck out his stumps to catch himself. The arms landed in the hot coals, the blood sizzled and the smell of burnt flesh filled the air.

"Jarmack'Trastibbik would truly be proud!" Airria exclaimed.

It was the first thing she had heard from him. It was the first sound other than the slaver's screams she had heard since the start of the fight. She looked at the horribly obese man writhing in pain next to the fire. She turned to look for Airria. It only took a moment to notice the man in black armor with a hole through him she recognized as being left by a magic bolt from her armor. Then she noticed the bodies of the guards, all twenty of them.

Airria was standing with eyes wide surveying the damage. Faith fell to her knees and began to cry. Every lecture she had heard given and she had given to Carrita about vengeance, pride and the need to justify her actions welled up inside. "He deserves it!" she screamed out loud. "He is a blight on humanity."

"So am I, by many accounts," Airria said in a gentle voice. "I've done bad things. Will I be next? And Carrita, the naga confirmed she used dark magic. Will she be next?"

"He put the darkness in her!" Faith shouted.

"We all have darkness in us," Airria's voice was now soft and calm. "Jammar, Kore, Bregette, Joskin and even Niesla have shown that they have some level of darkness in them."

"He brings it to the surface!" She was feeling as if she had become a monster and did not want to admit it.

Airria placed a hand softly on her shoulder, "We let it come to the surface."

She spoke more to herself, "He deserves the pain."

Airria knelt down beside her, "Now you have caused the pain, do you feel better?"

600

"Yes!" she shouted. The lie filled her eyes with tears.

"Really?" Airria asked. He put an arm around her.

She nestled in.

He continued, "I know how it feels, I've been there. Joskin was there for me, as I am here for you."

After she cried awhile longer, she crawled over to Henrik and used enough healing magic to stop the pain. She could not return the lost limbs or eyes, but took his pain. Then she grabbed some clothes from his wagon and helped him dress. She put his coin purse on his belt and helped him on his horse. "If this is the typical horse it will return to its home. You should be able to get help there." Faith's heart was halfway between bitter and caring. "If you do gain back what you have lost, might I suggest a new employ?" then she slapped the horse on the rear and watched it run down the road.

"I thought it would make me feel better, why didn't it?" Faith asked Airria.

"Vengeance consumes you and it takes hold of your heart. It is a heavy beast that can never be filled," Airria answered. "If you let it take control it will govern all your thoughts and feelings, but it never stops." He paused to raise her chin, "you made a good decision to let him go."

Faith examined Airria's face closely. The anger she had seen when they first met was gone. "What about you? Are you not on this quest out of vengeance?"

"To start with," Airria looked deep into Faith's eyes, "I've now had the opportunity to see into the eyes of pure goodness and compassion. It was looking into those eyes that brought me to begin questioning my need for vengeance. My quest has switched to one of rescue and aid to Carrita."

Faith blushed as she realized he was talking about her. "I think you see too much in those eyes."

Airria blushed slightly, "The actions carried through either of those eyes stayed true with only a few exceptions," he said.

His eyes shifted to the wagons, "We have some horses, wagons and people here." He walked over to the one wagon filled with people and picked the lock. Slowly the occupants began trickling out.

Faith was torn. She knew the greatest good was to move on to Derain, but she wanted to help these recently freed prisoners.

Airria spoke, "Take the wagons and the horses and head south. You will find the gates open to you. They will aid you."

Together Faith and Airria watched the wagon move south. It helped Faith to see the people free.

When she turned to start walking north her heart stopped. The morning light revealed a dark cloud, one so thick and black no ray of sunlight could penetrate. She took a deep breath, knowing they would have to pass through it to reach their destination and began walking.

Chapter 15 - Desperate Times

With the dark clouds overhead it was almost imposable to tell one day from the next. If it weren't for the crest of light to the south Joskin wouldn't know if the sun was even still rising.

Every day like clockwork the devils would send a carrier to the gate with a request to move up the day of negotiation. Every day the orcs would carry out a large, black palanquin with thorny bronze work around it.

On the fourth day Joskin noticed a very large army of undead moving into camp. This would also mean several lichs. If the undead were marching out of the Black Forest there were likely some vampires. Only the mistress of death, Rantail, or the high Black Dragon could coordinate this.

"This is not Rantail's work," Marren said out loud as if she could read Joskin's mind. "She wouldn't dare to interfere with this kind of force. No, only the oldest and most devious of the Black Dragons could achieve this."

"Then Jarmack'Trastibbik knows what we're doing," Joskin got a look of horror on his face.

"The devils would never agree to this peace talk without knowing that they could use it to their advantage." There was sadness in her voice. Not a selfish sadness, but a pity for Joskin. "I will do what I can, but my strength is spent. I fear that I will soon meet my end as well."

Joskin turned and stared south at the sliver of light peeking from behind the darkness. He wished he could have his cousin with him for the upcoming fight. "It has been two days since you said Carrita was up. Why haven't I seen her yet? I would like to consult with her on strategy."

Marren shook her head, "She rose from her bed and ran off. Only Niesla has seen her since. Now Niesla has disappeared as well."

Joskin looked back over the city. He was worried about both of them. Niesla had become his strength and Carrita helped him think. With both of them gone he was having a hard time planning anything, "Have you checked the library?"

Marren put a soft hand on Joskin's beard, "Carrita knows how much time we have. She knows this city better than anyone except her mother. I have checked her family library, but there are likely many rooms in her house I don't know exist. Carrita will be ready with the magic when the time is right. Niesla is likely helping her prepare. You must plan and do as you always have because Carrita knows your style and tactics and she will prepare accordingly."

Marren's words brought no comfort, but Joskin knew he had a job to do. He could again feel the stone wall forming around his heart locking out emotions. He knew Niesla hated it when he blocked out emotion, but it was the only way he knew to plan a battle where lives would be lost.

For the rest of the day he spent his time making sure they were ready. He offered transport out for all those who wanted to leave, though he didn't know any way to get them out. Even the old and the children offered to take up weapons. None were willing to abandon the city.

The southern light left and came again before Joskin was satisfied with the preparations. He had spent the night arming children and teaching them the basics of weapon use. He made sure all the oil kettles on the wall were filled and heated. The braziers were all filled and lit. Stones were stacked near the battlements.

Niesla's magical voice broke his focus, "I see you have been preparing as well."

Joskin spun around and saw both Carrita and Niesla standing there. Without thinking he gave them both a hug. He could feel a load lifting from his shoulders. "Where have you two been?"

Carrita smiled sheepishly, "My mother's laboratory. Although you are a very skilled warrior with superior armor and a powerful ax, this battle will require more. We have been working tirelessly to prepare for this confrontation."

Joskin looked over the army to the south. He knew Airria and Faith would have to fight their way through to enter the city. He had delayed this meeting in hopes Airria and Faith would be at his side, but there was no sign of their arrival.

He turned his attention to the north. His heart fell again. Keeping his eyes on the army he told the group, "I will need to meet whoever they send for negotiations."

Marren let out a long sigh, "Very likely you will be meeting the succubus appearing as a human."

Joskin's mind began swimming through all the tales he had heard through his life about the trickery of the devils. "I will do all I can, but I am afraid my pride has brought this city to failure."

"No!" Niesla protested.

"She is right," Marren said. "You're too important. You cannot go."

"I'm the only real option here," he said, feeling the weight of what he knew he had to do. "You three must hold the wall."

"We cannot hold it without your help," Niesla pleaded. "We need you on the inside."

"If I am successful, the army's strongest link will have been broken," Joskin replied.

All of them looked as though they were trying to refute his words, but none could.

605

Marren finally suggested, "Their leader will have an escort. It is only right that you should have one as well." Joskin began to protest, but Marren held up her hand to silence him. "Yes, I will go with you. I can make it back to the wall in time." She glanced over the army, "Yes I will go!"

Carrita chimed in, "We will also send three of the golems: the matrataur and two of the ship golems with swords.

Niesla added, "I will go with as well."

Joskin began to protest, but Marren silenced him again. She turned to Niesla and said, "If the worst happens to us, you and Carrita will have to command the efforts to save this city. You have the passion that will be needed."

Niesla looked from Joskin, to the army, to Marren and back to the army.

Joskin could feel a lump starting in his throat. He didn't want them to see him break down. For the first time he could remember he was going to fail to defend something he had committed to defend. He had fought many times believing he would not return, but had always believed his sacrifice would do the trick. This was the best chance they had, but it was a very small chance. Before now his life meant nothing to him, but at this point only his commitment to Niesla and protecting Carrita counted. He had to do his duty to them. He knew he would not make it out alive. He doubted if Marren would either. The golems would be a great loss. He knew what he had to do, but he didn't want to leave Niesla's side. In determination not to be seen with tear filled eyes, he turned, "I will ready my horse."

When he arrived at the stall his horse was ready in its barding. Persephone was also in her barding with Marren in the saddle. "Don't forget what I can do. If we can eliminate the devils, there may be a chance."

Joskin had to stare. Only Faith could ride her horse. Everyone who had tried to get near Persephone had been attacked. Since the teleport Persephone had been agitated. Now the horse was calm and Marren was on her. Finally he said, "Faith will be devastated if her horse is injured or killed."

606

Marren cracked a smile for the first time in days. "You know better than to try and stop this horse when she is determined."

Her words brought no comfort to him. He almost smiled as he looked at his armor. He remembered their trip across the ocean. His mind fell back to the orc smith. Then it passed through the mountains to the naga, to all their training and help. Then it went to the day they found Faith and Airria's armor and seeing the Guardian of Weapons, Salle'allak, in the cave atop the bitter mountains of the Arstock Range.

"There is more to this siege than just taking this city," the words escaped his lips without his thought.

"I believe you are correct. There's too much coordination, too many new alliances. Even Rantail could not coordinate this, too many conflicting interests. Only Jarmack'Trastibbik could bring together this army. She is operating outside the standards."

"Then I'll have to do the same." Joskin walked slowly over to his horse and ran a finger over the repaired armor. "What will they be expecting?" his hand slipped down to the hairless strips on the horse that only a few days ago were gashes.

Marren replied, "Likely an easy kill."

"Not if Jarmack'Trastibbik sent them," Joskin said with discouragement returning to his eyes. "If I can trust what I've learned from Airria, Carrita and every Guardian we have met, she knew this is the path we would take. She knew we would stop to help the siege. She sent these armies to stop us. She doesn't want the city. She wants me and Airria."

"What do you suppose she wants you for?" Marren said in a soft voice.

"From what I know of her she wants our souls," Joskin replied.

Marren responded, "If that's what she is after, she would've summoned you."

"Several of the Guardians have helped us along the way. I would guess the deities have some sort of watch a on us to prevent it."

"Time!" Marren exclaimed.

"What?" Joskin questioned.

"She will do what she can to slow you down. Destroying you and your cousin would give her all the time she needs."

"Then we can't allow them to delay us in the talks," Joskin said as he mounted his horse.

Marren agreed, "We'll have to start this battle as soon as we are within reach."

Together they quickly rode to the gate. As they approached it the people of the city lined the road. They all looked as if they were watching a funeral procession. Even with their speed, Joskin couldn't help but notice that everybody knew basically what was going on.

As the gate swung open they slowed the pace. The golems were already waiting next to the gate and fell in behind Joskin and Marren.

The enemy had brought out their palanquin. Today it was not guarded by orcs, it was guarded by what looked to be four well-dressed men and a guard in spiked black armor.

No other day had it been guarded by these. Joskin turned to Marren and whispered, "There will be no surprise attack."

Marren smiled charmingly at him, "When you get a chance, hit the palanquin. Do not enter it whatever you do."

Joskin responded with a nod and turned to face his doom. Side-by-side they walked their horses the rest of the way in silence with the golems behind them.

When they arrived at the wagon they were hailed by the man in long black robes. "You look as though you have come to fight, not to talk."

Joskin replied quickly, "Did you really expect me to come alone? All in your army are well known for their trickery. I only came prepared for traps."

The speaker promptly walked to the palanquin door, knocked once and said loud enough for Joskin hear, "My lady, they have finally come. Be warned they have come armed. What would you have me do?"

The door delicately opened, pushed by a gentle hand. Once open, a woman stepped out. She was wearing a long black satin dress with a slit on either side all the way up to her hip. She had a corset holding her dress tightly against her perfectly formed body. Joskin could not help but notice the movement of her cleavage as she breathed. Her face could not be more beautiful and was framed by long black hair which reached down to her knees. Joskin was completely mesmerized. Her voice was a bitter, yet welcome, song to his heart as she said, "Come now, there is no need for weapons. I have provided this place so that we could talk in peace. Let my guard hold your ax. You'll get it back when we are done."

Almost without thinking he dismounted and began to hand his ax to the black knight. *Niesla,* a voice said, almost as sweetly as the woman in black, except without the bitter feeling. Visions of his talks with Niesla came back to his mind. He remembered how her shiny, slightly curled hair would blow in the breeze. He withdrew his axe.

"Come now. We cannot talk peace with weapons of war between us." The woman in black's voice filled Joskin's mind with thoughts of pleasures he had yet to experience.

He was about to relinquish his ax when another thought entered his mind, the memory of the first day they arrived in town, he could even now feel the urgency and see Niesla's face. He withdrew his ax again. Visions of both Niesla and Carrita being killed, or worse captured and tortured, ran through his mind. A memory of Airria and the look on his face the day after he'd watched his father die flashed through his mind.

"You know you cannot win against my army, let us talk of your terms of surrender," the woman's voice once again almost erased any desire to resist.

He forced himself to remember Carrita's face the first time he saw her. He thought to himself, *That will be again, that will also be Niesla.* He looked the woman directly in the eye and yelled as he took two quick steps, "It won't happen!" His steps had brought the palanquin barely within striking distance of the long handle of his ax. His ax flew straight and true.

The woman moved with speed even Marren couldn't match, but missed stopping the ax by a fraction of a hair, her long black fingernails sparked as the ax handle slid by them. The wagon exploded in swirling flames of black and brown energy. The two men at the front of the palanquin almost instantly showed their true natures as vampires and then were incinerated by the blast. The two men in the back of the palanquin were blown several paces away and had transformed into their now bloodied demonic forms. The woman in black was blown only a few paces from where she was standing. She too had now assumed her full dark form; her dripping blood sizzled as it hit the ground.

She smiled a bloodthirsty smile, "I was going to let you be my slave. Now I will have to devour your soul and you will spend thousands of years being tormented by the very essence of me!"

Joskin took quick note that the blast had seemed to have completely missed him. He could feel the extreme magic in his ax; he could also see a bright violet light coming from it. He glanced back on a hunch, expecting to see pieces of stone and puddles of blood. The black knight was getting to his feet. Marren had backed the golems and the horses away in a pretense of peace and compliance. The knight had absorbed the energy that would have reached them.

Joskin felt the ax pull his arms to block a strike. He got his head turned in time to see the succubus' claws hit the weapon. As the creature touched his ax there was an explosion knocking her back several paces. Joskin knew he must strike now. The opposing army was bearing down on them and it would not take the succubus long to get to her feet.

Without noticing the other devils and with blood in his eyes, Joskin swung. The succubus was able to stand up and used her horn to block the blade. She reached for the handle with her rough claw.

Another explosion knocked her back to the ground. Her horn flew through the air out of sight. Joskin could hear a small battle behind him but did not want to take his eyes off the succubus. The glow in Joskin's ax was beginning to fade.

"Your power is beginning to wear thin," the devil's voice began to fill Joskin with an unbearable despair. "I will enjoy devouring your soul. Through my eyes you will get to see me tear your friends apart."

The words fueled the rage in Joskin's heart. He found himself wishing that he could place his rage into the ax. He stepped forward and swung again completely unaware of his surroundings. "No I won't!" he screamed. He only vaguely noticed a white glow intensifying around his weapon.

For the first time since their arrival the succubus had fear in her eyes. She desperately began to back away and brought her hands up to block the ax. Her efforts were to no avail, the heavy blade passed right through her stomach.

In the beginning the opening was small, but very quickly grew larger as souls began pouring out. Joskin could see gratitude on each soul's face as it left the devil. It seemed like he watched for days before the ground revealed a small crater, implying the souls were released in a violent explosion.

Joskin took quick note of what had happened on the rest of the field. It seemed that time had stopped when the ax struck the devil. In spite of the now charging army Joskin spun around to catch one of the incubus pouncing on him. He got his ax up in time to stop the huge jaws from clamping down on him. He could hear the hiss as the devil's blood dripped on his armor. The devil's teeth shattered on the handle and it threw the creature's head back hard. The small explosions didn't even seem to deter the devil. Joskin could feel the devil's claws digging through his armor. He could feel the venom from its touch burning in his veins. He could feel his arms growing limp as the devil's weight became unbearable.

As he was about to give up hope, Persephone smashed into the side of the beast, sending it tumbling away, but taking a vicious claw to the chest. His ax went flying away almost as far as Persephone's armor, but the horse jumped Joskin and stood between him and the incubus.

Joskin could see the large golem being chipped away at by the fighter in black. Marren was struggling to stay out of reach of the other incubus. His horse had been ripped in half. His limbs refused to move. He could only lay there helpless as the acidic drool burned into his shoulder.

The two golems with swords moved rapidly to Persephone's side. One of them barreled into the creature, the other grabbed Joskin and ran for the gate.

Pain overwhelmed Joskin. He could feel his mind going fuzzy. The dim light faded until everything went dark.

611

Chapter16 - Death Comes

Carrita was on the edge of tears as she watched Joskin and Marren lead the golems to the meeting. She had never feared for Joskin. He was always so sure of what he was doing. Now there was a complete lack of confidence in his eyes. Even Niesla's confidence and determination were gone.

Together the girls watched from the gate until it was closed. Then they both bolted to the top of the wall where they could watch what happened. When Joskin dismounted and began to hand his ax to a fighter in black armor with rigid bronze spikes at the shoulder Carrita panicked. Though the fighter was a head shorter than Joskin he stood confidently. She sent a small spell to him over the distance reminding him of Niesla.

He withdrew his offering, but began to hand it again.

Carrita prepared to send another spell, but noticed Niesla collapsed, leaning on the battlements. A strange type of astral energy was emanating from her soul. It was not magic as Carrita understood it. There was not a trace which Carrita could detect, but she could see a stream of thought and feeling flowing to Joskin.

When Marren stepped back, the golems followed suit. Persephone snorted and pawed at the ground.

Carrita could only watch breathlessly as Joskin drove his ax deep into the palanquin. The knight in black spun quickly, his shield blocking the tremendous release of magic, but he was knocked to the ground.

Persephone began darting around, weaving in and out of the incubi to stay out of their reach. The golems charged in. When an incubus was turned away from the horse towards a golem, Persephone would whirl and kick it, or Marren in her full demonic-vampire form, would swoop in and knock it to the ground.

When Joskin's ax landed a deep blow to the stomach of the succubus there was a sudden shift in astral energy, an explosion which did not seem to affect Joskin.

With the explosion Niesla jolted to her feet blinking, confused.

Carrita pointed her staff to use magic to help Joskin when the incubus landed on him, but Persephone charged it, knocking it to the ground before she could do anything. Persephone then positioned herself to guard him from the monster. The beast's claw drove through her chestplate and ripped it off; blood was spraying across the ground.

Both of the smaller golems darted to help. The corrosive blood from the devils now sprayed on the golems dissolving them quickly. One golem smashed into the incubus, the other grabbed Joskin from the ground and ran for the gate, while the third continued to fight.

Marren had focused her attention on the other devil. She was only barely able to keep out of reach. Through the air they spun. Finally Marren grabbed hold of the beast's wings and drove it into the ground.

Marren leapt off the beast and grabbed Joskin's ax. As fast as she could fly, she retreated for the wall. The devil darted into Persephone and ripped her in half.

The large golem was keeping the knight busy, but had lost several large chunks of itself to the dark blade. Its mighty ax, forged of pure darkness lay shattered on the ground. Nevertheless, the golem kept attacking.

The enemy army was almost to the battle when the incubi began chasing Marren toward the wall. Even with their gaping wounds they were much faster than Marren.

When Marren reached the wall she threw the ax and was grabbed by the succubi.

Carrita could hear Marren's voice in her head, *Are you ready?* Without waiting for an answer she said, *I will do what I can to slow the army.*

"Allan amis klairas!" Carrita yelled. For just a moment everything seemed to stand still, a beam of light streaked down to each of the three symbols in front of her. After a quick pulse of light, three glowing women in long white robes appeared. Carrita pointed to the devils and the oncoming army. As suddenly as time had stopped it began again.

The incubus let Marren go and tried to use their speed and size to force their way through the angels, but the angels together put up a magical barrier to keep the five supernatural beings separate from the rest of the battle. Their barrier made it so no one could see what was happening inside.

The golem carrying Joskin crumbled a few hundred paces from the gate. Marren, bleeding profusely with broken wings ran with only slightly more than human speed to grab him. She struggled but finally positioned him over her slender shoulders. Slowly she made her way to the gate.

Three soldiers met her halfway and carried Joskin the rest of the way to the gate. Marren took two swords from the soldiers and readied for a fight.

The enemy stopped its charge a few dozen paces in front of Marren. The enemy's front line was made entirely of skeletons in rusted armor. Marren tried to make a break for the wall but found her way blocked by three other vampires.

Marren's voice rang loud in Carrita's head, *Light! Don't worry about me! Destroy this army!* Without question and knowing she would regret her actions, she raised her staff in the air and created an intense ball of light. After so many days of such unnatural darkness even Carrita was blinded for a time. She could hear the crumbling of the skeletons and the hollow screams of the vampires and lichs.

When Carrita could see again she saw the black knight standing alone amidst piles of robes and bones. All of the dark bloods were cowering, but the commanders were already pulling out their whips. Carrita was now feeling weak from the magic drain. She could not stop this army. Commanders were barking out orders which sent the dark bloods charging the city again. They were carrying ladders and pushing catapults and siege towers.

The soldiers on the wall were careful with each arrow, every shot bringing down a foe. It became obvious the numbers were too great. The enemy's catapults began flinging balls of flame which seem to suck the mild light out of the air. The other mages did what they could to deflect the balls, but a few found their way through and started some houses on fire.

The black knight ran to the top of the siege tower and deflected arrows with his sword and shield. Before the tower touched the wall the knight leaped to the wall. His speed and skill reminded Carrita of Airria.

The tower crumbled on impact. Some of the dark bloods were riding ladders up and jumping before they touched the wall and crumbled.

Most of the wall forces concentrated on the knight who was too quickly disposing of them. A few of the orcs began to charge Carrita. She started to use magic to defend herself, but dared not to use too much. Niesla used a nice combination of magic and weaponry to knock them off the wall.

Soon her continued success gained the attention of the black knight who promptly cut his way through his own soldiers to get to her. Only a dozen paces before the knight reached Niesla a cry of pain came from the other side of the city. It looked like a lightning storm was taking place there, though the only sound was the bloody cries of dying orcs.

Without even trying to get past Niesla he turned his back on Carrita and ran across the city to the far wall, slaying anything which disturbed his path. Carrita followed though she was much slower. Because they went through the middle of town nobody stopped either of them. She watched the black knight slaughter his way to the gate door.

616

When the door burst open Carrita could see a clear path to Faith and Airria.

The knight let out a cry that made Carrita's blood run cold. She put the rest of her magic into a fireball to hit the knight in the back. She was only awake long enough to see the knight spin, absorb the magic and turn back around.

Chapter 17 – Reason

By the piles of bone and bodies on the road and the army of dark bloods pressing against the wall, Airria and Faith could tell the siege wasn't over yet. Large, two headed men-like creatures were pushing ladders with orcs to the top of the wall. Catapults were flinging groups of goblins in an attempt to get something over the wall.

Faith could not see any of the golems or Joskin on the wall. There was no sign of Carrita or Marren. "Do you think they are all right?" Faith asked.

Airria looked over the army of dark bloods. "The only way this siege would still be going is if they are." He stopped and smiled at Faith. "Should we see what trouble we can cause?" he said in a playful tone.

"Are you sure Jarmack'Trastibbik will not be impressed by the slaughter?" Faith questioned.

"We would be fighting the same army if we were on the inside of the wall," Airria said with a laugh. "The more damage we do here, the more lives will be saved in the long run." He paused to examine Faith's face, "Besides, it looks like the city could use the rest."

Faith was struggling inside, "If you truly believe it will help then we will need to make our way to the gate." She immediately began by shooting arrows as quickly as she could into the crowd of orcs, goblins and kobolds.

She did not care which arrow she used. Every once in a while she would pull her arrow in a direction which would almost hit her target, then curve its way back into her quiver. Mostly they hit with explosions of fire or ice sending small groups flying.

One of the two headed giants near the wall yelled something loud and rough. The battle stopped as all heads turned to face Airria and Faith. Weapons began pounding on shields. Finally a wave of orcs flooded toward them.

Airria stepped far enough away from Faith to give her room to work her sword dance. He raised his shield and started his own dance of death.

When they were within striking distance Faith's armor began shooting out bolts of energy at the orcs. Her blades found their mark on any who got past the devastation of her armor.

Side-by-side Airria and Faith cut their way towards the gate.

After a while the dark bloods realized they were fighting a losing battle and began to run to the nearby woods.

"You scared them off," Airria joked.

Faith was about to reply when she saw the gate door open and the fighter in black armor Airria had faced earlier in the week stepped out. "The Balance," Macron had called it. The armored figure let out a shriek which froze Faith to her core.

The knight spun around just in time to block a powerful fire bolt and turned back to face them. This person, with his armor, was Airria's equal.

Faith thought back to the last time these two had fought. Faith did not know what to do. If she and Airria were correct, her arrows would only energize this foe.

Airria stood his ground as The Balance rushed in. The fight quickly erupted into a sphere of pulsing black and white. The orcs and giants who had not yet run now ran in fear. The few orcs who had made it to the top of the wall were throwing themselves off in an attempt to run.

The flurry of the sparks and colored metal were throwing dust into the air. As they moved Faith did her best to stay out of the way. As the conflict approached vegetation on the side of the road it would shrivel and turn brown. The wounded on the road would shake and pass out when the fight came near.

Faith was so intrigued by the battle she didn't even notice the mild fluctuation in light as the sun set, nor did she notice the bright sunrise the next morning. The sun set again and still she watched. She could almost see two dragons locked in a flood of conflict.

The moon was high in the sky when she noticed the swinging swords slow. First she could see the blades as streaks, quickly they slowed to normal speed, finally both combatants collapsed unconscious on the ground. All Faith could do was stand there in amazement.

"Why are you standing there?" Niesla was standing over the body of the knight. "Should we dispose of this problem?"

"No," Faith replied softly. "There is a reason this warrior was sent. He's been looking for us. We need to know why."

"We know why!" Niesla said, far too bloodthirsty. "He has been sent to stop Airria from finishing his quest!"

"No," Faith's mind was swimming. She did not know how her voice was coming across to Niesla, but Niesla's voice seemed like a dream. She tried to put more emphasis in her words than had before. "This fighter has a special purpose. Greater than to simply distract Airria. This is not the first time they have fought. I am sure Airria is the primary target. One purpose of this warrior's trip is to slow us down, but I believe there is more to the conflict happening here." She turned her gaze to Niesla, "Use your bow to remove the dark sword from this fighter's hand." She remembered all of Carrita's warnings about dark weapons, "Do not touch the sword! Do not let any part of you touch anything on this knight!"

Faith did not even notice the shocked look on Niesla's face. "How do we take this armor off if we can't touch it?"

Faith pondered as she looked around. She was having a hard time focusing on anything except what she had recently witnessed. A few of the wounded orcs near the wall had been far enough from the fight to stay coherent, but were wounded badly enough to be unable to flee. "An orc should be able to do it. Yes. There are a few alive around here. We can compel them to remove it." Faith was lost in thought of what she had just witnessed.

It was finally starting to sink in, she was in a truly epic tale. She just stood in place staring at the two figures on the ground, both of them lying as if dead. She could see the destruction the small battle had caused. How much damage will a fight with the greatest of Black Dragons create? She thought back to the nights she had spent watching and admiring Airria's dedication. There was no way she could talk him out of his quest. She also realized how important it was to Jarmack'Trastibbik to stop, or at the least, slow Airria.

She was not sure if she wanted Airria to quit. *Maybe this responsibility could be taken by another. Why was Airria chosen for this quest?* she pondered. *All of this could not be an accident.* She knew much of her internal debate was based on her desire to keep Airria in her life, but she also knew in her heart that Airria was the only one that could do it. But from everything she knew of this dragon, it seemed as though even Airria might fail.

"You're in luck," Niesla's voice pulled Faith from her thoughts. "One of the wounded orcs says he will help in exchange for his freedom."

Faith looked up to see Niesla leading two soldiers hauling an orc, both of his legs were dragging behind him. The orc had several deep cuts on his arms and legs. To Niesla's obvious displeasure Faith approached the creature and began her healing spell.

First Faith used her magic to set the bone. She claimed all the pain for herself, as she felt numb it did not bother her much. Then she began healing the wounds and mending the bone.

When Faith was finished the orc stood proud in spite of his captivity. His eyes were filled with mistrust, but he stood in honor. He did not flinch as Faith ran her hand across his lower jaw.

"I have taken away your wounds," Faith could now hear her own voice as though she were standing outside her body. It was very calm and sweet. "I will return them with as much pain as I can if you do not help.

You know the rules of war. Right now you are nothing more than property, one of our spoils, if you will. How well you serve us will determine how you will be treated. You will receive kindness for kindness, pain for betrayal, but no death for your release." She was calm, believing her every word was correct to elicit the response she was looking for.

The orc's pride and confidence melted away.

Faith continued, "You can start now by removing this armor," she pointed at the black knight.

The orc's eyes danced nervously from Faith to the dark armor. "If legs break and crows eat eye of mine, still I not touch."

Without thinking Faith pulled and shot one of her marble tipped arrows at one of the orc bodies on the ground. The arrow seemed to melt into it as it turned to stone. The orc completely lost control of himself, a stream of fluid began running down his leg.

Faith said, keeping her voice soft, "So how will you spend your time for the next several years?"

The orc took a deep breath and slowly approached the fighter lying on the ground. He bent over and began undoing the buckles. Each time his hand touched it he winced in pain. Piece by piece he piled the armor on the road.

When the orc was finished Faith said, "You are free to go."

The orcs simply stood in amazement.

Faith looked him in the eye, "I give you your freedom."

The orc looked at her suspiciously.

"You can choose. You can live as a free person in this city or return to the slavery of your chieftain." Faith allowed only kindness to fill her voice, "Here you will have to earn your keep and the trust of others. There you'll have to do your chieftain's bidding," Faith left him with his thoughts.

She threw her cloak on the road and began using her sword to push the armor onto it. By the time she was finished the orc had already disappeared into the trees. She turned to Niesla who was standing there utterly confused. "Use your rope to bind this…" for the first time she noticed the figure who no longer had armor was not a man at all. "A

623

woman?" Faith heard herself say. She only stood in amazement as Niesla bound the woman. The part which had Faith's attention was this woman was absolutely identical to Tarmancia after a drastic haircut. If she hadn't seen this woman fighting Airria while Tarmancia was by her side she would have thought this to be her.

By this time a small crowd of guards had gathered. Many of them gasped when they saw the woman. Faith heard one man say, "It can't be!" Another added, "I knew she would betray us."

Without thinking Faith growled, "This woman is not Tarmancia!"

"I have known her since her father was made governor of Sarckran. This IS her!" one bold soldier said.

"This IS NOT her!" Faith screamed. Without thinking she placed her sword to the soldiers' throat.

"Your sword will prove nothing here," a deep, old voice growled from the back. A scarred humanoid covered in golden yellow fur, with a head of the brown and silvered maned lion stepped forward. "Whether she is or whether she is not Tarmancia, she will be treated with respect," the lion-man's voice made Faith want to duck her head. He commanded one of the soldiers to help him carry her to the prison.

Faith watched as the lion-man and the soldier carried the woman out of view. Then she ordered one of the soldiers to get a horse and to go get Sarckran's governor. "There is a reason for this," she said, more to herself than the lion-man.

Looking around the group for the first time, she noticed Niesla was alone. Neither Joskin nor Carrita was with her. She asked, "Where are the other two?"

"Carrita is resting in her own bed," Niesla answered. Her voice began to crack as she added, "Joskin is in bad shape."

Faith was torn, she knew she could not lift Airria and even with Niesla's help would have a hard time dragging him, but she also wanted to go check on Joskin.

After a moment the lion-man returned with a horse. "I would assume we are not to touch the armor," he said pointing to Faith's cloak.

"Yes," Faith said. She looked at the lion-man with a touch of suspicion. "Why are you so kind and how do you know so much?" Realizing her question was quite silly, she quickly tried to explain herself. "I mean, you quickly took charge and took her and…"

Faith was cut off by the commanding yet soothing voice, "You don't get to be my age in war without learning to think things through. I learned long ago that when a good person is adamant about something there is likely a valid reason."

Niesla introduced them, "This is Tesrik. He has been the captain of the guard since before Carrita was born."

Faith asked, "How do you know I'm a good person?"

The old lion-man shook his slightly silvered mane, "You know what you're doing with that weapon, but you did not kill the guard. If you are not as good as you are, your anger would have convinced you to take the guard's life." With a smile he added, "Your temper control is what you need to work on."

Faith blushed at the gentle chastisement, "I will work to control my emotions better in the future." Her thoughts returned to her friend lying on the ground, "Will you help us get both of these into the city gates?" she asked pointing to Airria and the cloak.

"I figured you might need some help," The lion-man's smile was strangely calming. "I would also guess you are concerned for your friend, but if this look-alike is as good as Black Dove, our prison will not hold her for long."

Faith looked at Tesrik and back to Niesla, "How do you know the name of Black Dove? Why do you associate her with our captive?"

Tesrik laughed, "She thinks she is so careful, but anyone who has seen her will know."

Faith had to admit the lion-man was correct. Tarmancia hid her alter ego poorly. Faith shrugged and turned to Niesla, "I do not know any spell to bind her so she will not escape."

Niesla turned to the lion-man. "Carrita is unconscious; she will be of no help for some time. What would you suggest we do?"

"If my Carrita has as much power as she seems to, I think this look-alike will wake up first," the lion-man suggested. He turned to Faith and said, "Either myself or you will need to keep an eye or her until the child wakes up." He easily loaded both burdens onto the horse and began leading it back into the city.

"Tesrik will take good care of everything," Niesla reassured Faith, pointing to the lion-man.

Faith hesitantly followed the horse and Niesla to the side of a well-kept yet small building. She watched as Tesrik opened a slanted door leading beneath the building. He took the dark-haired woman from the soldiers, threw her over his shoulder and disappeared into the cellar.

As Faith entered she realized this was a small prison. There were only two cages with bars reaching from floor to ceiling. There was a small bench against the wall. "What can we do?" she asked as Tesrik set the woman down.

Niesla just shrugged.

Tesrik closed and locked the cage, "Watch her while I go to help your friend."

After Tesrik left Faith pondered how she might prevent this woman's escape. "The bars are too close together for her to slip out. If we can break the lock she will be unable to pick it," she caught herself saying out loud. She turned to Niesla and asked, "Will breaking the lock accomplish our purpose?"

Niesla tapped her chin with her finger for some time. Finally she said, "It will only work if the cage were combined with the door to make it one solid piece."

Faith considered the various magical possibilities Carrita had taught her. She reached for whatever magic energy she could to help her. In her mind's eye she saw her magic peel strips of metal from the door and have it flow around the cage bars. She then did the same from the cage to the door. She kept her eyes closed long enough to see what it was supposed to look like.

When she opened them she noticed things did not go as she had planned. Absolutely nothing had happened to the doors, the cage or the lock, they were all intact. All she seemed to have done was make herself sick. Not as though her magic were depleted, but it was as if something

626

had happened to her by some uncontrolled magic. She looked to Niesla to see if she could tell what had happened.

Niesla's skin was a snow white color and she was crouching in a corner. Faith quickly examined herself, her skin was still the same color. When she turned to see if the cage had been affected, she noticed something dark in her peripheral vision. She spun completely around, prepared for something to be there. When she realized it was her hair she first raised a sigh of relief, then began to feel a touch of panic set in when she realized she had changed her own hair color. It was now raven black.

"Funny what magic can do isn't it!" the woman in the cell laughed.

Faith had not realized how much surprise and horror was on her face. "What do you know?" she snapped at the woman in prison.

"I know more than you would believe," the woman said mocking Faith.

"Obviously not enough to keep you out of this cage," Faith snapped back.

"Do you really think this cage will hold me for long?" The stranger teased back. "You really are foolish if you think such an ill crafted cage could hold me."

"Yes, actually I do!" Faith blurted out as confidently as she could.

The woman in the cage closed her eyes and seemed to be concentrating. Faith was beginning to worry until the woman in the cage began to strain. "That was not your magic that went awry." The woman almost looked scared, she was trying to hide it, but it was still obvious, "It is of no consequence. I will be out of here soon enough."

Faith could only think of one thing which could arouse such fear in this hardened fighter: the Dragon Council. Faith knew she did not have such command of magic. She did not know where she had got the magic, but she was sure it could not have come from dragons.

"I recognized your armor!" Carrita's voice was a welcome sound. "You are the extension, the mouth, the one who keeps Jarmack'Trastibbik's minions in line. You are the one who guarded the

627

mage who sold me into the slaver's hands. You are the one who sat and laughed the first time…"

Faith noticed Carrita's eyes had gone dark and hollow. They seemed to drain the light out of the room. In an attempt to change Carrita's train of thought she asked, "What are you doing up already?"

"You tapped into deep and hidden magic while you were fighting!" Carrita was addressing the woman in the cage. It seemed Carrita had heard the question from the stranger. "You shall pay as few have ever paid before!" Flames as black as Carrita's eyes, began to dance between her outstretched hands.

"Is this hidden magic so dark!!?" Faith shouted. She did not want to see her friend give in to torture. "Airria was there, too." She took a deep breath to calm her voice, "It could not be so dark." She very badly wanted to ask the stranger some questions. It also bothered Faith to see the woman become so excited to pay such a price.

The flame danced between Carrita's hands but they ceased to grow.

"Would you like to know what your mother looked like when I last saw her?" the woman in the cage taunted.

Faith gently placed her hand on Carrita's shoulder, "She wants you to try to torture and kill her." She was careful to make sure her voice carried none of the fear she felt her heart. "There are many fates worse than death. For this woman life is one of those. Her power is gone and her mother is soon to come to see what she has become." Faith could only guess the governor of Sarckran was this woman's mother.

Faith turned to the woman, "What would your mother say if she could see you now?"

The blackness and the flames began to give way to a brilliant white light. The black in Carrita's eyes began to swirl with brown, then white, until the blackness was gone. A single flame licked out and seemed to tickle the bars in the middle of the cage.

The woman in the cage began to scream as if her soul was being ripped apart. She threw herself against the wall and then the door of the cell. Then she tried to rip open her bare wrists with her own hands, only to watch the gouges in her skin heal behind her fingernails.

Faith was filled with terror, she couldn't imagine what horrible thing Carrita was doing to this woman. She wanted to interfere, but was afraid of what would happen if she did. She looked to Niesla for some direction of what to do, but Niesla merely looked confused. After only a few moments the sound of the screaming stopped. All of the sound from the cell ceased. Then the flames disappeared, drawn back into the fire between Carrita's hands. The flames seemed to dissipate as her eyes returned to normal. In a weakened state she said, "Here you shall stay unharmed and unheard until the day when love and mercy burn within you," then she collapsed on the floor.

She looked up to Faith, "I really have to stop doing this." She gave a weak smile and lay on the cold stone floor.

"Serenity?" Niesla questioned. After a moment she smiled and stated, "Peace is the worst torture for her. Her soul has become accustomed to pain. Now peace is the pain that will break the darkness within."

Faith did not really understand what Niesla was talking about and decided she would need time to understand. She gathered Carrita in her arms and asked, "Will you help me get her to bed?" She wanted to know what was happening and wanted to hear it from Carrita. "As fast as she woke up last time, it should not take long until she is awake again. Whatever this deep and hidden magic is, it seemed to bring her life force back very quickly."

Chapter 18 - A Voice from the Past

After putting Carrita to bed she asked Tesrik to watch her and went to look in on Airria. He was not sleeping the peaceful rest that depletion of his magic normally gave him. He was tossing and turning as he did when they first met. She was not sure whether it was something she had done or if it was a backlash from his fight. She did not like seeing him this way but did not know what to do.

Niesla's voice was a welcome distraction. "Come quickly," she said in an urgent tone.

Faith got up to see what was going on outside. People were sprinting from house to house. The guards were running across the wall. Not as if they were panicked, but as if they had too much energy. Now faith could see what Carrita had been talking about. There was magic in the breeze. The magic belonged to no element yet tasted of them all. It filled her mind with both peace and despair. It seemed wild and free, yet it had purpose with order.

"Carrita will understand this," Niesla said.

"I hope so," Faith replied. She could not help but wonder if she had contributed to this mess. She noticed that the walls somehow seemed new and strong. The government buildings seem to glow with energy. Looking at the town Faith could almost see its history. There it was in front of her, as if magic had pulled her through the stretches of time. It was a city ruled by a kindly woman, the Fairen, as they called her. She had two children by her side, one an elf, the other a dwarf. She was the woman Faith had seen in the shrines so long ago. She looked at them as if they were her own.

Faith could see something in this woman she had not seen before. The look of pride and excitement was eerily familiar. It was something in the woman's eyes.

Faith began to scan the town. Many dwarves were carefully constructing the wall. Her eyes were drawn to the way the dwarves were crafting each stone. They reminded her of the orc when he was crafting her sword. There was a definite love of their work, but also a love for who they were crafting for. They would look at the Fairen and smile. Her smile back seemed to be worth more than all the gold in the world to them.

Faith watched them for what seemed like months. She watched the sun come up and go down. She watched the dwarves as they squared each stone for a specific place and then hollow out two holes the size of her arm.

Every morning the Fairen would come out with several elves and buckets of crystals, crystals of all colors and shapes. She would take each crystal and melt it into the rocks, crafting a definite pattern. When the art was finished she would force the design deep into the rock so it could not be seen.

Elves were in the forge crafting long silver rods which were exactly the width of the holes the dwarves had made in the stones. These elves were every bit as careful and caring in their craftsmanship as the dwarves. When they had completed a rod it was set carefully in a stack.

Early on she could see the town was not on a mountain ridge but in fact it was a part of the planes. The humans, both male and female, both old and young, would go out to work in the fields and each night would bring home plenty of crops to put in the storage towers.

Faith stood and watched as the wall was built, stone by stone, until it was almost as high as the wall she remembered. Then the Elven mages would levitate the rods to the top and send them straight down through the holes until there was only a foot length on top. When the mages were finished the dwarves placed stones on top. From this point on the elves and dwarves worked closely together to make an equally sturdy structure on top.

Faith had lost track of the number of days which had passed watching this routine. They would smile when the Fairen or one of her counselors would come out to praise one of the craftsman for a job well done or a miner for large load of silver ore. She did not feel heat, hunger or thirst, she did not feel tired or anything else. No one seemed to notice her at all.

When the wall was finished and the final crop had been brought in, the Fairen called the town together. She told them, "Together we have worked to build this town. Together we shall enjoy peace within. After this night shall no dragon threaten us nor take anything from us. No giant or troll shall disturb our slumber. So long as free people are willing to defend these walls no tyrant will govern our town halls." After a short cheer she called out as Carrita had done on the ship. Faith could see the magic being pulled from each of the townsfolk. It was gathered around the Fairen then funneled through her staff.

Faith could see the crystal inside the stone light up as the magic was poured in. She could see the Fairen writing symbols of pure magic on the silver rods as if the stones were not there. She saw the magic carve symbols into the huge gates. She watched in amazement as the crystal filtered up through the earth, fused together into an enormous plate, reaching from one side of town to the other. She watched the plate sink back deep into the earth. Then the magic was placed within as well.

"I wish I could have brought my daughter to see this," the Fairen's voice surprised Faith from behind. The woman was standing near her, but was very translucent.

Faith looked at the woman leading the ritual then back to the one behind her.

"It was my crowning accomplishment!" the Fairen's eyes glistened with pride, but there was a touch of sorrow. "It was my greatest creation until her."

Faith could hardly breathe, "You are Carrita's mother?"

The Fairen smiled, "She is mine."

Faith was only slightly listening to the woman. "How are you here?" was all the thought she could force past her lips.

The woman put a finger to her lips and whispered, "Watch." Faith could not help herself, she turned back to watch the rest of the ritual. It seemed the woman took just a piece of her soul and placed it into the crystal plate and imbued it with the rest of her magic. She was the last of the entire town to pass up.

"I know the rest of my soul is out there!" the voice from behind said, pulling Faith's attention back. "This city is vulnerable until the rest of my soul is here to help protect it."

"Why?" was all Faith could mutter.

"When I lived to govern this town my soul was complete and therefore made the magic complete. With magic this powerful a soul must govern it. Only when I am returned will this city be able to withstand the trials which lie ahead." The Fairen smiled and said quietly, "You have seen the struggles to keep the city in my absence. Now see how it stands when I am here."

Faith turned back, knowing it was many years later and they were now on the wall. The town was surrounded by hordes of each type of dragon. A forest of Black Wood with leaves of black flame had crept up to the edge. It seemed there were twice as many Black Dragons as there were all the other dragons combined. They were facing each other in some sort of battle.

The Fairen, which Faith now recognized as Carrita's mother, Tarsella, said softly, "This town is at the corner of life and death. All the other elements have combined together to bring this wave of death to its completion."

"Why are there so many more Black Dragons?" Faith asked.

Long before the others, the Black Dragons realized their potential as a power of pure destruction. They also are the inventors of murder and seduction. They swelled their ranks to drive all life from this world, but on this day everything changed," Tarsella said proudly.

The walls were lined with archers and fighters. The dragons had trampled the fertile plane and it was bare as far as the eye could see.

Faith could make out the forest and the scorch marks covering the ground.

Armies of such power were not meant to fight on this world, she thought to herself.

Two dragons in particular caught her eye, the largest each of the White and Black Dragons. They were locked in an unending battle of speed of ferocity. The speed of claw, tooth and tail appeared to be an almost exact exaggeration of what they had witnessed earlier between the Airria and the strange woman.

"These two will fight like this many times in years to come," Tarsella said almost laughing. "They are perfectly matched and none of the others dare interfere. These two will in times to come lead the Dragon Council."

Faith turned to face the woman. She could not believe her ears.

"Yes, the black one is the one you are questing for," Tarsella said calmly.

"But she is so big! How..." Faith said. Somehow she had imagined the dragon more manageable.

"She is much larger now, nearly three times the size." The woman put her hand up to silence faith, "Watch."

As the battle continued Faith could see energy from the wall strengthening all of the dragons which fought in defense of life and every time a Black Dragon would get within a thousand paces it would explode.

"How?" Faith could not imagine such power.

"I tapped into the magic of an unborn child. A child who I carried for more than 50,000 years," Tarsella said, her eyes filled with tears. "I was pregnant with Carrita when we made these walls. The great White Dragon which you saw fighting earlier blessed my child for this purpose. She magically imbued her own blood into my unborn child and along with it much of her magic."

"Why did you have to carry her for so long?" Faith asked.

"Watch," came the reply.

As the battle raged the walls protected the city from the fight. With the strength the walls gave to the dragons fighting for life and the destruction they gave to the dragons fighting for death, the numbers began to even out. Soon the Black Dragons retreated back into the forest. Before the largest one disappeared she turned and shouted a curse which Faith did not understand.

"Her curse was not blocked by any around. It was meant to force me to carry my child for eternity, never to hold her." A hint of pure pride crept back in, "It only took me fifty thousand years to find a way around that curse. When Jarmack'Trastibbik learned how clever I had been she summoned the child and trapped her soul. I went to save her but never returned."

The remaining dragons began magically burying their dead, raising a huge mound to cover them. "They chose to conceal their dead in this mountain range. They made this town's foundation out of the dead bodies of several of the Black Dragons. They allowed me to keep a few shards of bone. Those arrows in your quiver are made from some of those shards." She then asked Faith to follow her and seemed to be walking through time and space as well. Faith watched as the Fairen opened a secret wall in a servant's quarters. Behind the thin stone slab there was an arrow, the shaft was of dragon bone. The simple tip was a dragon claw. Even the fletching were made of shavings of dragon scale.

"This arrow is the only one of its kind in existence. It is invisible to dragons; it also cannot be affected by magic. It can only be used by a dragon child, a descendent of one whose blood has been mixed with the dragons, one like you."

"I…" Faith tried to protest.

"You will soon understand," Tarsella held up a hand.

"But…"

"This is why you could tap into the magic. Your heritage is your strength."

"I…" Faith finally had a chance to protest and didn't know what she was protesting. After a moment of not finding anything to say she stumbled back to her question of so long ago, "What did we tap into?"

"Dragons are created of pure magic. You have tapped into the dragons buried in this mountain ridge. When the black and white knights fought they unleashed pent-up energy from the buried corpses."

636

Faith was still very confused, fortunately Tarsella continued, "When the dragons used their deceased kin as a foundation for this ridgeline they did not want their influence to alter the town so they took their hearts along with the dragons' soul gems. You see, a dragon's soul is kept within the dragon by the gems in its heart. Without a heart a dragon is the pure essence of magic."

On these words everything faded and Faith was watching the bustle she had been watching before she had left. She ran back in and removed Airria's armor so he could recharge his manna and wake up from his sleep.

She then ran to Carrita who was starting to wake up already. "It needs to be contained!" Faith exclaimed. Without waiting for a response she grabbed Carrita's hand and in her mind begged Tarsella to help guide them to contain the magic.

Carrita began chanting in the same tongue her mother had in creating the walls. The energy began to suck back into the ground.

Faith could feel the change. The magic was returning. Relief washed over her as the sickness began to fade.

After some time Carrita stopped chanting and looked up. She had tears in her eyes, "She helped me! She knew what to do. She always knows the truth."

Chapter 19 Dreams and Destinations.

The wind blew hot on Airria's face. The ground was covered in ash up to his knees. The trees looked as if a fire had raged through this place, except the trees still had their leaves. The leaves danced and beckoned to him like the flames of fire that had summoned that hideous dragon the night his father's soul had been ripped from its body. They seem more like black flames than leaves.

He looked around, he was alone except for a strangely familiar woman and a hideous Black Dragon. The woman spoke with an unfamiliar voice but with familiar emotion and command, "This will be our world if she succeeds." This was the woman from the dragon's crystal. This was the woman who stood so proud, the Fairen he had read about in the shrines. It was all he could do to turn his eyes from her.

He could see the Black Dragon clawing and casting spells at a wall of magic and stone. The dragon was unrelenting. He watched as her servants would pass through with ease, as she commanded them. She, herself, could not pass.

She kept clawing and casting spells trying to destroy the stones in the wall. He watched as the dragon ran through all of its magic until it would pass out. When she would wake up she would begin again.

Airria felt secure from the creature and only slightly nervous about her servants. Any of the creatures powerful enough to hurt him were locked outside of the wall.

After many months one of the stones in the wall cracked. Airria began to feel less secure. The dragon pulled the stone out of the wall and started on the next one. "Will she succeed?" he heard himself ask out loud.

The woman beside him had been silent after her introductory words. She now replied, "She will, if she is not stopped."

The gentle sternness in her voice told Airria that this was a good and important woman. "Why do the Dragon Council warlords not interfere?" he asked.

"They are bound by laws beyond this world. They can only directly interfere in their sphere," the woman's voice was calm, but there was panic in her eyes.

"Will she not destroy the sanctity and protection of this place?" Airria was showing his irritation. "Is not this the reason for the Dragon and Deific Councils? Is she not interfering outside of her sphere? Is..."

The woman cut him off, "No," she said softly. Even with her gentle tone her voice drove deep into his soul. "Their job is to teach and keep the elements in adequate balance. Death is a part of life. It is the completion of all living things. Therefore the death of all living things is well within this dragon's sphere."

"Can't the others in the Council do something, reset the stones or something?" Airria asked in desperation.

"They have done something," the woman said. "They have called on you to do what they are not allowed to do themselves."

"Why me?" he asked. "What am I that I should be called for such a task?"

"Why you, you ask?" The woman was almost smiling. "You ask the question and you hold the answer." She waved her hand and the dragon was gone and the wall was replaced by the home he was raised in. He could see himself as an eight-year-old child. His hair golden blonde with tiny streaks of bronze and red was blowing in the breeze. He and Joskin were standing side-by-side fighting several men to keep them away from their mothers. Airria remembered those days, his father was so proud of how fast he learned to use a sword. Though he was smaller, he was faster and stronger than any of the boys his age. He was faster and stronger than all of the men in town.

"Do you count this as normal?" the woman asked as if she knew Airria would not answer.

With another wave of her hand she brought him to his first battle alone. He was sixteen and his blade was already fast enough to keep three thugs' weapons at bay and allow him some blows of his own. In watching the scene his heart was filled with pride.

"You were so young and they were so much bigger than you," the woman continued.

Another wave of her hand and Airria was brought to the day he first saw Faith. It was the early hours of the morning when he was working to pick the door lock. He laughed at himself as he struggled to open it.

When the lock popped open the woman said, "A master thief would have had a harder time with that lock than you had."

Before the door of the wagon was open she waved her hand and he was brought to Jammar's place, to his training. He watched how clumsy and awkward he was then.

"It makes a large difference when you are trained by a Guardian," she said. "Do you believe it was an accident that you found Jammar?" She didn't wait for an answer, "Guardians won't train just anyone."

"What?" Airria said. He was starting to grow tired of what he felt were games. "Why me! Why does it have to be me! I don't want this task anymore," his voice trailed off in thought.

"I will show you why you were chosen," she waved her hand again.

Airria was now at a time he did not recognize, a time where dragons walked and talked with humans. He was in the street of a small village. A beautiful woman with long hair of gold and lightly golden skin came out of one of the huts talking to a much more mortal looking man.

641

She stopped in a panic and looked up. Without thinking Airria looked to see what had alarmed her. At the end of the street there was a woman badly beaten with torn clothes and a shattered look. The golden haired woman rushed to her aid. She picked up the woman gently, yet with ease, and carried her back to the hut. Airria followed her in. He saw the woman grab what looked to be a golden crystal and a bronze one off of the shelf. She smashed them together creating a magic stream into the wounds of the beaten woman who had been placed on the table.

"Bloodletting," his guide said, "that is dragon's blood she is infusing into the woman. It only works if opposing elements are used, in this case order and chaos."

Airria only halfway heard what the woman said, he was in pain. He could feel the burn of the magic blood flowing through him. He could feel the burn in the woman as her wounds were healed.

"Why was this woman chosen?" Airria winced.

The Fairen looked deep into Airria's eyes, "The reason she was chosen you will not know. Only know she passed this gift to you."

He asked, "Why did my father not have this GIFT?"

The woman smiled, "It is normally passed from woman to woman. Because I knew you would be your mother's only child I cast a spell to allow this gift to pass to you."

Airria could hardly breathe. He was seeing things he couldn't believe and hearing thing he couldn't refute. "You knew my mother."

The woman waved her hand, "Two rare orphaned sisters wandered into my home. I recognized them by their power. I sent them to Ramsal Island to be safe. Before they left I saw a glimpse of what could happen to them so I blessed them."

Airria could see the two girls. Even at their young age he recognized them as his mother and aunt. Their families had been killed and they had taken refuge in Derain. A very pregnant Fairen took them in. She assigned a kindly couple to take the children to the island Airria had been raised on. He watched them grow in Gentrail until they were in their mid-teens. They were kidnapped by a cruel man and forced into slavery. They were rescued by Joskin's father who claimed them and shared them with his little brother.

The Fairen smiled at him, "They raised you well. With all the pain they were put through they would not trade a moment of it if it meant you would be taken from them. They have had the chance to help dozens of children because you and Joskin have grown so well."

She waved her hand again, "I also knew I would need your help to free my daughter." Airria could see himself walking into a hut. A bruised and bleeding young woman was tied to a pole in torn clothes.

"I may have helped her get out of that hut, but she was the one who saved me. It was seeing her that helped me change so Faith could see any good in me."

"Would you like to see what brought her to this point? Would you care to see why Jarmack'Trastibbik has grown so bold?"

Airria numbly nodded his head.

He was drawn back to the wall. Jarmack'Trastibbik was sitting, caressing her crystal. Inside it Airria could see Carrita holding the hands of two women, two of the women Airria remembered standing by him when he dreamed about the crystal. His guide walked out of the wall and offered herself in exchange. The dragon agreed. Carrita was pulled out and his guide had her soul ripped from her body and placed in the crystal.

I was the one being with both the power and will to keep Jarmack'Trastibbik in check. I am not a Guardian. I am not bound by their rules. I can repair the wall, but I have to be freed.

Airria really didn't want this now. He only wanted to be with Faith, to spend the remainder of his existence with her. "Why did I have to be chosen?" he asked.

The woman got a concerned look on her face, "What you do with your life is your choice. Do realize your choice will affect many." Another wave of her hand and Airria was at a different time but still near the wall in the Black Forest. He saw the crystal Jarmack'Trastibbik carried. He looked deep inside. He could see his guide, his father, Carrita, Joskin, Niesla and even himself and Faith.

"Your choice is your own," he heard again and was left staring at the tortured souls.

Chapter 20 - Moving On

Airria awoke feeling tired, but more than that he felt weary. He hadn't found any peace in the things he'd seen and tried to excuse it all as a bad dream.

He found himself searching for Faith, looking for comfort in her eyes and arms. He jumped out of bed and ran for the door.

In the street he saw a dark-haired woman in memorable ornate white and gold armor comforting Carrita, with the white-skinned elf standing behind them. Somehow he knew something had happened. The dark-haired woman stroking Carrita's head had to be Faith. He had watched her too many times at night. He knew her by her every movement. The elf he guessed was Niesla.

He slowly approached the girls, Niesla was only ten paces away from them. "Something happened... I don't know what," She looked at Airria, "I don't think I want to know."

Airria looked around. The streets were empty except for the group. "Both you and Faith have changed appearance. Persephone, Joskin and Marren are nowhere to be seen and Carrita is crying. I would say a lot has happened."

Niesla scowled, "Both Marren and Persephone are gone. You'll not see them again."

Airria took a step forward, "Is that why Carrita is crying? And Persephone is dead? How?"

"She insisted on being a part of the battle. Marren rode her to the meeting."

"What meeting?"

"The one Joskin arranged."

"I am so confused."

Niesla closed her eyes and shook her head, "When we arrived the city was under siege. Three devils were leading the army to the north."

"Three devils would explain the reason Zerith was so determined to conquer, even when everything seemed to be going against them."

"Joskin arranged a meeting with them in hopes you and Faith would have time to arrive."

"If we hadn't stopped to help, we would have been here in time. We would have been able to stop this!" Airria chided himself.

"Persephone insisted on being at the meeting, as did Marren. Joskin slew the succubus, but was wounded by an incubus. Persephone saved him, but it cost her her life."

Faith slowly lifted her head and looked back to Niesla. "She was a fighter and loyal friend. I will miss her greatly."

Airria found it odd that her eyes were dry. He knew Faith loved her horse.

Niesla continued, "Marren was also wounded severely. She retrieved Joskin's ax and stopped the charging line giving us time to get Joskin inside the walls."

Carrita's sobs had changed. They were slower with a slight gurgle. "I killed Marren. It was what she wanted. I attempted to conceive of a way to destroy the army of undead without hurting her, but I could not shield her."

Airria was trying to find someone to blame other than himself. "Why didn't he wait for us?"

Niesla's voice was shaky, "Joskin waited as long as he could. We weren't sure you were even coming. Even Carrita had no idea why you weren't with us when we arrived."

Airria was filled with a sudden need to see his cousin, "Is Joskin dead, too? I haven't seen him."

Niesla looked down at the street, "No, but he is very hurt."

He could feel his stomach churning. He couldn't believe Joskin was hurt, but he was almost afraid to ask. He had never seen Joskin seriously hurt, at least not in a way Niesla couldn't heal him. "If he's hurt, why haven't you healed him?"

Niesla shifted her gaze to watch the two sitting in the street. "I don't know how. I was hoping either Faith or Carrita would know."

If Niesla didn't know how to fix whatever wound Joskin had suffered the situation was dire indeed. "Where is Joskin?"

Niesla looked up, a tear in her eye, "He is at the high shrine keeper's house." She began to walk away from the two in the street. "I will take you to see him."

"He has more strength than you know," Airria said comfortingly.

Together they passed quickly through the streets. The only house with the candles lit was the shrine keeper's house. The shrine keeper quickly ushered them to the bed where Joskin lay in furs soaked in his own sweat. He was shaking and pale. The priest's wife was mopping the sweat from his face as fast as she could.

For the first time since their childhood Airria was afraid for Joskin.

The priest was digging through old scrolls, sweat pouring down his face and a look of fear in his eyes. Piles of books, parchment and scrolls were covering the ground.

Niesla was the one to ask, "Will he be all right?"

Airria did not wait for the shrine keeper to answer, "Yes, he will be fine!" he yelled and stormed out to get Carrita.

To his surprise she was standing in the doorway, Faith was close behind her. She said without question, "Yes, he will be fine." Her gentle words brought comfort to Airria but not Niesla.

647

The keeper bowed deep, "I have searched all my materials. I have found nothing to help this man. His wounds were made by a devil and I fear no mortal can heal him. Perhaps you can summon an angel?"

Carrita let her hands hover over Joskin, passing up and down his body. Airria supposed she was analyzing the situation. There was something very familiar about the way she waved. It was not that he had seen her make the same motion a thousand times. He had, but the familiarity was something more.

I know of no mortal who can heal this grievous wound. Fortunately for him I am no mortal. I have been educated by two Guardians and have been granted immortality. I will start his healing and teach you what you will need to do to continue his recovery. I am not the same child whom you knew when I lived here.

After a moment it hit Airria. Her motions and tone of command were just like his guide. He realized what he saw while he slept was not a dream, but a communication from Carrita's mother. Somehow she had found a way to speak to him.

"I thought she was trapped, how did she show me all that?" he heard himself say out loud.

Faith's sweet voice broke his concentration, "She placed a piece of her soul in this city when she made the walls." She reached up and gently ran her fingers down his face, "You saw her too?"

Airria was torn by the touch. He wanted to feel the touch forever, but he knew he must go or he may never feel it again.

Faith continued as if she could read his thoughts, "Yes, we must go. There is no time to delay." She glanced over to Carrita.

Carrita responded without looking up, "Before you are ready to depart I will be finished instructing Garza in what he must do. It is time we finish this quest and bring my mother home!"

"There is no one to govern this town now, nor Sulitamis. We will need to fill those voids. I will stay to see what I can do," Niesla volunteered.

Airria looked at Carrita, "We won't be long."

Niesla gave Faith a hug, "I am sorry your horse died saving Joskin."

"Shall we prepare Joskin's horse?" Airria asked. A quick glance from Niesla told him that the horse was also dead. He had to ask, "The barding?"

Niesla actually spoke again, "Devil's don't leave much intact when they destroy something."

Faith smiled sadly, "It would appear we will be making the remainder of this journey on foot. Any animals remaining in this city will be needed to help rebuild the fields and repair the mines."

Airria ducked his head in mourning as he left. "I will do what I can. We won't need much."

Faith put a comforting hand on his shoulder as they walked to get his armor. Together they walked in silence until they were at the government buildings.

Faith stopped outside a large white house with gold vinework so real it seemed to be crawling out of the ground. Faith said, "There is something I must grab." She darted into the house and disappeared around a corner.

Airria went to the room he had awakened in. His armor was set neatly next to the wall. He picked up his chest piece and looked it over. He wondered if his being here would have saved Marren. If there was something he could have done to make the trip quicker so his cousin wouldn't have had to face those devils without him.

He threw the breastplate on the bed and sat down hard. It didn't matter what scenario he came up with in his head, both he and Faith had to ignore Sarckran or arrive to Derain too late to help. There was no middle ground. Neither he nor Faith would have given up the part they played in Sarckran.

He began donning his armor as he thought about the good they did, or more, the good Faith had done while in the town.

As he buckled his last strap Faith came through the door. She had a staff in one hand and an arrow in the other. The entire staff was made of violet crystal, but it appeared sculpted with vines. The closer Airria looked at it the more detail he could see. The arrow had white staff and fletching of multiple colors including black and white.

Faith placed the arrow in her quiver and tried to smile at Airria.

Airria ducked his head as he said, "I expected you would take the loss of your horse much harder. Are you all right?"

Faith looked out the nearby window. "I have been sold as property. I lost my parents and my brother. I left my sister with Jammar. I have cried too many tears. We have a job to do and I am not yet broken. All we have faced up to this time has brought me a new family. Persephone was a part of my new kindred, but I will not sit and weep for her until we are finished." She looked at Airria, "Then I will weep for all I have lost and rejoice in all I have gained." Her eyes sparkled brightly. "I will see my sister again and Persephone knew our task better than even Carrita. I will weep when we are finished."

Airria smiled at her determination. He felt a little uncomfortable that she was so resolute and he was losing focus. He glanced at the staff and asked, "Memorabilia or help?" He was trying to lighten the mood somewhat.

Airria marveled at himself. When he started out this quest he was different. Now he still wanted to see his father's soul freed. He still wanted more than ever to help Carrita free her mother's soul. The thing that amazed him was that his primary concern was to protect those around him. "Women," he said out loud. He knew in his heart the change was inspired by Faith. Her tenderness and beauty had torn the bitterness and anger out of his heart. She had filled his spirit with compassion and hope. Now he realized that it was seeing Carrita hurting for the first time that had opened the door to let Faith in.

Faith's voice pulled him out of his thoughts. "What did I do this time," she said playfully. She had her arrows. She had her bow in her left hand and the new staff in the other.

"Where did you get that?" he asked pointing to the staff.

Faith held it out for Airria to admire, "I believe this staff is a gift for Carrita from her mother."

"Apparently we saw different things," Airria said with a smile.

"Apparently. But we both got the same message," Faith said with a wink.

Airria said, starting to walk to the door, "Doesn't Carrita have enough staves?"

Faith cradled the staff and began walking. "I have a feeling she will leave the others behind for this one. After all, her mother made it and stored it for this occasion."

Together Airria and Faith walked back to the shrine keeper's house to say their farewells to Niesla and Joskin. As they walked, the streets felt so lonely, but filled with hope.

Carrita met them at the door, "Joskin will be all right. The poison from the demon made it deep into his blood, but he has a strength few others carry."

Airria smiled as he thought back to his vision. "Bloodletting," he said out loud.

"What?" Carrita stepped back, "Such a ritual would explain his strength, but how would you know about it?"

Faith and Airria looked at each other for a moment. Thankfully Faith spoke, Airria wasn't sure how much he wanted anyone to know about what he'd seen.

"I am glad he will recover," Faith said. "It is a great relief. We will have no worries while we travel," Faith's smile was unsure.

Carrita looked at Faith standing, holding the violet staff. Her eyes filled with tears again. "Where did you find this staff? After I returned, before I went to live with Marren, I looked everywhere I could think of to find it," she said, as she took it from Faith's hand.

"Your mother wanted you to have it," Faith responded.

Airria stood behind Faith admiring the child-like wonder as Carrita cuddled the srtaff as if it were her favorite doll. She held it in her arm and rocked it back and forth. With her other hand she ran her finger down the designs.

After a few moments he noticed Faith watching him. He blushed and said, "Well, we should be going." His voice was falsely deep and truly embarrassed.

Airria pushed past Faith and Carrita and went in to see his cousin. He was sleeping peacefully. Niesla was lying in a nearby chair with her head resting on Joskin's bandaged chest.

"They both need their rest." It was a relief to hear the gentle words from the shrine keeper's wife. "If what Carrita says is correct, he will sleep for some time.

Airria thought how maybe, if he had been quicker, he could have prevented this. Then he remembered the dragon bent on destroying all life. He wouldn't be too late to stop her. He placed his hand on Niesla's hair and whispered, "Take care of him." Fearing he might break down he rushed out hoping the girls would follow.

Chapter 21 - The Black Forest

Days melted into weeks. Time was forgotten as the group waded through knee deep ash which was constantly falling like snow from the trees. Sunlight had become an almost forgotten dream and the black trees became as familiar as a childhood playground. With no stars or sun to guide them, the only way they knew which direction to go was Faith's gray arrow. Faith would constantly throw it up in the air to check their bearings.

It had been so long since Faith had bathed. She horribly missed the feeling of being clean. The constantly falling ash from the burning leaves of the black trees had made its way into every crevice of her body. She had not taken off her armor in months. The magic allowed her to remain comfortable and, as far as she could tell, she did not smell bad. Still, she just wanted to be free of her armor, to feel a breeze through her clothes.

She just needed a break, a rest, a time to forget the weight of this quest. "We are stopping here for a short while!" She began unbuckling the armor on her legs.

Airria looked at her quizzically, "Are you hurt?"

Carrita, who had been wading through ash up to her thigh in a robe which reached the ground, said, "We really should keep moving. This forest is filled with creatures which could be in the service of Jarmack'Trastibbik."

Even the hot, dry air on her legs gave tremendous relief. "We have been in this forest for so long I can't even remember the feel of the sun on my face. We are taking some time for a rest. All we have done from the time we entered the port at Sulitamis is walk, fight and prepare for more fighting. We are going to pretend if only for a moment, we are not in this miserable place."

Airria began removing his armor. He carefully set it next to Faith's against one of the trees. Both of them set their weapons next to the armor.

Airria slid his hand into Faith's, "You know, my mother tried to teach me some dance. I was never very good at it, but it might be fun to try."

Dancing was forbidden where Faith was raised. The idea still bothered her, though it looked so enjoyable when she had actually witnessed it. She trusted Airria to respect her and her morals. "I know nothing of dance, will you instruct me?"

Airria laughed, "I really don't remember much, but what I do I will be happy to teach you." He pulled her around in a circle. "This really does work better if we have music."

"The only music I have ever enjoyed is the sound of things suffering," a surprisingly hollow and cruel feminine voice scoffed.

Faith looked to her armor but it was guarded by two incubi. Carrita reached for her staff, but it flew from her grasp.

"You will not need your weapons, nor your armor." A large, black skeletal matrataur strode out of the forest in tattered and rotten robes, "Her unmercifulness, Jarmack'Trastibbik, has demanded you be brought before her." The towering matrataur arc lich chattered its teeth together in laughter.

"She was never known for her patience," Carrita scoffed.

654

Airria attempted to dive around the incubi to retrieve his weapon, but a swift back-hand knocked him to the ground. He did not move.

Faith gasped and sprinted to his aid. He was breathing, but not moving.

Four succubae stepped out from behind a tree between her and the nearby weapons. Black drakes were flying overhead.

Carrita's eyes turned to a bright white and the flame of pure light began to form between her hands. "You will not leave this place!" she screamed.

The lich's voice chilled Faith to her bones, "I will leave this place and you will come with." The skeletal figure held up its black crystal staff pointing it towards Carrita. The staff began to glow the same color as the leaves on the trees. Faith noticed her hair lighten in the presence of the light sucking leaves and staff. As scared as she was at this point she was equally amazed. All the colors appeared as their complement, except around Carrita. The light between her hands intensified. In the trees nearest to her the flaming leaves began to go out.

A succubus threw a net over Faith and Airria. Another threw one toward Carrita.

Carrita waved her hand and the net flew back to the creature who had thrown it.

Faith tried to help, but found herself bound down to the ground unable to move or use her magic. She could feel the magic moving around her, but could control none of it. She could also feel the arc lich pulling Carrita's magic into his staff.

After what seemed to be days, but was likely only a few moments, the black staff shattered with tremendous energy. Though the lich, the devils and the group were untouched, the ground around them was cleared for a hundred paces. The trees had tumbled across the ground creating a huge ring.

"You have gained power since we last met!" the cruel feminine voice said. "You would have made a very powerful servant. Now you will spend forever as a powerless, mindless slave. Your soul will be trapped and tormented in your animated body!"

"You won't exist long enough to carry out your threat!" Carrita crackled with power.

Faith had been so intent on the magic battle and the banter she had not noticed the succubus walking up behind Carrita. Faith tried to scream, to let Carrita know, but she couldn't even breathe. With a quick hand the succubus in full daemonic form backhanded the child, knocking her unconscious.

Before Faith could even think to react she felt a collar slapped around her neck. She then felt her magic being bound, frozen in place. She could only watch as they placed a crystal collar on Carrita as well.

She tried to move, to fight, as they bound her hands and feet around a pole. Then once again she could only watch as both Airria and Carrita were bound to poles as well.

As the two incubi picked up Faith and Airria the lich mocked, "You should have listened to the child."

As two succubae placed Carrita's pole on their shoulders, Faith simply asked, "Why?"

"She demands it!" the succubus laughed.

Faith wished she could be unconscious. The ropes scratched and burned. The language these creatures spoke, though she could not understand it made her feel as though her insides we made of ice. The succubi seemed to find pleasure in bouncing the pole and watching Faith wince. When Airria woke up he began trying to struggle and yell. He did not yell in pain, nor plead, but struggled to free himself and mock the devils. "You are all cowards! I will tear you apart with my bare hands!" His voice faded into the woods.

The devils threw him to the ground and gagged him, "Silence rodent!" With a quick backhand Airria was silent again.

When Carrita woke up several days later, she didn't even struggle or say a word. For the first time ever she looked truly broken. She looked as if she had been reliving her worst tortures, as if she did not even care what happened to them.

Faith was not sure how long she hung from between the traveling devils. The creatures were relentless and cruel. They only stopped to heal the group enough to make sure they did not die in transport, then they would add a few more new wounds to each.

At one stop, there was a loud rumbling behind them. Then there was a loud crash as one of the sturdy black trees uprooted and flew away. At the edge of the clearing there was a matrataur with a white breastplate and a human-sized individual covered in black armor.

"I have waited a long time for this Mall'ice!" the voice coming from the armored figure was rich and commanding. "Today we get to see how good you really are."

"You know you are not allowed to touch me!" the lich screamed.

"That was only true until you interfered in the battles of mortals." The armored man pointed to the three lying on the ground, "In capturing these you have crossed the line. The council has deemed you fair game for me."

"Then that means I can finally rid this world of you!" the lich screamed as he raised his arms into the air.

Six black drakes came swooping out of the air at the knight. The matrataur reached out as if he were grabbing something and the drakes crashed to the ground.

The man in armor pulled his sword from behind his back. It was almost as long as he was tall and had a thin blade which ran crossways from the main waved blade. The part which drew Faith's attention was the flame. It was violet. Even in the deceptive light of the forest she could tell the color was true and she could see it emanating out for paces.

"You handle those well, let's see how you do with a real challenge!" Out from behind the trees walked twenty vampires in full daemonic form.

Neither the matrataur nor the man in armor seemed to deem them worthy of notice. They simply walked forward.

Faith heard the one in armor say, "The lich is mine!"

At the same time the lich said, "Damien is mine!"

The lich and the man in armor soon became a blur of black with violet streaks. Faith could almost make out the motions, though they were not as impressive as Airria's fight. She glanced over at the matrataur. He was covered in devil's blood and was using only his bare

657

hands and horns to tear them apart. He seemed to be playing with the devils as a cat plays with a mouse.

She glanced around to see what had become of the vampires. They were all gone, but there was a tall panther-looking humanoid.

A loud hollow scream of pain pulled Faith's attention back to the lich. One of its horns lay on the ground and the lich had backed away a few steps.

"Bal, it's time to stop playing around!" panther-man yelled in jest.

At this the matrataur yelled back, ripping the head off the last devil, "Show off!" There was definite amusement in his voice as well. The matrataur and the panther-man walked over and began untying Faith and Airria.

"Do you think he finally found his challenge?" the panther-man asked the matrataur.

The matrataur began to reply as he started removing Carrita's ropes, "Damien is having f…" He paused when he saw Carrita's face. He let out a wail of which shook the ground. His eyes turned blood red and he charged the lich.

It was as though Damien knew what to do. He simply backed away as the matrataur barreled into the lich. The matrataur's blood and hair misted the air as the lich clawed and tore at him. The sound of bone snapping was almost rhythmic as bits and pieces of the lich came flying out. From time to time flashes a magical energy flew out of the fight; the light and Damien's sword would flare as if the sword was absorbing any spells the lich was casting.

The panther-man looked at Carrita, "How do you know Balik'tars?'

"Of whom would you be speaking?" she answered.

The panther-man did not reply but turned back to the fight.

After half a day there was a flash of light and energy. Balik'tars was knocked to the ground, his breastplate missing and the lich was gone as well.

The matrataur simply bowed an apology to Damien and returned to the group. "Numbers are a dangerous game; don't let your guard down again," he said almost gently.

"You stole your friend's delight to seek retribution for me," Carrita said, then asked, "Why?"

"They call me Balik'tars or Bal for short," the matrataur said, gently removing the crystal collar from Carrita's neck. "I've been fighting the tyranny of my people for years. My past is a dark and twisted tale with only one true point of light."

Airria cautiously asked, pointing to the creature's scarred body, "Why don't you heal your scars? Do you keep them as badges of honor?"

"Few things in the world can leave lasting marks on me. These scars cannot be removed. They are from fights with creatures of truly intense magic: demons, devils, young dragons and even one rogue Titan. Creatures with power to create or destroy mountains," he said as he pointed to the scars. "In all my years, in all my battles, only one being ever defeated me, only one survived my wrath. She was the one who changed my outlook on life. She was the one who turned me from my sadistic ways. Now even she…" the matrataur stopped midsentence and looked at Carrita and asked, "You are the child of Tarsella, are you not?"

"How did you know?" Carrita asked.

Faith and Airria looked at each other. After all the people who had asked Carrita about her mother it was interesting to realize now how people who knew Tarsella, the Fairen of Derain, could recognize her daughter with only a glance.

"She gave me this," Bal said pointing to a particularly gruesome wound which ran from his ear to the corner of his mouth. The cut looked fresh.

It was only now Faith noticed that all of the matrataur's wounds from the fights had already healed.

"It will never heal," he continued, "this was a reminder to me that power is not obtained through aggression. Now I wish I could thank her for it." He glanced into the woods, "Many celebrated at the news of your mother's death." He smiled revealing his broad, fang-like teeth, "many died for their celebration."

"You're scaring the child," the panther-man said in jest. "Forget that, you're scaring me."

"It's all right kitty," Damien said running his hand across the cat's head, earning him a solid swat.

"Let's give them their stuff," the matrataur said with a laugh.

Airria put a hand halfway up and asked, "Will you help us?"

"We just did," the panther-man said sarcastically.

"You know where we are headed. Why you can't help us with that?" Airria asked almost pleading.

Bal placed his hand on his chest running his finger over a long scar. "You know what we are and how we are bound by laws beyond this world. Do not ask again."

Airria ducked his head.

"Here are your things, don't remove your armor or lay down your weapons again. Not for any reason," Damien said as he dropped them to the ground. He then turned and headed back into the forest. The others followed.

As the matrataur was at the edge of the clearing he turned back and said, "You are the children of power. You are the only hope we have for stopping the coming devastation." Without another word he turned and walked away.

"What did he mean?" Carrita asked.

"Bloodletting," Airria responded.

Carrita frowned, "This is the second time you have mentioned this ritual. How would you, with no magical training and almost no ability to read, know anything about a process lost for tens of millennia?"

Airria looked at them both in turn and then said with a playful smile, "I'm gifted. Just accept it."

Faith rolled her eyes at the comment.

"I guess we will soon see what he meant by his words," Carrita forced a smile, "or we will be joining the others in a crystal."

As excited as Faith was to remove her armor a few weeks ago she was just as grateful to be putting it back on. She took time to caress her swords before she sheathed them. While she waited for Airria to finish she cradled her bow. As they walked, she relished in the safety she felt.

Chapter 22 - Dark Places

The last three days had been relatively relaxing. The rescue and brief time spent with the Guardians brought back memories of the pleasantries of Jammar's place. Sadly the feeling was starting to fade and the agitation of missing the sun and constant threat of attacks was wearying. As nothing actually attacked, there was nowhere to vent their agitation.

Faith had accustomed herself to the strange light from the leaf-like flames constantly burning on the trees. The only variant in color came from the group; their clothes and their skin. From time to time Carrita would create a light globe to see true color, instead of the compliment, just to remind them what the truth was.

Airria stopped walking and pointed at a stone wall. It did not fit with everything else in this forest, it was gray. It was emanating strong magical energy. "I know this place. It's not far from here that Jarmack'Trastibbik is working to break into the protected realm." His words were very certain as he scanned up and down the wall, "Her den isn't far from here."

"How do you know?" Faith asked.

"I'm gifted," he said jokingly. "Besides, I can feel her." His smile shifted slightly. "Do you remember the potion Jammar gave me?"

"Apparently it bound you closer to the dragon than Jammar made it appear," Carrita said with a smile.

Airria smiled and gave her a wink, "Not too close though."

Faith's heart was even heavier now. Airria was trying to lighten the mood, but the reality, if not the enormity, of their quest was truly beginning to sink in. She looked at Carrita, how young she was. Yet though she showed amazing courage fear was sparkling through her eyes. Airria's walk was very confident, yet even with all the gifts he had been given his fear was showing through. "Then we can see the area where we will be fighting this dragon." Faith looked around. Both sides of the wall were surrounded by the black trees. This place did not instill confidence. "Perhaps it is time we talk of our tactics," she said trying to hide the shaking in her voice.

Carrita looked up at Faith, "She is very large and powerful. Even as rigid as these trees are they will afford us no protection. If she extends her wings she can create gale force winds to blow us around like leaves in the fall. She has an absolute mastery of the magics of death, but she likely will not use them because she does not believe we can win. She likes to feel extreme pain as her victim's life is ripped from their bodies."

"Jammar told me that she is fast and strong. In the open her size works for her, her wings give her advantage," there was a hint of hesitation in his words. "In a confined space there will be no retreat. It will limit her movement, but it also limits our retreat."

Faith asked, "Then where will we assume the best place for the confrontation to be?"

Airria looked at the ground, "It doesn't matter where we confront her, she will have the advantage. There will be no retreat in the open or in a cave. The best place will be where her advantage is the smallest. She won't track us nor come after us on her own. If we hide and wait for her all we will see are minions, so we cannot lead her into a strange cave. We will have to face her in her own den."

Faith felt a jolt run through her. "She knows her cave better than anywhere. I would think it the worst place for a confrontation."

Carrita grabbed Faith's hand, "Her greatest weakness is hubris. We are small and weak when seen though her eyes. The more comfortable we make her feel, the more she feels she has the advantage, the more we can exploit her weakness. Airria is correct. The best place for this conflict is inside the dragon's lair."

Faith had no gift for planning tactics. She had believed it folly to leave the safety for the wall in Sulitamis, but she realized looking back, it was the only way. Boarding the pirate ship she thought would be giving up the advantage, but if Airria and Joskin had not done so the group would never have acquired their ship and Carrita would likely be dead. No matter how ludicrous the plan sounded, if Airria and Carrita agreed it was the way they should proceed then Faith had to trust in them.

They walked in silence until they came to a break in the trees. There was no ash on the ground only uprooted trees and shattered stumps. The clearing looked as though a very large river had rushed through the area without mercy then vanished.

At the end of the valley-wide channel there was a monstrous cavern. The opening was far higher than any building Faith had seen and just as wide. For the most part the glassy black walls were worn and smooth. The group stood in awe for a long while at the overwhelming enormity of the cave.

When they reached the entrance Airria pulled out his sword and the flame of the blade burned bright enough that they could see clearly down the tunnel. The walls of the cave glowed with dark symbols. "It looks like this is the light we will be fighting by," he said with a halfhearted smile.

As the group proceeded down the tunnel several of the symbols exploded. Many others transformed into a streak of energy and were absorbed into Airria's shield. With each one Faith would jump and want to run.

Faith began to remember everything she had done wrong throughout her life. In her heart she believed the others knew all her faults and flaws. She began wondering how they could ever accept her, after a few moments she began to wonder how she could accept herself.

She found herself reaching for her dagger thinking to herself, *I should just end it now.*

"Concentrate on what's good, what you know to be truth," Faith heard Carrita say. "This is only the first one."

"But…" Faith found herself saying, "it is magic is it not?"

"Yes," Airria replied. "This is the magic Jammar spent many mornings training me for."

Even with this knowledge Faith had a hard time holding onto any hope. The harder she tried to think about something good, the more difficult it became to find anything to help. *At least I have good friends!* she thought to herself. *But,* her thoughts continued, *how can I trust them? There is a lot of treasure in here. They will kill me and take my share.*

"This is the magic they were talking about," Faith said out loud. She began to feel ashamed because she had thought the worst of such dedicated friends. *Why should they be faithful to me,* she continued in her mind, *what have I done to receive this kind of dedication? Why should they be here to help me! Why should I be here to help them?* These thoughts rattled around in her head. With each step they became more intense. She would bounce from hopelessness to fury to terror and back. When she thought she could not handle it anymore she finally screamed out loud, "WHY!?"

She noticed the concerned look on Airria's face. She could see he would do anything to help her, to make her happy. She realized he was fighting the same thoughts.

A tear ran down his cheek as he said, "I will tell you what I learned from Jammar, from my experience in the White Room." He slung his shield over his shoulder and put his sword away long enough to remove his left gauntlet. He gently grabbed Faith's hand, "At first I tried to overcome the White Room with thoughts of vengeance, happy thoughts of slaying the dragon and freeing my father. Then I realized that vengeance feeds these thoughts of fear and despair. I found that if I concentrated on the love and compassion my mother showed me I could deal with it. Now I have something stronger, something more helpful to me than any of the tricks I learned."

"What?" Faith asked in desperation, wiping a tear from his eye, "What is the tool you use?"

"You," he replied, rubbing the back of her hand with his thumb. "I remember the nights you stroked my hair as you helped me rest. I remember how excited I get just to talk to you. You have become my reason and my strength. Let me be yours."

Faith realized that it was not the voices in his head or the magically enforced despair that has caused Airria's tears. It was him seeing her hurt inside. "Hold my hand?" she asked, trying to find strength.

"Forever, if I have to," Airria replied.

Though the words sounded melodramatic and childish the sentiment made her feel better. For the first time since they entered the cave she felt a hint of peace. *They are true friends,* she thought.

It only took a moment before the negative thoughts took hold again. *They are mocking me,* she thought. *Why would they want me around? I am not special. I am ordinary. They need someone who can actually help them.* She began to let go of Airria's hand, but he gripped her tighter.

"Don't believe it," he said as if he could read her thoughts.

"Will the entire den torment us in this way? Will our minds be filled with thoughts of doubt and fear?" she asked apprehensively.

"Reach inside your heart. Find something to hold on to. Even your sister knew we would fail without you here. You have worked too hard to give up now. We have traveled together depending on each other through battles, heat, cold and pain. Hold on to the memories, how we have accomplished so much because we worked together. Hold tightly to those thoughts and do not let them go," Carrita said, grabbing her other hand. "Find your strength!"

Faith gripped both Airria's and Carrita's hands as they continued down the tunnel. The magic bombardments on their mental state continued. When Faith began to doubt her friends or herself she would squeeze their hands. Together they walked hand-in-hand until the tunnel widened into a huge opening.

"We could fit a whole city in here," Faith said in complete awe. She was feeling overwhelmed as it was, but now she was feeling utterly crushed. "How can we even hope to defeat such a creature as could create this place and needs so much room to live."

"I had forgotten how huge she is," Airria spoke very slowly. His eyes had grown large and his sword tip dropped to the ground.

Carrita frowned, "It would seem there are advantages to being the small one. Everything is huge to me. It comes to a point I don't notice anything more than just huge."

Faith was not sure why, but Carrita's statement was strange enough to make her laugh. She began to laugh so hard she fell to the ground. In this insane situation the youngest and smallest was the least scared. As she laughed she felt a barrier grow between her and the dark thoughts the cave was pouring down on her. She began to understand what Airria was talking about. It was not just enduring the thoughts; it was embracing the good she had received from her friends.

Finding this new strength she began to examine the area. There seemed to be buildings and walls made of gold, silver, armor and weapons. Gems and jewelry glittered in the strange light.

Airria's sword only lit a comparatively very small area now. It seemed to fade long before the distant piles. The rest of the cavern was lit by a large crystal at the top of the cave.

The crystal was absolutely mesmerizing in a horrific way. Even at its tremendous height Faith could see this crystal was fueled by the torment of the souls captured within. She could hear the cruel song of the souls crying out in torment, she could see the souls trying to escape in a gesture of futilely.

Faith let go of Airria and Carrita. She readied her bow. She drew one of her exploding arrows from her quiver, pulled it back and sent it sailing toward the crystal, "There is the crystal which needs to be destroyed."

The arrow flew straight and true. The explosion, for a moment, lit the entire cavern and temporarily blinded the party. The sound it made was deafening. When they regained their sight and their hearing returned they could both hear and see the crystal was completely untouched.

"This crystal is her pride and joy, it is better protected than anything else she has done," Carrita said in a frustrated, yet understanding, tone. "Even my mother could not shatter it."

"Let's look around, let's see what we can find, see if we can find something to help," Airria suggested. "There has to be something here to help."

Together the group started on the right side of the cavern. Each pile was organized by weapons, starting with daggers and working through spears, swords, axes, bows and all other manner of weapons. At the back of the cave was armor which was heaped in piles the size of large buildings based on color, material and gender. The left side of the cave was covered with piles of rings, amulets and other trinkets. Between a stack of weapons, armor and other items there were piles of gold, gems, silver and crystals, each reaching higher than an inn.

Airria yelled out, "She's here!" Then lowered his voice, "I will start alone," he said as he put on his helm.

Carrita got a look of protest on her face, but took position behind the rings. Faith climbed to a position near the top of the white, women's armor. Airria stood in the open on the floor of scaled gold.

Chapter 23 - Blackest Heart

It was not long before a woman no taller than Faith, stepped into the cave. She was seductively beautiful with long black hair and faultless tanned skin. Her hourglass shaped body was covered only in thin black straps of silk. Her voice was magically beautiful as she said, "You have come to destroy me. What a pity. My servants were sent to bring you so you could join me and my cause," she was biting her fingernail seductively. "The offer still stands for all of you." Her hand dropped, softly caressing each curve of her perfect physique until her arm relaxed at her side, her hand gently rubbing her thigh.

Faith was confused. She thought, *Was this woman really the great dragon Faith had heard so many terrifying tales about? Was this really the creature who had created this massive cavern?*

Airria's sword began to lower, but he shook his head, "Free my father, my uncle and Carrita's mother and I will let you live."

The woman took a short step forward, shifting her hips. "The young are often enamored by the little they have learned. Somehow they believe they know more than those who have been learning so long. They believe they can see so clearly what is happening. In truth they only see a small part of this world. You are very young. If you will let me, I will show you how little you know." She slowly turned around and started walking away.

Airria's head shook again and he raised his shield as if preparing to strike, "I said let them go!"

671

The woman turned far enough to look at Airria, "You are in my home at the request of the Council of Deities. Have you not wondered why they would send someone so young?" She raised her eyebrows. "They knew you were insufficient to stop me. They knew you would fail."

Faith could see Airria's shield and sword begin to lower. She could feel her own heart sinking. *Is she telling the truth? Were we really sent to our deaths?* Without thinking of the possible consequences she stood up and unleashed one of her petrifying arrows. She yelled, "You will never have us!" She continued in her mind, *Everything I went through to get here will not be for nothing!*

With unmatchable speed the arrow was snatched out of the air. "Foolish mortal!" the woman said in a cruel tone. "You cannot hope to defeat me. The entire Deific Council and Dragon Councils fear me enough to send you here at my bidding. They knew you would die. Everything has turned out exactly as I have planned!"

With the constant magical mental bombardment the woman's words were easy to believe and even though Faith had never felt an interest in women, she could feel the desire to be a part of this woman's existence. Optimism began bleeding from her heart. She looked around to find something to grab for hope.

"Your deception may work with common fools, but you forget I have already seen the truth of you. I know all you have to offer is torment," Carrita's voice seemed to shatter the despair Faith felt.

Carrita walked out from behind the rings. Her hair was dancing with white energy. She stood full of confidence.

Faith wished she could feel the same. She was starting to wonder if anything could make a difference.

"Oh yes, I was hoping to reunite you with your mother," said the woman. "She has been waiting patiently for you." Her smile only grew, "I enjoyed our first encounter. You gave me a gift I could not have acquired on my own. Now I will have the pleasure of your company again."

"Jarmack'Trastibbik, I will be reunited with my mother, but it will not happen by your will!" Carrita raised her staff, pointed it at the

672

woman and said something which sounded as if Faith should understand, but she did not.

The womanly form began to grow and erupt scales until the full size and cruelty of the dragon was revealed. Somehow, as the dragon grew the cavern seemed to shrink until most of the open area was filled. Even Faith felt as though she was smaller.

Jarmack'Trastibbik was bitter-black with eyes which glowed to match her crystal and two cruel ridges running roughly from her head to her tail. She had two oddly shaped twisting horns which were rooted at the back of her skull and curled almost to her jaw. There were four bone spikes jutting from her lower jaw, two in the middle and two at the back. At the end of her tail was a bladed ball the size of a warhorse.

"Child, you have gained power!" Jarmack'Trastibbik said. "You would have made a fine replacement for my servant which was destroyed in the Black Forest."

"The power I have gained has been a product of your attempts to torment me. I would never ally myself with you!" Carrita yelled and began chanting again.

Jarmack'Trastibbik waved a bone ridged claw at Carrita and she flew against the wall. Jarmack'Trastibbik taunted, "I said you have gained power, not become powerful."

Airria rushed at the dragon with all his might. His sword was blazing and his shield was glowing brightly. "You won't have them!"

Faith rushed to Carrita. She was sitting up scowling. "She will not throw me again." Her lip was curled in a determined frown and her teeth gritted together, her pride obviously more hurt than her body. She stood up and grabbed her staff.

Faith stopped the girl, examining her, "How are you not hurt?"

Carrita kept her focus on the dragon but responded to Faith, "My mother worked her craft well."

Faith relented and looked over at the fight. All she could see was a streak of light surrounded by pitch black inside of a white cloud. "What should we do?" she asked.

Carrita scowled, "Even I am not sure I can interfere. It appears I have lost my own chance for vengeance."

673

"He will stay near the ground," Faith said drawing an arrow. As quickly as she could she released random arrows, each one flew through the white cloud without reaction. She kept releasing them until she could feel the fatigue in her arm.

Faith quickly glanced over at Carrita. Her staff was glowing brightly. Her jaw was clenched tightly. Her eyes were narrow and mostly closed. She was shaking like a leaf in a storm.

"Something has got to break this up!" Faith said. She pulled the arrow Jammar had given her to guide the way. She took aim for the center of the dark mass. "Where is the dragon's heart?" she yelled and unleashed the arrow.

For a moment it seemed as though time slowed. She could see the arrow flying in a direct course towards the dragon's chest and no matter where the dragon moved the arrow pursued undaunted. Jarmack'Trastibbik tried to catch the projectile, but it slipped past her claw and shattered both the scale and arrow in front of her heart.

Faith could see the dragon as she looked down to examine the wound. This gave Airria a chance to strike. He drove his sword deep into the dragon's massive horn. When the sword was nearly halfway through there was a huge explosion.

The dragon reared back and screamed in pain. "You fools!" Jarmack'Trastibbik roared. "You shall pay prices you have not yet imagined!"

"You forget," Carrita shouted, now levitating, surrounded with energy, "I have endured you wrath before!" She then let loose a fireball of pure white energy which blasted into the dragon's chest.

Jarmack'Trastibbik took the blast as if laughing at a child's power. "I have only ever played with you, child! Now you will feel my wrath!" The dragon pointed a rough claw in her direction and Carrita, with her staff in hand, curled up on the ground and began chanting.

Airria swung his sword, slicing a large gash into the dragon's claw.

Jarmack'Trastibbik roared, "You will pay for your insolence!" and she swung her tail into Airria.

674

Airria, left with no options, braced for impact. The blade of the dragon's tail shattered on his shield, but Airria went tumbling across the floor. Jarmack'Trastibbik seized the moment and reached out to pin him.

Airria tried to slash at the oncoming claw but Jarmack'Trastibbik easily avoided the sword and used the momentum to pin Airria's arm against his body.

Faith froze with fear as the dragon summoned her crystal. Airria's soul slowly began to peel up from his body. He screamed in agony.

The arrow! she heard a voice say.

She did not care where the voice had come from. Filled with desperation she pulled the arrow she had picked up in Darian and aimed. The arrow seemed to be invisible to the dragon, for she did not react to it.

Faith's aim was perfect. The projectile flew directly into the crystal. The crystal shattered with a massive explosion ripping several of the dragon's scales off her body and slamming her against the distant wall.

Faith had expected the cavern to go dark, but it did not. She looked over at Carrita whose body seemed to have erupted into a bright white flame. The flame burned so brightly it lit the entire cavern. All of the symbols which had been glowing in deceptive light exploded at the same time releasing their energy.

For the first time since they had entered the Black Forest all of the colors appeared correctly. The wall looked black and the dragon's floor was revealed as being made completely of Bronze, White and Golden Dragon hides.

"You shall pay a price no mortal has in several millennia!" Jarmack'Trastibbik exclaimed. Then from her mouth erupted flame of such intense darkness it absorbed Carrita's light out of the air.

Airria had apparently seen this coming. With his free arm and all the strength he had left, he threw his shield to block the flames. It flew as if by magic. The force of the flames slammed the shield into Faith, knocking her off the mountain of rings she had climbed. She lay on the ground dazed, only vaguely hearing the sounds of the magical battle, the screams of Airria's pain and the roar of the raging dragon.

When she regained her senses she noticed she was on the rough scales of the dragon hides. She could feel the wild magic around her. She could sense the presence of mages and dragons commanding all of the wisdom from ages past. Even more importantly she could feel power and guidance far greater than all of the dragon's. She began to chant:

>blood and armor claim the flesh
>bring to life and mesh
>strength of ages rise
>magic and souls to guide
>bring our past in power
>in this time to flower
>from blood our bodies come
>dragon's form we shall sum
>from this dragon we find our curse
>from dragon's blood give us rebirth

Faith could feel her body changing. She could feel the dragon inside her. She could feel the magic of the arrows and the quiver absorbing into her body and focusing at her fingertips. She could see her fingernails change her right to rubies and her left to sapphires and her thumbs to marble. She could feel the power and ability to change to dragon form.

She glanced over at Carrita who was no longer the little girl Faith had tended to and learned from. She was a dragon as big as a small house. Her glowing white scales completely overwhelmed the darkness. Her eyes were pure violet crystal like her mother's staff. She had emerald green horns protruding up and back from her head with golden streaks running down her back fading into bronze on her tail. There was a silver and blue shimmer from her shoulders and she had flaming crimson teeth.

Airria also, had grown into a dragon. His scales were golden with swirls of white. His eyes, claws and teeth raged with the fire of the sun. He had four bronze horns protruding out of his head, two sweeping back and together and two curling smoothly to his lower jaw.

Even though both Carrita and Airria were now dragons the size of buildings they were still much smaller than Jarmack'Trastibbik.

"It was a mistake to believe the daughter of Tarsella would not be the more magical," Jarmack'Trastibbik growled. "It matters not, you shall all suffer pain beyond description."

Faith reached down to pick up her bow and she searched for an arrow. She noticed the dragon scales which covered the floor were now gone; all of them.

She did not have time to understand exactly what had happened. Nearby she found a small pile of arrows. All of them had wooden shafts and iron tips. Faith could feel no magic in them.

Jarmack'Trastibbik obviously had her attention split between Carrita and Airria.

Airria had already received many deep wounds, his blood was as white-hot as his breath. He was more agile than ever, but Jarmack'Trastibbik was no longer playing games.

Carrita looked as though she was concentrating with all her might. There was a sphere of white flame burning only a few paces in front of her face. From time to time the flames would flicker black or red and then fade back into white.

Faith looked at the simple arrow in her hand. She thought about running over to the mountain of magic arrows and grabbing one of those. *No,* she thought, *those are the arrows which I know have failed.* She looked at the simple shaft. *No magic, what can this do?*

"The dragon feels the magic, she is too skilled to let any magic arrow slip past her defenses," Faith heard Tarsella's voice instruct.

Faith shrugged and shot her arrow. It sailed uncontested into the Black Dragon's heart. *What was such a small stick to a heart so monstrous?*

Jarmack'Trastibbik roared in pain and turned her attention to Faith, "I may die today, but you will die first."

"Not if I have anything to say about it!" Airria said ramming his claws through the Black Dragon's chest.

For the first time the Black Dragon Lord had true fear in her eyes.

"Your heart will keep beating for years to come but will have no means to do anything," Airria said in a tone which made Faith shake.

"Your blood will be used to make creations of peace. When we are done, your heart gems will be crushed and you will cease to exist!" Airria pulled his claws out. His hand emerged with the massive heart still beating. Black streaks began to pulse down Airria's back.

Carrita sent her ball of fire to hit the heart. The heart exploded in a golden flame throwing Airria back into the mountains of armor. Carrita flew into the wall.

The light in Jarmack'Trastibbik's eyes faded. Her claws were buried by her massive frame. The black gems, the only remnants of her heart, fell to the floor.

Chapter 24 - New Beginnings

Airria couldn't believe the power he felt. He was as big as a house and had just ripped the heart out of the most fearsome dragon in history. He could feel the gifts of his armor melded into his scales. All the abilities of his sword had filled his teeth and claws. His head was swimming with thoughts of destruction. In his heart he felt the desire to kill.

He glanced around, looking for his next target. The first one he saw was Carrita. Even though she was as big as him and looked nothing like the child she once was, he still recognized her. She had taken away his vengeance on the dragon.

Before he made his first motion he noticed a small human. She was dressed in an elegant golden dress hanging off her shoulders with white lace and trim. Her hair was brilliantly white, his heart wrenched as she smiled at him. She was so beautiful, so elegant, like a dream come to life. He couldn't take his eyes off of her.

"Airria," she spoke his name.

All of the anger and desire to destroy faded from his heart.

"Faith?" he asked. He had recognized Carrita and she was a dragon.

Even though she was human and had the face he desired to always see something was very different. He felt as if he needed to bow to her.

He thought for some time on what he could say so as not to let this majestic woman know he hadn't recognized her, "How is it you aren't a dragon?"

Faith laughed, "I am a dragon. I have chosen to appear as a human. Do you not like the way I look?"

Now that his head wasn't clouded with thoughts of killing and fighting he understood that he could shift his appearance to whatever race he desired. Looking at Faith he realized he might not have a choice on skin tone or cloth color so he tried to imagine, based on what he knew of Faith, what she would prefer to see him in, something he hoped would leave her in as much awe as he was in looking at her.

He closed his eyes and felt his body adjusting. He imagined a plain tunic with solid shoulders and simple sleeves. He envisioned his trousers to have a crease running down them.

He took a deep breath and opened his eyes. For awhile he didn't know what Faith thought of him because she was not commenting. She only stood without breathing. Finally a smile crept across her face.

"You know me so well," she said. Her eyes traveled slowly up and down him. "Yes. You know me well."

Carrita also had shifted to human form. She had the biggest change. She no longer looked like a child, but she had become a full grown woman. She had chosen a very stately robe with varying rich colors.

After looking at the changes that had taken place Airria realized the cave should have been dark, but it wasn't. While the three had been looking around at each other they hadn't noticed that they were surrounded by thousands of souls of varying races, each of them with a soft glow of true gratefulness emanating from their incorporeal bodies.

Carrita's mother stepped forward, "We all owe you a debt which cannot be repaid."

Carrita had huge tears in her brilliant violet eyes. "Mom," she sobbed, "I have saved your body…am I too late?"

Tarsella looked lovingly at her daughter, "In truth I do not know if my body can be rejoined with my soul."

"Was all we suffered to free you in vain?" Carrita sobbed.

A voice came from the back of the crowd, "Not at all my dear." The voice was gentle, yet powerful. It was not loud or strong, but it did sink deep into their hearts. "Not one of these spirits would say that any of the price you have paid was in vain."

A man approached from the opening of the cave. He was plain looking yet his presence was enough to make every soul, and even the group, to bend a knee. "All of these spirits needed to be freed. None of them would say your efforts are in vain," he said as he picked up the Black Dragon's heart stones off the ground.

Carrita showed her impulsive childish spirit, "I came to get my mother back." Though there was defiance in her voice there was only humility in her eyes.

"She is now free from torment," the man said. "Is this not enough?"

Carrita only ducked her head and began to sob. Faith spoke up somewhat shyly, "Is there nothing you can do to help?"

The man smiled, "There is always something that can be done. Often we are unwilling to make the sacrifices necessary."

Airria could feel his own heart start to swell. "I only wished my father freed, but now I wish to see Tarsella restored."

The man softly wandered through the throng of souls toward the group. "How many have paid the price of death to allow you to become who I see you are? How much farther are you willing to go to bring Tarsella's body and soul to reunion."

Airria had nothing left to sacrifice, nothing he could think of. He had walked into this cave willing to sacrifice his relationship with Faith, but didn't want to take that risk again. He had brought his cousin and dearest friend on this quest, but had left him behind on the edge of death. He had left his mother, aunt and all the children he had grown to love.

After a long silence the man spoke again. "Tarsella, you have served as a protector. You understand better than most what awaits you if you choose to stay. You also know what will happen to so many others if

681

you go. I give you the choice. You can choose paradise and bliss or you can choose to stay and help your daughter through what is going to be a very rough transition."

Carrita yelled out, "Stay! Please stay." Even in the womanly body Carrita looked like a child. "I need you."

Tarsella reached out as if to wipe the tears from her daughter's eyes, but her hand passed through Carrita's face. "Oh child, I am with you always. Even if my body is not with you, our souls have been intertwined from long before there was physical form. You have been my reason for living for so long I cannot willingly leave your side. Long after this world has been destroyed we will still be together. Our spirits are eternal."

Carrita keep looking at her mother in sad silence.

Tarsella turned to the man. "Esnie, you gave me a similar choice tens of millennia ago regarding those I had created. This child means more to me than all the others combined. Do you think I will make a different decision?"

Esnie smiled with pride, "You have suffered so much since you first chose."

Tarsella reached to touch Carrita once more. "I would suffer it all again. More if necessary, to continue to provide a place for mortals to come and be safe. I have no regrets. You know better than I what is to come, what will be needed. My desire is to continue to help, to train my daughter, to be a part of her life. I wish to aid as many of those willing to allow me to. Nonetheless, I will do what you say is best."

Airria couldn't bring his eyes from the ground. Only Carrita's sobs could be heard. After a long moment Esnie spoke again, "I am sorry to put you through such a trial. I wanted you to see that you are all free to choose. Your decisions affect not only you, but others for generations. Your choices as a group have already cost many their lives and saved these souls from torment," he pointed to the group of races around them. "Know that you are not the only ones who paid a terrible price for what you love."

The group looked up and saw the crystal casket Carrita had stored her mother's body in. The man continued, "Our purpose is not fully accomplished." The body and the casket began to fade and disappear; Tarsella began to become more solid.

With a loud, "Thank you!" Carrita ran to hug her mother. "I missed you so much!" She held her mother tightly.

Esnie raised his hand and a small light formed. It began spinning and growing. As it spun the crowd began slowly wisping away. The last two spirits standing there were Airria's uncle and his father.

Unlike Tarsella these two didn't speak, they only bowed.

A tear ran down Airria's cheek as he muttered, "They are free."

Faith wiped the tear from Airria's face. She turned to Esnie, "I am grateful for your gifts, but I would like to know why?" She paused to look into the man's eyes. "I mean, I can see you know and love everyone who was in here. I can feel you had the power to take care of this problem without us. Why did so many have to pay such a high price to deal with the situation? Why did my parents and brother have to die? Why did I have to leave my sister behind?"

"It is easy to judge something as folly when you only see a small piece of what is happening. In all your travels you have viewed only a small part of this world. You have seen but a short while of existence. In time you will understand better the question you have asked." His eyes were filled with patience, "You know this is not about making people happy or making life easy. You are right, I do have the power." He smiled a fatherly smile towards Faith, "This existence is about making individuals more than they could be alone. This is about showing each individual what they are made of, who they truly are. I care too much to make it easy. I want to see each individual meet their potential."

"I do not understand," Faith said. "When I was little my parents did all they could to make my life as easy as possible. I want to make the ones I love as happy and comfortable as possible," she glanced at Airria. "If you care, why do you let bad things happen?"

The man smiled, "When you were young did your parents give you chores?" Faith nodded. "Did you enjoy them?" Without waiting for an answer he continued, "These chores your parents gave you were to help teach you, to help you be more. If they did not give you chores how could you have learned to be responsible, to use the powers they knew

683

you would acquire as your life advanced? How can you be more if you're not allowed to be what you are? How will you know what you can be if you are never tested beyond what you think is your limit? No being who has entered this world was meant only for the mortal. This existence is a test. A test to show you you are able to handle more. You have existed much longer than this world. You will exist long after it has gone."

Airria was feeling dizzy.

Faith collapsed on the floor, "I do not want to be something more."

"I believe you do," Esnie said with a grin. "You want to be a mother and a wife. In your desire you want to be a teacher and a protector. You see it is all connected. Many of your desires do not only affect your life they are joined with the wants and needs of others. You have the opportunity to make your own choices, but choices will affect others."

Faith looked up with a furrowed brow, but was cut off as Esnie continued, "How do you think your choice to spend time with Airria has affected Carrita?" He stopped for a moment to let her think on it and then continued, "What I have told you is more than I believe you wanted to hear. Just know it will make more sense in a few years."

Airria collapsed next to Faith. He bowed his head, feeling as if the weight of the world was upon his shoulders. He felt as if even the choices he had made were not his own, yet he knew that at any time he could have walked away from his quest. When he had started he chose to leave home to get vengeance, selfish vengeance. At the end, he had decided to continue to protect others. Now he was done, all he wanted was to be with Faith. Esnie had told them they all were free to do what they wanted, but made it sound as if there were more plans for them.

Faith looked up at Airria. She placed a hand on his cheek then glanced back to the man. "What other plans do you have for us?"

Esnie leaned in between the two of them, "Whatever plans or hopes I have for you, I will not force you to do my bidding any more than I forced Jarmack'Trastibbik to stop her attack. You make your choices and so far your choices have been, overall, very good," he smiled as he retrieved the Black Dragon gems off the ground.

He stood back up, "I do, however; have a proposition for the three of you." He looked around to make sure everyone was looking at him. "You have thrown the Council of Dragons out of balance. I have always made sure that I kept it in balance. Now a balance must be met." His face became more stern, yet non-demanding, "Will you accept the role of the Dragon Council?"

Carrita answered, "You are asking us to accept a tremendous responsibility."

"You have always understood more than others your age would." He looked kindly on Carrita's mother, "Your mother has done well." He turned back to Carrita, "You are right, I am asking a lot more of you than you realize, though I am asking no more than I believe you can handle."

Airria spoke next, "I don't believe I can fill the role Jarmack'Trastibbik was filling. I cannot be so cruel."

"I am not expecting you to fill in where Jarmack'Trastibbik left off," he explained. "I am expecting you will lead the others the best you can. The purity of balance has been forever destroyed. Dragons were put on this world to educate, to bring a balance of knowledge. There is a war coming. Many will be tested. It is for you to keep the knowledge and pass it on when the war is done. Thus you will maintain the balance of existence."

"I cannot stand by and watch others hurt when I have the power to stop it as I've seen so many Guardians do," Airria interjected.

"You have your choice. You can fight a few battles or you can teach tranquility. Sometimes you will save more lives fighting. Sometimes it is better to leave the battle and teach peace."

"I just want to be with Airria!" Faith exclaimed, then blushed and looked at the ground.

"Don't worry about that, I can join you together for more than just this existence, you can be together for eternity. As long as you work together, you will only grow closer until you will think and act as one. You are compliments of each other. Where one leaves off the other begins. This balance will make you an even better team to help lead. Believe me, I will always make it worth your while if you will do what I ask."

"You gave my mother the information she needed to allow me to be born?" Carrita asked.

"Yes," Esnie replied. "I needed you to be born when you were to help with this task. Your mother agreed and used the time you were in her womb to teach you."

Faith interrupted, "I thought she was cursed?"

"She was cursed far beyond what the council could undo," he answered. "As the Fairen, Tarsella had the opportunity to ask for direct help from me. It worked out better for her, the whole and every individual, thus I chose to help."

"Why don't you help more when asked?" Faith responded.

"I help more than you know, even when not asked," Esnie replied. "Can you so easily accept that your transformation spell was so within your abilities? Do you think a child remembers as much as Carrita was taught from before their birth? Do you believe that it was an accident that your ancestors were chosen for bloodletting? Yes I have helped. I have helped in the way that was best for all involved, both as a group and individuals."

The group fell silent. Esnie waited for awhile then asked, "Will you do what I ask of you, to the best of your abilities?"

Faith stood on shaking legs. She bowed, glancing to Airria, "Yes, I will do my best to make sure knowledge is spread with balance."

Airria didn't want to be left behind and Esnie had promised he could be with Faith forever. That was all that mattered. "I can't let you get that far ahead of me." He stood and grabbed Faith's hand, "I go where you go."

Carrita looked at her mother, then the man. She said with a torn look on her face, "I have had the opportunity to learn so much. It would be a shame for it to go to waste." She gave her mother one more hug and turned to face the man, "I will help, but I have only recently had my mother returned to me. Please allow me to spend time with her."

Tarsella stood tall and proud running her hand down Carrita's hair.

"Wonderful!" Esnie said. He held his hands up and the walls began to fade away into a huge white marble hall. Suddenly the group was surrounded by the entire Deific Council, including all of the remaining Guardians and the remaining Dragon Council.

Chapter 25 - Calling

Airria looked around the large white marble hall. He recognized each face from the statues and tapestries he'd seen at Jammar's. He recognized each dragon by its form and color. He had spent hours imagining what it would be like to meet these historic individuals. Now that he was seeing them in person he only wanted to hide.

Faith was squeezing his hand until a familiar voice yelled out, "Let me through!"

"Natalya?" Faith yelled back.

A small corridor opened up to reveal Faith's little sister. The child ran to Faith and jumped into her arms. "I have missed you so much. I wished every day you would return," the child said after a lengthy hug.

"You have gotten so big," Faith said with tears flowing down her cheeks. "I am sad I have missed so much of your growing up. I know it is imposable to retrieve lost time, but I would like to make up for as much as I can."

Natalya pulled away from Faith. "I know..." she stopped talking for a moment. Her eyes examined Faith from head to toe. "You have changed very much in appearance. Your hair, your eyes, even the way you dress is different." She put a hand on either of Faith's cheeks, "You have changed so much, are you sure you still want to be my sister?"

Faith brushed her sister's hair away from her face. "Dear Natalya, there is no change I could make to take my desire to love you out of my heart. You are my sister, you will always be my sister. Even if you do not want me in your life, if the changes in my life make me undesirable to you, I will forever love you and want you to be in my life."

Natalya hugged Faith tightly around the neck. After a short while she whispered in Faith's ear, "I will love you as long as you will allow me."

Airria could feel a lump forming in his throat. He tried to dislodge to discomfort, but it wouldn't go away. In an attempt to distract himself from the scene before him he looked for Jammar. At the end of the open line where the child had come from Jammar was standing.

Slowly he walked forward. When he was a few paces from the group he said to Faith, "She is every bit as amazing as her sister."

Faith didn't respond, but Airria asked, "How is my family? My mother? My aunt? The children?"

Jammar laughed softly, "It would appear that when you left the island your little group made quite an impression on the entire town of Tark-Ancia. A few agitators came through your home town, but none of them left. I didn't have to do anything. The usually selfish people have been protecting your family."

Airria snickered and said to himself, "They more likely wanted the money offered, but didn't want deal with us."

Jammar laughed again and turned around. "Order in chaos," he said as he disappeared into the crowd.

Thankfully the enormous White Dragon began making her way to the front. The movement helped Airria feel that fewer eyes were on him.

The gigantic creature spoke, taking Airria's mind off the scene of Faith's reunion, "In the beginning I was created as a partner, a compliment to Jarmack'Trastibbik. There can be no death without life.

690

Likewise there can be no life without death. The original essence of death has been eliminated, now my presence here disturbs the balance, my Lord Esnie." The dragon melted into a human woman with white skin and hair. She bowed low to the ground, "I have lived my life. It is time to pass my knowledge and essence to another."

"Your absence would also disturb the balance we have worked so very hard to maintain," Esnie said. "That is unless the entire Dragon Council is ready to relinquish their knowledge."

The Golden Dragon spoke from the back of the hall, "It was agreed upon in the beginning." She quickly transformed to a human with golden skin and hair and made her way to the front. She looked over the five humans near Esnie. "There are only five. How will you divide the knowledge? I can understand four. Will Tarsella or the child remain as they were?"

Esnie chuckled, "Tarsella already has her responsibilities and I will not burden the child further and ask her to carry such a load. Only the three shall shoulder this burden.

A woman who appeared to be made of bronze chimed in, "I like it. There is no way to divide eight into three. It should work out perfectly." She spun herself around and bowed low.

The white woman walked over to Airria and Faith. She put a hand on each and said, "Jarmack'Trastibbik was intended to be my partner. We were to work together, but our views differed so greatly we parted ways only to see each other in war. I hope you will be able to find the appreciation for each other we could not." She then went back to Esnie and held out her hand. One by one the white heart stones formed in her palm. When she was finished, she dropped them into Esnie's hand and faded away.

Before relinquishing her crystals, the golden woman approached Airria and Faith. "There is order in even the most chaotic of situations. All things exist in opposition. The pain you have suffered, the lives you have lost, it was all to bring you to this point."

After the golden woman disappeared the bronze one came up. "I don't know why they would talk to you before they go. You're going to know everything we know when we are done. Me, I'm here because it makes no sense. But you'll soon know what I mean." She smiled and danced over to Esnie to relinquish her crystals.

The other four only bowed to the group before giving Esnie their crystals. Once they were all finished Esnie turn to Airria, "You have already begun to absorb the knowledge of death; here are the rest of those crystals as well as the knowledge of order. After all you will need to know best the order of death so that you may understand when death is a good thing." With these words he dropped the golden gems in to Airria's hand.

As the gems melted into his hand Airria could feel twinges of knowledge flickering in his mind, thoughts driving his emotions a touch at a time.

To Faith he gave the bronze and white gems. "This will help you be Airria's balance. You will be the inspiration, the art and the forgiveness. You will have to temper his passion, as you have already done so marvelously."

"To you," he said in dropping the last four sets of gems into Carrita's hands, "I give the knowledge of fire, water, air and earth. They are inseparably connected yet eternally conflicted. You have already mastered these elements in combination better than any except me. Even your mother cannot understand them as a whole to the same extent as you."

Esnie then turned to address the Council of Deities, "Times have changed. The wall which protected so many has been breached. Even now the Titans, dragons and other powerful creatures fight for control of the opening. Those inside the sanctuary will soon be exposed to horrors and powers lost to them in legend. This is the time you have all awaited and feared."

He continued, "For tens of thousands of years this council has remained to govern the education of the people. You have had the power to shape the world, but have not had the opportunity except through mortal priests. Now is your time to walk and teach among the mortals."

"I give you this warning as I release you from your duties. Be careful where and how you use your power. Many of you remember the days of the Great Magic War. For those who do, you will also remember the fear and hatred which followed. So much knowledge was lost by the mortals. If you try to control the people with your power they will destroy you."

He looked Balik'tars directly in the eyes, "All of the items of power will be released and scattered across the sanctuary." Bal nodded as if he understood it would be his job to scatter the items.

"All in the Spirit Council will remain in place," he continued, pointing to eight beings of varying races seated around a large table. "You will have ample work ahead of you."

Turning his attention back to the entire council he said, "Each of you was chosen for your position based on who you were and what you have done. For tens of thousands of years you have served me well. Each of you has acquired items of power for your personal collections or have such items sacrificed to you. These items are yours to use as you see fit. Balik'tars will not take these items from you. Use them wisely."

Esnie bowed to them and added, "When you accepted your position you were given a ring to help you move from place to place with ease. You may use your ring to travel to a city of your choosing. Prepare them for what is coming."

One by one each council member disappeared with a final bow. Finally a portal to the judgment chamber swallowed up the Spirit Council. Soon only those who had been in the cave were left.

Faith spoke up shyly, "Though I feel the knowledge is in me I cannot access it. I still don't understand what we are supposed to do. I had hoped when we were finished here we would know what our responsibilities were."

"You have been given a tremendous amount of knowledge and understanding," Esnie said. "For now most of it is suppressed. As you live your life the knowledge will work its way to the surface of your mind. You will know what you need to do when the time comes." He smiled at all of them, "Until that time, just live your lives. You have a sister who needs to be raised up, you have a man who adores you. You are on the road to living the life you have always wanted. Just live it and trust I will help you to understand what you need to do."

"Marren?" Carrita questioned, "Will Marren be returning? My heart still aches for what I did to her."

"No, her time is done. She is happy where she is. All things have a course to run. She ran hers well." He paused a moment to look at the tears in the girl's eyes, "You made the right choice. Darian has its Fairen back. Sulitamis has a new governor. All is as it should be. All things change."

Carrita's eyes drooped, "I would feel better if I could hear it from her lips."

"My existence in this world was one of contradiction," Marren's voice came from behind the group.

Airria spun quickly around to see the woman he had known as a vampire.

Marren looked at each of them. "I am not as brave nor as giving as my dear friend Tarsella. I had grown weary of my station and wished for a way out. I did all I could to train my replacement. When given the choice to go back, I chose to stay."

Carrita stepped forward, dragging her mother. "Why would you want to die?"

Marren moved as elegantly as she ever had in life. "For the greater part of my life I was trapped, damned to an existence where I could not move on. Life is only one step in an eternal journey and I stayed to help a city remain free. Now there is another, I understand, willing and able to take my place. He will have abilities to help I could not, due to my dark circumstances."

Faith asked, "After so long worrying about an entire city what will you do?"

Marren reached out, her hand passing through Carrita's head. "For the first time in over a millennia I am able to converse with my father. I cannot express in words, Carrita, how grateful I am you did what you did for me. You saved the city and relieved me of my post. I do miss hugging loved ones, but I am happy here."

Airria asked, "Won't you miss touching people?"

Marren laughed, "There is still much you need to learn about what happens after your life. One such thing is to know this existence.

This part as a disembodied spirit is only temporary. When you know what I am talking about you will understand why I am not worried about such things." Marren bowed again, "It is time I go back to where I belong." Before any more questions could be asked, Marren faded way.

Esnie looked at each member of the group. "Change is coming and you are ready to help make the change better. For now it is time for you to travel. Visit your families prepare them for the wars ahead."

When he looked at Carrita he said, "You still have much your mother can teach you. Spend as much time as you can learning from her. She will help you find your strength."

Turning his attention back to the group in general he said, "Choose where you are to go. Close your eyes and think of whom you wish to see the most, aside from each other."

Airria closed his eyes and held tightly to Faith's hand. Even with Faith next to him he was divided. He missed his mother, but was very worried for Joskin. In the end he focused on his dear friend and cousin.

Chapter 26 – Peace

When Airria opened his eyes again all five of them were still together, looking out of a window of the governor's house at Derain. The streets were still bustling with workers trying to repair the damage to the city. Camps of refugees lined the streets.

"How? What? Who?" Joskin's voice was strong and only too welcome.

Airria turned around. Relief rushed over him as he looked at his cousin standing with only the aid of his large ax. "You are a welcome sight to these weary eyes."

"Airria?" Joskin asked and examined his cousin for a moment. "What happened to you? You look so different."

"I can't begin to explain everything that's happened to me since I left here." Airria took a step toward Joskin. He was going to give his cousin a hug, but Niesla entered the room.

The elf didn't look as elegant as she once had. Her hair was flat and oily. There were dark circles under her eyes. She stopped when she saw the group and asked, "How did you get in here?" She stopped and looked at Tarsella. "Fairen, you have returned." She dropped to one knee, "I am so very happy to see you back in this city."

Joskin turned to Tarsella and said, "I recognize you from the shrines we read on Ramsel Island," he also dropped to one knee.

Tarsella reached a hand out and lifted Joskin's chin. "Is it only through your education on the island which you recognize me? Do you not see in my eye the prolog for another?"

Joskin's focused on Tarsella. His forehead wrinkled and flattened. His brows shifted up and down. Finally his eyes grew wide. He lowered his head. "I did all I could to protect your daughter. As Airria has returned without her I would assume I have failed." He sheepishly glanced up, "I have more respect for her then any king or Guardian I have ever met. I am sad she hasn't returned."

Carrita burst out laughing. She began twisting back and forth in her robes like she had many times before. "Airria had no trouble recognizing me. I would have expected you to know who I am."

Airria smirked, "I do have the advantage that I was there when you changed."

Joskin's mouth opened slightly. After a long moment he dropped his ax and bolted from his knee to wrap his arms around Carrita. Leaning heavily on her he said, "I should have known, only you could have changed things so much."

Carrita kissed him on his cheek. "My heart is lightened by your continued recovery. I had hoped Niesla would have the strength to continue to heal you in my absence." She pulled away enough to look him in the eyes, "I am relieved to see she was amply strong enough." She turned and looked at Faith and Airria, "As to the alteration to our beings, I cannot take credit. It was Faith who cast the spell."

Faith's eyes shifted back and forth, "I did not know what would happen, I only wanted to help and my bow was not doing much."

Joskin rubbed the bandage wrapped neatly across his chest. "Niesla tells me I have you to thank for my recovery. She told me nothing of her own sacrifice." He looked back to the elf whose head was still ducked.

Carrita blushed and glanced back at her mother who was beaming with pride.

After some time of silence Tarsella walked over to Niesla and raised her up. "I can see you have sacrificed greatly for this human. I find it very odd to see someone who has the ability to live for hundreds of years be so dedicated to a human."

Niesla glanced to Joskin, "He has earned all of my respect and devotion. Though I may outlive him by centuries I will continue to be by his side, so long as he will have me. He helped save me when he had no reason to. He risked his life to save both this city and the city on the coast. I have never met an elf, dwarf, or any other mortal with such courage. Yet with all his skill in battle he holds fast to compassion. Yes, he has earned my devotion. When he is gone, I will remain alone."

Joskin opened his mouth in protest, but Tarsella spoke first, "What would you say if I told you there was a way for you to be with him for much longer, perhaps you could be together forever? Would such a proposition interest you?"

Niesla looked to Joskin, "Whether in the flesh or in the spirit, I am bound to this man. He has my heart. Where he chooses to go I will follow."

Tarsella turned to Joskin, "It would appear the choice is yours."

Joskin ran his hand over his smooth head. "I'm not sure what I did to receive such devotion from this elf, but I assure you the feeling is mutual. If there's a task you want me to do in order to keep Niesla in my life longer or, more realistically, to keep me in her life longer, then I will gladly do it."

Tarsella turned to Carrita, "Perhaps if I had found a man of such caliber I would not have taken the path I did. It was in my bitterness and hatred of men I created elves and dwarves."

Faith stepped forward, "Then perhaps it is best you did not find such a man."

Tarsella glanced from Airria to Joskin and then to Faith. "Perhaps it is best I did not, but I do envy you what you feel for these men. I envy your partnership. I tried for centuries to fill the void. Perhaps your stories will allow me to open myself up to such affection. For now I will relish my time with my daughter."

She walked over to the wall and placed her hand on it. A shelf opened up with a small, white, glowing vial in it. She pulled the vial out and handed it to Joskin, "Share this with your partner and live without fear of age."

Niesla held Joskin's hand, preventing him from drinking. "I know you are a good and noble ruler, but you have not told us what the price is for this gift."

Tarsella looked out the window, "Until now you have not asked."

Niesla let Joskin's hand go and joined the Fairen at the window. "It will not change my intentions nor will it prevent me from doing what I must. I only would like to know the price."

Tarsella glanced at Niesla, "My dear friend the Governor of Sulitamis is gone. She has passed from this life and has chosen to stay. The city she worked so hard to build and protect has no real leadership. I would ask that you and Joskin accept this position and make it your own."

"What can we expect when we drink?" Joskin asked. "I mean, will we feel different?"

Tarsella chuckled softly, "You will drink and sleep for a time. When you wake up you will feel the same with one exception, you will feel no hunger or thirst. I am sure you have noticed such a change in your cousin. This potion is only a more refined rendition of what he took at Jammar's residence." She waited for a moment and continued, "Niesla can show you to a room. She knows my house well. You both need rest. When you awaken you can prepare for your trip to the coast."

Niesla grabbed Joskin by the hand and led him out of the room. Faith opened her mouth to ask a question, but Tarmancia appeared in the doorway. "Fairen, I have come to ask your aid. I am told my sister has returned, but has been corrupted. My mother waits near my sister's prison in your own city. We can see her, but we cannot talk to her or even hear her. Tesrik will not let us near the bars. Will you come to help?"

"Of course I will assist you in any way I am able," Tarsella briskly walked out the door. Airria, Faith and Carrita were close behind. "Why would Tesrik not allow you near the bars?" she asked as they walked.

Carrita answered, "It was my command Tesrik is following."

Tarmancia stopped, "He said it was on the order of the Fairen's daughter and I know her well. She has been missing for some time. Where do you get the authority to give commands to a town guard?"

Carrita smiled brightly, "I knew your sister far better then I knew you. She betrayed all of us. She is trapped in a prison of rehabilitation. What I did, what I commanded, I did for her aid, not her punishment."

Tarmancia looked closely at Carrita. After a moment her head jerked to Airria and Faith. "What has happened? It has not been so long since I last saw you. Why have you changed so much?"

Airria and Faith laughed. Faith said, "There are more surprises to come, but for now let us help your sister."

Hesitantly Tarmancia turned around and led the group to the jail. Her mother was sitting on a bench, slouching with bags under her eyes. Tesrik was standing a half pace from the bars between mother and child.

Tarsella waved her hand and frowned. She turned to her daughter and asked, "What have you done? Why can I not open this door? Why can I not remove the spell or even understand what it accomplishes?"

Carrita paused for a moment, her eyes wide. Airria could almost see the thoughts in her head. Carrita was realizing she had cast a spell beyond what her mother could comprehend.

After a while her eyes began blinking slowly, "I balanced the forces of Fire, Water, Air and Earth to create a sanctuary from pain."

Tarsella began to wobble slightly, "Esnie was correct. Even before your transition you had a greater collective understanding of the essence of the elements than any mage or dragon has. You have discovered more about magic than I have ever known." She sat next to the other woman and let out a sigh, "There is nothing I can do here. Only these of the new council can help." Her hand waved, pointing to the three.

Carrita slowly approached the bars. She looked closely at the woman curled up on the floor. "She is still a danger to us. I cannot in good conscience let her leave her cage."

The first thought that went to through Airria's head was to let her die, let her accept her chosen reward.

Faith asked, "Is there nothing we can do. Can she not be redeemed? She has a family who loves her and will obviously do anything they can to help. Is there no way to aid her? Her very soul is in pain, as was yours when we first met," Faith addressed the last part to Carrita. "Someone helped you. Can you not do the same for her?"

A small piece of understanding was brought to Airria's mind by Faith's words and her desire to help was brought to his heart by the tone of her voice. "I believe I can assist. She doesn't want to be healed because she fears Jarmack'Trastibbik will find her and break her again. Let me show her that she is safe. Then and only then can she start healing," he said.

Carrita let Airria into the cell. He knelt by the woman and said, "She is dead. You know I wouldn't be here if I were lying."

The woman slowly looked up, "She is forever. She cannot die."

Airria placed his hand on her shoulder. He could feel the pain the dragon had caused. He could feel the torment the woman had endured. Slowly reaching in with his newfound magical ability he took the pain on himself. "You were forced to learn the power of a dragon. You know the feeling well. Now feel it again. I have the power of our master as well as the abilities of another."

At first the woman fought to hold on to her pain. Airria could feel she treasured it in a disturbing way. "It gives me strength."

"This is what your captor taught you." He bent lower and whispered, "You can feel I can take what I want. I received this from the one who taught you. Her strength was less because she didn't know what true power was." He turned to look at Faith pacing on the other side of the bars. "Your family will help teach you what will give you a strength that will far surpass what you have known."

The woman scowled, "You know nothing!"

In the woman's bitter face he could see he was getting through. He looked back at his friends and whispered again, "I knew enough to rip the heart from Jarmack'Trastibbik. All of her knowledge and power is mine. Additionally I received the gems from the heart of another dragon lord. It wasn't until I received it all that I realized it was those I care for and those who care for me that gave me the strength. The rest means nothing."

The woman let her head fall to the floor. She rolled to her back and began to cry, "I can't go back. They can't know what I've done." She repeated these words over and over, but reluctantly allowed Airria to slowly take her torment.

When he was finished he said, "Look at them. Look at your mother. For all she has been told about you, she still sits wanting to hold you. I'm not saying it will be easy, but if you let them they will accept you back. It is only you who still needs to forgive your crimes. It is you alone who has to make restitution to those you have wronged. We will destroy the armor and with it the knight who committed the crimes. No one outside of this prison needs to know you were the one in it."

She looked at her sister, then to her mother. She let out a long fluttery breath, "I don't know if I can face them."

Airria stood up, "It will take time, but if you are willing they will help you heal." He walked to the door and opened it, "Let them see her."

Airria didn't have time to get out of the way. The woman's mother pushed him to the side as she rushed for her daughter. Tarmancia was only a step behind.

Airria watched for a moment and then walked out to Faith and Carrita. "I made her a promise I don't know if all us combined can keep. I told her we would destroy the armor. Can it be done?"

Carrita shook her head, "The armor she wore was far more complicated and magical than even the dark armor knights of the Order of the Black Claw donned. I know not how to rid the world of the lesser armor, much less the greater."

Faith got excited, she grabbed the other two and dashed to where the armor had been kept, still wrapped in her cloak. She dragged the whole package to the center of the street and said, "Allow me to lead this time."

The armor began to float and churn inside a sphere of transparent white. As it swirled flakes peeled off and joined the motion. In time all that was left in the white sphere was a swirling vortex of dust and sand.

Faith threw her arms dramatically to side and yelled, "The dark warrior is no more. It is time to prepare for the future." She raised the globe high above their heads and let it explode. Soft enough that only Airria and Carrita could hear she whispered, "The magic used to create this armor will help heal the city." She drove every particle of armor deep into the ground.

Tarsella spoke from behind them, "There is much we need to prepare for. Change is upon us. This change will be for the good of all. I look forward to your reign."

Airria's heart fell as he was reminded of the responsibility he had accepted.

Faith grabbed his hand. He turned to her and looked in her eyes, "At least I will have you to help me."

Faith smiled and brushed his hair behind his ear, "Always."

Made in the USA
Columbia, SC
26 May 2024